Southern Legacy

A Novel by Jerri Hines

http://jerrihines.org/
http://twitter.com/jhines340

Copyright 2015 by Jerri Hines
Cover Art by Erin Dameron-Hill
Edited by Faith Williams, The Atwater Group

ISBN: 978-0-692-55871-3

DEDICATION

To my husband, Bob, for allowing me to follow my dream.

In Memoriam

To two lovely Southern ladies who were major influences in my life.
My grandmothers
Mamie Lambert Dotson and Ruby Lee Caveness.

.

CONTENTS

PART ONE

BELLE OF CHARLESTON

Chapter One

"It is your duty as a Montgomery to protect your legacy."

Lieutenant Cullen Smythe observed the head of the Montgomery family expound on the obligation that being his heir apparent meant to his cousin, who promptly drank down another shot of whiskey.

Clayton Montgomery would have none of his grandson's blatant disregard of the responsibility that had been placed upon his shoulders. A tall man, the elder Montgomery used his height to his full advantage. He walked over to his grandson's side and slapped the glass out of his hand, crashing it to the floor in a million pieces.

Wade leaped up into the old man's face. For a brief moment, Cullen thought he would have to step between the two. Thankfully, Wade lowered his gaze and stepped back.

Cullen shook his head. When he rode up the winding road lined with massive live oaks with their waving curtains of gray moss, he had not pictured his return to the home of his youth to have gone as it had.

For well over a hundred years, Montgomerys had lived along the Ashley River. Sitting back from the river's bank, the brick house reigned over the plantation. A brick arch centered the home with two sets of curving wrought-iron staircases that led up to the entrance.

To the side of the entrance, columns ran up to the covered porch that wrapped around three sides of the house. A veranda of considerable proportion sat in the back and faced the grand garden. The smell of heady, fragrant jasmine, roses, and magnolias encompassed the early spring air. Magnolia trees flanked both sides of the garden, giving to the magnificent plantation its name.

This was the place he considered his home. His heart belonged to Magnolia Bluff and his Southern family. He had been raised here alongside his cousins, Percival and Wade. How many days they had spent along this riverbank!

His mother had given birth to him in the room that overlooked the river. Even after his mother died from the fever, Cullen had stayed until his father remarried. Situated seventeen miles outside of Charleston, it had been a perfect place to spend his childhood. He had thought of it often on the *Cayne*.

Memories comforted him on those long voyages. How vivid the pictures in his mind of the sights of the river: fishing in the overgrowth under the live oaks, canoeing on the river, and racing their horses through the gray beards of the Spanish moss on the giant oaks along the little-used river road. The trouble the three of them found—it had always been the three of them, until now—Percival was gone.

"Good Heavens, Cullen, talk some sense into your cousin!"

Cullen didn't move a muscle in his face, but looked directly at his grandfather. He stared into the cold gray eyes of a man whose orders rarely got questioned. Clayton Montgomery's heritage gave credence to the man's arrogance...generations of Montgomerys living off the South Carolina soil.

"I believe Wade understands exactly what is expected, Grandfather."

Cullen glanced over at his cousin, whose eyes bored into the man in front of him with a hatred Cullen had never seen from Wade. Where had the carefree, fun-loving soul gone? Had it died with his brother?

Wade's appearance hadn't changed. He was an exceptionally handsome man. With thick, golden hair and clear blue eyes, his face bore a cool recklessness that females found wildly attractive. He had only to smile to have them flock around him, but he wasn't smiling at the moment.

Lieutenant Cullen Smythe was twenty-five years old, the same age as Wade...a year younger than Percival had been. Cullen stood six feet, the same height as Wade, but that was where the similarities ended.

Cullen had dark brown hair with long sideburns and a mustache, neatly trimmed. His nose was narrow, slightly aquiline, and his jaw, firm and angular. His face was bronzed golden by his time in the sun.

He was a deliberate sort, never one to make an impulsive decision. He had an air of authority, a quality that served him well in the Navy. No one dared question one of his orders, not with his eyes boring into them. He had been told they seemed to pierce into the depths of one's soul.

It had been Percival who had been fearless and brave. More than once had his older cousin stepped between him and Douglas

Montgomery. Cullen's uncle—Wade's father—had been a mean drunk. Percival thought nothing of protecting the younger ones from his father's wrath when the man would drink himself into oblivion.

Percival had become his father's target during those times. Percival had not shirked from his father's hand. Cullen understood the way Percival thought: as long as his father's rage was directed at him, the others—Wade, the girls, his mother, and Cullen—would not be harmed. Percival's scars, the black eyes, a broken arm, and bruises from those confrontations, served as a badge of honor to Cullen.

Clayton hadn't turned a blind eye to his son's irrational behavior. Many times Douglas had been thrown into the guesthouse set off to the left of the main house until he slept off the effects of his binge drinking. But Clayton could not always contain his son when Douglas went on one of his rampages. He had allowed the boys to hide in his room if he wasn't home when Douglas's temper exploded.

It had been here, in his grandfather's study, that Cullen had always felt safe. It seemed to be a fortress in his young mind, formidable with its dark, heavy furniture and the realistic mural of horsemen in battle with swords drawn. Tonight, the room had lost its appeal, replaced with a morbid foreboding.

The darkness that had invaded Magnolia Bluff since Percival's death over a year ago had not faded. Percival had been the chosen one: the darling of his mother, the successor to his grandfather, the invincible brother…for that was what they were…the three of them, Percival, Wade and himself—brothers.

Cullen remembered well the anger that filled him with the news that Percival had died. Thrown from his horse! The drunken fool! No one had to tell Cullen that Percival was drunk. There had been no better horseman around these parts. Cullen could still hear Percival brag that he was a better horseman drunk than sober. The reality…he hadn't been.

"Explain to Cullen why you won't hold to your word! I doubt—" Clayton was ruthlessly cut off.

"I told you, Grandfather, I would take care of the situation. Surely, Randolph Wragg does not hold to our conversation after Percival's death."

"Confound it, Wade! Don't take me for a damned fool. You know well that there was and is an understanding. You gave him your word."

"Word? He came to me while I was grieving and laid guilt upon me about Percival's honor…"

"He asked you to hold to Percival's engagement to Clarissa. Hell, all of Charleston knows that you are engaged to the lady and was waiting only for an appropriate time to announce it. It has been over a year. It is time. Where is your honor? Your sense of duty?"

"By God! What more do you want from me? Did I not give up my commission in the Navy because of my duty to Magnolia Bluff?"

Cullen took a deep breath. Wade had resigned from the Navy shortly after the news came of Percival's death. It cut him deep to see Wade depart. They had been back together since the day they entered the Naval Academy.

Cullen had little memory of his mother. Dolly Montgomery Smythe died when Cullen was five from the fever. His father, Jonathan T Smythe, had seen fit to leave Cullen at his mother's Southern home until he remarried.

Shortly after Cullen had turned thirteen, he left to live in Philadelphia and had not returned until after he had become a cadet in the Naval Academy, alongside Wade. The dream of joining the Navy had been Percival's...the three of them together against the world.

When it had come time to apply to the Naval Academy, Percival held back, allowing Wade the opportunity. Guilt gnawed at Cullen at times, knowing that Percival sacrificed his dream for his brother. Both brothers could not leave home. One had to stay and look after the family.

Wade had met up with Cullen at the Naval Academy in 1852. The next four years had seen the cousins side by side in Annapolis while school commenced and the summer cruises aboard ship.

Leave saw Cullen in Charleston; only brief periods did he return to Philadelphia. His heart pulled him to the place he considered his home. After three years on duty, Cullen's father requested he return home for family issues that had developed in Philadelphia.

Cullen had complied and resigned from the Navy. It would be official as soon as he returned to Washington. But he had not passed up the opportunity to return to Charleston when his ship docked in port. He had not seen the family since Percival's death.

"Come, Wade, it could not be that bad. Clarissa Wragg is a lovely creature," Cullen said in hopes of calming the tension.

The response was a glare. Wade shrugged. "Doesn't matter. Not now."

Clayton's color heightened. "He fancies himself in love with none other than Josephine Wright."

A sudden frost hung in the air on Clayton's words. The venom in his voice couldn't be denied, uttered as if the girl was a leper. An awkward silence ensued.

Finally, Wade smiled, his normal charismatic smile twisted. "Josephine Buchanan Wright, Grandfather."

Good Lord! Understanding suffused throughout Cullen as he recognized the name. He stared over at Wade. Had his cousin lost all his good sense!

"Wade!" escaped Cullen before he had time to contemplate his utterance.

"Don't look at me like that, Cullen. I know better than anyone whose daughter she is, but she is also Henry Buchanan's granddaughter. Is not the Buchanan name as old and respected as ours?"

"Watch your tongue, Wade Montgomery. Montgomerys don't go back on their word. At least honorable Montgomerys, like Percival..."

Wade flew into a rage. "Percival was given the opportunity to choose his bride. Why do I have to honor his engagement?"

"You know well the reason," Clayton shot back with the same passion. "How long have I covered for your father's ill-fated judgment? Only to discover Percival inherited one of his weaknesses. I have kept nothing back from you. Percival accepted Wragg's dowry before the marriage."

Unbelieving what he heard, Cullen broke into the conversation. "Percival gambled?"

A look of anguish crossed Wade's face. He ran his fingers through his disheveled hair and shook his head. "Tell me there is another way."

Clayton said nothing and settled back into his chair behind the desk, confident he had won the argument. He lit up his pipe, took a puff and blew smoke up in the air.

* * * *

In the early morning haze, the water of the river was placid. Live oaks and pines lined the banks in the undergrowth. Birds woke with a song; frogs chirped; the wind rustled through the leaves. The familiarity of the sights and sound gave him comfort. Love of this place bore deep in his soul.

Heavens above! He believed he was drunk.

Cullen chugged down the rest of the bottle. He drew back and threw it into the water, disturbing the quiet and waking his sleeping...unconscious cousin.

"Don't be so loud," Wade uttered with the greatest of difficulty. Squinting, he stretched upward. He held his head in his hand.

"It's dawn. We need to return to the house."

"Dawn be damned!" Wade groaned.

Cullen had never seen Wade wallow in self-pity. He hadn't been the sort. The Wade he had known was a man of action: one to plan and manipulate to get his way, usually by the skin of his teeth…living on the edge…pushing the limits. He always had managed one way or another until now.

Cullen glanced back over the water, and then back at Wade. His expression had changed. One corner of his lips drew upward and his right eyebrow arched.

"You could do it."

For a moment, Cullen didn't comprehend Wade's meaning. He grimaced. "For the love of God, Wade! Are you trying to pawn off your fiancée on me?"

"Would it be the worst? You need a Southern woman to keep you warm at night, not one of those frigid beasts in the North. Why, Clarissa is one of the loveliest women in all of South Carolina…"

"I couldn't care less if she was the belle of Charleston. I'm not intoxicated enough to consider taking a wife."

"She is rich as well."

"I have no need—"

"Ah, yes. I know well enough. The Smythe money! You are a free man to choose who to spend your life with. You have no obligation to uphold the honor of the Montgomerys!"

"You talk nonsense, Wade. You make it sound as if a gun was held to your head. We have kept in correspondence. You sounded as if you were satisfied with the arrangement. Out with it. Have you compromised the lady?"

"Josephine? No…" Wade stammered, shaking his head. "You wouldn't understand."

"Try me," Cullen shot back. "I would love to understand why you have fallen for the daughter of the man responsible for your father's death."

"Father killed himself—"

"After he was bled dry by Brantley Wright. The man is a professional gambler. Grandfather says he is a cheat."

With an unsteady hand and confused expression, Wade waved Cullen off. "Grandfather blamed Wright for Father's shortcomings. You knew Father as well as anyone. It was not only his drinking. Father gambled away a fortune, cut to the quick of the Montgomery's heritage…I believe more so than Grandfather has admitted. Percival…Percival alluded to it when he informed me of his choice of bride."

13

"And yours."

"Ah, yes." Wade chuckled to himself. "My choice."

Wade rubbed his forehead and looked up at Cullen. The years between them gave credence to an understanding of what it meant to be a gentleman of the South. A gentleman's reputation was his lifeblood.

A Southern man's character could never be questioned—loyalty, honor, duty to one's country, God, and family. It was the tie that binds, but he saw that Wade was deeply troubled. It disturbed him.

"What is it, Wade? Tell me. Are we not brothers?"

Wade pressed his lips together tightly and nodded. "Always. You, Percival, and me. Now it is only us two. I trust no one as I do you."

Cullen said nothing. He did not mention Andrew, Wade's younger brother. It was not only the four-year difference in their ages, but their views on life that separated the brothers. Wade had always been one who lived life to the fullest; Andrew, the silent, studious sort. He was attending medical school in Philadelphia.

"As I do also, Wade."

"Since Percival's death, I have done all that Grandfather has requested. He is determined that I replace Percival. He has told me more than once that the whole of Magnolia Bluff will go to me. I will be its master."

Cullen remained silent. His grandfather believed in the sanctity of the family. That meant the name Montgomery, which he did not carry. The rebuff annoyed him beyond measure. Was not he as much blood as Wade?

Yet, Magnolia Bluff would never be his because of the name he carried, no matter how much he loved the place. He carried a good name, but one that wasn't Montgomery.

"I'm not Percival nor will I ever be," Wade confessed. "I fear I will be a disappointment to Grandfather. I have been already."

"Come, Wade, do not cloud the issue. It is not Grandfather who bothers you. It is the girl. I have never seen you in such a state about a woman."

Wade turned from Cullen and stared blankly across the river. "Charlotte became fast friends with Josephine at Madame Tamline's French School for Young Ladies. They have become inseparable...I saw her for the first time here at Magnolia Bluff. I mean, the first time since she was grown...a far cry from the time you rescued her down at the Battery. Do you remember?"

Cullen nodded. It seemed a lifetime ago, but he remembered pulling a young girl from the water. He had been so angry with the child that she had put lives at risk until he learned it had not been her who had done so...

"It doesn't explain why you pursued a relationship," Cullen pressed.

"Christ, Cullen! You never have been in love, have you?" Wade glanced back over his shoulder, and then turned away again. "I knew I was committed. She knew. I didn't mean for it to happen. We both...both understood about my situation with Clarissa. Josephine refused to meet with me. But I would arrange a meeting whether she wanted it or not.

"I convinced her I would make it work...I lied." Wade paused and choked back his emotions. "Somehow she knew about the debt Percival left. She told me her father had arranged a dowry for her...that maybe it would cover what was owed. I told Grandfather I was withdrawing from Clarissa.

"He flew into a rage and laughed at me. Told me that the account that Wright set up for his daughter held no more than twenty-two hundred dollars. A far cry from Clarissa's. It would leave the estate with a debt it cannot pay and a blemish once more on our honor."

A silent breeze swept over the river, a chilling one in the early morning air. For a time, neither said a word.

"You are holding to your engagement." Cullen said it as a statement, not a question.

"Yes," Wade admitted in a voice no louder than a whisper. "I have to find the courage to tell Josephine. I fear I'm not brave enough. I don't know how to walk away from her..."

Cullen clasped his cousin's back. "Then, I will do it for you."

Chapter Two

The early spring morning gave way to the promise of a warm day. A puff of a breeze came over the still pond and stirred the water ever so slightly into a ripple. Cullen stood at the foot of the elongated bridge that connected the garden in the Groves, the Buchanan family plantation, to the meadow where the cows grazed.

It was here that Wade told Cullen to meet Josephine. It had been their spot. A perfect place for lovers to rendezvous. Hidden away from prying eyes, huge live oak trees dripped with Spanish moss that shielded the view around the pool.

The lush garden filled with blooming azaleas wove around the banks of the pond. Its touch gave way to a sense of peace and tranquility Cullen had rarely experienced. For a moment, he soaked in the beauty, a façade of the world around them.

Cullen had accepted this life…this belief that his people were God-ordained in so much that their wants and needs came before all else. It wasn't until he moved North that doubts emerged, doubts that he could no longer ignore.

But today…today wasn't to question the life around him. He had a mission. He pulled his pocket watch out of his pocket. He was early.

A rustling sound interrupted his thoughts. He looked up over on the other side of the bridge. A woman ran down the slight incline. She held up the hem of her skirt while the low grass whipped her ankles. Her hair ribbon blew off as she hurried, giving way for her raven hair to tumble down her back.

She wore a rose muslin gown, with a high collar and puff sleeves. Her cheeks blushed from her exertion with the warmest of smiles. She had the look of one rushing to her love. He could not take his eyes from her.

The night of his return, he had attended a dinner party of Charleston elite. Beautiful women at every turn of his head, none more so than Wade's intended, Clarissa Wragg. Clarissa was a stunning woman, her dark hair upswept with ringlets that framed her classical oval face. Her brilliant blue eyes sparkled in the candlelight. Beaus surrounded her and waited on her every whim.

Yet she had done nothing for him, not like the one who ran toward him. She was breathtakingly beautiful.

Laughing aloud, she hurried across the bridge and called out, breathless, "Wade. Wade. I'm here."

Screened from her view by some overgrown azaleas and trees, Cullen stepped out. Startled, she stumbled.

He reached out instinctively and caught her by her shoulders. In his grasp, she gazed up at him and met his eyes. Her dark eyes widened, but slowly the fright subsided with a flicker of recognition.

He had seen those eyes stare at him years before when he had saved her from drowning. Lord, she had been only a child. She was a child no longer. The eyes that flared back at him were fully a woman's.

Red-faced, she pulled back and glanced around him. Troubled, her smile disappeared. "I am afraid I have made a mistake. I was—"

"Expecting my cousin," Cullen offered. Bowing his head slightly, he continued, "Wade could not make it this afternoon. I came in his stead. You may remember me, Cullen… Lieutenant Cullen Smythe."

She shrugged in a self-conscious way. "I remember you. One doesn't forget being pulled from the depths of certain death."

"An over exaggeration."

"Not to me," she said in a low voice. Her chest heaved as if she regained her composure. "Wade was looking forward to your visit." She looked him over in his blue uniform. "You are in the Navy. Wade said you served together until he was called home after…the unfortunate incident. I did not realize you had arrived."

Her voice faded and left an awkward silence. She broke her gaze and glanced around the grounds; then back at him. "Wade is not coming?"

Cullen had never been one to panic. Moreover, this task had seemed so simple. Yet, he could find no words. He stood there dumbfounded on how to handle the words he had to utter.

"Again, I need to apologize. I thought my note…"

"Note?" She glanced back over her shoulder. Only then did either of them notice a petite mulatto girl, a pretty thing, stood on the edge of the bridge with a letter in her hand.

"Miss Josephine, I tried to tell you when you dropped the note in your bedroom. You left in such a hurry. I had no time to stop you without drawing attention."

A look of panic flashed on Josephine's face. "Oh, Gillie, did anyone...?"

Gillie shook her head. "I do not believe so."

"Your girl reads?" Cullen asked the question without thinking of the consequence of putting Josephine on the defense.

Cullen had sent a note in Wade's usual manner to inform Josephine of his arrival, but it had not been Wade, but Cullen. Cullen had only requested a moment of her time. Obviously, Josephine had not read it, but reacted only to the note being delivered.

But the girl had to have read the note to realize Wade would not be waiting for her mistress. Slaves were not allowed to read...or most were not. It, also, did not pass his notice that this girl, Gillie, seemed quite fluent in her speech.

Josephine snapped her head back around to Cullen. Her eyes hardened. She said coolly, "Gillie is not *my girl*. She is my companion."

Cullen let it go. It would serve no purpose to dispute Josephine's claim. He, too, had been raised here in the South. He had heard all the justifications for keeping the institution: the slaves were content; they would not know how to take care of themselves. Moreover, Southerners hated being told what to do. That in time, they would resolve the slavery issue themselves.

The question became when that time would come. Only when he moved up North did he understand the magnitude of the cruelty and injustice of slavery. He supposed everyone had their own way of dealing with the issue. If Josephine felt this girl was her companion, he would not argue, at least not at this moment.

Cullen stepped toward Josephine. "Again, I apologize. I need only a moment of your time."

Her eyes were solemn, without any show of emotion. She folded her hands in front of herself. "What has happened?"

"I'm afraid I'm a bearer of bad news, Miss Wright. I have been asked by my cousin to extend his deepest regrets, but he is breaking off any further communication or meetings between the two of you. He understands that you may have misunderstood your relationship, but he needs to uphold his responsibilities and hold to his engagement to Miss Wragg.

"I am certain you will understand his position. He doesn't want to cause you harm by a continued association…"

She looked mortified. Her bottom lip trembled. She stumbled over her words. "He's not coming…ever? He is holding to marry Clarissa?"

"He hasn't done anything to compromise you, has he?"

"Compromise?" she gasped, visibly shuddering. "Oh, Mother in Heaven! Did he say he had?"

"No, no," he assured her. "He said he had not. It is only you seem distressed."

He did not add that although Wade gave his word he had not compromised Josephine Wright, looking at her in this light, in this place, doubts emerged. Wade had never had an issue bedding a lady on his choosing…unless Wade had other plans.

Slowly, the realization sank within him Wade had had honorable intentions in this less than proper courtship. Wade played with fire and got burned, but it was not his cousin who held his sympathy.

Josephine stood there as she came to her senses. She fumbled to get herself presentable. The girl, Gillie, ran over to her mistress and twisted Josephine's hair back into a bun.

"Miss Josephine, we need to return to the house. Oh, my, you don't even have your bonnet," Gillie said in a nervous manner. She shot Cullen a look of suspicion from the corner of her eye. "Your grandfather requested your presence down in the parlor. He wasn't happy…far from it. We have a visitor."

Josephine gripped Gillie's hand while the girl pinned her hair in place and wheeled around to face her. "Who?"

Gillie hesitated. "Mr. Wragg."

Josephine covered her mouth with her hand. Shocked. "Oh, Heavens to Betsy! Why does he want to see me?"

Cullen's head snapped to the sound of hooves crossing the bridge. His attention upon Josephine, he had not observed two horsemen who headed toward them. He recognized them readily even though he had not seen either for years: Henry Buchanan's grandsons, Harry Lee and Buck Haynes.

He held no doubt that they recognized him as well. There was contempt in their eyes. The elder, Harry Lee, rode ahead. He wore no hat, exposing his deep auburn hair, tousled back from his sunburned face. Tall and lean in the saddle, he rode with an arrogance that illuminated his fine horsemanship.

19

The shorter one seemed content to follow in his brother's shadow. His hat sat snug over his large ears. He reined in beside Harry Lee and leaned over his saddle.

"Well, well, well, what do we have here?" Buck asked with a contemptuous smile. "Here we thought our dear cousin was rendezvousing with Wade."

"Doesn't mean he's not here. Look over in the undergrowth. Don't trust any Montgomery."

Harry Lee exchanged looks with Buck. Buck nodded and maneuvered his mount around the small group.

"My cousin isn't here," Cullen said coolly. "I was out for a morning ride. Thought I would ride by the Groves and pay my respects."

"I had heard you were on leave here in Charleston. A lieutenant now in the Navy!" Sarcasm oozed in his voice as his eyes raked over Cullen. "Come for Wade's wedding? Should be a doozy. I hear Randolph Wragg is sparing no expense on his only daughter."

Josephine's face drained of all color to a whitened ash. She had lost the tears welling in her eyes, replaced with a blazing anger. Her hand whipped around Gillie and pushed the girl behind her. The action didn't go unnoticed by Cullen.

Cullen stepped forward, hoping to take the disgruntled pair with him and away from Josephine. "Perhaps you can ride with me…"

Harry Lee pressed his lips together with a gleam in his eyes. "Don't think so, Yankee. We came down here on business. Grandpa Henry sent us to find Josephine." He looked directly at her. "Going to tan your hide."

"Get going, Harry Lee," Josephine demanded. "You got no business here. Take Lieutenant Smythe up to Grandpa Henry. He'll be quite mad if you offend a guest."

"Is that what you call your visitors…guests? Think there are other words I would use."

Josephine reddened. Buck laughed on his return to the group. Cullen felt his hand clench tight.

"Here we thought you were only entertaining Wade."

Cullen's hand tightened together into a fist.

"Guess they share more than just blood." Harry Lee tossed his head back and laughed.

In one quick motion, Cullen jerked Harry Lee off his horse. He had enough of the insinuations. He pulled back his arm and punched Harry Lee, first with a right, and then a left. The next, Harry Lee lay sprawled on the ground. Behind him, Cullen heard a horse neigh and a thud.

He spun in response to see Buck befuddled, crawling to his knees with his horse running away down the path. A gun sat on the edge of the bridge, flung from Buck's fall. To the idiot's back, Gillie silently dropped a fallen tree branch she had used to swat the horse.

"Son of a bitch," Harry Lee cursed under his breath and rubbed his jaw.

"Next time watch what you say in the presence of a lady." Cullen stood over him. He glanced back at Josephine, who started forward at her cousin. Cullen seized hold of her. "No need, Miss Wright."

"Ain't gonna do any good. Not after Grandpa Henry gets hold of her. She's done gone and hurt the Buchanan's name like her mother," Harry Lee uttered.

The words hit Josephine harder than if he had physically hit her. She started to speak, and then stopped. Cullen saw the turmoil boil within her, the pain that flashed across her face.

"What kind of nonsense is that?" Cullen demanded. "How can her reputation be ruined by an accidental meeting? Ask her! She did not come to meet me."

Josephine shook her head in a dazed manner. "I have done nothing to be ashamed of, Harry Lee. I will explain to Grandpa Henry. He will understand."

"Not after this morning. Mr. Wragg is waiting to get your word you won't do anything foolish to stop Wade and Clarissa's wedding," Harry Lee growled.

"What kind of men are you?" Cullen demanded. Infuriated, he took hold of Josephine's arm and pulled her to him. "You would let someone tarnish Miss Wright's good name on a rumor. For I know for a fact that it is all there is. Hell, it's your name. You are out here taking it out on me when it is not I who pose a danger to Miss Wright or my cousin."

"What do you expect when we find you here alone with Jo?"

"Do you feel that I have compromised Miss Wright? Is that your issue?" Cullen's voice rose. His anger ran high. "Do I need to make an offer for her hand? Is that your mission?"

Josephine gasped. Her eyes widened. Obviously, the utterance was not what she expected. In truth, it was not his intention, but he would not let her suffer for his cousin's foolishness. Wade had asked him to offer for Clarissa. The thought horrified him beyond measure.

Yet, he would do so now for Josephine? Damnable guilt weighed upon him. It was not only honor that brought him to this point, but a strong attraction he had never felt for a woman.

He had never been like his cousin, with a woman on his arm at every turn. A foreign feeling surged through him. He had made love to many women, but had never fancied himself to be in love nor did he now. But he was overcome with a sudden need to protect this woman.

Thunderstruck, Harry Lee stood and dusted the dirt off his pants. He shook his head and retreated. "Do not be hasty. There's no need. The matter could well be cleared up. You are right. It is not you we have issues with at the moment."

"Then I will escort Miss Josephine and her girl to the house. The matter will be settled, I assure you."

Harry Lee mounted up. Buck ran off after his horse, which had stopped at the bend and grazed.

"I will inform Grandpa Henry."

Cullen watched Harry Lee ride off, and then turned to a stunned Josephine.

She made no movement other than a slight shake of her head. "Are you mad? Do you have any idea of what you have done?"

He shrugged and eyed her with a sudden found amusement. "I have attempted to protect your honor. Do not be concerned. I doubt that your grandfather will see the need to take the matter further."

"But what if he does? Where will you be then?"

"With a distressed wife, it seems." Cullen joked, but the look on Josephine's face told she was not amused.

"Don't tease me, Lieutenant Smythe. You do not know my grandfather. If it is as Gillie and Harry Lee have indicated, my grandfather will be on a rampage. He has warned me of what is expected of me, no matter the arrangement he made with Papa."

"Arrangement?"

"When Papa left me here with Grandfather, he made an agreement with Grandfather. Grandfather disowned my momma when she married Papa. Papa wanted me raised in Charleston and to become a lady. It was why I thought I had a dowry that would satisfy you Montgomerys. Did Wade…?"

"Wade looked into what your father left you." Cullen's tone sobered. "It was not enough to pay the debt owed he is expected to cover."

Josephine lowered her gaze and pressed her lips together in a manner to keep control of her emotions. "Papa didn't leave me a dowry?"

Cullen hesitated. It pained him to confess his knowledge. "A small one only."

22

She looked back up at him with her large telling eyes. "How much?"

"Twenty-two hundred, from what I gather."

"No, no, no, it can't be." She shook her head. "It makes no sense. Papa has been most adamant about me marrying a gentleman. He gave Grandpa Henry instructions. I wasn't to marry before eighteen. Said that we marry too early down here in Charleston. But I thought…he wanted…me to marry…"

"Perhaps you should talk with your father," Cullen suggested.

"Yes, of course, I will write him immediately," Josephine said, her voice unsteady. She glanced back at Gillie. "Come, Gillie. We may need to pack to return to Charleston."

She stepped onto the bridge, but turned once more to Cullen.

"Do not repeat your offer, Lieutenant. I will take care of the situation."

"I can assure you, Miss Wright, I am capable of handling myself. I ask you only to trust me."

"But…"

"It is a matter of honor, Miss Wright. I will not let my family's name be tinged. My cousin cannot rectify this situation without causing a larger scandal. I promise you I will not let that happen."

"I cannot ask you to make such a sacrifice," she said in a soft whisper.

"Please, Miss Wright, all I ask of you is to trust me." He offered his arm to Josephine and strolled toward the house through the lovely gardens. Behind them, Gillie led Cullen's horse by the reins.

Chapter Three

In the library, Josephine Buchanan Wright waited to be summoned by her grandfather. Most days, Jo loved the quiet hours she spent in the warm and friendly room. She would lose herself in the pages of one of the many books lining the shelves.

The book she was reading now, *The Personal History, Adventures, Experience and Observation of David Copperfield*, lay where she had left it, on a table beside the oil lamp. The pages were well worn; it was the third time she had read it.

The heavy mahogany desk with accompanying leather high back chairs filled the far corner. A large cream area rug covered the shiny wood floor; the walls held a wallpaper of a floral design of blue and brown flowers.

She sat in her usual spot on the worn sofa in front of the jib windows. With the sun filtering onto her back, she would enjoy a book for hours without being disturbed. This was her escape away from the family. Today, though, she felt suffocated within the walls.

Upon her return to the house, her guest, Lieutenant Cullen Smythe, had been shown into her grandfather's office by Lucas, the house butler. Harry Lee stood outside the open door until Lieutenant Smythe entered. He followed and the door was shut.

She expected to be called into the room at any moment, but moments became minutes and minutes into…oh, she didn't know how long it had been. It felt like an eternity.

Gillie had brought her refreshments and had hurriedly addressed Jo's appearance. Her unruly hair had been pulled back off her oval face with a ribbon. She examined herself in the gold-plated mirror over the fireplace.

Her face was still flushed from her earlier exertion; her eyes, swollen, but there was little she could do about them. In the privacy allotted within the confines of the library, she had succumbed to her emotions and wept. Wade had deserted her.

How she loved him! It was not what it seemed… Oh, for Heaven's sakes! Who was she trying to deceive? She had known he was forbidden. Like others before her, she surrendered to his charms. She had allowed him to convince her he would marry her…that he loved her.

Wade was ever so handsome: his golden-brown brows straight and thick, heavily lashed blue eyes. His hair, soft and blond streaked with sun highlights, was kept short. Unlike the fashion of the day, he had a clean-shaven face, void of mustache or beard. He had only to smile at her to have her swoon at his feet! *Oh, what a ninny I am!*

She had thought she was different, but she was no different than any other he had set his eyes upon. Her heart ached.

"Miss Josephine, your grandfather is ready for you."

Jo dabbed at her eyes with her handkerchief and rose. She followed Lucas down the hall to the office door, which was ajar.

"Come in," her grandfather called to her.

She went into the office. He gestured for her to sit in one of the high back chairs across from his mahogany desk. The room was filled with heavy, dark furniture. His desk was strewn with newspapers and letters; the rug was a gloomy wine color.

"Do sit down, Josephine. Your aunt and I have been discussing this situation that has arisen. You must understand we are quite displeased."

A solemn look came into his eyes. She glanced over at her aunt, who sat tall in the chair next to hers. Jo was fully aware of a wave of apprehension within her. Instincts told her it was best to comply.

Aunt Sybil, her mother's sister, wore her usual black skirt and white lace collar and a cameo pin at her throat. She refused to come out of mourning even though her mother, Jo's grandmother, had passed away over two years ago.

Her hair, pulled back in a strict bun, was streaked with gray, though she had only turned forty-five last month. Her face conveyed a strong strength of will, the same strength of will that ran through Josephine's blood.

"I thought, Josephine, that you understood that I would not abide another scandal. When I took you into my household, I made that plain."

"Grandpa Henry, I assure you I have done nothing…"

"Josephine," Grandpa Henry said bluntly. "Randolph Wragg would not have appeared on my doorstep this morning without reason."

Josephine lowered her gaze. This had been her biggest fear before she had lost Wade…

"Josephine, look up at me."

She looked back up at her grandfather. He had not changed over the years. Not overly tall and on the stout side, he walked with a noticeable limp. But his appearance had always been immaculate. He had a neatly groomed beard and finely combed hair.

He eyed her with an intensity that told her the seriousness of her circumstance, tilted his head to one side and then the other. His lips pressed together tightly.

"Grandpa Henry, Wade wanted to marry me." She tried not for her voice to quiver…to show more courage than she felt.

"You knew well beforehand he had already spoken for Miss Clarissa Wragg."

"He assured me that it was rumors."

"It was not," Grandfather said.

Jo sensed his stirring frustration. Her mother before her had disappointed him by running off and marrying one far beneath her while engaged to another. Her grandfather was a prideful man and not a forgiving one.

Suddenly she could picture his anguish of being told her mother had eloped with the most distasteful man. His youngest…beloved daughter, had betrayed him by marrying a gambler! Oh, the shame! At least, it was what had been told by Miss Hazel.

On her mother's marriage to her father, Lucinda Buchanan had been disowned by her father. Never again would she see her family. Jo had seen her mother's torment by being cut off from her family.

Jo assumed it had been one of the reasons her father had brought her back to Charleston… her mother's dying request. Her father had never been the indulgent sort toward her, but her mother had been a different matter. Her mother wished her daughter to be accepted by her family; her father had made it happen.

Jo often wondered how her father had done so. Her grandfather had been steadfast in his refusal to see his daughter…even while she lay dying. Now she, too, had disappointed him.

A lump in her throat grew as she confessed, "Grandpa Henry, I have not done anything to disgrace our name. I met with Wade only with Gillie by my side. He was a gentleman. If now his engagement is official, he would not make his presence known to me."

"But you did meet with him."

She wanted to say that she had done nothing wrong. She loved Wade, he loved her…but the words she wanted to utter didn't emerge. So she said nothing.

She watched Grandpa Henry and Aunt Sybil exchange looks. He frowned.

"Josephine, there was a huge breach between your mother, Lucinda, and myself. I don't want to have it repeated."

"I love my home, Grandpa Henry. Please do not throw me out."

A hush fell over the room. Aunt Sybil gave Jo a sympathetic eye. The petite woman sat with her delicate, aristocratic features and her finely shaped hands crossed in her lap. "No one wants to see you go, Josephine. There is a remedy."

"It will not come from Wade Montgomery…that is a certainty."

Josephine glanced over at her grandfather. He looked at her with a bleak expression. Oh, good Lord! They were going to marry her off!

"I will inform your father. He had instructed me not to give my permission without his consent. Now, I do not think we can wait."

"Papa? Where is he? Can I not go to him?"

The sudden sharp memory of his face swept back upon her. A tall figure of a man, he carried himself with airs of a position in life that had been denied him in Charleston. She thought her papa rather handsome with his dark sideburns and goatee.

A gambler by trade, her father had a gallant manner that put most at ease, but behind his appearance was a man bent on getting his way. She had long realized that her father was a shrewd and, at times, ruthless businessman.

That is what plagued her now. How could he have thought twenty-two hundred could have been dowry enough for a gentlemen of Charleston? With the scandal attached to her name, any respectable gentleman would demand quite a large sum…much more than twenty-two hundred. Her father was no fool…if it was his intent for her to marry into Charleston gentry.

"The last letter I received stated he was on his way back to Charleston. He was held up in New Orleans, but acknowledged he was traveling overland. He informed me to forward any letters to an address in Atlanta until further notice."

"To Aunt Cora's?"

Her grandfather's translucent gray eyes narrowed. Immediately, she regretted her question. Grandpa Henry was already greatly troubled. She supposed she should have hidden her knowledge of her father's *special* friend. Better yet, not to reveal the lady who traveled with her father and herself for years after her mother passed away…before she came to Charleston.

She sat back in her chair. It would be best to remain silent at this point.

"Of course, there is the younger brother, Andrew," Aunt Sybil said.

"I would never!" escaped Jo. "He hates me!"

"Then that dreadful Yankee cousin…"

Jo glanced furtively at her grandfather. He frowned.

"Holt Miller has expressed an interest. He may be the best choice," Grandpa Henry said. "But I will present it to your father. Perhaps it will not fester."

"It will fester, Father," Aunt Sybil said pointedly. "I know the Wraggs. Tongues have already begun to wag. We need to react promptly."

Jo felt she couldn't breathe properly. Holt Miller! Andrew Montgomery! She could never marry either. But neither could she cause a scandal. Relief flooded her when her grandfather dismissed her.

She wasn't thrown out, but her future looked bleak indeed.

* * * *

Josephine tossed and turned. No matter how hard she tried, her eyes would not open. Water. She felt water was rising around her. Fear gripped her.

She had nowhere to turn. Desperately, she tried to find footing in the stone wall. The wind ripped against her. Thunder roared; a wave slammed her into the wall. Banging her head, she released her hold.

She fell backwards and she splashed into the unmerciful tide. At her gulp, storm-ridden water filled her mouth. She fought against the current, but wave after wave pounded her body. Her head throbbed. A suffocating feeling overwhelmed her. She couldn't breathe.

Suddenly, strong arms grasped hold of her, carried her out of her nightmare…brought her back to life. Gasping, she opened her eyes. He stared at her with his dark, brooding eyes.

"Josephine Buchanan Wright, what in the world are you still doing in bed!"

Startled, Josephine bolted upward. For a moment, she didn't know where she was. Slowly, her room came back into focus. She was in her bed. Taking a deep breath, the scent of dried rose petals and lavender of her bed linens calmed her. She sank back onto her pillow.

"Josephine, up!"

Jo squinted her eyes at the noise calling to her. Good Gracious! It was Grace Ann. What had her grandfather gone and done? She took the edge of her cover and pulled it over her head. Immediately, a hand jerked the blanket back.

28

"Don't you think you can get away from me that easily! Now, get up! I have a lot of work to do here." She paused and stared down at her cousin. "What's wrong with you? You look like you haven't slept in a month."

"I haven't slept at all," Jo retorted. She reached up and grabbed back her cover. "I had a dream…"

"The one that haunted you for years? I thought it had stopped." Grace Ann retreated a step to sweep the curtains back. The room filled with bright sunlight.

"As did I," Jo answered with her hands covering her eyes. "Grace Ann, please. I'll get up. Give me a moment."

"It is almost nine o'clock."

Jo rubbed her eyes in an effort to hide from Grace Ann's hawk eyes. She had no desire for Grace Ann to know the effect the dream had upon her. How vivid the remembrance. She shouldn't have been surprised. Seeing Lieutenant Smythe brought back the memory. He had saved her then and he seemed intent on doing so now.

Cullen Smythe scared her, never more so than yesterday when he appeared out of nowhere. Tall and intimidating in his Navy uniform, he looked much as he had seven years earlier. With her child's eyes, he appeared as a knight in shining armor, having whisked her out of the ocean and certain death.

Only then he had been angry, staring at her with those…those eyes. She shivered as she recalled being laid on the rain-soaked ground. Her head hurt. She could barely make out the others ranting around her.

Not understanding the words, she understood the meaning. They were mad, furious…at her. It seemed they blamed her for the mishap. Being new to Charleston, she had little bearing of where she was or where she would head. She didn't care.

With their backs to her, she crawled to her feet and took off. Afterwards, she pondered her move. Being a tiny thing, she had little chance to outrun a grown man. She made it only to the edge of the Battery before he caught her.

"Little one," her rescuer said, exasperated. "I am in no mood to be racing around in the midst of a storm. I have already jumped over a wall and into the ocean. My clothes are drenched. My boots hold more water than you weigh. So do not try my patience."

Later, she comprehended Cullen thought her responsible of the accident. Harry Lee had blamed her, but it had not been her. It had been him…Harry Lee. Even now, the remembrance of his despicable act made her stomach churn.

That day had started off with such promise. Her father drove her around the Battery after he had first taken her to Miss Hanney's Fashionable Wears. Papa had bought her an assortment of garments she hadn't an idea she had need of…drawers, petticoats, chemise, garibaldi blouses, walking dresses, a double shirt with a corselet, everyday dresses and her favorite, a zouave suit made up of a jacket over a dress with a full skirt.

Up until that moment, it had only been the two of them, her father and herself—along with Miss Hazel, her mammy—after her momma passed away from a miscarriage. Jo had been there when it had happened. She would never forget Momma passing away in front of her eyes…she had been only seven.

After her mother died, Jo had ventured with her daddy to many cities: New Orleans, New York, and London. She had been under no illusions. Her father hadn't kept the fact he was a gambler, an extremely competent one, a secret. It was how he made his money. She never could remember wanting for anything. He rarely lost.

"Do not listen to those who say I cheat. I do not. I am a gentleman. Honest and true," Papa informed her as the two played cards as they traveled to Charleston. "Here, let me show you."

She had been truly amazed. On every hand, Daddy recited every card played and in order.

"It is skill, my dear. I tell you, for I do not want you to be ashamed of what I do."

At the time, she hadn't understood his meaning. Now, she had no doubt, especially when she heard others speak with such acrimony.

"I won't have it, Jo. Mr. Whitney and I were in Charleston preparing for a trip to Philadelphia until he got the note from Grandpa Henry. Then, Mr. Whitney canceled everything. Said we needed to lend a hand or my family's name would be dragged through the mud." She turned abruptly with hands on her hips. "Wade Montgomery…I swear, Jo! I thought you had better sense."

Jo scowled. She had no desire to talk of her situation, especially to Grace Ann. Her cousin would have never found herself in a situation such as hers. Grace Ann had tried in vain for years to mold Jo into a true Southern lady.

Grace Ann was a woman who few would fail to notice. She had a rare pale beauty, ivory skin, golden hair, and fiery brown eyes. She carried herself with an elegance that couldn't be taught. She had often teased Jo about her lack of poise.

Less than a year older than Jo, Grace Ann had married Theodore Whitney eighteen months ago, a rich widower twice over. Jo often wondered why Grace Ann had chosen such an older man for her husband, when she had her choice of any beau in the county.

She supposed that although an older gentleman, Theodore Whitney could offer the gregarious Grace Ann the life she craved. Undeniably rich, he owned plantations in north South Carolina into North Carolina.

"Tell me, Josephine, that you haven't gone and got yourself in trouble."

"Grace Ann! Why, I would never!" Jo said crossly. She swung her legs off the bed. "Don't even know why you are worried about me. Thought you would be basking in my disgrace."

"It would not only be your disgrace," Grace Ann said.

Though, Jo saw Grace Ann's gaze brightened at the thought. Her cousin had never been good at concealing her feelings toward Jo.

"You're family. Mr. Whitney has made it clear we will not let you be shunned for something not in your control. We can't have a Buchanan not received! Besides, everyone knows how Wade is."

"It wasn't like that," Jo protested. "Wade is caught in a proposal not of his making…"

"I'm sure he is." Grace Ann laughed. "I can imagine it would take only one of his smiles with you. Ever the innocent."

"You don't know Wade." Indignation echoed in her voice. "He doesn't love Clarissa. He loves me. He's only marrying her because of Percival."

"It well may be, but he's promised and good girls don't associate with men who are taken. Especially men like Wade Montgomery. Don't know what you have done to Wade, my little mousy cousin, but it has Clarissa Wragg all in a dither."

"You're telling me that bothers you? As I recall, you can't abide Clarissa Wragg."

"It's not Clarissa I'm concerned with at the moment."

Jo looked at Grace Ann in surprise, who in turn gave Jo a pleasant smile. Immediately, understanding suffused through her. Family…the string that binds.

"Don't worry. I won't embarrass the family. I will go visit Aunt Cora's in Atlanta."

"That won't ever do, Jo! Clarissa won't be happy until your reputation is so terrible that no door will open for you. I heard it said she has told everyone how fast you act toward Wade. The rumor will erupt into scandal if you leave. It is what Mr. Whitney believes. As do I."

Jo wanted to ask why her husband was so concerned with her. In all the time she had known him, he barely paid any attention to her. The thought swept through her that the situation was worse than she had imagined. It was not only her broken heart that weighed heavily upon her.

"Jo, we'll fix everything. Grandfather sent for me to prepare you for the wedding on Saturday…"

"Oh, Grace Ann, I can't. I couldn't. I won't."

"You must. Mr. Whitney agrees with Grandfather. Though, I thought Mr. Whitney was going to have a heart attack when Grandfather said he was going to give permission to Wade's cousin…what's his name, Lieutenant Smythe…for your hand. Mr. Whitney put a stop to that."

There was a long pause. "Cullen…Cullen asked for my hand?"

"Lord help me! You didn't know. What did you think Lieutenant Smythe did when Harry Lee caught you two in the garden? He done it all proper like."

Jo eyed her cousin, confused, but she shouldn't have been. For as long as she had lived under this roof, it had seemed others knew more about her life than she did herself. She shook her head. "He shouldn't have. I told him not to…we met by accident."

"Well, Grandfather told him he would give it consideration, but Mr. Whitney said your papa would be fit to be tied. A Yankee. Never."

Jo pictured the Navy lieutenant in her grandfather's study, explaining his position. Lieutenant Smythe had a manner about him that few would question, but she did. Why would he do so? It only magnified her problem.

Seeing him again, she realized time had not eased his manner. Solemn and serious, smiling did not appear to be one of his natural qualities. Unlike Wade, Cullen would not be considered good-looking. Tall and lean, he had acquired a slight scar under his left eye since she had last seen him, but in a way it added to his appearance. No, she thought him ruggedly handsome.

His eyes…brooding dark eyes stared into hers as he had her in his grasp in the garden. Something when he held her mesmerized her being.

It touched her that he had offered for her hand, but it was quite out of the question. She could never marry someone out of obligation. Though, she feared that a husband would be found for her quickly after this incident…if one could be found for her.

She fumbled with her wrap and hugged it close to her. "I would not suppose it was a true proposal...he is a gentleman whether he is a Yankee or not. He felt it was his duty. Nothing more."

"I will say that it is what a Southern gentleman would do." Grace Ann shrugged and gave Jo her sad eyes. "But I'm afraid it will never do. Now where is your Gillie? We don't have time to have a gown made. So I have brought a trunk of my gowns that we need to sort through...I have a green silk I believe would be most becoming, but it will have to be altered."

Jo nodded silently. It mattered little what she said or felt. Her course had been set.

Chapter Four

A hazy sun shone in the early morning sky. Jo rode onward, determined on her path. She didn't look back. She didn't dare.

She chose the path that ran straight to Miss Hazel's house. Most times when she called on her old mammy, she would take a roundabout way to disguise her visits. It had been another place Wade and she had met each other.

Oh, how she longed for Miss Hazel's arms about her. When her father had left her with Grandpa Henry, it had been the only comfort she had for such a long time.

Her father had left the older black woman in Charleston when he departed the city. He had no need for her with Jo firmly set within the Buchanans' household. Since her grandfather had emphatically refused to take Miss Hazel within his home, her father had set up his old servant not far from Jo…close enough for Jo to visit.

Little less than three miles down the road toward Charleston, Miss Hazel lived in a log cabin. It sat a stretch from the road's edge. On her right, woods crowded the view filled with oak, maple, and walnut trees, covered with Spanish moss. On her left, there were unawakened fields. Within the next few weeks, slaves would litter the area and plant for the new harvest.

A little farther on, the dirt road opened to a small clearing. The sight of Miss Hazel's home bought her to a halt. Not much to look at: just a whitewashed wooden house with chickens running wild in the front yard. A water barrel sat out by the porch and clothes hung on a line out back, far from the outhouse.

This was Miss Hazel's home, of which she took great pride. The elderly lady had grown up in a small slave hut on her master's property. Like most slaves, the cabins had been shared with others. Crowded and filthy, it had only one room with a dirt floor and open windows…a miserable place in both the winter and summer.

Miss Hazel now lived in a house with glass panes and wooden floor. An iron stove and a dry sink comprised the kitchen. A brick chimney in each room warmed the cabin during the winter. A quilt she made with her own hand covered her bedstead. A table with two straight back chairs and a semblance of an old settee filled the living area.

Most Sundays found Miss Hazel fixing fried chicken dinners for her company, mostly visiting slaves from the neighboring estates, which included the Montgomerys'. There was a reason Miss Hazel lived here. It was near her son, Heyward.

Her master sold him when he was only ten to the Montgomerys. Miss Hazel never talked about that time in her life, except her heart soared when Papa bought her this place to be close to Hayward.

"Life's been good to me…I get to watch my family. Most don't get that."

Jo knew that Miss Hazel considered her family, too. Jo found solace with that fact.

Jo dismounted and walked up the three planked steps. Most days Jo would find Miss Hazel rocking on her rickety old rocking chair. She wasn't there this morning. Too early.

"Miss Jo, think. You still have time to get back to the house before anyone misses you."

Jo glanced back over her shoulder. "I've quite made up my mind. I won't be humiliated in that manner. To…go to Wade's wedding! It is something I could not bear…"

Her voice faded as she choked back tears. The sudden sharp memory of her loss swept back upon her. The hurt Wade had inflicted in her was a fresh wound that only time would heal, if ever. She knew only she had to leave…no matter the cost.

"Miss Jo, I helped you in this madness. I helped you deceive Mr. Temple, but this has to stop. I had Eudgo deliver your message about withdrawing your money…never did I imagine the wild scheme would work. I liked to have died when Eudgo brought back the satchel filled with what you requested."

There was more than a hint of reproach in Gillie's words, but Jo ignored it. She had been desperate for money. For what she had planned, she would have need of it…at least until she found her papa.

Moreover, it had been a calculated risk. Hadn't Charlotte teased her so, going on that she was too clever by half?

"Momma says gentlemen don't like clever women and Jo, you act too clever most of the time. Momma says a girl should be ignorant and act more ignorant than she is."

At Madame Tamline's French School for Young Ladies in Charleston, she had excelled in the schoolroom. She had heard, at times, one would wonder who was teaching the class. Why, it was the reason Charlotte Montgomery had become her best friend. Charlotte hadn't the aptitude in the classroom. Jo offered to help Charlotte. They had been friends ever since...until now.

Gillie had been with her at school, also. Gillie had been at her side since that awful day she had almost drowned. Papa had been outraged at the stunt Harry Lee pulled. So livid, he bought the small imp outright and gave her to Jo.

Gillie was an orphan slave of her grandfather's at the time she had almost drowned. Her mother had been a house servant in the Charleston household. From rumors, Jo gathered Gillie's mother had been disturbed for a time before she walked in front of a carriage. Grace Ann whispered it hadn't been an accident.

Having only been a toddler, Gillie had been an outcast in the house. She hadn't talked for years. When Jo had met her, she spoke sparingly and only when spoken to...the poor thing. She had been a tiny mite, but such a lovely, sweet child.

The day Harry Lee held Gillie over the railing at the Battery was etched into her memory. Her heart froze at the sight. It had been the first day she had met her cousins. She remembered the excitement playing on the Battery until that moment...when Gillie's scream ripped through her when Harry Lee dropped her...

Moreover, Harry Lee made no apologies for his behavior.

"She's Grandfather's. One day she'll be mine. I can do what I want with her."

Jo had been sickened. Gillie had been nothing more than a piece of property. But her papa had remedied the situation by giving Gillie to her...not as a slave. Papa had such strong feelings against slavery. He would never have given her a slave. She remembered clearly her father's words.

"She is your companion," Papa said.

"As a friend to be with me always," Jo reasoned at the thought.

"Yes, Jo. So you may never be alone."

Then he had left. She may not have been alone, but she felt so lonely, if not for Gillie and Miss Hazel. It was the reason she couldn't leave without seeing Miss Hazel...the reason she was taking Gillie with her.

Jo reached back and squeezed Gillie's hand. "Gillie, I told you that Mr. Temple wouldn't question the note. All I had to say was that I was certain he would understand the need to be discreet and the rush of the matter."

Gillie looked at Jo. Gillie didn't have to say she was worried. It illuminated from her large, telling eyes. "You're going to find yourself in trouble. That you are."

"I have it planned out. I just...I just need time away from here..."

"Child, child, what have you gone and done now?"

Jo turned to see Miss Hazel emerged in the open doorway. Jo didn't hesitate. She ran into her old mammy's arms.

The weight of the world lifted and Jo lost control of her emotions. She sobbed, uncontrollably. Miss Hazel held Jo for a piece until she took Jo by the shoulders.

Miss Hazel wasn't a small woman, but rather tall and big boned with huge, shrewd eyes. Time had whitened her hair, which she kept pulled back tightly in a bun. Despite her years, her dry wrinkled hands held Jo strong and firm in her grasp. She shook her head sadly.

"Tell Miss Hazel about it. What has happened?" Miss Hazel looked around Jo at Gillie, who held a wicket valise in her hand.

"I'm going away...to Papa...I can't stay here..." Jo swallowed back her tears. "Oh, Miss Hazel, Wade left me...he lied to me...he told me he was going to marry me...but he's not...he's...he's marrying Clarissa Wragg tomorrow!"

Again, Jo burst into tears. This time Miss Hazel would have none of it.

"Dry those tears, child. Ain't gonna bring him back. He's not the first lying, deceitful man and he won't be the last. Now sit down here and tell Miss Hazel all about it. From the look of ya, you haven't eaten a thing. You must be hungry. I'll make some breakfast while you talk."

Jo helped Miss Hazel fixed biscuits and gravy. Miss Hazel made the best biscuits for miles around. As she took the biscuits out of the stove, Jo wiped beading sweat from her brow. It was going to be a hot one today.

All her instincts told her she needed to leave promptly to make the train to Atlanta, but she hesitated. It was so hard to leave Miss Hazel.

"Honey child, sit down. There's ain't no need to rush. I smell a storm coming. You don't wanna be out in the middle of it. So sit right down there. Won't hurt nothin'."

"I have to go soon, Miss Hazel." Jo eased down into the chair. "I have to make the afternoon train. I'll eat and then I'll have to go. I'll be back as soon as I find Papa. He'll fix everything for me when he hears what happened."

The old lady's sharp eyes looked directly at Jo. "Ya only fooling yourself if you think your Papa is going to be happy. He wanted only one thing when he left you with your grandfather and that was to see that you were married all proper."

"Gracious, Miss Hazel, what did you expect me to do?" Jo defended herself. "Everyone hates me. Clarissa Wragg is telling lies about me to excuse Wade. Grace Ann says she has called me a trollop…"

Jo found her voice shaking, and then faded to nothingness.

"Oh, honey child, you have made a mess of things, but it happens. If ya run now, it will only get worse. Everything that lady is saying will be believed. Ya won't be coming back."

Jo found she was unable to speak. Miss Hazel's words sunk deep within her. She lowered her head and whispered, "I can't. I can't take their accusing eyes on me."

"If ya go, ya'll never be able to show your face in these parts again. Ya know how it is. Besides, child, I ain't raised no coward."

Oh, Jo wanted to say, *but you have. I'm a coward.*

Suddenly, Jo heard horses riding up. She glanced around. Where was Gillie? Where was Miss Hazel's boy, Lark?

"Miss Hazel, what have you done?"

Miss Hazel didn't answer. She didn't have to…the door swung open.

Startled, she watched Lieutenant Smythe walk into the room. He wore no uniform, but fitted trousers and a blousy shirt. He ran his hand through his disheveled hair. His dark eyes flared his anger…at her. In that instant, he seemed unnaturally big, as he had years before…

Jo took a step back. Her hand covered her mouth in disbelief. She didn't know why but her every instinct screamed to run. This man was a danger to her.

She forced herself to breathe. Her focus was so intent on Cullen, she barely saw the other who walked in with him. His companion was shorter and walked with a slight limp. His face had a semblance of a smile, which softened his gray eyes. He wore a hat, which he took off when he entered into the home, exposing his much lighter hair, almost white.

Jo knew him well enough: Wade's younger brother, Andrew Montgomery.

"Miss Jo, I couldn't let you leave." Miss Hazel's irritation flared. "It ain't right. It ain't!" Directing her attention on Gillie, who silently eased back into the cabin, Miss Hazel snapped, "I told you, girl, we needed Master Wade!"

Oh, Good Lord, Miss Hazel had sent for Wade! Wade, who had deserted her! Oh, she had disappointed Miss Hazel! Her mammy wanted her to marry the man who would be master of Magnolia Bluff.

Jo pressed her lips tightly together and closed her eyes. She wanted nothing more than for the ground to open up and swallow her. Voices surrounded her, but she couldn't make out who said what… Her chest heaved heavily…

Noises blended all together. For a moment, she was back in time…on the Battery the first day with her cousins. There had been a parade. Drums beat in rhythm; the excited rambling of people around her; the horses' hooves clicking over the stone streets; the barking of orders from the man who led his regiment sitting tall upon his white horse. The soldiers rode in sync with each other. Nary a head of a horse hung down, as if they themselves served in the regiment.

After it passed, Papa let her play with the other children…strangers who were her kin and their friends…laughing, giggling, and singing at the top of their voices. Grace Ann was there with her pretty set curls, sitting in a wooden railed wagon pushed by a couple of young blackies. Charlotte joined in along with a bunch of happy, fun-loving children, made of black and white.

It was the first time Jo laid eyes on Gillie. Smaller than the rest, she ran behind everyone, but the little one laughed…Jo remembered her laugh. Then the clouds darkened, threatening rain…and Harry Lee appeared.

The tallest in the group of boys who walked down the Battery toward them, his thick auburn hair escaped out from the bottom of his hat. His mouth frowned with the subtle evidence of facial stubble, as if he attempted to grow out a mustache. His eyes glared at Josephine, cold and dry.

Jo sensed the stirring of anxiety with his presence. She had no memory of how or why Harry Lee grabbed hold of Gillie and hung her over the railing. Cruelty…nastiness…downright meanness…some kind of sport to impress his friends. He seemed to take great joy in Gillie's screams.

No one attempted to stop him. No one seemed to dare. She would never forget the look on his face…pure evil…he laughed and then released the defenseless girl.

"Miss Hazel, it wasn't my fault. I went to Heyward like you said…"

Gillie's voice brought Jo back to the present. She watched Gillie edge back behind the men to be by her side.

"He refused to get Master Wade…"

"Well he should," Cullen said bitingly. There was a cold glitter in his eyes as he glanced around the small room. His eyes lit upon the valise, and then back at her. "I had thought you innocent in this whole mess. Only now to discover, you are a vixen. This is what you had planned? Enticing Wade to leave with you?"

There was a long pause before she uttered, "Vixen?"

Vixen! Jo suppressed the flash of anger that went through her. It would do no good to explain to this man what she had intended.

"You had me, Miss Wright. I believed you had been wronged. You must have thought me a fool for defending your honor in the manner I did."

"I had thought you a gentleman. It shows how wrong one can be." Her tone was steady and cold. She glanced over at Andrew, who had remained silent.

Andrew's gaze lowered at her glare. He seemed disturbed. She wasn't surprised. Charlotte had told her that Andrew blamed her for his limp. It had been her fault. He would never have broken his ankle if she hadn't insisted someone jump over to save Gillie.

Andrew had been with Harry Lee that day. He had watched Harry Lee without a word. Jo screamed, cried and rushed to the railing. Irritated, Andrew pushed Jo aside. He crawled under the rail and jumped down onto the beach. He had fallen on a rock and collapsed down in excruciating pain. He rolled on his side and clutched his ankle.

His ankle had been broken. It had been a bad break. Even after it healed, Andrew walked with a limp. He had never forgiven her.

"Could you not resist coming to humiliate me, Andrew?" Jo asked. "The Montgomery boys have come to save the family from little old me?"

"It was not like that, Josephine," Andrew said in a low tone. "We only want to stop you from ruining your life…"

"Don't! Don't say that!" she cried. "I'm tired of hearing that everyone is trying to protect me! I am not a nitwit! No one….no one is worried about me…only themselves. Be honest! It is your family…Wade…that you are concerned about. Not me."

"We want only to contain the situation."

Jo stared at Cullen. His voice was so icy it chilled her soul.

"Ain't right. Master Wade promised her he married her. He did. I hear' him myself right out there." Miss Hazel pointed to the porch; her hand waved at Cullen in a mad fashion. Jo had never seen her so worked up. "Ain't right. Master Wade wanted to marry Miss Josephine. He said so…"

Suddenly, it was not herself that was of concern. The old lady's voice shook. Her blurred eyes betrayed her misery. Then her feeble hand gripped tight to the table. It cut Jo's heart to the core.

"Miss Hazel!"

Jo started toward the woman, but her progress was halted. A firm hand gripped her elbow. Cullen wheeled her around to face him.

"Let your girl see to her," he demanded. He gestured for Gillie.

Distressed, Jo watched Gillie obey the man few would question. Gillie wrapped her arms around the old woman and led her to the back room and her bed.

Jo wanted nothing more than to jerk her arm back, but she didn't dare. He appeared quite displeased.

Cullen glanced in the direction of Andrew. "Stay here a moment. Let us know if Miss Wright is needed while she shows me around the farm."

* * * *

Cullen fell into step behind Jo as she walked down the steps.

"You didn't send for Wade?" he asked.

Jo paused and looked back at him. His face was void of emotion, but his actions told more than words. Her answer held importance to him.

"I came only to say goodbye to a dear friend. It seems that Miss Hazel held to Wade's word more than I."

"You have no intention of disrupting Wade's wedding?"

Her eyes flamed. "Why do you insist it is my intention? Do you not think I have some pride? Wade lied to me. He made promises he could not keep. I want nothing more to do with him…ever!"

She briefly thought of running from him, but it would be a useless gesture. *Why did he keep pressing her so?* The answer, though, appeared to please him that she had not sought out Wade.

"Come, let us talk." He extended his arm. "Tell me, how is it that your mammy lives close to you?"

41

Given no choice, she accepted and walked down the dirt road with him. "The farm is hers. It was payment from Papa. Miss Hazel said it was perfect, being between her two babies."

"You confuse me, Miss Wright."

"Miss Hazel considers me hers as well as her son. Heyward, Wade's man, is her son. Miss Hazel came to Papa when her master lost money gambling to Papa, but Papa couldn't free Heyward. He had already been sold to you Montgomerys. Papa was quite upset that you Montgomerys wouldn't sell him."

"Your father freed your mammy?"

"Papa hates slavery, Lieutenant Smythe. Miss Hazel was never a slave to Daddy. I told you it is the same with Gillie. She is my companion."

"Miss Wright, it is not my intention to dispute your claims, but this farm is owned by your father, not Miss Hazel. Though I admire your stance on slavery, I would ascertain that neither Miss Hazel nor your companion are free."

"Then you have been misinformed." Jo halted and pulled back her arm. Her nerves frayed. She could take no more. "Why...why, Lieutenant, do you feel the need to bait me? If you believe you know the answer, why ask me? Why...why do you feel the need to interfere with my life?"

"My actions are intended to help, not harm."

"You feel guilt because of Wade? Well, I release you from any guilt you may feel. I am leaving...I am going to find Papa...I want nothing more to do with any Montgomery...," she lashed out, frowning with suspicion. "You...come bounding into Miss Hazel's, with Andrew of all people."

"Andrew came because he thought he might reason with you. Nothing more."

"You should know better than I that he hates me."

"Why would you say such a thing? His foot? You believe he blames you for his limp? It would be foolish to do so, to blame another for one's own actions. It was an accident. Nothing more."

"Were you not angry with me that day also? Do not lie to me. I remember well your words and your eyes...you frightened me. You were so irritated with me."

His tense expression eased...softened. "I suppose to a child it might have seemed so. You have my heartfelt apology for my actions. I had thought you acted recklessly, endangering others. I had not recognized the circumstance until much later."

"Since you returned, I have dreamed of it often…of you rescuing me…of Andrew agonizing in pain. I meant no harm to anyone. I wanted only to save Gillie…"

"Miss Wright, if Andrew holds resentment about his accident, it is not you he holds responsible."

She glanced askance at him. "What do you want from me?"

"Miss Wright, you must be aware that I have presented myself to your grandfather. I have asked for your hand. It does not bode well to discover that the woman I have offered for is running away."

"Do not distort the offer. You did so—"

"I did so with the utmost sincerity and seriousness. I am not in the habit of offering for a woman's hand, since I have never done so before you. Do not take it lightly."

She could tell he was most serious. "I'm afraid you have me at a disadvantage. You must realize that only a couple of weeks ago I believed I was to marry your cousin…I…"

"You believe yourself in love with him," Cullen said with a sudden smile that told her he thought he had her at an advantage. "Tell me then why I do not believe that you even know what love is. My cousin has a reputation for accumulating hearts. Most females cannot see behind his smile.

"Granted, you fascinated him more than any other. Do you want to know what I believe? I believe that marriage scared him and he sought an escape."

Temper flashed again. "You believe I was no more than a diversion."

"I believe he convinced himself you were more."

"That is why you have offered to sacrifice yourself. To fall on your sword to save your family face."

He stepped closer. She retreated a step and readied herself to bolt, but he didn't permit it. He caught her arm and pivoted her around abruptly.

"Miss Wright, you have the most annoying way of antagonizing me."

His arms wrapped about her and pulled her into an embrace. She had no time to protest. His lips were upon hers. She made no resistance, being taken by complete surprise. Her frigid response thawed in the warmth of his arms.

Her body reacted in a way most worrisome. Tentative. Curious. Then with a primitive instinct. The war between her mind and body was lost. Her lips softened under his and he ravished her mouth. Shock tensed through her. Every fiber of her being was encompassed by this man.

Slowly, she realized his lips had released hers. The world once more became reality. Her eyes opened to find him studying her face.

"If I am to fall upon a sword, I will do so willingly," he whispered so close she felt his breath against her. "Now tell me what you had planned, Josephine."

Her name rolled off his lips as if he sang a song. Mesmerized, she didn't want him to talk. She wanted him to kiss her again, but it would never do…

"I can't." She pushed back out of his arms. She shook her head, fighting back emotions that welled within her. Her life had spiraled out of her control. "You shouldn't have."

This man…had kissed her in the middle of a road without a thought they could have been seen. Moreover, she hadn't cared. She had enjoyed his kiss…reveled in his arms.

A tide of feelings stirred within her. Bewilderment…helplessness…longing. What had he done to her?

Wade had never kissed her in that manner. Their meetings had been arranged with the utmost care. His kisses had been stolen with the fear of being caught weighing on both their minds. She realized that Wade hadn't wanted this for her…for her reputation to be tarnished, for he had known that he would have to leave her in the end.

Lieutenant Smythe…Cullen gave no thought to what could be said. The arrogant cad!

For a moment, they faced each other. Neither moved, but his eyes bore into hers as if he could read her thoughts.

"Is it so hard to believe I am to visit my papa?"

"Do not lie to me, Miss Wright. If you leave today, nothing but scorn or worse will await your return."

Her eyes blazed at his assertion. His expression remained firm, but he did not accuse her of sending for Wade again.

Jo's pride emerged. "Perhaps I will not return."

"It will not be a choice if you go on this foolhardy venture. You run, then all of Charleston will believe the rumors."

She wanted to hit him for the insult, but it would be a useless gesture. He spoke the truth. She lowered her gaze to hide the angry tears welling…angry at the world…Wade…Cullen… but none more so than herself.

Her weakness had stained her family's name as her mother had done years ago. The difference, though, was her father had married her mother. She stood alone in her disgrace.

Suddenly, he reached over and lifted her chin upward, giving her no option but to look at him straight in his eyes.

"You have been compromised by your relationship with my cousin. Miss Wragg has made it a vendetta against you. She will not cease her ramblings. Though it is his character that has raised suspicions about your relationship, not yours. You understand that the only way to quiet the talk is an honorable marriage."

"If I am not here…"

"It will not cease. Do you find me so disagreeable that you choose to run?"

She could not find words to answer him. She tried to turn, but he held his grip firm.

"You will want for nothing, Miss Wright, with your marriage to me. I believe you are not adverse as you might think."

His look affected her in a manner she hadn't expected. His fingers lightly touched her cheek. A shiver swept through her body. His head dipped again and he kissed her.

"Tell me, my sweet magnolia."

"It is not you," she whispered with the greatest reluctance. "They aren't going to accept your proposal. They…they are trying to arrange a marriage to another. I heard them talk of Holt Miller. I cannot take that. I have heard how he treated his first wife."

She shuddered on the thought of that man touching her in the manner that Cullen held her.

"So it is he who you are running from," he breathed. Something flickered behind his eyes that told that the answer pleased him. "Why do you suppose that your grandfather will turn down my offer?"

She hesitated. "You're a Yankee. Mr. Whitney told Grandfather it would never do."

"Yet, I'm good enough to save face until Miller can be convinced to take you as a bride." He laughed. "Devil be had! You are a little vixen. You took your money to keep from having any dowry…"

"It is not funny!" she cried. "I need the money for the journey. I will not have you making a joke of my life…"

"But you will have me."

She stared at him, completely mystified on how defenseless she felt against him.

45

"Look at me, Josephine. You will attend the wedding festivities tomorrow and stop all this foolishness. It will only make matters worse."

"It will be you who will make it better?"

He ignored her question. "We will escort you back to the Groves. I will keep your valise, of course."

"Of course."

At this point, she hadn't another choice. She needed to think. She couldn't do so with him so close.

Chapter Five

Jo ran along the edge of the garden. The rain had stopped much earlier, but the ground was wet. Moreover, the sun cast a reddish tinge to the sky as it lowered over the horizon. She hadn't much time.

She glanced back over her shoulder nervously. Behind Jo, Gillie nodded to her mistress. No one was following. Jo breathed easier. She didn't need any more difficulties. She had a need to talk to him before…before the morning…for answers…closure…she wasn't sure.

As she rounded the bend, only stillness greeted her. She was alone.

"Heyward said Master Wade would be here. He will come, Miss Jo."

Jo made no response, but wandered over to the garden bench. Doubts crept in that he would truly make an appearance, but there again, it had not been her who asked to meet. He had.

When she returned to the Groves, Gillie relayed a message from Wade to meet one last time. Heyward had given it to her as she waited for Lieutenant Smythe and Master Andrew to ready to go to Miss Hazel's.

Her heart sank. She must be mad to be here, waiting to see the man she once loved. Loved…because she would not allow herself to feel anything other than anger for him…not after the hurt he had inflicted. Moreover, the thrill of a clandestine meeting with Wade was gone, replaced with a turmoil of emotions.

She had always prided herself in her ability to reason her way out of a situation. More than once, she had been told she was too much like her father. She had always taken pride in being like Papa, though she realized most had not meant it as praise. But it did not take intelligence to decipher she would not be walking away from this unscathed.

47

She should never have allowed Cullen to talk her into staying. *Oh, whatever was she going to do!*

How foolish she had been to believe Wade's assumption that they could have been married. She reprimanded herself greatly for allowing her heart to rule her good sense. It gnawed at her soul…for no matter how foolish she had been with Wade, never once did she suspect the scandal exploding around her.

How had it happened? What had they done to raise suspicions? The whispers that circled her were bad, far worse than anything that had really occurred. This Jo knew, even though neither Grace Ann nor Gillie had hinted to what was being said…she saw it in their eyes.

Jo had dealt with that look in the past…after she had leaped over the wall to save Gillie. Grandpa Henry had said she had caused a spectacle of herself; Aunt Sybil said she needed to learn to be a lady. But back then, Papa had been by her side.

"Jo reacted to someone in need, not only a small child, but Mr. Andrew Montgomery. I agree that the proper etiquette did not occur to her at that point…for both survived."

Papa had been her protector…*Oh, where was he now?*

She had never considered that it would have been frowned upon to make that leap. Why had she not stopped to think of the ramifications of her actions? When she was a small child, her mamma said Jo reacted with her heart.

Miss Hazel said it was more that Jo saw the world as she wanted it to be. "Ya always thinking others think like ya. Ain't that way, Miss Jo."

Was that still her problem?

When she made the leap over the wall, her one thought was to help the little one sprawled out on the ground as the water rushed over her. She remembered praying she was still alive—her heart pounded so hard she thought it would burst through her chest—and then Gillie choked and coughed.

Andrew had dragged himself to her side by that time, his ankle swollen and disfigured. It hurt to look at, but he made no complaint. A wave broke over them and drenched the small group. Andrew had hold of both of them and refused to let go.

Spitting out the taste of salt water, Jo helped drag Gillie back to the wall. Andrew lifted the small one up to waiting arms, but it left them with a problem. The storm worsened and brought in rough waves, along with a riptide that wanted to pull everything in its wake out to sea.

When Harry Lee returned to pull up the next one, Jo understood only one thing. Andrew could not fight against the storm, not with his injury. He needed help up. This she did over his objections.

"Do you want to die a gentleman?" she questioned, as the water rose higher. "It won't take a moment for someone to pull me up once you are set. You need help."

She had seen his reluctance, but he could not argue with her reasoning...only...only Harry Lee hadn't saved her. He missed her hand and she had fallen back into the sea; Cullen leapt into the storm-ridden waters to pull her out to safety...

Now...she was drowning again.

"Miss Jo, I don't mean to add to your issues, but Heyward asked me—"

"You do not have to say the words. I understand—truly I do, Gillie. I will discuss your intentions. He will understand."

"It's all I ask, Miss Jo. I know everything you're going through. Truly I do," Gillie said. "I don't want to add to your troubles. I know you will try. It is only we had hoped..."

Gillie's voice faded. Guilt cut through Jo like a knife. To give hope and then so cruelly take it away was unforgiveable in Jo's eyes. Gillie asked for so little.

She had known there had always been an attraction between her Gillie and Heyward, but Heyward staunchly refused to act upon it until Wade had begun courting Jo. It had been one of the reasons Jo had thought Wade would never have deserted her in this manner—Wade had told Heyward he was going to marry her.

Finally, Heyward felt safe to commit without fear of losing the one he loved. It was a fear most slaves experienced. The law stated slaves could not marry in the same manner as whites.

Grandpa Henry had declared it was God-ordained. It was worrisome to Jo. Slaves *married* only by permission of their owners, reciting promises instead of vows not of "until death do us part" but "until distance."

Miss Hazel had told her that was how it was with Heyward's father. Her master sold him out of state. Forcibly separated, she had never seen her *husband* again. Now, Heyward faced the fear he had fought so hard not to face: losing Gillie.

"I will fix it for you, Gillie," Jo promised. "There is no reason to keep the two of you apart."

Gillie grew pallid; her eyes drooped. "I fear there's nothing you can do, Miss Jo."

Never in her life had Jo felt so helpless, ashamed…and embarrassed that her reckless behavior had caused Gillie pain.

Jo straightened as a horse and rider emerged out of the wooded area. Wade had come. She had thought she would not have been affected by his presence. She had been wrong. One look and her heart stirred.

He was dressed formally in mustard-colored trousers and black coat. His squared jaw shadowed with bristles of his unshaven face. He thrust his hand through the thick blond hair; his pale blue eyes stared at her in a cool, distant way.

Suddenly she had doubts about the meeting. Had he come to torture her? Could he not leave her alone to reconcile her fate? She watched him dismount. As he stepped toward her, she rose and held her hand up in front of her to halt his progress.

"Why are you here? Have you not done enough damage to me?" The bluntness of her voice relayed her seriousness.

"I beg your indulgence. Heyward gave me the message from Miss Hazel. You cannot hold it against me if I profess I was concerned."

His words poured out in a charming, well-bred Southern drawl. How handsome he looked. It tore at her heart.

"Then you would have also known that your cousin, Lieutenant Smythe, handled the situation." She tried to sound calm. "He kept me from running, if that is your concern…which it should not be."

"I came to soothe your fears." He gave her a slow smile. "You must know how it pains me to see you treated in such fashion. I had no wish for you to have to endure this wrath."

"Is that the reason you came? To ease your conscience? Have you convinced yourself that a few pretty words will relieve you of any culpability?"

"Dammit, Jo, I know it will not. I came because my cowardice has made matters worse. I should have come instead of Cullen—"

"You have never been a coward, Wade. So do not insult me telling me so," she interrupted coolly. She glared at him suspiciously. "Perhaps, though, now I see the reason for your presence. You have come to save your cousin from me."

"It should have been me to have come. Cullen should not have been involved."

Jo sighed heavily. "Why? If it had been you, Harry Lee would have called you out. It would have only been made worse, for one of you would have been killed. At least…at least Cullen could offer what you promised."

Wade was strangely silent for a moment. He pressed his lips together tightly as if in thought.

"Say what you have to say, Wade," she insisted. "I do not need to listen that I'm the cause of this pain."

"It is not the reason I sent Cullen," he said in a hoarse, ragged voice. "If I came, I would not have walked away from you."

He reached out and touched her hand, and then her face. She caught her breath. For a moment, time descended into a reservoir of memories. Her soul ached for what had been lost…one touch unlocked the forbidden passion. She had no will to stop him as his arms rounded her…something too strong to resist. His mouth found hers…the hurt and pain momentarily vanished in his embrace…until in the far reaches of her mind, she rebelled. He belonged to another; to be married on the morrow.

"Wade, no," she choked out. "I can't do this."

"I need you, Jo," he implored. "Come with me. I know of a deserted house not far from here where we can be alone. Let me love you as I desire…I know you desire it also."

"To become what, Wade? A common doxie." Shaking, she pushed against his chest. She whispered, "It's over. Us. It should never have been. It was a mistake."

"It was never a mistake." He caught her hand and held it fast. "It is what gnaws at my soul for what we could have been." His eyes beseeched her, but he released his hold. "I told you I am a weak creature, but you…you have my heart. I will always love you."

"But it will not stop you from marrying another."

"Duty and honor bounds me to another. This I know you understand, for you are as I."

She wished she could have protested…to say family and honor meant nothing. But in truth, it meant everything.

Shaken more than she cared to admit, she lowered her gaze and took a step back.

"I have upset you further. It was not my intention, Jo. I want to ease your burden." He paused. His voice altered. "I want to address the rumors of the marriage that is being arranged for you."

She looked strangely at him. "It is not your concern."

"Please, Jo, listen. I won't allow you to marry that brute Miller." He cleared his throat and scowled. "I have met with Taz Foster. He is willing to offer for you."

She stood very still, unbelieving his gall at such an action. She said stiffly, "It is not yours…"

"It is," he said forcibly. "I know that my cousin has acted on behalf of my family. He is an honorable man, but it is not his to shoulder. I don't believe your family will have an objection to Taz. He comes from a good family. He will be at the ball tomorrow night."

She fell silent, fearful she would show her emotions. He remembered that Taz was her friend, but for him to have made such an arrangement! He looked upon her with more compassion than she was willing to accept. How dare he pity her! Her temper rose at his arrogance.

She shook her head. "So you have set in mind for me a husband. Not you...not your cousin. Why ever, sir, I believe you find me beneath you!"

"It is not like that. Taz is a good man. I imagine you will find satisfaction in helping with his endeavors. He has plans for his school."

"That is how you see me? A schoolteacher?"

"I see you content, surrounded by children," he said. "Clarissa thought..."

Jo whirled and strode angrily away on his utterance. What a ninny she had been! He had talked of her to Clarissa! He was as Grace Ann warned. A manipulator! The scoundrel!

She wanted to scream! He had left her for a woman who had branded a scarlet letter on Jo's forehead. It was this woman he talked to her about. The nerve!

Instead, she suppressed a sudden need to lash out at the man before her. His instinct to protect the woman who would soon be his wife weighed heavily on his heart. The realization cut her to the core...that damnable honor.

Then suddenly, comprehension sank deep within her. It was not her he had come to shield from scandal. He had come to contain the scandal. He had come to contain her!

"I'm not your concern, Wade. Go home and prepare for your day. Ease your mind. I will not make a scene. I refuse to disgrace my family further."

She looked back at him, hoping he did not see her pain. She drew in a deep breath. "But the reason I came to meet with you was not about us, Wade. I came because of Gillie and Heyward."

His eyes hardened. "What of Gillie and Heyward?"

"You know what I mean. Don't pretend you do not." She glanced back at her companion.

Gillie stood at the end of the bridge, loyally waited. Jo watched the wide-eyed mulatto girl cast down her eyes demurely. Beside Gillie, Heyward reached over and took her hand in his, gently touching her.

Jo looked back at Wade. "They are in love with each other. We promised them a life together..."

"There is little we can do about that now."

Jo lifted her chin. "Surely there is something...Wade. I gave my word to Gillie. I refuse to go back on *my* word."

"Tell me, what would you have me do? Do you want to rid yourself of Gillie? Have her become a member of my household?"

"You promised me that Heyward would be freed." Her gaze pierced into Wade, unflinching in her desire to see to the happiness of the couple. "Gillie is already free."

"Josephine, you are being childish. Have you not comprehended that Gillie is not free, but a slave as much as Heyward?"

"You lie," she cried. "My father..."

"My dear, your father is a liar and a cheat. You have been misled."

She crossed over in front of him and slapped him. "How dare you! Papa is a gentleman."

He grabbed her wrist and pulled her to face him. "I dare...yet knowing everything I do, I still fell in love with you. Do you know what is wrong with you, Jo? You live in a fantasy world where everyone thinks and feels as you...it is not like that. I wish...I wish I could have given you the world as you see it.

"Now, though, you need to face reality. If we had married, Heyward and Gillie could have well married if they felt the need. It can't happen now, for I know you will never let Gillie leave your side."

"You won't release Heyward?"

"You silly fool!" His frustration showed. "Heyward isn't mine. As is everything around me, he is Grandfather's."

"Your words have flowed like honey this day, Wade Montgomery. I was foolish to ever have believed you. Now, you insult Papa, yet have not looked at yourself." She jerked her hand back. "Leave. Do not return. I don't want or need your help."

He hesitated. Then reluctantly, he walked to his horse and mounted. "I am sorry, Josephine. I never meant to hurt you. Tomorrow I will wed another. I will honor my commitment, but not without cost. I will live with the regret it is not you."

It was a declaration of his pain, but she refused to give to him the forgiveness he sought. She remained silent and watched him ride out of sight.

Chapter Six

The hour was late. Night had crept in with its stealthy cloak of darkness. Cullen sat alone on the veranda and smoked a cigar. Wade had not returned to Magnolia Bluff…where he had gone, Cullen hadn't a clue.

Matter of fact, Cullen hadn't seen his cousin since he had taken care of the incident regarding Josephine. He grew concerned. The façade Wade had created around himself that he had accepted his fate stood in question. Cullen worried that second thoughts about the lifelong commitment Wade had promised to a woman he did not love had emerged.

He had assured his grandfather and Andrew there was no cause to be alarmed. He only wished he was as confident as he sounded.

Ebony shadows bustled around him as they prepared for the activities on the morrow. Magnolia Bluff would be seen in its glory, hosting the ceremony. Neither Clayton nor Wragg had spared any expense in displaying the union between their families.

Despite their magnificent home in Charleston, the Wraggs owned no plantation. The affair had need of open spaces to celebrate to the fullest, giving that the whole of Charleston would attend the grand celebration.

Taking a puff of cigar, he released a circle of smoke over his head. Deep in his thoughts, he didn't hear tiny footsteps walking toward him.

"Wade has left me, hasn't he?"

Cullen glanced over his shoulder in the direction of the feminine voice. He shouldn't have been surprised to see Clarissa in the open doorway into the parlor. The whole of her family had been at Magnolia Bluff for the last few days in preparation for the wedding.

The dark-haired beauty walked toward him in her night robe and wrapper. Her long hair twisted into one long braid. He studied her for a long moment. Even in the dimmed light, he saw her puffy, reddened eyes.

"Wade. Are you talking of Wade?" Cullen faced her, but made no attempt to stand. He spoke without formally addressing her presence. He hadn't the energy to give false greetings. He was too tired.

"He hasn't returned and neither has his man."

She stared at him. At most times, she would have given him a dazzling smile, but she wasn't smiling. Gone was the mask she hid behind; fear illuminated in her eyes. Her frustration made known.

"It seems strange a bride to be questioning her husband before they have exchanged vows." Cullen shrugged casually. "I would have believed you would be sleeping, contemplating your day in the morning."

"Will there be a day?" In dramatic fashion, she fell down on her knees beside him. She grasped his hands and pleaded. "Find him. Please. Lieutenant, I have already lost Percival. It would break my heart to lose Wade also. I love him so."

"Love?" Cullen arched his eyebrow toward her. There were many words he would have used about his cousin's association with this woman. Love had not been one of them. Obligation. Duty. But not love. He withdrew his hand and rose. "I do not know what I can do for you, Miss Wragg."

"Clarissa, please, Lieutenant. We are to be family," she said in a voice which Cullen was certain often gave her the results she desired. "You have to find him. Convince him it is—"

"You want me to tell him he needs to hold to honor and duty." Suddenly, a perplexed frown crossed his face. "You are not considering threatening me. Tell me, what lengths would you go to get your way?"

She hurled a glare at him, immediately on the defensive. "How dare you! Have you forgotten that I am the injured party?"

"Please forgive me if I do not see it that way," Cullen said tersely and wondered why he even bothered to reply.

"Oh, you cad!" she declared. She raised her eyebrows sharply and looked at him through narrowing eyes. "I suppose I should not expect more from a Yankee—"

"Now you have resorted to explain my actions by calling me a Yankee," he cut her off abruptly. "May I remind *you* that I was born and raised here on this plantation. I am as much a Southerner as you. If, on

55

the other hand, you call me a Yankee because I dare to question what is going on around us…then I wear the title with pride."

"Oh, Good Lord! Don't let Papa hear you! I swear you are deliberately provoking me!" She rose and stood defiantly before him.

Cullen came to the conclusion that the lady feigned the innocence of a simpleton, ready to defend her belief in the Southern way of life with only the standard boring answers repeated a million times over the last few years.

"You may find me confused at your assertion. I know it has been you to have gone after Miss Wright in your mistaken belief she has done you harm, when in essence it has been you to have caused her grave damage." Cullen offered his perception freely. "It is what concerns you now…that Wade knows what you have done. That he may have gone off to find the happiness you fear you cannot give him."

"I wanted only to save him from that woman. Nothing more. My Aunt Sissy told me that some men need to be saved from themselves. That is what I intended to do."

"To save him from Josephine with vicious rumors? Do you understand the harm you have done to an innocent?" he chided her.

"Forgive me, Lieutenant, but it is my understanding that Miss Wright is far from innocent."

For a moment, he almost forgot it was a lady before him. His temper raged. "Explain yourself quickly, for my patience has been worn thin. I know Miss Wright and she is a lady…much more than the one before me."

Indignant, she sneered, "Then it is you who has been misled. I have it on good authority of her actions."

"Please enlighten me," he retorted. "For the way I see it, it could be no worse than you being alone with me at the moment…late at night…dressed…"

"Oh, Heavens!" She gasped in shock and clutched tight to the collar of her wrapper. "You could not think…believe…I would never! How dare you compare me to…to Miss Wright! Why, I was told she…she has...known a man!"

The declaration hung in the air. Good God! Someone had riled her to the point where the green-eyed monster surfaced within her and her claws emerged…riled her enough to have torn into Josephine's reputation.

"I do not know who told you such a vicious lie, but I assure you the lady I know would never compromise herself in the manner you believe," he snapped, exasperated. "You must know I have offered for the lady. I would not do so to one such as you suggest."

She refused to comment but stared at him in mute surprise. Her face paled; her breathing quickened. He saw readily she had not contemplated the consequences of her actions. She had thought only of herself.

"Calm yourself," he said finally. "I believe someone has purposefully given you false information."

"Are you certain?" she asked in a voice lower than a whisper. "Aunt Sissy says that devil women cast a spell on men when they use their feminine wiles upon them."

"Go to bed, Miss Clarissa." Cullen shook his head. "You are needlessly worrying. Wade will not disappoint you. He has given his word and without question will hold to it."

"It is only my nerves, I am certain," Clarissa conceded. With her lips pressed together tightly, she had the look of one wanting to ask one more question. Instead, she turned and walked back into the house.

* * * *

A short time later, Cullen walked toward the river. Each step reminded him of another time and place, the times in his youth when the three of them would sneak out of the house in the dead of the night. Lord, the things Percival had them do.

Cullen found Wade at the river's bank. He sat down along the roots of an old live oak and stared blankly in the darkness. The slow lapping of the water sent ripples along the Ashley River. The rain had stopped hours ago. Now, a bright waning moon hung high in the night's sky. Strange. He sensed a calming... a peace here.

Wade made no effort to acknowledge his presence, though Cullen knew full well he had to have heard him. Not far from his side, his loyal man, Heyward.

Heyward stood and made his way to Cullen. "Ain't doing nothin' but sitting thar, Lieutenant."

Cullen nodded. "Go back to the house and wait for him. I'll bring him up shortly."

"Yes, sir," Heyward said dutifully.

Cullen walked over to Wade. He said nothing, but took in the view. How many times aboard ship had he dreamed of this spot? He could still see Percival, standing buck naked along the edge of the water, taunting them to come for a midnight swim.

"Percival. He would have wanted me to marry Clarissa."

57

The silence broken, Cullen said, "Without a doubt, the family honor meant much to Percival. He did everything in his power to maintain it. That I know."

"He wanted to go into the Navy worse than either one of us," Wade said thoughtfully. "He wanted adventure. Instead, he stayed here to pacify Grandfather. Ironic, isn't it? That he should have died and we lived."

"Life is full of ironies."

"I suppose." Wade sighed heavily; then chuckled to himself. "When Clarissa professed her undying love to me, I found myself wondering if she had said the same to Percival. Then I came to the conclusion, it was only my being heir to Magnolia Bluff that she loved."

"It is not Magnolia Bluff she fancies herself in love with…it is you. You know she loves you. I don't believe her feelings are in question."

Wade made no concession to Cullen's statement. Instead, he said, "She will be a perfect mistress here at Magnolia Bluff. She has already had Grandfather give her a tour of the duties he wants her to perform…much to the chagrin of Mother. Mother told me later she would be returning to White Oaks after the wedding."

"It is that way with most families. No different than how most women feel. Moreover, I have found Clarissa to be no different than most belles in Charleston, except she is the most lovely."

"Grandfather tells me I am indeed fortunate. I could not ask for more."

"A beautiful wife who loves you. A large estate. Many envy you."

"I know…I know," Wade conceded. "I am not one to wallow in self-pity. I needed only a moment here…it is where I find peace when I think of Percival."

"Then it is a good thing. He should not be forgotten."

Wade rose. Taking the rock in his hand, he threw it far into the river. Both men heard it splash into the river's waters. Wade turned to his cousin.

"Grandfather will never forgive me. He holds it against me that Percival died…he wishes if it had to be one of us, it should have been me. Percival would never have disappointed him."

"That's not true, Wade…" Cullen protested.

Wade laughed a harsh snicker. "It is, Cullen, but know, I won't disappoint either Grandfather or Percival on the morrow. I will leave my melancholy here along the river bank and face my fate in the morning light."

"Wait." Cullen halted Wade. A devilish grin emerged on his face. "Does the rope still hang on the wide elm over the river's bend?"

Wade shook his head. "You're not thinking of…"

Cullen didn't wait for Wade to finish. He took off down along the river's edge. Wade was only a step behind his cousin. A sight to behold: two grown men running…laughing…playing as children would have done…one last time.

* * * *

In a small chapel on the grounds of Magnolia Bluff, the handsome and gallant Mr. Wade Montgomery exchanged vows with the ever lovely Miss Clarissa Wragg. A match ordained by the heavens above. Money and an old respected name united as one.

The sun climbed over the treetops in the east when bride and groom emerged from the church as husband and wife. Cullen's eyes followed the couple as they basked in the glory of their moment.

Wade kept his word and left the night's disillusionments behind him. Cullen stood up for Wade during the ceremony and watched his cousin proclaim his love for the woman by his side. His cousin had not faltered.

Later, outside of the church, Wade accepted congratulations with a smile and all his Southern charm. Clarissa looked radiant. Cullen was certain she had never looked more beautiful. Her happiness irradiated from her being.

She wore an exquisite ivory-colored silk with a wide gathered skirt that had been brought in from Paris for the occasion. The lace veil was edged with a floral motif. Her hair had been uplifted in the most fashionable of styles. Around her lovely neck, a cascading pearl necklace hung…a gift from her groom.

A buggy brought the happy couple up to the main house. After he stepped down, Wade turned and offered his arm to his bride. She looked up at him lovingly as she hung on his arm in a newly acquired confidence that came from being his wife.

Fine carriages and saddle horses filled the side of the front lawn by the time the church party returned from the ceremony. The house itself had been swarmed with a crowd of people. Guests waved to each other and called greetings. Children, white and black, played on the lawn. Pavilions had been placed near the magnolias and the giant oak.

Overhead, the sun shone down brightly on the gathering. When the reception line formed, Cullen stood close to the end and studied the proceedings. Wade placed one of his arms around Clarissa's waist, a loving gesture that was not lost upon his bride.

Cullen wondered at the complicity of the guests who seemed content to accept the happy couple. The whispers of Wade's misadventures were forgotten. Wade played his part; he would play his. If all continued as planned, soon the tongues of Charleston would be stilled.

Smoked pork and beef barbeque welcomed the wedding guests in the afternoon. The celebration ball would commence later in the evening with an elaborate dinner of turkey, ham with molasses, breads of all sorts, jams, jellies, fruits and gelatin. Clarissa had herself decorated the massive white wedding cake. Randolph Wragg had even arranged for ice to be delivered for homemade ice cream.

Cullen noticed that the Buchanan family had arrived, except for Grace Ann and…Josephine. Her arrival had been arranged for later tonight. A brief moment in the celebration, but one that held significance for both families involved.

He soon fell out of the reception line. He had heard the utterance Yankee one time too many after the guest stepped away from him. Shrugging it off, he found refreshment and took refuge under the giant oak.

"There he is."

Cullen turned. His grandfather strolled up with Thurman Bowdre, a representative of the South Carolina state assembly. Cullen recognized the man readily enough, one of the many outspoken orators of this state.

Bowdre held a reputation of being a younger version of the state's revered late senator, John Calhoun. Cullen had heard Bowdre held to Calhoun's beliefs in a state's rights to secede from the Union. Bowdre promised to follow in Calhoun's footsteps. He had already challenged the rights of the Federal government, much as Calhoun had done early in his career.

The balding Bowdre was a rather portly gentleman, whose stride carried with it an arrogance and conceit Cullen had seen many times with politicians. Neither was Cullen surprised to find that Bowdre greeted him with one of those false smiles that seemed to be plastered upon one's face.

"It is a pleasure," Cullen said after introductions, acutely aware that the man observed him.

"Your grandfather said that you are visiting Charleston before returning up North. I'm sure your family is glad you are here for the happy occasion." Bowdre positioned himself to gain all of Cullen's attention. "You are in the Navy?"

"Only until I return to Washington. My service is complete. Shortly, I am to follow my father into his shipping business in Philadelphia."

Bowdre nodded. "It is what I understand. I have been searching for one such as yourself—someone with Southerner roots…that has an understanding of our ways. Your father has influence in Washington?"

Immediately, Cullen was put on his guard. "I'm afraid I haven't seen my father while I have been at sea. Our letters we have corresponded have not ventured toward politics."

"Ah, Cullen, Mr. Bowdre wants only a small favor."

Cullen eyed his grandfather with reservation. Although he was confident of Bowdre's motives, he was unsure of his grandfather's. His grandfather knew well that his stepmother, Monica Ross, came from a long line of politicians. Her great-uncle had served an ambassador to Spain under John Quincy Adams's administration; her father, George Ross, had served as an advisor to Pennsylvania's governor, James Pollock.

"I am unsure if I'm in a position to dole out favors."

"Did I not tell you, Thurman, that you will know where you stand with my grandson? He has within him the Montgomery integrity."

"It is a quality to be admired," Bowdre said in an exaggerated manner. "I ask only if I might impose upon you an introduction to your father, Jonathan T. Smythe, on my trip to Philadelphia next month. Nothing more. Your grandfather informs me that your father is expanding his shipping business and has invested in the railroads."

"I have not gone into details with my father about his intentions, Mr. Bowdre," Cullen said tersely.

The audacity of the man irritated him. Again the puppet strings that tied him to the South pulled upon him…and Bowdre wanted him to be that puppet. Cullen was no fool. He suspected Bowdre wanted to influence the eastern terminus of the transcontinental railroad to be a Southern city…Charleston would be Cullen's guess. The logistics of such a move made no sense.

There had been enough trouble with the railroad concerning the turmoil surrounding expanding slavery out West. The South felt threatened by the expansion…that they would lose the power they wielded.

For years, Cullen heard the rumblings. South Carolina delegates had been quite outspoken in their never-ending contestation over states' rights. Moreover, their incessant proclamation of succession was heard upon every slight the Southern state felt came their way.

He supposed it made little difference this day whether he gave Bowdre an introduction. He had no worries his father would be easily influenced.

"You are returning soon?"

"Soon enough." Cullen felt it best to maintain a politeness. "Send a note over on your arrival."

Bowdre smiled broadly, content with his mission. "God bless you. I had been afraid that you would have turned into one of those red Republicans. I'm glad your Southern blood runs strong in your veins."

"Meaning if I had not agreed with you, I would not have a Southern connection?"

Bowdre's lips twisted. An odd expression altered his face. "Lieutenant Smythe, I only expressed my gratitude for your kindness. It is not often that kindness has been extended to us Southerners. I am so tired of hearing self-righteous Yankees criticizing our way of life."

"I consider myself a Southerner." Cullen's words rang clear.

"But of course. Being Clayton Montgomery's grandson, there is no question. But living up North, how frustrating it must be. Secession is in the air. The time will come when all men will have to choose a side. It will not dissipate until the Northerners stop their insufferable interference. I can well imagine those damn Yankees must put you on your defenses with their smug condemnations of the South."

Cullen kept his eyes on the man. "I would not condemn the South, Mr. Bowdre, but I would hope that we would find our way around this escalating conflict. It is time to address our own issues instead of letting others point out our faults."

"Come, Lieutenant, do not skirt the issue you have addressed. Am I to understand you side with the Yankees concerning the provocation of the South concerning slavery? The North should keep to their own problems, of which they have many. They shouldn't stick their noses into our affairs. It is an insult to the South, trying to prohibit what they do not understand."

Cullen realized it would have been wise to say nothing in return, but the man had not relented upon him. He snapped, "Do you not believe that view is short-sighted?"

"Look around you, Lieutenant. The economy would falter…there would be an uprising and thousands of whites would die. Then who would look after the Negros? They can't look after themselves," Bowdre declared.

"I feel you are pushing me into a debate, Mr. Bowdre." Cullen glared coldly at the man. "Debating is for politicians, not I. I know only what I feel and let my conscience dictate my actions."

"It is divine. Did not Abraham own slaves? Does not the Ten Commandments say 'Thou shalt not covet they neighbor's house, nor his manservant, nor maidservant'? Never once did Jesus speak out against slavery, even though it was widespread within the Roman Empire. It has been ordained by God."

Cullen didn't flinch. "Whose God?"

"Cullen!" Clayton Montgomery interrupted. "I believe it is best to leave this discussion for another day."

It was a notice that Cullen wouldn't ignore. He suspected that his reaction had nothing to do with his frustration about the growing tension in the country. He had long learned to keep his feelings to himself. It did no good arguing…not here at the wedding.

Cullen glanced over at his grandfather, who walked away with the good Thurman Bowdre. He was under no delusions about his grandfather's stance.

He had always considered his grandfather an intelligent man, but he suddenly discovered his grandfather was no different than any other Carolinians he had met. As the others around him, Clayton Montgomery followed blindly, led by tradition and loyalty. Cullen found it was a flaw within the Southern code—not to question those who led them.

If some leader did not emerge who was willing to compromise, Cullen feared conflict was inevitable.

"It is good to see you haven't changed."

Cullen turned to find Wade leaning against the wide berth of the giant oak's trunk. Cullen walked toward him as Wade pulled a couple of cigars out of his waistcoat pocket. He handed one to Cullen. With one quick strike against the bottom of his boot, he lit it up with a burning match.

Wade took a puff and nodded to Cullen to join him. "I promised Clarissa I would only be a moment."

Cullen walked over beside his cousin and accepted. They stood there side by side and observed the guests.

"I should have warned you what Grandfather had planned. He does so only because he wants you to be thought of as one of us."

"It matters only that my family believes I'm one of them."

For a moment, there was a silence. This growing conflict had been an unspoken barrier between them. With all that had surrounded both during his time here in Charleston, Cullen hadn't broached the subject with Wade.

The Navy Lieutenant Wade had been would never have considered South Carolina seceding from the Union would be an answer to the escalating conflict. But this was not the Navy man he had once been. He was a man prepared to protect what he considered his birthright.

Wade exhaled and left a trail of smoke. "You are and will always be my brother."

Cullen understood. Nothing would come between the bond they shared. The two stood silently for a time. Cullen finished his smoke and dropped it to the ground. His foot stomped on it.

"You seemed content this day, Wade. Only one look tells Clarissa seems greatly enamored of her husband."

"It has been a good day." Wade smiled and looked over in the direction of his bride. She glanced up at him and returned it. He turned to Cullen. "I'm glad you were here. Thank you for standing up for me."

"As you said before, we are brothers. It is what we do."

Wade nodded and walked back over to his bride.

Chapter Seven

The jangle of the harness seemed to resound within the carriage. For well over an hour, Josephine heard it each time the horses stamped on the ground. It had begun to wear on her frayed nerves.

The sun set low in the sky. Soon it would be dark, but she would reach her destination well before darkness. Magnolia Bluff was around the next bend. She had visited the plantation several times in the past, but never had she been so nervous. She sat back against the cushions.

"Oh, for Heaven's sakes! Jo, your hair!"

Jo glanced over at Grace Ann, who gave her a disapproving look. She turned to Gillie.

"Don't look at me," Gillie said. "I spent the whole of the afternoon preparing you for this night."

Jo sighed. Never had she taken so much attention to her appearance. She wore Grace Ann's emerald-green taffeta with its layered ruffles and puffed sleeves. Her breasts were pushed high in her stay, but Grace Ann said it gave the desired effect, flattering her curves and fullness of her bosom.

A new set of long white gloves had been acquired, along with a lace fan attached to her wrist by a matching ribbon. Small yellow rosebuds graced her raven hair caught up in fancy combs. Around her neck she wore a family heirloom that once had belonged to her great-grandmother, a glittering emerald necklace: cascading emerald drops surrounded by clusters of diamonds. Aunt Sybil had insisted.

Jo wanted nothing more than to be a wallflower this night, but it was far from Grace Ann's intention.

Grace Ann's mouth grew firm. "Remember what I've said. If you believe we will let these Wraggs tarnish our good name, you would be quite mistaken. You need to show these leeches that you are a Buchanan."

"Grace Ann, I don't think I can do this…see Wade…at his wedding…" Jo's voice faded. "It was supposed to be my wedding…"

"This won't ever do!" Grace Ann declared. "Where is the Jo I know? I have never seen you back down from a challenge."

"I've had my heart ripped out."

"Oh…no, you don't, Josephine Buchanan Wright. I am not going to let you wallow in self-pity…not for this Wade Montgomery. You are going to be swallowed alive by those vultures if you arrive holding your head down."

"I can't help…"

"Do you want to be humiliated? Embarrassed? Be subjected to a wall of contemptuous glances? It is all his fault…Wade's. He led you on to believe something that could never be. Do not let him see what he has done to you."

Jo straightened herself up and stared at Grace Ann. Her cousin had struck a nerve…realization suffused through Jo. Wade had lied to her…made promises that he had no intention of keeping…then her reputation had been torn to shreds while he himself was not touched by scandal…making her miserable while he celebrated.

Jo's shoulders squared and her jaw locked indignantly. If she had nothing else, she had her pride.

"Hold that chin up," Grace Ann encouraged. "Wade Montgomery will rue the day he messed with a Buchanan."

"I will try," Jo said. "It will help to know that I have only a few hours of this torture."

"It won't be all torture. You have Lieutenant Smythe, who has given his word to see to your comfort this evening."

"I thought you said that he would never do…being a Yankee and all."

"Mr. Whitney said your daddy would never agree. I myself think it would be a splendid arrangement."

Jo eyed her cousin dubiously. At first, she thought perhaps Grace Ann teased her, but the look upon her face said otherwise.

"I do," Grace Ann reiterated. "I believe the two of you would make quite a match. I met his parents in Newport last summer when Mr. Whitney and I visited the Dunlaps."

"I thought he lived in Philadelphia."

"You silly goose! The Smythes have a summer home in Newport."

"A summer home? Why then did you call him a poor relation?"

"I said a poor Yankee soul. Heavens to Betsy, Jo! To be so intelligent, I do wonder about you at times."

The news struck Jo as strange. It bothered her. Why, she wasn't certain. It shouldn't matter to her a twit what Lieutenant Smythe's financial status was. She doubted that his offer for her was nothing more than a moral shield for the Montgomerys' honor…especially if he was as well-off as Grace Ann indicated.

Of course, the lieutenant had said her dowry mattered little to him…but she had taken it to mean that it mattered little because he had no intention to marry her either…like Wade. It was no more than a game to either of them!

Then how could she explain her dreams, once filled with Wade, were now replaced this arrogant lieutenant? Deep in the darkness he came to her, embraced her, whispered words within her ear, his lips upon hers. She forgot everything around her when she had been in his arms…even Wade.

Guilt raged within her. Shame. She was shameful to have allowed him to kiss her in that manner when she was heartbroken for his cousin! When had her life become such a tangled mess?

Only a few days ago, Harry Lee had warned her. "Them Montgomerys are up to no good. I'm telling ya, Jo. Out for revenge they are. They blame your father for Douglas Montgomery's death. Can't trust 'em, not a one."

Of course, Harry Lee had been drinking when he uttered the warning. She didn't trust him—she would never trust him—but there was truth in his words she couldn't ignore. She had heard the rumors of Douglas Montgomery's death, but had paid them no mind. Perhaps she should have.

The carriage slowed to a stop. She had arrived, leaving her no choice. She would have to face the world in which she lived, pretend to be resigned to her fate and lull them with sweet sincerity.

She thought her heart would burst it beat so rapidly. She whispered a prayer. She would need all her strength and courage this night.

The door opened. Grace Ann exited first. Jo stepped out, and concealed her anxiety behind a façade of charm and smiles. Her cousin interlocked her arm with hers and the two walked up the steps together.

* * * *

The house had been transformed. The mansion shone brightly; candlelight illuminated from every window, carried outside with strings of Chinese lanterns. Laughter and merriment teemed throughout the mansion. It seemed the whole of the Low County had been invited for the event. The house brimmed with a bounty of guests, who trickled out into the lawn and beyond.

A wide spread of food had been placed outside on the piazza for the convenience of the guests to eat and drink at their leisure. Tables and chairs had been arranged out of the flow of revelers. The elaborate meal had extended into the night.

French champagne flowed, along with imported wines. The house blacks served the immediate needs of the guests, filled up empty glasses. A group of young slave boys paddle-fanned the food to keep flies and insects away from the food.

The rooms carried the fragrance of all the potted plants that had been brought in for the occasion: gardenias, roses, hydrangeas, geraniums, and oleander plants. On the first floor, the furniture had been cleared out except for the chairs to allow room for guests to dance the night away. Old ladies had already staked their place to overview the entertainment. They prepared themselves to guard the young ladies for the evening, much like bears protecting their cubs.

A bevy of maidens swirled around in their multitude of colors with lace shawls hanging around their arms. Fans spangled and dangled from their wrists. Their hair amassed on top of their heads in only the most fashionable chignons. Necklaces and earbobs glittered in the candlelight. Men attired to match their elegance for the occasion.

In the first drawing parlor, a raised platform had been placed in the far corner for the orchestra from Charleston, a group of black musicians. Their mesmerizing music, a sweet melody, floated throughout the home. The room was crowded, hot and muggy. The players' grinning faces already shined with perspiration.

Cullen stood against the back wall and watched the dancers waltz. He sipped his champagne in a bottomless glass. No sooner had he finished his drink, one of the black servers would fill it. Lord, help him. That woman had his head spinning…though it well could be the champagne.

His eyes fixed upon Josephine dancing with…what the hell was his name?… Taz Foster. She looked stunningly beautiful, all dressed in her glory. Her head tilted back as she laughed. The willful, stubborn woman!

He drifted outside and leaned against a white pillar. He reminded himself to be patient. She had a part to play this night and had come well prepared. It became quite obvious that the Buchanans had circled around their own.

A hush descended down on the festivities the moment the Buchanan cousins entered the house. It seemed that a sea of souls ebbed closer to observe the exchange between the newlyweds and the hussy who tried to steal the groom.

Clarissa greeted her in the most stilted fashion…one that would have evoked more whispers…retreating from Josephine when she stepped up to congratulate the two. Wade watched helplessly.

Cullen thought Mrs. Whitney was going to slap the woman, not that the woman didn't deserve it. Clarissa well understood the ramification of such an action, but he had suspected she would have done so after their conversation last night.

His words had fallen on deaf ears. She cared only that Wade had returned. Then the tears and fears of the night before were forgotten. Clarissa let her jealousy override her good sense. Instead of quietening the rumors, she was in danger of inciting more with her greeting of Josephine.

It was an ill-thought-out revenge against Josephine. Clarissa underestimated a Southern family tie, for it was not only the Buchanans she had set to tarnish, but the Montgomerys as well. The Wraggs had maneuvered this marriage between their families, but Clayton Montgomery would not soon forget the manner in which it was forged…neither would Wade if Clarissa did not learn to contain her emotion.

It was then that he strolled to Josephine's side. "My dear, I have been waiting patiently for your arrival. You have been missed."

Her chin went up in defiance. A fire lit in her eyes and she smiled at him. "I'm sorry to have been delayed, but we are here now to enjoy the celebration."

Only when he leaned down to kiss her cheek did he notice her visible tremble. "Show no fear," he whispered in her ear. "I will be by your side."

Her eyes softened on his utterance, but it had not come to be. His intent to escort her to the dance floor had been thwarted. Before he could speak once more, a group of young ladies swarmed Josephine.

"I thought you would never get here!" His cousin, Charlotte, pressed through the people, along with Wade's younger sisters, Jenna and Amy. "You look enchanting, I must say."

Josephine was swept away by an army armed with giggles and laughter, far stronger than whispers and rumors. Clarissa surrendered, having been given no other option, though Cullen noticed her grimace at the sight.

He watched Josephine from afar. She had been surrounded by beaus on every side. It had not been as he had expected. The latent hostile crowd seemed bewildered, and then oblivious of her.

Clayton Montgomery wandered up to him, drink in hand. "Come back in, enjoy yourself."

"I need some air." Cullen stared down at his glass.

His grandfather shrugged. "Do not frown. It seems the issue with that woman will soon be behind us."

Cullen's head snapped up. "You arranged this?"

"It needed to be handled. I won't have one of my grandsons burdened with Brantley Wright's daughter."

"No matter if it was your grandson who ruined her reputation."

"If it was not Wade, it would have been another with her sort," Clayton went on. "Don't fret. I will see to it that she is not shunned, if that weighs upon your conscience."

"With Taz Foster?" Cullen asked with thick sarcasm.

"Much better than Buchanan's solution of Holt Miller."

Unblinking, he stared at his grandfather. Taz Foster was a decent man…a teacher, Cullen thought he remembered. They were of the same age. He had heard the man had started up a school in Charleston for boys. A far cry from the landed gentry's life Josephine had been accustomed to.

There again, Holt Miller owned more than a couple of plantations, but he was a drunk with a temper. It was rumored his first wife's death was no accident as Miller claimed…that in a drunken rage, he had pushed her down the stairs to her death. But no one dared challenge him on his assertion she had tripped and fallen.

"I believe it should have been her decision. It will now be forced upon her."

"It is for the best. Your cousin, Andrew, isn't hankering for it to go further and you can't tell me that your father would be pleased if you brought home that vixen for a bride. I know you are an honorable man. I thought if I smoothed the horde of people readied to stone Miss Wright, you would be able to walk away with your head high."

Cullen studied his grandfather for a moment. There was more…Wade. He was protecting his own…Wade.

"Grandfather, I believe I am capable of making my own decisions."

"You have always been pig-headed stubborn," Clayton exclaimed, quite loudly…too loudly. Heads turned. He pointed his finger with the hand he held his glass. "I have always felt responsible for you…I want only to save you from a lifetime of regret."

70

"I don't need you to do so," Cullen said in a low, frosty tone. "I am my own man."

"As you will," Clayton returned with the same coldness. "I raised you and failed."

"Why, Grandfather, why? Because I don't believe in secession and won't listen to such nonsense!"

"When have you become an expert on the matter?"

"Has it gone that far that we can't disagree?"

"Your mother…God rest her soul…wanted you raised as a Southern gentleman. I gave her my word."

"You kept your word, Grandfather," Cullen said. His voice calmed at the mention of his mother. "I am who I am because of you…of living here at Magnolia Bluff. Give me credence."

"I do, Cullen. It is what I fear."

Cullen found he had no words. He downed his half-filled glass and walked away.

In the midst of all the gaiety and music, Cullen drifted back inside to the dance floor. All the way across the room, his eyes lit upon Josephine. He grinned to himself as he watched her talk to Charlotte and her cousin, half-smiling behind her fan.

Having felt his gaze, she looked toward him. Something in her eyes challenged him. One he would not ignore, though somewhere in his mind, a voice told him he should. Lord, he must be mad, but he had no willpower to stay away from her.

A reel had only moments before ended. To his glee, the music began again…a waltz. Then from the corner of his eyes, he saw another man…that fool Holt Miller…walk toward her. He had enough with proprieties.

With an air of utter assurance, he made his way through the crowd and stepped in front of Miller. With a slight bow, he extended his arm to Jo. Without a moment's hesitation, she swept him a low curtsy and accepted his offer.

His arm went about her waist and she smiled up at him…a dazzling smile. Her soft eyes gleamed with a mischievous twinkle. In the candlelight, they seemed a multitude of colors: green, brown, or were they dark as night?

"I thought you had forgotten me."

"You have not been out of my thoughts all night. I have not been able to find a moment that you have been free."

"I am on display this evening, sir. Have you not noticed?"

He glanced over her shoulder. She was not mistaken. The eyes of the ballroom were upon her: the pursed-lipped chaperons, anticipating any misstep; the ill-tempered girls, callously waiting to repeat malignant whispers; the gentlemen, biding their time in hopes of a brawl that would ensue.

"I have eyes only for the most beautiful lady here tonight, my dear magnolia."

She blushed. "My word, Cullen, I did not realize you were such a sweet talker."

"Usually, I am not. It is the company I am keeping that has inspired me in a way I can't explain." He pulled her closer to him. "You dance divinely."

"Now I know you are teasing me," she said, with another smile. "I do so enjoy the music. It is not often that I have been able to enjoy the activity."

"I cannot imagine you sitting alone on a night such as this."

Immediately, he regretted his words. He had no desire to distress her. Had she been kept back from social functions? How little he knew of her upbringing…

"I do declare, Lieutenant Smythe." She laughed. "You must know by now that I have two left feet. At least, it is what Grace Ann has told me. I have not minded watching others. As a child, one of my fondest memories is hiding on the banister and watching the dancers whirl by in our home in London. I remember Momma looking so beautiful and happy on Papa's arm. It is one of my last memories of her."

"You surprise me. You do not seem the sort to sit back and let others enjoy life while you only observe."

"How well you read me," she said. "I believe we all have our talents. Unfortunately, dancing may not be my best, but I have not despaired. I have been told my horsemanship is excellent."

"I would not disagree. I have seen you upon a horse. Perhaps we can go for a ride later next week."

"Are you asking whether I want you to come calling?"

"Is it scandalous to say I would love to spend more time with you? Do not fend that you do know I find you fascinating. There are so many things I want to learn about you."

"You want to know more about little ole me? Most would rather I not mention the time I lived away from Charleston."

"Come, Miss Josephine, I eagerly await your tale. You forget I dragged you out of the Charleston Harbor at one time. I know what most do not."

"You are being quite wicked, mentioning—"

"Perhaps I see you with different eyes than others in this room. I see a compassionate, lovely woman, who has more courage than most men I know."

"Oh, Cullen, I fear that courage is not a virtue that most mommas inspire to their daughters."

"I find I disagree with you. I believe that Southern women are not only born with beauty, but the same innate character as Southern gentlemen, only they do not flaunt this ability. Women do so with grace and style."

"You did not mention bull-headed."

"It is not a word I would use, but, yes, I have found a certain lady quite stubborn."

He drew her tighter to him. For a moment, neither spoke. Warmth surged through him with her in his arms. He wanted this lady...of that he had no doubt. He had from the first moment he saw her.

What he was feeling he could not put into words: desire, passion...lust...he felt all of those, but this was more...it was a need. For once in his life, he accepted what he could not explain.

The music faded. Cullen slowed his steps to a stop, but he did not release Jo.

"I'm not letting you go from my side. I fear you will disappear," he said. "Would you, my lady, care to dance the night away with me?"

"You, sir, are indeed a brave man. I will confess I have enjoyed myself immensely. I cannot think of a more enjoyable way to spend the rest of my evening."

"It will be my pleasure. Come, let us rest a few minutes before the next dance." He moved her through the crowd. "I believe I see a spot..."

A sudden jolt halted their conversation. Jo gasped. The front of her gown had punch running down the bodice. Cullen recognized the girl who held an empty cup in her hand. Maybelle McIntosh...one of Clarissa's friends.

"Oh, my goodness, Jo. I'm so sorry," the girl uttered. "I should have been paying attention to where I was heading. I was deep in discussion with Peggy about the beautiful wedding. Such a handsome couple. Don't you think?"

The other girl beside Maybelle covered her mouth in an effort to contain a giggle, but not well enough.

"Here, let me help..." Maybelle brought out a handkerchief.

Jo pushed her hand back harshly. Cullen stepped between them.

"I will see to Miss Wright's needs. I believe you have done quite enough."

Cullen took Jo by the elbow, but not quick enough.

Maybelle hissed, "The nerve she has! She lost one of the Montgomery men and has turned upon the other. Hussy!"

Cullen glanced over to see Clarissa watching the exchange. She made no movement, but he noticed a slight smile emerge on her lips. Angered, Cullen would have liked nothing more than to wipe it off her face, but then it would cause more of a spectacle than had occurred.

Momentarily, self-consciousness flashed across Josephine's face. Her confidence shaken…the incident reminded the lady of her indiscretion and shame. On every step he took, he saw the light dim in her eyes; her face whitened.

"Are you okay?" Cullen looked down at her with concern.

She tried to smile, but failed. "Can you not see? They are whispering behind their fans." She glanced in the direction of the old biddies who sat in chairs against the wall. "This is the moment they have been waiting for…to see my disgrace."

"They will see nothing of the kind," he assured her. He whirled her through the door and into the foyer. "If they want something to talk of, they can talk of us. Come."

He took her hand and pulled it through his cocked arm. At the far end of the foyer was their escape; the door was opened to the rear of the veranda.

A full moon shone down on the pair. Cullen had only taken time for Jo to clean the spot on her gown. One of the house girls brought out a cloth and a bowl of water. It wasn't as bad as it seemed in the ballroom. Most of the punch had missed its intended target, but it would assuredly leave a stain.

He didn't care. Once they were married, he would buy her a hundred gowns if she wished.

"It will dry," he stated. "Let us take a stroll."

She made no objection, allowing him to take a discreet path that ran between the giant live oaks and the formal garden to the river's edge. A sultry breeze flowed along the water; gray beards of Spanish moss stirred on the trees. He caught a scent of crab apples and roses.

Behind them, the sound of the party dimmed. Instead, sounds of frogs and crickets made their own melody. She broke from him and sauntered over to a clearing under one of the large trees.

She silently stared out into the nothingness. He walked up behind her. "Plotting your escape?"

She shook her head, but made no movement to look back at him. "I fear there is none. You should have let me leave to find Papa. How could being shunned be worse than this...pretending to be something I'm not?"

"I thought we had this matter settled, Josephine," he said. "It is becoming most bothersome."

She turned and stared at him. "Why do you persist? Do you not know I have been told you have been released of your obligation?"

He reached for her. She pushed back. "Don't," she cried. "I can't take this...I can't pretend anymore. It would have been best if you had let me run."

"Listen, Josephine, I have not withdrawn my offer...nor do I intend to do so."

"Don't do this to me, Lieutenant. I am tired of being a pawn where I don't understand the rules of the game." She clutched her hand to her chest. "I can't smile another minute when all I want is the earth to open and swallow me. I have tried to do as they wanted...it is my fault for believing Wade...I accepted my punishment...but this is cruel," she rambled, not knowing—not caring—whether her utterances made sense. "I am to laugh and smile...not to let any see my heartbreak...and still they whisper."

"Is it...is your heart broken?" He put his hand firmly about her waist, pulled her to him. He remembered the defiant young girl drenched in the pouring rain. Those eyes...those eyes stared into his. He saw the scared little girl he had pulled from the water.

She hesitated. "What do you want me to say?" Her voice quivered. "My world has collapsed around me. I have disgraced my family...now I have to pay the price. I am no fool. I was invited here tonight to be paraded around to be ridiculed."

She reached down and touched his hands in a vain effort to release his hold. He had no intention of letting her go.

"You knew what was expected before you arrived. You have performed admirably. Don't come at me now and tell me you have lost courage."

"Let me go!" she cried. "I came only to save my family's face. My family does not deserve to be humiliated..."

"It is not the only reason."

Her eyes suddenly flamed and body tensed. "Why do you do this? Provoke me to no end."

He smiled, a mocking smile for no other reason than her anger made her eyes come alive. It inflamed her further.

She went on, "Perhaps it is more...perhaps I wanted to lash out at Wade...to hurt him as he hurt me. I wanted him to see that I do not need him..."

"You have seen Wade," he said not as a question, but a statement. "Your temper has been aroused. You are no longer subdued when you talk of him."

"He came after I returned home yesterday." She lowered her gaze. "He told me I should accept what we had is over and move forward. It will be for the best for both of us. It was he...it was he who asked Taz to offer for me. He told me he is looking after my best interest...to soothe his conscience."

Her voice was laced with thick sarcasm. The news irritated him...more so even than it obviously had Josephine.

"He is ever the gentleman," Cullen said stiffly.

"Is it not you also he is looking after? To save you from marrying me...to keep you from being indebted to him for life?"

He chuckled. His playful mood returned; his eye cocked upward in amusement. "Don't hold it against me if I don't give Wade's opinion much credence. You need to understand before..."

"Before...I'm married off, Lieutenant Smythe."

"Cullen."

"Cullen," she repeated. Her eyes softened, but carried a worried look. "It won't be to you. You have to know that. I do not hold to Wade's wants, but I won't go against my family. I have hurt them too much already. They have protected me..."

"It is what a family does," Cullen acknowledged. "But they have no need to protect you from me."

"I have told you that other plans are in place. Taz Foster will make a good match. He comes from a good family and he is a friend. He knows of my dowry...he said...he said that it would be enough to add another wing to his school. He seemed quite happy with the thought...only..."

"Only what?" he pressed. Not waiting for her to answer, he said, "Only he cannot make you feel what I do. What you felt when we kissed...like this."

He felt her change within his grip. She looked up at him; her red lips trembled. His lips met hers with his overwhelming desire unleashed. Forgetting everything but her, he embraced her, unrestrained of the boundaries between them. Beyond lures and subtlety, he took her mouth hard, releasing a hunger that had built within him. Her hands pressed against his chest but not in resistance.

His arms rounded her tighter, pulled her instinctively to his body. Her body melted into his as his lips took hers hungrily. A gasp of pleasure escaped her lips and rid him of any restraint. He ravished her with his kisses.

She wanted him as he wanted her. She closed her eyes as he pressed fervent kisses down her ivory neck to the swell of her breasts. The urge within him to have her completely drove him...compelled him to claim what he desired...and he desired her worse than he had ever wanted a woman.

In the distance, sounds emerged; they both were reluctantly brought back to reality. He drew back and gazed into her eyes.

"I have to go. I hear Grace Ann," she said. "Oh...but...Cullen..."

"Ssh, my sweet magnolia." He placed his finger over her lips. "I want you to know that a marriage to me won't be so bad. I know...I know it has not been easy these last couple of weeks, but tell me that you don't feel something between us."

"What do you want me to say...I'm so confused...I can't do this..."

She stumbled backwards, her eyes fixated on his. Abruptly, she turned and ran down the lane. He displayed no astonishment, but he followed. He watched her talk with her cousin, who waited at the end of the path.

Grace Ann wrapped a shawl around Josephine's shoulders. Cullen's brows came together in a harsh scowl. His ire grew as he watched Josephine ushered back into the main house and disappear from sight. *Lord! Now what was his next move?*

Honor and duty drove him to offer for her...to accept her grandfather's decision to call upon her until Brantley Wright made an appearance or a letter came to dictate his wishes. It would not come to that, Cullen realized.

Despite the shame that had befallen Josephine, her family had swooped down and shielded her from the fate bestowed upon one who would have to marry one of those *damn Yankees*. First the despicable Holt Miller, then this Taz Foster...why then could he not walk away?

"Lieutenant Smythe, I wish to have a word with you."

Cullen hadn't noticed Wade had joined him. He expected Wade to be enjoying the festivities alongside his bride. Moreover, his cousin seemed outraged...mad as an old banty rooster and...drunk.

"What's the matter? Why are you not inside?"

"Matter? You asked that after that display…dancing with Jo in the manner you did…defending her…drawing more whispers with your exit. The question becomes why do so? Your obligation has been lifted. You could have simply walked away…"

Without warning, Wade pivoted around and swung his right fist into Cullen's jaw. Cullen staggered backwards and held his hand up to his chin in disbelief.

"Christ! Wade, what the hell is wrong with you?"

Wade lunged again; Cullen spun in response. He shifted and caught Wade by the collar. He swung his fist back…but halted. Instead, he jerked Wade up to his feet. He got in his face.

"You bastard! You are angry with me for upholding your indiscretion…your indiscretion!"

Wade pushed Cullen back. Incensed, he lashed out, "I asked you only to tell her…to tell her I had to marry Clarissa…I didn't have a choice. I didn't ask you to offer for her…I begged you to offer for Clarissa…"

"Go back into the party, Wade, before you do something you will regret in the morning."

Wade stumbled and almost fell. He caught himself, holding his head as his dulled and confused senses tried to grasp his actions. He glared at Cullen; color suffused his face.

Cullen moved to offer help, but he halted when he saw Heyward. Heyward met Cullen's eyes as he slipped his arm around his master's shoulder. The tall, dignified black gestured he would care for his master.

Cullen didn't attempt to speak to Wade. It would do no good. There was no reasoning with a drunken soul. He turned and walked back to the house. His shadow swayed in the moonlight as he mounted the steps up to the veranda.

The compassion and pity he felt for his cousin faded, replaced with a despairing impatience. He was at the point he didn't care whether Wade knew it or not.

* * * *

Nightmarish as the night had become, Wade had forgotten he had his bride waiting for him. Heyward reminded him as he walked him back into the house. The thought sobered him quickly.

He had been raised in a culture of expectations. To walk away from Josephine, he had to draw from his strength of character. He had been foolish to have ever courted her in the manner he had done.

True, he had shown her only adoration. He had not crossed the line until last night. But he should have never gone to her…no, he reprimanded himself, he should never have allowed Cullen to have gone for him with what was his to tell her. But the question remained: would he have been able to walk away from the one thing he truly loved...

Last night, he had wanted nothing but to have taken her in the moonlight...to make her his...even if he could never give to her his name. What a fraud he was! Behind his impeccable manners...his charm...laid a person who wanted nothing more than to have forsaken all of it if she had allowed.

Jealousy ripped through him when he saw her with Cullen. The way she looked at him and he her, gnawed at his heart to the point his anger grabbed hold of his good sense. How thankful he was to Heyward. At least, he had not made a fool of himself in front of the guests...or Clarissa...his wife.

Heyward had found him a quiet spot to sit and compose himself before he made his way up to his room...*their* room. Wade rose. He had delayed long enough. She would be waiting for him.

As he walked up the staircase, he thought of the woman he married. Clarissa had loved Percival. While in the Navy, he remembered the letters that his brother sent him about her. Now, he feared he was a disappointment to his new bride compared to Percival.

Clarissa would make a fine wife. Such a lovely lady, exquisitely so, but he also ascertained she had another side...the one that lashed out at Josephine, set to destroy the woman who stood between her and the man who was now her husband.

With each step, he came to the realization that the two were a great deal alike. Duty and honor bound them together. Each would have rather had another, but were fated to be one.

He turned the handle of the door, and he entered into a dark room. The lamps had been extinguished.

"Wade? Is that you?" a tiny voice asked.

"But of course, Clarissa. Time is growing late." He moved across the room. "Why are you here in the dark? I will light..."

"Don't!" she cried. "Aunt Sissy said it would be best...if it was dark."

Her voice faded into the darkness, but her nervousness could not be denied. He walked to the bedside. His eyes, adjusted to the dim light, saw her eyes large and terrified. It became obvious Clarissa had not been told what occurred between a man and a woman could be a wondrous thing.

"I had an amazing day. Did you not?"

"Oh, yes, Wade. The ceremony was so touching. I believe the whole of Charleston turned out for our celebration. Why, everyone said it was the best barbecue ever! They meant it too! It was the grandest day until..."

Once more her words faded, but it was not nervousness that halted her. He realized Clarissa was thinking of Jo.

They sat in silence for a time. He decided he would not force her to consummate their marriage this night. He had never forced himself on a woman; he would not start with his wife. Even with the realization that most welcomed the opportunity to share his bed.

Clarissa needed to be wooed; then seduced far away from the influence of her stuffy old Aunt Sissy. He could well imagine the old biddy told Clarissa to lie on the bed and endure the pain and humiliation that was part of marriage.

His attention now upon his wife, he would make the effort needed to have a successful marriage. He was certain he would have her most willing in the days to come.

Taking the sheet, Wade pulled it up around his wife and tucked her into bed. He leaned over and kissed her cheek. "Sleep, my dear. I will take to the chair. When you are ready, I will take my place alongside of you in our bed."

He only wished she hadn't seemed so relieved.

Chapter Eight

Scandal created the strangest trepidation, Jo thought as she sat in the parlor with Grace Ann and Charlotte. Over the last week since Wade's wedding, the household had become lugubrious and energized with purpose at the same time.

Aunt Sybil and Grandpa Henry had sat in the study for hours and debated her fate. Mr. Whitney consulted on the issue before he left for Charleston. Uncle Vernon declared there was no need for a deliberation. It was plain and simple. It was a disgrace for the family, which required Jo to marry quickly and without fanfare.

No one asked Jo her preference. It became apparent that her opinion mattered little. She just waited to be told her fate while she lamented the disaster her life had become.

Callers trickled in and out of the Groves, among them the Fosters. It had been quite uncomfortable. Jo had known Taz since she arrived in Charleston. They had a long-standing friendship, but it had never been more than that.

Taz was of short stature. His brows were black and thick above deep-set eyes fringed with dark lashes. He was an intelligent sort. In her youth, Jo and Taz had spent many hours playing chess and contemplating books along the Battery. He hadn't been the sort to have many friends.

His parents seemed none too happy at the change in events of their son's life. Mrs. Eliza Foster greeted her with a chill that never melted during the visit. Jo observed that not even the prospect of her son marrying into one of the prominent families in Charleston overcame the stigma of the scandal attached to Jo's name.

"I fear she has reservations, Jo," Taz said. "She worries about the reputation of the school. I have told her of your intelligence, but if not for the promised dowry, I do not feel I could make the offer."

Jo wanted to retort that marriage would quiet the scandal, but found she hoped that Taz would not make a formal offer. She liked Taz well enough, but did not love him. The thought of a lifetime of reproach from his mother was enough to sour the contemplation of marriage.

There really was no good outcome to the dilemma she faced. If it wasn't Taz, Holt Miller loomed on the horizon. God help her! She could not face a man such as he! She had heard he had been a handsome man in his youth, but his looks faded with years of drinking. His flushed, ruddy face…a gut that hung over his tight pants…mean-spirited.

"Calm yourself, Jo. I assure you that it will be over soon enough. Of course, the wedding will be small, quite understandable," Grace Ann complained. "But afterwards, I will talk Mr. Whitney into a large celebration in Charleston. A grand affair, I imagine, as long as you are not expecting too soon. It would only stoke speculation."

"Grace Ann!"

"Oh, Jo, don't fend innocence. You know the way of the world. You are not one of those naïve young things like Charlotte here."

Charlotte turned twelve shades of red. Uttering under her breath, she said, "I know things."

"Dear Charlotte, you're too sweet," Grace Ann mused. "Jo, on the other hand, has always been a curious thing."

Jo flushed with the remembrance of interrupting two of her grandfather's slaves when she had been on a ride. She had only been thirteen, but it was embedded in her memory. She had been racing Harry Lee, Buck, and Grace Ann along the back roads to the fields.

At first, she thought the naked buck was hurting the girl. Lord, she hadn't an idea what was going on…grunting and panting…the sweating, gleaming back of the man covered the woman. Jo screamed.

Then the buck stood…she had never seen a naked man before…she did that day. Later, she could have sworn Harry Lee had known what had been occurring. She had been kidded endlessly since that moment.

Jo frowned. "Don't tease Charlotte, Grace Ann. She will think less of me."

Grace Ann shook her head and waved her hand in front of her face. "Look at me, Jo, and tell me that you have not shared more than a hand hold with Wade. Do not lie. His reputation precedes him."

"I don't need to defend myself. I told you he had been honorable," Jo protested. She allowed her gaze to drop. Grace Ann always had a way of pulling the truth out of her.

"Momma says that people spread a scandal far faster than any truth. It is a shame, she says, for this scandal is based only on unfounded rumors."

"Charlotte, my innocent dear, it matters not how the whispers began, but how to still them which leads now to Jo's dilemma. I believe that Lieutenant Smythe will be a good fit."

Jo raised her chin ever so slightly. "It is not fair to expect him to pay for something that was not his fault."

"The world is assuming more than the truth…far more," Grace Ann said directly. "It matters little what happened, but that you were alone with him and everyone knows."

"I wasn't alone with Wade. Gillie was always by my side!"

"My dear Jo, I say this with love, but you have been compromised." Charlotte tilted her head to the side. She patted Jo's hand and went on. "It is unavoidable. Andrew would step up, but since Cullen has so adamantly insisted, Andrew feels it will suffice."

"Charlotte, I wish I saw the world as you. Andrew would offer for me only in the most dire of circumstances. We both know it," Jo said, followed by silence for a long moment. Then she shrugged. "I'm not so confident as either of you of my future."

"I believe if I had my choice, it would be Andrew. Cullen does so make me nervous with his looks. I swear they could melt ice," Charlotte offered. "Moreover, Grandfather and Cullen are constantly at each other, especially about succession. They breathe fire and fury. At least that is what Momma says. Cullen said that it will not bode well for the South if they make the move to break from the Union. Momma almost fell off her chair. Blasphemy, she says!"

Charlotte cocked her head toward Grace Ann, who nodded in agreement.

"Pity. I thought him the best of the lot."

Jo gave the two a dubious look. They talked to her as if she had a choice…as if she was picking out a dress.

"Do tell, what do we have here?"

Jo looked up. Harry Lee entered the parlor and smiled, not sweetly, but tight and hard at her. He appeared quite pleased with himself, which in itself worried her. He turned his attention to Charlotte and sent her a brilliant smile.

"You look quite lovely this morning, Miss Charlotte. Have you come to visit for a while…I hope."

Charlotte glanced at Harry Lee, red as a beet. Adoration and tenderness flickered over her face. The girl was sweet on her cousin! Good Lord! How much worse could it be!

"Um…" Jo's sharp eyes noted Harry Lee giving Charlotte a gentle touch on her shoulder.

Harry Lee smirked at Jo. He sauntered over to the tray of cucumber sandwiches and took one. With one in his hand, he pointed over to Jo. "You amaze me, Josephine. Truly you do."

"Pray tell…how exactly have I impressed you, Harry Lee?"

He chuckled and plopped down on a chair across from her. "Ya done gone and got Grandfather all riled up with Abraham Foster's demanding your dowry upfront before any formal announcement with his son. Then…" He paused, almost choking to contain his laughter. "Then he begins ranting about it only being twenty-two hundred and to make—"

"There's no need to continue, Harry Lee," Jo interrupted. "It's not funny. Grandpa Henry has already talked to me."

"I do declare, Josephine Buchanan Wright, what have you done now?" Grace Ann asked.

"Nothing…not much," Jo stuttered. Flustered under Harry Lee's watchful eye, she squirmed. "Don't look at me like that. I only took what was mine."

"Your dowry?" Harry Lee asked with a cynical smile. "I have to hand it to you, Jo. You have gall. Tell me how you did it…I mean, withdrawing the money."

"Why on earth would you do such a thing?" Grace Ann glanced over at Jo, puzzled.

"I was going to find Papa." Jo glared at Harry Lee. "But I changed my mind."

"So you still have the money," Harry Lee pressed.

"I've already told Grandpa Henry."

"Hope you have all of it if you want to pull off your marriage to Taz Foster," Harry Lee said. "Abraham Foster pressed for more, you know."

"It is not your concern."

"Oh, Jo, you do have it, don't you?" Charlotte cried. "Oh, Heavens to Betsy!"

"Calm yourself, Charlotte." Jo glanced over at Charlotte, and then back at Harry Lee. "I have it. I need only to retrieve it."

Harry Lee sat back. "It will be a relief to Foster. Sometimes, Cousin, you outsmart yourself."

"Oh, do be quiet!" Jo hissed. Her temper was beginning to rise.

"You do have it, then," Charlotte said, relief evident in her tone. "You had my heart fluttering so. I would hate for all the news for you to be so bleak."

"News?" Jo questioned. "You have news for me?"

Charlotte glanced nervously over at Harry Lee and pleaded with her eyes. He grinned, but he shook his head.

Jo felt her heart race. Something was wrong. She turned to the only one who would tell her the truth. She stared at Harry Lee.

"What is it that you all know that I do not?"

"Good Lord, Jo. You live in a little world that you create for yourself. You see only what you want," Harry Lee began. "You wear your heart on your sleeve and take in every stray thing you encounter…your little entourage. Yet, you are not a fragile thing."

"I do not need to be lectured, Harry Lee. I know what you think of me. Tell me. Tell me now!"

"Do not get high and mighty on me, Miss Wright. You have brought this upon yourself …"

Somewhere down in her soul, she feared what was going to be said, but she feared more not knowing. "What has happened?"

"Harry Lee, watch your words. Our Jo has a good heart…that is all," Grace Ann said and her face was suddenly quiet and somber. "It is only because we know how close you are to your Gillie and Miss Hazel…"

Charlotte reached over and took Jo's hand into hers. "Oh, dear Jo, I wish you could understand that Grandfather didn't have a choice. Clarissa was livid when she discovered that Wade's man, Heyward, was seeing your Gillie…she went wild, crying that Heyward would want to see Gillie and in turn Wade would be forced to see you…She forced Wade to leave Heyward behind on their trip. Then…then Grandfather sold him."

Jo went silent and her heart sank. Oh, Heavens Above! Whatever was she going to do? It was going to break Miss Hazel's heart…and dear, sweet Gillie. She swallowed. "Who was he sold to?"

Harry Lee answered, "Holt Miller."

* * * *

Beaufort was the first stop on their wedding trip. Wade had chosen it, remembering the feeling of tranquility the place evoked within him after Percival's death. Once more a wave of nostalgia overcame him. He wondered at times whether the feeling would ever leave him.

Wade Montgomery looked over at his wife. Clarissa was beautiful this morning, dressed in a pale pink flowered muslin dress with a delightful matching bonnet and new white gloves. Her blue eyes sparkled as they rode around Beaufort in an open carriage. Everyone in the streets paused to watch the lovely pair from Charleston as they rode along the narrow streets…such a handsome pair.

The happy newlyweds had arrived at Wade's Uncle William Martin's a week ago. His mother's brother gleefully welcomed Wade and his bride. Uncle William's home was grand and spacious. Situated along the sea coast, the house offered everything for a young couple to enjoy.

The grounds of the plantation were magnificent. Large oak trees covered in Spanish moss lined a path down to one of the most eye-pleasing beaches Wade had ever seen. He had already found himself enjoying the fishing it offered. The cove, also, lent to privacy, which Wade planned to use to his full advantage.

The time away from his immediate family and Magnolia Bluff had been a welcome relief. The issues upon him faded the farther away from his home…the farther away from Grandfather, Cullen, and…Josephine. Though, some concerns he couldn't distance himself from…the cry for war never faded. Dinners had been filled with the ramblings of secession and rants against the cowardly Yankees. But, somehow, here in Beaufort, war seemed a distant threat.

He snapped the reins and glanced over at Clarissa, who batted her long black lashes at him and smiled ever so prettily. She sat demurely with her hands folded in her lap, like a proper Charleston belle had been born and bred to do.

This time together had been good for the both of them. He had not pressured her on consummating their union. He discovered she had a real fear of making love. He was certain it came from listening to her aunt telling her to *endure* the primal needs of her husband. It was her *duty*. Never would he forget the look on her face when he kissed her lovely ivory neck as his hand cupped her breast over her nightdress. Shocked. Stunned. Mortified.

He was on a mission and found himself enjoying his seduction of his wife. He was an accomplished lover and needed only to wait until her fear subsided. He was making progress…he was no longer sleeping on the chair. Moreover, her body ceased to stiffen on his touch when they were alone in their room.

That she cared for him, he had no doubts. He had seen it in her eyes. He had caught her several times watching him as they sat on the veranda with their mint-garnished drinks. The lazy days…time alone, just the two of them. The time approached when she would welcome his presence.

Soon…soon he would have her naked body under his, crying out his name.

Uncle William and Aunt Lydia had been the most gracious hosts, seeing to their every need. Wade found himself greatly enjoying his time with his uncle. Uncle William was a renowned horseman and bragged he had the finest horses south of Virginia. A fact Wade would not dispute, especially his uncle's eye for the finest horses. Uncle William had just bought an impressive stallion, a big brute…a winner for certain.

The ride back to the plantation from Beaufort was no more than half an hour. Wade smiled when Clarissa eased close to his side and squeezed his arm. As they rounded the bend, Wade noticed excitement down by the barn. His uncle stood by the wagon and nodded approvingly.

"God bless him. Wonder what he's done gone and bought now."

"Oh, goodness! I believe your present is here!" whispered Clarissa excitedly. "Your uncle handled my request so quickly. I hope you are pleased."

"I'm certain whatever it is, I will be," Wade answered her enthusiastically, certain it was a racehorse. "You should not have done so, my dear."

"But I did. It is my fault Heyward is no longer with you—"

Immediately, he reined in the horses and brought the carriage to an abrupt halt. Clarissa caught herself falling forward. He gave her no support. Instead, his eyes bore into her.

"Heyward has only stayed at Magnolia Bluff while we are traveling because Grandfather requested he do so. Make no mistake about it— Heyward will become a member of our household on our return."

Color rose in her cheeks; she shook her head.
"Wade…Wade…please do not be mad. It…was only…only…"

"What do you know that I do not?" he demanded.

She lowered her head and visibly shook. "Surely, you will not be angry…he is only a slave…"

He gripped her shoulders and forced her to look up at him. "Tell me now."

"Your grandfather sold Heyward. Oh, don't look at me like that, Wade. You could not expect me to accept Heyward, knowing that…that woman would use him to get at you with her disgusting little maid of hers."

"You know that Heyward is attached to Gillie?"

Her lips pressed together tightly, she said nothing. Her silence answered his question.

Outraged, Wade released his wife and pushed her away from him. The next few hours were a blur. He remembered distinctly walking down to his uncle, who showed him his new man much like Uncle William had shown him his prize racehorse.

Wade thanked his uncle for his hospitality, but explained he had been called back to Magnolia Bluff. He packed in the midst of Clarissa's cries.

"Don't leave me, Wade. You can't. We have only just begun our wedding trip."

He wrenched her hands from his arm. "My dear, I had been willing to start a life with you…you. I was willing to forget all the harsh things you said and did before our wedding, the scandal you almost created. I thought you manipulated by circumstances.

"I have been a fool, for it is you who is manipulating me." He laughed harshly. "You continue on the trip…by yourself, because I go to rectify your actions."

"Please, Wade. I love you so."

"Love? Truly? If you loved me, you would not recoil at my touch. You would trust me. I am your husband, Clarissa. No matter what you have been told…no matter what has happened in the past…I married you. Know it is you who is destroying whatever we had begun."

"Take me with you. I will change. I will…"

"I can't deal with you at the moment, Clarissa. You tell people whatever you will. I don't care."

He left her in tears and rode back to Magnolia Bluff…alone, without Clarissa or his *new* man.

* * * *

Jo stood quietly in the open-way of the barn, trying to think. The stable boy, Boyd, hurriedly saddled up her horse, continually glancing back at her. No doubt nervous to do as she bid. She had never ridden this early in the morning…with only Gillie by her side.

A rain-driven gust swept through the unlatched barn doors. She shivered; from the rain or her nerves, she didn't know. She had quite made up her mind the best course of action to take and was fully aware of the danger her plan of action presented. Now she had only to find her courage.

She looked over at Gillie. Gillie gave her an anxious smile, but it was a smile. The first she had seen since Heyward had been sold, a semblance of hope in a desperate situation. Good Lord! The mess she had made of not only her life, but poor, poor Gillie…her heart was broken, for more reason than an affair of the heart gone astray.

Never had the chains of slavery bore upon her. They did today…she hated it. She hated that slaves were not thought to have hearts. How could men be so cruel to each other?

She fought back her distress. She needed her concentration on her journey—first to retrieve her money, next to retrieve Heyward. She had lost her innocence of the world around her. She realized that retrieving Heyward would cost more than money…that was her fear.

In the midst of the rain, she saw figures emerge and walk into the barn. Oh, for Heaven's sake! It was Harry Lee and Buck.

"You could have waited until after the weather broke."

"Harry Lee, you are not going to stop me—"

"It is not my intention. Buck and I are going with you."

Startled, Jo could not believe her ears or eyes. Harry Lee took his hat off and slung off the water. He looked up at her and smiled. Then he ran his hand through his hair and placed his hat back on top of his head.

Buck yawned with an annoyed expression plastered on his face, but said nothing. He tucked his loose shirt into his pants.

"What are you guys doing?" Jo questioned.

"Helping you, Josephine," Harry Lee said, and gestured to the stable boy. "Boyd, saddle up our horses as well."

"I'm going—"

"I know exactly what you have planned. You are as easy to read as a child who wants candy. You want to go *save* that slave of Wade's for your precious Gillie." He turned and gave Gillie a sly grin, and then turned back to Jo. "I told Grandpa Henry I figured you have your money somewhere and knew you would try something. Just had to wait until you did."

"Don't try to stop me. I promise you—"

He laughed. "I will tell you again, Cousin; we are here to help you. Do you think we would let you go to Miller's by yourself? We are Buchanans."

Harry Lee was never one to waste his time. Jo suspected he had an alternative motive, but at the moment, there was something comforting with his presence. She mounted up and rode into the rain.

* * * *

"It is a hell of a thing. I'm surprised the Buchanans haven't called you out. Harry Lee is a hothead. I can't imagine how you have avoided a duel to this point. Thinking on it, it is odd."

"It will not come to that." Wade's response came after a long pause. The conversation had gone awry…again.

Cullen's own mood was foul. Frustrated and exasperated, the answers he had sought in Charleston had not materialized. He had returned to Magnolia Bluff last evening, only to discover Wade's unexpected presence.

The time in Charleston was not all wasted. His papers had gone through. It was official. He was no longer in the Navy. He needed only to make one visit in Washington to put this Navy career behind him.

Cullen realized it was time to leave the Navy, but it was not without reservations. He loved the ocean. He could never explain his comfort on the water. Nothing in his transient life seemed very important when he stood on the deck of his ship. The ocean transformed the world around him, made his troubles minuscule in the galaxy of stars above him and the water below.

He walked along the beach for hours and contemplated his life. He had always considered himself a logical man, but there was nothing logical about what was going on around him. He had written his father, who responded with a request for him to withdraw himself from the situation.

It is not yours, Son. There seems to have been a web that has been dropped. Don't get tangled up in the mess.

He couldn't deny the words his father wrote held truth. His father had always been the voice of reason, not prone to emotions that seemed to run rampant within his Southern family.

The offer for Josephine's hand had been refused. His obligation paid, he was free to return back to Philadelphia to begin a life out of the Navy and follow his father into his business. Why then could he not bring himself to depart?

Perhaps she was nothing more than a distraction, a need to grasp hold of meaning in his life. He held to the beliefs that were instilled in him in his youth. It was how he lived his life. Had not his strong sense of duty and loyalty led to the offer?

Then why couldn't he get her off his mind…her eyes staring at him, her body against his, his lips on hers…

He had come to one conclusion. He needed to return to Philadelphia, away from this madness that had gripped Magnolia Bluff…but not alone. He intended to return with Josephine as his bride…over the rejection of his suit from her family…over the objections of his.

He had not told anyone, including Wade, of his intention. He had enough with all the fuss. It should not be so complicated. He was confident if he spoke to Josephine's father, he would convince the man of the viability of the marriage. He wanted no more talk of scandal or Wade…not of Josephine contemplating marriage to any other man…not Holt Miller…not Taz Foster.

Now, he needed only to convince Josephine…which was his intention this morning. He had not wanted to get into another discussion with Wade, especially not about his slave. Last night, he had interrupted an argument between Wade and Grandfather over the fact that Grandfather had upped and sold the slave, Heyward.

The argument carried over into this morning. Cullen wanted no part of it. He wanted only to call upon Josephine. Wade still fumed. Granted, Cullen agreed, it was all a little odd, but it meant little to him. Moreover, if his man meant so much to him, why had Wade not brought him along on his wedding trip?

Cullen was tired of regressing backwards in discussions with Wade. Nothing seemed to appease his cousin. There was no purpose arguing further. Annoyed and frustrated, Cullen strode toward the door.

Wade followed and called out, "Leave well enough alone, Cullen. Go home. I should have never pulled you into this mess. I apologize, but I will see to it now."

"The hell you will," Cullen snapped. He halted and stepped up into Wade's face. "I've seen how you have handled it."

"What's that supposed to mean?" Wade's aggravation emerged. He pushed Cullen back as his eyes bored into Cullen.

"You know well what I mean! You are trying to maneuver this thing to your advantage …instead of looking after her best interests…tell me that you don't have plans for her after she bores of this schoolteacher." Cullen laughed at Wade's silence and took a step back. "I'm right. I knew it."

"You're an ass!"

"Perhaps." Cullen reached for the handle to the front door. He turned back to his cousin. "Look, Wade, you said you came to see if you could retrieve your slave that Grandfather sold behind your back. Do that. I will do what I…"

Behind Cullen, Wade abruptly slammed the door shut with one hand. "It's what I've been telling you. It's connected. You don't understand any more than you understand Josephine."

Cullen stopped abruptly. "Then enlighten me."

Wade swallowed hard. "Heyward was with me when I met with Josephine. He began a courtship of sorts with her maid…companion…Gillie. Clarissa confessed to me that she made a request of Grandfather…to sell Heyward because she feared it would be used by Jo to meet with me."

"It makes no sense."

"I told you that you don't know Jo."

Wade's tone said much more than his words. *I know her better than you ever will. She loves me. You are going in blindly in a place you have no purpose.*

Wade went on. "You have insulted me without cause. I would never treat Josephine in that manner or Clarissa. I understand only too well when I wed Clarissa, Jo is out of my life. It does not mean I do not care, but I would never compromise her…again. She does not deserve this."

"You realized that you brought this whole thing upon us with your foolishness. Remember the night of your wedding—"

"I was drunk," Wade didn't let him finish, "and jealous…of which I have no right." Wade's manner eased; his voice lowered. "Know now, I'm here only to rectify the damage done. Clarissa knows I'm here and why, as I know what she has done.

"That is the reason I have returned. My conscience gnaws at me. I can't begin my new life. I need to rectify the wrongs done. Clarissa was the one to demand Heyward be sold."

Cullen looked at Wade coolly. "Then do what you need to do, as will I."

He swung open the door and descended down the stairs. The rains had eased, at least for the moment. His horse waited, tied to the hitching post. It was only then he noticed they had visitors; Wade had already seen them.

Harry Lee and Buck rode up the lane and halted in front of Cullen.

"Morning," Harry Lee greeted them with a broad grin. He tipped his rain-soaked hat toward Cullen.

Cullen studied the two for a moment. Finally, he said, "Morning. What brings you our way?"

Harry Lee leaned back on his horse. "You do, Lieutenant Smythe."

* * * *

There was more to Miss Josephine Buchanan Wright than Cullen had imagined. Wade had known, which aggravated him to no end. When Harry Lee informed him he had come for the valise, Cullen's temper flared.

He thought Jo had sent for her dowry to marry that schoolteacher, but it had not been the case. It was painful for him to acknowledge, but Wade had been correct in his assumption.

The distance from Magnolia Bluff to Miss Hazel's cabin was no more than half an hour in good weather. But the darkened heavens burst forth with a downpour. Lightning lit up the sky; thunder roared. It took over an hour.

The small farm lay eerily silent as they rode up. The dogs and chickens seemed to have found shelter from the storm. A door creaked open and broke the quiet. Josephine appeared. She stood motionless for a moment on the porch.

She looked as if she had been caught out in the storm. She wore a rain-soaked navy riding habit under a cloak: her hair disheveled; her eyes reddened; her face flushed.

"You came?" She looked at Cullen, puzzled and nervous. She glanced over at Harry Lee. "I thought you went to get the valise."

"He didn't give it to me. Insisted on seeing you. Both of them did."

Cullen watched her eye Wade. She was clearly upset. Moreover, she seemed quite anxious. Her gaze shifted back over her shoulder. He dismounted.

"What are you up to, Josephine? Harry Lee says you have a wild scheme about getting Heyward back," Wade admonished as he jerked the reins back on his horse. "Surely you aren't that foolish to think Miller will sell him to you!"

"It is not your concern, Wade Montgomery!" she cried. Her dark eyes snapped with fire at Wade. "It was you who sold him! I asked you only for one thing…one thing…to see to Gillie and Heyward's welfare and you had him sold! To Miller!"

"Good Lord, woman, I have ridden half the state to rectify the misunderstanding."

She stood there defiant, yet something was amiss. Cullen sensed it. Behind her bold claim, he could hear a quiver in her voice. Her hands trembled so bad she clutched to her skirt.

"You are frightened," Cullen said as an observation. He walked up the steps. She looked at him, and then at the others still on their horses. She retreated a step. He would have none of it. He grasped hold of her arm and forced her to look at him. "Tell me what is wrong."

Her eyes widened; her body shivered. Lord give him strength! She had ridden here in this weather. Her clothes were still soaked. She was going to catch her death!

"Look here, Smythe…" Harry Lee leapt off his horse.

Cullen held his hand up, warning Harry Lee not to advance. He wasn't going to let her go until he had answers. Josephine lowered her gaze, but said nothing.

"Josephine," he began.

"Please, Cullen," she pleaded. She looked up and pressed her lips together as if finding it difficult to find the words she wanted to say. She reached over and laid her hands on his chest, fumbled with the lapel of his coat. Her bottom lip trembled.

"You have not called upon me. Grandpa Henry said your offer is no more." She paused, and choked back the tears that welled in her eyes. "It would not matter if it had been accepted. I have need of the money far more than for a dowry. Tell me…tell me you brought it."

He shook his head. "Not with me. I took it to Charleston and placed it into an account…"

"Oh, no…no," she cried. Her hand covered her mouth. For an instant, fear flickered in her eyes. She clutched Cullen's hand. "Get it. Oh, please…you have to."

Behind her, he heard moaning…movement. Drawn to the sounds, he released Jo. Opening the door wider, he saw her distress.

A fire burned in the fireplace. Beyond it, Miss Hazel and Gillie stood beside the bed. They leaned over and wiped the tattered back of a black man who had been soundly whipped. He lay on his belly, naked and unconscious. The injuries oozed with a dark red fluid. From his view, at least fifty slashes. Both women looked up, justifiably nervous.

Cullen needed no other explanation. The women harbored an escaped slave… Heyward had run away from Miller.

Chapter Nine

"Dammit, Jo! What have you gone and done now?"

"Harry Lee, do not use that language with me," Jo retorted. She did not need to be told the severity of their situation. "You cannot believe I knew Heyward would have escaped and ran back to Miss Hazel."

"Think now the position he puts you in," Harry Lee said.

Jo shot Harry Lee a reproachful glance. She would have liked to have told him he was overreacting, but knew he was not. Miller would never allow Heyward to be sold after he ran away. Jo feared a far worse fate awaited Heyward. She understood the code of slavery only too well.

Growing up, she had been instilled with pride for her ancestors' fight for freedom, but that freedom hadn't extended to slaves. Freedom of slaves scared the good plantation owners in the South. A slave uprising was a constant fear. A way of life threatened meant that a runaway slave had to be found…had to be punished. Hope of freedom was not allowed for any slave.

On their ride toward the Montgomerys', Jo had confessed where her money was—her own attempt to escape—to Harry Lee and Buck. Harry Lee seemed quite amused by the tale. A short time later, he suggested she and Gillie stay at Miss Hazel's until he retrieved the valise.

She hadn't argued; rather, she felt relief. She had no desire to go to Magnolia Bluff. Strange, but at that moment, she felt trusting Harry Lee was the right thing to do. She had never done so before, but he had never shown this much compassion for her.

The group broke off at the lane that went up to the cabin. Gillie had gone into the dwelling to ensure Miss Hazel had a fire; Jo had taken the horses out to the barn. She was miserable, wet to the bone, and wanted only to return to the cabin to dry by the fire.

It was then she saw him…Heyward. In the stillness of the rain, the motionless figure looked like a fallen log. Then it moved. Stunned at first, she was too tense to move. Edging closer, she noticed light convulsions shook the figure.

Horrified, her heart froze as she recognized Heyward. His back was ripped, striped with whip lashes. His arms and legs were scratched and bruised; his feet cut up from running through the woods barefoot.

She had never seen a whipping, but she had heard they stripped the slave and tied them to a post. Heyward was a proud man. She could only imagine the humiliation of the punishment. The torture…pain. A sick sensation overwhelmed her at the thought.

The shock didn't hit her until they had him on the bed. She watched Miss Hazel hover over her son and whisper to him lovingly; tears streamed down Gillie's cheeks. Everyone in the room understood the magnitude of Heyward's actions. Then she broke down and wept, for there would be no sympathy for the suffering of a slave. It was not allowed.

Cullen walked across the room and brought her back to the present. The fire burning in the fireplace illuminated a small aura around him. Her heart stirred with his presence…a strange comfort. Oddly, it carried no sense of disloyalty to the memory she once shared with Wade.

How short a period of time her heart had swelled with feelings for the man in front of her. The girl she had been with Wade had matured. She had lost her naïve view of the world.

"Tell me what you would have me do," Cullen said simply.

She wished she might go to him and find shelter in his arms. But he had said the words briskly…bluntly, reawakening her resolve. Swallowing back her selfish need to be loved, she must not betray her weakness.

"So you want your valise back to save this slave," Cullen said "You should have come to me yourself and explained. I do not like you are here."

She considered his declaration. "I did send you notes. I received no response. Charlotte said you had gone to Charleston. Grandpa Henry told me your offer had been refused. What did you expect me to do? I had no choice but to handle this myself. I do not expect any more from you than to return the valise…that is all I want."

"It is not here. Moreover, I wouldn't give it to you even if it was here."

"It is the only thing that will save Heyward now." Panic grew within her. If she could not convince him to buy Heyward, then the poor man's future looked bleak indeed.

"Don't know if you can save him. Not at this point," Cullen said frankly. "But he cannot stay here. Wade and I agree that the best course of action is to get him back to Magnolia Bluff. It's our best chance in dealing with Miller."

"What if…." She wanted to push to get them to help Heyward escape…to go against their upbringing…against the law. Moreover, it would be a great risk to their own lives.

He made a quick, despairing gesture, his frustration evident. "I have told you I will do what is necessary. You will stay here and wait."

She nodded solemnly. She did not need to be told he echoed the sentiments of the men in the room. It was not only Heyward who was endangered. If he was found here, Gillie, Miss Hazel, and she would pay a steep price for giving refuge to an escaped slave. She had known the risk the moment she saw Heyward. Yet she refused to do nothing.

She had never been so scared in her life.

* * * *

Time passed slowly. Josephine sat beside Miss Hazel; strange, for she had a need for her mammy much as she had when she was a child. Miss Hazel held her against her bosom, gently caressing Jo's head.

"Ya are so much like your father," Miss Hazel rambled on in a nervous way. "Ya used ta get so mad as a young girl when I told you. My, oh, my! What a temper ya had. Your little lips would pout. Ya'd stomp your feet. Ya wanted to look like your momma.

"Oh, ya loved your momma. Ya'd tell me that one day ya would grow up to look just like her, always bragging ya had the most beautiful momma. Ya did. Miss Lucinda looked like an angel. I can see her now, with her sunflower hair and brilliant blue sparkling eyes. How she loved your papa and you. I remember once you held a cocoon in your hand. Ya told me that you figured that was how it was going to be—that one morning you were going to wake up and have golden hair.

"You waited, so confident it would happen." Miss Hazel sighed. "Of course, it never did. I stopped telling ya that ya looked like your papa, acted like him too. Oh…you two butted heads even when ya was just a mite ca'se you both so alike…two peas in a pod, I'd say.

"Now ya gotta find it within yourself to act like him now. Your papa…now he has a talent… All them people gettin' mad about losing money to him…accused him of all sorts of things. Cheatin! Lord A'mighty! The man would never stoop so low…not your papa. A gentleman, he is." She chuckled to herself. "It's his ability to recall every card played—in order. He used to practice with me and your momma. Amazing...watching him, but his talent...his real talent is his temperament. Nobody can read his real feelings, like a mask...that's what ya hafta do...dig deep within yourself and find that in ya now. It's there."

Jo pushed upward and looked into Miss Hazel's face. "I won't let you down."

Miss Hazel pressed her lips together tightly, choking back her emotions. Jo had never seen her so.

Suddenly, boots pounded across the porch and the door swung open. Buck raced inside.

"It ain't good. There's riders."

From her vantage point, Josephine could see the group of riders draw near. The storm had broken, but a gray haze encompassed the rain-soaked ground. The men rode up. Their faces betrayed their angry purpose; their hands held tight to their pistols.

"Damnation," Buck stated. "It's the special patrol."

Suddenly, Jo's stomach ached; her head hurt. Fear churned inside her. *Heaven above, don't let me get sick.*

She glanced behind her. Miss Hazel looked so vulnerable...so helpless, scarcely able to draw a breath.

A deep-toned threat from the depths of hell stood at their door. Her blood pulsed faster. Through the glass pane, she saw the stocky, middle-aged man dismount. He was coming inside.

Buck cocked his pistol. Jo stepped forward. She warned, "Don't."

The next instant, the door swung open. Jo whirled around. In walked Holt Miller; behind him, a couple of his men, armed and looking extremely dangerous.

"Well...well...well. Look what we found, boys."

"What are you doing here?" Jo asked when she found her voice.

The moment was tense while Miller looked around the small cabin. Then he broke the quiet. "Searching for a runaway."

"Got no runaway here," Buck answered in a gruff voice. "Now it's best you leave."

"Don't tell me what to do, Buck," Miller warned. "I will leave when I get answers."

His pudgy red face smiled at Jo, a scornful smile. His expression remained imperturbable; a pistol readied in his hand. His gaze sent a chill down her spine. He hated her. There was no mistaking it. It was in his eyes.

"Tell me, Miss Wright, why you are here."

From the corner of her eye, she saw Miss Hazel, her eyes pleading with her. *Don't make this worse!* She swallowed back her retort and smiled. This was going to be difficult.

"Why, Mr. Miller, I swear, I do believe you are mad at me."

"Ain't the time or place to get into that, Miss Wright," Miller said. "Reckon you got about a minute to answer me before the men start taking this place apart."

She laughed. "You aren't serious? Please tell, why you would ever think such a thing?"

"'Cause that nigger wench is his mother...'cause something stinks about the whole thing." His voice had a cold edge. Jo's heart churned at the unfeeling man...the man who inflicted the suffering upon another human being.

"You're a funny man, Mr. Miller. You sounding so nasty and all." She glanced over at Buck, whose finger lay on the trigger of his pistol. His eyes bore into the man. Her cousin sensed the same as she: the man was on the edge. "Here I was thinking when you rode up, that my little old prayer had been answered."

"Like most women, ya ain't makin' no sense," he quipped.

Her fear became overwhelming when she looked into his eyes. Fear was replaced only with an emerging anger as comprehension sank deep within her...he had come to destroy not only Heyward, but everything attached to his slave. She would not allow that to happen...ever.

"I want your runaway," Jo told him. "I will pay you for him whatever you have been out...perhaps I should say, Grandpa Henry will pay. I know he will."

"You must think me a fool."

"Would it not ease your frustration?"

"That nigger deserves what is coming his way. The penalties are known to all."

"Oh, come, Mr. Miller. Let us lay our cards on the table. You know well Miss Hazel was my mammy and my papa set her up here. It is why I'm here today—because she called for me. It's his property you threaten. When he returns—which will be soon enough—he is going to be angry if Miss Hazel is upset and all.

"Already his ire boils at the Montgomerys. A while back, Papa tried to buy Heyward and had been refused. Now with the whispers about me…and a Montgomery…then they up and sell him to you," she sucked in air and continued, "I believe it's you who has a choice to make."

His eyebrow rose. "That would be?"

"Sell Heyward to me—or keep him and then answer to Papa. You know Papa, don't you, Mr. Miller? His reputation is well earned. He may not run you through with a sword, but he will ruin you…you know he will."

Miller ran his hand over his bristled face. With a grave nod, he shrugged. "Got no quarrel against your papa nor he with me. He knows our laws."

"I'm sure he does," she agreed. She met his eyes. "I'm sure he will be quite understanding, Mr. Miller, Papa being who he is. You go ahead and have this slave die by your hands. You do what you believe is best and hold to the fact that you have the law behind you. All I will ask— don't sell him back to the Montgomerys."

She saw a flicker in his eyes.

Behind her, a voice called. "Found him, Miller. Just got word. He made it back to Magnolia Bluff."

"Mount up," Miller commanded. He said nothing more.

Josephine watched the group ride off. Buck never took his finger off his pistol. The immediate danger dissipated, but there would be no rest.

Jo couldn't deny that hope rose inside her. Miller wanted no trouble from her papa, but, there was no mistake that he wanted to humiliate her for her refusal of him…hurt her. She had just given him a way to do so. She only prayed he took it.

* * * *

Cullen rode back to Miss Hazel's. The day hastened to dusk. Above him, drab skies gave promise of a dark night. There would be no moonlight to light a journey after the sunset. After this day, he doubted many decent folk would be making their way about until morning.

It was over, but the fever pitch of the escape would not simply vanish. Tempers had run high. That damn patrol had wanted blood…wanted to have seen Heyward strung up. Their appetite had not been satisfied…at least not on this day.

His heart caught in his throat when Miller rode up and stated he had left Josephine back at Miss Hazel's cabin. A million thoughts ran rampant in his head…one he had not— Miller calling for him after ascertaining Heyward's condition.

"God Amighty, where is that smart-ass fucking Yankee!"

Soon after, the threat had been averted. Heyward would remain at Magnolia Bluff, at least until he recovered…if he recovered. The slave had been badly tortured; his wounds extensive. He lay in the sick house. When Cullen departed, his aunt had been tending to his injuries.

Behind him, a carriage rolled down the road, set to take Josephine back to Magnolia Bluff. It had been deemed the safest place. Charlotte had wanted to come to retrieve her friend, but had been denied permission. She would see her friend soon enough.

The muddy road made for a slow pace. Deep in the woods, he heard the sounds of life emerging after a storm: chickadees sang, crickets chirped. He prayed that Buck had seen to Josephine's safety.

As he rounded the bend, Cullen caught sight of Buck on the porch, gun in hand. He gestured to Cullen.

Relief flooded him. One worry averted; now, his attention to the other battle he was assured was about to take place.

* * * *

"I'm not going."

"It isn't a choice." Cullen spoke the command. Annoyance etched into her face told she would ignore his warning. "Why won't you listen to me?"

"I have heard every word you have spoken," she started. Anger was there in her voice. "I want only to go home."

"I don't understand, Josephine. I thought you would be pleased."

"Pleased?" She shook her head. "Relieved, but not pleased."

He watched her in wonder. She had no reaction when he told her that Heyward had been spared. Instead, she had comforted Miss Hazel. Overwhelmed, the old woman collapsed on the floor. Jo's companion had been of no use, for she herself wept in the corner.

Jo untied her horse and walked it out of the stall. She gasped as he caught her hand when she went to tighten the strap of the saddle. *The stubborn woman!* He forced her to look at him.

"Do you not want to see for yourself Heyward is safe?"

"Safe? Is he? Truly?" Her voice quivered; she lowered her gaze. "Miss Hazel and Gillie are set to go in the carriage. I hope you will not refuse to transport them. They have a strong need to see Heyward. I have given Gillie permission to stay as long as she deems necessary."

She drew in a breath as if she had the weight of the world upon her shoulders. "I have much to do. Grandpa Henry, I fear, will be disappointed once more with my actions, but I will need to smooth out today's events to gather his permission for Heyward's presence. I fear—"

"You want to take him to the Groves?"

101

She looked back up at him and nodded. "But of course. I will take responsibility for him."

She did not appear nearly as angry as he first thought. More thoughtful than annoyed.

"Jo, do you understand what transpired?"

"Miller sold Heyward to you. For that I am grateful. Truly I am. It is only now…" A sudden tide of conflicting emotions seemed to rage within her. She reached over and touched his hand that held her arm, warm and tender. "Now, I will have to face my disgrace. You do not have to tell me that my dowry is no more. I have had to contemplate the circumstances. Miller would have wanted to have been well compensated."

She did not have to say few men would want to wed her now. He understood she had clung to the hope that the semblance of a dowry her father had left her would suffice to save her reputation and an honorable marriage.

She had sacrificed it all for the life of a slave. Few would give her accolades for the action. Moreover, it would be held in contempt by those who held to the stiff, unforgiving rules of Charleston society…the same rules that dismissed another human's worth simply by the color of their skin.

Josephine understood the consequences. She had lived her life under the shadow of scandal. It was the only world she had lived…a world she loved despite everything. It ripped at the core of her being…just as it had his.

"Let us talk. Give me but a moment to see to the others."

* * * *

They stood on the porch and watched the carriage disappear around the bend. He had done as she requested: first sending Buck along his way and then Miss Hazel and Gillie to see their loved one.

Foolish. For now, Josephine was alone with him, compromised once more and vulnerable. He looked over at her and a memory flashed vividly in his mind, of holding her in his arms and tasting her lips. It was decidedly difficult not to take her in his arms again.

She moved back a step. "I need to leave myself. So tell me quickly what it is you want to say. It will be dark before I get back to the Groves."

He held back on his instinct to refute her intention of riding alone back to her home. He had intended to make it quick, not to linger. She had an effect upon him that no other woman had ever had. Her mere presence distracted him.

102

"I did not use your money. As I told you, I have kept it safe for you."

She eyed him suspiciously. "You told me that you bought Heyward. That he was no longer a slave under Miller."

"I did not lie. I bought Heyward, Josephine. I bought him with my money, not yours. Miller wanted assurance that Heyward would no longer be in South Carolina. He did not want a reminder that a runaway slave evaded his punishment."

"You are going to take him North?"

"It is what I have planned. Prepare yourself, though; he is greatly injured."

"I know only too well." Her voice faltered. "Your compassion overwhelms me."

"There is one thing more. I freed him. Heyward is now a free man. He will have to accompany me up North and his freedom will not be widely known. There is no need to rile Miller back up in arms. Heyward will have a position in my household if he wants."

She reached for his arm and halted his words. "You freed him?" she gasped. "Why did you do so? The money you are out...all for..."

"For you."

Time stilled. He pulled her to him, no longer resisting his repressed need for the woman. Nothing mattered in that moment, only his intense desire for her...for Josephine. She moved closer, allowed him to press her body to his. The need was not his alone.

Behind her, the sun lowered on the horizon, tinged the sky a brilliant red, and highlighted her beautiful face. Her hair, once held up in a bun, had loosened, feathering against her pale skin; her eyes softened.

Lovely...simply lovely.

Lowering his head, he inhaled her being. Her breath quickened with the beat of her heart as he leaned down his lips to hers and touched them softly. He felt her tremble beneath his kiss.

Her lips lingered a moment, long enough to tell him everything he wanted to know. She wanted what he offered...he had no need to ask permission or to be afraid of her refusal.

Her hands clutched his coat's lapel. She opened them, pressing against his chest, but not in resistance. She had surrendered to his desire.

He pressed her back through the door, kicking it with the back of his boot, and slammed it shut. They would not be disturbed. He laid her down on the bed, the one only hours before held a runaway slave. Remnants of the man stripped away, it held only a bare mattress that sank with their weight.

103

He cupped the nape of her neck so she could accept his kisses. He seduced her mouth open. His need drove him to taste, explore and possess the woman, while her gasps and breath spoke of her own passion.

In his grasp, her body molded to his. He grew bolder. He touched the buttons to her jacket…buttons never meant to be touched by a male's hand, undone to expose the swell of her breasts. Her hand went to his to halt his intent.

"I can't," she whispered.

His gazed locked on hers. He could not allow that…not now. He was in a situation in which he had lost his control.

"My sweet magnolia, are you going to deny us what is inevitable? It has been this way since I first lay eyes upon you. You are mine and no other's." He breathed the declaration against her mouth.

His mouth crushed against hers, giving her no time to answer, only respond to his kiss. She melted with his touch, and then circled his neck with her arms. With abandon, he ravished her mouth. Never had he been so completely besotted.

He finished unbuttoning the last button. He paused a moment only to see if she would stop his intent. She did not. Instead, she leaned up and took off the confining material. She looked back up at him; her corset barely covered her breasts. She reached for him.

Images of her naked body compelled him. He wanted so much to bury himself inside her. Somewhere…something deep within him…urged him caution. She was a virgin. A gentleman would never take advantage of her…but he simply could not contain his desire.

The feel of her body against his compelled him…the taste of her lips, her gasps of first known pleasure…the promise of wanton passion. He kissed her while his hands loosened the corset and pushed it down far enough to free her breasts. She closed her eyes and sighed deeply. His lips moved down her slender throat.

He had never made love to a virgin, but her body moved beneath him in a gentle arch that maddened him. Any nervousness she felt faded, replaced with an eagerness that astonished him…sent him over the edge from seduction to sheer madness.

His gaze fell upon her full, round breasts that beckoned him. He cupped her firm breast and caressed. Her nipples hardened against the gentle kneading. He watched her as his fingers circled the tip, touched lightly, teasing her ever so gently. The barest smile emerged told of her pleasure.

He lowered his head and used his tongue ever so wickedly to madden her. He heard her breath quicken…as he slid his hand down under her skirt… under her pantalets.

Wicked sensations cascaded through her body, pulsated, titillated every inch of her sensitized skin. All of her was alive. The stunning shock of his breath against her breast—suckling one, and then the other—left her craving pleasure her body sensed his touch promised.

The hurt and pain of the day's event seemed distant. It had no place in this moment. He pushed back every thought she had except one…this aching need that had enveloped her. She was not ignorant. This was wrong…so wrong…but she had passed the point of caring.

She could not stop her body's response to his caress and found she had no energy or want to do so. Desire crashed through her wall of conscience. Her need held no reason, only longing.

He looked up at her. His eyes told her he was fully aware of her awakening passion. He watched her as his hand slid down her stomach and gently nudged her legs apart.

"Do not be afraid. Trust me, Josephine," he whispered. "I want only to love you."

She had no voice, but nodded. She was nearly mindless, wanting only to be in his arms, ready to beg him to continue. He responded, gliding her along this journey of discovery.

Once more, his mouth found her breast, suckling until she was mad with want. His hand caressed her thighs and moved to where it covered her mound. His fingers touched her and stroked her being, prolonging each deliberate stroke. Deep warmth flowed within her, stunning her.

Suddenly the sensations within her grew to a point of alarm, as if she balanced on the edge of an abyss…falling into the unknown. Somewhere in the far reaches of her mind, she heard herself call out his name.

Lost in this world, she surrendered to his command. Then abruptly he stopped.

Jo opened her eyes to find he stared down at her. She grasped his arm, looked down at her naked breasts…shocked by her loss of control.

He gave her a small smile.

"Oh, my!"

Reality suffused through her of what had occurred. As if only realizing she lay exposed to his view, she wrapped her jacket over her breasts. Her face flamed.

"Do not be embarrassed. As much as I wanted to take it further…as difficult as it was to give pause, I did so. We will have time enough."

"Time enough?"

"My darling Josephine, you think now I will simply let you go? I have come to the conclusion we are fated to be together." He leaned over and kissed her lips lightly. "I will not fight fate. I want you to revel in our love, not to regret an impulse."

Slowly, he eased off the bed. She gazed at him as he walked toward the door. Fully aware of what had happened, she blushed hotly.

He paused and looked back at her.

"I will leave you to your privacy for a moment. When you are ready, we will talk."

Chapter Ten

Sweat streamed down Wade's back. Good God! It was so damn humid and hot. The small cabin, which served as the sick house of the slaves on Magnolia Bluff, had only one tiny window.

"Get some boys in here to fan him," Wade commanded and wiped his mouth with his hand. He had half a mind to send for Andrew. He was still in Charleston.

His anger mounted at the sight before him. It hadn't been a good day. He would have liked nothing better than to have run through Holt Miller for what he had done to Heyward. Lord have mercy!

Not one of the slaves at Magnolia Bluff had a scarred back. To see this...the whole of Heyward's back torn up—it was enough to make him vomit. Miller could have easily killed the man.

His anger was not only directed at Miller. His grandfather held his wrath along with... Clarissa, his bride.

His mother had instructed Old Olivia, the healing woman, to stay by Heyward throughout the night. Old Olivia sat there now and sporadically washed the wounds gently with a wet cloth. Heyward unconsciously grimaced in pain.

Wade had been prepared to negotiate with Miller for Heyward. If necessary, take the exchange to court. It had not been necessary. The man had one objective when he had been shown Heyward stretched out naked on a cot in the sick house.

Miller had been satisfied that there had been no aid given the slave to help in his escape. After Miller concluded that Heyward had come back to Magnolia Bluff to seek asylum and beg to be taken back, he wanted only to make a deal with Cullen.

While Cullen sat in negotiations with Miller, Wade had prepared for the worst, even to the point of arming some of his most trusted slaves. He was not about to let Miller get his hands on Heyward again. Surprisingly, his grandfather made no objections and toted his pistol in his belt under his waistcoat.

It had not come to violence.

"Wade."

He looked up to find his wife. She was dressed in one of Charlotte's old day gowns with a kerchief wrapped around her head. She had come to nurse the wounded slave. He had not expected the reaction from Clarissa...moreover, he hadn't known she had come to Magnolia Bluff.

"I have brought your man some opium. Your grandfather sent a message to Andrew, but he had already departed back to Philadelphia. But Dr. Jameson, my father's doctor, sent the medicine out. He said he will be here by morning if needed." Clarissa handed it to Wade. She took in a deep breath and entwined her hands together in a nervous manner. "I know you are annoyed with me, Wade, but I thought I would come to show you that I'm sorry not only by my words, but deeds."

Wade set it down on the table, then he took her by the elbow and led her out the door. "My dear, do you have any concept of what nursing a wounded man means? There's nothing romantic in the work and it is work. There are no comforts here in the sick house. It's hot and sweaty. I would think it would go against your sensibilities."

Wade stared at her. Her face was paper white; her eyes narrowed. She lowered her gaze. He had never seen her so downcast.

"It is my fault. You told me as much. I will not be able to live with myself if he dies," she said in a low, trembling voice. "I came because I do not want you angry with me. I want to be the wife you want."

"I told you we can have no marriage if you do not trust me...if you don't take me on my word."

"I'm ashamed of what I have done, truly. I thought upon what you said and found I could not disagree." Her lip quivered. "I have been selfish and ever so jealous. I want to show you that I can be mistress of Magnolia Bluff."

Wade suddenly laughed, a low, soft laugh. "Hon, you have taken me by surprise. I did not expect you to follow me."

"I told you, Wade, I love you. I have always loved you. It was only...when I heard those rumors...I got so afraid you would leave me. My heart could never bear it." Her voice, barely a whisper, faded into the air. "Then to hear that you pressed Cousin Cullen to offer for me..."

He slowly raised his eyebrow. "I did what?"

"I have reconciled that our marriage was forced upon you. It was only being told that you did not want me..."

He gripped her arm and whirled her around her to face him. "Who told you such?"

She had no time to answer, for at the moment, rapid footsteps approached. Wade looked up to see a distraught Miss Hazel and Gillie rush to the entrance of the cabin. Wade released his grip on Clarissa.

"Calm yourselves. He is resting. Clarissa has brought some opium for his pain."

"Thank you, Master Wade." Miss Hazel hurried by him. "Lieutenant Smythe told us. He did. My heart sings. Thank ya...thank ya all."

Wade let Miss Hazel pass into the cabin. He paused Gillie. "I expected to see my cousin and Miss Josephine. Are they up at the house?"

Gillie shook her head. "No, sir. Miss Josephine refused to come."

"My cousin?"

"He stayed with Miss Jo. I think he wanted to convince her to come back to Magnolia Bluff...he did let Master Buck leave beforehand."

Wade shrugged indifferently. "I'm certain Cullen will take care of Miss Jo. Go see to Heyward."

Gillie hesitated a moment, and then rushed by him. Wade turned back to his wife. A strange expression came over her face as she regarded him.

"Something wrong?"

"It may be nothing, but did the girl say that Buck was with Josephine?"

"Does it matter?"

"No, I suppose not." She hesitated, and then she said, "Odd, though. I thought there was a rift between Josephine and the Buchanan brothers."

"They are still family. Family stands by family."

"Then why would they...Harry Lee and Buck...have been the ones to tell me the sordid tales of you with Josephine."

* * * *

Sounds of the early night surrounded the couple who sat on the porch. Their legs dangled over the edge; their hands entwined. From the corner of her eyes, she saw him smile at her. He pulled her hand to his lips.

"I will miss this." She turned to face him. Gone were the reservations she held. She was ready to face a new life Cullen promised to her. "You will be there with me?"

"I will be by your side," he assured her. "I haven't been home in over two years, but I doubt it has changed much. I believe you will enjoy it. I have a house, Rosemount, outside of the center of Philadelphia in Fairmount Park. It's a home I inherited from my grandmother, my father's mother.

"She left it to me so I would feel the *pull* back to Philadelphia. She had been extremely upset with my father for letting my mother raise me in Charleston. She feared I would not become a true Smythe. You see, it is not only my grandfather and yours who dictate to those they love. My grandmother did so from the grave."

"By leaving you a house?"

"Besides my father, I'm the last of the Smythe line. My father remarried after my mother died, but I have no siblings, only a step-sister. My grandparents' estate was left to me. She cut my father from the will."

"I don't understand."

"It is not complicated." He shrugged. "In honesty, I have given it little thought. I handed over my financial holdings to my father. I gave my father the rights to what should have been his."

"He will not be angry with you for choosing me?"

"I admire my father more than any man I know. He is honorable and true. When he meets you, he will understand."

His dark eyes gleamed. She felt her face warm.

"He will know that I love you," Cullen said. "It will be enough for him."

He drew her to him and embraced her closely. "My father married my mother against his parents' wishes. Mother hated Philadelphia and was so unhappy. When she announced she was with child, he consented to her returning to her home while he traveled on business.

"Father never saw her again. He blames himself for her death, thinking she would have survived if she had been in Philadelphia…if his mother accepted her. That is the reason I know he will accept you."

She leaned up and kissed him. "You have never said you loved me."

"I thought my actions said more than words," he said. "It is your commitment I have not heard."

"I said those words not long ago to another and he left me. My heart reeled from the hurt and betrayal. But you were there." Her heart rose in her throat. "You stepped into his place to hold to the honor of the Montgomerys. You did not have to do so. You watched over me, all the while knowing you were being used by my family, only to have your proposal slung back in your face. There were no strings to tie you to me."

The intensity of the moment grasped hold of her. Only this morning, she thought herself doomed to be shunned by good society, never to have hope for a life she yearned to have. She choked on her emotion. "You asked if I love you. Cullen...you flow through my heart. My feelings deepen every moment we are together."

He kissed her hard. "You have made me a happy man." He released her. "It's best we return to Magnolia Bluff before I change my mind and ravish you completely."

"I do declare, Lieutenant, I believe you have compromised me," she teased.

"Without question, Miss Wright. I believe now the only recourse is to marry you."

He gazed down into the warm, brown eyes. It was easy to become mesmerized in their clear depths. Then slowly, he lowered his mouth to hers. For a moment, the world was theirs. Passion burst forth, all his good intentions forgotten as his desire owned him.

She met his mouth eagerly and unafraid. Every fiber of their being yearned for each other— here and now.

"My...my...my. Josephine Buchanan Wright, why ever are you in the arms of that damn Yankee?"

Abruptly, Cullen broke from the kiss and whirled Jo behind him. He stood and faced Harry Lee and Buck...once again. This time, he looked down the barrel of a gun.

The night's darkness gave way only with the lamps lit in Miss Hazel's cabin and the lantern Cullen had sitting on the porch. But he could see clearly the cocked gun that bore down upon him.

"Harry Lee, have you done gone and lost your mind?" Jo asked incredulously. "Put that gun away."

Harry Lee's eyes narrowed and glared. "Never been more serious. Now step away from the good lieutenant."

Cullen refused to have her move. Suspicion became realization for him. His mind raced with the events that had led to this point. There had to have been someone to rile up the rumors surrounding Jo and Wade...but why protect Jo afterwards...why help her save Heyward? Unless...

"It was you...you were the one who started the rumors about Wade and Jo?"

"'Course it was." Harry Lee smirked. "Who else could have riled up Miss Clarissa where she badmouthed Jo to the point where Jo was on the verge of being shunned by any respectable family in Charleston...to a

111

point… Almost over did it a bit. Had to add disreputable details because just meeting each other didn't send her over the edge. You should have seen her when I told her I caught Wade humpin' ya.

"Gave her vivid details no lady should ever hear…Didn't realize she was such a little hellfire."

"You bastard!" Jo cried. Stunned, her hand went over her mouth. "You hate me that much! Look at the damage you have done to the family's name."

"I'm saving the family, Jo," he sneered. "Otherwise, do you think I would have gone to all this trouble…for you?"

"For me?"

Oh, Good Lord, he wants Jo for himself! Cullen glanced over at the porch, where his pistol lay. He had to distract the boys long enough to ease over close enough to lunge for it.

"So you knew about Jo's dowry. You didn't help her this morning to save Heyward. You wanted her money. A mere twenty-two hundred?"

Harry Lee swung his head back with an uproarious laugh. "You're a fool…much like your idiot cousin, Wade. He doesn't even know what he walked away from. Duty and honor. Thinking his sacrifice will help the Montgomerys hold on to Magnolia Bluff!"

"Sur' was dumb when he had it in his hands," Buck offered with a snicker.

Wade's hands? Magnolia Bluff? Josephine? Made no sense. Cullen eyed the brothers. Harry Lee and Buck exchanged pleased looks. Cullen was openly confused. He grasped that Harry Lee had been behind the vicious rumors that threatened Jo's reputations. He had even suspected the scoundrel of being the cause, but he had thought it malicious, not with purpose.

No matter the reason, he sensed the immediate danger. He pushed Jo down on the ground and lunged for his gun.

Harry Lee nudged his horse forward in response. With the heel of his boot, he smashed his right foot to the side of Cullen's head. Whipping around, he spun Cullen until he lay sprawled on the grass.

"No! Don't hurt him!" Jo cried. "For God's sakes! What is wrong with you?"

Cullen pushed himself up on his knees. Blood trickled down from a gash on the side of his head. His head hurt; his vision blurred from the warm fluid oozing over his eyes.

Jo rushed to Cullen's side. Harry Lee leaped off his horse and jerked her away.

"I can't have that, Jo. Ain't right," he taunted her and gripped her arms tighter. "You're going to hafta learn some manners."

Jo tried to wrench free, to no avail. Cullen rose and contemplated his next move.

Buck maneuvered his horse in front of Cullen and cocked his gun. "Don't go trying anything, Yank."

"Keep your gun on him. I have what I want. I'll get Jo back to the Groves. You know what to do when I'm gone."

"Cullen."

Her voice cut through his pain. He wiped his eyes with the back of his hand. "Damn you, bastard! Let her go!" Cullen roared, "If you lay a hand on her, I swear I will kill you."

"I ain't gonna hurt Jo…not yet. There are things we are going to hafta do first, like get married," Harry Lee laughed as he told Jo. "Now, mount my horse. Don't trust you on one by yourself. If you give me any trouble, I'll shoot lover boy between the eyes right in front of you."

Jo complied. Her hand reached up to swing her leg over the saddle. Harry Lee extended his hand to help her. Without warning, she kicked him once and then across his face. She swung her leg across and tried to gain control of the horse, grasping for the reins.

Harry Lee grabbed hold of the reins in one hard motion and abruptly yanked her off the horse. She stumbled backwards, unable to stay on her feet. Harry Lee reached down for her.

"I wouldn't do that if I was you." Cullen held tight to his pistol and aimed straight at Harry Lee. "Jo, come here."

"Goddammit, Buck! I told you to keep an eye on him! Lord a'mercy, you let him saunter over and pick up his gun!" Harry Lee fumed.

Jo scrabbled to her feet and raced to Cullen.

"Are you all right?"

She nodded. "I just want to get out of here."

"Ain't gonna happen," Harry Lee said. "Buck, shoot Jo if he makes a move on me."

Cullen wrapped his free arm around Jo and pushed her behind him. "Go home, you two! I don't know what has gotten into you, but your game is over."

Harry Lee shook his head. "But it ain't. You can't marry Jo. I won't let it happen. I've gone through too much to let her simply slip through my fingers now."

"It will be over my dead body," Cullen answered him. From the look in Harry Lee's eyes, Cullen saw that would not be an issue for Harry Lee. Cullen pressed, "Why? Why are you doing this?"

Suddenly in the distance, Cullen heard horses that sounded as if they were coming their way. He felt Jo's hand grip the back of his shirt.

"That would be my men." Harry Lee chuckled deep in his throat. "I suppose it won't hurt to tell ya now, considering you won't be able to tell anyone. Everyone's got it all wrong when it comes to Jo. She ain't a poor relation. She's probably the richest heiress in Charleston."

"You lie, Harry Lee," Jo murmured. "I don't have anything except what Papa left me for my dowry."

"You little imbecile. That was your pin money for your gowns and such," Harry Lee scoffed. "When I found out that you thought it was your dowry, Pa allowed you to withdraw the money. How do you think you got it so easily?"

"It makes no sense," Jo said, puzzled. "What good does that do you?"

"Convince you, you had no choice but to marry me," Harry Lee acknowledged. "It would have been so much simpler if you had just accepted your fate. I had the tongues of Charleston wagging about ya. Made you think you had no dowry. I would have swept in and saved the face of the family from the scarlet hussy all of Charleston thinks you are."

"You have roused my curiosity, Harry Lee. What do you hope to gain?"

"Not that complicated, Lieutenant," Harry Lee snarled. "Seems Jo's Papa is a mighty good poker player. In one night, he not only wiped out my grandfather, I would guess Douglas Montgomery lost a mite bit. So much so, Clayton Montgomery had to mortgage Magnolia Bluff. Want to know who bought out the mortgage?"

"Brantley Wright," Cullen replied as if digesting the information.

Harry Lee smiled smugly. "Seems he made some sort of deal with you Montgomerys. Somewhere in the middle of all of it, Clayton Montgomery tried to outsmart Wright. How or why he thought he could, haven't a clue, but Wragg is in the middle of it.

"Grandpa Henry and Pa figured it out quick enough." Harry Lee shrugged. "Clayton Montgomery forced Wade to marry Clarissa Wragg and in the end it will cost him Magnolia Bluff."

"That day in the garden, you were set to find Wade…you were going to call him out?"

114

"It would have been the simplest thing. Since then, Jo has had me on my toes, trying to keep one step ahead of her… and you."

"Even if you are telling the truth, I will never marry you, Harry Lee." Jo shook her head violently. "Nothing on this earth will force me to…I will tell Papa…"

"If he's alive, Jo. Have you wondered where he is?" Harry Lee asked contemptuously. "The last Grandpa Henry heard was that he was high 'ni sick with the fever in New Orleans."

"No…Papa is on his way here."

"He's had plenty of time to get here. I wouldn't be surprised if he hasn't been dead for weeks now."

Cullen held Jo back from lunging at her cousin. Harry Lee had hit a nerve.

"Papa's not dead. I would know…I would…"

"See, I tol' ya. Got no choice with Grandpa Henry being your guardian. Now come along with me and be a good girl."

"She's not going anywhere with you." Cullen aimed his pistol straight at Harry Lee.

Harry Lee's confidence grew as the mounted men rode in and reined in their horses. He uttered in a crazed voice, "Be smart, Yank. Nobody's gonna help you out here. If you wanna make sure Jo gets out of here unharmed, lay down your gun."

"Wade! Cullen! It's Wade."

Jo's voice resonated around Cullen. He looked up to see Wade headed a group of men from Magnolia Bluff.

"Don't mean to rush you, Cousin, but let's get the hell out of here."

* * * *

"Bastards," Cullen snarled, watching Harry Lee and Buck walk down the road in the darkness. Their horses had been taken from the brothers, along with their weapons, but the threat of Harry Lee's men still loomed. He looked over at Jo, who sat mounted on her horse. "You ready to ride?"

"The sooner the better." She nudged the side of her horse. "I just want to get as far away from here as possible."

"At this point, Magnolia Bluff is the safest option," Wade offered, trotting up to the two. "Don't want this to escalate further. Knew Harry Lee was mean as they come, but never figured him to act so brazenly. I have questions."

"As do I." Cullen reached up to wipe back a trickle of blood that still oozed from his wound. Time enough to see to it when they reached safety. "How did you find us in time?"

115

"When Clarissa arrived at Magnolia Bluff, she admitted it had been Harry Lee who incited her anger toward Jo. Got a bad feeling, especially when I got back up to the house. Charlotte was in tears. Harry Lee hadn't even come to see her after the danger passed. Disappeared without a word to her. Never trusted the bastard. Figured I had already armed Saul, Woody, and Iggy in case there had been trouble with Miller. Relieved my worry to come out here and check on the two of you."

"Owe you one, Cousin. Now we need to get the hell out of here. We'll discuss the rest back home."

No more words were uttered. The next moment, the whole of the group galloped down the road toward Magnolia Bluff.

Chapter Eleven

The slaves sung hymns throughout the night for Heyward. The melody came clearly through the open windows in Charlotte's bedroom. It did little to ease the tension, nor would there be sleep.

Jo had heard Wade give orders for the men to stand guard outside the main house. Cullen hadn't even let her go to the sick house, though he sent a man to check and watch over Heyward.

Relief flooded Jo when she discovered that Heyward had greatly improved; scarred for life but he would live. Miss Hazel and Gillie had been allowed to stay by his side. *Oh, she wished Gillie was with her now.*

Charlotte lay on the bed. She wasn't asleep. Tears streamed down her cheeks, heartbroken. The poor thing was in love with a fiend, who had used her unmercifully...not only for information.

"Oh, Jo, he promised we would marry...can you forgive me?" Charlotte choked on the words.

The devil! Jo took her in her arms and rocked her friend. How well she understood what her friend was going through at this moment!

"Don't think of him," Jo urged. "It will do no good. We are friends. Nothing...nothing...will change us."

"But you don't know what I told him..."

"It does not matter. I know him only too well, Charlotte. It was not you."

Charlotte sobbed in Jo's arms until the early morning rose over the horizon. Thoughts ran rampant in her mind, to the point her head hurt. What if Harry Lee was right? What if Papa was dead? Whatever was she going to do?

The door creaked open. Clarissa strode inside, holding a breakfast tray. She looked lovelier than Jo had ever seen her, dressed in a baby blue watered silk dress edged with cascading lace. Her thick dark hair hung loose down her back, as if she had just emerged from a bath and was letting it dry. Even in the wee hours of the early morning, she was a sight to behold.

She greeted the girls with a warm smile. "I hope you don't mind. I brought you up something to eat. I know you probably haven't had a thing to eat. I should have seen to you last night but…it was so chaotic."

Suddenly, Clarissa blushed a million shades of red. Abruptly, she took a deep breath. "Oh, come, now, Josephine, do not look at me so. I will send in my girl promptly to see to your needs. I know your girl is down with Heyward. I can lend you a gown…"

"I will borrow one of Charlotte's," Jo said. She released Charlotte and rose. Charlotte pulled up the covers and looked at Clarissa strangely.

"Thank you for breakfast." Jo took the tray, dismissing the need for Clarissa's presence. Instead, Clarissa slipped into the high back chair by the window.

"Is there something else, Clarissa?" Thunderstruck at Clarissa's audacity, Jo stood frozen to her spot. Her tone was hardly cordial and she made no effort to extend a superficial courtesy.

"Why, yes, dear, there is." Clarissa looked imploringly at Jo. "Wade has told me that I have shamed him with my behavior. I want to extend an olive branch to you. Quite sincerely and with my deepest regrets that my actions caused you any harm."

"You have taken me by surprise."

"Wade has been quite direct in his address of the circumstances before our marriage," she went on. "I will confess I may have encouraged unfounded whispers. But for the life of me, you did nothing to defend yourself…and now look at yourself. Inviting scandal again."

Taken back, Jo managed to keep her voice steady. "Why, Clarissa, what a sacrifice you have made to attempt such a heartfelt apology! Here I imagine you would rather ask if Wade has been honest with you."

"You have the nastiest way about you, Josephine. *Here I thought* you would be undying grateful that the lieutenant wants to marry you. He declared to the family his intentions last night…despite the unwanted attention you have called to us."

By your hand! She caught a glimpse of the hoity-toity girl who had always gotten her way. Bullying. Mean-spirited. Manipulating. But in that moment, Jo also saw Clarissa's desire to know that Jo posed no threat to her relationship with her new husband.

Clarissa loved Wade. She had gone to great lengths to ensure her marriage. Guilt weighed upon her soul, Jo was certain…and well it should. Now her petty jealousy threatened what she had fought so hard to attain.

Had Wade called his wife out for her actions? Had he told Clarissa the magnitude of damage her harmful words had done?

Wade's face flashed before her. He had come to save Cullen and her on a hunch. The anger she held against him dissipated, leaving her only with the hurt. How easy it would be to whisper to Clarissa that Wade had been quite passionate with his proclamation of love toward her.

She wanted to hurt Clarissa the way she had hurt her, leaving Clarissa with doubt. Doubt that would gnaw at her for years to come. Eat away any chance of happiness the couple had. It would be so easy…

Then she thought of Cullen. He had proclaimed his intentions openly to his family last night. Suddenly, nothing else mattered but being with him. He would protect her and make her forget Wade…forget all that had happened before they met.

Jo turned her attention back to Clarissa. "If you have wondered about Wade and myself, there is no need. My association with him deems from my friendship with Charlotte. I accept your apology with hope we will put it all behind us."

Clarissa's face softened as she heard the words she desired. "But of course." Clarissa stood and hugged Jo. "We are to be sisters. Wade says he looks upon Cullen as a brother."

Jo could not deny a source of anxiety was alleviated with the hope of leaving scandal and whispers behind her.

"Do ready yourself quickly. I so want Wade to see us together," Clarissa declared. "As well as your lieutenant. The men will be so happy!"

Charlotte exchanged looks with Jo. Both repressed the sudden impulse to giggle until Clarissa departed. Then the two collapsed into a cascade of laughter.

* * * *

After breakfast, Wade walked back into his brightly sunshine-filled bedroom. He had left his wife to refresh herself and now found her taking down one of the pictures on his wall. Her thick dark hair hung long down below her waist. She had dressed for the day in a becoming gown that flattered her coloring. She made an enchanting picture.

Clarissa whirled around. She leaned against the heavy chair by the window and pressed her hand against her chest. "Good Heavens, Wade! You scared the wits from me!"

"It was not my intent," he answered. "I see you are rearranging our room. I will admit I like what you have done."

"Why, Wade Montgomery, I haven't done a thing except take down that old picture!"

"Perhaps it is the feminine presence that leans to my admiration."

He saw a warmth capture her expression. The night had lent to a new beginning…new hope that their marriage had not been a mistake…with the agreement that the past would stay in the past. There would be no more mention of Clarissa causing a malicious scandal or the words Clarissa had overheard him utter in a drunken state that he had wanted Cullen to offer for her so he could marry Josephine.

There had been so much strife between them, Wade now wanted nothing more than to have harmony between Clarissa and himself. The wall between the two crumbled in the night air. With the morning sun came the realization they were truly man and wife.

Almost shyly, she slipped her arms about his neck. "I have done as I promised. After my bath, I went to Josephine and made peace."

"On your word."

Smiling, timidly, she kissed him. "We are sisters."

"That is good," he said with disarming charm. He reached over and ran his hand through her hair. "You look quite lovely with your hair down."

"It won't dry if I braid it while it's wet."

Leaning down, he whispered, "I would love to see you with it down."

"You see me now…oh…"

Wade raised a brow wonderingly. Her face flamed red, but she did not recoil.

"It is broad daylight, Wade," she said in a shy, soft whisper.

"It is."

Wade released her to lock the door. He turned back to her; she reached out a hand and stepped close to him. His arms embraced her with a fevered eagerness and swept her up in his arms. The bed beckoned.

* * * *

Cullen chewed on the butt of his cigar and considered lighting it. The smoke-filled library had seen an endless stream of one after another over the last few hours. Now, morning was upon them and still no answers.

Looking refreshed, Wade strode into the room. He had left the discussion shortly after it began. He had no patience for what he heard.

"Has anything been settled?"

With his legs outstretched in front of his chair, Clayton shot his grandson a stern look. "We have pieced it together as nearly as we can."

"Except..." Cullen's word hung in the air. *Except* his grandfather's part in the whole of the mess. "I told you, Grandfather, I'm not leaving until I have answers. I'll be damned if I let you evade my issues. Neither should you, Wade. Tell him...tell him."

"Tell me what?"

"It was something Harry Lee told me last night, but I wanted to confirm it before you were informed. Grandfather refuses to talk of it."

"I told you, Cullen, it was all lies...a pack of lies."

"Tell me, sir, why I don't believe you. Can you not see that it's time for the truth?"

"Truth!" Clayton's voice rose higher. "Truth! The truth of what it takes to protect this family! You stand there now ready to condemn me for things far beyond your comprehension."

"I understand what I have been told."

"Do you? You are no better than any other Yankee. You want to blame someone else without looking at yourself first."

"Damnit! I'm not a Yankee. I was born and raised here in Charleston. Hell, you raised me. My blood bleeds Southern, but it doesn't mean I stopped thinking for myself because of my love for my home."

"You have turned your back on your Southern roots, Cullen." Clayton sounded stern. "I've heard you talk."

"Why? Because I don't believe in this call for succession? The whole idea has taken grip of the whole of South Carolina like a fever during sick season. Listen to the irrational rantings of those around you.

"I've heard them all. I've had them slung at me, for Heaven's sakes. Saying Carolinians have no choice. We have been insulted for the last time. We need to show them Yankee devils!

"I ask you—insulted how? Because our way of life is built upon the backs of slaves. You know it. I know it. You also know that it's our stubbornness and stupidity that won't admit we need to address our own problems instead of lashing out at the Yankees for pointing them out to us."

"Hush your mouth! It's about states' rights! It will be a cold day in hell before I let a damn Yankee tell me what to do."

"You would rather secede? Secession will lead to war. No one will win if it comes to that."

"There is a time and place when a man has to take a stand for what he believes in. Loyalty...honor...duty—that is what Southerners hold to..."

121

"Christ Almighty! What is going on in here? What has this got to do with our problem at hand?" Wade interrupted. "We could have the Buchanans at our door any minute now with Jo under our roof. What will they find but our voices raised in enraged anger! Have we forgotten we are family and are not enemies?"

"Ask Cullen." Clayton looked at him steadily. "The time is coming when sides will have to be chosen."

"Is that what you want me to do, Grandfather?" Cullen asserted. "There are times when you have to fight. Are you sure this is one of those? Are we protecting our lives and homes or a way of life that should change? Where are our leaders who should stand up and demand that common sense prevail? They need to be heard before we launch into a path of no return."

"We can take care of our own. Don't need or want any Yankee interference! Do you believe that Yanks want our Negros if we freed them? You fool yourself if you believe they are interested in their welfare. Their leaders want only to hold power over us. It is their one intent. So, yes, Cullen, we are protecting our lives and homes from an enemy."

"Protecting how? With commitment and honor? I know no better men than those I call my friends and family here in the South. Truly men of character, but the truth is character will not protect one from cannon fire. Have you considered what you will face?"

"Beyond your indignation and outrage…behind the cotton, slaves, and a whole lot of puffed up arrogance of Southern gentleman…the North holds the factories, foundries, shipyards, iron and coal mines."

"Blasphemy! I will not have it in my home!"

"Hold!" Wade demanded, coming between the two with arms outstretched to keep his grandfather from physically trying to remove Cullen. "What has brought this about?"

Cullen made a quick, despairing gesture. "My purpose was to address the issue with Josephine. Grandfather chose to turn the conversation, diverting my attention. But ask him…ask him what his arrangement with Randolph Wragg was before you married…when Percival was alive."

"Of course there was an arrangement. You know that, Cullen." Wade threw a quizzical look at Cullen, and then his grandfather, only to have his grandfather stare back at him in defiance. Wade's eyes narrowed. "What the hell have you done, Grandfather?"

Clayton's voice was filled with a pain that would never fade. "Do you know what it is like to find your son dead…shot in the head? His

122

brains splattered against the back of the wall and know…and know…" His face hardened as he choked on the words. "That he pulled the trigger himself because of one man…one man…Brantley Wright."

A hush fell over the room. Clayton lifted his chin and met his grandsons' stares. "I have done nothing to be ashamed of protecting my family's name and honor. Nothing."

"Grandfather," Wade said at last. "I know you have long held it against Brantley Wright, but I looked into it myself. Do you not believe I, too, wanted to blame someone for my father's weakness? I even told Josephine her father was a liar and a cheat. Sometimes the truth hurts, but we must face it.

"I talked with Samuel Padley, father's best friend…his only friend at the end. He said that Father was depressed, wouldn't quit drinking, couldn't…"

"Stop gambling. Is that what you're going to say?" Clayton muttered despairingly. "Douglas wanted only to pay back what he lost that night. He kept trying but it was never enough. Douglas swore he would pay me back, but…he kept losing. If not for that one damn night, he would never have taken his life. Wright took him for every cent he was worth."

Wade did not relent, but pressed forward. "Tell me, Grandfather. Tell me something I don't know, because I can tell you all I have learned. I know well the night you talk about…the night after the New Market race. Father won big at the races. When he went over to Lester Dengate's, he was looking for a bigger score. His mistake—he sat at Wright's table."

"Cheated him…Wright did," Clayton snapped. His shoulders drooped; his breathing labored. "By the time I got there, Wright had that godforsaken snake smile plastered on his face. Oh, Wright won big that night."

"I understand that Wright is a skilled gambler, Grandfather. I would wager he knows well how to play people. It is foolishness and arrogance to sit at his table. I take it Henry Buchanan was also there that night?" Cullen asked.

Clayton nodded. "Shortly after, Henry took in his granddaughter. Then slowly…little by little, Brantley Wright began manipulating the world around us."

"Harry Lee said that Wright holds the mortgage on Magnolia Bluff," Cullen said.

"What?" Wade looked stupefied with surprise.

123

The conversation went no further. A commotion in the foyer disturbed the discussion. A moment later, the door flew open. A man dressed in a black broadcloth suit with a white ruffled shirt and black tie walked into the room.

Despite not being overly tall, he carried himself with an air that gave weight to his presence. His hair, black with streaks of gray, lent to a distinguished look; his goatee was closely trimmed. Cullen looked into his face and met his dark black eyes.

Brantley Wright had come to Magnolia Bluff.

* * * *

In the privacy of the parlor, Brantley Wright showed little emotion in greeting his only child. He was ominously silent when he kissed Josephine.

Jo cared little about her father's subdued response. She wrapped her arms about him and kissed him warmly on both cheeks.

"Oh, Papa!" Jo's tears threatened. "Harry Lee said you had died! Do not scare me like that! I wrote and wrote—"

"Jo." He glanced behind her. "Are you going to introduce me to your beau?"

Jo's spirits soared. He wanted to meet Cullen! She reached behind her and grasped hold of Cullen's hand. "Lieutenant Cullen Smythe, this is my father, Mr. Brantley Wright."

Cullen bowed his head slightly. "It is a pleasure to finally meet you, sir."

"I have heard a great deal about you, Lieutenant," Wright said. "My father-in-law told me that you asked permission to call upon my daughter."

"I would like the opportunity to talk with you also."

Wright raised his cold, bright eyes and nodded stiffly. A frown flickered across his face. "I will arrange a time. Would it seem rude if I ask but a moment to speak to my daughter…alone… for a few minutes?"

"Not at all." Cullen took a few steps back toward the door.

Jo caught her breath. Oh, Papa had dismissed Cullen! She looked over, apologetic, at him; he simply winked and pulled the sliding door together. The room took on a somber air with a heavy, stern gloom about it.

"Now, Josephine, I am greatly disturbed to hear of your conduct. You have incited another scandal to our name." Brantley Wright looked directly at his daughter. "I'm disappointed that you forgot your rearing. It is shameful…disgraceful."

Jo's instincts went on alert. This was not the reunion she had hoped. Suddenly, she felt like the child again who had leaped into Charleston Harbor. A cold pang of guilt assaulted her that she had disgraced her father by her scandalous conduct.

"I wish I could defend myself properly, but I fear you have heard the worst. I'm ashamed that I have caused you hurt. It was not my intent."

"I could excuse your impropriety if you had been raised differently. Your poor momma wanted you to be accepted. It was her dying wish. I have gone to great lengths to hold to my promise to her."

Jo lowered her head. She had failed her momma. She choked back her tears.

"Look at me, Jo. Do not hide behind tears. It will not work. You are not a fragile flower that wilts on the vine. You are too much like me." He scowled. "I want to know what happened from your lips. There will certainly be recourse."

Her head snapped up. Did he mean he would call out those he felt offended her? A duel over her honor?

"Papa, there is no need. Truly. Cullen…Lieutenant Smythe offered for me. He asked Grandpa Henry all proper and such. There again, Grandpa Henry turned him down when Taz Foster asked to call upon me…but after yesterday…" she rambled. Nervousness gripped her. "Yesterday, Lieutenant Smythe bought Heyward to save him from that nasty Miller…he freed him."

Brantley stared at his daughter. He had always been a hard man to read, more so at this moment. "Lieutenant Smythe wants to marry you? That was not my understanding."

"Oh, yes, he does," she added hastily. "He would have certainly talked with you first, but you were not here. You will like him, Papa. I know. He stepped in when those awful rumors of Wade began. Then he stopped me when I was leaving to look for you. He took the money from me…"

"My God, child, what is in your head?" he roared. "Is that where your account went to? I was notified it was closed."

Taken back by his intensity, she nodded. "I'm sorry. It was only…only I didn't have anywhere else to turn. Grandpa Henry wanted me to marry that awful Mr. Miller. I couldn't have that…I couldn't. I took my dowry…"

"Your dowry? You think that account was your dowry?"

"I thought so until yesterday. Harry Lee…Harry Lee said some confusing things, Papa. Truly, he did. Why, he said I was an heiress of some sort…Papa, he wanted to shoot Cullen and…Papa, he wanted me to marry him. Harry Lee! I would never!"

Jo was scared, her heart heavy with fright. Her father's face turned a million shades of red. His temper flared.

"It is obvious that I'm hearing two different tales." Frowning, Wright raised a severe eye at his daughter. "There is a carriage waiting for us. I need to speak to the Montgomerys for a moment. Then we will depart immediately for Charleston."

She wanted to protest, but her father was not one to be questioned. "Gillie and Miss Hazel?"

"I will see to their welfare."

Jo hesitated before she left the room. "Papa, I'm sorry for the pain this has caused you, but for the life of me, I understand none of how it got so out of control. I will confess to seeing Wade, but only with Gillie present. He had thought…" She paused. It seemed so long ago now. "It does not matter what he thought. It was not meant to be. He was a gentleman, Papa. It was less than Grace Ann ever did."

Her father's frown deepened, but he made no attempt to halt her. She went on, "I have tried to be the lady you wanted, Papa. Truly, I have. It pains me to have hurt you so."

"Tell me only this, Josephine. Wade Montgomery wanted to marry you?"

Confused, Jo nodded. "It was what he told me…only his family made him hold to Percival's commitment. He—"

He raised his hand to halt her thought. "It is all I needed to know. Go wait for me. I won't be long."

Chapter Twelve

Charleston in the early afternoon was a splendid place to host a garden party. It was a fine May day with flowers in their full glory: azaleas, gardenias, and roses. The magnolia tree held magnificent blooms. A nice sea breeze cooled Grace Ann's back lawn.

The house was on Water Street, right around the corner from the Montgomerys' Charleston residence. A typical home for the area, it had three floors with a piazza on each level covered in ivy. A wrought-iron fence surrounded the property.

When the visitors were announced, Jo, Grace Ann, and Aunt Sybil had already begun entertaining on the veranda. Jo glanced up to notice Phyllis Wilder and her mother entered the room. Jo picked up her skirt and walked over to greet them.

"Why, Josephine, how sweet you look in that dress," Phyllis exclaimed as she kissed Jo's cheek. "The color does flatter you so."

"I do believe that I have never seen such lovely creations. The poor butterflies won't know where to light with all these beauties in the garden. Look over your shoulder, Phyllis. Why, Lora has on a gorgeous pink silk with a garland of tiny matching rosebuds. Have you ever seen such a sight? I must ask her how she entwined the buds in her hair. Don't you think, Jo?"

Jo turned to her companion and smiled. Clarissa had been by her side since she arrived in Charleston four weeks ago. She had learned quickly that one didn't have to answer Clarissa. A simple smile would do.

Charlotte came up beside her and squeezed her arm. She whispered, "You have company."

Jo glanced back beyond Charlotte to the back of the garden. He was there under the magnolia tree. Immediately, she slid back from the group.

She slipped down the stairs and made her way to Cullen. She had not seen him since the day her father arrived at Magnolia Bluff. He had departed to Philadelphia for a brief visit. Letters had been exchanged, but nothing more. Now he had returned; her heart fluttered.

How everything had changed since her father's appearance! Not one whisper of her adventure had emerged into the winds of Charleston society. Jo learned quickly the influence Brantley Wright's presence wielded.

"You have returned!" Jo cried, a little too loudly. She gave little thought to the old matrons' eyes. Surely nothing would be deemed inappropriate, not in plain view of all those in attendance. She refrained herself from doing what she really wanted…to have slung herself into his arms.

"Only this morning. I came first to my grandfather's house to refresh myself," he said with a wide grin. "Then I had to see you."

He looked quite handsome and, oddly, relaxed. Dressed in tan breeches and a fine white linen shirt, he took his hat off. "You look breathtaking," he went on. "I have missed you."

"Oh, Cullen, I can hardly contain myself. I have waited for this moment."

"Be patient only a little while longer. I go to meet with your father down at the Pavilion."

He did not have to say the words. He was going to ask formally for her hand! Papa would have to say yes. She hadn't a doubt he would consent. Had Papa not told her to be prepared?

Jo clutched her heart. "I cannot believe it is real."

"I informed my father of my intentions, who gave his blessing. I told you that he would. My family cannot wait to meet you. They wished only it would not happen so fast, for I told them I could wait no longer. I want a small wedding in Charleston, but I fear a large reception will await our arrival. Mother…my stepmother…Monica, will insist upon it."

"I do not care if it is only us. I have told Papa I wanted nothing more than to be your bride."

"I go to make it a reality." He reached in his pocket. "Before I forget, I have correspondences for your girl, Gillie."

"Heyward." She took the letters. "Gillie will be so pleased. He is well?"

"He has recovered fully and accepted a position as my father's man. I will admit that Father was impressed. A former slave so…what was the word my father used…educated."

Jo lowered her gaze. Warmth flood her face. "It was me…well, not so much. It was Gillie…Miss Hazel was so proud her son could read and write," she stuttered.

"Jo, look at me," Cullen commanded. Slowly, she lifted her eyes to find his smiling warmly at her. "Father was pleased with Heyward."

"Are you? To have a wife who so clearly ignores the law." Her voice faded for fear someone would overhear. "What you must think of me!"

"I find myself the luckiest of men." He grinned. "Go enjoy your party. Meet me here later, before supper. I like this spot. Under a magnolia tree. A fitting place, for every time I see one, I think of my magnolia."

She watched him slip out of the back of the garden. Her heart filled with joy. She turned and rejoined the party.

* * * *

The Pavilion Hotel sat on the corner of Meeting Street and Hasell in the heart of Charleston. It had not surprised Cullen that it was here that Brantley Wright had arranged his stay. It had surprised him that it had been Brantley who requested the meeting.

Cullen had planned on calling on him upon his return, but he had barely placed his foot again on Charleston soil when he received a summons. A summons he would not ignore.

The peal of bells from the church steeple resounded out the open windows. Cullen sat and awaited the man's entrance. Having met the man at Magnolia Bluff, Cullen understood his grandfather's intense dislike for the man.

Brantley wasted no sympathy for Clayton Montgomery. Moreover, the man had taken a pompous attitude with his grandfather. Cullen half-expected the man to be thrown off the property, but it had not happened. Brantley Wright had left on his own accord and in his own time.

Cullen had spoken only briefly to the man. Brantley had cut off Cullen's attempt for a discussion concerning Josephine.

"You have my heartfelt thanks for seeing to my daughter's welfare. I want only to take care of certain arrangements before this talk. As you well imagine, I have many affairs to attend to. I will admit I have been caught off guard."

To Cullen's amazement, Wright had also thanked him for freeing Heyward and insisted on repaying him. Cullen discovered he was not a man to be refused.

"Go do what you must to see to Heyward's arrangements. If it is my daughter that is your concern, you have my word: my daughter's future will not be announced until your return."

He had not been allowed to see Josephine, but letters flowed freely between the two without incident. Cullen realized that a step back was not uncalled for at this point. Brantley seemed to have a wisdom about him, understanding that love found in the midst of danger lent to a strange excitement...felt more deeply...more intensely...for the moment.

Cullen reasoned that Wright wanted to know how Cullen felt once the danger faded. Would his interest flame out? It had not; his feelings had not diminished. Moreover, he felt them more deeply.

"Lieutenant Smythe, it is good that you have come."

Cullen stood on Wright's entrance. The man gestured for Cullen to sit. "There is no need to be formal. I hope that your needs were seen to while you waited. I was about to have a drink. Would you care for one?"

"Certainly."

Wright walked over to the cabinet and brought out a bottle of whiskey. He filled up two glasses. He handed one to Cullen. "It is the best in Charleston."

Cullen held no doubt it was. He took a sip and gathered up his courage to address the issue at hand. "I want to talk to you of your daughter."

Wright took a seat across from Cullen. "I expected as much." He gestured with his hand for Cullen to wait for a moment. "First, before you say a word, let me explain my position."

Wright stared at Cullen. Cullen sat, confused for a brief moment for the reason he would have fallen under the scrutiny of the man across from him. Confused until he remembered who Brantley Wright was...a professional gambler.

A skilled poker player could read his opponent, wasn't prone to emotions and took an opportunity when it presented itself. Cullen wasn't in the mood to get played.

"Relax, Lieutenant."

"It is simply Cullen. I have resigned my commission."

Wright nodded in a way that told Cullen he was digesting the information. He tilted his head to the side and pursued his lips together in thought. "I like you. Truly I do, Mr. Smythe," he added. "I don't like many people.

"You have shown yourself to be a man of character. A true gentleman. You have protected my daughter's honor. You have shown yourself to be compassionate to a fellow human being, even if he was a slave. You have stood up to your grandfather. That alone tells of your courage."

"It is who I am."

"Yes, I suppose that is true." Wright's words hung in the air for a time. Finally, he went on. "Tell me what you think of me."

"I know what most know, sir. You come from Camden, South Carolina, if I'm not mistaken. Made your way being a gambler. Then married Josephine's mother, Lucinda Buchanan."

Wright smiled. "I loved that woman. Really loved my wife. They buried my heart when they laid her in the ground. Can you understand a love like that?"

"I believe I can."

"I hope so, Mr. Smythe. I hope so," Wright repeated. He swirled his glass and stared at its contents. "Lucinda wanted her daughter to be brought up surrounded by those who loved her. Her reasoning had been she had been loved greatly; in turn, her daughter would be. When I left, I imagine Josephine was lonely and often frightened, but hoped she would be loved as Lucinda wished.

"I know my daughter well enough to know, no matter what, her courage would prevail to face the life I left her to have. I knew well that Charleston waited only for an opportunity to shun her. She is my daughter and I had insulted the good people of Charleston by daring to marry one of their own."

Wright sat back and looked up at Cullen. "Most of the good people of Charleston believed Henry Buchanan took in his wayward child's daughter out of the goodness of his heart. Why would he not? Living in the land of plenty, his plantation was large and sheltering a young girl presented no problem. That was not the case."

Stillness lay heavy in the room. Cullen eyed the man questionably. Of course, Henry Buchanan took Jo into his home.

"I'm afraid you have lost me."

"Henry Buchanan did not take Josephine in out of the goodness of his heart," Brantley repeated. "He had to be persuaded."

He set his glass down. "I was not born a rich man, Mr. Smythe, but I was born with a gift. I have used that gift to my full advantage. Make no mistake about my claim that I am a gentleman. Despite what you may have heard, I am no cheat. There has been no need.

"When you are in my profession, you learn to read people as I have read you as being honorable. I hold that you will not repeat what I tell you now."

"You have my word," Cullen said, fascinated by now of the tale unfolding before him.

"I have never been a doting father, but I love my daughter. I wanted her to have what I had not…what her mother wanted for her. Lucinda desired for Josephine to be raised here in Charleston as a lady, part of her family…the Buchanans. When I first presented the idea to Henry Buchanan after Lucinda's death, he refused. Not that it should have shocked me. The man had refused to see his dying daughter when I sent for him."

Anger took hold of his voice. He rose and walked to the window. Composing himself, he turned back to Cullen.

"While my wife was taking her last breath, I told her that her father had tried to be by her side. I told her that her father begged forgiveness and that he wanted her to know he loved her. He would take Josephine to raise. It calmed her before her death, but it was all a lie. But I pledged to keep my word."

"You beat Buchanan on a wager to convince him to take in Jo."

Wright laughed—a harsh, cruel laugh. "At the time, I came back to Charleston for one purpose. I came back for revenge, using their arrogance and greed against them."

"Them?"

"The Charleston elite," Wright said with indignation. "They shunned Lucinda for marrying me. They shunned her."

Wright took a sip of his drink and stared off into nothingness. Composed a moment later, he turned back to Cullen. "What you need to know is that the stakes were high. I played with only one intent, knowing well who I played against. Men who carried themselves like they were holier than God himself. In truth, nary a one of them had a white soul.

"Buchanan lost enough to agree to take Josephine until her marriage while Douglas Montgomery…"

Cullen couldn't refrain himself. "You broke my uncle, Mr. Wright. He killed himself."

"If he killed himself, it was not over his loss to me," Wright countered. "I gave him an out. I offered him a deal."

Cullen realized that this story held importance. An ominous feeling enveloped him.

"I want you to understand my intent, Mr. Smythe. I didn't want his money. I wanted for Josephine to be accepted. The best way that could happen would be as a member of one of the oldest, respected families in Charleston. She herself comes from one...except for my black mark against her. For her mother's sake, I wanted Josephine to be mistress to a grand plantation."

"Magnolia Bluff."

Wright shrugged lightly. "In exchange for the money he owed me, Douglas agreed we would arrange a marriage between his eldest boy and Josephine when she was old enough. Then Clayton Montgomery decided to interfere with our arrangement.

"Clayton tried valiantly to *save* his plantation. It is expensive to maintain a large household while your son is out drinking and gambling away money he doesn't have. Douglas kept on gambling to the point where the only option was to mortgage Magnolia Bluff."

"Harry Lee said you held the mortgage on Magnolia Bluff."

"Harry Lee is another matter...one, I assure you, that has been addressed."

Cullen realized that Harry Lee had disappeared. Where he had gone was a mystery, but it was a mystery Cullen wouldn't pursue. He had faith Brantley Wright had taken care of the situation.

"But Harry Lee wasn't wrong. You do own the mortgage on Magnolia Bluff."

"Yes. Your grandfather went to Wragg's bank, where Wragg arranged a mortgage. Shortly after, your cousin was engaged to his daughter. After his death, it seems your other cousin married her. I'm afraid your grandfather was under the impression that the marriage would save his precious Magnolia Bluff. He is no longer under that impression."

Good Lord! All this time...the scandal...Josephine was supposed to have married Wade? Instead...

"Wait. This makes no sense." Cullen's voice waned. "Something is wrong."

"You must realize by now that upon my daughter's marriage she will become mistress of Magnolia Bluff. I truly wish it could have been you."

Shocked by Wright's utterance, Cullen said, "It can be, sir. Surely you don't want your daughter in the middle of this madness. I can well support your daughter in the manner you desire. I will take her away...."

"Up North? While I acknowledge you make a compelling argument, you are a Yankee. It will never do. Josephine has been raised to be a Southern Belle. A Southern Belle she will remain."

"I must strongly protest!" Cullen stood in disbelief.

"It will do no good. It has been set."

"I love your daughter. I will see to her welfare and happiness. This I promise—"

"Let's not make this harder than it has to be," Wright said. "Tell me you don't feel the political landscape. The political rhetoric is hard to ignore on either end. South Carolina wants to secede. If the dispute widens, my presumption is that your loyalty would lie with the North."

"It makes little difference to us. Our—"

"Love? You believe that love conquers all. Don't be a fool. My wife was disinherited from her father. It was a hurt that never healed. I know your history, also. Your mother returned home to have you. Tell me why she did not return?"

Silence encompassed the room. A hopeless silence. He would not accept it. No...he would not lose the woman he loved.

"Don't, Mr. Smythe. Don't consider going against my wishes. If you love her, let her go. Trust me. It will be for the best. If you do not believe me, ask your grandfather."

* * * *

A puff of sea breeze swept through the garden. Night had fallen and still she sat. She had not moved from the bench despite the darkness...despite the words her father had uttered. She pulled her shawl around her shoulder. She felt a chill, but not from the gust of wind...from her heart.

He had not come. He promised, but he had not come. Her heart had been ripped from her, leaving only a void.

"Jo, it's time to come inside."

She glanced back to see her papa walk up beside her. She said nothing. He sat down with her. Silent tears streamed down her face.

"Why, Papa, why? I love him so."

He placed his arm about her and she laid her head on his shoulder. She wept.

"In time, you will understand."

She wanted to scream; she would never understand! She understood only one thing. Her need for Cullen.

"I will not leave you until everything has been settled. I should have never left the last time. I should have ensured that the agreement was carried out to my satisfaction. I let my disdain for this place influence my decision. It reminded me too much of your momma."

The mention of her mother softened her heart. "I loved her, too, Papa."

"Then know this was her wish: that you be accepted here in Charleston. It was her biggest regret that she was outcast."

Jo pushed back against his chest and looked into his eyes. "Papa, I know you love me, but don't do this. Momma may have wanted to come home, but she never regretted marrying you. She told me so many times. I understand. I do, for I will never be happy without Cullen."

He shook his head. "You are wrong. She never complained, but I saw the hurt and pain in her eyes. I was the reason for that pain. I promised her on her dying bed. I have held to that promise."

"Oh, Papa, Momma would have wanted me to be married to a man such as Cullen. He loves me...oh, please, Papa..."

"Josephine, it is settled. When you have married and the children come, you will forget him."

"Married?" Jo bolted upward. "Married? To whom?"

"Andrew Montgomery."

Stunned, Jo stared at her father. She shook her head. She murmured, "No...I could never...I will never."

"You are a dutiful daughter and will do as you are told."

Jo stood. Panic surged through her. "Papa, I love you. Truly, I do, but I cannot do that. I could never marry Andrew Montgomery."

Retreating a couple of steps, she turned and bolted out the back gate into the street with only one thought in mind. *Cullen.*

* * * *

Night had fallen. Drink in hand, Cullen stood with his back to the window. Moonlight streamed into the room, touched his shoulders, and cast a forlorn shadow. He looked over at Wade. His cousin had down the contents of his glass and prepared to pour another.

"I'm sorry, Wade."

Silence crashed around them. Wade seemed lost for words. It had not happened often. Only one other time had Wade been this quiet...when he had been informed of Percival's death. Uncle Douglas's passing had not been the same, even with the method of his demise.

Years had prepared them for the path of destruction his uncle had journeyed. The grieving for the loss of a man haunted by demons began when Uncle Douglas drowned his problems with the bottle.

The three of them—Percival, Wade, and himself—had tried to live up to their grandfather's expectations, having held the man in high esteem. His word was law. It had been how they had been raised—striving to hold to the honor and duty their name demanded. Clayton Montgomery's son had failed.

The problem with holding a person high upon a pedestal: it makes for a much larger fall when the realization that the man is only human suffuses through you, thought Cullen. Never had he seen Clayton Montgomery so desperate, trying frantically to hold to the old world he had known. Cullen imagined his grandfather felt his control slip away from him.

After his talk with Brantley Wright, Cullen had a confrontation with his grandfather…one that had not gone well. His grandfather confessed he had made an arrangement with Brantley Wright for Andrew…Andrew to marry Josephine…the last-ditch effort to maintain his plantation.

Wade shook his head. "What is this world coming to, Cullen?"

"It is changing. We can't let it change us, Brother. I don't know much at the moment, but I do know that."

"I'm so angry, but it is not directed at you. For the life of me, I can't get the image out of my head of what Grandfather has done to me…to you. I could have everything I wanted in this life…and saved the family's honor, had Grandfather not allowed his prejudice to ruin everything!"

"What's done can't be undone."

"But, Cullen, what has been done?" Wade faced Cullen. "There's more to this, Cullen. I feel it in my bones."

"I agree." Cullen let the words hang before he went on. "Grandfather had to realize the chance he had taken to have gone against a man like Brantley Wright. I cannot help but think that Wragg is mixed up in this business at the bank."

"It is my fear," Wade agreed. "It would mean that I won't be able to protest without placing not only Grandfather under scrutiny but my father-in-law."

"It will leave you with little recourse. If Wright and Grandfather get their way, Andrew will have control of what you thought would have been yours."

"Ironic, for Andrew wants nothing to do with what has been given him. Magnolia Bluff. An heiress for a wife. He is the one who feels he is making the sacrifice for the family." Wade sighed. "My brother is as upset as we are about the set of circumstances, but there is another piece that disturbs me. Harry Lee."

The words reverberated in the room. Cullen had been told that Harry Lee had left Charleston, but no one seemed to know where or when he would return.

"Wright contends that Harry Lee is no longer an issue. I assure you I will look into the matter," Cullen promised. "Moreover, Wade, I need you to know I haven't made up my mind what I intend to do. I know you still care for Josephine, but you have started a new life...one that I will help, if you allow."

"I don't understand."

"Wright refused to sell Magnolia Bluff, but it does not mean that Andrew will not," Cullen stated soberly. "I will help you secure the plantation from Andrew if it becomes his. I know what it means to you."

"I cannot accept a loan from..." Obvious relief flooded Wade's face despite his surprise at the offer.

"From your brother...of course you can," Cullen said. "My own grandfather condemns me as a Yankee. He did not look to me as an heir despite my claim as his grandson, but surely you do not disinherit me."

"I know you have a Southern heart. Grandfather does also. It is only he cannot control you like he does Andrew and myself."

"I'm afraid I have no control myself. It gnaws at my soul and crushes me."

Silence again. Both men felt the weight of the truth while neither knew how to ease their pain.

* * * *

Jo raced to the Montgomerys' home. She cared little what the neighbors thought if they saw her. She had to see him. Out of breath, she banged on the back door until one of the house blackies answered it.

"Master Cullen. I need to see him." She gulped for air.

A new fear gripped her. What if Cullen wasn't home? Whatever would she do? She paced outside the door for what felt like an eternity. The door opened.

"Cullen!" she cried.

He stood for a moment and stared at her. His eyes grieved. Understanding his hesitation, her eyes widened. "Oh, Cullen, tell me it is not so."

He rushed toward her. Taking her by the elbow, he uttered, "Come. We will find privacy."

Jo hurried beside him, her small steps barely in step with his. He did not slow until they reached the Battery.

Standing against the backdrop of the Charleston harbor, utter wretchedness assaulted her, physically weakened and mentally broken. Her nerves were shaken; she made no effort to conceal her feelings.

His eyes lit upon her. She could take no more. "Don't leave me," she pleaded. "I can take anything but the knowledge you don't want me."

He reached over and caressed her face. "It has nothing to do with my feelings toward you."

"Papa...Papa wants me...to marry...Andrew," she said, desperately trying to find her words. She clutched his hand. "I cannot...not when I love you."

"Oh, my sweet magnolia, I wish things were different. Your father took a great effort to explain your situation. It is complicated. It tears at the ties that bind between honor and duty. If I gave in to my desires, I would sweep you up North."

"Please, Cullen, I will go."

He shook his head. "Our love would change. Over time, our passion will turn to resentment, then, God forbid, apathy. I could not live with that. It is best if what we had becomes a remembrance."

A sudden anger surged through her. She pushed away from him. "Go then! I care not. You are no more than a coward. No better than anyone else in my life. Promises made, only to be broken. Hold on to your honor and duty and know I will give myself to another!"

For a breathless moment, the world stilled. The ocean waves pounded against the stone wall, spewing water all around them. She became oblivious of everything around her except Cullen.

Suddenly, she felt his hand around her waist. He drew her into his arms. He leaned down and kissed her. He deepened the kiss. She couldn't think; she could only feel...

"I'll be damned if another touches you," he whispered against her lips. "I can't fight this. I choose you, always you."

"Everything will be all right as long as we are together," she answered. She kissed him, sliding her fingers into his hair.

Lost in his touch...his kiss...she didn't hear another approach, but she heard a scream. Abruptly, Cullen broke from her lips, but did not release his hold.

Running up to the couple, Gillie slowed only when she reached her mistress's side.

"Oh, Miss Jo, you have to return. Immediately. It's your father...he's collapsed. Miss Grace sent me for you. You need to come...he looked...oh, Miss Jo!"

Jo stared at Gillie in disbelief. She had just been with her father. He had seemed so alive. Slowly, ever so slowly, she stepped back. Tears welled in her eyes…for her father…for Cullen…for herself, she didn't know. She was only aware of an overwhelming ominous feeling that enveloped her.

She looked at Cullen, a pleading look. There was no need. He took her hand and together they made their way back to the house.

* * * *

The room took on a gloomy frost. Brantley Wright laid deathly ill in bed. Jo watched him sleep. He seemed at peace, but she refused to leave his side. He would waken and immediately ask for her.

The doctor had come and gone. There was nothing more to be done. It was her father's heart. The fever he had contracted had weakened it.

"With the heart, it is hard to say," Doctor Jameson informed her. "But, Miss Wright, be prepared. I doubt, even if he survives this bout, that he will live through the year."

Jo refused to believe the doctor. Not her father. He was so strong…invincible.

"Jo." Her papa opened his eyes a slit to see whether she was still beside him. He closed them again. Then with effort, he said, "You gave your word."

"Yes, Papa."

"It is for the best. You will see."

She gulped back the tears she didn't seem to be able to contain. She could not deny she was truly Southern, instilled with virtues of loyalty, honor, duty to God and family. It was the tie that binds. She would not break her word.

"Rest, Papa." She gave him the comfort he sought. "Your lawyer has already been by the house. It has been arranged. I will not fight it. I will marry Andrew."

Content, he slept once more. She rose and walked over to the window.

Outside, life went on as it had always. The sun shined, the birds sang, and the tide came in and out. When she told Cullen her decision, his expression had not altered. He had expected it and made no objections.

She had not seen him since the night her father collapsed. Charlotte had told her he had withdrawn back to Philadelphia.

Presented to the world surrounding her, she now had all anyone could ask for—wealth, privilege, and the promise of marriage to one of the oldest, respected names in Charleston. Why then did she feel so utterly alone? She wondered forlornly however was she going to survive each day. Cullen was gone!

Suddenly, the indomitable spirit that lived within her surged forth. Oh, good gracious! She could not afford to wallow in self-pity. Was she not her father's daughter? She would never let the world see the pain that tore at the core of her being. No…Never. She would hold her head high like a true belle of Charleston.

PART TWO

SHADOWS OF MAGNOLIA

Chapter One

A warm, southeasterly breeze sprang up just before Josephine Buchanan Wright walked out of St. Philip's Church. She paused in the portico and enjoyed the gentle caress. A much-needed reprieve from the hot, sweltering heat of August.

She had only recently returned to Charleston, having spent the early summer on Pawley's Island. Papa had rented a fine, airy house down along the shoreline, private and perfect for his recovery from heart failure. With having only to throw back the shutters and inhale the cool light ocean wind, Jo found it a temporary escape from the tangled web her life had become.

Long, lazy days, she cared for her papa. The time spent lounging on the beach under a large parasol and sitting on the side porch sipping on mint lemonade, enjoying visitors that came and went.

Charlotte visited briefly, and then journeyed with her momma over to Columbia to see relatives. Grace Ann followed Charlotte's stay accompanied by Mr. Whitney.

"Mr. Whitney is taking me to London!" Grace Ann informed Jo. "It is a shame that I won't be at your wedding, but Mr. Whitney felt it only proper to see you before we departed."

Jo had no desire to even think of her upcoming wedding to Andrew Montgomery. Charleston was miles away; the wedding, not until the end of the summer. She had decided to live in the moment.

It had been a delightful stay. Alongside Grace Ann, Jo seemed to relive days gone by of childhood. She laughed and giggled with Grace Ann like they had done when they had been children, enjoying picnics on the beach and wading in the surf. It was good to laugh. She thought she had forgotten how.

Papa spent a great deal of his time in talks with Mr. Whitney. Jo suspected it had to do with her grandfather and cousins. Papa steadfastly refused to discuss it with her, assuring her she had nothing to fear.

Grace Ann hinted that Harry Lee and Buck had been exiled from their home state.

"I swear I don't know what got into their heads, but now they are heaven knows where assuredly regretting their behavior. Why they can't set foot back in Charleston, not without fear of repercussions from your papa!" Grace Ann tried to make light of it. "Momma is saddened by their actions. She believes they did it to save the family. I honestly believe that was purely selfish on their part. Men are selfish creatures, but they most assuredly would not have done you harm."

Jo made no argument. It would serve no purpose. Grace Ann wasn't responsible for her brothers' faults. To Charleston society, the bad blood between Grandpa Henry and Papa had been whitewashed, dealt with between the men themselves. The final resolution seemed to satisfy her papa, and she took heart in that fact.

Initially, Jo was saddened to leave the shore, but her mood altered when she returned to the city. A warming sensation swept through her as the wheels of the carriage rolled over the narrow, cobbled streets, and passed by familiar sights. This is what Papa understood.

The houses surrounded by lovely gardens and giant oaks and palmettos, the shops along King Street, the salons where political rhetoric flowed over into the streets, the view of the ships in Charleston Harbor. Everything was as it was before she left as she had always known it to be. It was home, a part of her.

The peal of the church bells announced the Sunday sermon had been brought to a close. She could not deny the affect the familiar sound had upon her. Memories disturbed the smooth peace she had found away from this city—assaulting her casual acceptance of the events that had unfolded over the last few months.

Her sensibilities ruled her heart, not allowing her the ability to mourn what she had lost. She could not afford to release the wall she had erected. No, her fate lay with the man her father had arranged she should marry. She would not contemplate a different path. She would behave in the manner demanded of a good Southern woman.

Releasing a pensive sigh, she moved along side of her fiancée. Surreptitiously, she studied the man who would be her husband within the week.

Andrew Montgomery leaned against his cane. Handsome enough, Jo supposed. Not as tall as the other Montgomery men, his dusty blond hair was cut short along with his sideburns. He had grown a goatee but kept it neatly trimmed. His stance lent to the conclusion his leg pained him.

He was a quiet, studious man. His soft brown eyes rarely sought Jo's, but she had seen compassion in them toward others. His time devoted into becoming a doctor. He, too, had only recently returned to Charleston, having finished the last of his studies in Philadelphia.

Jo assumed he would set up his doctor's practice here in Charleston, but he had not yet stated that fact. Neither had he talked of the plantation that would be theirs, Magnolia Bluff. In truth, he had told her little. Their marriage was born of obligation, not love.

Papa's lawyers had met with Andrew immediate upon his arrival. The settlement between Papa and the Montgomerys had been finalized. It would not be the wedding of her dreams, but drawn from a legal agreement.

Her reluctant fiancé had been the epitome of politeness, but she sensed his repulsion. The man, who soon would be her husband, hated her, more so now than ever. He would marry her to save his family's fortune. She would marry him to be her father's dutiful daughter.

Oh, what might have been…if only Cullen… No, no, no! She pushed the memories from her mind, if not her heart.

At the foot of the church steps, Jo instantly recognized the lady heading their way. The mother of one of Clarissa's friends, Deborah Wilder. The older heavy set woman greeted the couple with a warm smile.

"Was it not a wonderful service? One leaves Reverend Riley's sermon feeling vindicated," Mrs. Wilder said, stepping closer to Jo. "It makes me feel good knowing God is on our side."

Jo sensed the woman wanted to continue the good reverend's sermon and condemn all Yankees. Jo was not one to run from a challenge. She would have like nothing more to point out that in the northerner churches, they, too, were preaching the same, except, she was certain that they thought God was on their side.

"I enjoyed it greatly," Andrew offered. "Reverend Riley is a fine speaker."

"I have said it many times…you have only to ask Mr. Wilder that I have…we are indeed fortunate to have Reverend Riley here in Charleston. They tried you know to convince him to go to Savannah, but he would have nothing to do with it. Said his home is here. Did my heart good," Mrs. Wilder went on. "Of course, I assume he is marrying you two on Saturday."

A small smile emerged on Andrew's lips. "I asked him myself."

Jo couldn't remember Andrew smiling in her company. It was only then she noticed the tight lines around his mouth ease; his eyes held a softness she had never seen. *For Heaven's Sake! He can be pleasant when not in conversation with me. He is just as miserable as I about our union!*

"Josephine," Mrs. Wilder said as she reached over and squeezed her hand. "I have a confession…I saw…"

Jo exchanged a confused look with Andrew. She looked back at Mrs. Wilder. "Saw? I'm sorry…"

Mrs. Wilder took in an exaggerated breath. "Your gown. I swear I have never seen a gown so breathtaking! Why Ellie…Miss Haney… told me, it had come from Paris."

"Papa surprised me with it when we returned to Charleston."

Papa had seen to it that the whole of her wardrobe had become most fashionable. Why she wore the most flattering rose floral print this morning. The skirt was tied back to show the tiers of elegant white ruffles and her bonnet matched the lovely pink in her gown. Her dark tresses gleamed richly, drawn back from her face in an openly woven white silk net.

"It is quite exquisite, especially the pearls beaded into the gown and the lace!" Mrs. Wilder exclaimed, then abruptly her voice lowered. "I declare, Josephine, I was shocked though. Did I see your girl getting fitted in the back room? At first, I thought I was seeing things. Of course, I cornered Miss Haney…she didn't want to, but eventually she confessed you ordered the girl several items from her store. All hush…hush."

"If you mean…"

"I understand," Mrs. Wilder released Jo's hand and patted it ever so gently. "Truly I do. You have a compassionate heart. I say this only because your poor momma is not here to do so. God bless her soul." Her voiced hissed underneath her breath. "But you can't have a blackie in our dress store…shopping!"

Immediately, the woman straightened herself. "Of course, I would never say a word about what I saw. Poor Miss Haney would suffer so if everyone knew she serviced slaves. What else could I do? Phyllis is such good friends with your Clarissa." She glanced around. "Where is the lovely girl?"

For a brief moment, Jo considered the unfairness of it all. She wanted to retort that Gillie was no longer her servant or *slave*. Jo had only wanted Gillie to enjoy the moment. The courts had finalized the official papers that freed Heyward and Gillie. Gillie would travel with Jo to Philadelphia after Jo's wedding to enjoy one of her own; a true wedding stemmed from the love Gillie and Heyward had for each other.

Jo had not asked much for her own wedding. It was deemed best to have a small affair, immediate family only at the ceremony at the Montgomery's house on the Battery. A far cry from Clarissa and Wade's grand affair. She did not care for herself, but she wanted more for Gillie. She wanted Gillie to enjoy her moment.

Papa had been indulgent toward her since she agreed to marry Andrew. In so doing, when Jo insisted that she give Gillie a wardrobe for her wedding gift, her papa obliged by convincing Miss Haney to fit Gillie for her travels.

What on earth was Mrs. Wilder doing in the back of the store snooping? Why the store had been closed when Gillie had been fitted! The nosy thing!

"Who?" Jo asked. Lost in her thoughts, she had quite forgotten what the woman had asked.

"Why that sweet thing, Clarissa! I don't believe I saw her at service."

"Clarissa is feeling a bit under the weather, Mrs. Wilder. I am certain she will be able to attend the ceremony at week's end. I hope to see you and your family as well," Andrew's brow was harshly furrowed. "I thank you for your concern with my Jo. I can assure you it will be addressed."

Mrs. Wilder clutched her bosom. "Thank the Good Lord you know now. I had been so worried. I knew you would want to know."

Andrew waited until Mrs. Wilder walked away before he grasped hold of Jo's elbow. She wanted to protest, but it was not the place to do so.

Warily, she allowed Andrew to guide her to the carriage. She wished that Grace Ann had not traveled to London with Mr. Whitney or that Charlotte hadn't gone to visit family in Camden. She felt so alone.

Jo found Wade and his mother waiting patiently for them in the open carriage. She paused before accepting Wade's assistance up into the forward seat. He startled her when his blue eyes locked on hers with a frowning intensity.

Wade Montgomery. The man who at one time she professed her love gave her a reproachful look. He had changed. Not his looks. He was still undeniably handsome, tall and lean with streaked blond hair and deep, blue eyes.

No, it was his feelings that had altered. He hated her because he had lost the one thing he loved more than he did her—Magnolia Bluff.

She smothered her growing misery, happy only that Papa was not beside her to endure the ire of her new family. He had looked so pale and tired this morning, she insisted he rest.

It had been Papa who had stubbornly held to the promise he made his wife before her death. Ruthlessly determined, Papa had succeed in maneuvering Jo into becoming a lady accepted by Charleston society…mistress of Magnolia Bluff, but it came at a much higher price than what her papa imagined. Papa handed her over to a family that held little love for her.

She wanted nothing more than to make them understand that as much as they hated Papa, if not for the marriage, they would lose everything…everything. Not by her Papa's hand, but by the actions of Douglas Montgomery, father, husband and son of those who now resented her intrusion into their household. Now, it would not happen because of her union with Andrew.

Andrew settled himself beside her, but it was not her fiancé that irritated Jo. Wade had not taken his eyes from her.

Wade drew a stiff smile. "I told you, Drew that you needed to talk with her."

Jo had no need to ask the reason for his statement. It was obviously he knew exactly the topic of conversation with Mrs. Wilder. She was not quite sure how to react to Wade's hostility. Her chin tilted upward in defiance.

In the far recesses of her mind, she could hear Grace Ann exclaiming, "Smile. Nothing like a bright smile to confuse your enemy. Charm the stars, Josephine. Charm the stars."

Jo's lips curved upward. "I'm sure that you are over reacting to Mrs. Wilder. It was not…"

"Your papa did not arrange a fitting for your girl in one of the most exclusive dress shops in the city? Once more, your dear papa gave no thought to the consequences of others when enacting his will."

Stubbornly, Jo shook her head, rejecting his statement. "It is not fair to blame, Papa. It was my gift to Gillie. She is accompanying me to Philadelphia after the wedding but is leaving me afterward. She is to marry Heyward. He has found a house for them to live…"

"I can assure you it means little to the good folks in Charleston what Gillie's plans are," Wade's voice was calm, but chiding. "You will soon be a Montgomery. You have an obligation to uphold our good name."

Jo's face burned at his statement. An awkward silence ensued. Jo glanced at Andrew, who lowered his gaze.

"Andrew!" Her voice rose higher than she intended. How could he sit there and let his brother reprimand her? "Are you going to let Wade talk to me in this manner?"

"Jo, dear, Wade means only that perhaps you are too close to your girl," Marie Montgomery looked straight at her future daughter-in-law with sympathetic eyes. "Understandable. We all become close to our servants at one time or another, but there is a line we cannot cross. You are much too smart a young lady not to realize there can be ramifications."

Flushed with frustration, Jo sat back. She was not willing to accept Wade's rudeness so readily. To let him treat her in this fashion was unacceptable. Strangely, at that moment, she felt Andrew reach over and grasp her hand in a reassuring way.

As the carriage slowed to a stop in front of the house, Andrew gestured for her to stay by his side while his mother and Wade walked up the steps into the entrance.

"I know you are upset with me," he said. "and with good reason. I have not been fair to you. I do not need to mince words to tell you I have met our engagement with the greatest reluctance."

"I have felt it," Jo acknowledged, eyeing him curiously. His words seemed sincere, almost repentant.

"These last few months, I have felt I was nothing more than a puppet being led around by my strings," he went on. "I realize, though, you too have been forced into this arrangement. I have treated you abominably even knowing you have made *sacrifices*."

His last word hung in the air. He paused and swallowed hard. "Be patient. It will take time for my family to adjust. I do owe you an apology for not defending you with Wade. He had no right to address you so harshly. But…Wade is upset, not at you, but Clarissa."

"Clarissa?"

Andrew lowered his gaze and pressed his lips together tightly as if contemplating his next words. Looking back up at Jo, he said, "Clarissa has miscarried."

* * * *

The late afternoon threatened a summer thunderstorm. Showery with thunder rumbling, Jo walked back over to the Montgomery house along the Battery. She should have stayed home and read to Papa. Instead, she had braved the elements and came back to see Clarissa.

The men had gone out for the afternoon while Mrs. Montgomery sat down in the parlor with her embroidery. Her future mother-in-law looked at her oddly when Jo announced her intent to visit Clarissa once more, but she made no objections.

Before she had left earlier in the day, she had visited briefly with the ailing Clarissa. The poor thing hadn't said much but looked so peaked...and sad. The beautiful woman, who only the day before looked so vibrant, so full of life, now lay pale and listless in her bed.

Propped up by pillows, one long dark braid fell over her shoulder as sunlight from the window filtered about her, giving her an aura, a heavenly radiance. Her face was pallid. Gone was the glow of her warm cheeks, the sparkle in her eye and it concerned Jo.

She couldn't quite understand herself why she had returned to visit Clarissa. They had never been close. Perhaps, it was compassion for the loss Clarissa had endured. Jo didn't know, but something pulled Jo back here...something felt wrong, ever so wrong.

It took effort for Jo to find the courage to walk up the stairs to Clarissa's room. Knocking lightly, Jo didn't wait for an answer, but gently opened the door. She wasn't going to disturb Clarissa, but leave her a vase of freshly cut gardenias with soft pink roses.

Jo entered the lavish bedroom with its rosewood furniture, rose brocade draperies and large French Aubusson rug. The darkness from the storm had invaded the room, leaving it in shadows.

She saw Clarissa's servant girl, Rosa, shut the window. Jo heard the patter of raindrops against the windowsill and the howl of the wind. The clouds had opened.

The dark girl with aquiline features and crisply waving hair tied up in a kerchief gestured she would take the flowers.

"Why them gardenias will soothe her."

"It is what I hope, but I see she is sleeping. So I won't disturb her," Jo said softly. "She worried me after I left. I thought these might brighten the room a bit."

"I am worried too, Miss Josephine," Rosa said in a low whisper. "She done gone and sent Master Wade away. Told him she just needed sleep. But I think she don't want him to know how poorly she feels. She won't let me send for the doctor neither."

Glancing over at the sleeping woman, Jo nodded in understanding. Womanly ailments were not talked of in Charleston society. Frowned upon to be acknowledged. She could well imagine Clarissa would suffer before admitting her issues.

Clarissa opened her eyes briefly and then closed them again upon seeing who it was. "Jo."

Jo walked toward the weaken voice and sank down on the edge of the bed. Clarissa looked worse. Her closed eyes were sunken; her face whitened. She grasped in the open air until Jo caught her cold hand and held it gently.

"I brought flowers for your room."

"I can smell gardenias. I do so love them," Clarissa uttered in a whisper. "Oh, Jo, I'm so glad you came back. I don't want to be alone."

"I will send for Wade."

"No, no…," she broke down and wept. "He is already worried enough. I can't let him see me like this…Oh, Jo, I've lost the baby. Wade is going to be so upset with me. He was so happy…as was I. I could give him something to love…"

"Clarissa, he already has you. He loves you. You will have other children."

"Does he? Does he love me, Jo?"

"Yes, Clarissa. He has been a bear all day because of his concern for you."

After a pause, she drew a breath and whispered, "Don't leave me, Josephine. I am scared ever so scared."

In the far recess of Jo's mind, the words echoed—I'm scared, ever so scared. She had heard them before, another time and place. The fear growing inside of her turned to panic.

The image of her mother lying on her death bed swept before her. Remembrance of holding on to her cold…cold hands. How pale she looked as her life was ebbing out of her…

Jo looked up to see Rosa on the other side of the bed. "Go get the doctor," Jo ordered. "And send for Master Wade."

"But Miss Josephine. Mistress…"

"Get him now!" Jo's voice rose in a sea of alarm.

Suddenly, Clarissa clutched her stomach. Grimacing, she cried out. "I hurt. Oh, Jo, I hurt so."

Jo wrapped her arms about Clarissa, as the poor woman's gripped Jo's arms tightly. Pain shot through Jo's arms, but she refused to move.

"Don't leave me."

"I won't," Jo promised. Suddenly, Jo felt warmth oozing around her. Looking down, she watched blood covered the sheets, spreading quickly. She screamed.

* * * *

The heavens cried and the rains came; a torrential downpour burst upon the funeral procession. It had slowed to a light drizzle, but Jo refused to leave the grave site. Not yet. She couldn't leave until she told Clarissa that she was sorry, so very sorry.

Haunted by Clarissa's face, Jo remained by the grave site. The poor dear wanted nothing more than to live, but it was not meant to be. The miscarriage had caused bleeding that couldn't be stopped.

Staring down at the fresh, wet dirt, she thought of what Papa told her.

"Death transcends all barriers and shows no mercy. The rich, the poor, young, old, free or slave. It is a fate that none of us will escape."

Papa's presence gave her strength. He held to his belief in God and life after death. He clung to the promise of seeing his beloved Lucinda after this life was done. She wished she held his faith.

St. Philips Church had been crowded for the funeral. Such sadness. An assembly of slaves sung mournful hymns. Their strangely soothing melodies filtered in through the open doors.

Condolences did little to comfort Randolph Wragg, Clarissa's father. Distraught, Jo worried that he would succumb to his grief. He looked lost and ever so alone. Slumping over, he lost his composure more than once. Wade sat next to his father-in-law in shock. He showed little emotion as if unbelieving the sight before him.

"Andrew said you were still here."

Jo looked up. Wade. His cravat was loosened; his shirt untucked. He held his hat in his hand, twisting the rim one way than another. When his eyes met hers, she could have wept.

"I haven't had the opportunity to thank you for being with her at the end," he said in a solemn voice. "Doctor Jameson said there was nothing that could have been done. It was good that you called for him when you did because now we can live with that knowledge."

"It happened to my mother."

He nodded. Pressing his lips together, he drew in a deep breath. "She...Clarissa...didn't want me there. Doctor Jameson said the night before for her to stay in bed. It would pass...."

His emotions swelled and he quieted. Jo wanted nothing more than draw him into her arms and comfort him, but it would never do. Clarissa's death had not changed their relationship.

Her marriage to Andrew had been postponed but only for a short period. Andrew would return to Philadelphia within the week. He was set to study surgery with one of his former professors, Dr. Nathaniel Halcoyne.

Papa had no objections. Andrew had arranged to return at Christmas. The marriage would commence at that time. Jo discovered through the tragedy their relationship had evolved, but there was still no love.

Jo realized that it would never be a passionate affair of the heart. But a friendship had been forged. Andrew offered her a shoulder to cry upon, comforted her, and for the first time, they had talked.

"You will make a wonderful doctor's wife, Josephine. Compassionate and caring. I foresee us working well together."

He made no profession of love. She had not expected any. She hoped only to create a home where she could raise a family safe and loved. She wanted children, lots of children.

Moreover, Andrew took it upon himself to see to Gillie's welfare, overseeing her journey North to Heyward. It pained Jo not to go with Gillie and see her married, but it was for the best. Jo could not leave her father nor could she bear to see Cullen. The hurt of losing him had not eased with time.

Jo's gaze lowered to the fresh grave. She wished there was some way to relieve Wade of his grief, but only time would ease his sorrow. She sighed.

"It was not your fault, Wade."

He shook his head. "It was. It was my fault, Jo. Clarissa never wanted…you wouldn't understand. She should never have been…"

"Don't do this to yourself. It will do no good. She loved you greatly."

He collapsed down on his knees, "I cared…I did not want this…"

"She knew, Wade. Take comfort that you made her happy."

Jo glanced over to the other side of Clarissa's grave at a tombstone. *Percival William Montgomery. At least, Clarissa would not be alone.*

She leaned down and placed her flowers on the raised plot of dirt. The bouquet of gardenias paled in comparison to the massive amount of flowers covering the grave.

"Gardenias," Wade said, reaching over and smelled the blooms. "She was very much like a gardenia, beautiful and delicate." He looked up at Jo. "You, though, are more of a magnolia."

He gave a small smile with a faraway look in his eyes. "Mother could never grow gardenias in our garden. No matter what she did the magnolias always shadowed the gardenias."

Jo said nothing more. She left Wade with his grief.

Chapter Two

Walnut Street Theatre at Ninth and Walnut Street in Philadelphia hosted a grand production of Othello. An impressive performance by a young actor, Edwin Booth, held most of the audience's attention. Cullen Smythe wasn't among those mesmerized. No, his thoughts were miles away in Charleston.

When he first returned to Philadelphia he had buried himself in his new position at Smythe and Company as one of the directors of acquisitions. It was a position that suited him.

The family business had become one of the largest investors into the Philadelphia Railway Line and wanted to expand further. It was one these challenging projects along the railway that he was put in charge of; he had to learn quickly how to secure financing for this venture.

Only recently had he begun to socialize. Tonight, he sat in the box stage with his former Navy Academy classmate, Gavin Mitchell, and his wife, Diana. To their side, was along Hugh McFadden, Diana's brother. Also in the Navy, Hugh had served with Cullen aboard the *Cayne.*

From the corner of his eye, Cullen observed his escort for the evening. He had to admit when he was introduced to Ophelia Harding he found her devilishly good looking. She had dark brown hair and vivid blue eyes. Tonight, she wore an expensive green bell-sleeved gown. Lovely. Except every time he looked at her, it was another he saw.

Josephine. He remembered her in a deep green gown which fitted closely over her breasts… Damn. Damn. Damn.

Damn Andrew for appearing less than a week ago. Now he lived in a special hell knowing Josephine was left in Charleston with a grieving Wade. Why it bothered him so he could not put into words.

Had he not accepted that she was to marry Andrew? She chose to be the dutiful daughter; he chose to let her go. He left her knowing she would never be his. Never.

He had come back determined to forget everything about her. Wipe her from his memory. But there were some memories that never faded.

At least, Philadelphia did not remind him of her until tonight. Damn Andrew.

Philadelphia was a far cry from the coastal city of Charleston. Philadelphia boomed with industry and commerce located along the Delaware and Schuylkill Rivers. Clusters of mills and factories lined the streets of the city dominated by heavy industry. Shipbuilding. Textiles. Locomotives.

The one common factor between his northern and southern home was the political unrest concerning the South's peculiar institution of slavery. Cullen found public opinion here in Philadelphia increasingly hostile toward the practice.

"I'm glad you are home, son," Jonathan Smythe told Cullen on his final return. "I fear the tension is going to escalate. Selfishness and lust for political power on both sides will not allow for another outcome except a violent reaction."

"Stubbornness to a fault," Cullen acknowledged with reluctance. "There are no wise and prudent minds calming the flames, only the foolish and irresponsible fanning them."

Philadelphia was a political hotbed itself. There was a growing population of enthusiastic and determined abolitionists, which was met with opposition. Abolitionists had long been looked down upon by the other groups within the city: the Irish, the Germans, and the elite.

The free Negroes added to the labor market which competed directly with the Irish and Germans. There was little sympathy for the free blacks. The Fugitive Slave Act had given leverage to those who gave aid to abolitionists efforts to free the slaves.

Law enforcement officers were encouraged to arrest not only a runaway slave, but anyone who helped in the attempt. Odd that the feeling of animosity toward the south grew, but it did not ease the vindictiveness toward the runaways and their supporters.

Tonight, though, the unrest was the furthest thing from his mind. He stared across the stage to another box stage. His cousin, Dr. Andrew Montgomery, sat in the box with his mentor, Dr. Nathaniel Halcoyne and his daughter, Kathleen Halcoyne.

Kathleen Halcoyne would never have been called a beauty. Her light brown hair had been arranged with a fashionable flare. It did little to soften her features. Her chin was too pointy; cheek bones too wide, but she had other attributes that men admired. Well-endowed, her elegant gown with a low bodice accented her best quality.

Cullen watched with dismay as Kathleen leaned over and whispered to Andrew. Her hand touched his and …Good Lord…caressed it! His cousin responded with a laugh and the two exchanged lingering looks.

The nerve of the woman! Even from this distance, he recognized the two shared an intimacy well beyond acquaintances, well beyond proprieties when one was attached to another.

Anger surged through Cullen. He had been rendered powerless by the events beyond his control. He had sacrificed what he wanted the most in the world for the betterment of the family, not to have Josephine hurt in this manner.

His family here in Philadelphia had been informed of Clarissa's death by telegram. Cullen felt Wade's pain. To begin a new life and have it cut short so quickly! Cullen had sent correspondence to Wade with a heartfelt invitation to visit.

He had not heard back when Andrew appeared at Rosemount, who relayed the sorrowful details. Cullen had not been surprised to discover Josephine's compassion or the fact the wedding had been postponed. It had stunned him, though, that Andrew had returned back to Philadelphia so quickly.

Cullen's gaze fixed firm on Andrew. His futile fury contained but raged inside of him. Something was amiss.

"Cullen, my boy. You coming?"

Cullen slowly turned his gaze. His friends had risen from their chairs. The play was over. He glanced over at Andrew once more. Kathleen had entwined her arm with his.

He had no choice but to leave with his friends. He had no time to question Andrew about his *friend*. Not tonight…damn.

* * * *

Flanagan's Olde Ale House was not busy at two o'clock. Cullen received his drink quickly and drank down his first sip before he made his way to a booth. Mitchell had sent word to meet. At last, he hoped he would have answers.

The last couple of weeks, his suspicions toward Andrew had only grown. Why only the night before Andrew had been over for dinner in the company of Miss Kathleen Halcoyne. Granted his sister Elizabeth said that she had invited her friend, and Andrew had only escorted her. It did little to alleviate his questions.

155

He took another sip of his drink thinking of his sister. Elizabeth was odd. He couldn't think of another way to describe her. Ever since he had met her, she had been the quiet sort. He had been thirteen when his father brought him to Philadelphia.

To be honest, he had not looked forward to having a sister. Moreover, he hadn't wanted to leave Magnolia Bluff and his cousins, the only family he had ever known. His father was almost a complete stranger, his grandmother overwhelming. It wasn't until he met his new step-mother that he began to feel at home.

A warm and lovely woman, the former Monica Ross Marlowe seemed to know his apprehension. His step-mother welcomed him and gave him space needed for him to accept this different life. Gradually, he began to feel part of his father's home.

His step-sister, though, kept to herself. Perhaps it was the six years difference in their ages with Elizabeth being the senior. Elizabeth Marlowe was a contrast to her mother. Whereas Monica was confident and sophisticated, Elizabeth was exceedingly timid and shy.

The poor thing was not attractive, nor did she make any effort to improve her looks. Her dull brown hair pulled back giving her face a strained look without her hair to soften her eyes, which were quite small. Rarely did she smile, but when she did her eyes were lost in her face. Moreover, she was painfully thin to the point Cullen worried a strong wind could do her harm her.

At times, Cullen felt pity for Elizabeth, but any compassion, he showed, was met with open hostility. He learned to keep his distance. That was until his father wrote him of her predicament. It was not a new story, but one of old. A lonely woman desperate to feel love was taken advantage by a despicable man.

Elizabeth had been badly used by a man that Kathleen Halcoyne introduced her to—Jeremiah Lowney.

"Sorry, I'm late. I had one more thing to attend to, but it is all set now."

Cullen watched Mitchell eased into the seat across from him and gestured to the man behind the bar for a mug. Cullen added another to the order.

Not much was said while they waited for their drinks. Cullen assumed Mitchell hid his disapproval of Cullen's strategy. Mitchell had said as much on their last meeting when Cullen revealed his plan.

"You are still insistent on processing?" Mitchell finally asked. "You want to go down this road."

"I thought I had made myself quite clear. You have made known your reservations. I know you can't understand my position, but it is essential to me that I know Andrew's actions. It is not that I don't trust my cousin as much as I distrust that woman."

"My concern lays with you, my friend. I know you still hold feelings for his fiancée," Mitchell said bluntly.

Mitchell had always been forthright and frank. It was the reason Cullen had always relied on his friend's opinion, but at the moment, though, his manner irritated Cullen to no end.

Cullen ignored his friend's insinuation. It would do no good to deny what he felt. Mitchell could never understand the sacrifice he had made; Josephine had made. He would be damned if he allowed it to be for naught.

"It has to do with my family. Kathleen Halcoyne is a woman bent on mischief. How else do you explain her introducing Elizabeth to a married man? Why Mother allows Elizabeth to hold the friendship still is beyond me."

"Perhaps it is because Elizabeth is a grown woman."

"In age," Cullen argued. "But she has a vulnerability. She was ruined by Lowney. If I ever lay eyes on him again, I will forget the agreement that was made."

Anger oozed from Cullen's tone. It was not clear how exactly the whole of the episode developed. What Cullen had inferred quickly was that the man had made Elizabeth's life a living hell. First, Lowney convinced her to elope with him, and then afterward confessed he was already married. Then it, the blackmail, began. It had destroyed Elizabeth's delicate soul.

On his return, he had helped his father hunt Lowney down. A one-time payment ensued with the promise if he ever returned or made contact with Elizabeth again, he would be arrested and held accountable for his crimes. It had been the only way to avoid a scandal for Elizabeth.

Cullen's instincts told him there was more to the story than what Elizabeth acknowledged. He sensed that Kathleen had more to do with the affair than was recognized. Now the devil woman had set her eyes upon Andrew.

"You believe it stems from your rejection of her."

Mitchell leveled his gaze upon Cullen. Cullen looked straight back. He realized that Mitchell believed it to be absurd that Kathleen Halcoyne would be that vindictive, but Cullen suspected that Kathleen had not taken well to his rebuff, no matter that it had been years ago before he had entered the Navy Academy.

To this day, he remembered well the shock of discovering his sister's friend naked in his bed. He had said nothing, but left the room with only the demand she remove herself. He said nothing to his father or step-mother.

Looking back, he regretted keeping silent. He had been young and inexperienced, but he knew instinctively he wanted nothing to do with the woman. Yet, he did not inform his father. He felt he could not.

Elizabeth seemed so excited with her new friend, her only friend that Cullen had been aware she had. Moreover, Kathleen had been engaged since that time. Unfortunately, her fiancée had passed away shortly before her marriage.

"I do not believe she is vengeful toward me," Cullen said. "I simply do not trust her motives."

Mitchell shifted his position. A pursing smile tightened his face. "I did as you requested and had your cousin followed."

"And?"

"You were right that Andrew has kept a secret from you," Mitchell offered. "Finish your drink. Hugh is waiting for us."

* * * *

Overhead a flock of migrating geese gabbled in the brilliance of the serene sky. The blushing leaves of vivid red and gold told of another change of season. The horse trotted onward, rustling through dried fallen foliage.

Rounding the bend of Park Road, Cullen inhaled the smell of the ripe earth. Before him, he caught a glimpse of his grand country estate, Rosemount. His great-grandfather built his home in the midst of a hundred and fifty acres of farm land. Situated atop of the high cliffs overlooking the Schuylkill River, the impressive house was flanked by a pair of matching outbuildings.

There was nothing nostalgic in the scene to Cullen.

The bold mansion was two and a half stories of stucco masonry with a horizontal belt of red brick runs, the elaborate summer residence of the Smythes. In a way, the Georgian architectural reminded Cullen of his Southern heritage, but no magnolias bloomed on these grounds.

Mitchell and McFadden rode beside him, but no man spoke along their journey after Cullen was informed the answers he sought lay within the walls of Rosemount.

Along the miles traveled toward his destination, Cullen restless thoughts overwhelmed him. An odd sudden remembrance surged forth of a conversation he held with his step-mother here at Rosemount shortly after he arrived back from Charleston without Josephine.

"I see the hurt within you, Cullen," she said in a sympathetic tone. "I wish I could take the hurt away, but it is a part of life. The truth is, she will never leave you and will always be a part of you, the part that brings warmth."

"Forgive me if I don't see it that way, Mother."

"No, I don't suspect you do at the moment, but in time, it will come. Love never leaves you. It may fade like an ember, but to be love is precious. It holds meaning whether you recognize it or not."

"Nothing holds meaning at the moment. I am a gentleman and will accept my fate, but don't expect me to embrace it."

"You are so much like your father. Men do not express their feelings as we women do, but you must know that your father loved your mother very much. Her death wounded him gravely," she went on. "When I met Jonathan, he was confused. He wanted you by his side…you were a part of her…a part of himself. He needed you to remind him of his love. I sent him to retrieve you because we all need to be reminded that we are loved. Bitterness will tear at your soul."

Her words weighed heavy on his heart. He could not explain what he himself did not understand. How at times, minutes seem like hours and hours an eternity away from her.

A gust of a chilling wind reminded him that he was not in Charleston. The autumn evening was upon him, cool nights and the smell of fire from the chimneys.

He reined in his horse in front on Rosemount. Standing in the front entrance, was a tall, handsome middle-aged man. His black hair speckled with gray had been slicked back from his face, and side-whiskers accentuated his prominent profile.

Cullen nodded in acknowledgment. "Good evening, Father."

* * * *

The dull ache brewed in his head, progressed to a constant throbbing as Cullen followed his father down the basement steps. He felt betrayed. His anger directed at his father, the man he had trusted and handed over control of his estate without a second thought. He now understood his grandmother's reason for leaving the estate in his hands.

After dinner, Mitchell and McFadden departed back to Philadelphia. Neither discussed the purpose to their visit during the meal. The conversation consisted of the tension building in the South, not the matter at hand. No, his father waited until their guests left, but Cullen saw it in their eyes. They both knew what he was about to be told.

In the library, Cullen gave his father his undivided attention. A million thoughts ran rampant in his mind while his father talked. He said little throughout the discussion, but every word suffused through him.

Cullen walked behind his father on the winding staircase. His eyes struggled to conform to the dimming light. He had not used these stairs before. The secret staircase lay behind the bookcase across from the fireplace in the library. So many secrets…

The largest loomed before him. His father, Jonathan T. Smythe, the respected member of Philadelphia Society was an associate of the Underground Railroad and had been since before Cullen was born.

* * * *

The basement to Rosemount was dry with a high ceiling, making for substantial headroom. Perfect for storage and hiding runaway slaves. The whole of the area had been converted into a shelter for the passing fugitives.

In the far corner, a row of cots lined the side of the wall. A brick fireplace burned to the right of Cullen, vented into the existing chimney on the upper floor. A dining table was also within the large room. At the moment, it held a single occupant, a well-dressed black man.

He wore a black suit with a high collar white shirt and a black bowtie of velvet. His shoes were laced with a broad heel. A dark hat lay to his side. The moment Cullen appeared, the distinguished man stood.

"Cullen," Jonathan Smythe said. "This is my friend, Mr. William Still. When McFadden followed Andrew and discovered our little hideaway, William offered to talk to you to help you understand what we do and why."

"Your father informs me that you have only just resigned from the Navy," Still said solemnly. "It is a comfort to Jonathan to know you are home."

Cullen had already realized by the looks exchange between the two men that each held the other in esteem. A sudden resentment surged through him with the knowledge that this Still seemed to know his father better than he did, but perhaps he didn't know his father at all.

Observing the black gentleman, Cullen surmised that the man was older than himself. He estimated the man to be in his mid-to-late thirties, intelligent with a mild, confident manner. There wasn't a fanatic feel to his tone or mannerism. No, the man carried himself with a quiet dignity that came from living a life with purpose.

A frown crossed Cullen's face and shrugged. "It seems obvious that you both are intertwined in the Underground Railroad together. While I sympathize, don't expect my support. It's against the law."

160

Still sat back and nodded. The man needed no reminder of the Fugitive Slave Act of 1850 or the notorious slave catchers that hunted down slaves that escaped. The law imposed stiff penalties including high fines and imprisonment for help given to any runaway.

Furthermore, society frowned heavily on abolitionists. The Underground Railroad had been the epitome of secrecy well needed to be successful.

"Cullen," Jonathan said. "Don't be under the illusion that I'm apologizing for my actions. It was necessary. When you were younger, I kept it from you for your own protection."

"Now it would seem it would be so you can keep financing your little venture."

The harsh words cut through the thick tension. An awkward silence ensued. Cullen shook his head. There was no reason to stay in this room. He turned to leave.

"I want you to understand. That is all I'm asking."

Cullen stopped and looked back at his father. "I believe I understand well enough."

"Please sit," Still requested, calling attention back to himself. "I ask you to listen to my story. I understand your anger for I have my own. But your father does not deserve your animosity."

"I do not need to be told how to feel," Cullen shot back his growing rage at the man.

"It is not my intention," Still said. "Your reputation for being a fair and honest man has preceded you. I know what you did for Heyward and his wife, Gillie."

"It was not I," Cullen snapped. He wanted to say it was Josephine who had risked her welfare, but instead he said, "Brantley Wright saw to his freedom, as well as the girl."

"You saved him," Still said simply. "It showed you looked at him not as an object but a human being."

Cullen made no response. Still continued. "My parents were born slaves, but yearned to be free. My father bought his freedom by hard work. My mother didn't have that opportunity. Instead, she fled with her four children only to be caught and brought back. She was not content. She escaped again. This time she was successful, but it came at a price. She had to leave two of my brothers behind who had been sold to slave owners in Mississippi. It tore at her heart. It is the reason I do what I do.

"Her sacrifice gave me the chance to make something of myself. I swore it would not be wasted. I have devoted my life to helping those kept in bondage."

Still rose and walked over to his father's side. He clasped the back of Jonathan's shoulder. "This is a good man." He took a deep breath as if affected by his own words. "I have been fortunate to have become a successful business man. It gave me the opportunity to help the Underground Railroad more efficiently. It is how I met your father.

"I could stand here and tell you story after story of the brave people who have helped those in bondage. I can tell you the tales of those that have escaped—hiding in crates and ships for days on end without food and water. Crawling through briar patches, cut and wounded, risking their lives to gain freedom. But I know I don't have to tell you for you know the hardships.

"What you need to hear is only this. Jonathan Smythe has done what his heart has called him to do. Do not let your wounded pride come between your father and yourself."

Still picked up his hat. "It has been a pleasure to meet you. I hope it will not be the last we will see of each other. I bide you good night."

He said nothing else but left Cullen alone with his father.

* * * *

A long silence followed between father and son. Cullen contemplated the man who had rejected society's stance of turning a blind eye to the horrific institution of slavery. Deep within him, he comprehended the strength and courage it took his father to do as he had done, but his father had kept it secret from him. His own father did not trust him!

In his youth, good and evil was as clear as night and day. Now, it seemed to have merged into a dull gray.

"I never meant for you to find out this way. For that I am truly sorry," Jonathan broke the silence. "I should have told you immediately upon your return."

Cullen stood indignantly looking at his father. Unsmiling, he said, "Grandmother found out. That is the real reason she left her estate to me and excluded you."

"Your Grandmother felt I was going to bring shame upon the family. Already your mother had left me. She felt I had dishonored our family."

Suddenly a realization suffused throughout Cullen. His body tensed. "Good Lord!" he cried. "Mother knew!"

"It was the contention in our marriage," Jonathan acknowledged, pain in his eyes clearly visible. "I cannot deny that the fault lies with me. Guilt has gnawed at me since your mother left me."

162

Loyalty toward his mother surged through him. It was not only him his father had betrayed. "How could you, Father? How could you?"

There had been so many years lost to them in his youth. Cullen had thought the two had mended that bridge, but he had only realized that the gulf was too wide.

Jonathan moved across the room to the table and sat. For a moment, he leaned his head into hands. After a time, he looked back up at his son. In the dim light, the basement offered, Cullen saw water well in his father's eyes. Emotions overwhelmed the man. He had never seen his father cry.

"Dolly was my weakness," Jonathan said in a softened tone. "I should have never married her. Looking back now, I see that, but at the time, I couldn't live without her. I deceived her and in the end, lost her."

Cullen watched his father take a deep breath in as if contemplating his next words carefully. His father pursed his lips and slowly began his tale.

"When I was young, I was bold and adventurous in my efforts to make a fortune. I was determined to show Mother that I could make it on my own. By the time I was twenty, my venture into shipping had been fruitful. I had arranged a triangular trade arrangement through South America and China. I bought the cotton and had it shipped.

"It was on one of my voyages when I laid anchor at St. Augustine along the northern coast of Florida. During the layover, one of my men, Al Renaud from the area, invited me to go on an alligator hunt. Late that night, Al took us into the marshes. As we made our way along the water's edge, we heard a baby cry. Worried because we were in the middle of a swamp infested with alligators and snakes, we rushed to the cry. A full moon illuminated the sight that would be etched into my memory forever.

"Across the inlet, a black baby was tied up with a rope around its neck and its torso screaming and thrashing in the water. Before I could make a move, a gigantic alligator lunged out of the water and clamped down on the child. Immediately, men emerged from the overgrowth and roped in the alligator, killing it. Al grasped hold of me and refused to let me interfere. There was nothing we could have done at that point.

"It was a group of alligator hunters using black slave infants as alligator bait. I was aghast and appalled. Al explained that he had heard rumors of hunters that stole slave babies to use them as bait. We reported it, but nothing was done except notify the plantation owners to be aware that men were stealing black babies, only to protect their property. Property!

163

"Babies! They were killing babies! Thinking no more of it than if they were a chicken or rodent!" Jonathan paused and collected himself. "It was then I did my own soul searching. I had as most turned a blind eye to slavery. It did not affect me personally. After witnessing the barbaric act, I swore I would be silent no move, not so much with my words as actions. I gave up my own ambitions and went to work for the family business. Smythe and Company. It made Mother happy, at least for a time.

"I'm no politician. I could not change the laws, but I had the means to help. In the beginning, Al and I helped smuggle escaped slaves onto our ships. It was dangerous, too many eyes in a contained area. Eventually, we found others like us and became associated with the Underground Railroad. On my trips, South, I helped arrange safe houses and routes for the fugitive slaves to take."

"You met Mother on one of those trips?"

Jonathan nodded. "Yes," he answered. "She had no knowledge of my actions until after she came North with me. To be honest, I never intended to tell her. She was Southern and held her father in high regard. She was a gentle soul but believed as her father taught her that the slaves were better off as they were. She thought they couldn't take care of themselves without guidance. The night she discovered my deceit cost me dearly. It cost me her love, my mother's and you."

"Yet, you have not stopped."

"Nor will I."

Cullen rubbed his forehead, trying hard to comprehend all his father was telling him. Thoughtfully, he said, "You use the railroad here at Fairmount to help I would imagine. Curved the line to slow it at a certain point so the escapees can jump off, where they are collected and taken to Rosemount."

"If you want, I will give you all the details of the operation," his father said. "I don't want you to be angry."

"I am angry, Father," Cullen lashed out. "How could you? How could you not tell me— your own son! You let me discover this on my own and expect me to be fine with it! You keep it from me, yet Andrew must know everything."

"Andrew became a necessity," Jonathan said. "I told you I never meant for you to find out this way."

"Or at all!"

"Perhaps the thought crossed my mind," his father acknowledged. "I know how close you are to your Southern family. Andrew…Andrew had his own reasons for doing what he has done. I did not recruit him. He came north to medical school searching for a way to help. He...held suspicions."

"Suspicions?" Cullen looked at his father, confused. Then slowly once more he grasped his meaning. No, his father would not have had the nerve. "Magnolia Bluff! You run the Underground Railroad through Magnolia Bluff?"

Cullen listened in complete disbelief. His father held nothing back, telling of the integral parts of a well thought out system.

"You have to know that we abhor violence. Our actions are only to withdraw slaves that desire to be free, not to instigate a rebellion against their owners. It is a dangerous path for them to take. The dangers are made quite clear."

With a stubborn frown on his face, Cullen folded his arms and stood in a defiant manner. "You let Mother return to Magnolia Bluff and kept..."

Jonathan shook his head quite vigorously. "It was not like that. Dolly knew. I told her as I am telling you. She never said a word."

Being so young when his mother died, Cullen remembered nothing that would have contradicted his father's account. But why had he kept this information from him?

"I know this is a lot for you. I don't expect you to forgive me yet, but in time, I hope you will understand."

Cullen's brows drew together in irritation. "I fear that my temper will allow only my ire at the moment. That you help slaves escape is not the issue as much as you did not trust me...even after I saw to Heyward's safety. You must have realized my position."

"I fear that was my doing, Cullen. I advised Uncle Jonathan to wait."

Cullen turned to face his cousin. Andrew walked around the table and settled a chilly stare upon his cousin.

"Come, Cullen, do not begin to tell me that you are annoyed with me? It was you that had me followed."

"With reason," Cullen replied icily. "You are an engaged man flaunting another woman around Philadelphia."

"It is what I thought," Andrew sneered. "Then this matter can be cleared up promptly. Miss Kathleen Halcoyne is a friend. Lest I remind you, it is not your concern, and neither is Josephine Wright. She is my fiancée."

"I will not have you..."

"That is where you are wrong," Andrew retorted. "You have no say in anything associated with Jo. I would strongly advise you to leave her well alone. Do I make myself clear?"

Anger gripped Cullen tightly. Fury choked in his throat, making it impossible to respond. It took all his willpower to overpower the urge to punch the snide look off of Andrew's face. He looked over at his father, then back at Andrew.

"It will not be a concern any longer," Cullen stated, turned abruptly and walked out of the basement and up the stairs. He asked only for his horse and rode back to Philadelphia.

Chapter Three

By late fall, Josephine had returned to Magnolia Bluff. It was different this time. She was welcomed into the house as its future mistress. The knowledge did little to alleviate the gloom that enveloped her spirit.

The oppressive heat of the late summer had broken, replaced with much cooler weather. With the coming of the shorter days, a gray dampness invaded the plantation. The fields had been harvested, lending the time for other activities to be enjoyed by the men of the family. Hunting and fishing became a daily occurrence.

Papa enjoyed the time outdoors and had regularly participated, but these daily undertakings had taken a toll on his well-being. He began to go less frequent. The decline in Papa's health had become more apparent.

Jo worried about him. In all her life, she had never known him to be anything other than the imposing, yet charming figure of a man he presented to the world. His dominant personality had never been questioned. Now, he had begun to question himself. That alone scared Jo.

Away from the bustle of Charleston gave Jo time to contemplate the changes in her live in a relatively short time. She had come to the conclusion she needed to immerse herself into the affairs of the estate.

Andrew's mother offered to show her around, not only the house but the whole of the plantation. Jo learned quickly there was more to running the plantation than maintaining the household.

167

The responsibilities were enormous. Thankfully, Marie Montgomery had been the embodiment of patience. She set to train Jo in becoming a competent mistress of the grand plantation.

Descending the staircase the first day she was set to shadow her future mother-in-law, Jo discovered a present on the side table. Opening it, she was deeply touched. It was a receipt book filled with detailed instruction for medical care for the inhabitants on the plantation. It held vital information for Jo to be able to perform her duties from preventing miscarriages to killing rats. Most times, it was handed down from mother to daughter.

"Oh, Mrs. Montgomery!" Jo cried and clutched it to her chest.

Smiling broadly, Mrs. Montgomery said, "My dear, I think it's time to come up with something less formal. Please call me Mother Montgomery."

"Mother Montgomery," Jo agreed, wondering how something so simple as a name warmed her soul. Looking at the woman, she could see the world Papa wanted for her—to become the lady of Magnolia Bluff. Finding happiness in a home filled with lots of children. She wanted lots of children. Perhaps it would fill the void within her.

Alongside Mother Montgomery, she began making shopping list needed for the upkeep of the plantation and keeping a ledger of housekeeping accounts. She had even accompanied Mother Marie to the sick house when one of the field slaves, Jolene, leg became infected from a spider bite. Jo watched the compassion Mother Marie showed and was impressed with the skill she treated the infection.

Her work kept her busy. She couldn't stop, if she did memories, would seep into her consciousness. She couldn't allow that to happen.

Time was passing ever so quickly. Christmas would soon be upon them, but she held none of her usual excitement for the holiday.

Since she had first come to Charleston, she had celebrated the season at The Groves surrounded by her family. Those she thought loved her. She wondered if she would ever set foot again in what had once been her home.

The rift between Papa and Grandpa Henry had grown wider. Over the last few weeks, Papa had cut ties with her momma's family and steadfastly refused to talk of it to her, only demanding that she obey him. It frustrated her to no end. She wanted to tell Papa that she knew the argument stemmed from Harry Lee and Buck's actions against her because Rosa told her.

With Gillie's departure, Clarissa's maid had become hers. Rosa had the necessary skills to be an excellent maid. Unlike Gillie, Rosa did not invite confidences, but Jo discovered Rosa rarely kept an opinion to herself. She did more than hint to the rumors surrounding her cousins. She talked openly about the whispers.

"Harry Lee and Buck are on the run from your papa with good reason, Miss Jo. It's said that your papa wants to string them up for what they did to you. He has warned them if they come back it's what will happen. It serves them right," her maid carried on. "Caused a ruckus, they did with them lies. Told Miss Clarissa not to listen to the oldest one. He's got the devil in him, he does. But ya got nothing to worry about now. Your papa is taking care of you."

Jo took comfort she was beyond the reach of her cousins. They could not do her more harm, but she missed Aunt Sybil and Grandpa Henry. Though, she admitted it pained her to know that Grandpa Henry had used her unmercifully.

She was relieved that Papa's anger had not extended to Grace Ann. Jo supposed that it had more to do with Grace Ann being the wife of Theodore Whitney than anything else. The older gentleman had been the epitome of graciousness.

Mr. Whitney's kindness extended far beyond his hospitality of using his Charleston home. After his return from Europe, Whitney helped Papa with his business dealings and managed to keep the peace between Papa and the Montgomerys.

Miss Hazel told Jo that Mr. Whitney was repaying a kindness to Papa because of his parents. The Wrights had done Whitney a favor in his youth that Whitney hadn't forgotten. While it explained why Whitney had offered his help, Miss Hazel irritated her. Jo sensed there was more to the story, but Miss Hazel refused to acknowledge anything else. She only shook her head when Jo pressed her.

Her old mammy moved back to her farm when they arrived at Magnolia Bluff. It had distressed Jo, but Papa insisted he was well enough for Miss Hazel to return home. Jo realized that Miss Hazel was not far away, but it dismayed her. She had taken comfort with having her mammy a constant in her life again.

She had lost so much over the last few months and had become consumed with worry about Papa's health. She fought against the wretchedness that was encompassing her, but it seemed endless. Miss Hazel had given her a semblance of normalcy with her presence.

Jo had enjoyed sitting with Miss Hazel and reading Gillie's letters. It gave them both joy to read of Gillie's happiness with Heyward. Gillie wrote in detail of their lives. She had gotten a job at a local bakery within walking distance of her new home. Heyward this, Heyward that. Jo smiled looking over the letter. Every other word reflected what Heyward thought or had done. *At least one of us is happy.*

Miss Hazel made regular visits to ensure Papa's was not pushing himself too hard. She was the only one he seemed to listen to when it came to his well-being. She did not cower when his temper exploded but forced him to keep it in check.

Papa remained a man possessed. His desire to see Jo settled had not lessened. Growing up, Jo had been used to living in the backdrop of society. His reappearance had pressed her into the glare of Charleston's elite. She sensed their resentment yet at the same time the outward appearance of respect. She was under no illusion. Her every movement was under observation to maintain a proper reputation. She held no doubt if she made any misstep she would feel their wrath.

For Jo, it had become a constant fear. She had never been good at concealing her emotions, but she wasn't given a choice. She aspired to erect a wall around her wounded soul. It had not worked. She was consumed with an overwhelming melancholy when the memories assaulted her...painful ones that tortured her.

Faces haunted her at night when she closed her eyes. She saw Papa pleading with her to fulfill his promise to her dying momma; Cullen saying nothing, but seeing the hurt in his eyes she had caused when he walked away and then there was Clarissa dying in her arms.

How helpless she felt and powerless to give the desperate woman what she wanted the most—to live. She could still feel Clarissa's hands clutching tightly to her as if Jo could stop her life from ebbing away. How fragile life was!

Jo was caught in a whirlwind of sadness. Despite Grace Ann assuring her that her heart would mend, it had not. She had been the one to turn from him, but it was Cullen that was never far from her thoughts. She could not confess the truth to anyone.

It was not all that disturbed her. The entire time she had been within Charleston, the talk of secession intensified with constant threats against the North. The people were intoxicated with enthusiasm to the point where it would have been impossible to ignore the restlessness of the South. Everywhere Joe went it was proclaimed over and over again. Upon the lips of every man, they talked of nothing else.

No one was louder than old man Montgomery. "Damn Yankees! Need to mind their own affairs instead of sticking their nose into ours!"

It shocked Jo that Clayton Montgomery was so open about his hatred toward the North. She had known he was an opinionated and outspoken man. He resented the audacity of the North dictating to him what to do on this own land and telling him the horrors of the practice that his ancestors had built their fortune. She wondered had he considered one of his grandsons was one of those *painted devils*.

"We will take care of our own! 'em Yanks need to leave us the hell alone, or they will awaken within us a fight that they will regret soundly!"

Unlike most around Jo, the thought of secession confused her. Confidence exuded from every Southern man, woman and child that the South would not be bullied but would make a stand, even Papa. A deeply felt hatred strengthened each day against the North.

Perhaps, though, it was the fact that the wedding was upon her that depressed her. Once again, arrangements had been put into place. The ceremony would take place Christmas Eve, a private affair with only family in the drawing room.

In the low country, Christmas was a time for celebration for everyone with all the slaves included. It was a time of goodwill and reflection. The perfect time to enjoy nuptials. Grace Ann and Mr. Whitney had shown respect for Papa and postponed their plans to return to his plantation in Camden to attend the ceremony.

The only other person, Papa invited, had been Clyde Morgan. Papa had arranged for his attorney to attend to ensure that the contract was upheld before he released his hold on Magnolia Bluff. A reminder of her fate, but she needed no reminder. It was of the utmost important to Papa for her to become the lady he envisioned.

Despair overwhelmed Jo. In a few short weeks, she would become the wife of a man she did not love, entrapped within the boundaries of loyalty and duty. But that was not today.

Today she found refuge in riding, a pleasure she had not enjoyed for months. She looked over her shoulder and saw a figure riding towards her.

Jo had been at Magnolia Bluff only a few days when Wade returned to his home from his uncle's in Beaufort. It had been impossible to ignore each other, quite impossible.

Before her, Wade reined in his horse and smiled. "I'm glad to see you decided to join me."

She nodded. Without another word, she nudged her horse forward into a gallop. Behind her, he followed.

* * * *

Undoubtedly inappropriate, her morning rides with Wade became a routine. Neither spoke of the impropriety of riding alone. Joe had no desire for it to end.

171

Cutting through the undergrowth, Joe ducked under the Spanish moss and laughed when Wade caught up with her. Reining her horse to the right, she prepared to bolt, but he was too quick. He had hold of her rein.

She screamed with a laugh, not realizing that in the shade of the woods she illuminated a beauty surrounding her with her eyes beaming, but the look on his face said it had not escaped his notice.

"You should always smile."

"Oh, you say!" She tried to jerk her reins back. "If you give me but a minute…"

"Don't think so," he laughed himself. Her eyes burst forth with a mischievous sparkle. He reached for her, and she took off again.

For the first time in such a long time, Jo wasn't thinking about tomorrow. Her only thought was riding and leaving everything else behind her.

Jo realized Wade had his own demons. He had not spoken of Clarissa since the burial nor had he talked of Magnolia Bluff. The loss of what he thought would have been his had to weigh heavily upon him.

He had done as she and lived in the moment. She wondered if he sensed the danger. She could never confess she enjoyed the thrill of the forbidden, not daring to consider the ramifications if they were caught.

Once more, Wade caught up with her while she rounded a bend. This time he reached out for her and peeled her from her horse. Unbalanced, the two toppled down in a pillar of tall weeds.

Jo scrambled to her feet. Her hands flew out in the direction of her horse.

"Wade Montgomery!" she cried, watching her horse ride off without her. "Look at what you have done!"

"I see well what I have done," he said in a low tone, but clear, so clear to her ears.

She turned back to him to find that he made his way to her side. He seemed not to have a care in the world…what if her horse arrived back at Magnolia Bluff without her?

Wade stepped even closer to her. She didn't move but stood mesmerized by his gaze. As if she had no will of her own, she fell into his arms. She had no recollection of how he molded her to him or when his mouth found hers…but for a moment the world around her disappeared.

Trembling, her lips pulsed gently against his. A forbidden passion was unleashed, freed of its restraint. Something too strong to fight overwhelmed her. He kissed her long and passionately. Her mind inflamed with a growing desire, a need to feel desired and refused to hear a voice within her telling her she belonged to another.

Somewhere in the back of her mind, she knew she needed to stop him, but she didn't. She kissed him back. Her body took over wanting what he had to offer. She uttered a faint helpless sound. He seemed not to notice. His lips descended down her neck.

Her senses came alive with his touch. No, no, no! She couldn't, but her body responded to his touch seemly unaware of how wrong this was. The voice became louder. *I am pledged to his brother.*

"Wade," she gasped and pushed back from him. Her hand covered her mouth, grasping for a breath. "Why did you do that?"

Brazenly, he looked at her without a tinge of remorse. He said simply, "You had the look of one that needed to be kissed."

Shaken, she had no retort and thankfully he didn't press her. Instead, he walked down the trail for a moment and returned with her errant horse.

* * * *

It had come. Christmas was upon Magnolia Bluff. Scent of evergreen and freshly baked gingerbread swirled throughout the house. The rooms were decorated beautifully with holly and bows.

Most years, the holiday lent to visits of family and friends, including dancing and partying into the wee hours of the morning. Feasting, drinking, and carols sung would go on for days, climaxing with a show of fireworks on Christmas Night.

Jo remembered the impatience as a child hanging up her stocking for St. Nicholas, waiting to discover what he had left her. It was a shame the Montgomery's had no little ones this year to enjoy the practice, but the swell of excitement of the slave children gave Jo heart.

The little ones seemed so happy with the smallest of things and eagerly awaited the day. At Magnolia Bluff, Jo learned that the slaves were given clothes for their gifts, shirts and pants for the men, dresses for the women and shoes for everyone. The young children, also, received candy in their stockings.

This year the festivities had been curtailed with the family being in mourning. The Montgomery's merriment would be contained to only close relatives, including guests to her wedding.

Rebelliously, Jo had pushed the contemplation of her wedding from her mind. Now, anxiety riddled her. Over the last few weeks, she had given little thought to the fact that she had not received a letter from Andrew, knowing he was expected at the Magnolia Bluff within the next few days.

She realized Andrew held his own reservations about their union. Had she not her own? Even now guilt weighed upon her for allowing Wade to kiss her. She had been foolish to believe she could share a friendship with him giving their unresolved feelings for each other.

Reason returned to her. She had not ridden since that morning and tried her best to avoid Wade. It was impossible to avoid him completely, given they lived under the same roof. At times, she felt his eyes upon her. Looking back at him, he would have a small knowing grin on his face. It bothered her to no end.

Wade had to understand she had quite made up her mind to marry Andrew. She had lived on the edge of scandal for so long. She refused to do so any longer. She would not shame Papa with her actions. Thankfully this morning, Charlotte had arrived at Magnolia Bluff.

The last Jo had seen of the dear girl, the poor thing had been downhearted with Harry Lee's betrayal. Upon notice of her friend's arrival, Jo raced down the stairs in a new deep rose velvet gown that was only half-way tied up the back because of her exhilaration. She found Charlotte smiling up at her at the foot of the stairs, fidgeting so.

Charlotte looked most fashionable with her brown tresses woven into swirled buns on both sides of her head. Her own gown looked festive, a royal blue dress with a button bodice and ruffled skirt. She wore a matching jacket trimmed in navy velvet. But it was her twinkling eyes that betrayed her excitement. To Jo's delight, Charlotte had transformed into a dreamy trancelike state. Immediately Jo realized the girl was in love.

Interlocking her arm through Jo's, Charlotte strolled into the parlor with Jo and sat beside her on the settee. More than once, she hugged Jo tightly.

"I do believe you will like him, Jo. He's a planter outside of Columbia…of course…you must have guessed he would live there since I was visiting Aunt Vera."

Charlotte rambled on, incoherently. "He is a widower…and is an older gentleman, but not that much dreadfully older than I. The first time I met him he told me I looked like a daisy in the meadow. I was wearing that butter-yellow taffeta…did I say that already?"

"Yes, darling," Jo said. "He sounds wonderful, except you have not told me his name."

"I did not? Oh! I did not!" Charlotte exclaimed, blushing profusely. "Arthur Bowles. Aunt Vera says his family is well-respected…they moved down from Richmond. He told me he was going to speak with Papa. Oh, Jo, I think he is going ask Papa for my hand. Why else would he want to speak with Papa? He said he is coming down after the new year with Aunt Vera and his parents."

"I am so happy for…"

Abruptly the serenity of the reunion was broken. A roar erupted upstairs. The distinct sound of Papa's voice echoed throughout the house.

"Hell's Fire! This will never do! I will not be played!"

Immediately, Jo bolted up the staircase leaving Charlotte in her wake. *Papa! What had happened?* Her heart raced. How selfish she had been! *If anything has happened to him because he discovered my adventures with Wade, I will never be able to live with myself!*

"Does he take me for a damn idiot?" Brantley Wright burst from his bedroom with a letter in hand. The gaunt man strode angrily down the hall. Until that moment, she had not notice how his once tailor fitted clothes hung loose about him. He halted in front of her. "Have you seen this? Do you know?"

Bewildered, Jo shook her head and took the letter Papa swung wildly in front of her. "Calm yourself, Papa. Your heart," she pleaded.

His cheeks reddened. Tenseness strained his face and the heaviness his chest breathed told of his difficulty inhaling. Fear gripped her that he would keel over in front of her.

She gripped his hand. "Please, Papa. Let's go back into your room and lie down."

He did not argue, which worried her more. Rosa appeared in the doorway.

"Get me his medicine and send for Miss Hazel," she instructed. Then she turned her attention back to her papa.

Papa slept while Miss Hazel sat with him. He seemed to have calmed, but Jo was worried. She had never seen Papa in such a state. He had always been a man in control, confident and assured. Today, he showed his apprehension.

"Call for my attorney, Jo. I need him here today."

"Papa, I will send a note but I don't know how soon…"

"Do not delay," Papa rasped. Lying down on his bed, he reached up and gripped her hand so tight it hurt. "Morgan will come. He will know what will happen if he does not. Send the note requesting his immediate presence…"

"I will. Rest. Please, Papa. For me."

Jo eased out of his room. Confused, she retired back to her room and took Papa's note that had greatly disturbed him out of her skirt pocket. It was from Andrew.

175

Her eyes flitted over the written words. Thunderstruck, she sank into the chair by the window as understanding suffused within her.

Dear Mr. Brantley Wright,

Due to unfortunate circumstances, it is with the utmost regret that I must postpone my journey home at this time. My mentor, Dr. Halcoyne has fallen ill. He has asked me to cover for his surgical practice until his recovery, which forces me to cancel my travel plans. It is a deep regret. I want you to convey my sincere apology personally to you. While it may delay my wedding plans with your lovely daughter, it will not keep our nuptials from being undertaken at a future time. I understand you want the ceremony to commence in short order and have committed myself to making this happen as soon as possible.

As a show of my intentions, I had thought of inviting Josephine and yourself up to Philadelphia for the ceremony to be held here. Then I understood it would be selfish of me to cause Josephine the distress of not having our wedding surrounded by family and friends.

The air of turmoil is brewing around us. In Charleston, the air breaths for secession; here in Philadelphia the tension holds against us. I do not want to subject Josephine unduly to the hostility. It hurts me to delay the wedding once more. I know the pain it will cause, but it will only be temporary. I believe because of the atmosphere here in Philadelphia, it is my belief that is best to postpone the wedding. I will immediately return the moment Dr. Halcoyne recovers. At that time, the marriage can commence. I will leave the details in your hands.

With heartfelt regret,

Dr. Andrew Montgomery

Jo rose with the utmost feeling of helplessness and stared blankly out the window. She had long since lost track of time. She had stared disbelieving at the letter until the words held no more meaning to her. She let the letter slip from her hand.

Leave the details in your hands! Empty words! She had nothing in her hands, only a bitter void. Even in her naivety, the excuse sounded lame. She clutched her stomach. Oh, how she ached!

Now Papa's concern became clear. *"Do they suppose I bluff?"*

She may not have understood the arrangement fully, but she knew that her father wasn't bluffing. Far from it! She knew Papa was deathly serious in his intent and feared it would kill him.

Anger surged forth. Andrew understood the precarious health Papa was in! Had not the doctor in Charleston given him only until the end of the year? Stubbornly, Papa clung to life to see his promise fulfilled.

Deep in thought, she did not hear the door creak open and shut or the footsteps walking toward her, but she felt the arm that encircled her from behind. Startled, she turned. Wade!

Glancing around the room to ensure no one else was witnessing this breach of propriety, she pushed him back and hissed, "Whatever are you doing in here?"

"I was worried about you. How is your papa?"

Jo met his questioning stare. "Papa is resting, but his health, as you well know, is waning." A prolonged silence passed, widening a gulf between them before she found the voice to speak. "I suppose Andrew wrote to you also that he has been delayed in Philadelphia."

"Unfortunate," Wade said, but he did not have the look of one distraught over the fact. His eyes never wavered from hers as he once more stepped towards her. "I know that it has distressed your Papa."

She gazed up into his warm blue eyes, sensing his intentions. It was easy to become mesmerized. Leaning down, he pressed his lips on hers. She gasped at his boldness and yet they felt so warm and tender. Open-mouthed, the kiss vividly revealed his desire, weakening her resolve.

A sudden urge wrestled through her conflicting emotions. She wanted to be loved, not to be used as some pawn in a game she no control, but this would never do. No matter their past, it would never, ever do. Not now.

Fighting desperately against her own growing desire, she twisted away. Shaken and shocked by her wanton act, she staggered back a step. "Oh, why do you hate me so much you would blatantly disgrace me? It will certainly be the end for Papa or is that your intent? Your brother has done his best!"

Wade scowled. "You don't know what you are saying. I would never harm you or your papa.'

"Then why are you here? You must know Papa is beside himself. It will kill him. It will certainly kill him."

"It is not my intent to do any harm. This is the only room in the house where we will not be overheard," he said bluntly. "But you should well realize what I want. What I have always wanted—you."

Her eyes widened and snapped with a sudden ire. "You know that is impossible," she uttered under her breathe. "That decision was made long ago. You made your choice. I made mine. It cannot be undone without harsh consequences. Have you forgotten you are a widower of less than a year, or I am engaged to your brother?"

"What if I don't want to proper? If I wait the allotted time, I will lose you. I refuse to lose you again."

For a brief moment, she wanted to believe him; wanted to believe she did not have to live her life in a loveless marriage. But Papa's words echoed within her. *They are playing us for fools, Jo.*

Oh, what a mess her life had become! Society had a set of rules to follow she could not ignore. She had skimmed along the edge of society for so long; lived in fear that she would disgrace Papa. Already the matrons of Charleston eyed her suspiciously. The old ladies were sharp. They would never forgive her selfish actions if she gave in to the man before her. Entrapping a man in mourning while engaged to his brother! She would be labeled a Jezebel.

Shunned! No, they would not blame Wade. He would not feel their wrath, but she held no doubt she would for the rest of her life.

A resolve emerged within her. She would never allow that to happen. She was no simpleton. Her life had become a charade, but no more. She had fallen into a dark abyss, allowing others to dictate her needs, but had not the last few months taught her she could trust no one?

Lest she forget her own grandfather betrayed her!

Beneath his critical gaze, she summoned her courage, "You are not trying to manipulate me, are you, Wade? Playing on my emotions to get what you really desire—Magnolia Bluff."

Wade flung his hand back derisively. "Have you forgotten you once said you loved me? I thought, perhaps now, I would be the better choice than Andrew. I cherish you."

"At one time, I would have believed every word you said. It is not the case now."

She left her words hang in the air. Wade, too, had betrayed her. He lied to her, telling her they could share a life together. Then it all fell apart. So much had happened. She didn't even know if she believed in love anymore.

Only Papa had her best interest at heart. He wanted her to have what had been lost to her momma. There had been Cullen, but it had been her to walk away from him. Taken in account the arrangement that Papa had laid out, the terms had not been met, only constantly postponed. To what purpose?

There was only one answer. Clayton Montgomery was playing a game of his own. He had already made clear he had no desire for her to marry Wade. He had forced Clarissa upon his grandson. Had he now employed Wade into his ploy? To delay a union until the time when he could challenge Papa without fear of repercussions? Could she trust Wade or anyone?

They believe I bluff?

Wade's frown was fierce. "Can you deny what we feel for each other? The last couple of weeks we have only grown closer."

From perplexity, he changed swiftly to a decisive lover. Suddenly, he caught her by the shoulders and forced her gaze up to his. Jo found herself captured in his arms. His mouth found hers, and for a moment, she forgot everything except being in his arms. Her breath caught in her throat…she fought against the rising passion.

"Let me love you as I yearn to do," he whispered against her lips. "We can marry quietly with your Papa beside you."

Her mind rebelled. If she allowed this, she would be lost forever. "Wade, no," she gasped, turning her face from him. "We can't do this. I can't allow you to lose everything."

"I will gain the world if you marry me."

"Oh, no, Wade, do you not know? The contract. It is not only Andrew that has to hold to it. I do also. If he refuses me, then everything will revert to my dowry for me to marry one of my choosing, but if it is I that breaks the terms, I get nothing."

He stiffened. Then he released his hold. "Why do I not know of this?"

"Why would you? You were married when it was drawn up," she said. Her voice quivered. It was harder than she imagined. "When you came into the room, I was preparing to go wake Papa. He was upset with his letter from Andrew, but it is not all for naught. In my letter, Andrew pleaded with me to come to him. We will marry in Philadelphia. He did not press Papa to allow me, not wanting to force upon me a decision I did not want to make if my one desire was to marry here in Charleston. So you see, I have no choice."

The look of desolation crossed his face. It tore at her soul.

"I beg your pardon, Jo. I will not force myself upon you again."

Jo watched him ease out the door. She followed and latched it, barring anyone from entering. Reaching into her skirt pocket, she pulled her letter from Andrew…his letter to her. It had not been opened.

She stared at the closed door. A feeling of wretchedness engulfed her. The Montgomerys would learn they were not the only ones to run a bluff.

Chapter Four

The relatively mild winter had taken a turn in Philadelphia. The new year had brought with it brutal freezing winds and intermittent snow squalls. This evening, the bitter cold kept most within their warm homes.

Dark and dreary, one lone carriage trudged through the back streets of Georgetown. It rolled through a section notorious for its connection to the underworld. But the occupants rode through without a thought to their safety, not with their armed footmen. Kathleen Halcoyne had selected the footmen herself for this specific purpose.

"You don't need to say anymore," Kathleen assured Elizabeth, thankful the carriage was dark and her friend could not see her eyes rolling at the question. The woman had more than played upon her nerves this evening. It took all her will not to scream at her.

But it would never do, she reminded herself. She needed Elizabeth for her scheme to work. Never in her life had Kathleen found it this difficult to keep up this façade with this poor pathetic creature sitting beside her in the carriage. Moreover, she had done it for years. It had been a necessity.

Elizabeth had been her only link to the society she so desperately wanted to be a part. That was until Andrew fell into her hands. There again she had need of Elizabeth.

"I do not like this part of town at night. Moreover, the weather is bitter. Are you certain you want to go in alone? Suppose we come back in the morning light?"

Granted, she understood Elizabeth's nervousness. The back alley behind the shady hotel would put most gentle born women on the edge. It excited Kathleen.

"He is expecting me now."

"But am I to sit out here in the dark and cold and wait. It has begun to snow."

"For heaven's sake, Lizzy, I cannot go back home alone. It will be brief."

"It is never brief."

Kathleen ignored the last statement. Elizabeth would do nothing. She would sit and wait no matter how long it took Kathleen. Elizabeth was loyal to a fault. Kathleen would not even need to remind Elizabeth that not long ago it was she who had waited on her.

Of course, that too had been of her invention, Jeremy Lowney. It had been quite cruel to poor Elizabeth, but quite necessary. Kathleen would have her revenge. She would make Cullen Smythe rue the day he refused and humiliated her.

Kathleen had never been a patient person, but this scheme she had hatched years ago, since the first time she laid eyes upon Elizabeth's stepbrother. How smitten she had been with the tall, broodingly handsome young man from the Deep South! More importantly to her— rich.

The deception had been perfect. No one suspected her sinister motive for befriending poor little Elizabeth.

She had dreams, unfulfilled dreams. She would be damned if anyone stood in her way. It was close. She could taste it. Finally after all this time, she would have what she had always wanted but was denied.

Kathleen had grown up the spoilt daughter of one of the leading surgeons in Philadelphia, Dr. Nathaniel Halcoyne. Unfortunately, his skill with the knife did not extend to his finances. Her father indulged his only child, but he also extended his generosity to any misfortunate soul he encountered, which frustrated his ambitious daughter to no end.

She had long lived on the edge of proper society. Her father's practice catered to the wealthy, but she had only been allowed a glimpse of their lifestyle. What she saw she liked and wanted! Oh, how she hated the snobbish looks bestowed upon her by his clientele. As if she was no better than a lowly servant, merely the daughter of their doctor, nothing more. She vowed one day she would reign over Philadelphia high society.

Long ago, she had come to the conclusion she would never be considered a classic beauty, but she had other attributes she used to her full advantage. Wit, charm, and a low cut dress gained the attention of more than one wealthy beau.

When Cullen stifled her attempt to trick him into marriage, she swore she would make him regret the day he turned her down in such a humiliating fashion. She had learned from her mistake. She had been young and naïve. But no more.

She had come close once with dear Maynard. The fool. Maynard Richards had come to Philadelphia in search of a cure. Her father had been highly recommended, and the sickly young man sought out his help. A thin, gangly man, he walked with a limp. His face tinted with a pale yellowish color; his fingernails dry and brittle: his health was fragile at best.

Her father diagnosed his sickness, finding the cause of his illness to be a large tumor in his stomach that caused excruciating pain, lack of appetite and constant vomiting. Surgery was risky. There had been no guarantee Maynard would survive, but her father performed a brilliant operation.

Along with a successful surgery, her father insisted the young man recover at their home. Soon, Maynard became enamored of Kathleen. She, in turn, encouraged his feelings. Why would she not? His family was one of the wealthiest in Boston. Maynard professed his undying love to Kathleen, and she was thrilled when he proposed. She would have the wealth she had dreamed about! That was until his parents interfered.

The scene those dreadful people made! Threatening to disinherit him…then promptly kept their word. It was a ploy for Maynard to withdraw his offer and the weak bastard wavered. He caved. Oh, how he cried. Telling how he could never live with himself, knowing he disappointed his parents so! It was then a plot took hold. How dare he put his parent's needs before hers!

Why her father had only just spent a fortune on the engagement party. Maynard had not even considered how he had imposed upon her father's hospitality. If she allowed Maynard to leave her, she would have become the laughingstock of Philadelphia. She would never allow that to happen. If he could never live with himself if he married her, then she would see to it he would not live.

She pleaded with him to give her time to find a way to tell her father, knowing how bitterly disappointed her father would be. Maynard agreed. It had been his doom!

It was easy, much easier than it should have been. As the daughter of a physician, she had learned a few things about certain drugs and poisons. It had been so simple. Two weeks of adding arsenic into his morning coffee, and Maynard died. Not even her father could save him.

She became the grieving fiancée. Sympathetic to society. It was then she discovered she enjoyed the power it gave her. The thrill of getting away with the unthinkable. There was no remorse, only exhilaration!

Soon, a list formed within her mind and Cullen Smythe was at the top of it. She wanted him destroyed and everyone associated with him. She had got bored waiting for him to return from the Navy. So her attention turned to Elizabeth. Public disgrace of Cullen's stepsister, his family, would suffice until his return.

Introducing Jeremy Lowney to Elizabeth had been a stroke of genius! She enjoyed leading her lovesick friend around in a circle. How desperate Elizabeth had been for love. Her game changed when Cullen returned.

Elizabeth's insufferable stepfather, Jonathan, and Cullen Smythe had cut Jeremy Lowney off from the troubled woman without the public embarrassment. It left Elizabeth with heartbreak and, unbeknownst to anyone but Kathleen, in the family way.

With her focus redirected back at Cullen, she encouraged Elizabeth to handle the problem in the back alley. Kathleen had gone with the distraught woman and held her hand while she aborted Lowney's spawn.

The emotionally disturbed Elizabeth hadn't wanted to abort the baby, but Kathleen couldn't have it. Not with Lowney running away like a dog with his tail between his legs. Kathleen couldn't trust Elizabeth wouldn't give her up about her association with Lowney. Moreover, the abortion was leverage against Elizabeth if Kathleen ever needed it.

Frustration weighed upon Kathleen until Andrew Montgomery returned from Charleston. Her father had always held Andrew in high esteem, his prize pupil. Although she had always been aware of Andrew's attraction toward her, she had given him little thought. He had nothing more than a son of a Southern planter, stating more than once that he was seeking his own way in the world.

Her interest flared when Andrew lamented his fate was tied to an unwanted fiancée, an heiress who was giving him the whole of his family estate, an heiress who was in love with another—Cullen.

Her interest piqued, but it had been Elizabeth who had brought her what she had been looking for. The piece she had missed in her quest for vengeance.

"For the life of me, I don't know why he demands you meet him here. It is not safe. I tell you, you should be wary of him. I wish I had never introduced you to him. I don't know what you hope to accomplish."

Kathleen smiled as her hand lay on the door handle. She knew exactly what she had in mind. She had found Cullen's Achilles heel and intended to use it to her full advantage.

"Hush, my dear. There is another blanket behind you to keep you warm. I promise I will be out shortly. I need only to ensure he understands exactly what he needs to do. We are close…so close."

She exited quickly; she didn't give Elizabeth a chance to protest. Grasping tight to her cloak, it was so cold she could see her breath. But he was there at the back door, waiting.

In the shadows, a tall, lean figure walked toward her with a swagger that came from confidence. His hat tilted low and made it difficult to see his eyes. His lips curved upward into a wide grin.

"Miss Halcoyne, I wondered whether you would brave the weather tonight," he said with an exaggerated gallantry and offered his arm.

Walking beside him, she smelled liquor on his breath, mingled with his musky odor she had come to know so well. He led her up the dim back stairs, and stopped at the first room on the third floor.

"You need to have better accommodations."

He laughed and opened the door, to allow her entrance. "You know well why I do not. If I'm at a reputable place of business, Wright would surely find me. I told you he has eyes and ears everywhere. I haven't had a good night sleep since I've been on the run."

"Do not attempt to tell me the man scares you, Harry Lee. Are you not the same man who came north to redeem his family's honor by killing poor little Andrew?" She took off her cloak to reveal a low-cut gown. It had its desired effect.

His bold eyes raked over her body, from the tip of her slippers up to up her cleavage. A savvy smile emerged on his lips.

"I'm still not convinced it is not the best course of action to take."

"What? Are you planning on killing all the Montgomery men? I tell you once more you will obtain all that you want and more if you stay true to the plan."

She looked at him defiantly, daring him to question her scheme. It had taken all her wiles to convince him not to outright kill Andrew like he wanted to when she first met him. Why, he and his brother had the nerve to show up knocking at her house, knowing that her father was his mentor.

Thank goodness it had only been Elizabeth and herself at home at the time. If not for Elizabeth recognizing the men from one of her visits to Charleston, this opportunity would have been lost, along with it a plan that would work to both their best interests.

"You see, my love, I have been thinking about it. It would be so simple to slit his throat. Then the bastard Wright's desire to see his darling daughter the belle of Charleston would be foiled."

"And where would you be then? No better than you are now. Exiled from your home without a cent to your name. The Groves would still be lost to you forever. I tell you, Harry Lee Haynes, you do not think a foot in front of you…"

He laughed and took her into his arms. "I am jesting. Have I told you I like it when you get all riled up?" He untied the laces on the bodice of her dress.

She glanced around the room. Anticipation surged through her veins. In a breathless voice, she asked, "Where is Buck?"

"Out," he answered bluntly.

What a deliciously wicked thrill to have him take her here. She felt his hands hoist up her skirt. He was the most satisfying lover she had ever had. Rough and violent, he brought her to a climax in a bellow of cries.

She halted his progressive briefly. She had almost forgotten the reason she had come.

"She's coming," Kathleen whispered. "Andrew received her letter earlier today announcing her intention. Josephine Buchanan Wright is coming to Philadelphia."

He did not have to tell her that the news excited him. Wild with passion, he slammed her against the wall and had his way with her.

* * * *

The falling snow glittered in the new morning light. Josephine leaned against the forward railing of the upper deck of the steamer, fascinated by the frozen precipitation. She had never experienced this weather. Strange how the sparkling white gave a façade of tranquility and calm. She wished she had some semblance of serenity. She had none.

Her stomach turned in anxious turmoil. Informed that her destination lay less than an hour ahead, she suppressed her growing panic. The confidence she exhibited to her papa faded as quickly as the warmth of the Southern breeze.

When she departed Magnolia Bluff, she ached inside. She had no desire to leave Papa, but she saw the glimmer of hope in Papa's eyes.

"You have made your papa proud, my dear." He kissed her cheek, and she was gone.

She held back her tears with a face of anticipation and excitement, and concealed the truth from all eyes upon her. No one would see the

185

hurt that lived within her. She swore she would give him the peace of knowing he had fulfilled his promise to Momma.

The night had been spent in a restless sleep, tossing and turning. The closer she came to her destination the closer she came to being exposed for the fraud she was. In Charleston, she had been successful in her ruse. She had convinced Papa and the Montgomerys that Andrew had sent for her. Why even Mother Montgomery and the girls, Jenna and Amy, accompanied her north!

She came boldly to Philadelphia with a façade of happily looking forward to her marriage. Rosa had packed her Paris gown for the ceremony, which she had tried on twice to show the girls. She chatted endlessly about seeing Andrew and the thought of having them for sisters.

Now, she couldn't contain her nervousness. The snow had begun to fall harder as they neared the shore. Through the flurry, clusters of buildings came into view. The city of Philadelphia lay before her.

The captain came out of the pilot house and shouted instructions to the deckhands, and then to the helmsman. Jo felt a jolt as the steamer docked against the wharf. A single, sharp piercing whistle blew; the paddle ceased, and movement halted.

Her eyes skimmed the docks for any sign of Andrew. He had to be here. Had she not pushed him into a corner? He would not dare leave his own mother, sisters and fiancée to fend for themselves in an unfamiliar city! She did not see him!

Alarmed, his absence threatened her mission. This was her biggest fear—her bluff was about to be called.

"Josephine, whatever are you doing on deck? It's freezing!" Jenna cried, as she gestured Jo toward the stairs. "I declare we haven't come prepared. Why I don't even have a muff! Momma is frantic we will get frostbite."

A sudden gust of snow swept across the deck. Jo turned and allowed the wind to die back before she walked to the stairwell. With her arm wrapped around Jenna, the two huddled close and descended the steps.

"Momma and Amy are waiting for us."

Josephine clutched her cloak tighter. She swore the temperature must have dropped ten degrees. On the lower deck, they were joined by Mother Montgomery and Amy.

"I'll be happy to get to a nice warm place with a fire. I hope the hotel is not far away," Mother Montgomery said. The older woman walked in front of the girls while their trunks were being unloaded. She looked around the docks and suddenly waved back at a large figure of a man; apparently she had been expecting the man.

It certainly wasn't Andrew, but there was something familiar about him. As she neared the man, she had a moment of relief. It came to her. She knew him a long time ago when she was a child. Back then, the brawny Irish man seemed larger than life. A friend of her papa...Joshua Finn.

Josephine's attention was drawn to Finn. Memories flooded back of the time before Charleston. Traveling city to city, night after night, Papa attended to his business with Finn by his side. She remembered his kindness to the shy child of his employer.

"I trust you had a comfortable journey," Finn said in his thick Irish brogue. He flashed Jo a brilliant smile with a twinkle in his eye.

"It is a pleasure to meet you, Mr. Finn. Josephine's papa spoke highly of you." Mother Montgomery glanced around and grimaced. "Andrew isn't here? I thought he would greet us."

"When Mr. Wright telegrammed me to oversee the necessary arrangements for his precious daughter, I agreed without hesitation. I will handle all the necessary details. I met briefly with the good doctor yesterday. Sadly, Dr. Montgomery has agreed to consult with a Dr. Levine in New York City on a patient who needs immediate surgery. He left late last night. I assured Dr. Montgomery I would see that you are settled at the hotel. I would assume he will present himself later in the week."

The answer seemed to satisfy Mother Montgomery. Finn gestured for the ladies to follow him to a brougham. A frigid gust of the wind took Jo's breath away. Gasping, she quickly accepted Finn's hand for assistance into the carriage.

Jenna and Amy followed, with Mother Montgomery climbing in beside Jo. The women slid in beneath a warm fur throw.

"I will see to your trunks and follow behind you," Finn offered. "The driver will take you to the Girard House. I will meet you there. The rooms are already set. A representative from Gimbel Brothers will meet with you ladies this afternoon to supply you with the necessary garments for this weather."

"It is much appreciated, Mr. Finn. I'm certain my father-in-law will—"

Finn grinned. "Beg your pardon, ma'am. Mr. Wright has seen to all of your needs."

"But there are so many of us," Mother Montgomery protested.

"Mr. Wright gave me clear instructions, Mrs. Montgomery. It is his daughter's wedding. He feels it his obligation to see to your welfare while you are in Philadelphia."

Mother Montgomery said nothing more but settled in beside Jo. Soon, the brougham moved, rolling through the newly fallen snow. Jo could hear the driver shouting at the traffic the weather had caused. With a whistle and a crack of the whip, the pace steadied for a time. It halted before a sandstone building on Chestnut Street. A sign on the corner labeled it the Girard House.

As she stepped out of the carriage, Jo immediately recognized this hotel was a spacious and lavish establishment. Papa had spared no expense. Glancing back over her shoulder, she was relieved to see that Finn was right behind them.

Whisked into the richly ornamented interior, Finn paused Jo for a moment.

"Your father asked me to look after you in his absence. We need to talk."

His words were crisp and direct. She understood his meaning. "But of course."

"Your father wrote me in great length of your situation. There are immediate concerns."

"I am aware there may be a few obstacles."

"He's gone," Finn stated flatly, not letting her say another word. "Your fiancé has gone missing."

Chapter Five

The bitter cold had broken. The snow had melted into a slushy mess making it challenging to negotiate the streets. Jo glanced out the curtained window as the carriage approached a line of private houses. The brick buildings held numerous apartments with the only distinguished features being the different colored doors and shutters.

For the last two days, Jo had been kept busy. She hadn't the energy to contemplate her absentee fiancée. At least on the surface, she fended belief in Andrew. On his part, Andrew had sent notes to both Jo and Mother Montgomery, assuring them both that he would be back in the city in a few days. The message sent with his deepest and most sincere apology for not being able to postpone his trip to New York.

Finn had been true to his word. He had seen to their immediate needs. The chambers were large and accommodating, made up of two bedrooms in each suite. Jo shared her suite with Mother Montgomery; the girls adjoined theirs. Moreover, appropriate garments had been delivered promptly for the harsh weather; fur line cloaks, boots, muffs, and scarves.

Last evening, the Smythe family joined the women for dinner. It had been pleasant enough Jo supposed. Upon entrance, into the dining room, she immediately recognized the tall, handsome older gentleman, Jonathan Smythe, as Cullen's father. There was no denying he had the same eyes. To his side was a striking lady with dark streaked hair. Cullen's step-mother, Monica Smythe, had the grace and poise of one used to wealth and status.

To her surprise, she found Cullen's father quite charming. It was his sister, Elizabeth that Jo sensed, held animosity towards her, but Jo expected nothing less…not after what had occurred. After all, Cullen was her brother. Thankfully, Cullen was not among the group. She could not have dealt with seeing him.

Jo had worn a mask, never betraying her true feelings. She had downplayed Andrew's actions. She smiled and talked about the preparations for the wedding she held doubts would ever take place. Never letting down the wall she had erected around her heart...

This afternoon, she had arranged to talk to Finn freely. She was to meet with him over lunch once she had called upon an old friend. The only bright spot to her visit—Gillie. She would be reunited with her dear friend, one she had missed so terribly. It warmed her heart.

The driver pulled to a stop in front of Gillie's address. Disembarking from his seat, he opened the door for Jo and her companion, Rosa.

"I'll wait right here," he said.

Jo held no doubt Finn had given firm instructions that she was not to be left alone. She accepted the man's hand and stepped down into the mud and slush the sidewalks had become. Lifting her skirt, she walked over to where planks had been placed.

Outside the door, Jo smelled the aroma of freshly baked goods. Smiling, she knocked ever so gently. The door opened, and she faced her beloved friend.

"Gillie!" Jo exclaimed. "Oh, Gillie!"

"Come in, Miss Jo. It feels like it's been forever since I've seen you."

Smiling broadly, Jo walked in and waited only until the door closed behind Rosa before she embraced Gillie warmly. Jo broke from Gillie and held her at arm's length.

The girl, Jo had known, had blossomed into a lovely woman, prim and ever so proper. She wore a long sleeve blue calico print dress with a white collar. The sleeves widened at the wrist, and the waist was long and narrow. It looked as though it was an older gown which had been altered to accommodate the changing styles.

Jo wondered briefly why Gillie had not worn one of the gowns she had made for her back in Charleston, but it mattered little. Gillie's eyes shone with a light that only happiness brought.

A lovely cameo was pinned to the neck of the collar and matching earring dangled from her ear lobes. Jo reached over and touched the cameo.

"How lovely."

"It was Heyward's wedding gift to me, Miss Jo. It is my treasure."

190

"Indeed it should be," Jo said and released her hold. "I do wish I could have been there for the wedding. Was it as wonderful as I imagined?"

"Miss Jo, it was the best day of my life. It is legal and binding, Heyward says. None of that jumping over a broom. We were married in a church all proper. Why Dr. Montgomery served as one of the witnesses!"

The mention of Andrew took Jo back a moment. She was glad he at least had seen to Gillie's welfare.

"Why whatever kind of hostess am I? Come into the parlor. I have a nice fire and have prepared some tea and biscuits."

Gillie took Jo's coat and gloves and left him on the hall table, then led Jo into a small quaint room. Jo glanced around curiously. The furniture had been well worn; the curtains faded, but it was tidy and warm. A brilliant fire burned in the hearth.

"I hope you don't mind I brought along a companion. Mrs. Montgomery would have frowned upon me if I had not. You remember Rosa."

"I do," Gillie said, glancing over at the woman who had taken her place. "Please, make yourself comfortable as well."

Jo sat down on the chair in front of the fire. "Gillie, it is so good to see you. You are content? Oh! I can tell you are!"

"Ever so, Miss Jo," Gillie answered, untying her apron. "Let me go get the tea."

Everything seemed in order, Jo thought, surveying the room. A far cry from the lifestyle she had lived within Charleston, but there was no mistaken her friend's happiness.

Gillie returned bearing a tray and set it down on the table. She seated herself, poured a cup and added sugar and cream. Handing the cup to Jo, she said, "The way you enjoy it, Miss Jo."

Jo accepted the cup. "Is Heyward still employed by the Smythe's?"

"Yes, except now he's down at Mr. Smythe's office. Mr. Smythe is training him to be a clerk. I'm right proud of him. He's going to be a business man. Wants to start a business himself. Mr. Smythe says he'll help him."

"That's wonderful."

"Now, Miss Jo, tell me why you are here. I'm happy to see you, but it is quite unexpected. In your note, you said you have come here to wed Dr. Montgomery. I would have thought your papa would have demanded the ceremony be held at home."

"It is a matter of contention," Jo confessed. "But at least it permitted me to visit you."

Jo sipped her tea. A strange uneasiness emerged; a sudden reluctance to admit her purpose. The mantel clock chimed half-past ten. Jo placed her cup down.

"I've missed you, Gillie. So much. I was wondering if perhaps, you could…"

"I told ya it was why she was coming."

The harsh voice resounded throughout the room. Jo looked up to see Heyward standing in the hallway. His scowl deepened as he strode to Gillie's side. From the hapless look on Gillie's face, Jo quickly accessed that Heyward was not happy with the reunion.

"Heyward, I did not expect you to be home," Jo said in her most pleasant tone.

Silently, she chided herself for not asking about his health. The last she had seen of him, he had been quite ill. Today, though, he carried himself as the epitome of health. He bore no visible sign of the beating that almost killed him. He looked as he had, except he had grown a beard.

"You have a nice home. It is good to see Gillie so happy."

"She is not going with you." His tone was sharp and direct. "Can't just come in here and disrupt our lives with your appearance."

"It was not my intention," Jo protested, taken back by his intensity. "I had thought…that perhaps she might accompany me while I was here in Philadelphia. I have so much to accomplish, and I do so need my Gillie."

Jo looked over at her former companion and smiled. Gillie blushed and glanced over at her husband, then gazed down on the floor.

"Gillie?" Jo questioned with a small laugh. "You do realize how hapless I am about details. I thought it would be such fun." Suddenly, she had the urge to beg her. Instead, she added, "I will see that you are well compensated."

"Miss Jo, I'm not sure I can. I have a job…"

"Which she lost a day's wage, I might add, to see ya this mornin'," Heyward snapped.

Much to her chagrin, Jo noted the deepening darkness of his mood and watched him apprehensively. *Where had the animosity come from?*

"Perhaps it is for the best if I didn't," Gillie said in a low, timid voice. "Besides, I have nothing to wear. Since I worked at the bakery, I have no need for formal wear."

192

Jo stared incredulously at her friend. "Where are the beautiful gowns I had made for you?"

Silence fell upon the room. Gillie looked up at Heyward. Her eyes appealed to him in humble entreaty.

He sighed heavily. "Look around ya, Miss Jo. Where do you suppose she was supposed to wear such finery? They came to better use. She sold 'em. We live a simple...but contented life."

Aghast, her face fell. Quickly, she recovered. "It was not my intent to insult you. You must know I would never do anything to hurt Gillie."

"I do, but ya need to understand that the two of ya live in different worlds now."

"You cannot suppose to tell me that I can have nothing to do with my dearest friend anymore."

"Friend?" he corrected. "Miss Jo, Gillie was your slave."

The words hit her harder than if he had slapped her. She felt everyone eyes upon her. The meaning sank deep within her consciousness. As much as she thought of Gillie, the poor thing had no choice in the matter. Gillie had been bound by chains of the dreadful institution.

Words choked in her throat. The exhilaration of seeing Gillie dwindled, replaced with an overwhelming sense of humiliation and sadness. She rose.

"But of course. It has been good to see that Gillie is well looked after. I won't impose on you further." Jo made her excuses and walked toward the door.

"Miss Jo," Gillie said, rushing toward her.

Jo forced a force smile. Reaching over she squeezed Gillie's hand, she asked, "You are happy?"

A sadden look reflected in her eyes, but she nodded.

"It is all that matters. Take care of yourself."

Jo leaned over, kissed Gillie's cheek, and she left.

* * * *

"Look, Lass, we don't have time to dawdle back and forth. I remember when ya was just a wee little thing. Ya wasn't much of a liar then either."

Jo gathered her composure. The morning visit with Gillie had disheartened her greatly, but she didn't have the time to wallow in self-pity. Was it not what she wanted for Gillie? She had only her own foolishness to blame.

Finn had asked Jo to meet him at Parkinson's, the best café that Philadelphia had to offer. The restaurant was set in a handsome row house, which held a ladies' saloon, as well as a confectionery shop. They met in the garden, barren and cold, but it allowed the privacy needed.

Exasperated, she stared at him. "What do you believe I have misled you in, sir?"

"I have been making the arrangements that your papa requested, but ya and me both know things aren't like ya told your papa. Dr. Montgomery seems to have become quite a reluctant bridegroom."

She choked back the urge to tears and shrugged. "You must have figured out that my engagement is not all it seems. It was arranged by Papa…"

"Ah, lass, it didn't take long to figure out your papa has made a play. The question becomes what is yours?"

Pressing her lips together tightly, she thought briefly of denying knowledge of what he alleged. She suppressed her pride. It had become a useless sentiment in her quest to accomplish her objective.

"I am determined to see that Papa's wishes are carried out. It is imperative that the ceremony commence quickly, Mr. Finn. You must be aware of my papa's fragile heath. He wants my future settled."

"Ah, well then, settled it will be," he informed her imperiously. "I found your Dr. Montgomery."

She stared at him in bewilderment. "And?"

"Well, lass, I spoke to him and laid it out as I seen it."

Questions arose of where Andrew had been; more importantly why he had abandoned her. The expression upon Mr. Finn's face did not invite those inquiries.

"You believe that my engagement can be salvaged?"

"This I will promise you. It will be dealt with to your advantage. Dr. Montgomery has a fine reputation from my understanding. A gentleman. But gentlemen have their secrets, too," he nodded, undismayed by the fact. "I informed Dr. Montgomery that you have come to Philadelphia for one purpose. If the ceremony is not preformed, then the agreement will be void, and you will be freed. I will personally make it known of his failure to uphold his word."

"But…but then Papa…" her words faltered. "I will disappoint Papa…I can't."

"There you are wrong, Miss Wright," he said   "Your papa has been a gambler all his life. He knows that there comes a time in a hand to call. It's that time."

Chapter Six

The Smythe house in Philadelphia sat on the west side of Seventh Street. The red brick mansion was a splendid home, three stories high with accompanying dormers. White marble steps led up to the black entrance door with prominent matching shutters. A couple of gas-lit lights lay on either side of the entry. A quite elegant dwelling.

The chilled January wind greeted Cullen when he stepped out of the carriage. With the greatest reluctance, he had accepted the invitation for dinner, mostly because he had run out of excuses. He had moved out of his own house over two months ago and had only returned for the holiday.

He had taken an apartment over his office. He had told his father it was for convenience. The truth was he needed to be on his own.

Burying himself into his work had not dulled the pain. He stilled lived in a special hell where her face haunted him. The image had not faded no matter the hours he spent behind his desk, the amount of brandy he freely downed when alone or the late nights he kept. He had found no peace.

He prayed the dinner would not run long. He had plans this evening with a young lady. Maude was not suitable to introduce to his family, but she suited him at the moment. She seemed content with what he had to offer and made no other demands.

Dressed for the theater, he looked confident and superb in his black frock coat, open to a single-breasted waistcoat that matched his trousers. The black satin cravat magnified his dark eyes. His hair had grown to the point it curled behind his ears. He had kept his mustache neatly trimmed and hadn't allowed it grow out in a flowing manner as was fashionable.

The smell of freshly cooked roast rose out of the kitchen. Good. Dinner seemed prepared to be served. With a little luck, he would be out of the house within an hour. Disposing of his coat, hat and gloves to the butler, he entered the drawing-room

His father stood on his appearance, but his eyes fell upon the other occupants. Mother sat next to Elizabeth, but to his surprise, he discovered his aunt and cousins.

"Aunt Marie, what brings you to Philadelphia?"

* * * *

"I personally cannot believe the audacity of the woman," Elizabeth began before the main course was served. "To come all the way to Philadelphia without cause. It does give the impression of desperation."

"Elizabeth," Monica reprimanded. She threw a sympathetic glance toward Cullen. "Miss Wright has every right to visit her fiancée. It is understandable with her father in ill health she wants to ease his mind. It has been unfortunate that the nuptials have been postponed."

"Wanton if you ask me," Elizabeth uttered under her breath, not caring if anyone heard.

"You have not met Josephine, Cousin Elizabeth," Jenna said. "She is quite kind. Why she insisted upon buying Amy and I…."

"I'm certain we do not have to expound upon Josephine's virtues," Mother Montgomery interrupted her eldest daughter. "I will welcome her as a daughter. To be frank, it is not Josephine that causes me concern."

Jonathan placed his fork down and looked over at Cullen. "Marie was wondering if you knew where she could get in touch with Andrew."

Cullen scowled. His father was well aware he had had no contact with Andrew since the day he had found out about the Underground Railroad. "You have me confused."

"I'm afraid I'm embarrassed," Mother Montgomery said with a forlorn expression. "When Andrew wrote to delay his wedding because of his obligations to Dr. Halcoyne, he invited Josephine to Philadelphia. We arrived fully expecting he would meet us. Instead, he sent a note of apology stating he was out of town briefly, but he promised would attend the dinner tonight."

"And he has not made an appearance," Cullen finished his aunt's train of thought. "I suppose Josephine is in her room lamenting the fact."

"Oh, Josephine is not here. We are staying at a hotel," Jenna said. "She refused tonight's hospitality extended, saying she was giving us time together as a family and as she is not family, she won't impose upon us. She said that Andrew knows she is at the Girard House and when or if he appears, he can seek her out."

"Josephine is quite upset. She worries about her father as do I. Brantley Wright is in failing health. I fear he will not last much longer," his aunt said. Her face reflected her dismay. "Father Montgomery sent me along to make sure that Andrew holds to his word."

"I say again that Andrew is not behaving like a man in love," Elizabeth exclaimed with venom. "It is not fair to pressure him into a loveless marriage."

"Elizabeth, do be quiet. It is not our affair," Monica said firmly.

Cullen picked up his glass of wine and took a sip. He offered no more to the conversation. He understood. The carefully laid plan, to ensure Magnolia Bluff and the estate tied to the plantation stayed in Montgomery hands, was unraveling at the seams.

Monica was quite right. It was not their affair. Moreover, the theater awaited his presence.

* * * *

Cullen strolled over to the table across from his desk and poured himself another brandy in a futile attempt to dull his mind. He had left the play during the intermission. He couldn't even remember the name of the show. Maude...he wouldn't be seeing her again. He seemed to remember she was quite irritated with his behavior.

He had dropped her back at her apartment and returned to his office. He walked back over to the window and stared blankly out. All, he could see, was her face; all, he could hear, was his father saying Josephine was in Philadelphia. *Lord, what was blaring so loudly?*

He rubbed his forehead. Tick...tick...tick...the damn clock! He wanted to throw something at it, but the glass in his hand held the only substance that would see him through the night.

Loosening his cravat, he unbuttoned his shirt and pulled it out of his trousers. His waistcoat already lay somewhere in his office. He supposed he should make his way up the stairs to his bed, but he couldn't.

"Is this how you spend your evenings?"

Slowly, Cullen turned his gaze to the doorway. The room silenced except for the ticking of the damn clock. Josephine stood before him. For a moment, he thought her a hallucination, and then she stepped towards him.

He took in the lovely sight. In the dim lit room, her glossy dark hair curled beneath the crepe bonnet's amethyst brim; her large dark eyes gazed at him, reflecting the vividness he remembered. Her expensive bell-sleeved gown fitted closely over her breasts with a frilled lace bordering the bodice. Her voluminous skirt clung tight to her tiny waist then flowed down over the hoop with crinolines trimmed with deep purple satin with pleated taffeta. She undid the hook and placed her outer cloak trimmed in fur over the back of a chair. She seemed to be warm enough on this cold and frigid night.

Time stretched. Finally, he spoke, "Josephine, I heard you were in Philadelphia. Honestly, I did not think I would see you."

"Or you did not want to see me," she said. Sauntering around the hard back chair, she sat. "It was not my intent."

"No?" he questioned. "You come to my office and the thought did not occur to you that I might be here."

"I was invited here. I had no knowledge this was your office."

"Come, Josephine. Do you expect me to believe this a coincidence? You here…now with me…alone? What game are you playing?"

"I'm afraid it was I, Cullen. I apologize, but I did not know where else I could meet with Jo without interference."

Cullen turned to the voice. Momentarily taken aback, he had not heard the approach of the man. He stared, completely astounded. In the doorway, his errant cousin stood! *Hellfire, what on earth possessed him to meet Jo here of all places!* Furthermore, Andrew did not have the look of one apologetic. No, he seemed perturbed in fact.

Chugging down the last of his glass, Cullen sat it down on his desk. "I suppose the two of you would like to be alone. Since this room is occupied, I could offer you my apartment upstairs."

"Confound it! Cullen, you must know this is a delicate situation," Andrew snapped. "I would never have imposed this meeting upon you if I had known that you were already done for the night. I was told you were at the theater. When this meeting was compelled upon me, this place came to mind. I needed privacy to explain my position to Jo."

Cullen was going to retort if Andrew knew he was at the theater. Then Andrew would have had to be told by one at the dinner tonight. He held no doubt of who would have delivered the message—Elizabeth, which meant Andrew had to have been in the company of Kathleen. No, he would not press *that* issue at the moment.

Jo smiled, but Cullen could see her face clearly. Her eyes blazed; she wore a mask of fury. Coldly, she said, "I did not come for you to clarify your position, Andrew, but mine. If it was up to me, I would be done with the whole lot of you Montgomerys, but it isn't. Do you suppose that Papa believes it was impossible for you to come home at Christmas?"

Ignoring Cullen, Andrew entered the room, hat in hand, but made no effort to remove his gloves or coat. He walked over to Jo. "I wrote to you and explained that I could not leave Dr. Halcoyne. If you are to become a doctor's wife, you will have to be more understanding. I have my reasons. Quite good reasons! Additionally, I specifically asked you to be patient. Why on earth have you appeared in Philadelphia? Do you understand the confusion you have caused?

"Why I believe Mother is ready to go to the authorities because she believes I am missing!"

"Not avoiding your fiancée?"

"What if I am?" Andrew fired back. "I will not have this, Josephine. I refuse to be threatened and bullied! Sending that *hoodlum* to confront me!"

"Mr. Finn is not a hoodlum. He is a business associate of Papa's. He is overseeing the details to our wedding because Papa cannot. I do not believe he was happy having to hunt down my *bridegroom*."

"That remains to be seen."

An unnatural silence descended. Josephine went white. Her smile lost; she retorted, "I came to give you one last chance to rectify the mess you have made. Make no mistake, my efforts are for Papa. He was prepared to call in his debt. I asked him to wait until my return.

"Understand clearly, if the marriage does not take place by week's end, I will return to Charleston and leave you to deal with the consequences."

Andrew winced, but quickly composed himself. Pressing his lips together tightly, he responded in a serious tone, "You are your father's daughter."

"Was there a question?" she answered. "I assume you will see your mother in the morning to tell her your intentions."

Andrew said nothing for a time. He took a deep breath as if the thick tension had made it difficult to breathe. He conceded. "I will do so, since I have little choice in the matter."

"You are wrong. You did have a choice as did I."

Resentment, anger, hatred illuminated from his eyes. Slowly it ebbed, replace by a small smile. "Of course, you are quite right, Josephine. I will make amends." He ran his hand across his brow. "I suppose it is settled. Come. We have imposed upon Cullen long enough. I will see you back to your hotel."

She recoiled back from his extended hand and shook her head. "I have already seen to the arrangements. My carriage is waiting with Rosa to take me back."

Andrew turned to Cullen and gave a polite bow. "Please accept my apologies for this inconvenience." Then he started toward the door. A sudden hesitance made him pause. He glanced over at Jo as if his conscience gnawed at him.

"For God's sake, Andrew, go!" Cullen had had enough. "I will see that Jo gets back to her hotel safely."

Easing back toward the door, Andrew took his leave. Cullen closed the door soundly behind him. Jo made no protest to stop him. Instead, she rose and strolled over to the window. He watched her stare out into the street.

Beneath her anger, he saw something else while she observed Andrew's departure. Her manner bore an edge that suggested her actions had been quite deliberate. For a long moment, her eyes were fixed on the street below.

He had not expected such a reaction. Andrew's odd behavior would have most women in tears. Not Josephine. She had come to confront him…to deliver a clear message.

Pouring himself another drink, he said, "It seems you are having your fiancée followed. I would have to agree with the sentiment that your marriage seems doomed from the start. Truly, Jo this is what you want?"

Jo faced Cullen. "None of this is what I wanted."

"Neither was it my preference."

Her chin came up in defiance. She met his eyes, and her gaze softened. He saw something deep in those eyes—raw anguish.

Lowering her gaze, she said, "You must believe I never wanted to cause you distress. I have found it best not to think of what might have been. It may be the best for you as well."

Swirling his drink in his hand, he laughed. "Madam, I have not given you advice on how to live your life. Please, do me the same favor."

"Sir, I have no control of my fate. You do."

He cut her off with a snarl. "As you told Andrew, it was your decision."

"It was for the best."

"Do I dare defy you? Because in my eyes, I cannot see for the life of me how it is for the best."

Jo looked at him askance. "Convince me otherwise."

Suddenly, his pent up frustration overwhelmed him. He had not expected the effect she still held over him…driving him to such a violent reaction within him. How dare she!

"I offered you a life beside me. I offered you my heart."

"Did you?" She raised her eyebrows and stared at him. "Or were you caught up in the moment? I do not deny we shared a tenderness, but when life stepped in-between us, where did you go?"

200

"Woman, are you mad? Do you not recall…"

"Recall that you made no protest when I told you I had decided to honor Papa's wishes… or that it was I that begged you to take me away before Papa fell ill."

"Because I put your needs before my own," he said before he considered his words.

"Because you came upon the realization that it was not meant to be," she said softly, calming the rising tension. "There was too much against us. You are a proud, honorable man, Cullen Smythe. You could never have lived with your family losing their heritage. I realize that Papa played upon your feelings, also."

"And now you are to live with your Papa's arrangement?"

"Papa is dying." Her tone betrayed welling emotions. "He devoted his life to fulfill his promise to my Momma. I will see that it is fulfilled. It is why I am here!"

Cullen cut her off with a snarl as he slammed his glass down. "My God! You are committed to marrying a man you do not love!"

"You understand nothing!" Her voice was sharp and pointed as she whirled to face him. "I came to discover what secret Andrew is keeping."

"Secret?" His voice faded. Her confidence dealing with Andrew had given the distinct impression she had arrived with a plan. "Why on earth would you think he has a secret?"

Her face expressed her sorely strained demeanor. "You Montgomerys meddled in the arrangement thinking I am only a pawn, mistakenly assuming I'm desperate. There is only one of two outcomes to my appearance here in Philadelphia. Either Andrew and I marry or we do not. If I do not, the arrangement is no more. Papa has already taken measures if that is the case."

"He will take Magnolia Bluff."

"Need I remind you, it is his already," she countered.

"I can't imagine Wade would simply let…"

"No," she laughed caustically. "He tried to persuade me to marry him. He even professed his love. Perhaps there are some deeds the matrons of Charleston would overlook, but marrying Wade less than a year after Clarissa passed and being engaged to his brother are not among them.

"My reputation would be ruined beyond repair. Shunned for a lifetime. Moreover, he withdrew his offer when I told him that if I disgraced Papa I would receive nothing. Magnolia Bluff would be lost forever."

"Ah, the golden ring—Magnolia Bluff. May it be damn!"

Lost in a darkness that raged within him, he closed the gap between the two of them. Dangerous in the state he was in. It was Josephine before him, the woman who haunted his dreams.

He had tried to fill the void, but only she could quench the urge within him. Her eyes blazed fiercely at him. A gentleman would step back. Let her leave to savage the life she envisioned, but tonight he was no gentleman.

"You are no more than a sacrificial lamb, my dear," he said harshly, showing no mercy. Ignoring the voice within him for caution, he responded to the sexual aura surrounding her and sensed her own need.

"I know," she whispered. "Do you not know I realize it well? Why do you press me so?"

"Because," he said in a low, hoarse voice. "You are here."

He reached across and untied the ribbons of her bonnet. He removed it and set it down on the desk. She made no movement to leave, though her eyes said she was befuddled.

Given her no time to bolt, he lowered his face to hers, kissing her in a way that told he was not playing games. He desired her. Wanted her. He did not care about any agreement that would separate her from him with the morning light. Tomorrow was another day. Tonight she was his.

He kissed her again and submerged himself in that abstruse world where the past and present fused. It was all too vivid in his memory of the passion they shared. It flamed once more. She returned his embrace.

It felt good. The pleasure offered a blissful escape from the reality around them if nothing else. Her lovely sighs resounded as a melody in his head. He cupped her breast with his hand. She arched into him welcoming his touch.

He felt for the laces that tied her gown in the back, loosening it enough to caress her bare skin. Kissing her hard, he pressed her back against the wall. He made quick work of the bodice of the dress, exposing her to his view.

"You are so very lovely."

He kissed her neck; her bare shoulder. He wanted to taste all of her. His lips moved down, savoring each kiss. He buried his face in her soft breasts and brushed his thumb over her erect nipple. She cried out in delirium of pleasure arousing him to the point where he could barely control himself.

His mouth suckled her breast and pleasure surged through him at her gasps. He was lost in her essence, caressing her silken skin halted by her gown. This would never do. The damn hoop interfered with his intent. He needed it off. She was not naked.

202

He whispered, "Come with me upstairs. Don't leave me this night."

Cullen overwhelmed her. With one touch, one kiss, he brought down the façade she presented to the world. Peeling away the layers until all that was left was her bare emotions and the all-consuming need to be loved by him.

His warm breath on her skin sent delicious shivers through her; his mouth seared flames against her breast. He made her forget everything else, and she melted into him, creating rapture within her she had never felt. It would be so easy to accept his offer. To take this night and make it their own.

Somewhere deep in her consciousness, the voice of reason emerged. Softly at first, then roaring...*He's a Montgomery! Despite the label, as one of those dreadful Yankees...he was as much a Montgomery as Wade...as Andrew. They protect their own!*

She had taken so many precautions not to see this man, knowing the affect he had upon her. She had let her guard down. Reprimanding herself for not knowing that this was Cullen's office, she fumed at Andrew! At all the Montgomerys!

Her ire stirred. She pushed back against him, but he would have none of it.

"Ah, no, my love. Do not leave me like this."

He ravished her with kisses, urging, compelling her until her resolve weakened. His hand slipped down her body and lifted her up into his arms.

Abruptly in the distance a sound resonated in the room. Louder and louder the noise intruded into her consciousness. Slowly, she recognized the knock on the door.

"Miss Jo, Miss Jo," Rosa's voice carried through the closed door. "Mr. Finn is asking where you are. We need to return to the hotel."

"Good Gawd!" Cullen rasped hoarsely. Primitive fury erupted. Cullen grounded his teeth as he released her. The moment shattered and with it the knowledge his desire would be denied.

Stumbling slightly, Jo regained her footing and pulled at her gown to cover her naked breasts. Her face flamed a deep red; she lowered her gaze.

"Go away, Rosa," Jo said in a weak whisper. "I will be down shortly."

"I ain't going, Miss Jo. Don't trust 'im. I don't," Rosa stated firmly. "I'll wait right here."

"Get back down stairs," Cullen growled. "She is unharmed if that is what is worrying you."

Jo heard no footsteps walking away. She realized Rosa was true to her word and stood outside the door.

Reason returned as Cullen withdrew from her side. What had she almost done! A weakness, to be loved by this man, overcame her good sense. She needed to leave…immediately.

Disheveled, she tried to regain some of her composure. The back of her dress loosened. There would be no doubt of her actions once she left the room if the gown was not tied and her hair down.

Clutching her gown over her bosom, she turned to Cullen. Her lips quivered, unable to form the words she needed to ask.

"Don't look at me." His nostrils flared and glared her down. "I refuse to help you walk away from me."

"Cullen, I never meant…" her voice faded.

His face tense and unsmiling, he stepped back to table with the decanter. "Impulsive actions can lead to more than just a kiss, Josephine. I make no apology. You choose to leave me again, do not believe I will play your fool any longer."

"I wonder who is the fool," she replied with a bitter laugh. "I wish…"

"Stop! It doesn't matter anymore," he cut her off sharply. "Go. Go live your life, and I will live mine without you. As far as I'm concerned, whatever has been between us is done."

She watched him grab his glass and refill it. His words stung like salt to the wound, but she refused to let him see the hurt. She wanted to feel anger and rage at him for treating her in this manner, but she only felt disheartened.

Saying nothing else, she picked up her cloak and walked out of the door with all the dignity she could manage. Rosa fell in behind her in silence. Confused and daze, Jo climbed into the carriage.

Her maid sat beside her mistress and gently began tying up the back of her gown. There was nothing they could do about the bonnet she left, but otherwise she was quite presentable by the time the carriage rolled in front of the Girard House.

Her reputation was intact. Her emotions, though, toiled to a painful depth for it had taken all her willpower to walk out that door. Her heart wrenched. She had nothing left, but to fulfill her papa's desire and marry Andrew at week's end.

Chapter Seven

Rosa dressed Jo for the evening. Her maid had an amazing ability in styling her hair in an upswept coiffure. Her dark tresses were artfully interlaced into a swirled grandeur. It was a luxury that Jo admitted she enjoyed.

Gillie had been the best companion. She had shared everything with her Gillie. Alone together, the two would talk for hours on end. Rosa was not like that. Efficient in her duties, her new maid did not invite an intimacy that Jo shared with Gillie. It had surprised Jo that Rosa had retrieved her from a compromising position…grateful, though, Rosa had.

Her heart ached, but if she had stayed in his arms, she would have been ruined. A weak moment would have destroyed her life. Cullen was too dangerous to be around alone. She would not let it happen again.

She had taken great care in her appearance this night. Andrew had been true to his word and called upon his mother yesterday morning. Cordial if somewhat distance, he had presented himself the epitome of a doting fiancée, inviting the small party to the theater this evening.

Jo labored deciding which gown to wear, pondering whether to be demure or bold. She chose her midnight blue velvet gown with a low cut neckline. The skirt was domed with two tiers. She was determined to make an appearance.

She donned a matching hooded cloak with an exquisite fur trim along with a hand muff. She took one more glance at herself before exiting her room. Mrs. Montgomery and the girls had already headed to the lobby to meet Andrew.

At least, Jenna and Amy were excited about the performance. The two seemed to have been making the most of their adventure north.

Hurrying down the hall, Jo slowed on her entrance into the well-lit hall. She spotted Andrew standing by Cullen's parents.

"Oh, Jo! There you are!"

Jo smiled at Mother Montgomery. The woman walked with spry in her step since Andrew had made an appearance. A worry alleviated, Mother Montgomery had relaxed and began to enjoy herself. She gestured for Jo to come to her side.

"I was telling Monica how we are looking forward to this evening. Jenna swears that Edwin Forrest is doing a reading."

"If you haven't seen one of his performances, you will be impressed, Miss Wright," Monica Smythe said looking at Jo with a stiff smile. "We were disappointed you were not able to come to our dinner the other night. I was afraid we would not see you until the ceremony."

"I did not want to impose," Jo said in her soft Southerner drawl. "I, too, am disappointed we have not spent as much time together as we might wish. I had hoped Andrew's extended family would have been able to accompany him down at Christmas, but then Andrew himself was unable to attend."

Jo turned towards Andrew. Her lips curved graciously at her fiancée, but his eyes bored into hers for a moment. There was a whiteness about his tense lips at told he had not appreciated the comment. She wondered if she had gone too far in needling him about his absence.

He limped up to her side and extended his arm. "Come, my dear. Let us go and enjoy the evening."

"Do not be such a bear, Andrew," his eldest sister reprimanded. She rushed up to his other side and slipped her arm through his. "It is going to be such a wonderful evening. I have heard marvelous things about Mr. Forrest. Do you suppose we can meet him? Oh, the girls will be so envious back home if I tell have met the infamous Edwin Forrest!"

Exiting out of the hotel, Jo noticed the look Andrew gave his sisters who were laughing and giggling. She found herself envious. He had never looked at her with such ease or caring.

"Miss Wright?"

A strange man repeated her name twice before Jo realized that the man was speaking to her. She looked around to find two men staring at her. The larger one stood with his feet spread wide and his hands in his coat pocket. He wore a wide brim hat, dirty and worn as were his clothes.

His mouth twisted a smirk of a smile. Then he turned his head and spit, wiping his mouth with the cuff of his coat. "You be Miss Josephine Wright of Charleston, South Carolina."

206

His accent bore from the South, but Jo could tell nowhere near Charleston. There was an arrogance in his demeanor that immediately annoyed her.

Andrew pushed her ahead. "Get into the carriage, Jo. I will deal…"

"Now…now, don't be rushing her off. Only have a question for the lady." The other man walked out of the shadows and nodded to Jo. "Won't take but a minute of your night. I'm Constable Leo Channing, and this here is Mister Earl Mann."

"Ain't necessary I tell ya," Mann complained.

"Calm yourself, Mann. Want it done all legal."

Jo halted. "What do you mean all legal? What is the matter?"

"About a slave of your grandfather's, Miss Wright," Constable Channing stated. He held up a poster. "Mr. Mann here thinks he's found the runaway."

Comprehension dawned upon her. Earl Mann was a slave catcher. She shuddered at the thought and wondered who had run from The Groves.

"It has nothing to do with you," Andrew whispered in her ear. "You don't need to deal with these men. I will handle the situation."

She nodded and took a step forward, only to be halted once more.

"Miss Jo! Miss Jo!" Rosa rushed forth and wrapped a lace shawl around her head. "You will freeze."

Leaning down for her mistress' ears only, she said in a low voice. "It's Gillie, Miss Jo. The men are talking about Gillie."

The name struck a cord, and Jo stiffened. She retreated a step and grabbed the poster from the constable. She stared at it in outraged disbelief.

$100 Reward. Ran away from my farm, near Charleston, South Carolina, my servant Gillie. She is five feet, slight built. Tiny weighs no more than a hundred pounds. Mulatto. Talks refine and walks with an attitude. I will give One Hundred Dollars reward to whoever will secure her in jail, so that I get her again, no matter where taken…Harry Lee Buchanan.

She squared in front of the men and demanded, "Tell me where is she?"

"Miss Wright, you need to understand what you face."

"I am listening," Jo answered.

The carriage rolled along the stone street. She sat across from Jonathan Smythe. Cullen's father had offered to take her down to the courthouse. Andrew had argued there was nothing to be done until the morning, but Jo refused to listen to him. Gillie had been arrested!

With Rosa beside her, Jo breathed deeply. She needed to calm herself. She would be no use to Gillie if she let her nerves weigh upon her.

"Please, Mr. Smythe, tell me what I face."

"I'm not certain, but I know that after the 1850 Fugitive Act, no freedman is safe on the street if a slave catcher decides they want them. It was set up to let slave-owners reclaim what they thought was theirs. But it has been abused. From what Andrew has told me, it seems your cousin, Harry Lee, has decided to use it to get back at you. It would be best if you let me handle the situation."

Jo shook her head. Everything was going too fast. She was openly confused, but she understood one thing. She would not abandon Gillie. She said, "She is my responsibility. It is my fault."

"It is late, Miss Wright. Andrew may have been correct that we might not be able to do anything until morning," he said. "I requested one stop before we arrive at the jail. My son may be of help."

She wanted to protest, but a lump of sadness thickened her throat. She watched him in silence as he left the carriage when it stopped.

"You're doing right, Miss Jo."

Glancing at Rosa, Jo had almost forgotten her maid accompanied her. Heaving a laborious sigh, she said, "I almost ignored those dreadful men. How did you know it was Gillie?"

"Heyward sent word. I ran for you as soon as it came. I thought I was going to be too late."

"I almost was gone," Jo replied and eyed her maid suspiciously. She had the distinct impression that Rosa knew more than she said. "After our last meeting, I'm surprised Heyward came for me. I would have thought I would have been the last person he would have sought help from."

"Heyward don't hate ya. Ya hafta understand. Heyward was protecting his own. Ya being a sweet thing and all, but neither Gillie or you have a clue what the real world is like. He may have seemed harsh, but he knows what is out there. Gillie has always been too naïve. It's dangerous in this time and place as ya see now."

"It is my fault."

"No, ma'am. It's the way ya been raised. You are better than most. I can tell ya I've never seen a lady and her maid as close as the two of you. Why it was talked of back in Charleston more often than naught."

"Talked of…Gillie and I?"

"Why Miss Clarissa would say it was like you had a little doll you would dress up and play with."

Jo felt a tightness in her throat that signaled tears. She could ill afford to show weakness. She swallowed them back. In a low soft voice, she said defensively, "I...I never..." She paused. Then words flowed from her heart, "I love her as a sister. After Papa left me in Charleston, she was the only one I had...I thought it was the two of us always...I didn't realize...she had no choice in the matter...it never occurred to me..."

Her words faded into the dark. Suddenly, she felt Rosa pat her hand.

"My, my, Miss Jo, don't ca be crying. Ya a good person. Guess Gillie feels the same about ya or else Heyward wouldn't have sent for ya."

The door of the carriage opened. To Jo's surprise, Cullen entered behind his father. She thought he would refuse to help, but he proved her wrong.

He had the look of one that had rushed to ready himself. His shirt still hung loose over his pants; his tie undone.

Plopping down across from her, he tucked in his shirt and tightened his belt. His eyes, though, lay on Jo. Despite all that had transpired between them, she felt her spirits lift.

Cullen set about to tie his cravat. His voice low and serious, he said, "Father told me what has transpired. If you are willing, I have a plan."

* * * *

When at last they reached the jail, Jo was thankful that the Smythe men had accompanied her. It was no place for a lady, especially at this time of night. The three story red-brick building sat on the town square and seemed to be surrounded by police men and scruffy, dirty delinquents.

Cullen exited, leaving the others to wait. It seemed an eternity. The silence was broken only by a police wagon, which rolled to a stop beside them. Two officers unlocked the barred door. Three men emerged, bearded, tipsy fellows singing loudly.

Then she saw Cullen returning. He opened the carriage door and offered Jo, his hand.

"It is set."

Jo walked up the steps, gripping tight to the railing. Cullen pushed open the front door and allowed her entrance. The corridor was dark and cold. Her heart beat rapidly but calmed when Cullen took her arm.

"This way."

She let him led her into a dimly lit room. She flushed at the sight and was overwhelmed by the close, stuffy smell. An assortment of smells riddled the air between the smoking fire, tobacco fumes, and, she swore, the foul odor of liquor.

In the smoke-filled haze, a lone officer sat behind a desk littered with unread papers. A lamp sat at the edge. He looked up at her.

"You're the one?" asked the pudgy man whose uniform jacket was unbuttoned. He pulled the top drawer out and grabbed a cigar. Lighting it, he puffed the smoke up in her face.

Coughing, she fanned the air around her and found her voice. "Yes, I am. I understand from that dreadful man you might have my girl. I do hope so, and that man hasn't ruined a perfectly good night on a fool's errand, especially with him barging into my hotel and announcing to the world I have lost one of my girls. It is embarrassing enough."

"Sure it is, ma'am," he uttered uncaringly and looked through the pile of papers. He grabbed one and read it. "Says here the owner is a Harry Lee Buchanan."

"Well, I'll be. So it was Harry Lee who has seen to my needs. I will have to thank my dear cousin, won't I when I return?" She smiled at him pleasantly. "I can assure you if it's my Gillie, she is mine or should I say my papa's. He will be so pleased."

"What proof do I have that she is yours?" he asked, leaning back in his chair with a cigar in hand.

Her smile widened. "Why what do you need? I arrived from Charleston last week and am staying at the Girard House. I'm to be married. Dr. Andrew Montgomery...he's under the direction of Dr. Halcoyne here in Philadelphia. Do you know of him? Well, Andrew wasn't able to return home for Christmas... It was absolutely horrible. I had to come all the way up here for the ceremony. I'm..."

"Ma'am," he interrupted. "The runaway says she was freed."

"Dear Gillie!" Jo went on. "We had talked to Papa about it, but I doubt Papa will agree now, not with her running like she did. Shame truly."

The officer looked over at Cullen, who simply stated, "I imagine, a simple telegram would sufficient to Mr. Brantley Wright back in South Carolina. Granted, it will take time and Miss Wright was hoping to have the girl back by her wedding that is if it is her girl."

The man grimaced. "Think you will have to wait until the hearing in the morning."

"Oh, pooh!" Jo pouted. "Here I was set to pay you the reward."

"Reward? That goes to the slave catcher, ma'am," he said, taking another puff of the cigar.

"But if she wants her girl back tonight?" Cullen pressed and reached into his pocket. "I could give it to you to give to him. A hundred, wasn't it? I'll add another ten for your trouble."

The man's eyes bulged. Taking the cigar from his mouth, he laughed. "You will sign for the girl?"

Relief flooded her; she answered, "Why of course."

The windows were lightening; morning was on the horizon with a promise of a new day. Jo had not slept. She waited now on a pew in Mother Bethel African Church to say goodbye to her friend.

Gillie had been freed, but she wasn't out of harm's way, not with Harry Lee bent upon revenge. He would not stop at one attempt. Cullen, his father, and Heyward discussed the situation in length and came to the conclusion it would be the safest course of action for the couple to leave Philadelphia and head north to Canada.

To Jo's amazement, the hurried arrangements had been made with astonishing efficiency. There had been no confusion in the preparations, only the urgent need to leave before that slave catcher, Mann, realized Gillie had been released.

The side door opened quietly, and Gillie entered. Jo rubbed her puffy, reddened eyes. It had been a long night.

"You are ready?"

"Yes, Miss Jo. Heyward has packed all we can bring."

A hush ensued. Jo moved over, and Gillie sat next to her. Gillie reached across and took Jo's hand.

"Thank you," she choked on the words as silent tears streamed down her face.

Jo hugged her tightly. "There is so much I want to say and no time to say all that I feel. I'm so sorry. You wanted to start a new life here, and now you have to leave. It's all my fault. Harry Lee..."

"He is the evil one, Miss Jo. Not you. You saved me again."

"Yes, but...Heyward..."

"Heyward is scared and angry. It should not be like this. We are free, and yet we have to run. How can a free person fear as we do?"

"I'm sorry...so, so sorry," Jo uttered between her breaths. Her composure lost. "I want you to go. Truly, I do, but I'm going to miss you. It already pains me. Before when you left Charleston, I knew I would see you again...now I am so afraid I will never see you again. I don't know what I'm going to do without you."

211

"You are the strongest person that I know. I, too, am lost for words," Gillie leaned back and touched Jo's cheek. Through her tears, she smiled, "But we do not need to say words, because we feel it in our hearts."

Jo nodded. From the corner of her eye, she caught sight of Heyward walking in the room. He motioned for Gillie. It was time.

Gillie didn't look back but fell into her husband's strong arms. He looked at Jo and said simply, "Thank ya, Miss Jo. Thank ya for my Gillie."

Holding her hand over her mouth as if it could keep the flood of tears welling within her, Jo watched the two depart. Suddenly, she wasn't alone. Easing in beside her, Cullen wrapped his arm around her shoulders. She leaned her head down against him and wept.

* * * *

In a patch of shadow, the burly man watched patrons exit the tavern. Most swaggered down the street, latching onto their companions in drunken laughter. He gave no notice to most of them as he emerged silently from behind the pillar, turning up the collar of his wool coat to help hide his face. He walked at a slow pace, unhurried.

His eyes fixated on the man in front of him, the tall, lean one with the wide brim slouch hat, who ducked into the dark alleyway. He followed and watched the man slip into the backdoor of the broken-down boarding house.

He had obtained a reluctant forced piece of information that led him here tonight. It was a welcome relief; especially since he hoped to eliminate the threat against Josephine without her even knowing she had been endangered.

He paused long enough to take his gloves off and pull his derringer out of his belt. At the door, he listened for a moment and glanced back over his shoulder. Nothing. He turned the handle and entered.

At the bottom of the stairs, he halted. His instincts sensed a presence. It was too late. He felt a sharp edge slice across his neck. He reached up to his neck, only to feel warm red liquid ooze out in-between his fingers. He felt nothing else.

Harry Lee took out a thin silver flask from his inner pocket and gulped down the brandy. Wiping the knife against his pants leg, he replaced it back into its sheath, then stepped over the lifeless body.

That took care of one problem. Kathleen's plan had worked. Couldn't accomplish their objective with Finn in the way. He was getting too close.

212

"Ready?"

Harry Lee looked up at his brother. "Yep."

With a bag over his shoulder, Buck tramped down the rickety stairs. "Got everything."

"Good. Let's get out of here. We have a busy day tomorrow."

Harry Lee took one last look at the dead man with satisfaction. He was going to make Brantley Wright rue the day the man stole his heritage and ran him out of the state.

Everything was falling into place despite Gillie slipping through his fingers…that would be remedied soon enough. Kathleen Halcoyne had manipulated that fool Andrew into believing he was doing the best for his family.

By tomorrow night, he would have Josephine. With that knowledge, he smiled. He was tired of running. He was ready to go back home.

Chapter Eight

The late January morn found Philadelphia a cold and barren city. Jo had wakened to a dark threatening sky and a whistling north wind. When the staff girl came to build the fire in the hearth, she mentioned a winter storm lay on the horizon. By nightfall, it was expected the streets would soon be filled with a mantle of white.

It mattered little to Jo if it stormed outside. No, her only concern was that she fulfill her promise to Papa. This was her wedding day. Before breakfast was served, she had received a telegram from her papa wishing her well. It served as a reminder of what she was doing; it gave her fortitude.

Furthermore, Andrew would not be disappearing. There was nowhere for him to hide any longer. For better or worse, they were about to be bound together as husband and wife, if not for the love they shared between each other, for the love they had for their families.

The suite had been prepared. The ceremony would be a small affair with only Mother Montgomery, the girls, and Finn in attendance.

Finn had offered to give her away in place of her father. Jo hadn't a doubt Papa had requested it from his friend. The thought touched her. She looked up at the clock on the mantle. Strange. With only a few hours before the event, she thought she would have heard from Finn by this time. She shook away her uneasiness. She was letting her nerves get to her.

She stood in her lace pantalets and linen corset, which covered over her three billowing lace petticoats. Her wedding gown lay on the bed. Exquisitely beautiful. So soft to the touch. The bodice was of sheer ivory striped silk with pink taffeta, beaded in pearls. The sheer ivory striped

214

skirt lay over a triple-layered skirt worn over crinoline, elaborately trimmed with delicate lace. Miss Haney called it a crinoline silhouette.

Rosa had diligently worked on a fashion for her hair, cascading it down her shoulders. Staring at her reflection in the mirror, Jo had to agree it was most flattering. Papa surprised her with another gift, a stunning set of culture pearls: the single droplet earrings set off by four strings of pearls around her ivory neck.

A slight knock on her door deflected her attention. Smiling sweetly, Mother Montgomery eased in the room bearing a tray of tea, ham, and hot biscuits.

"Rosa said that you ate no breakfast. You will need your strength, my dear. I know you want to enjoy this moment," she glanced over at the gown and set the tray down on the table by the settee. "Come and sit. There is time."

Jo obediently seated herself in a high back chair across from Mother Montgomery and accepted the porcelain cup filled with hot tea. She stirred in a teaspoon of sugar and took a sip. The warm liquid felt good going down, relaxing. She hadn't realized how tense she had become.

"You are going to make the most lovely bride, my dear. Andrew is lucky to have found you, as am I to have gained you for a daughter-in-law."

Mother Montgomery's sudden expression choked Jo's already frail emotions. She fought to maintain composure.

"I know you young have your ideas of what life will be. You, though, have experienced the brutal truth of the world. Most of us don't realize it until much later in life. Know that despite all you have gone through, have faith it will lead you to where you need to be. You are exactly what Magnolia Bluff needs for its mistress. Don't mistake Andrew's reluctance for a character flaw. He is a good soul and a good man. You will have a happy life together and be blessed with many children. Believe in it and hold to that belief."

"Do you...hold on to that belief?"

"Yes," she said simply. "Sometimes it was the only thing I had to hold to..."

Mother Montgomery stared blankly out into an empty space and seemed lost in another time and place.

Jo studied the woman. She was the epitome of a Southern wife, compassionate and kind, supportive...setting an example for her daughters to follow, including Jo.

"Now," Mother Montgomery leaned forward, her blue eyes softened. "The girls have been so appreciated of your generosity."

"It gives me pleasure."

"I know." She reached over and patted Jo's hand. "You have been a dear. But today, we have a surprise for you. The ceremony is going to be moved to the hall downstairs, followed by a reception. Your Mr. Finn thought it a splendid idea when the girls came to him with the idea. Elizabeth helped to invite all of Andrew's friends he has made in Philadelphia and, of course, the Smythes." As if remembering that Cullen was part of the family, Mother Montgomery quickly added. "There will be no distractions. You deserve a day to remember."

"Truly, I am touched," Jo said. A sudden warmth enveloped her. Papa would be so pleased. "It worries me, though, that I haven't heard from Mr. Finn this morning. Have you seen him today?"

Mother Montgomery shook her head. "I will send Rosa downstairs and ask. I would not worry. I'm certain he is overseeing last minute details. It will be a wonderful day."

Jo smiled. The day had certainly brightened.

* * * *

The darkened sky had made the day seem as night. A storm lay on the horizon much like the storm that raged in his heart. He sat across from Hugh in a game of chess, but his mind was not into it. He had already lost three games. Good Gawd! He had lost her, truly lost her. He had hung onto a semblance of hope, but it was over.

He pulled his pocket watch out. The ceremony was in less than two hours.

"Checkmate," Hugh said, leaning back in his chair. "I think we have time for another game before we need to get ready for tonight."

"I know I agreed to go out, but I don't think..."

"Oh, no, my friend. You are not backing out on me this evening. Diane is expecting us both. I refused to let you abandon me in my time of need. If I go alone, I'm certain I will hear a lecture on my deficiencies about not calling on our mother. Since Gavin has departed, I do not even have him to serve as a go between my sister and myself. Besides I know, my nieces will be terribly disappointed if you do not make an appearance."

Mitchell had left Philadelphia over a week ago having been recalled early for a special meeting in Washington. Hugh's leave was almost up as well. Despite having carefully considered his resignation from the Navy, Cullen suddenly found himself envious of his friends. He wanted to be anywhere but here.

"I have the whole of the night planned," Hugh went on. "After dinner with Dianne and her brood, I have made arrangements for us down at O'Gradys."

A knock on his door interrupted his reply. Cullen glanced up in surprise as Andrew walked into the room. He looked like hell. Unshaven, his eyes drooped from lack of sleep; his hair disheveled; his clothes wrinkled.

"Cullen, Cullen," he repeated. "Your man, Paddy, let me in. I told him…I told him I had to see you."

Immediately, Cullen pushed back his chair and stood. "What is wrong?"

"I have made such a mess of things," he mumbled incoherently. Raising his head up, he looked Cullen straight in his eyes. "I don't know what else to do. I need your help."

Unbelieving the tale that had been told, Cullen paced a path in the rug. Andrew sat on the sofa looking strangely defeated. Cullen held no sympathy. He exploded, "How could you? How could you do that to Josephine, to the family, to yourself? What the hell were you thinking?"

"I'm well aware of what I have done. It will be difficult for you to believe me now, but I had only the best intentions for all involved."

"You are correct on that point. I think you only had yourself—Kathleen's best interest at heart."

"What more do you want me to say?"

"Do you not think Jo deserves an explanation? You have betrayed…"

Andrew shook his head. "Stop badgering me, Cullen. If Josephine was a docile, quiet thing, all of this would have been avoided. I tried to work it out to everyone's advantage…truly I did."

A moment of enlightening suffused within him. The words escaped him, "You thought Jo would marry Wade."

Andrew did not answer, lowered his gaze. *Oh, Good Lord!* His cousin had lost all his good sense!

"You…intentionally thrust the two together at Christmas in hopes she would *have* to marry Wade! You even made moves to keep her from me!"

"Wade marrying Josephine would have been the best solution," Andrew muttered. Then suddenly, he stood. "Would it have been so bad? Wade has never had an issue seducing a woman…especially one he wants…one that has Magnolia Bluff attached to her.

"Yes…yes…yes…I thought when I delayed our impending nuptials she would have found comfort in his arms. Her father would have been content. Wade is who Wright wanted to begin with."

"You fool! Sit down!" Cullen roared. "Who have you been listening to that suggested it would have been the best for Josephine? She would have been shunned by all of Charleston society! Don't answer— Kathleen."

"God forgive me, Cullen, but Kathleen isn't wrong. I could never have been happy with Jo, nor she with me." Andrew threw back his hands. "I can't abide her. Now it's said. It will be for the better."

Cullen laughed harshly. "Better? You have just lost the family's heritage. Explain to me how that is better."

"But how could I marry someone feeling as I do?" Andrew said in a low, firm voice. "You think I don't know what kind of woman Josephine is. She is a far better person than I. Do you know why I joined the Underground Railroad? Josephine."

He stared at his cousin skeptically, wanting nothing more than to shake some sense into him. But he saw a need in Andrew that sparked an ember of pity. His cousin had a need to expel a demon that gnawed at his soul.

"Do you remember down at the Battery when Jo leaped over the railing to save Gillie?"

"Very well. I was there. It was the day you broke your ankle in your attempt to help. The day I got soaked dragging Jo out of the bay."

Andrew sighed. "I could have stopped Harry Lee before he dropped Gillie. I knew what he intended. I did nothing thinking my friends would think me weak. Instead, it was this small irritating waif that called Harry Lee out. I watched her doing what comes so natural to her. She places honor and duty higher than most men.

"After I was recovering, I thought about what happened. As horrific as it was, knowing Gillie could have died, nothing happened to Harry Lee. It wasn't deemed criminal because Gillie was nothing more than a slave. I made a vow that day. I have kept it."

"Commendable, but it does not explain why you can't marry Josephine?" Cullen snapped.

"Do you think it's easy for me to admit that I'm not man enough to handle her? She needs a strong hand. I don't have the time nor the energy to contain her spirit. Oh, God. Do you think I want to hurt her?" He pushed his hands against his forehead tightly. "I can't. I can't do this. I fended her off as long as I can."

"Don't give me this nonsense! Sounds like nothing more than Kathleen's prattling."

"You don't understand, Cullen...I couldn't even if I wanted to marry Jo," Andrew confessed.

"Good Lord, man, what have you done?"

"You have to understand. It wasn't until after Clarissa passed away. Kathleen reasoned that Wade loved Josephine...they would be happy together...as we are, Kathleen and I. And...Wright would have Jo as mistress of Magnolia Bluff..."

Comprehension sank deep within him. It explained Andrew's strange behavior over the last few months. He knew, but he had to hear him say it.

"Tell me, Andrew."

"Kathleen discovered she was with child. My child," his cousin uttered. "We married. Kathleen is my wife."

Cullen stared at his cousin in stilted silence. No...no, Andrew would never have done this, not the Andrew he had known growing up but as he spoke the last months flashed before him. Did he not know the pain and anguish of giving up someone you loved? How hard it was to walk away...

It did not excuse his behavior, only explained his actions.

"Why, in Heaven's name, have you let the engagement go on if you were already married?"

"I told you. Magnolia Bluff. For God's sake, the family stands to lose..."

"When you married Kathleen, the family lost everything. You fool!" Cullen growled. "What kind of man are you?"

Andrew ran his hand through his hair and shook his head. "I wanted to believe everything would work out. Kathleen said it would, but it has only gotten worse. I need to make this right. I don't know how..." His words faded into the thick air.

"You haven't a choice. You have to man up and face Josephine."

His cousin walked over to the window and gazed out at the threatening sky. He nodded and took a deep breath. "I need to explain to Mother. At least, it is only family today gathered for the ceremony. I don't know how I would face..."

"Only family?" Cullen cut him off abruptly. "Oh, God, you don't know."

Cullen didn't have time to explain. Grabbing his long coat, he shuttled Andrew out the door with a confused Hugh following.

219

As the carriage neared Girard House, Cullen battled his temper. It would do no good to lose it. He gritted his teeth.

His stupid...stupid naïve cousin! Kathleen, the she devil! Cullen cursed himself for not doing more. He knew she was up to something. Even now, it hadn't occurred to Andrew what his bride was capable of doing.

When his father had told him of the wedding, of what Elizabeth insisted upon doing for Andrew, he should have been suspicious. Elizabeth had been quite open with her hostility toward Josephine. He had thought it was because Jo had turned him down, but now he realized it stemmed from Kathleen.

That woman had an uncanny ability to get others to do her bidding. He wondered though if Andrew had informed his new wife that the family's fortune was no more. Somehow he doubted it.

Why had Kathleen allowed the façade to go on as long as it had? What was her purpose? He was certain she had one. To humiliate Josephine? For what reason? Just downright meanness. Spite. Or simply because she could.

The reason mattered little. The plan had been put into place to humiliate Jo in front of all of Philadelphia. It would not take much. Kathleen probably even had the press within the hotel for the event. The tide of public opinion rode high against the South...this would serve only to fan the flames of hatred.

A Southern belle after a married man with an expecting wife! He could read the headlines now—*Southern Adulterer!*

The carriage rattled along in the crowded streets. As it rolled to a stop, Cullen climbed out in front of the hotel. He lingered a moment surveying the entrance. It was as he feared. He recognized many of the guests arriving.

He walked up the steps behind Andrew and Hugh. He hadn't a plan, but his intuition told him he would be needed. Kathleen was determined to cause drama this day. He wanted Josephine far away from it if he could help it.

Making his way through the crowd, he caught sight of his father. Tapping Andrew on the shoulder, he gestured for Andrew to follow him to the rear of the room.

"Father, Andrew needs...," Cullen began but was immediately cut off. His father's expression altered.

"Cullen, I'm glad you are here. The wedding has become a disaster," Jonathan glanced over at Andrew and Hugh. Surveying his nephew, he grimaced and continued. "Mr. Finn, Miss Wright's friend, was found dead early this morning in shantytown. His throat was slashed. He was identified only by papers he had in his pocket. The sheriff arrived here only moments ago. Finn's housekeeper said he was expected here today."

"What was Finn doing in shantytown?" Cullen asked, but then a thought struck him…one his father had already formulated. "You suspect something underhanded is going down."

"Finn has seen to Josephine's welfare since the moment she arrived. It would be too much of a coincidence if his murder was not linked to Josephine in some manner." Jonathan looked over his shoulder. Ignoring Andrew, who stood in silence, he grabbed Cullen's arm. "I fear that Miss Wright may need to leave."

"Why Andrew Montgomery where ever have you been? Why are you not ready?"

All four men turned to the feminine voice. Jenna smiled, a wide broad grin. "Tell me you have another suit. Of course, you must. You can use my room upstairs to change. I told Momma there was nothing to worry about despite what that hideous Kathleen Halcoyne was telling Momma…you would not believe…"

"Ssh, Jenna, I can't take your babbling at the moment. Kathleen has reason, more than you understand at present to be upset, not with Josephine, but me."

Jenna eyed Andrew suspiciously. "What is wrong with you? All of you? Oh, do not tell me that really was Buck Haynes I saw."

"Buck is here?" In an abrupt fashion, Cullen grasped Jenna by the shoulders. He questioned, "You saw Buck?"

Jenna recoiled from his intensity and nodded her head slowly. Uncertain of what he wanted her to say, she whispered, "I thought it was he, but Momma said it was an impossibility."

Upon the utterance, Andrew lost his forlorn expression. Cullen looked over at his father, from the look on his face thought the same. Cullen turned his attention back to Jenna and demanded, "Where is Jo?"

"Rosa said she was about to make her entrance…"

Cullen didn't wait for Jenna to finish her thought. He had to get to Jo. Pushing back any in front of him, he rounded the stairs and froze at the sight. Walking down the steps, Josephine paused. Her gaze caught his.

She took his breath away. Oh, my lord, she was breathtakingly beautiful. She wore a sheer pink striped ivory gown which set off her ivory skin. The whole of the gown shimmered in the light. The dress hung low off the shoulder accentuated her full bosom. The skirt gathered at the waist, and delicate lace flowed downward in three elaborate layers.

Strands of her dark hair weaved back in a fashionable twist while the rest cascaded down her shoulders held back with pearl combs. A layered pearl necklace fell down to the neckline; matching earrings dangled from her ears. Lovely. Simply lovely.

"Cullen."

His name escaped her lips much like a cry. Breaking from the trance she had cast upon him, he rushed up the stairs. Taking her arm, he said softly, "You need to come with me."

A protest lay on her lips. He shook his head. "Trust me."

She made no other resistance, but gave a troubled look at Andrew who followed the pair back into her suite.

Jo sat down abruptly, crushed…stunned as she listened to their tale. Her eyes wide in disbelief filled with tears. She covered her hand to her mouth in a vain attempt to keep the dam from bursting. Unheeded the tears fell, not for herself, but Papa…and Mr. Finn…he had been so kind.

Words assaulted her from all sides. *Finn found dead…fear the Haynes brothers are about…need to withdraw her back to a safe place.* But it was Andrew who spoke with a tongue sharper than a knife plunged into her heart. He was married…his wife was with child…All she comprehended—the news would kill Papa.

"Jo, I deeply apologize," Andrew cleared his throat. "I did not mean to cause you pain. I know I cannot undo what has been done, but I will return to Charleston and explain it to your father. I will do whatever it takes to rectify this situation."

Unmoved, she said nothing but glared at him.

"Say something for God's sakes. Yell at me! Tell me what a coward I am…what a miserable excuse for a human being I am."

Andrew fell to his knees beside her and took her hand. She jerked it back.

"Get your hands off of me!" Jo cried with fire in her eyes. "Did you ever think of talking to me? To be upfront with me, instead of something so devious. Now I will have to live with your lies…I hope one day to forgive you, but it won't be today."

"Please, Jo, understand I panicked. I had to do something. Kathleen…she comes from a well-established family. I couldn't disgrace her. I tried to…take care of the situation…and then it all fell apart with your appearance…I don't know what more you want me to say."

"Nothing. I don't want you to say anything. Leave me, just leave me alone," she replied caustically, feeling hurt and degraded. "Only think about how selfish you have been. I agreed to marry you, not for me, this was never for me. I wanted to give something to my papa. I hope what you gained in your betrayal outweighs what you have lost."

She turned her head away from Andrew. Her eyes fixed on the men across the room deep in discussion. Cullen lifted his head and glanced her way. Suddenly, an ominous feeling swept through her.

Worry. Concern. Anxiety. She saw it all in his eyes. He stepped toward her and extended his arm.

"Come. We are leaving."

"With you?" Jo decried. Her mind hardened. "I want only to go home to Papa, away from any of you!"

"You have little choice," Cullen said softly. He fumbled in his pocket and pulled out a handkerchief. He handed it to her. "Now, dry your eyes. There is a danger here. Your papa would never forgive me if I did not see to your welfare."

She startlingly noticed her hand was trembling; her lip quivered. She looked at him with a sudden feeling of utter helplessness. She was scared and so alone…ever so alone.

He took her hand in a strong grasp. She rose.

"I need my trunk and Rosa…"

"We will worry about that later. Now we are leaving."

He gave her no option other than taking her fur-lined cloak and muff. She went out of the room without another word.

Chapter Nine

Joe sat in silence. The carriage had long lost the smooth ride along the streets of Philadelphia. The wheels jounced along a rutty road, jarring her back and forth against the cushioned sides. The winds of the snowstorm howled and rocked the occupants. Pulling back the curtain, visibility had greatly diminished. The snow was all she could see blowing hard on the window.

Cullen watched her; she could feel his eyes upon her. She wished he wouldn't do so. She didn't want him to see the tears she couldn't contain, not him, not any Montgomery.

Since the day she had agreed to become Andrew's wife, she had prepared for her life. She had denied her heart. Instead, she walked the path Papa laid before her; one that would lead to a happy, content life, a life of redemption for her mother's indiscretion. There would be no salvation.

She had fought her own feelings when every fiber in her body wanted to be loved. She doubted she believed in the emotion anymore. How foolish she had been to have allowed herself to be used in this manner!

Wade…who had pleaded with her…*I need you, Josephine*. Oh, what a fool she had been! He must have known. Had Andrew asked him to seduce her? Had they conspired against her to the point where she had blindly walked into the fire?

Moreover, there was the one sitting across from her. There was little doubt he had always considered her fast. It is how he had treated her. Touching her, kissing her until all she wanted was for his to take her and forget the consequences!

She felt tears welling once more. Her pride shattered; her heart crushed.

The carriage slowed to a stop. Only when she accepted Cullen's hand stepping out of the carriage did she noticed their destination. It was a home…far from Philadelphia.

The wind whipped around her. Gathering her cloak tighter about her, she turned to Cullen. "This isn't an inn."

"No," he said simply. "I said only I had made arrangements."

"This isn't acceptable. Take me to an inn."

"This will serve your purpose. It is away from your cousins. Make no mistake, Josephine. They mean you ill."

Suddenly she hated him, hated him with all her might. She realized he had momentarily saved her from humiliation, disgrace and Harry Lee, but she hated him, irrationally blaming him for the events of the day. Her eyes flared. "I demand you take me back to an inn!"

He ignored her outburst, extending his arm for her. Servants had emerged, standing in confusion on the front steps.

"You are mistaken if you believe I'm going anywhere but into the sanctuary of this house. We are fortunate that we have made it to Rosemount."

"You can stay," she looked up at the coachman. "Take me…"

"Ah!" she cried.

Cullen wasted no more time arguing. He swept her into his arms and carried her up the steps. He didn't pause entering the foyer but began ascending upward. Her feet kicked violently, and she pushed against his chest.

"Let me go, you brute!"

Pounding down a corridor, he halted long enough for a servant to open the door. The next moment, he placed her door on the floor of a bedroom. Stumbling backward, she regained her footing. Her hair escaped its hold and fell disheveled about her face.

"Stay here while I see to our needs. Try anything—anything at all and I will tie you up. Try me, Josephine. I have lost all patience with this mess, of which was none of my doing."

"I didn't ask for your help, nor do I want it! I want only to go home to Papa and never see another Montgomery ever again!"

Standing defiantly, he ran his hand through his hair, having lost his hat somewhere along the path to this room. Tension filled the air. His jaw clenched with his own frustration.

"I will send someone up to tend a fire and bring you some dinner. Heed my warning. Try anything foolish like running away in a snow storm, I will carry out my threat."

He walked out, slamming the door behind him. A minute later she heard a click. She ran to the door and tried turning the handle. He had locked the door.

* * * *

The fire burned brightly, fed by a steady placement of logs. The servant girl, Hannah, had come back like clockwork on the half-hour to ensure the room's warmth. Each time, she locked the door back behind her.

Jo had refreshed herself. The girl had helped her take off her petticoats and hoop. Jo had kept the gown on even though she had been offered a nightgown. It wasn't hers and for some foolish reason, it gave her a sense of security.

Hannah had brushed out her hair and plaited it into one long braid. The tray of food had remained up touched. She had no appetite.

The storm had not ceased. She had never experienced a blizzard, but she had to admit that she was glad to be inside and not venturing to some unknown inn. Not that she would concede Cullen was right...not tonight.

Her mind reeled with worry. Papa! Oh, however was he going to take the news of the misadventure! She had a need to return to Charleston...away from this horrible, horrible place.

Standing at the window, she heard the door rattle, open and close again.

"Deceptive is it not? It seems so calm and serene, yet it can be deadly if trapped out in the middle of it."

She said nothing but kept her gaze out the window.

"Josephine," Cullen said in a low, husky voice. "We need to talk. I find I would rather you look at me to do so."

She looked around crossly. His manner had eased and seemed more relaxed, having changed to more informal clothes. His shirt hung loose over his pants; his feet bare.

"There is nothing to discuss. I want to go home."

"It is the plan," he said. "I want to ease your mind. Father has already telegraphed your papa and briefly explained what happened. He will know you are safe."

She grabbed his arm. "He will know what Andrew has done...it will kill him." Looking up at him, she felt nauseated.

A small smile emerged as his eyes bore into hers. "No," he said with unexpected tenderness. "I told Father to tell him it was no matter that Andrew had not married you."

"How could you, Cullen?" she wailed. "How can you be so mean?"

He took her hand up to his lips. "Because now you are free, Josephine Buchanan Wright. We do have much to talk about but at the moment, all, that matters, is that you are free…free to marry me. That is what I told him."

"I…don't understand," she said, stumbling over her words, but she did. She understood clearly his meaning for his lips climbed up her arm until they found hers and he kissed her with a completeness that wiped out every conscious thought except his lips upon hers.

Suddenly, he released her and turned her around. Gasping, she questioned, "What are you doing?"

"What I have wanted to do since the first time we met."

He undid the hooks of her gown and it flowed down her body to it lay on the floor. Then he whirled her around to face him in her chemise and pantaloons. Physical desire made her breathless as he slowly began untying her laces.

He pushed down the loose material exposing her perfect breasts to his view, but he wasn't done. He had to have her naked…fully totally naked. Nothing was going to come between him and his desire this night.

Gently, he eased off the last of what lay between him and all of her. Her clothing littered the floor. She stood before him, bare and lovely in the firelight. His arousal hardened to the point he didn't know if he could take her the way he envisioned, slowly savoring every moment.

"You are beautiful," he whispered, kissing her lips lightly. "I want to make love to you all night long…I won't let go of you…ever."

"Cullen," she uttered, betraying her own need with a plea to complete the love they shared. "I…want you to know…I never stopped loving you."

"I know, my love, as I know that my heart beats for one purpose— you, Josephine. Nothing matters but you."

Dropping back her head, she bared her creamy throat to him. He buried his lips on the pulse that made her body melt to his. He bent down and picked her up, sitting her down long enough to pull back the covers of the bed. Then he placed her within the sheets.

She would not be lonely long. Stepping back, he began to undress. She watched him and stared at his masculine firmness without a tinge of embarrassment. Smiling, he climbed onto the bed beside her and propped himself on one elbow to look down at her.

He gazed upon her as if he wanted to say something, but at that moment her hands wrapped around his neck. The hurt she had longed felt, she pushed away accepting what he had to offer. For so long, he had wanted this from her, and now she was giving herself to him completely. She made no resistance, wanting only his hungry kisses, bold caresses and craving his most intimate touch.

He lowered his mouth on hers once more. Her consciousness lost in the titillations sweeping through her body. Rational thoughts dissolved with his touch. He consumed her. They blended with an impatient urgency, a fierce tide of desire that enveloped them both. Outside laid a cold and empty world. Together there was only a fire that burned, flamed with each kiss shared.

The whole of her body shuddered with sensations he had created, robbing her of all but one thought. She needed him, wanted him desperately. Instinct drove her to fulfill the ache growing within her. Her breasts tingled for attention. As if reading her mind, he complied. She felt his mustache scrape along her ripe fullness until his mouth clamped over her nipple, suckling her until she cried out in pleasure.

The whole of her body shuddered with a sensation he had created. She needed him, wanted him desperately. Instinct drove her to fulfill the ache growing within her. Her breasts tingled for attention. As if reading her mind, he complied. She felt his mustache scrape along her ripe fullness until his mouth clamped over her nipple, suckling her until she gasped in pleasure.

His hands caressed her body, down her leg, then up her thigh until they touched her most secret softness. She parted her legs so he could touch her, so the moist warm ache would be relieved. His firm and sure caress claimed her for his own.

Waves of pleasure cascaded through her until she was devastated with want of an unknown release. Her body would deny itself nothing of the wicked sensations he created…demanded. She clung to him, spiraling out of control into a madness only he could abate.

She cried out at his touches designed to craze her. Her eyes opened to find him watching her and seemed to revel in her distress.

"Are you torturing me?"

"Oh, no, my magnolia, come with me," he beckoned. He spread her legs and kept her wanting with those devastating caresses at the core of her being. "So slick and warm and ready."

"Cullen, please," she begged. The intensifying hunger became almost insatiable, clutching the sheets beneath her.

He took her just as she was. His naked body covered hers. Her eyes widened when his blunt hardness invaded her. With a single breath, she surrendered to him.

The moment he sunk into her a burning pain exploded within her lions. She felt her every muscle stiffened as her cry was muffled with his mouth upon hers. He kissed her until the ache dulled and she began to feel his fullness again as he plunged deeper within her. He slowed his play as if savoring every moment of pleasure he was obtaining. Within her a new sensation overwhelmed her as he began to move, a feeling she could not deny smothered her.

A budding rapture of which she could only respond to, her hands wrapped around his neck, returning his wild, ardent kisses. Unrelenting passion tore through her. His touch brought heat to cold places as if she had only half lived before his touch. His strokes quickened and became more aggressive to where she thought she would explode.

Each thrust brought her to a new plateau of pleasure. They became as one in the mix of unrelenting passion, fiery unrelenting desire merged together and gushed forth in a torrent of scintillating ecstasy.

She felt warmth fill her and welcomed it, knowing she was part of him for always. Slowly, he relaxed and released her. He rolled back against at pillow and pulled her to him.

"Cullen, don't leave me..." she muttered against his bare chest.

His arms slipped around her and kissed the top of her head. "I won't, Josephine."

Jo had never known what it was like to give herself freely to a man until Cullen. He came pressing himself into her life. She hadn't wanted him to and yet he hadn't stopped, making his presence dominate in her existence, and she wanted him.

She wondered whether she should confess that his kiss lingered on her lips and in her heart; that she shivered with his merge touch and yearned for it; that he haunted her dreams...

Her heart raced, frightened of words he would speak or those he would not. She did not know how long she lay quietly in his arms. She didn't move. She had no desire to disturb the peace she had found in the stillness of his arms.

"Josephine." Cullen broke the silence. "I have the need for you to know I have never been so content. I love you. As I breathe, I will love you always."

She tilted her head towards him and accepted his kiss and love.

229

A white covering dressed the landscape and glittered in the morning sun while a crackling fire danced in the hearth. Jo rushed back across the cold wood floor. Cullen raised the bedcovers, and she slipped in beside him.

"Cold?" he whispered against her neck before he kissed it.

"The bath was lovely," she answered breathlessly. Her whole body shivered, not from the freezing temperatures outside, but from his touch. He stirred her blood with desire.

The night had been heaven. She had never known such contentment as lying in his arms until the morning light. He had seen to her every need, including a steaming bath. She felt rejuvenated and refreshed.

Promises had been made in the heat of the night…promises that had not faded in the bright light of day.

Jo had soaked in a steamy bath while memories of the night lingered, unforgettable, heavenly memories—pure bliss. Outside was a wintery wonderland. The storm had closed Rosemount off from the rest of the world. The road had been snowed under at least for a few days, and she planned on savoring each precious hour.

The world forgotten while in his arms, she lost herself in his presence. Her worries seemed distant and far away here within these walls. There was nothing here that wished her harm or wanted to humiliate her. No, she had Cullen to protect her.

He had made no attempt to conceal his suspicion that Harry Lee was bent on doing her harm. A pistol lay on top of the nightstand and, if by chance the scoundrel appeared at Rosemount, he had in place a plan of escape.

"The servants are on alert if there is any sign of his appearance. You would follow our butler, Lawrence, to the basement. He will know where to take you from there," Cullen spoke, holding her tightly in the dark. "It is the winter season. We have only a minimum staff working, but they are loyal and trustworthy."

"Are they not appalled by my being here with you…like this?"

"They are too well trained to say, Jo, but I doubt it will be an issue since I informed them you are to be their new mistress. I would have married you last evening if I could have gotten the Reverend here, but there is little doubt now that you will soon be Mrs. Cullen Smythe."

"Papa…"

"Your papa has no quarrel with me. He said as much when I asked for your hand. It was only circumstances that kept him from giving me his blessing. Now there is no choice." He leaned down and kissed her.

"Lest I remind you that you are quite ruined for marriage to any other. You are all for me…all that I want…all that I need."

His words rang in her heart, confident that Papa would accept Cullen.

He reached down. With a single tug, the belt of the robe loosened enough to spread wide the garment and hug her close. The heat of their bodies blended as she wrapped her arms around his neck, lost in the essence of their love.

Chapter Ten

The weather warmed, and the sun shone, but the thaw had flooded the roads. It took over a week for Cullen to get Josephine back to Philadelphia safely. There had been no rush on his part. The time together with the woman he loved allowed for endless days filled with games of chess, reading and talks of their future together. But it had been the nights, the unforgettable, tantalizing nights that had been burned into his memory.

It was late afternoon before the carriage arrived at the townhouse. Jo wasn't happy he had brought her to stay at his Philadelphia house. He understood her reasons, but the residence was large enough for everyone. More importantly, safe.

"I will feel their eyes on me," she said as the carriage slowed to a stop in front of the residence. "I don't want to be pitied. What they must think!"

"They know I care greatly for you," he answered her in a tender voice. "Besides, Aunt Marie and the girls are here. They moved out of the hotel after the incident." He paused for a brief moment. "You realize that this will be our home. My family will be yours."

Her eyes widened. At first he thought she would protest. Instead, she asked, "You will be by my side?"

"Always, my love." He leaned over and gently kissed her lips.

"Then I will do as you wish."

His eyes met hers, and though unspoken, the meaning was clear. She had managed to maintain an outward show of calm, but she was scared. She had not expressed that sentiment, but she was. He wouldn't fail her.

Cullen stood alone in the library with a drink in hand one hand, cigar in the other. Jo had been shown upstairs to rest after their journey. He was worried about her. Her life had been upheaved once again. He realized she needed to see her papa…she needed his blessing. She wanted to return to Charleston. It was the last thing he wanted.

The door creaked opened. Cullen had been standing with his back to the fire, but he turned to face the door. He glanced up to see his father walk into the room, followed by Hugh.

"It is good that you are home," Jonathan said, walking over to the decanter. He poured a drink for Hugh and himself. "Hugh has been busy."

Taking a puff of his cigar, Cullen directed his attention to his friend, who had accepted the glass from his father.

"I went down to shantytown myself and talked to others who boarded at the same house. Two men fitting Harry Lee and Buck's description. Southern drawl, tall, lean, auburn hair. Little doubt it was the two. They rented a room for the last few of months."

Cullen released a trail of smoke. "Did anyone see anything?"

"No one I found. The men disappeared at the same time of the murder. It is disturbing, though, they were here for that amount of time."

Jonathan took a paper from his coat's inner pocket. "A telegram arrived yesterday. It is from Brantley Wright."

Cullen placed his drink down on the mantle and took the telegram.

Josephine,

It was disturbing to hear the details of the wedding. I take comfort that your young gentleman has looked after your welfare. I understand his desire to marry you quickly. He expressed it clearly in his telegram. I ask only you do so here in Charleston. Come home. Let me ensure you are safe and well. I need to see you.

Your Loving, Papa

"Be cautious, Cullen. Remember the last time you traveled to your Southern home. You were confident that Josephine would be your bride. Do not underestimate your grandfather."

"Josephine is not Mother."

"No," Jonathan conceded. "But Clayton Montgomery will not sit idly by and allow his heritage to be lost."

Tapping his cigar ashes, Cullen laughed, "You forget I am blood. I will assure Grandfather I won't make changes in Magnolia Bluff."

"Clayton might say tainted blood, son. I only say be prepared."

233

"I can assure you, Father, I know what I face. I can't be manipulated. If there are any questions about Jo's inheritance, we will simply walk away from it. It is Harry Lee that is my immediate concern. Allowing Buck to be seen at the Girard House tells me that Harry Lee is getting bolder in his attempt to kidnap Jo."

"I believe it went deeper than an attempt to kidnap Josephine," Hugh offered. "I think his plan was to foil the wedding publically in the most humiliating fashion. Word would get back to Wright. If his health is as fragile as reported…"

"The news could have killed him," Cullen agreed. "Harry Lee must be under the misguided impression that Jo would be under her grandfather's guardianship. I know that Wright changed it to his friend, Whitney, but guardianship will matter little after we are married."

"It is a relevant fear. Have you considered leaving Josephine here in Philadelphia while you settle issues in Charleston?"

"More than once, Father. She will have none of it, especially after she sees this telegram. She is deeply concerned about her papa. Granted, I wanted to be married before we depart for Charleston, but now…"

"Tear it up."

Cullen was stunned by his father's utterance. "I could never do that to Jo. She has been deceived by everyone she has known. I refuse to do so to her."

"Tear it up," Jonathan repeated. "You do not know your grandfather…"

"What can Grandfather do, Father? This is now out of his control."

An awkward silence ensued. For a brief moment, he considered doing as his father suggested. But he didn't.

"Andrew has already departed to rectify the situation the best he can. Wait to see what he has to say."

"It is always, Andrew, with you, Father. May I remind you that it was his reckless behavior that led cause this whole diabolical."

"He is remorseful for his actions and is taking responsibility for them."

Resentment, frustration, anger raged inside of Cullen. Andrew, who chose to go against the establishment that had long been the South, ; Andrew, who devoted his life to helping those in need; Andrew, who almost let Harry Lee, get his hands on Jo…

"Cullen, are you planning on visiting Washington on your return?" Hugh questioned, directing the rising tension to another subject. "I was told you have not responded to Commander Davis' correspondence."

Cullen shot his friend a hard look. "Hugh, I told you before I'm not reenlisting."

"I believe that Commander Davis wants to convince you otherwise. Feelings are escalating on both sides. If it doesn't calm soon, Davis wants to be in readiness to make a show of force to discourage further threats of seceding. He believes your knowledge of the area would be an advantage."

Cullen frowned. "I'm well aware that the talk in Charleston has intensified. The people are fueled with secession enthusiasm and threaten more often than not to secede from the Union, but don't ask me to take arms against my brothers. And God have mercy on our souls if we are pushed to that point."

* * * *

Harry Lee heard the key turn and the door open. From the corner of his eyes, he saw who it was. He made no effort to greet his guest, only felt to make sure his pistol was secure in his belt. He didn't trust the bitch, not after the botched attempt to get Josephine.

Thankfully, he had had luck with that slave catcher, Earl Mann. Earl sure had been fired up after he had been duped by sweet little Josephine. He was willing to do almost anything to help Harry Lee in his venture. Mann had gone out of his way to complete their special project to the satisfaction of all parties.

He had even found Harry Lee another apartment. This one was down at the docks away from all prying eyes. Temporary, but their work was completed.

At the moment, Buck was out finalizing the details with Mann. The brothers would be gone in the morning.

Finally, he turned around. Chewing on the wad of tobacco in his mouth, he spitted into the spittoon beside the door. "How did you find me?"

"You know you are the most disgusting man," Kathleen said, smoothing her skirt and smiling. "Buck sent me word. I should have my feelings hurt that you would leave without a goodbye."

"Spare me the dramatics," he sighed heavily. "I don't have the time. What do you want?"

"Oh, lover, you sound so gruff."

"I am," he snapped. "Things didn't exactly go the way I wanted. I've had to…"

"I know what you have done. Buck told me," she said without betraying any annoyance. Matter of fact, she appeared quite smug. "Calm yourself, Harry Lee. All is not lost. For Heaven's sake, all of this can work to our benefit. I promise you the Montgomerys are fighting among themselves."

Harry Lee stared incredulously at Kathleen, restraining the urge to strangle her. He would have Josephine now if she hadn't signaled Buck to make his appearance at the reception too early. The plan fell apart with Buck being recognized. It allowed Josephine to slip through his fingers...once again.

Moreover, Kathleen had foolishly miscalculated her husband. Overconfident, she had discounted the man's conscience.

"Tell me, my dear, exactly how to do you see us turning the events into our favor," his voice was flat and deadly. "I don't have Josephine...Cullen Smythe does. He probably has already married her!"

"I know he has not," she said with a sneering grin. "I told you the Montgomerys are as desperate as you. Elizabeth told me that the Smythes received a telegram from Brantley Wright requesting Josephine return to Charleston. The dutiful daughter will wait to marry until after she sees her dear papa.

"Andrew has already left to go home in a vain effort to repair the damage done. You need to do the same. Go home. Get down there before Miss Wright. Set in motion the wheels of justice."

Her eyes narrowed dangerously and stepped towards him. He stilled as she wrapped her arms around his neck and kissed his lips. "We both know that Wright couldn't have sent the telegram, which means trouble brews within Magnolia Bluff."

He jerked her back roughly. "Do not attempt to play your games with me. I promise you I'm not your sniveling husband."

"I know," she uttered in a low seductive tone. She took his hand and placed in on her stomach. "You have to suspect the child, I carry, is yours. It is all that has gotten me through the last days, knowing it is yours and not Andrew's."

Withdrawing his hand, he suddenly laughed, "You do not stop."

"Never," she said, tracing her finger around his lips. "Do you want me to? We have so much to look forward to. You reclaiming the money that Wright stole from your family. I...you know what I want."

He snickered. The woman had gall, but if what she said was true, if Jo wasn't married to Smythe, he had a chance, especially with the little surprise he already had in store for Jo. He was anxious to get back to Charleston.

"So, your husband has left town?"

Kathleen smiled, took his hand and led him to the bedroom.

* * * *

Cullen watched the dolphins leap alongside the breaks from the coastal steamer. He loved the sight; he loved the feel of the ocean's breeze against his face. He felt at home; he felt like he was going home.

The steamer cruised into the harbor with a barrage of travelers standing along the railing. The familiar sight of the white church peaks signaled the return to Charleston along with a warm breeze. They had already passed Fort Sumter and Castle Pinckney.

Soon the ship would be docked. He looked forward to it. All the turmoil of the last weeks would end. His plan was simple. He would escort the ladies to their Charleston residence. Then, he would accompany Josephine to her father at Magnolia Bluff and send for the reverend. By evening, she would be his bride.

He had dismissed his father's concerns. His father had been an outsider here in the South; Cullen was born here. His blood was their blood. It was the tie that bound him to this place.

His attention turned when he caught sight of Jo. Walking beside his aunt on the deck, she gave him a mischievous smile. Her mood was gay, which, Cullen was certain, confused his poor aunt.

He supposed most would have expected Jo to be desolate. Her fiancée had secretly married another, leaving her in the most humiliating fashion. Yet, she strolled alongside the Montgomery women with a brilliant smile. Happiness radiated from her being.

Watching his aunt leave Jo at the side railing to talk with Jenna, he strolled over to Jo. Smiling broadly, he was amazed that he found himself more enamored with her every day. The woman took his breath away.

"We're home. I've missed it so," she said, gripping the rail. She tilted her head and looked up at him with impish eyes. "I'm wicked, but I do not believe I have ever been happier. Papa will see..."

"It will lift his spirits, I'm certain, because I do not know a more beloved lady, even if it is by one of those damn Yankees."

"Adored Yankee," she corrected, glancing out at the pier where Negro stevedores waited to lift the gangplank in place.

He laughed soundly, "I will do my best to convince your papa of my worth, my darling, but know if he doesn't agree I will take things in my own hands."

"But of course, Papa will have to after..."

She lowered her gaze and blushed so prettily. He knew exactly where her mind had wandered; where his was also. He was most anxious to get her back into his bed, ached if the truth be known.

"Cullen," his aunt said behind him.

Cullen turned to acknowledge her, reprimanding himself. He had quite forgotten he needed a chaperone to talk with Jo in public. "Aunt Marie, I beg your pardon. With docking, I got caught up in Jo's excitement of returning home."

She shrugged in a self-conscious way. Her smile had faded; she seemed tense. "Dear Cullen, do you suppose I could bother you for a moment and impose upon Josephine to keep my daughters company? I need to talk to you before we disembark."

Cullen lifted an eyebrow. The seriousness of her expression conveyed she had something important on her mind. He turned to Jo. "Wait with Jenna and Amy. I will come to escort you as soon as we are finished."

He watched Jo sauntered over to Jenna, who wrapped her arm about Jo's and commenced chattering. The girls were giddy and animated, but his aunt...A look of panic flashed across her face. Quickly, she suppressed it, but she frowned as if carrying about a great worry.

"I'm glad you sought me out," Cullen began. "I assume you realize my intent towards Josephine. I want to assure you that I have no desire to..."

"Oh, Cullen," she shook her head. "It was obvious that Jo and Andrew should have never become engaged. I am happy that it did not turn into the catastrophe it could have become. That is not my concern...not really."

A sudden ominous feeling replaced the hope he held for the day. He questioned, "Aunt Marie, what is wrong?"

"Everything, Cullen. Everything."

* * * *

Jo glanced over her shoulder and watched Cullen talked with Mother Montgomery. Immediately, she noticed Cullen's expression alter. Something was wrong. Lines tensed on his face.

Puzzled, she watched him look out across the pier, and then back at her. Mother Montgomery gripped his arm and said something. Cullen nodded impatiently and started toward her...almost running.

Not even bothering with a semblance of politeness to his cousins, he took her arm. "We need to leave immediately."

He gave her no time for protest. Her feet floated over the gangplank and stone pathway until she stood in front of one of the Montgomery carriages. She recognized the footmen. Her heart pounded wildly.

Pivoting back around to face Cullen, she was about to question what was the matter when Andrew emerged from the other side of the carriage and gestured for them to follow him.

"I have another carriage waiting for you," he said, pointing to one to the far corner of the street. "Come. You need to hurry."

Cullen scowled but wasted no time in ushering Jo forward. "Andrew, what is going on? What have we walked into?"

"It is confusion," Andrew began, looking anxiously behind them. "You need to go home. It will be explained in detail. Know, though, I had nothing to do with this. I came back only to undo the damage I had done. I sent a telegram warning you, but you must have already left."

"The Buchanans know we have returned?" Cullen asked when his hand gripped the handle of the carriage door.

"It is worse," Andrew informed him crisply, holding the door open wide of Jo to enter. He motioned for Cullen to do the same and waited until Cullen sat to answer fully. "Harry Lee has also returned. You need to hurry. Trust me, Cullen, I want only to right the wrong. Go now. Wade is waiting at the house. Hurry."

Andrew promptly shut the door. The carriage swayed rolling away from the pier. Jo fell back against the cushions. It would not be a long ride, but she was well aware of the Cullen's scowling brow. Her heart pounded so hard it felt as if it would burst out of her chest.

Cullen sat solemnly; his breathing became rapid.

"Cullen," Jo found the courage to voice her concern. "What has happened?"

Her question hung in the air. Something within her told her not to ask…she didn't want to know. For once in her life she was happy, truly happy. If she didn't ask…

He grimaced, taking her hands in his. "The news isn't good, Jo. I'm afraid it couldn't be worse."

"You are scaring me."

"Josephine, I'm sorry. It's your papa." He wrapped his arms about her. "He has passed away…"

Jo heard nothing else he said. She was lost in a spiraling abyss.

Chapter Eleven

It took an effort of sheer will for Jo to follow Cullen around to the garden's rear gate. He had the carriage driver dropped them a street away from the Montgomery Charleston house. Her mind reeled.

She had come to know a strong, determined, courageous, and loving Cullen. Something was different with him at this moment. She saw fear.

He stopped abruptly in front of the back door. He did not speak but took her by the shoulders, forcing her look into his eyes. Finally, he said, "I don't know what we are walking into. Aunt Marie confessed that Grandfather intentionally kept back the information that your papa passed. Jo...Grandfather was the one that sent the telegram."

Jo's confusion ran deep; barely comprehending she had lost Papa. "I don't understand."

"I would never have allowed you to return if I had known of your papa's fate. Father warned me about the lengths Grandfather would go. I refused to believe my own grandfather would do something so underhanded. He has put you endanger."

"Andrew said Harry Lee..."

"He won't harm you. I swear."

A cold, tight feeling formed in the pit of her stomach. She clenched her jaw tightly to keep it from trembling. She uttered in a low voice barely above a whisper, "Don't leave me, Cullen."

"I will do anything to keep that from happening."

He released her, turned and knocked on the door. His hand went behind her and steered her through the back entrance, up the servant stairs to the second floor. Emerging from the study, Clayton Montgomery gestured for the two to enter.

"Miss Wright, let me offer you my condolences. Most unfortunate state of affairs," Clayton said. "Come in. Cullen did right by bringing you here."

Jo raised her eyes and met the man's gaze. She did not trust him and wanted nothing more than to refuse, but Cullen ushered her into the room. His arm rounded her waist and kept her tight against him.

"Be quick with it, Grandfather. I'm in no mood to be trifled with. You have tricked Jo into returning," Cullen snapped.

"Hold your tongue. It was necessary. Sit, and I will explain…"

He hadn't the opportunity to finish his train of thought before Wade rushed into the room. Hat in hand, relief flooded his face when he caught sight of Jo.

"They are here," Wade announced. "Cullen, for God's sake keep her out of sight."

Clayton followed Wade from the room. Cullen walked to the door and closed it enough to peer through to the stairs.

"Cullen, what is going on?"

"Ssh, my darling, there are men at the door," he said in a soft voice. Taking her hands in his, he kissed them.

Suddenly, she heard voices, loud and boisterous. *Oh, Good Lord, are they after me?*

"I know she is here. She arrived back in Charleston on the steamer."

"Calm yourself, Vernon," Clayton asserted in a firm voice. "You have quite lost your manners. I have not invited you into my home. The last we spoke a few days ago, I thought I made it clear we are not on speaking terms."

"Can't say this is a social call, Clayton. Don't usually bring the sheriff with me when I go calling."

Confused and frightened, Jo shivered at her uncle's voice. *The sheriff? What was going on?* She felt Cullen's arm tighten around her.

"I know well what you are trying to do Clayton Montgomery. It is not going to work. I received word she arrived back with your grandson. Produce her immediately or…"

"Or what, Harry Lee, or what?" Wade pressed.

"Now…now…gentlemen. This can be settled quietly and quickly. Look, Clayton, is Miss Wright here? With her father passing like he did, it leaves her grandfather as guardian. You got no right to keep her."

"Come now, Lucas McCoy, if you knew Josephine Wright, she would make her presence known if she was here. Do you not believe it is a little suspicious that Vernon there and Harry Lee brought you along?

From what I hear, Whitney is her guardian. Wright didn't want those two anywhere near his daughter."

"Look, Wade, I've got a paper here that says she is the ward of her grandfather. All, I know, is the law. If you feel different, you will have to take it to court."

"I will. That paper, you have, is worthless. You have it only because Buchanan called in a favor with old Judge Simmons. Everyone knows they're kin. Simmons married Buchanan's second cousin," Clayton fired back.

"Gentlemen, gentlemen," another voice emerged. Jo recognized it readily enough. Andrew. "I have just come from the docks. I picked up Mother and my sisters. They are waiting to enter their home. If you would be kind enough to back away and allow them entrance."

"Not going anywhere without Josephine."

"If its Josephine you are looking for here, then you will be sadly disappointed. We dropped Josephine off at the Pavilion," Andrew said. "She checked into the establishment. I'm afraid she is still perturbed by my actions. When she saw me, she refused to come with us."

A long moment passed. Then Harry Lee's voice resonated throughout the house, "Jo has been devastated by your behavior, Dr. Montgomery. I want only to protect her from you Montgomerys. I warn you not to try anything…"

"Warning me?" Wade matched Harry Lee's intensity. "I think not. Don't come here and try to threaten me. It is I that has the law on my side."

"The hell you do! You try and marry her…"

"I will do more than try," Wade asserted. "Wright's will is firm and direct. Theodore Whitney is Jo's guardian. Wright made sure that his will was filed all proper and such before his death. Go see his lawyer, Clyde Morgan. Furthermore, Wright gave his blessing for me to marry Jo. He amended his will with the necessary stipulations. It is I that warn you to leave Miss Wright alone. Now, vacate my premises!"

The door slammed. A moment later hurried footsteps took to the stairs.

Jo fell back to a chair and sat. Cullen knelt beside her, holding tight to her hand. The door slung back as the Montgomery men entered.

"Andrew has sent them on a fool's errand. Hopefully, it has brought us enough time to depart."

"I'm not going anywhere, Wade…not until I understand what is happening," Jo's voice cracked with pain.

"I will tell you everything, but not now. We don't have time."

He reached down for her hand. She recoiled back.

"Don't touch me!" she cried. Looking over at Cullen, she pleaded, "Take me away."

"I'm afraid he can't do that," Clayton stepped in front of Andrew and walked across to his desk. "I will be blunt for we don't have time for niceties."

A scowl crossed his face. Jo sensed that the day had become a steady stream of disastrous events. She watched Clayton sit and reached for his pipe. She had no patience.

She glared at him. "Tell me what you want and be done with it."

Cullen would have none of it. He flew into a rage. "You lied to her, Grandfather! You have put her life endanger. I will never forgive you for this...never!"

Clayton filled his pipe and lit it. "A necessary evil, Cullen. It was Wright's last wish. I gave him my word on his death bed. I will hold to it."

"Wright would never have placed Jo in this position!"

"There you are wrong." Clayton went through a stack of papers and pulled out a letter. "The letter was written in a shaky hand, but it is his."

Reading it over quickly, Cullen grimaced and flung the letter back down on the desk. "It means nothing."

"It means everything," Clayton's lips twisted, greatly agitated. "When Wright discovered that my grandson fell short of his obligation, that Andrew had deceived everyone, he collapsed. He lived long enough to state his wishes. Legally, he already had it set after the last stunt Harry Lee pulled by cutting off Buchanan from Josephine. Vernon and his boys can bellow all day long...he hasn't got a leg to stand on."

"You make no sense," Cullen declared.

"Brace up and listen," Clayton said with a jeering note in his voice. "Wright left the whole of his estate to Josephine with Theodore Whitney as her guardian. Which means includes everything that was Wright's— Magnolia Bluff and all that goes with it along I suspect much of The Groves. The way Buchanan is acting it would have to be. Buchanan will use everything at his disposal to challenge the legality of the guardianship.

"If he wins, we lose most everything that has been ours for generations, but there is a simple solution. Wright stipulated his desire for Josephine to marry a Montgomery. No court will overturn Josephine's marriage to Wade."

"Over my dead body! She is to marry me...we would have already wed if not for that false telegram. You knew that it would work..."

"Do you want Josephine to be harmed?" Wade questioned coldly. "You know as well as I what Harry Lee will do to her if he gets his hands on her. Do you not understand if you marry Jo, Buchanan will challenge the legality of it? You will lose in any court within this state. There is no way you will win, not now in this turbulent atmosphere of hate toward any Yankee. The outcome would send Joe back into their hands."

"If Jo was your concern, you would never have tricked her into returning!" Cullen retorted. "What of proprieties?"

"It is at a point where proprieties be damn," Wade said crossly. "And it was not I that sent that telegram. I did not know she was returning until after Andrew came home."

Jo was lost in the debate. Her heart choked in her throat. A dreadful feeling enveloped her that she was losing Cullen. How had everything gotten so confusing?

"I don't give a damn about the will or Magnolia Bluff. We will wed and return to Philadelphia without delay," Cullen said in icy fiercely. "We are getting the hell out of here."

"It is quite the quandary, Cousin, but there is not another way."

"We will see."

An unsettling quiet descended the room. Cullen rose pulling Joe up with him. She clung tightly to his arm and began toward the door.

Wade stepped out in front of her with a hard penetrating look. "Ah, if it was only so easy as to run," he said with a sardonic grin. "You won't get escape Harry Lee on your own. The only way, to solve this, is to marry me."

"Step aside," Cullen commanded.

Wade lunged at Cullen. Dazed, Jo fell back against the wall. Wilting to the floor, she watched in horror as the two unleashed their pent-up anger. Cullen slammed his fist against Wade's jaw. Wade stumbled momentarily; then answered with a punch of his own.

She could take no more. Curling her knees into her, she hung her head down in her hands. She dared not look up. The day had become a nightmare.

"Enough! Enough! We are family."

Slowly, she raised her eyes. Andrew stood between the cousins with his hands spread.

"We are not enemies!" Andrew contended, shouting at the two. "If you want to be mad at someone, be mad at me. It does no good saying what should have happened. It will change nothing."

"Andrew is right," Clayton said. "Cullen, you want time to come up with another plan. I understand. Give it to him, Wade. Right now it will be safer to get Miss Wright out of the city. Saddle up the horses, immediately without delay. Understand eyes will be upon you. Leave for Magnolia Bluff. Leave now. Andrew and I will stay here to hold them back as long as we can."

Too stunned and weary to move, panic and confusion churned in her. Strong arms rounded her, lifting her back to her feet.

"Come with me. I will help you ready."

She clutched his arm. "Cullen. Oh, Cullen…" Tears sprang to her eyes.

He embraced her and whispered, "We will find away."

She needed to change. Clothes were brought to her, boys clothing along with a hat and boots. Clamoring in boots too large, she once more found Cullen waiting for her outside the door.

Seeing the clothes hanging loose about her, he tied a rope around her waist as a belt. Her body trembled uncontrollably. She was frightened, more frightened than she had ever been in her life, not for her life, but the thought of being ripped from her lover's arms.

He gazed into her eyes and caressed her cheek. The tears began; he wiped them off, kissing her gently.

"Promise me…promise me that you won't leave me…ever."

He breathed out deeply but said nothing. Instead, he kissed her again.

"Can you ride?"

She nodded uneasily. He took her hand, walked down the stairs out the door to the stables where Wade waited. Mounting up, she followed Wade's led with Cullen at her side.

The three rode in silence. She was exhausted, sore and emotionally drained, but she made no complaints. She had to get out of this mad town. It was as if she woke up in a nightmare. As soon as they were on the outskirts of Charleston, they broke into a gallop.

After riding for a couple of miles, Cullen motioned for Jo to slow to a trot; then a walk. Soon, Wade disappeared from view. Startled for a moment, she caught sight of Wade hiding in some overgrowth on the road side. *Was he hiding in wait?*

Cullen gestured for her to continue onward. Rounding the curve of the dusty road, a shot rang out behind them. Alarmed, she glanced back over her shoulder.

"This way, Jo," Cullen said, directing her to a clump of young saplings. "I have to go back. If we don't come back in a few minutes, ride and don't stop until you get to Magnolia Bluff." He handed her a pistol. "Use it if you have to. Understand? They can't take you."

She saw the fear his eyes held for her; heard the trepidation in his voice. He tethered back his horse, his gun in hand. "I love you, Josephine."

He reined his beast around and spurred the horse back toward Wade. Frightened beyond measure, she hadn't long to wait as horses' hooves bore down the road, fast approaching, slowing only when coming upon her.

Cullen paused only long enough to utter, "Ride."

Chapter Twelve

A canopy of Spanish moss arched high overhead served as a shield to the light rain that had begun to fall. It had been a long, tiring ride. The horses had been pushed to their limit; their sides flanked with sweat. Shadows of the day bored down upon the riders. Before long the sun would set.

The road twisted through a line of live Virginia oaks, opening up to a view of Magnolia Bluff. None seemed to notice the signs of early spring around them. Tree sprigs sprouted buds that promised the birth of another season. Soon azaleas and camellias would bloom and engulfed the grounds with rich, vibrant colors.

As Jo neared the brick residence, she saw Cullen and Wade exchange looks. She breathed easier. It was good; all was quiet.

Neither man took to the entrance but rode over the lawn to back. Jo followed. A giant black man ran out from the cookhouse, halting when he saw Wade.

"Amos, take the horses down to the stables," Wade demanded. "We are not here…do you understand?"

"Yas'm, Master Wade."

"Come back quickly and met me in the study," Wade ordered.

Jo took no notice as Cullen's arms opened to help her dismount. Unsteady, her legs wobbled when her feet touched the ground. Without hesitation, Cullen wrapped his arms under her and lifted her up. Hiding her face against his chest, she felt him carry her upstairs.

"Miss Wright needs attention. A warm bath, clothes, and food."

His voice resonated in the room. She heard feet scurrying away. Jo doubted anyone would dare defy his orders.

He sat her down on the bed. Pulling off her hat, her hair fell loose down her back. The sight she must look! Dirty…filthy from the ride, dressed in boy's clothes…a far cry from the lady, her papa, envisioned.

Oh, how I disappointed Papa! Her throat tightened with contained grief.

"Jo," Cullen said. He cradled her face in his hands. "Jo, listen to me. You are safe. Nothing is going to happen to you here. I need to talk with Wade about the situation. I want you to rest. I will be back shortly."

She heaved a tremulous sigh. "I'm scared."

"No harm will befall you, my darling."

A protest lay on her lips but was interrupted by two house girls struggling to haul a small brass tub into the room. She watched Cullen walk out the door, closing it soundly on his exit. She stared blankly at the vacant space he once stood until one of the girls announced the bath was readied.

She dismissed the girls. She had no need of assistance nor did she want any. Slowly, she dispensed with the boyish garb into an indiscreet pile on the floor and eased down into the tepid water.

Closing her eyes, she let the heat seep into her tired limbs, rising only from the tub when her fingers became water-wrinkled. Toweling herself dry, she eased the nightgown over her head and straightened it out as it clung to her wet figure. She managed to walk over to the dresser for a comb to fight the tangled mess her hair had become.

She stared at the woman in the mirror who seemed like a stranger. Suddenly the comb caught in the snarled hair. She fought it for a moment. Freeing it, she flung it across the room.

Standing, she walked back to the bed and grasped hold of the post. All the emotions she had dammed within her burst forth. Papa's dead. *Oh, my God! He's dead. I failed him! However am I going to defend myself against Harry Lee…he is after me… for my money…then he wants me dead! Worse…Cullen…they are going to take Cullen from me!*

Tears, welling in her eyes, fell unheeded as she slid down upon the floor.

Cullen found Jo slumped down clinging to the post. He lifted her, pulled back the covers, and gently placed her within the bed. Frantically, she reached for him, clutching his shirt in a tight grip. He needed nothing more than to pull her to him. He let her cry.

Sniffling, she rubbed the side of her face, wiping her eyes dry. "I'm sorry. I shouldn't be this way. I don't know…"

"Hush, my love," Cullen whispered, but the words she wanted to hear, longed to hear, needed to hear didn't come. Where were the words that everything would work out—no matter what they would be together—nothing would stand in the way of their love?

He kissed the top of her head and released her. "Give me a moment."

Sitting on the side of the bed, he kicked off his boots and pulled out his shirt from his pants. He leaned back against the headboard, drawing her into his arms. Somewhere in the night, she slept.

Jo woke several times, and Cullen held her. At times, he too slept, leaning his head against hers. At others, she would wake with him staring at her as if he was memorizing every inch of her face. She woke long enough to eat a tray of food, which had been left for them.

The door was kept open. She remembered for she woke. Cullen had slipped out into the hall. She heard Wade's voice whispering to Cullen. There were no harsh words, only mumbling she couldn't understand, but it was clear. They weren't leaving her alone.

Suddenly, Jo woke startled and bolted upward. Her heart pounded madly. She had a nightmare, a terrible nightmare. Harry Lee stood outside the house, laughing, taunting her. "Got nowhere to go, Jo. I'll find you…"

Arms tightened around her and pulled her back to his chest. "You're safe. It was only a dream."

In the meager light of wee hours of a new day, she looked so incredibly lovely. Her dark hair hung loose and ran down the curved ripeness of her body; her large telling eyes beckoned to him.

He never thought he would be holding her like this thinking about losing her. The threat was real. For so long he had lived with his life holding to what was right…he didn't want to be right at this moment.

She needed him; he wanted her. It had taken all his strength not to take her as he desired. He didn't want to be strong any longer and deny what was his. He shouldn't, not knowing what the future held.

He resisted no longer. He eased off the bed and crept to the door. Slowly, he closed it and turned the lock. Pausing, his eyes fell back on the beautiful lady. She understood. Reaching down to the hem of her nightgown, she pulled it over her head.

He crawled back in under the covers. He kissed her, gently at first and then as she began to respond to him, his kisses became more passionate. Forgetting everything else, their bodies melted together, enraptured, reaching into their very souls to fulfill the burning desire they held for each other.

In the stillness of the early morning, he held her tight. Both sensed the urgency of their need; neither wanted to let go of the other.

"Tell me, Cullen," she whispered. "Say the words that will ease my worries."

Emotions tore at her heart, overcome with love for the man who held her. Overwhelmed with the sensation she was about to have her heart ripped apart.

"If you are asking if I will fight for us…as long as I breathe."

His ragged whisper echoed in her heart, but his words held pain…pain she felt also.

He slipped out of bed and put back on his pants; his shirt he pulled through the arms lay unbuttoned. He grabbed her gown and handed it to her.

There was no need to tell her that he had to leave her before they were discovered in such an embrace. There was no need to tell her that once he stepped out of the room, the world would enter, a world that had spiraled out of control.

He leaned over and kissed her. Lingering on her lips, he whispered, "Know you are loved."

* * * *

Listlessly, Jo readied for the day. She had been brought a wardrobe, and the girl helped her with her hair to make it look presentable. But Jo found she had no energy, wanting nothing more than to hide in the corner.

From her window, she watched activity swirl around the plantation. Men arrived. Most she did not know, but they were all armed which frightened her. In despair, she sagged back to the bed.

Then, she straightened fearfully as the door creaked opened. Apprehension faded upon recognition of her guest. She ran into the open arms and burst into tears.

"Now, now, sweetcums, your mammy is here," Miss Hazel said, choking on her tears. "I'm here."

"Take comfort he went peacefully." Miss Hazel held Jo as if she would have a child with Jo's head leaning against her bosom. She went on, "Nothin' nobody could have done. Mr. Whitney. He took your papa to his final resting place. Took him home."

"Mr. Whitney?" Jo sniffled. "I don't understand."

250

"I told Mr. Wright to tell ya. I did, but Hon, you don't need to hear it today. Mr. Whitney owed the Wrights a favor. He made a vow and kept it. He did. In time, Mr. Whitney can tell ya the story."

Silence ensued. The old woman sighed, patting Jo's back. "Master Wade came himself to get me. He cares for you."

Jo stiffened and drew back. "He cares about Magnolia Bluff. It is his love. I am only the string that ties it back to him."

"It is not what I remember."

"A lifetime ago," Jo said laboriously and eyed Miss Hazel confused. "Don't dawdle if you have something you want to say. I've had enough of riddles, but I will say I am surprised Wade sent you to be his ambassador."

"Child, he ain't using me for nothin', except seeing to your needs," Miss Hazel chided Jo. "I saw ya with him before this whole mess exploded. I saw how you two looked at each other."

"Before or after he married Clarissa," Jo shot back quite out of temper. "He chose Magnolia Bluff over me then as now."

"And what did ya do when ya agreed to marry Master Andrew? I wonder how that was different. You left your Yankee."

Stunned, Jo noted the disapproval in Miss Hazel's face. Instinctively, she distanced herself from her mammy. "I don't know what you believe I should have done differently. I tried...tried to please Papa. I..."

"Hush, Hon, don't rile yourself up. Ya no more wanted to marry that man than him you. It's what I'm trying to say. Ya and Master Wade are cut from the same cloth."

"Don't you do this to me...not you! I feel like I have been a pawn in a game of chess being moved back and forth in one strategic move after another. No more! I'm going back to Philadelphia with Cullen."

"Ya think it's as easy as that. It always seems that way, but it ain't. Never is. Look at my Heyward. He thought all he needed was to be free," Miss Hazel said in a rather brittle tone.

Jo had no need to ask if Miss Hazel had been informed about the attempting kidnapping of Gillie. It was apparent Heyward had been in correspondence.

"Shouldn't it have been? All, they wanted, was a chance to live their lives the way they wanted...it wasn't fair for them to have had to leave everything they dreamed about. The law didn't protect them even though they had papers," Jo rambled, shaking her head in confusion. "I didn't understand. Heyward was so angry when he saw me in Philadelphia...so angry."

"It ain't you, it's the world. He got no control. He feels he's still in chains."

She studied her mammy with the sudden realization that perhaps Miss Hazel too felt the chains. Oh, good lord, what if Miss Hazel didn't truly return her love? She gazed down at her hands with a sudden sickening feeling.

"Now don't ya go questioning me, little lady," Miss Hazel gently reproved her. "I know ya better than ya know yourself. I ain't going nowhere. This is my home. It's in my blood as much as any white man. Home calls to ya no matter where ya at."

"This whole thing has gotten out of hand, Miss Hazel. I want you to come with me when I leave. Maybe not when Cullen sneaks me out of South Carolina. But I will send for you. I'll find Gillie and Heyward and…"

"Child, you are living in a dream world like Heyward. Ain't going to happen. I know ya not going to go against your papa's wishes. It was always Master Wade he wanted you to marry."

"Papa told you this?"

"Yas'um, he did, Hon," she said bluntly. "And I listened while others talked him. I heard Master Wade promise your papa he would look after you despite losing this place."

Jo stared at Miss Hazel in astonishment. "Wade said that? He would take me as his wife even losing everything?"

"He did. Heard him myself trying to calm Mr. Brantley after reading that letter. Never thought he would survive the night, but Master Wade sat by his bedside until Mr. Whitney arrived."

"Letter?"

"The letter that woman sent…the one that Master Andrew married," Miss Hazel said in a harsh voice. "She devil, she is if there was ever one. She wanted your Papa to know that ya would never marry a Montgomery and she was going to see that all of Philadelphia knew what kind of hussy ya were and Charleston as well."

"No…no, she couldn't have," Jo uttered in disbelief. Why ever would Kathleen have done so? Why would she have been so malicious? It made no sense. Jo didn't even know the lady.

"Ask Master Wade," Miss Hazel said, slightly miffed that Jo would question her. "I heard, too, Mr. Brantley telling Master Wade there was no stipulation in his will that kept you from inheriting his whole estate. Where would have Master Wade have gotten that idea?"

Kathleen forgotten for a moment, Jo, herself a trifle insulted at Miss Hazel's insinuation, said, "This conversation is going nowhere. None of it matters. I'm marrying Cullen. We have already done so if not for what we thought was Papa's telegram…it was a trick, a mean bitter trick. But it won't stop me, not this time not after…"

Miss Hazel stared at her. She saw. She knew. She cried, "Oh, Lordy child what have you gone and done?"

Horrified she had been so foolish as to let down her guard, Jo heaved a long sigh, "I love him, Miss Hazel."

"Hush your mouth and never mention say it again," Miss Hazel shook her head ominously. "Poor child, I tell you it will make matters worse."

Jo scowled, started to speak again and then caught herself. It would do no good. Miss Hazel didn't understand. She wasn't going to marry Wade. She couldn't. She had done her due with her responsibility to Papa.

Andrew had been the one to betray her. Wade had let her leave Charleston. Cullen, who she had rejected because of her duty, had saved her—loved her. She would not forsake him again.

Chapter Thirteen

The sun had burnt away the mist as another day had dawned. With all the tension and quarreling that had taken place, they were no closer to a remedy. Cullen was at wit's end trying to come to some rational conclusion to this horrendous state of affairs.

Last night, Clayton Montgomery arrived with the reverend at his side. It enflamed Cullen with rage. In his arrogance, his grandfather assumed that Jo would simply accept the fate he had laid out for her. Clayton cared nothing about her, only what she could give him—Magnolia Bluff.

Cullen sensed that Clayton Montgomery felt he had regained full control of his precious estate, no matter the cost to Cullen, his own grandson he had sorely used. Clayton's confidence lay with the comprehension of Josephine's character and the supposition that Josephine would never allow others to suffer for a selfish need on her part, being with Cullen.

Moreover, Cullen realized that Clayton thought he knew his grandson, that Cullen would back off for the good of the family. If he married Jo and smuggled her up North, they would leave his family to deal with the perplexity of the consequences. It would not only be Jo that would be unable to live with that decision.

His grandfather did not know him as well as he thought. Cullen would have no issue taking Jo away from this madness! He had no intention of leaving her behind.

But there was one thing that kept from him from taking Jo immediately away from here. Cullen realized his grandfather had not exaggerated that there was no court in South Carolina that would rule in a favor of a Yankee, not in this atmosphere of secession. And he would never allow Jo to go back to the Groves, to Harry Lee, no matter the personal cost to himself.

There had to be another way. Perhaps if he got a court in Philadelphia to rule on her guardianship? He needed to talk to his father…he needed time.

There had to be another way…

Walking out the back door, Cullen caught sight of Wade coming up the path that led to the riverbank. It did not take much to surmise his cousin had come from the pier. Cullen concluded aid was coming in from Charleston by the waterway.

Frowning, his grave look betrayed his frustration. Other arrangements he had not been party too since his grandfather had made his appearance.

The morning had found the plantation crawling with activity. Neighbors and friends had rallied on the call from Clayton to protect his home. Sides had been drawn. Men, Cullen had not seen for years, had come armed and prepared to fight.

His cousin headed toward the stables where the men had gathered. Crossing through the dormant garden, Cullen gestured for him to stop.

"Wade, a moment."

Wade paused and looked back at Cullen, obviously on edge. "I'm not sure we have anything to talk about."

"I believe we have everything to talk about," Cullen stepped in front of him and blocked his path. "I want to sneak Jo away. I need your help."

"Help take Jo away?" Wade scoffed. "Into the hands of Harry Lee? I think not. Look around you. You see everyone that has gathered to help us. The Buchanans have done the same."

Wade pointed to a tall man, wearing a long, broad coat and cocked hat, leading a cavalry unit. Cullen recognized him from his youth, Ambrose Reynolds.

"You have called in the militia?"

"Had no choice. The Buchanans have McCoy in their back pocket. Grandfather petitioned Governor Gist. We have sent word to Whitney to return to take his place as Jo's guardian, but it won't solve the issue at hand, not with old man Buchanan challenging guardianship. It would go to the courts, and there is a chance that the courts would overrule the will with Buchanan being her grandfather.

"Grandfather presented our case. The governor agreed and has sided with us. He sent the unit to uphold the law, but they won't act until it is deemed legal."

"What does that mean?" Cullen snapped.

255

"It means that Jo has to marry me," Wade said sharply. "It is the only clear cut way to halt any legal proceedings from the Buchanans."

Cullen glowered at Wade, stunned by his animosity toward him. "How can you ask her to do so after all you have put her through? What Andrew has put her through? Let me take her. What kind of life can you offer her after tricking her to come down here to begin with? You placed her endanger. She…we trusted you."

"It was not I!" Wade replied furiously. "I did not even know she was returning. I was preparing to go North myself. I would never do her harm. I know what she faces, but this is the only way."

"The same as becoming engaged to Andrew was the only way. The same as lying to her while he married another."

"Do you not know I see my brother's failings? That I suspected, something was amiss. I let her go because of proprieties, because I understood what was driving her. Duty and loyalty. I would not have ever phantom such a deception from Andrew. If I had, I would have never let her go. Now, I will have to live with that decision. What could have happened…"

His words faded; his anger dissipated. But not Cullen's.

"Wade, do you not remember the day you asked me for help with your dilemma concerning Jo? You choose *Clarissa*. I gave you that help. I ask you now to help me in mine. You say you are not responsible for calling her home…prove it.

"Help me get her back to North. I will fix this. I will take care of the legality. I will not see the ruin of my family…we are family…you and I…you are my brother!"

Wade stared at him. Cullen saw the conflict in his eyes, the sadness, the pain. The tie, that bound them together, was strained; stretched to a breaking point.

Nothing was said for an endless moment. At last, Wade spoke, his voice low and deep with emotion. "I love Josephine, Cullen. You may feel I have no right, but I do. I won't allow harm to come to her. If Harry Lee gets hold of her…"

"He won't," Cullen swore, grasping onto the resignation he heard in his cousin's voice. "We will take care of the legality of the will. I will not allow anything to happen to Magnolia Bluff. I will ensure Jo's happiness."

Wade stood in the stillness that developed. He drew in a deep breath. "It won't be easy."

Relief flooded Cullen. He clasped Wade's shoulder tightly in exhilaration, but Wade was staring past him. He saw his cousin's expression alter; he turned.

Stunned, he watched a black man burst out of the tree line. Stumbling forward, he scrambled to his feet and ran. He fell as he reached the lawn. Cullen rushed forward with Wade by his side. The scruffy faced Negro pushed on his arms and tried to stand.

Cullen reached down to help the man up. He had a swollen right eye; his lips puffy, and he had burnt welts up and down his extremities. Staring at him, recognition suffused through Cullen. Good Lord! It was Heyward.

"Mr. Cullen," Heyward gulped for air. "Save her…save her."

"Who?" Cullen asked, exchanging unbelieving looks with Wade. "Who?"

"Gillie. Harry Lee…he has Gillie. He's going to kill her."

* * * *

Cullen bent down and took Heyward's arm over his shoulder. Allowing the injured man to lean against him, Heyward sucked in deep breaths. His eyes blazed with fire. He pushed against Cullen with shaking hands and stood weakly on his own.

Tears welled in the proud man as words seemed to choke in his throat. "I have a message for you," he looked at Cullen. "And Master Wade. He knew…he knew."

"Knew what?" Cullen asked. Confusion weighed upon him while he stared at the tortured man. A million thoughts ran rampant through his head. "Harry Lee knew what?"

Heyward swallowed hard. "He had us hunt'd down. That monster, Earl Mann, the slave catcher kidnaped us. He sprung a trap when we got to Elmira. Must have discovered we were to travel through the town and bribed neighbors to betray our guides. We spent the night in an old barn. They came while we slept. Hadn't a chance."

Wade had signaled to his man Saul. The black man came running with a ladle filled with water. Heyward rapidly gulped down the offered relief.

Looking up over the dipper, Heyward went on, "He took me and Gillie back to Philadelphia…to the docks…Harry Lee and Buck met us…they beat the shit out of me and took Gillie from me…"

His voice faded off. There was no need for more words. Heyward rubbed his forehead, pained in his thoughts.

"He tole me..to go to Ma's. Wanted Ma to get Miss Jo to…come to him," Heyward said in a broken voice. "She wasn't there."

"No, Miss Hazel is here with Miss Jo," Wade answered him solemnly. "You understand we aren't going to let Miss Jo go anywhere."

"I figured as much…I wouldn't let Miss Jo go myself…He's the devil…he is, but I need help, Master Wade. Help to go get my Gillie." Heyward searched both men's eyes. "I heard 'em talking…Mr. Wright he is dead?"

"Yes, he passed away while Miss Jo was in Philadelphia," Wade concurred.

"But…the wedding with Dr. Montgomery did not happen…he was already married?"

"Yes, Heyward. It is why Miss Jo returned."

Heyward reached across and gripped Wade's hand. "The one…Buck laughed about it. Said it worked…to make Wright so mad…so angry…that it he would go ove' the edge an' die. That's what they said…"

"Go on," Cullen encouraged. "What of his plans?"

"Harry Lee hear' there is a reverend here. The man's gone plum crazy," Heyward uttered in a low cry. "He sent me here with a warning. He wants Miss Jo in his hands before night fall or…or he will kill Gillie. Dear Lord, he said he was going to stake her head for everyone to see."

* * * *

"You can't go. It's what he wants."

Cullen rubbed his palm over his mouth and took a deep breath. Both had listened to the horrid tale Heyward had recited of how Harry Lee had hunted down the couple like animals, kidnaped and brought them back to Charleston as criminals.

"I'm going to kill him," Cullen struggled to maintain his composure. "It is the only way to truly end this. He is not going to stop until he is dead. You can come with me or not, Wade. I'm not debating the issue. There is no time. I need men…"

"Who, Cullen, are you planning on recruiting? Who out there is going to save a black woman, who most will say is his slave, from a white man?"

"It is not the only thing that bothers me. He planned this, Wade. Don't you understand? He knew of the letter, which means he had a hand in sending it."

"Perhaps," Wade acknowledged. "But it was addressed from your house."

"But sent by Andrew's wife, Kathleen."

"Hellfire, who has Andrew married?" Wade exploded. "Do not tell me that she is mixed up with Harry Lee?"

All eyes fell on Heyward, who shook his head. "I hear' nothing about a woman."

"True, I could not see how she could be," Cullen acknowledged. "How would she know of Harry Lee? But the woman is not to my liking. I do not trust her and fear what she is capable of. I have no doubt she manipulated Andrew and that she meant Jo harm by humiliating her at the farce of a wedding."

"To write such a letter as to try to provoke Wright's death would imply she had knowledge of his health, which could have easily come from Andrew lamenting on the mess he had gotten himself into," Wade deduced. "But to what end?"

"Kathleen is a vindictive woman, but she is also ambitious. What would she gain by Wright's death? It makes no sense,"

"Then possibly she had nothing directly to do with it. Harry Lee could have bribed a servant to tell the actions of those within the house, and he used the information for his benefit," Wade thought out loud. "Harry Lee may have intercepted the letter or sent his own. I would not put anything above Harry Lee at the moment. I remember how he fueled Clarissa against Jo."

"It is nothing we can prove. Besides, we have more immediate concerns. It doesn't matter at the moment what he has done, but what he has planned," Cullen snapped with a sudden impatience. "Hell, Wade, you know why he's doing this! He wants to flush Jo out...he's not going to stop by only sending Heyward to us. He is sending us a clear message. If he can't have Jo, no one will."

"Don't you think I know that he is desperate?" Wade's expression hardened. "I see only one recourse—for you to let go of Jo. Give me the power to end this for good."

Cullen fought back his rage. Never would he would tell Jo to marry another...She was his...his life. Neither would he sit idly by and let Gillie die.

"I'm going with or without you," Cullen declared. "I will make Harry Lee rue this day."

"If you leave now, it will be without me," Wade said firmly. "I refuse to ride into an ambush. You must be aware he will be prepared. We must be also."

"We haven't time," Cullen asserted, ignoring Wade's assertion. His instincts told him to react swiftly.

Heyward straightened himself and winced with his pain. "Take me, Mr. Cullen. Not going leave without me." Gripping for Cullen's shoulder for balance, he continued, "I know others that will help if we got nobody else. Iggy and Woody."

"If you must go now, take Saul also. He is a sure aim," Wade offered. "I will follow as soon as I can."

Cullen watched Wade depart and head straight toward the house. He comprehended Wade's course of action as well as he understood his own. He turned to Heyward. "Prepare. There is no time to waste."

* * * *

Restless, Josephine rose and strolled over to the window. She had already stuck herself three times with the needle while trying to embroider. Miss Hazel suggested it to keep her mind busy, but it was useless to try to divert her attention. What she needed was to get away from Miss Hazel's accusing eyes.

Her mammy had not left her side since she arrived two days ago for more reasons than one. She had not allowed Jo to be alone with Cullen, much less talk with him. *Well, I will just ignore her. I refuse to be bullied. And if she says one more word commending Wade's virtues I will scream!*

Outside, there was a scuttle of activity…activities that put her in a state of nerves. She could not very well overlook the seriousness of her circumstance, not with armed men patrolling the lawn. Oh, she wanted to ignore them all except Cullen, but it was an impossibility!

Even her conscience aggravated her, gnawing at her soul. Why…why could she not dismiss her papa's wishes? Had she not tried to fulfill his request? It was not her fault that Andrew had betrayed her. Should that not relieve her of her obligation?

Her heart ached. Her life had become a hopelessly tangled mess. She wanted Cullen, needed him as much as she needed the air to breathe. But then if she truly loved him how could she ask him risk everything for her…to turn his back upon his family? Irrational in her thoughts, she wanted him to; she wanted to return with him to Philadelphia. She wanted a miracle and time, precious time, was running out.

Sounds of hard footsteps pounded along the marble corridor disturbed her peace. Turning, she saw her guard, Amos, stand in the doorway, then step aside. Wade stormed into the room and immediately, his eyes fixed on her. Serious and intense, he wore no smile.

She read his intent and wanted nothing to do with it. Lowering her gaze, she walked slowly back over to the sofa and perched herself in a ladylike poise. Prepared to do battle, she returned his glare.

"You have something on your mind?"

"What in the devil is wrong with you?" His eyebrow raised; he pressed, "What else has to happen before you understand the magnitude of your refusal? How many will die?"

"Die? Surely you jest!"

"Die!" he cried. "Cullen told me to stand back. Let you decide, but you haven't made a move. Make no mistake—your hesitation will cost lives. What do you think is happening outside? Everyone we know has been called upon to defend you…to keep you out of the clutches of Harry Lee. It could be so easily solved."

"What? Marry you? You forget yourself," she said curtly. "You asked before, then married another. Then I was forced into an engagement to your brother. I held up my end of the arrangement. I am not the one who didn't hold to the commitment. I was set up to be humiliated and scorned. I didn't ask for this! I don't want this upon me!"

"No, but it is yours to own," he knelt down and faced her. "Josephine, don't look away. You know as well as I what you will do. Delaying will only cost lives. Why is it so hard? I thought at one time you wanted to be my wife."

"Do you have to ask? Do you want me to say the words?"

"No." His voice softened. He took her shaking hands into his. "You need to realize something has happened."

"Happened?" she murmured. She saw something in his eyes. Frightened, she swallowed back her tears. "I want to talk to Cullen."

"He is gone."

A crashing silence ensued. Suddenly, Jo realized they had been joined in the room. She glanced around. All eyes lay upon her. Miss Hazel. Amos. Clayton Montgomery. Men she didn't know, uniformed men. *Why was everyone in here?* Her emotional dam collapsed. She could stand it no longer. She had to get away from their stares.

She tried to rise, but Wade halted her.

"It is bad, Jo. Harry Lee kidnaped Heyward and Gillie when they tried to escape Philadelphia and brought them back to Charleston. He released Heyward to send us a message. He wanted you to exchange yourself for Gillie."

"I have to go. I have to save Gillie!"

"You are not going anywhere," Wade stated firmly. "Cullen and Heyward are attempting to rescue Gillie as we speak. Not only will the law consider Cullen a fugitive if he attempts this as it stands now, he is walking into a trap. I know it. He knows it. Blood will be spilled."

"Help him, Wade. Oh, God, help him," she pleaded.

"I intend to, Josephine. There is a militia unit waiting."

261

"Waiting?"

"There is no more time to debate the issue. The will needs to be upheld."

Chapter Fourteen

Harry Lee had Gillie held up at the Davis farm, consisting mainly of an old abandoned house. Two miles beyond Goose Creek. A dangerous place to strike for the small group for several reasons. It sat on a small, cleared hill, giving it clear visibility to any uninvited visitors.

Cullen had been well aware of what the penalty would be for his attempt to free Gillie if caught when he rode off with Heyward and the others. The law would not be on his side.

Arming slaves and allowing them to attack white man would lead only to one conclusion, unless Cullen considered Gillie property. Then the southern law changed. That, though, would not be a consideration, not given the fight for Wright's estate, despite the fact that Gillie had been freed. Cullen allowed his conscience to rule his decision, much as he supposed his father had becoming a part of the Underground Railroad.

As well as he could figure, Heyward reckoned Harry Lee had ten to twelve armed cohorts. The farm itself sat straddle to The Groves, which held the threat of reinforcements. There would be no element of surprise. More or less a suicide mission for the four men.

Cullen had no doubt of the heart of the men he rode beside. It was their ability to fight which he held misgivings. Heyward was a man possessed by hatred that in itself posed a problem. Cullen needed Heyward to focus on the task.

At Moure's Corner, Cullen reined in his mount. It was as far as they would ride. Overhead, the sun bore down on him. Sweat from the tension as much as the heat poured from his being.

He figured it had to be one or a little after. There would be no cover of darkness or the time to wait for it.

Iggy tapped his shoulder. Glancing to his right, Cullen saw what had drawn attention. Behind the tree line, a man sat hat down over his face, legs propped up. The lookout had fallen asleep. Thankful for a small stroke of luck, Cullen crept up quietly behind the man.

It did not take long to subdue the man without calling attention to their actions. Gagging the guard, they left him tied up to a tree.

The house sat half a mile up the road. He could see it from his view on the edge of the bend. It did little for his confidence. They could go no further without some semblance of a plan.

Staring at the farm house, it wasn't large. Three…four rooms at the most with a barn a hundred yards to the right. The house had an unobstructed view.

Placing his hand up, he couldn't permit Heyward to react haphazardly. "Just a minute," he said. "Heyward, you need to understand that our odds aren't good. We are outnumbered and outgunned. I see only one plan that might work."

"Tell me, Mr. Cullen. I'll do it."

A loud excruciating scream resounded a female screech. A wild expression crossed Heyward's face. He prepared to rush toward the house. Cullen pushed him back.

"I swear I will tie you up, and you can keep that fellow down the road company," Cullen threatened. "You will certainly get yourself and Gillie killed if you run in blindly."

"I can't stand here…"

"You're not. We are going to get her. Trust me."

The big black man's eyes watered. Cullen reached over and clasped Heyward's shoulder. "I will make him pay."

Cullen glanced around. Damn, he saw no dust on the road behind him, no riders coming to help in the rescue. Wade hadn't changed his mind, steadfastly refusing to make a move until he could legally.

It was too late to consider he had reacted irrationally in this attempt. Cullen motioned for the other men to huddle.

"I see no other choice but to cause a diversion. We will get only one chance."

An hour had passed. Piercing screams ripped through Cullen. He was sickened by the sounds and drunken laughter.

He checked his guns one last time. Taking a deep breath, he waited for the signal. Where were they? They had enough time to circle around and come in from the back of the house.

It came. A billowing smoke emerged behind the house. The moment had come. He kneed his mount and rode toward the front porch with his revolver over his head and fired.

At the sound of the shot, Cullen heard a commotion within the house. Men rushed out, including Buck followed by Harry Lee. All eyes and guns trained on Cullen.

"Well, well, well, what have we here?" Harry Lee shoveled his way forward. His grin widened. "Where is your cousin?"

"Just me," Cullen replied stiffly. "I want you to release Gillie."

"And why would I do that?"

"You want me to recite the law to you," Cullen taunted. "She is a free woman."

"Not according to our law here, Yank," Harry Lee scoffed. "She's mine now. Wright's dead. Grandpa Henry gave her to me being that all that is Josephine's is ours. If Jo wants her free, she needs to come here herself and tell me. I'll listen to her."

"How stupid do you think we are, Harry Lee? How stupid do you suppose Wright was? After all he did, he would make the mistake of giving Buchanan Jo's guardianship."

"Its you that ain't that bright," Harry Lee replied and nodded to two men to his side. "Bring him in. McCoy can explain to him how that last will won't be upheld…"

A shot rang out.

From the back, Heyward and his friends attacked. The plan had been set in motion. Carrying torches and revolvers, Iggy and Woody would move in first while Heyward went for Gillie and Saul covered their escape. If everything held to the plan, in and out swiftly.

"Fucking nigger!" "Get 'um." Another shot and another. "Shoot the nigger, damn it!"

Cullen watched as the house was torched. Ablaze, panic set in. Shots whizzed by his head. He slid off his roan and fired backed, fired until he had no more bullets. His horse bellowed and stumbled backward, hit numerous times, and fell dead pinning him down.

Looking up, a gun pointed straight to his head.

"You want me to finish him off, Harry Lee."

Somewhere in the midst of smoke and confusion, he heard Harry Lee growled, "I have something better planned for him."

He felt arms pulled him from under his horse and instantly felt something hard hit him from behind into darkness.

* * * *

Jo had read Shakespeare's tragedies. For the life of her, she never comprehended how everything ended in heartbreak. She reasoned that it could have been avoided. If only Hamlet had reacted quickly and decisively; if only Romeo and Juliet had been more patient...if... if only... Today she understood.

She concluded that everyone has a tragic flaw—a force that drives one's life. Within their life, a choice, a decision would be made; a life changing decision where there would be no turning back. She had made her decision. She loved Cullen; nothing else mattered except that he lived.

Standing now in the middle of the drawing room, the Reverend Stanley Ripley recited the wedding vows. She repeated them in a low, firm voice. It all seemed so surreal.

There would be no reception; no flowers; no friends and family. The couple stood in the middle of witnesses. Some Jo loved; others she hadn't the foggiest idea who they were.

Clayton Montgomery sat with an expression of satisfaction. He had expected the outcome. Had he not brought the good reverend with him when he rode out to the plantation the night before? Everything had been set for the wedding; given only the façade that she had a choice.

"You are now husband and wife."

After the pronouncement, Wade leaned over and kissed her cheek. She whispered, "Save them."

"I will."

She caught his hand. "I'm going with you."

"Don't be a fool. It's not safe..."

"You got your way, Wade," she said, maintaining her composure with great effort. "I'm going whether I go with you now or behind you after you depart."

A compromise of sorts had been made according to Wade as he dragged her toward the stairs. He would go; she would stay. She cried out; he picked her up like a sack of potatoes and carried her into the bedroom. She hit his back over and over with her fist until he put her down within the bedroom.

"Wade, don't do this!"

He gave her no answer but locked the door upon his exit.

"Amos, stay in front of this door. Do not move!" His voice carried soundly through the wooden entrance. "I swear it will be your hide if you let her leave this room."

Jo tore over to the window. She watched Wade mount up. True to their word, the unit of South Carolina's finest Calvary Division followed behind him.

Her vision blurred. A frightened feeling overwhelmed her. Thoughts rambled quickly through her mind. *Will I ever see Cullen again...Gillie? I didn't even get to say goodbye to Cullen! Will Wade get there in time?*

Watching until they faded from view, she collapsed onto the floor and prayed.

* * * *

Startled, Cullen woke on the ground drenched in water. Another bucket of water thrown choked him as he swallowed half of it. Pushing upward in a daze, a form emerged in his view. Harry Lee.

A humorless smile looked down on him; behind the culprit, flames engulfed the house. Smoke billowed around him; panicky voices resonated. From the chaos ensuing and Harry Lee's expression, Cullen surmised Heyward had been successful.

"Wake up, you fucking Yankee!" Harry Lee kicked him. "Get up. I want you to know you're going to die."

"What's wrong? Things not going like you planned," Cullen sneered. "Let a few Negros get the best of you."

Harry Lee kicked him again. "Shut up, you smart ass Yank. You won't be saying much soon enough!"

"It's funny. Ain't it, Harry Lee. He thinks he saved that bitch," Buck uttered a wicked laugh. "He wouldn't think that if he saw what we did to her."

"Get him up and let's be done with it. I don't want to see any more of them Montgomerys riding in on this mess."

"Just do your damn job, McCoy," Harry Lee barked. "Get him strung up. We'll leave him dangling to greet 'em if they make an appearance. If they don't, let the birds peck his eyes out."

Cullen felt hands gripped his shoulders and dragged him to his feet. Looking around, he stared down at Lucas McCoy. He jerked back away from him, only to be restrained from behind by two more of Harry Lee's men.

"In a hurry?" Cullen taunted. "Scared yellow-belly!"

A punch into his stomach doubled over Cullen. He gasped for breath. "Killing me not going do you any good. Grandfather got a court order to uphold Wright's last will. It's over. You lost!"

McCoy stepped in-between Harry Lee and Cullen. "What do you mean?"

"Exactly what I said. Grandfather got the governor to have a special hearing called. It is done. Whitney is Josephine's guardian. You Buchanans were cut off," Cullen expunged his knowledge. "You say this is all legal, but you will have to answer for this. You're stupider than a wild hog tying your coattail to this crazy bastard."

Harry Lee rushed him again. This time Cullen pivoted, taking his guards by surprise. Breaking their hold, he leaped out of the way as Harry Lee crashed into the bungling idiots. Stumbling back, he felt the heat of the smoldering building; saw his roan lay where it fell.

Buck pulled out his pistol from his waist and fired straight at him. Cursing, he dove behind his dead horse. He was surrounded and unarmed. He hadn't a shot out of hell of getting out of this alive. *I'll be damn if I go down without a fight.*

He glanced over the belly of his mount. Harry Lee grunted and straightened himself out to full height. Pushing his brother to the left, he gestured for the others to go right.

Driven by the instinct to survive, he leaped over the legs of the dead animal and lunged toward Harry Lee. He caught Harry Lee by the arm, spun him around in a choke hold, using him as a shield. Suddenly, behind his head, Cullen heard the distinct click of a cocked gun.

"Let him go, Smythe."

"String him up!" Harry Lee squeezed out the words through Cullen's chokehold. "Hang the son of a bitch!"

McCoy sidestepped over in front of Cullen, keeping a steady aim. It was then Cullen saw the makeshift gallows. Hanging from one of the higher limbs of the Virginia Live Oak, a noose dangled in front of him.

Cullen eyed McCoy with a raging fury. He had to act quickly. With a firm, strong thrust, Cullen slung Harry Lee directly at McCoy and gripped McCoy's arm. Wrestling for the gun, it fell, loose, on the ground.

A shot rang out hitting the ground beside the revolver, then another.

"God Damn it, Buck, don't shot blindly you'll hit me."

"Ain't me. They're here. The militia!"

With great reluctance but understanding he had no choice, McCoy recoiled back. Harry Lee's men took off, running for the barn and the horses.

McCoy shook his head at Cullen. "Not going to make any difference. They'll let Harry Lee have his quick justice for what you've done..."

Another shot fired at McCoy's foot. Cullen glanced over to see Wade ease his revolver down. It answered McCoy's question.

Not for Harry Lee, he snarled, "This ain't over, Yank."

Stumbling back, Harry Lee reached behind his back and withdrew a Bowie knife from its sheath. Slashing wildly, he surged at Cullen.

Maneuvering out of arm's length, Cullen retreated a few steps, trying to regain his footing. He couldn't form a clear thought, his mind muddled from exhaustion and pain. The glitter from the sun blinded him for a moment. Harry Lee stabbed, sinking into Cullen's left arm.

Cullen groaned in pain, reacted spontaneously. He gripped Harry Lee's lower arm blocking another thrust. Pulling back on his grip, Harry Lee scrapped across Cullen's bare palm.

Blood oozed down his wrist dropping unheeded on the ground. Frantically, Cullen pushed back. Harry Lee stumbled backward; his eyes widened with crazed madness. He slashed the knife violently in the air, possess with the intent to kill.

Cullen attacked and caught Harry Lee's arm in a cross hold. Using his remaining strength, Cullen pushed Harry Lee back. Stumbling, Cullen maneuvered himself in position. Taking hold of Harry Lee's grip on his knife, Cullen forced the knife down, back into Harry Lee stomach, thrusting harder and harder until Harry Lee collapsed.

The wounded man's eyes glazed over. Peering up at Cullen, his lips moved but no sound came. He gripped his side as blood oozed between his fingers. Silent, he fell forward.

Harry Lee lay motionless on the ground when the militia rode up to the burnt out house. Cullen sank down to his knees, holding his injured arm. He stared up at Wade as he rode up beside him. A spasm of sickness assaulted him. He comprehended clearly the only reason the militia had come to his rescue.

* * * *

The full moon reflected off low-hanging clouds, giving off a silvery halo in the night's sky. Eerie shadows lengthened over the laborious flow of the Ashley River. Cullen heaved a long sigh as he waited.

They had retreated back to the Bogart Farm, an old family friend. Old man Bogart had lived on his small plot of land for the last sixty years, much to the generosity of Clayton Montgomery. Cullen's grandfather had helped the man more than once save his farm. Now, Bogart was called on to return a favor.

The farm was situated down below Magnolia Bluff, along the river. The small group sought sanctuary in his barn. Moreover, the farm had its own dock which made it easier to travel by river down to Charleston. It had been deemed the best course of action to have Heyward, Gillie and Cullen leave at the soonest possible time.

Sheriff McCoy had not been wrong in his assumption that the good people of the low country wouldn't take too kindly to Cullen's actions—saving a black woman with the use of Negros...armed Negros.

Clayton Montgomery had ridden out to tell Cullen himself that his grandson needed to depart for Philadelphia hastily...and to say good-bye.

It was too hard to take...this ending. A bitter gall to swallow.

"The boat should return within the hour."

Turning, it was Andrew.

"Let me at your arm," Andrew said. "Blood has seeped through your bandage. Come back up to the barn. I'll dress it again."

Cullen shook his head. "You can see to it when we get to Charleston."

"You look like hell."

"It's how I feel," Cullen acknowledged. "Is Gillie well enough to move?"

"Don't have much choice," Andrew's face contorted in disgust. "We don't want to be anywhere near here if Harry Lee dies. The story will be twisted so that we'll have half the low country after us. Won't matter, he's crazy as they come.

"If anyone could see what he did to that sweet little thing, they probably run him through themselves. Time will tell if I can save her life, but what he, they did to her, will be hard to ever get over. She won't look at me or Heyward. Her gaze is unfocused. I'm not sure if she knows she is in the world. She shrieks at anyone's touch and recoils back into a ball. He mutilated her face, her body. The pain she endured, what she is in now, is unbearable."

"But that's not what they will hear."

"I know what will be said," Cullen said abruptly. He had no desire to hear it again. "Have we heard anything from Buchanan?"

"Wade should be back before we depart. He will know more."

Cullen buried his head in his hands and paused for a moment of deep reflection. His eyes closed; he saw her face. Those eyes...Oh, damnit...those eyes. How was he ever going to walk away? But honor dictated he would do exactly that—walk away. Hell, he had a pounding headache.

"Andrew, can leave us alone for a time. Cullen and I need to talk."

Looking over his shoulder, Cullen watched Wade stroll up to his side. Andrew hesitated and then complied. Silence ensued for an endless moment.

Finally, Wade spoke, "Harry Lee is clinging to life. It is best for you not to be here whatever the outcome. The matter will be handled. Trust me."

"He deserves to die," Cullen snapped. His tone reflected his testy mood. "If he lives, Jo…"

"I told you I already have the situation in control. I will protect Jo. This vendetta will end…today. I now have the law behind me. A plan has already been put in motion to have the feud cease, or the consequences will be dire for the Haynes men. It is not plain to know whether Henry Buchanan had his hands in the plot against Jo, but Vernon Haynes and his boys greatly underestimated Brantley Wright and the Montgomerys."

A helpless feeling stabbed at the core of his being worse than the knife Harry Lee used on his arm. He eyed Wade, confident and assured, and found himself envious. Wade had the one thing he loved more than anything else on this earth, the one who had married Wade to save him. It cut him to the quick.

"I won't let them target you, Cullen."

He scoffed, "I don't give a damn what you do. I can take care of myself. You go back and play master of your desire—Magnolia Bluff."

"It has come to this," Wade said it not as a question, but a statement.

"It seems it has," Cullen stood, glowering. "Leave me alone, Wade. I have no patience for anything that has transpired. You stand before me so damn smug. I thought we were family. Instead, I was tricked into bringing Josephine down here. You…you placed her endanger. So do not come to me and pretend to be my brother."

"I have already denied those allegations. I doubt you will believe me if I repeat them. Know though, I harbor you no ill will."

"Because you have Josephine!" Cullen cried in outrage. "Am I now nothing more than an outsider? Do you believe you can dictate to me? I think not!"

"It is best now for you to leave before we both say things we will regret," Wade said stiffly. "I owe you a debt of gratitude, but make no mistake, I realize that things have changed between us. Josephine is my wife. I will see to her welfare and happiness."

"I need to see her before I go. I can't leave as it stood."

"No," Wade said flatly. "She has had too much to deal with and accept. She doesn't need you to pull at her heart strings. She needs time to bury the past and begin a future. If you care for her, give her peace."

Wade said nothing else, pivoted and walked back toward the farm leaving Cullen alone in his thoughts. How Wade dealt with his actions against Harry Lee mattered little to Cullen. He would be long gone.

The atmosphere here in South Carolina was already riddled with tension against any Yankee. For so long, he had straddled the fence; he wasn't anymore. He discovered he was his father's son.

Anger and fury consumed him. He had failed her. She had held out waiting for him and believed they could become what he had promised. Briefly, he thought back to the day Wade had asked him for help with Josephine. He should have known they had been doomed from the start.

He had been ill used by the family that had raised him. Now, they were safe from the wolves at their door. The legacy of the Montgomerys of Charleston intact, but at what price?

Josephine would always be a ghost within his heart. Feelings that would never fade. He never understood how strong his love ruled him until this moment.

Given little choice, he would take Heyward and Gillie back to Philadelphia. He would not abandon them. Josephine would want that. In the end, Cullen realized he would leave with his frustration and ire, not caring if he ever returned.

PART THREE

BORN TO BE BROTHERS

"Why do men fight who were born to be brothers?" ~ *General James Longstreet, Battle of Gettysburg*

Chapter One
Magnolia Bluff, Charleston
Winter, 1860

A light mist had settled over the dreary rain-swept landscape. Josephine leaned against the windowsill of the room that Wade had locked her into...so long ago. She had lost track of time. It seemed an eternity while the hours slowly ticked away and still no word had come.

Her eyes skimmed over the panorama of the plantation, but she was keenly aware of each rider who came up the long winding lane. She watched as one mesmerized, lost in her thoughts.

Lifting her head up to God, she prayed. *Oh, Lord, in your mercy, don't let them die!* Nothing mattered except that Cullen and Gillie lived. There would be no peace until she knew they were safe.

Where...where had everything gone so wrong? She had been so anxious to return to Charleston after Andrew Montgomery had jilted her at the altar. On the journey back home from Philadelphia, she should have felt desolate. She hadn't—no, far from it. She had never been happier because of Cullen Smythe and the love they shared.

She had returned to Charleston with the bright hope and dream of the life before her. She had only herself to blame for the dilemma she found herself in now. Cullen wanted to marry before they had departed Philadelphia. It was she who had delayed the wedding ceremony because of that *telegram*!

How was she to have known that Clayton Montgomery would have been so devious and cruel? The imposter had pretended to be her sick papa and tricked her into returning before she married Cullen.

Upon her arrival, she had been devastated to discover that her papa had passed away. Clayton Montgomery had manipulated the situation to his advantage and his desire to keep Magnolia Bluff in his *Southern* family.

Jo rose and walked over to the door. When she turned the handle, the door rattled, but did not budge. Locked.

"Miss Jo, do ya need something?" a voice asked through the barrier.

Smothering a frustrated gasp, she pleaded, "Amos, it has been long enough. Master Wade will understand if you let me out. I need to find out what is happening."

"Ah can't, Miss Jo," Amos answered. "Master Wade don gave me orders."

She grimaced; she wanted nothing more than to scream. Instead, she pounded on the door until her hands hurt. It got her nowhere. She had only succeeded in scaring the servants. Moments later, Jo heard a timid knock from one of the kitchen girls, who asked whether she had need of anything.

Jo wanted nothing more than to retort she wanted out! She had to see whether Cullen and Gillie were safe, but she realized she would only exude wasted energy. She was trapped in her room. Wade had seen to that.

Her desperation worsened; she found it hard to breathe. How had it come to this?

Only hours before, she had placed her faith in Wade's word and married him. She hadn't time to contemplate her actions. She had reacted in the only way possible to save Cullen and Gillie.

Now Wade had his precious Magnolia Bluff. And…well, she would deal with her loss. Knowing that somewhere in the world, Cullen was...alive.

With a heavy sigh, she remembered a time when marrying Wade Montgomery would have made her the happiest woman in Charleston. So handsome and debonair, he had completely disarmed her with his engaging smile and charm.

She had fallen under his spell and thought herself in love with him. But that was before he deceived her…before he had married Clarissa…before she had met Cullen.

Cullen! Her heart fluttered at the thought of the dark and brooding man who she loved…who had saved her more than once from certain scandal. He had been so certain that they would be together forever. It had not been meant to be.

No one had foreseen the inconceivable actions of her cousin, Harry Lee—kidnapping Heyward and Gillie to force Jo's hand. Why, in God's good graces, would Harry Lee attempt such a thing?

The answer came readily enough—revenge! Harry Lee wanted to inflict as much damage and hurt to Jo as he could. In the past, Harry Lee had tried schemes to get her inheritance. He wanted her dowry. He realized she would never agree to marry him on her own accord and wanted to force her into a marriage she would never survive…of that fact, she had no doubt.

Harry Lee scared her. He held little regard for human life and thought only of his selfish needs, no matter what he had to do to obtain them. She had known that the first time she had met him when she first arrived in Charleston. Harry Lee had almost killed Gillie.

Her cousin had taunted the tiny slave girl before he dropped her over the railing at the Battery. It nauseated her even now to remember.

Aghast at the scene, Jo had tried to save the helpless young girl. Her efforts had almost cost her her own life, but Cullen had saved her. Brave, courageous Cullen…oh, how her heart wept at the thought of the danger he now faced.

Outside, she heard a commotion and raced to the window. The lateness of the hour had cast shadows over the old oaks draped in gray moss. Caught in the time between dusk and dawn, the plantation stilled, like the quiet before a storm.

A group of men had gathered around a rider in an intense discussion. Within minutes, Clayton Montgomery had mounted his horse and led a group of riders down the road. Something had happened!

Jo shivered uncontrollably with the deadly worry that Cullen had been killed—or Gillie. Her stomach churned; her head throbbed.

Anger swelled within her to be locked up in this room. She should be there. What if Gillie had need of her? What if Cullen was injured? What if? Oh, she was sick with worry!

When she was a child, she hadn't an inkling she was an heiress. No, while she lived under Grandpa Henry's roof, she believed herself a poor relation and forced to live on the edge of the society her momma so desperately wanted her daughter to be a part of.

She had known it had been her momma's dearest wish for her to grow up to be a lady. But she had been quite unaware that Grandpa Henry had been forced into caring for her.

Moreover, Grandpa Henry greatly resented Jo's presence, having disowned her momma, Lucinda, for marrying her papa, Brantley Wright, a notorious gambler. In all that time, Jo had never figured out what Harry Lee had known all along—her papa had made a deal with Grandpa Henry.

Darkness descended with a silent somberness that shrouded the house. The rains dissipated, allowing a full moon to shine down on the quiet grounds. Jo stood longingly at the window. Closing her eyes, she could see his face so clearly.

His dark eyes stared into hers as if he could see into her soul. One look…one touch was all it took for her to melt into him…for his lips to claim hers. She still felt his kisses and the hope that lingered long after his lips broke from hers.

It seemed like another lifetime. Now, Cullen was lost to her forever. Wade had to get there in time.

Wariness and exhaustion overcame her. Jo lay down upon the bed. Her eyelids drifted closed, but it was a fretful sleep.

Miss Jo…I hurt so…help me!

"Gillie!" Jo bolted up. "Gillie, I'm coming!"

Abruptly, two strong hands grasped hold of her shoulders and gave her a slight shake. Consciousness returned as a face emerged from the haze. Wade.

"Jo, Jo."

"Let go of me. I have to go. Gillie…she needs me. Don't you hear her?"

As she pushed back against Wade, she rose and stumbled. He immediately caught her and whirled her around in his arms.

"She isn't here, Jo."

Her limbs felt leaden. Not able to lift her gaze, she asked urgently, "Dear God, don't tell me…"

"We got there in time. Cullen and Gillie live."

Jo knew a moment of immense relief and collapsed against his chest. She wept. A minute…two—she had lost consciousness of time.

"Cullen." Her lip quivered at the mention of his name. "Oh, thank the good Lord! I have to see him! Where is he? Downstairs?"

For a moment, Wade said nothing. She lifted her eyes to find his blue eyes reflected his concern for her. Slowly, the realization dawned upon her there was something wrong. She wrenched herself out of his arms. She moved toward the door, but he would have none of it. In one quick movement, he blocked her exit.

Confused, she studied him. From the corner of her eye, Jo caught her reflection in the dressing mirror. What a sight she looked! Disheveled, her hair had fallen down around her face. Her eyes were reddened and puffy; her dress wrinkled. She'd scare the saints.

"Give me a moment and I'll ready myself."

Wade's brow was harshly furrowed. "Jo, stop."

"Wade, I swear if you don't let me leave this room, I will scream. I have waited all day. I need to see them…to make sure they are—"

"Listen!"

She froze. Her tears ceased as a semblance of rational sense returned. *Oh, Lord, Wade was her husband!*

Everything had changed. Suddenly, her hands shook; her legs trembled. In the crackling silence, she felt that urge once more to weep.

He moved to her side and led her to the edge of the bed where they sat. He cleared his throat apologetically. "For all intents and purposes, it is over. As I promised, they are both safe, Cullen and Gillie."

To Jo, his voice resonated a calm, stabling force in a tone much like one talked to a young child. Sudden apprehension swept through her that there was more to his tale than he wanted to admit. "Tell me everything, Wade. I have a right to know."

In a slow, methodical manner, Wade began. "Gillie was rescued but not before she was gravely injured. I'm sorry, truly I am. Andrew has seen to her injuries. He is with her now. I sent her to Charleston."

"Wade, I have to go to her…I have to tell Miss Hazel. What of Heyward? Oh, this is all so confusing!"

As she attempted to rise, Wade grasped tight to her hand. She settled back down. He loosened his grip as he went on. "Miss Hazel has gone with her family into Charleston. I won't lie to you. Harry Lee inflicted damage to Gillie long before we realized she was within his control. Trust that Andrew is seeing to her welfare. She is in good hands. Andrew believes she will recover…but not here. It's imperative they leave Charleston immediately."

"For goodness' sakes, you can't mean without me seeing her. That will never do—"

"There is little choice, Jo. Gillie wasn't the only one gravely injured. In his rescue attempt, Cullen stabbed Harry Lee, critically wounding him. He is hovering between life and death. I have been told they doubt Harry Lee will survive the night. If he dies, Cullen will be a wanted man. There aren't many in these parts who will take kindly to what he did."

"He can't leave…he wouldn't just leave me. I have to go."

"No," Wade stated in a firm tone. "You aren't leaving the plantation as it stands. Not until I get the matter settled. I have to make peace with your family. For everyone's sake."

"I am to be a prisoner? I think not."

"You are not a prisoner in your own home. You are understandably upset and need to rest." He took her by the shoulders to force her to look at him. "I will stay with you until you sleep. We will talk more in the morning before I leave."

Recoiling, she hissed, "This is your doing! You have what you want…your precious Magnolia Bluff, but I won't have it. I'm going to them. Gillie needs me…Cullen…Cullen would never leave me. He will come."

"Have you lost your mind? You are now my wife. Cullen will not come. I made certain he understood my position. I suppose now I need to make myself clear to you. You will have no further contact with Cullen," Wade commanded. "You may write to Gillie, of course."

Jo was speechless. Her heart sickened while anger churned within her being. Her tone went cold, and her body stiff. "You are too kind. Now please leave me with my grief."

"Josephine, you know I will never leave you. Given time, you will see that everything will work out for the best. This is what your papa wanted. He realized that you and I are cast from the same mold…the same viewpoints and traditions. I gave your papa my solemn word that I would look after your welfare." He reached for her. "I know you are hurt—"

"Don't touch me! You don't know my pain…being ripped from the arms of the man I love. No one will love me the way Cullen did….touch me the way he did…no one…" Suddenly, she saw Wade's expression harden.

"Love you? Touch you?" Wade drawled slowly. "Tell me, my bride, how exactly did my dear cousin touch you?"

Unable to find her voice, Jo lowered her gaze, experiencing the chill of a sober consciousness of the reality of her new world. It saddened her more than she ever expected. Cullen was gone…he wasn't coming back. She was left alone to face her husband…Her husband!

There was no way to avoid the inevitable. *Oh, Lord, he will shame me when he discovers the truth!* She looked back up at his cold glare.

"Cullen touched me deeply…he touched my soul. We had planned to spend the rest of our lives together," Jo whispered as she tried desperately to contain her welling emotions. "And we would have if I hadn't been so cruelly tricked. Is it not enough you have gotten your precious plantation? Do you want to know if your wife is chaste? I'm afraid in that you will be disappointed." She swallowed hard. "Moreover, the thought of anyone else touching me in that manner disgusts me."

Wade's temper flared at the obvious insinuation. His eyes blazed and teeth bared, betraying his fury. Frightened, she edged off the bed and stumbled back against the wall. Immediately, he closed the gap between them.

Her arm gripped tightly, Wade jerked her into a rough embrace. "You gave yourself to him," he growled under his breath. "For shame, after all your father did for you to be thought of as a lady."

She pushed back against his chest and slapped him, hard across his face. She lifted her head in defiance. "Shame is not what I feel. It was not that way."

"What way is that, my dear? The way a man will tell you anything to get what he wants? You think he loves you? If he did, he would never have left you. Cullen rode out knowing you would marry me…knowing he had lost Magnolia Bluff."

"You lie," she cried. "Cullen had no desire for Magnolia Bluff. He loves me!"

"You silly fool! You do not know my cousin as well as you thought, for Cullen craved Magnolia Bluff as much as I." Wade laughed in a harsh manner. His hard gaze made her step back. His cruel words had hit their mark, but he did not relent. "He left you when he recognized he had no chance of winning. If he cared for you as you insist, he would never have taken your virtue…never left in disgrace to face your husband. So don't tell me that he loves you."

"You...that...that has to be a lie." Jo's voice cracked. Wade had cut her to the quick. She wanted to defend Cullen…to declare that he did love her more than anything…but...had it truly been a lie? She had wanted Cullen to take her away from this place. He had hesitated and now was gone. Her heart ached. Had she been deceived?

"My poor darling, sacrificing herself for the man she loves…"

Jo turned away as a terrible void filled her, heartbroken with the comprehension she had no one. Silent tears streamed down her cheeks. "Leave," she said in a voice no louder than a whisper. "You have what you want. Now leave me with my memories of what I have lost."

For a moment, she thought he would protest, but he pivoted on his heels and left her alone with tears and doubts and too many questions. She flung herself upon the bed and cried herself until she finally slept.

Chapter Two

Despite the rumblings of secession, Charleston was more alive than ever. The apex of the winter season had commenced, Race Week. Most years, Wade would have found himself in the midst of all the activities. Hell, he would have been the center of attention.

Race Week officially began the racing season, which ran from the early Charleston spring into the summer in Virginia. The love of horses ran in Wade's blood. Outside of Beaufort, his Uncle William had maintained a stud farm of some of the finest breeding stock in the Carolinas.

As a boy, Wade, Percival, and Cullen had spent many a day at the horse farm, where they had learned to ride. Wade had always strove to better Percival's horsemanship. Although more than adequate in the saddle, he never surpassed his brother's skill on a horse, but no one had a better eye for racehorses than Wade. He had become renowned for his uncanny ability to pick horses that would be developed into winners.

However this afternoon, horse racing was the furthest thing from his mind. Only minutes earlier, Wade had left his lawyer's office. After much debate, the decision had been made to extend an olive branch…a legal contract…to the Buchanans. Wade was determined that this vendetta would end—today.

He had given his word to Wright that he would give Josephine the life Wright envisioned for his daughter. If nothing else, he had always been a man of his word…ordinarily.

"It is more than a generous offer, Wade," Morgan said. "And one I feel Mr. Wright would be in total agreement. It will allow Henry

Buchanan to live out his days, managing his estate as if it is his. The strong language in the document will leave no doubt that if the Buchanans fail in the terms, the Groves, along with one hundred thousand dollars, would immediately revert back into your hands."

"I trust you have made it clear that if any harm befalls my wife, I will demand not only the Groves but the income from the estate in that time span, along with interest."

"Read over the document slowly. It is plainly stated," Morgan advised. "I will take it myself to the Groves this evening. I realize the urgency."

Wade read it over twice and everything seemed in order. He looked up at Morgan. "The last word I received said that Harry Lee was barely clinging to life. I want this signed whether or not he survives. The rumors need to be smothered. Henry Buchanan needs to understand the consequences if he doesn't comply."

"The arrangement is a benefit to both parties," Morgan said. "I will make sure he understands. I don't foresee any issues. Mr. Whitney has returned to Charleston and offered to come with me to help convey the importance of ending this once and for all."

Confident one obstacle had been hurdled, Wade now had to inform his grandfather. He held no doubt that his grandfather would not be happy. Grandfather wanted to ruin Henry Buchanan, but, in Wade's opinion, that action would only serve to facilitate the feud.

After the meeting, Wade decided to walk back to his Charleston home. He needed time to think. Josephine worried him. To be honest, his mind was never far away from his bride, whom he had left at Magnolia Bluff alone.

He felt confident she was in no danger at the plantation. He had made certain of that with his trusted servants and the guards he had hired to oversee her welfare. Her safety wasn't what troubled him, but how he was to bridge the wide gulf that had emerged between them.

Cullen had departed Charleston, along with Miss Hazel, Heyward, and Gillie. Andrew had seen to the arrangements. Though Cullen had honored Wade's request and had made no effort to see Jo before he left, a fear surfaced that Cullen would always be a ghost between Jo and himself.

For the past year, Wade had been so engrossed in his woes. His every waking moment had been filled with Magnolia Bluff...he had felt it so close within his grasp. It had been his sole intent to have the estate back in control of the family.

Magnolia Bluff had been the reason he had let Josephine leave for Philadelphia. The little conniving thing had tricked him. Anger gripped the core of his being. If he had called her bluff…if he had done what he had desired and taken her in that moment, none of this would have happened.

Fear was the reason he had let her go…fear that the family would lose Magnolia Bluff… their heritage, not because he didn't love her. God in heaven! He loved the woman! Even now, that love tore at his soul. He should have said proprieties be damned! He should have…

As he turned the corner, Wade walked toward the house. He heard voices…feminine voices on the portico. He strode up to the door to find his sister, Jenna, sitting beside the new addition to the Montgomery household, that *Yankee* woman his brother married, Kathleen.

Impatient to see Grandfather, Wade glanced over at the woman. She was beautifully dressed and expensively, if not somewhat warm for Charleston's climate. She wore a deep purple gown accented with black stripes. The large ostrich plume hat drooped quite fashionably over her crown. Her pelisse matched her gown trimmed with black fur.

He cared little for her before he met Kathleen and less now he had had the pleasure. Never would he consider her a beauty, seeing little reason his brother would have fallen under her spell. He sensed an intrinsic coldness and self-absorption about her. Not to mention, he had not seen a sign of affection toward her husband.

"Why, Wade, I'm so glad you are here." Jenna almost leaped from her chair. "You gotta talk some sense into our new *sister*."

He grimaced and turned to Jenna. "What are you talking about?"

"I truly don't see an issue." Kathleen rose up to greet Wade. "Do tell Jenna that it is perfectly appropriate for Andrew and me to attend the Jockey Club's dinner tomorrow night and then the ball on Friday night. Though, to be honest, I am so looking forward to attending one of the Montgomery's Saturday night dinners I've heard so much about. I'm assuming you begin during Race Week."

Wade exchanged a look with his sister. Her eyes pleaded with him for help. This was the last thing he needed to deal with. "Kathleen, you are new to Charleston. Given the circumstances of your nuptials, it may be for the best to be introduced to Andrew's friends slowly and quietly." His voice was sharp. "Moreover, you have to understand that my wife's father has recently passed away. It would not be respectful to host a dinner party so soon after his death."

"Oh, you are quite right, Brother Wade, and I don't want to seem unfeeling, but your marriage hasn't been announced. All so hush-hush.

Why, your dear bride isn't even in Charleston." She smiled sweetly to dismiss the objection. "I had thought the dinner here on Saturday would serve as a wonderful introduction to all my husband's friends and relatives. You have such a lovely home."

Wade realized that Andrew must have talked of the renowned family dinners held in the blue parlor twice a month when the family resided in Charleston. The feasts were grand affairs that most of the wealthy and distinguished families of the low country had enjoyed at one time or another.

Held underneath the sparkling crystal chandelier, a table would extend across the room, filled with assortment of delicacies from shrimp pare to coconut pie. The Montgomery's prosperity was displayed conspicuously for all to see. Beautiful damask linen lay on the table set in Staffordshire bone china, crystal glasses, and their silverware. Decanters were filled with various kinds of wines and Madeira flowed freely.

He shook his head at Kathleen's insistence. "You need to talk with Andrew."

Jenna grasped his hand and turned her back to Kathleen. "Stop her, Wade," she whispered. "Momma has already told her it would not be proper."

"It's not my problem." Wade maneuvered around his sister and went into the house. He didn't need anything else to handle.

Wade slammed the door, moved across the high-ceilinged central foyer and up the stairs to the study. He walked into a fog of pipe tobacco smoke that hung over the room. As he expected, his grandfather sat in wait.

Wade glanced toward the man and made his way to the liquor cabinet. Despite the early hour of the afternoon, he needed a drink. He grabbed hold of the Irish whiskey and poured two glasses.

"Is there trouble?"

"At the moment, only Andrew's annoying wife." Wade pivoted around with the drinks, and handed one to his grandfather. "I thought Mother was going to talk to her and explain how things are done here in the South. Seems Kathleen wants to celebrate Race Week. Not to mention her desire for us to hold a dinner in her honor."

"Your mother has talked to her. More than once. Afraid it has done no good. That woman's got nerve. Does whatever she damn well pleases. It is evident that Andrew has no control. I told him for God's sakes stop being such a spineless wimp. Man up and show a fucking backbone."

Exasperation apparent in his face, Wade scowled deeply. "I want her out of this house. I won't have her upset Jo. It is no secret she sent the letter to Wright that caused his heart attack."

"Andrew knows he needs to find another place to live. I heard him tell her myself that they were going to have to find a house of their own. She doesn't want to leave."

Clayton Montgomery accepted his drink in one hand and flicked ashes off his cigar with the other. "Coldhearted bitch. She doesn't care one iota how it looks for the family. In her condition, she's out parading about town. Bad enough she's a Yankee."

Somehow Wade got the impression that Andrew's bride couldn't have cared less about the delicate situation the family was in at this time. Surely, Kathleen would have to realize that it would not be easily forgotten she had maliciously married an engaged man. People around here wouldn't take too kindly to her actions nor would they soon forget.

"Andrew made his bed. He will have to sleep in it." Wade drank down the contents of his glass, and then turned to pour another. He needed something to knock off the edge.

"Enough about Andrew. Out with it," Clayton Montgomery demanded, his impatience worn thin with talk about the youngest grandson's mistake. His jaw tightened as he squared off with Wade about the problem…the only problem…that mattered to him. "Is it settled?"

"By sunset, the agreement should be signed. Whether Harry Lee lives or dies, this vendetta is done."

"At what cost?"

Wade watched his grandfather release another puff of smoke. The man sat back, smug, as if he had already assumed Wade had made a colossal mistake. It kindled his anger. After years of being in Percival's shadow, he had come to the conclusion that nothing he would do would ever be enough for Grandfather…He was not Percival. Even in death, he'd never equal Percival in his grandfather's eyes.

With a small shrug, he sighed. "None to you, if that is your fear."

"It's not, Wade. I had a long talk with Whitney this morning while you were with Morgan. He said that you had put together an interesting proposition. That it was Wright's wish."

"I told you that myself," Wade snapped. "Wright had no desire to hold on to the Groves and bankrupt his wife's father. He only wanted for Buchanan to care for Jo, but I made certain there was a stipulation that Jo inherits the estate after his death in the agreement. So in reality, Grandfather, I have lost nothing."

"That is what Whitney explained to me in full detail, but I didn't think you could pull it off." Clayton stood. He was a tall man, the same height as Wade, and looked eye to eye with his grandson. Over his lifetime, he had used his height to his full advantage when the circumstance allowed, intimidating those who he felt was beneath him...which, accordingly, was most everyone.

Wade had seldom seen his grandfather smile, but a small smile emerged as he held up his glass. Today, though, his old, gray eyes flashed a different sentiment. *Was it admiration?*

"Well done. A Montgomery through and through."

Initially shocked at the response, Wade stared suspiciously at the old man. Some of his reservations yielded to his grandfather's obvious elation. "I will feel better when I hear back from Morgan. I want those papers signed. Then I will feel safe that the Buchanans won't retaliate no matter what happens to Harry Lee. I want peace. This whole state is already riled up against the Yanks. I don't want Charleston to turn against us."

"Not going to happen." Clayton's answer was sharp and direct. "You have made sure of that. Cullen's gone."

The words cut through Wade and pierced his soul. He lowered his eyes and studied the floor, as if contemplating his next move. Slowly, he met his grandfather's gaze. "All I have ever done, I have done to save Magnolia Bluff."

With his cigar in one hand, Clayton pointed at Wade with the other and laughed. "Ain't gonna argue with you, boy. It was good to know that you are more like me than I thought."

"A chip off the old block," Wade answered with gruff sarcasm. "God help me."

Clayton shook his head and waved his hand. "What's wrong with you? You got what you wanted...all that you wanted."

"Maybe...maybe it's how I got it. What I have had to do and knowing I wouldn't have had to do a damn thing if you hadn't interfered to begin with," Wade stated with a sudden flare of temper. "If you had left well enough alone, I would have been married to Jo before Cullen got involved. All this could have been avoided if you hadn't tried to outsmart Wright!" His voice rose higher. Suddenly, he threw his empty glass into the fireplace. It shattered into a million pieces. "I wouldn't have had to mislead Cullen!"

The old man walked back around his desk and sat. "It was a hard call and you made it." He took a puff of his cigar. "Can't look back, now. It was the right thing to do."

287

"It could have gotten Jo hurt or worse!" Wade took a deep breath and regained a portion of his composure. Guilt…it was the guilt that gnawed at him.

"No way you could have seen that son of a bitch, Harry Lee, returning like he did," Clayton said. "You didn't do anything Cullen wouldn't have done himself."

"No, you're wrong. Cullen would never have done what I did to him." Wade shook his head. *Lord! His head pounded.* "Cullen…he was closer to me than Percival. He trusted me."

"You did what you had to."

"I did what I had to get Magnolia Bluff, no matter the cost." Wade broke his gaze from his grandfather and stared hard at the fireplace. "Lord Almighty! You know I almost helped him sneak Jo out of the state. He came to me right before Heyward appeared. I would have helped him then. Even after all I had done to get her back to Charleston…but it changed when he went to save Gillie…ever the hero."

"In whose eyes?" Clayton snarled. "A fool in mine. Never took him as one, but not only could he have lost his life, he could have cost the family dearly for that act. Lest I remind you, it was you who saved him. Going to save some Negro! The boy has lost his mind!"

"He was going after Harry Lee," Wade replied in defense of Cullen. "Harry Lee was bent on revenge—"

"For God's sake! Cullen armed blackies. There is no defense."

"I helped him, Grandfather. We have armed trusted slaves before—"

"To defend ourselves…not to free a slave of a white man!"

"You and I both know that Gillie was a freed woman. He had no right to her—"

"In the eyes of our neighbors, neither did Cullen," Clayton shot back. "Only you did after you married Josephine."

Wade forced a laugh. "Because then Gillie was considered my property! Do you not know how absurd that sounds? Is there any wonder the Yankees consider us barbarians?"

"Hold your tongue! No loyal Southerner would utter such blasphemy!" Clayton's manner turned cantankerous. "Montgomerys don't speak against our own."

"Maybe someone should!"

The room stilled as if all the air had been sucked out of it. Clayton sat his glass down and leaned forward. "Don't say things you don't mean, son. What's eating at you?"

Wade stopped short of saying the truth. What weighed on his soul—guilt on tricking Cullen and in the same breath anger at his cousin for making love to his wife...his wife! No gentleman, no matter the circumstance, should ever leave a woman in a compromising position. Never!

But, if the truth be known, he was angrier at himself because he loved Jo. Had always loved her, even when he was married to Clarissa and Jo loved Cullen! For heaven's sake, she only married him to save her lover. Now, he had everything he desired except her love. No, Wade could never admit that to his grandfather.

Clayton studied his grandson. "You have done what you had to do. Don't you know I understood well why you sent that telegram pretending to be Wright? It was the reason I gladly took the blame for it."

Wade made no response. He had no defense for sending that telegram pretending to be Brantley Wright...asking Jo to come to home to marry Cullen, wanting only to ensure she was safe and happy. It had been a cruel trick.

He had no excuse. Jealousy had overridden his good sense...he wanted Josephine...he wanted Magnolia Bluff. He had been desperate, knowing that Josephine was with Cullen. He had no doubt Cullen would not wait to marry Jo after Andrew's fiasco. He had to do something and quickly.

His stupid...stupid brother! Andrew should have told him. He could have convinced Jo to stay... had he known...had he not feared losing Magnolia Bluff.

But he would have never intentionally put Jo in harm's way. He had not taken in account Henry Buchanan's attempt to reclaim Jo's guardianship. It had almost cost Jo her life. He would have never forgiven himself if anything had happened to her.

"The good Lord leads us down the path we are to take," Clayton went on. "Anyone with any common sense knows she will be happier with you than up North. She is a highly principled and resilient young woman. This is her people."

Wade looked back at his grandfather. There it was...that arrogance. He sneered. "You didn't think that about Jo a year ago."

"It takes a real man to admit he was wrong." Clayton took a puff of his cigar and released the smoke over his head. "I was wrong. I shouldn't have tried to outmaneuver Wright. He just got under my craw. I knew his ma and pa up in Camden. They were nothing more than poor white trash. And him wanting to marry his daughter to a member of my family! My family!"

"Her mother was a Buchanan."

"Made no difference to me," Clayton went on. "It was her daddy who riled up my bad side. His highfalutin ways. Took advantage of my boy. Then Wright caused me to make mistakes and compound them by making more. But it was you, Wade—you have restored Magnolia Bluff to the Montgomerys and upheld our legacy. You've done the Montgomery name proud."

Wade said nothing for a long moment and considered the words of praise. He shook his head and walked toward the door. "I'm going back up to Magnolia Bluff after I hear from Morgan. When I return, tell Andrew I want that woman out of my house."

Chapter Three

Outside, erratic gusts of wind rustled the branches of the old oaks. Josephine woke, not from the noise, but from the nightmare that plagued her. Her eyes widened as she stared into the darkness that surrounded her. A sudden realization swept through her that there was no nightmare; she was living in her own special hell.

A strange chill stabbed at her heart. She shivered with the understanding that nothing would ever be the same. Her papa was dead, Cullen was gone, and Gillie was terribly hurt... Although no one had confirmed her suspicions, Jo knew Harry Lee and the harm he would not have hesitated to inflict upon her dear Gillie.

Self-pity surged through her. Cullen should have never attempted to save her after Andrew's betrayal. It would have been best for everyone involved. Then, she would have never known what it was like to feel for another as she did for him: to be swept up in the glory of their ardor and then to have her beating heart ripped from her body.

Gillie...poor, sweet Gillie...suffered because of her! Guilt overwhelmed Jo; guilt few would understand. Jo well knew the whispers behind her back about Gillie. No self-respecting white folk gave one of their servants...a darky...the dignity and respect that Jo had given Gillie. It was unheard of, but she could never explain their connection to anyone.

Society may have shaken their heads at her for her treatment of her servant, but what would they have done if she declared she loved Gillie as a sister? Rebuked, no doubt. How could they have ever understood that for a time it had only been Gillie and herself?

Jo had had no one else. She had been the poor relation and had endured the lowly looks of those who thought themselves better than she because of their birth. Now, the forces against them had intervened and kept them apart when Gillie needed her the most.

Trapped in a web of honor and duty, Jo surmised there would be no happy ending for her. Cullen had left without a word. Why could he not have come to her? Maybe then she could have coped with the loss.

A wave of hurt so great enveloped her. Why…why hadn't he swept her away when they had a chance? Leaving her here, he had accepted what she would have to do…expected her to do. *Oh, what was to become of me now!*

She was a married woman, not to Andrew, the man she had been promised, or Cullen, the man who she loved beyond her own life. No, she had married Wade to save the ones she loved: one she loved beyond measure and the other, a kindred soul.

There would be no sleep.

Jo lay in her bed and watched the lightening of the sky. Another morning dawned. She looked over at her mourning weeds laid out for her to wear. Rosa had brought them from Charleston when she arrived at Magnolia Bluff two days ago.

Left on the plantation with no other family, she had tasks to perform. It would be expected. The mistress of a plantation's lot was not an easy one. Her responsibilities were never-ending. It was ironic. Only a short time ago, she had been a sought-after heiress with no thought of the drudgery of everyday life as a married lady.

That life ended and a new one had begun. She would no longer be courted in any fashion. Wade had what he wanted. She would only serve as a reminder of what was.

This was a man's world. Jo would do as he bid. Had she not been reared as a lady? She slid out of bed, donned her clothes and prepared to face the day.

* * * *

The sun had set long before the wheels of the buckboard ground sharply over the gravel road as it headed to the main house. From the drawing room window, Wade watched the wagon stop at the front steps.

A moment later, he heard the door open and close. He walked out to the foyer to greet his wife's return. "Good evening, Mrs. Montgomery."

From the expression on her face, he had startled her. Rightly so. He had not sent word of his intent to return tonight.

Untying her bonnet with the dark crepe veil, Jo pulled it off along with her black gloves and placed them on the foyer table. She was suitably dressed for mourning her papa in a black dress with a dark floral lace collar. When she looked up at him, she wore a somber, tired expression.

He moved closer and inhaled her fragrance, the light scent of a lavender sachet. For so long, every time he had caught a whiff of lavender he had thought of her.

"Wade. I...I wasn't expecting you," Jo stammered. "I would have had Millie prepare a dinner."

"Dinner was an hour ago."

She gave a small shrug. "Then you are set. Now, if you will pardon me, I will retire for the night."

Annoyed with her dismissal, he said coldly, "Pray, join me in the parlor. We need to talk."

Jo advanced toward the stairs, but paused. Glancing over her shoulder, she said stiffly, "I don't believe we have anything else to say that wasn't said the other night when you left me here alone."

"I had matters to attend to in Charleston," he said curtly. "Of which, you were fully aware. I came to relieve your worries. Surely, it will ease your mind to know that there will be no retaliation from your family."

"Is that all? You could have simply sent a note."

"What? You do not care for the details of the agreement?"

"No," she said simply, but clearly. Jo met his glare with her own.

He stared long and hard at her. She was aggravated, but so was he. His patience had worn thin. "Where have you been?"

"Cora Randolph called on me this morning. Old Miss Heddy is laid up. Fell and broke her leg. I went to visit and brought her a basket."

"Cordial of you, but I don't think that Barclay would have greeted me in the manner he did on my arrival if you had just went calling on a neighbor."

"Why on earth would the overseer...?" Her voice trailed off as if suddenly she comprehended. Her expression cleared. "He has a problem with my having Amos see to Miss Hazel's place while she is gone."

"You should have come to me."

Jo shot him an angry look. "Perhaps I would have if you had been here...if anyone had been here."

"Barclay runs the plantation."

"You are to tell me I have no say?" Her chest heaved; her eyes flared. "But of course! I should know my place."

"You are mistress of the house. You are well aware of the expectations."

"Of being a Montgomery?" Jo took a couple of steps up the stairs and then abruptly pivoted around. Her eyes narrowed. She said with ominous calm, "Behaving like you and yours? Celebrating your good fortune! I heard how you Montgomerys are living it up in Charleston— welcoming Andrew's bride with open arms. So tell me again about your expectations of me. How I cannot even request help for my old mammy?"

"Where did you hear such nonsense?"

"Cora." Her eyes blazed with anger directed at him. "Cora said while I am here mourning my papa's death, the rest of you Montgomerys are enjoying yourselves with your newfound fortune. That is what is being said." Her voice was sharp and true. "I know…I know that I am not the woman you thought, but I did not deserve this. Go back to Charleston. Celebrate your victory. I don't want you here."

Taken aback by her claim, Wade had no defense. He made no effort to stop her as she rushed up the stairs without even a glance backward.

* * * *

Josephine had taken a long warm bath to ease her anger and…oh…she was angry. *How dare he question my behavior!* What of his? What of the Montgomerys? A sudden wave of despair swept through her. *By heavens, what am I going to do?* She didn't know much at the moment, but she knew she couldn't stay—no matter what her papa wanted. He had been wrong, ever so wrong.

After her visit with Miss Heddy, she had ferociously labored most of the afternoon at Miss Hazel's home and expelled most of her ire cleaning and caring for the farm. Miss Hazel would have never forgiven her if something happened to her home. Jo thought miserably she should have stayed at the cabin.

Rosa had brought up a tray for her supper, but it remained untouched. She had no appetite. A knot pitted in her stomach. She needed time alone to contemplate her next move.

Having dismissed Rosa for the night, she stared blankly at her reflection in the mirror. How long she sat, she hadn't a clue. Lost in her thoughts, time had no meaning.

The last year, she had endured the desolation of contemplating failing Papa and facing the wrath of Charleston society. Her every action had been designed to uphold the façade that she was a part of that world. *How useless it had been!* All of it had been for naught.

In the distance, she heard a noise grow closer…uneven footsteps came up the hall and halted at her room. To her dismay, she heard a key turn. *Oh, good Lord! He had a key to her room!*

She had no chance to barricade the entrance, but she tried. As she bolted upward, she raced across the room and had barely gripped the handle when the door jerked open. Stumbling backward, she watched her husband enter.

His hair was tousled. Heaven knew where his waistcoat was, but his shirt hung loose over his breeches. Wade leaned casually against the doorway with a decanter under his arm and a half-filled glass of brandy in his hand. The fact that the other half seemed to have been spilled over his shirt did not seem to disturb him.

His blue eyes caught hers and then moved unabashedly over the full length of her body. Her dark, shiny hair fell loose down below her waist, having been washed and left down to dry. His eyes lingered upon her high, full breasts.

Her cheeks warmed under his gaze. She wore a practical dressing gown, but it was light, sheer and revealing. She immediately regretted not wearing her wrap, which lay across the bed, but she had not expected his company.

Straightening himself out to full height, he maneuvered into the room and slammed the door behind him with his foot.

"You're drunk." Her voice carried a sharp tone of rebuke.

"Not quite, my love, but I'm getting there. Would you care to join me?" He raised his glass and sipped slowly as he eyed her from over the glass.

"Get out!" she demanded and pointed at the door. "You have come to the wrong room."

"On the contrary, madam," he replied in a long drawl. "I am exactly where I want to be. You refused to talk to me…and I refuse for you not to." Wade drank down the liquor and then pounded the glass down roughly on a nearby bureau, along with the decanter. He turned to her and stared, once more scrutinizing her.

She stared at him and shook her head in disgust. "You've gone and lost all your good sense."

"I believe I passed reason on my last bottle." He laughed, seemingly quite amused. But something beneath the mask he wore told her otherwise. "I'm working up to atonement."

"You need forgiveness?"

"More than you know." Wade flung up his hand derisively. "But not for the idle gossip you repeated. Do you not know me better than that?

At one time, you professed love for me. Do you believe I'm capable of doing such a thing to you?"

Indignation overwhelmed her. "Remind me of that love, Wade. For what I remember is betrayal. You lied to me then, as you are lying to me now. I will not play the fool any longer. Your one desire has always been Magnolia Bluff. You have it. Now, let me go."

"Go?" he questioned with a sudden soberness. "Have you forgotten you are my wife?"

"It does not have to be. The marriage can be annulled and declared void. You can have Magnolia Bluff. I want nothing of it."

The room suddenly felt very small. A core of fear shifted within her heart. The whole of her surroundings disappeared and all that remained was Wade, serious and subdued.

He caught her arm and pulled her to him. "Even if that was a feasible option, which it isn't, I would never allow that to happen." His icy-blue eyes cut through her; his jaw tensed. "I made a vow to your papa. I will hold to it despite your feelings. I came back to Magnolia Bluff to tell you everything that had been arranged. I spent the whole of my days ensuring your safety and caring for your welfare. I would *never...never* allow you to be disgraced."

Rendered speechless by his intensity, she stared at him in confusion. She had the urge to run, but his grip on her arm tightened.

"By God, you will listen to me!" he said in a caustic tone. "Andrew and his wife have been instructed to leave our house...*our home* in Charleston. I have made it clear *she* is not welcome. You have convicted me unjustly!"

"Unjustly," she murmured. "How else can I see what has happened? You left me here alone...alone!"

"You were well looked after. There was no place safer for you than here at Magnolia Bluff."

"By whom? Servants and hired guards! Is this what you want from me? To remain as a prisoner, hidden from the world? Does it ease your conscience after taking all that once was mine?"

"You are being absurd, Josephine." His face flushed with anger, his eyes ablaze. "You need only to accept what has happened. It is yours as it is mine. You are now my wife...my wife. You need to trust me."

"Trust you, a drunken fool!"

His frown was fierce. "My poor Josephine. The quandary you have been left with me as your husband."

Slowly, his hand caressed her face. She stiffened with the contact, wary of the intent she saw in his eyes as his gaze fell down upon the curve of her breasts. "You look beautiful. I have never seen your hair down," he murmured huskily as his hand tangled in her thick, long hair. "I ache for you. It is well that we are married."

"Married?" Her ill-concealed ire spewed out of her mouth. "This is what you call a marriage? An agreement so you can claim Magnolia Bluff. Have you forgotten why I married you?"

"It is never far from my mind." Clearly agitated, a savage curse escaped his lips. "My damn cousin. Nor will I forget what you gave him so freely...what is mine." His voice faded into the night as his mouth covered hers.

She felt his anger at her and Cullen in his kiss. She tasted the whiskey on his lips, but beneath her bosom, her heart pounded wildly as she found herself caught up in his touch. The kiss deepened as a tense awakening arose in her, astonished that her own anger seemed to fuel his.

He broke free from her lips and his gaze drifted over her, thoroughly. "You are enough to drive a man insane," he breathed. "You were made to love."

"You talk nonsense." She pushed back against his chest, but his strength held her firm. Jo looked up defiantly and declared with venom, "I hate you!"

"Hate me all you wish, my love. It changes nothing. I am your husband, with wants and needs." His expression hardened. Tension sparked. "Do you think I have ever stopped loving you?" With his hand clamped behind the nape of her neck, he brought her lips back to his.

Her world spun as he embraced her with another savage kiss. The hurt and pain she had so long held within her exploded. Jo struggled for air when his lips released hers.

Cullen was an all too vivid memory. He had left her...he was gone...gone...and she was so angry at him...at herself...at Wade. She didn't want to hurt anymore. She needed to draw away from him. Instead, her arms slipped up around his neck and pulled him even closer. Jo kissed him back.

Fast and hard, Wade's kisses came to satiate the greedy hunger that vibrated through Jo's body. His mouth took possession of hers. Unbridled passion burst through the anger and demanded gratification. His lips moved down her neck. Her breasts tingled with a maddening desire to be devoured. There was no pretense to where this would lead.

Somewhere in the frenzy, he shed his shirt and pants and wasted no time disposing of her gown. His long, sleek fingers untied the ribbon around her neck and slid the thin robe down her thighs. He paused only a moment when he cast it aside and sat on the bed to pull off his boots.

In the candlelight, she gazed upon his naked body. Lord, he was so handsome with his broad shoulders and muscular frame. He returned her look with a frank gaze of his own that made the whole of her body tremble, but he was too far away. She had time to think and she didn't want to think. She wanted him close, touching her…making her forget everything but this moment. He complied.

Her breath shortened as he drew her back into his arms and laid her down on the bed. Kneeling on the mattress, he straddled her body and pinned her beneath him. He unsettled her…she was at his mercy, but he had no mercy to give.

His hot, pressing kisses told he was bent on only one thought—her complete and total surrender. A reawakened vitality emerged; her body came alive with his touch. Her breasts grew heavy and full. Her nipples hardened more, sensitive to his caress…his kisses as he used his teeth and lips to tease and taunt them.

Her world spun. The power he held over her strangely excited her. Sensations cascaded throughout her body, leaving her breathless. He kissed her mouth and rubbed his body against her. She felt the hard ridge of his arousal. Impatient, she arched up to him.

He wasted no more time. He parted her legs and his fingers pushed deep into her. She clutched her hand on his shoulders; her hips pushed at him. Wild and frantic, she submitted to the intimate caresses that brought her to the edge of rapture.

She needed more. She needed him to take her now…The whole of her body was about to explode…and then suddenly he paused.

In the dark, she looked up at him. In the shadowed intimacy, the world beyond the door did not exist, obscured into the darkness. He caressed down her body, reminding her she was under his control.

Roughly, he gripped her arms and lifted them over her head.

"Stay still."

It was an order that would not be disobeyed. He had a power over her that frightened her. She whispered, "Please, don't hurt me."

"I would never hurt you, my love," he whispered in her ear. "I'm about to make you purr like a kitten."

His voice calmed her fear… He bent over and began to kiss every inch of her naked skin. His lips crossed over her lips, downward along her creamy white neck to the swell of her bare breasts, where he paused, suckling until new sensations emerged…more intense…more powerful.

Tremors palpitated through her as he continued his journey, kissing her skin down along her flat stomach, over to one thigh and then the other. He slid his hands under her, cupped her bottom and slid her forward. He kissed her at the pulse of her desire. A primitive ferocity overwhelmed her, overriding any objections she had to utter at such boldness. Shocked, never had she imagined such an act.

She should have recoiled at his wicked behavior, but she could not break the spell she was under while he did unspeakable things. His tongue flicked over the core of her pleasure. Powerful sensations possessed her...madness overcame her.

Mindless of anything but the want within her, cries escaped...the sound of her complete surrender. He moved over her and entered, filling her throbbing need. Passion saturated her body as he thrust into her, harder and harder, dominating...commanding her on every reentry.

Their bodies strained and cleaved together until her world shattered into a million pleasurable sensations. It seemed to last an eternity...waves of ecstasy, one after another, surged through her until she climaxed into mindless release.

Wade collapsed on top of her; the sweat from their bodies glistened in the afterglow of their lovemaking. A moment later, he rolled off and fell back on the pillow, smiling broadly.

Slowly, the aftermath of her climax tremored through Jo. As she regained a semblance of reason, she scooted over to the far side of the bed. Catching her breath, the reality of what she had done suffused through her. She glanced over at the man in her bed.

She had meant every word that spewed out of her mouth at Wade when she said she had no desire to be touched by another man. Even then, she had known it was a ridiculous assertion. Wade was her husband. But she had not meant for this to happen...not yet.

His eyes caught hers and reflected the physical intimacy they had shared. He reached for her hand and kissed it.

"Lord, woman."

Words caught in her throat, unsure of what to say. She felt exposed and vulnerable. When she reached for her gown haphazardly thrown across the foot of the bed, he grasped hold of her hand and halted her progress.

"Oh, hon, I don't think so," he chided her with a twinkle in his eye. "We aren't done yet."

When Jo awoke the next morning, Wade was gone. He had left only a note that stated he had urgent business in Charleston. Interestingly enough, he had placed correspondences from Grace Ann on her bureau that contained an invitation to visit her in Camden. It seemed Wade had even accepted the offer and expected her to leave within the week.

Jo read through the invitation while memories of the night lingered…memories she would not soon forget. Whatever problems they had between them, it did not extend into their bed. He had taken her at his will and left no doubt that she was his and only his.

With the greatest reluctance, her gaze pulled away from the tumbled bed linens and she readied for the day. No, she thought, staring at herself in the mirror, it was good he was gone. She needed time to heal…not only from the bruises on her body, but from the conscience that gnawed at her soul.

Guilt suffused through her. She wondered how she could feel shame lying with Wade. He was her husband. Her lover—the man whose face haunted her dreams, Cullen—had deserted her.

Chapter Four

The Whitney family had been in the state a long time and had a quite distinguished pedigree. Unlike the Buchanans and Montgomerys, their fortune had increased tenfold over the last decade. Theodore Whitney's wealth stretched over three states, six plantations and owned over eight hundred slaves.

Whitney Hall was the personification of the Whitney family's wealth and prestige. Situated outside of Camden, the two-story wooden house built on brick pillars was massive. It had black shutters with a green shingled roof, along with a double-deck porch. Climbing ivy covered the white pillars where French windows opened to the porch.

The large porch allowed for a line of rocking chairs and small tables for family and guests to enjoy the late afternoon view of the grounds. The finely manicured lawn was scattered with large live oaks and magnolia trees. On this day, the fragrance of crabapple trees, yellow Jessamine, and Cherokee rose embraced the air.

Josephine looked over the scene and sipped lemonade. She had been given a warm welcome when she arrived a few days back.

"I swear it is all they ever talk about…secession." Grace Ann sighed heavily and glanced across the porch at the men who talked in a circle about the growing unrest.

"Wade believes it will depend upon the upcoming election later this year," Jo said absently. At least, it was what Wade had written to her in his last letter. Elections and politics filled his pages…how his presence was needed in Charleston for one meeting or another.

In her mind, the letters held nothing more than useless excuses. She shook off her melancholy at the thought of her husband and looked over at her cousin. It had done her good to visit with Grace Ann.

Grace Ann looked as lovely as ever, dressed in a flattering blue day gown. Her blonde hair glistened in the sunlight, pulled up in a decorative hairnet constructed of gold-thread mesh and cream-colored silk ribbons.

The two sat with the other married women at Whitney Hall, the wives of Theodore's sons. Sarah and Peggy were quiet, but hospitable, though neither compared to Grace Ann in their appearance. Moreover, both were older with a brood of children of their own.

Jo had never questioned her cousin's decision to marry Mr. Whitney, but she had wondered. Theodore Whitney was a distinguished man of fifty-eight. Handsome for a man of his age, Jo supposed. His hair was streaked with gray; his eyes were strong, vital. A man of medium height, but carried himself tall and walked with a brisk purpose. But there was over a thirty-year span between their ages.

Grace Ann had her pick of eligible bachelors in Charleston and she had settled upon Theodore Whitney. It had been a surprising choice to Jo, but Grace Ann seemed quite content with her marriage. Never had she given any indication to Jo of dissatisfaction with the union.

Louis and Peter were sons from Theodore's second wife. He had three daughters from his first. They, too, often made appearances at Whitney Hall with their own families. In total, Theodore Whitney had five children and twenty-one grandchildren.

At the moment, Jo watched quite a few of them running around on the lawn, playing alongside of the slave children. Laughter and giggles echoed around the grounds until one of the youngest Whitney children fell. A cry burst forth.

"Elijah Whitney, do not play rough with your sister," Sarah demanded and scooted back her chair. Shortly, she was down on the lawn, looking at a skinned knee of her daughter.

Jo smiled at the scene when the small girl seemed all better when her momma kissed her scratch. The other children had already run off, but one stayed behind, a small slave boy.

He was dressed in a loose, dirty white shirt and wore no shoes. A wide smile crossed his face as he waited for the return of his playmate. Jo took another look. She swore the child looked white.

"Grace Ann," Jo whispered behind Peggy's back. "That child looks…"

Ensuring she would not be overheard, Grace Ann glanced over her shoulder and leaned over to Jo before she answered. "It is Louis, if you must know," she said in a low voice. "Mr. Whitney has reprimanded him numerous times. Louis has shown only arrogance and takes whatever slave whore he chooses. Shameful. He doesn't even acknowledge them. Sarah has no choice but to turn a blind eye."

Peggy looked oddly at the two. Jo inclined back and gave her a small smile. Covering the whispers, Jo turned the conversation. "I was inquiring of my cousin if she had knowledge of any of my relations in Camden. While I am here, I thought I would reach out to them. Do you know of them...the Wrights?"

"You want to visit the Wrights?" Peggy questioned.

"They are my family," Jo answered, but quickly concluded that Peggy did not believe it would be appropriate. Making light of the situation, she went on, "I traveled many places with Papa. London. New Orleans. New York. But, I fear, Papa never brought me to his home. Even while I stayed with Grandpa Henry, I never traveled to Camden. So I have never made the acquaintances of Papa's family."

"Of course, you shall."

Surprised by his interruption, Jo watched Theodore Whitney rise and cross over the porch. She asked him, "You will take me?"

"In time," Whitney replied. "First, allow me to take you to your papa's grave. Say, tomorrow afternoon."

"I would like that very much." She had wanted to visit Papa's grave the moment she had arrived. It would be good to go with someone who shared her grief and something told her that Whitney had been touched by her papa's death. "I will wait most patiently."

* * * *

A spectacular sunset loomed over the grand oak trees and cast a reddish tinge over the pond. The small graveyard nestled along the hillside within a black wrought-iron fence, a quiet, peaceful place. It had served as the final resting place for the Whitney family for over a century.

Josephine knelt beside her papa's grave. It sat to the far corner, away from the immediate family...unmarked and alone. Whitney had assured her that the marker would be engraved and placed on Papa's grave before the end of her visit.

She supposed it was strange that she had never been to her papa's birthplace, but he had not even talked of his home or invited questions about his childhood. What she had discovered had come from Miss Hazel, which had not been much.

Her grandparents, Lucas and TaeLynn Wright, had come from humble backgrounds and lived on a small farm in Camden. It was rumored that Lucas Wright had risked his own life to saved Whitney from drowning. Whitney then swore he was in debt to Wright and held to it by seeing to Wright's son after his father's death.

Jo had always believed it had been the glimpse of the life Whitney lived that had been the motivation for Papa to succeed. Fueled by being an outcast in the world he wanted so desperately to be a part of despite his wealth and marriage, his hopes had fallen upon her, his only child.

She laid a black wreath down on the solemn spot and whispered a fervent prayer, a final farewell. She hoped now her papa had found the peace he had not found in this world.

Behind her, she heard Whitney move to her side. For a time, he said nothing. In this light, he looked older. Tense lines formed around his eyes; his shoulders drooped slightly. An aura of sadness surrounded him.

"It is a tragedy that your father could not have seen you married to Wade and are now the mistress of Magnolia Bluff," he said. "If you had any doubt, know that it was his wish."

Emotions swelled, but words caught in her throat. The last month, her world had collapsed around her. She had been left confused and bewildered with little to cling to…she had strived so hard to please her papa. The knowledge that Wade had not lied to her gave her a semblance of strength.

Jo sighed. "Thank you for your kindness. I know Papa came to depend upon you. He must have admired you greatly because I can't ever remember Papa relying on anyone the way he did you."

"Over the last year, we formed a strong bond," Whitney conceded. "It is that bond that I wanted to address with you."

"Mr. Whitney." She looked up at him. "I know he was grateful for the opportunity you gave him as a child…"

"Was he?" Whitney scoffed. "I provided for him, gave him shelter, offered him an education. It was he who grasped the opportunity. I did little else. I barely noticed him when he was here at Whitney Hall."

"Why would you? It mattered only that you looked after his welfare and kept your word to his father."

"Is that what you truly think? Have you not heard any of the whispers about your papa?"

"Whispers?" she questioned, once more bewildered. "I am afraid you have me at a loss. I thought you one of the few people who held Papa in esteem?"

Whitney broke his gaze and stared out across the pond. "Esteem? I admired him more than I do any of my other sons." He turned and faced her. "He was my son, Josephine, as you are my granddaughter."

The woods became deathly still as Josephine listened to a man expel his demons. This…this was what Miss Hazel had tried to keep from her. Her father was a *bastard*! Her stomach churned! *No…no…no! Papa may have been the son of a poor man, but he was no bastard.*

"Brantley never meant for you to know," Whitney confessed. "He did not want your name tarnished, but I'm afraid that my sins have fallen not only upon my son, but you as well. A child branded by not actions of his own, but would be shunned for a lifetime."

"I do not believe it…" Her voice quivered. "Papa would have told me."

"It was his shame, Josephine. It was what drove him to prove to everyone he was a gentleman."

The truth suffused within her. She was going to get sick. All she had done to have kept the dowagers' tongues from wagging and all this time, they had been correct. She would never be part of their society…

Then suddenly, a thought hit her hard. Grace Ann had complained about Louis…the mix-raced slave children. If the Whitney men gave no thought where they planted their seed…

Jo drew in her breath. "My grandmother? Who was my grandmother?"

"Her name was Eloise. She was the daughter of a small store owner in Nashville. She had come to visit her sister here in Camden after her mother passed away and her father had remarried." Whitney paused, as if reliving a different time. He shook his head slightly. "We were young…too young. She was no more than fifteen when Brantley was born. My father out-and-out refused for me to marry one he thought so beneath us.

"It was then that Father made arrangements for Brantley. When Eloise decided it would be for the best to give up the child, Father took him and gave Eloise enough money to return home. In turn, Father paid the Wrights to take in my son. Father made up the story of me being grateful to Lucas Wright after he passed so it would explain why we took Brantley into our household. Father took quite a liking to Brantley…he had charm and intelligence even then."

Josephine shook her head. "Why? Why are you telling me this? I do not want to know…You had to know it was better for me to think him the son of a farmer than a…*bastard*." The word spewed out harsher than she wished. Her poor papa! The whole of his life he had strived to overcome the social stigma.

305

"I was proud of my son, Josephine. He overcame much in his life. Know I would never have told you if I did not believe it necessary," he said.

In spite of her shock, Josephine had a need to know his purpose. "Then explain to me why you think it is important to me...now."

"Don't go visit the Wrights. It will only stir up unnecessary trouble. Leave it as it is."

"Am I to live a lie?"

"It is not a lie, Josephine. My son...your papa was a fine man. I wish men were judged by their deeds and not by the labels placed upon them, but you know as well as I that is not the way of the world."

Jo rubbed the pain from her forehead. Her lips pressed tightly together, she pushed back her toiling emotions. "I am so confused."

Whitney reached over and squeezed her hand tightly. "I am certain you are. This will be our secret, but know you are not alone. We are family."

She thought of Papa and the man beside her. She realized that Whitney had long looked after her and wanted only her to know of his love of the son he had lost. Strangely, she took comfort with the knowledge and took it to heart that he would never confirm the rumors. Suddenly, she didn't feel so alone in the world.

* * * *

A canopy of moss-covered branches arched over the long avenue of oaks. It gave way to a pasture where the horses were stabled. Alongside the stables were the dog kennels where Josephine found herself this morning.

Her slippers were wet from the dew as she kept up to the little feet of the child in front of her. Unable to sleep, Josephine had risen early and, as had been her habit of late, she walked. This morning, Mirabella, Sarah's youngest girl, had joined her.

"Coosin Joosphin," Mirabella, a pretty little thing with natural blonde ringlets falling haphazardly around her smiley face, called to Jo. "See!"

Josephine smiled at the small one, who had her pudgy little fingers between the opening in the fence and played with a litter of puppies being weaned from their mother. Seven whiny pups gathered around the girl.

"I see, Mirabella."

"Want 'em out." Mirabella pointed to the momma dog, a large, powerfully built bitch pacing in another pen.

"Sweetie, we need to leave them where they are and ask your papa when you can get them out."

"They cry."

"It may not seem so, but it's for the best for the momma and the puppies." Jo knelt down on one knee to face the little girl.

Suddenly, she caught herself. Oh, it was happening again...the dizziness, the stomach upheaval. Covering her mouth with her hand, her stomach churned and her head spun.

Jo opened her eyes. She was on the ground with a tiny hand patting her face, trying to wake up. As she looked up, she saw Mirabella crouched down beside her.

"Coosin Joosphin'...you okay?"

Faint, Jo sat. Almost immediately, she saw an entourage come toward her, Grace Ann leading the way. Not even waiting to dress for the day, she still wore her nightclothes.

"I'm fine." Jo attempted to stand. Embarrassed, she waved back those who had rushed to her aid.

Grace Ann would have none of it. "Oh, pooh! It is only us women, Jo. Not like we haven't seen it before. The sickness will pass in time."

"It's not that, Grace Ann," Jo protested. "I just haven't slept."

Grace Ann smiled, a knowing smile exchanged with Sarah. "Of course it is. Hon, you married a couple of months ago."

With her arm wrapped about Jo's shoulders, Grace Ann walked with her back to the main house while Sarah had Mirabella's mammy look after her daughter. The women ushered Jo back to her bedroom and into bed.

Oh, mother of all! She couldn't be expecting! She fought against welling tears—the tangled mess that had become her life. *Whatever am I going to do!*

"I'll see to getting you some tea," Sarah offered. "It helped me in your condition."

The moment Sarah left the room, Jo gripped her cousin's hand. "I can't be expecting...I just can't be. Wade..."

"Hon, he will be thrilled, I'm certain. Men are, you know."

"He won't be...he only married me because..." Jo couldn't finish the words. She burst into tears and wept.

Sitting down on the bed's edge, Grace Ann pulled Jo into her arms and rocked her. In the silent room, she asked, as if contemplating the worst, "You did have relations with your husband?"

Jo nodded. "Yes...but..."

"Then there are no buts," Grace Ann stated plainly, dismissing Jo's fears. "Honey, it ain't right the way you've been treated. Engaged to one brother, then marry the other. But you need to write Wade. He needs to know—"

"No," Jo said emphatically. "I'll die first. He wants nothing to do with me. Why else would he send me away? You don't know…Andrew is in Charleston with his…his wife. I'm left out…they only wanted…"

"Nonsense, you silly girl," Grace Ann said. "Mr. Whitney says that Wade has done a grand job of negotiating peace between Grandpa Henry and the Montgomerys. Now that Harry Lee is recovering nicely, it is well that there are no ramifications from that awful incident."

"You don't understand. Wade is not happy with me to begin with…now this."

"Now what? A baby? Are you not happy with the thought? Do you not understand how much I would love to be in your place? You have to realize how much I would have loved to have a child."

"You never have said."

"I have maintained my dignity." Grace Ann heaved a tremulous sigh. "Mr. Whitney does not care. Our marriage has been a happy one for us both. He has children from his other marriages and does not feel the need for more. It is my loss."

The idea that Grace Ann felt the sting of being barren had never occurred to Jo. Grace Ann had never been the mothering sort, but Jo understood the reproach of an unforgiving society.

"I have always yearned to have a child…it is only…what if Wade doesn't want it…or me?"

A laugh escaped Grace Ann. "Then we will do it together. You and I…and Mr. Whitney, of course. We have a plantation over the border in North Carolina. It's small. I have only been there once, but thought it would be a lovely place for a child."

"Do you think we could?"

"I would not have said so, if I didn't know we could," Grace Ann assured her. "But I doubt it will come to that. I can't believe Wade would ever let you go. You forget I was there when the two of you were on the verge of scandal, proclaiming love for each other."

"I'm not so sure."

"Well, I am. Truly, though, it is of no matter, for I'm quite excited to be an auntie."

Jo eased her head against Grace Ann's shoulder and listened to her cousin talk. She needed to be distracted for despite the confidence Grace Ann displayed, Jo held none. She was worried, terribly worried.

* * * *

It was a quiet afternoon. Josephine sat out on the porch and enjoyed the peace and serenity of the moment. Sarah and Peggy had taken the children to visit Peggy's sister, who lived over in Chesterfield. It was good to have this time.

Somehow, she had to come up with a semblance of a plan. Despite Grace Ann's support, she couldn't impose on their hospitality much longer. She had heard Whitney talk of returning to Charleston. Jo held little doubt Grace Ann would be by her husband's side.

Jo had let Grace Ann ramble on about their wild fantasy of going to the plantation in North Carolina to raise her baby. Her cousin meant well, but Charleston was brewing with the thrill of anticipation of the upcoming presidential election. Anxiety would riddle Grace Ann if she missed a moment of the excitement and celebration, especially with the news filtering in about the escalating tension against the North.

The question had become not if she was going to leave South Carolina, but where was she to go. She had few options, but she couldn't stay. However was she going to carry on?

Instinctively, her hand went to her stomach. The local doctor had confirmed she was to be a mother. She had long dreamed of having a child, but not like this. Not with a husband who hated her…not knowing… Oh, she could die!

"Josephine."

Slowly, Jo turned and uttered under her breath, "Wade."

Her first impulse was to run. As she stood, she readied herself to bolt, but he caught her hand and held it firm.

"Calm yourself, woman! My Lord! One would have to wonder what you think of your husband!"

Her eyes flicked over him. By heavens, he looked handsome! His face bronzed golden by the sun; his blonde hair gleamed; his clothes were immaculate, with not a button out of place; his boots brightly shone. He carried himself in his crisp manner, which was evidence of his good breeding…but he had taken her by surprise.

"What are you doing here?"

"I've come to take you home."

She stared at him in silence. She didn't know for how long. Finally, she said, "Surely, you jest. I haven't heard from you in the last couple of weeks. Then you show up unannounced. Why?"

Wade closed the gap between them. "I have behaved abominably. I have no excuse except I let my anger…jealousy get the better of me. It was not my finest hour. I have come here to beg your forgiveness."

"Don't do this to me. I can't take it from you…not now."

"Take what? An apology?"

Her dark eyes snapped with fire. "Your lies. I don't know what game you are playing, but I want no part of it."

She pivoted around with every intention of leaving him where he stood. He seized her by the shoulders and maneuvered around to face him. "I asked you to listen to me, Josephine."

"Why? In your eyes, I have shamed you. I can't undo what has been done. I didn't ask for any of this…" She pulled away from him. Her voice trailed off. "I don't know what you could say that would change anything."

"I love you. I've always loved you." His words silenced her. He took advantage and swept her back within his arms. "I do not deserve your forgiveness, but it is what I ask." His declaration and soft words gave her pause. He pressed on. "I was angry, but not at you, but myself. I should have never let you go to Andrew."

"But you did… How could you?"

"I didn't know he was married. If I had, I would never have let you go. Remember it was you who lied to me that he had called for you."

"With reason." Her eyes burned into his. "You chose Magnolia Bluff over me."

"I, too, had reason. Do you not realize that I know you better than you know yourself? You…who holds to family honor and duty! You told me that Andrew was holding to your engagement. How could I ask you to sacrifice a part of yourself?"

"I can't think," she whispered. "What more do you want from me?"

"Before God I declared myself to you, Josephine. You are my wife. Have you no sense that it is you who has consumed me?"

"Then why do you hate me so?"

"Hate you?" he asked. "Can you not understand I love you? Everything I have done is for you. I have the matters settled with your grandfather. Andrew has gotten his own house in Charleston, with strict orders to keep that woman from you…"

"That should be easy enough since I'm not in Charleston."

"But you will be," he uttered thickly as his disarming smile emerged. "I have no excuse for leaving you as long as I have other than I hadn't the courage to face you. It was easy to get lost in the happenings in Charleston. It is no excuse, but I have come now to repair the damage."

"I don't know if you can."

"I ask only that you give me the chance to try." He took her hand and fell upon one knee. "Josephine Wright Montgomery, we can spin in a circle all day, all month. By God, I believe we could do so for the rest of the year, but it will not get us to where I want us to go. I have come to take you back and I will make up to you all that I have failed to do. Give me a chance to show you of how I feel."

He reached in his side pocket and pulled out a ring. "It's about time I put a ring on your finger. What I would like to do when we return is have another ceremony. A large one in Charleston. We will invite the whole of the city, if you want. I want to give you the ceremony you deserve…"

She shook her head as she looked down at the ring, not a simple gold band, but a band encased with an emerald surrounded by a diamond on each side. "I can't…" She desperately searched for her courage and control to tell him the words that needed to be uttered.

She wanted nothing more than to tell him of the child…to tell him the child she carried was Cullen's…to make him wonder if her words were true. Would he love her then…would he still promise her the words he uttered here today?

She had a desire to hurt him as she hurt. But to what end? Her hand went upon her stomach once more. It was not her life, but her child's she had to consider. She could not play with the future of her child. *Words uttered cannot be taken back.* Once they are said, the damage is done.

She withdrew her hand and said simply, "I can't… I'm with child."

* * * *

From the look on Wade's face, the news was not a shock. Instantly, she knew Grace Ann had interfered and written him of the circumstance she now found herself. She saw it in his eyes.

Over the last year, she had lost her youthful innocence. She had become suspicious of everyone…trusted few…questioned the man she married, even the man she loved. She had spiraled down an abyss to where there was only a faint light in the distance.

She waited for the accusations. He had come to torture her…humiliate her further…label her a hussy…her child a bastard.

At the time, God forgive her, she had no remorse for lying with Cullen. Had they not loved each other…planned for a future together? She had given herself freely…but he had left her.

No matter the reason, she had to fend for herself and a child…a child…God help her…she didn't know what to do.

That last night she had spent with Cullen, words were never spoken, but each had known she had no choice. She would marry Wade. Why

311

then would Cullen have made love to her, leaving her to deal with the possible consequences of their actions?

Surely, Cullen had known that Wade wouldn't be patient toward exercising his connubial rights and where would she be? *Where I am now—at a loss and terribly alone.*

She shook her head solemnly and stepped back. She wanted nothing more than to withdraw back to her room, but he halted her progress.

"Don't leave, Josephine. We need to talk without other ears listening."

Hesitantly, she looked up at him through blurred eyes. She could take no more, but he held her firmly.

"I can't allow you to turn away from me after uttering those words."

"What do you want from me, Wade?" she asked amid simmering frustration. "Do you want to taunt me as I try to defend myself? You know as well as I, I have no defense. Tell me what you want me to say. Do you want to hear the child is yours? Would you believe me if I declared it was?"

She jerked back her hand. Tears she had fought so hard to contain fell silently down her cheeks; her legs weakened. "I can't," she cried. "God help me, Wade. I can't live with your accusing eyes upon me, knowing the question that will always dwell within you."

"There is no question, for my eyes hold only the love I feel for you," Wade stated firmly as he took her back into his arms. He tenderly wiped away her tears, so confident...so assured. "I have been frothed with jealousy...besides being a complete ass...but this child is mine."

Befuddled, Jo shook her head. "I refuse to play games with you, Wade. You so as much as called me...," she stuttered over the word, "a...a whore when you discovered I had been with Cullen and now you know for certain the child is yours? I refuse to live this way, Wade, with suspicion upon me and my child. I can't—"

Wade leaned over and silenced her with a gentle kiss. "You are my wife. The child is mine...as is his mother. You are coming home with me."

He gave her no time to protest as his lips descended upon hers again. Within her the urge to correct him, to tell him he was wrong, emerged, but she hesitated and with hesitation came silent acceptance.

* * * *

Rain pounded against the pane of the window. Josephine lay in bed and listened to the wind howl, thankful that Wade had decided to stay at the inn in Orangeburg on their way home to Charleston.

Since his declaration, Josephine's heart had warmed toward Wade and she discovered herself falling under the spell he wove around her. He played the gallant husband in front of the Whitneys and waited upon her every need.

Thanking the family proficiently for taking such care of his bride, he made arrangements for their return to Charleston. He professed his impatience to have Jo by his side, and the couple departed Camden less than a week after his arrival.

When she said her good-byes, Whitney gave her pause. "Wade is a good man. Don't hold to the past. Take this moment and move toward the future. May God be with you."

She wanted to believe she had a future with Wade, but doubts gnawed at her. There had been no more intimate discussions between them. He had given her time to contemplate his words, but she had only become more confused.

"You are supposed to be resting. Rosa said you haven't eaten today."

Jo sat up with a smile as Wade entered with a tray of tea and cucumber sandwiches for her dinner. "I'm fine. The queasiness comes and goes. It is to be expected. Truly."

"It won't hurt to take it easy. We are not in a hurry. I want you to take care of yourself."

She wondered whether he was remembering Clarissa...that he held fears. "Wade," she whispered. "Are you scared?"

As he sat the tray down on the nightstand, he looked at her strangely. "No, should I be? You're not feeling—"

"No, no," she quickly assured him. "It's only...Wade, I don't know about any of this...I am...I am scared." Sudden emotion overcame her. She didn't know what was wrong with her as a dam of tears streamed down her cheeks. "All you have done, you have done for your family...and now you have me to content with..."

"Ssh, Jo, I'm afraid I'm not much of a nurse." He slipped in bed beside her. "What is wrong?"

"Everything...I have not heard from Gillie. I fear for her. In my sleep, I hear her calling to me. I know she needs me...and I can't get to her..."

"Don't do this to yourself, Jo. You are putting yourself through needless anxiety. Though, I will not make light of her injuries, which were severe," he said in a solemn voice. "But it is my understanding that Gillie is recovering—slowly. I give you my word it is all that I know. I would imagine that is the reason your Miss Hazel hasn't returned to

Charleston. I know how much you need your mammy, but I would not expect her back in the near future."

"I know Gillie has need of her. I worry…that is all. I wish I could see Gillie."

"I understand your need, but, I'm afraid, I would insist you not travel in your condition. I assure you I will see to it that all her needs are met."

He wrapped his arms about her and kissed the top of her head in a comforting manner. "But allay your fears about Harry Lee. He may live, but your grandfather has banished both your cousins to his plantation in Mississippi. They are not to return."

She could not contain the shiver Harry Lee's name sent through her. "Truly?" she questioned anxiously. "He is not the type who will give up."

"Trust me, Jo. It will not be worth his effort. I have made certain of it," he stated emphatically. "I will protect you. You are safe."

Her hands clutched tight to his dampened shirt. "There is more," she rasped as she choked back her tears. "There is a fear within me for my child. God help me, Wade, I won't have my babe called a…bastard."

He reached down and brought her chin upward so she could see his eyes. "Neither will I, my dear. I told you there is no question."

"But—"

"No question," he said adamantly. "I love you, Josephine. You are my wife. I will be by your side always. I have much to make up for." He kissed her gently. "And if I have to spend the rest of my life to convince you of my love, I will."

Jo could hear the steady beat of his heart under her ear. She was comforted by his gentle stroking of her hair. Her tears dried, her eyelids drifted closed. When the mattress moved, she was startled. "You are leaving me?" She grasped his hand.

Wade eased off the bed and gently laid her head on the pillow. "Only so you can sleep. I will make a pallet on the floor."

"Don't," she pleaded. "Don't leave me."

"Honey, I'm not going anywhere. I will be right beside you."

"I don't want to be alone. I need you, Wade."

He gave only a short pause before he eased in beside her. His lips found hers. She responded as her body trembled against him and passion stirred.

The rain fell in a steady rhythm deep into the night, but in the morning, the sun rose and the birds sang. Josephine woke in the arms of her husband, oddly content. She smiled up at him as he rose from the bed they shared.

"What a beautiful day." He leaned back to kiss her. "I'll see to our breakfast. I find myself quite hungry."

Jo watched him leave the room. Wade seemed happy…happy that she had accepted the life he offered and offered no more resistance.

During the night, she had come to the realization of her need for Wade and she clung to him. Her silence upon the matter of the child had sealed her fate. She chose not to question Wade's proclamation of love and faithfulness. She accepted all he seemed so willing to give to her now. Wade gave her hope. She was going back to Charleston with her husband and the bright promise of their life before them.

Chapter Five
Philadelphia

The summer found the presidential election on the mind of everyone in Philadelphia. There were a few people with other matters of importance. Insignificant in the eyes of the world perhaps, but within one small apartment, the world the family had known had fallen apart.

Dreams of a better life…faded, as did his wife. Heyward watched helplessly the small, fragile woman collapse into a world of her own…one that didn't include him. God, he had tried, but she recoiled at his touch…at his voice.

Gillie only allowed his mother to care for her. The only name she cried out for was Miss Jo, occasionally recognizing *Miss Hazel*. It tore at his heart and soul.

"Ma, what am I to do?"

"It is not you, son," Miss Hazel said in a solemn voice. "It is like she has regressed to her childhood."

He agreed, having wakened to Gillie's scream, loud and shrill. Then the sobbing began. It gnawed at him that he could not give her comfort, but watched his mother tend to her.

"Miss Jo? Where is Miss Jo?" Gillie asked in a timid, frantic voice.

"I will go and get her. Now, ya just lay yourself down."

"Ssh, not so loud," Gillie whispered in a plea. "Master Buchanan can't know."

"Know what, child?"

A small smile crossed Gillie's lips. "Miss Jo. She lets me sleep in her bed. Says she has plenty of room."

"I'm sure she does."

Gillie lost her smile. Her eyes bulged as terror gripped her. "Miss Jo holds me when I wake. She keeps the dreams from coming. I need her."

316

She looked around frantically. "Where is Miss Jo? Master Buchanan didn't find out. Did he? He would whip her for sure."

"No, child, all is well. Miss Jo will be back in a minute. You sleep now."

Exhausted, Heyward sat down at the table. He swore he had not slept since the night Gillie had been arrested. Nothing had been the same.

A slight summer breeze moved the curtain. It promised to be a nice, lazy Sunday. Soon, the streets would be filled with churchgoers. Sunday mornings had been Gillie's favorite. She so enjoyed to socialize at church. He loved how her face lit up talking with her newfound friends… Now he hated Sundays.

He wanted for her to wake up from the nightmare she was living in and be the Gillie he loved. He hadn't a clue how to make her better. Where had *she* gone? Would she ever return?

Rage shook his core, not at Miss Jo. No, she had sacrificed herself to try to save Gillie. His all-consuming anger was directed at the man who had done this horrific act. A man who gave no thought to a human life. One day…one day he swore he would make Harry Lee pay for the damage he had done.

While her physical wounds had healed, she was left with terrible scars. All the mirrors in the apartment had been hidden. He couldn't allow Gillie to see herself. The right side of her face had been sliced; her eye drooped. The nerve had been cut, leaving the cheek sagging. Her beauty left only in an echo of what had been.

Heywood's anger roiled. That bastard Harry Lee had cut her breasts. Then he had mutilated her to where she would never be able to have any relations with any man…if she ever wanted to have them again, which he highly doubted. Gillie lived but she was only a shell of the woman she once was.

"Heyward, I was thinking about Miss Jo."

He looked up at his mother, who sat down across from him. "Miss Jo?"

"Now don't ca get upset, but I wrote to her and asked her to come. Master Wade answered. He said that Miss Jo has been deeply worried about Gillie, but is unable to come to Philadelphia. I thinks she's with child. He hasn't let her know how bad Gillie is, but Master Wade made a suggestion."

Heywood's forehead furrowed. "What kind of suggestion?"

"I told him that Gillie needs Miss Jo. It's the only way I see her coming back into the world. You may not like it, but Master Wade offered to take Gillie back to Charleston. He is certain Miss Jo would give her the best care…I would return with her."

God, he felt awful. All that the two of them had gone through to leave the South behind! His first instinct was to say an emphatic no…but something in him told him that it would be the best for Gillie. "But that bastard…Harry Lee?"

"He's dun gone. Ain't coming back, Master Wade said. I believe him. I do. Master Wade won't let nothin' happen to Miss Jo."

Suddenly, an abrupt noise interrupted their conversation. *Was it the back door slamming?* Heyward rushed up and looked quickly into Gillie's room—she was gone! Panicked, he ran outside and down the back alley into the street.

He got there too late…too late to stop his wife from walking blindly into the road…too late to save her from the oncoming carriage that was unable to halt before it swerved into her. But he was there to hear the screams of the onlookers…to see his beloved wife lie motionless on the cold ground…to hold her as she took her last breath.

Miss Hazel hurried behind her son. She found him with tears streaming unheeded down his face, cradling a lifeless Gillie, barefoot and in only her nightgown. A sad sight…such a sad sight.

* * * *

Thick tension cut the air. Cullen held no doubt that changes were coming. He was just concerned whether it would be a change for the better.

Cullen had finished attending a Republican political rally for Abraham Lincoln and had retired back to his hotel, where he had agreed to meet with his former Navy commander, Charles Davis. His work for Smythe and Company had taken him to Chicago. He had made a brief stay over in Washington before his intended return to Philadelphia.

Most times, Cullen did not revel in politics. It was nothing more than a necessary evil of expanding his business. No matter the outcome in November, this election would undoubtedly have widespread consequences. It was inevitable.

The 1860 run for president had come down to four candidates. In the beginning, Cullen believed that the Democratic entrant would have been the Little Giant, Stephen Douglas. Although Douglas held no opposition to slavery, he had not given his support for the expansion of slavery in the West, wanting instead to give the people of those territories the right to choose whether or not to have slaves. It was not enough for those in the South who demanded there not be any limitations

318

to the practice. The South had become radical in their approach to what Lincoln called a *peculiar institution.*

The Southern voice accepted only those who supported the spread of slavery. When the Democrats held their convention in Charleston, it was evident the party was divided. After fifty-seven ballots, no solid candidate was endorsed. When they met in Baltimore a month later, Douglas was finally nominated by the Democrats, but not with support of the whole party. The Southern Democrats emerged with a candidate of their own, John Breckinridge.

As it had been from the beginning of presidential campaigns, Lincoln's run for the country's highest office had been conducted from his hometown of Springfield, Illinois. Rallies held in his honor across the country were done so with Republican representatives reading from Lincoln's published speeches, such as the one that Cullen had just attended.

Tonight, Cullen listened to Lincoln's Cooper Union address being read.

"There is a judgment and a feeling against slavery in this nation... Nor can we justifiably withhold this, on any ground save our conviction that slavery is wrong...Let us have faith that right makes might and in that faith, let us, to the end, dare to do our duty as we understand it."

Cullen held no doubt of whom he would vote. His vote would be cast for the Republican, but not without reservations. He had been raised in the South. Despite the rage he held toward his Southern family, he understood their concerns.

But unlike his Southern family, he questioned the South's claim that their contention was about states' rights. Although, he conceded that Northerners held a certain superiority toward their Southern brothers.

But now he comprehended only too well that it wasn't states' rights that were the basis of his support to the Republicans, but human rights. He had learned that fact...after what he had seen with his own eyes...what Harry Lee had done to Gillie...

"Lieutenant Smythe..."

Cullen stood on the address. Commander Davis, a man of average height, graying hair, and a well-groomed mustache, had arrived as arranged in the lobby of the Willard Hotel. The overly large room exhibited the luxury of the grand establishment, with great columns, huge chandeliers, plush rugs, and high carved ceilings.

Cullen had chosen the seats in front of the large fireplace to hold the intended conversation. While in service, he would have given his superior a salute. As a civilian, Cullen extended his hand. "Simply

319

Cullen Smythe now, Commander Davis. You forget I resigned my commission over a year ago." Cullen gestured for the distinguished officer to the seat across from him.

"I beg to differ. I know well you resigned. It is why I am here." Commander Davis smiled and sat. "If I have your permission, I will be direct."

"It would be best, sir."

"I would like for you to reenlist."

Baffled, Cullen shook his head. "Commander, in our last correspondence, I politely refused. McFadden and Mitchell's arguments did not change my mind. I doubt anything you say now will make me feel any different. Why are you being so persistent?"

Davis laced his hands together and leaned back in his chair. "I believe in being prepared, Smythe. It was why I asked you to attend the rally tonight. What was your impression?"

"I found the speech to be insightful, but in honesty, I have already made up my mind who I will cast my vote for."

"As has most in the nation," Davis acknowledged. "Saying that, it is my belief that Lincoln will win every free state. It will be all that will be necessary for Lincoln to become the next president. I ask you, what do you believe will happen when that occurs?"

Cullen fell silent for a moment. He realized exactly where the commander was headed. It was a thought he had refused to contemplate… The commander, as did he, didn't feel that the South was making idle threats.

"Old Abe is not beloved in any of the slave states. I would not be surprised if there is a call for secession, at least by my home state."

Davis nodded. "It is my conclusion as well. In this political climate, I believe it would be foolish not to consider that is the option the South will likely take. Even more foolish not to prepare for it."

"I don't disagree, Commander, but I still am confused."

"It is not that difficult concept, Smythe." Davis's smile faded. "One has to consider that the lines will be drawn. There is a potential of losing a great deal of our Navy officers to the South if that occurs. If it becomes a rebellion, the Navy will be in need of good, qualified officers."

A somber, ominous feeling encompassed the air. Cullen sighed. "It saddens me, but while I hold to my country, what you are asking me is to potentially take up arms against my own family."

"Look, Smythe, you were one of our finest young officers. Mark my word, you will be needed, especially because you are from South

Carolina. You, more than anyone, should understand that they are preparing themselves for a war."

Cullen fell silent, his silence acknowledging the truth in Davis's words. He understood all too well his Southern brothers and the pull of loyalty upon them to their home. He could well imagine the resignations that would follow if the South called upon them.

Davis's eyes filled with an intensity Cullen had rarely seen in the commander as he continued. "You are not the only Southerner I have held this conversation with. Not every Southern-born gentleman will be led blindly into the fire. Commander Farragut, a Southerner himself, has made it well-known that he regards secession as treason."

"I have long admired Commander Farragut," Cullen said in a solemn tone. "But what you are asking of me, I don't know if I can do so."

"Smythe, if it is as I predict, it will be asked of every man in this nation."

A dark cloud of gloom descended upon Cullen; his conscience weighed against him. His heart was Southern. Of that fact, he had no doubt. His anger against his own family also tore at his soul, but he did not want to let his ire over his personal life lead him to a decision that would have devastating consequences.

Growing up, he remembered the stories his grandfather told of his family battling for independence against the British. Pride burst forth in what had been accomplished to create the United States. The cost had been high for that freedom…how quickly it seemed to have been forgotten.

If he let reason rule him, Cullen comprehended that the country was a democracy where the minority could not dictate to the majority. It was his heart…his love of the people…the land that made him hesitate. The realization swept through him that he would not be able to postpone his decision much longer…as well as he could no longer emphatically state he would never stand against the place of his birth.

"Commander, I appreciate you reaching out to me," Cullen said with more confidence than he felt. "I will give the matter deep consideration."

"It is all I ask." Commander Davis rose. "It has been good to see you, Smythe."

Cullen watched the commander depart with the comprehension that if the situation was as laid out before him, he would have no choice but to choose a side. But it was a decision he could not make in haste.

* * * *

"I have tried so desperately to follow the rules that society and God has dictated. Now look at me."

"Could not most men and women complain of the same?"

Cullen had been awakened early this morning by his father's unannounced visit. He had only arrived back in Philadelphia late in the night. "Father, do not tell me you woke me this early to discuss the meaning of the world?"

"If it is bothering you." Jonathan stood in the middle of the room. He hadn't even removed his hat. He gestured toward the door. "Would you care to have breakfast with me?"

"I rather you tell me why you are here." Cullen tucked his shirt into his pants and combed his disheveled hair back with his fingers.

Jonathan nodded. "As you wish."

The slight grimace on his father's face did not go unnoticed by Cullen. He walked over to the window. The sun had barely risen. He turned back around and faced his father. "What is wrong?"

Jonathan pressed his lips together tightly and swallowed hard. "I thought it best to tell you myself instead of writing. Shortly after you left for Chicago, Heyward's wife was killed in a terrible accident."

"Gillie? How?"

"She walked blindly into an oncoming carriage. From what Heyward said, she had never fully recovered from the attack upon her."

His heart sank. Josephine would be devastated… A deep frown emerged. For a brief moment, he had forgotten it was not his to share with Josephine…she was not his to comfort. "It is sad, Father, but it has nothing to do with me. I have done all that I can do."

"That is not in question," Jonathan said. "Your actions were to be commended. It is only… there is more."

"Father, don't. If this has anything to do with my Southern family, I can assure you I have no interest." Cullen waved his hand in front of his face to halt his father. "I have, though, made a decision I want to share with you. I have decided to reenlist in the Navy."

"The Navy?" Jonathan said, taken back. "I thought you had no intention to serve again."

"That was when I had other plans for my life, before the threat of war loomed on the horizon."

"Do not do so because of anger, son."

Cullen shook his head and shrugged. "I have been trained to serve, Father. I feel strongly that the Union should not be divided. Do not question my patriotism."

"Of course, I do not, but do not expect me to exhibit happiness with the thought of you being drawn into a war. Although, it will not dim the pride I feel for having you for a son." He sighed heavily. "Still, you need to listen to me."

"What, Father? What could possibly be so important that you are pressing me so?"

"It may be nothing, but I thought you needed to know," Jonathan said. "Andrew wrote to me directly. Josephine is with child."

Chapter Six

A light ocean breeze swept through the veranda, giving a brief reprieve to the sweltering day. Josephine breathed in deeply. She would talk Wade into a long walk after dinner. She so enjoyed the evening strolls that had become their habit as of late.

How she loved Charleston! How happy she was that Wade had brought her back to the city...she had come home.

Charleston had become alive and vibrant with the constant ramblings of the election. The people were abuzz. Secession seemed inevitable if Lincoln was elected and Wade believed he would be.

"Lincoln's election will spur secession. We will have no choice," Wade informed her after one of the addresses supporting Breckinridge. The meetings down at Institute Hall had become more frequent.

Jo believed her husband, though she didn't understand why the city took such joy in the thought of breaking away from the rest of the United States. The rants against Lincoln echoed along the streets. Lincoln had been the butt of many jokes. No *damn* Yankee was going to tell the fine people of South Carolina what to do...

Hatred toward the man chilled her bones. She supposed it had a lot to do with her condition. The one thought that consumed her was her child and nothing...nothing was more important.

Wade had spun a cocoon around her, insulating her from the world. A smile formed on her lips as she felt the baby move. Oh, how she loved the feeling! She loved that Wade had cared for her in such a tender, loving manner. He had made her forget her life before...she thought only of her future...their future.

A burst of laughter came from the French doors, along with a mixture of voices chatting gaily. Josephine turned to see her sister-in-law walk onto the veranda.

324

Kathleen Montgomery was dressed in a lovely blue gown with a lace split. A matching white lace shawl wrapped around her shoulders. Quite lovely…and expensive. Jo knew because Wade was paying his brother's bills.

Andrew spent above his means, courtesy of the demands of his wife. Wade held no sympathy toward his brother until the birth of their child. Kathleen had delivered a sickly little girl, Fannie. And with her birth, Jo's anger toward Andrew melted.

She could not take her wrath against an innocent child. When Andrew asked Wade for financial help, Jo urged Wade to do so. Not for Kathleen, but for the baby. Kathleen had taken full advantage, to the point, she had moved back into the Montgomery Charleston house.

Jo simmered inside as she watched the woman manipulate the situation. Why, the woman left the poor babe in the care of the mammy most days while she socialized! Jo didn't even think the woman looked into the nursery and the care of Fannie fell upon Mother Montgomery and herself.

Behind Kathleen, Charlotte swept through the doors and entwined her arm in her newfound friend. Much to Jo's chagrin, Charlotte had seemed to take a fancy to Kathleen.

"Jo, I do wish you could accompany us this evening." Charlotte squeezed Kathleen's arm playfully. "It promises to be quite enlightening."

"Another rally?" Jo eyed her friend suspiciously. Something about Charlotte worried her. She looked the same, but something…something had changed since Charlotte married. Was it her eyes…where was the spark that used to light her eyes?

"I do wish you could go with us." Charlotte glanced down at Jo's stomach. "You are feeling well?"

Jo felt her face flush. No one in polite society talked openly of a confinement, only whispered tellings when one was alone, never in front of others. She had no objection to Charlotte or Mother Montgomery…it was Kathleen. "Yes. To be honest, I have never felt better."

"I may be biased but I do not believe Jo has ever looked more beautiful."

Jo smiled at her husband, who walked to her side and placed his hand protectively on her shoulder. She reached up and held his hand.

"Dear brother, you seem to be leading a charmed life," Kathleen said sweetly in her newly inflected drawl. "If only Andrew could be so fortunate."

"I am charmed, dear sister-in-law." Wade flashed a disarming smile. "And fortunate enough to have shared in my good fortune, even with my errant brother."

Kathleen gave no sign she had heard Wade's barb. Instead, she returned his smile. "I feel exceedingly fortunate myself. Charlotte and I are going out this evening. Our husbands are treating us to entertainment over at the Crockers'. Are you going to be in attendance...oh...I forgot you would have to go without poor Jo." Kathleen glanced over at Jo and smirked. "Still in mourning?"

Breathing in deeply to contain her irritation, Jo said nothing. Kathleen did not seem to understand the standard mourning in the South. Her father had passed less than a year ago. She had changed the lace around her collar to white, but she had no intention of changing out of black until a full year had passed. Papa deserved her respect.

"I have plans with my wife tonight." As Wade eased down in the chair beside Jo, he kept her hand in his. "Go and enjoy yourselves."

Wade waited only until the women disappeared back into the house before his hand went to Jo's stomach. The baby moved again. "He knows it is his father." Wade chuckled.

"You are certain it is a boy," Jo teased.

"Without a doubt, my love," he said. "As I also know his name."

"Oh, really. Are you going to let me know?"

"I was thinking of Percival. Would you find it acceptable?"

She brought his hand to her lips and she kissed it. "A perfect name for our child."

"It was my thought," he said in a tender voice. "Are you ready for our stroll?"

She nodded and allowed him to help her to her feet. Arm in arm, the two started toward the Battery. Jo leaned her head against his shoulder. She was content as long as she ignored the guilt.

Jo's conscience plagued her; her deep sense of righteousness gnawed at her. What right had she to accept this happiness? She had made love with Cullen...and now she accepted Wade's contention that the child was his...pushing back the possibility that the baby was Cullen's.

Aunt Sybil had talked to her once about what a woman should expect from her husband— that it was to be endured and bore with dignity and fortitude. That there were embarrassing intimacies between a husband and a wife which must be tolerated. Perhaps it would have been so if she married Andrew, but not with Wade.

Those few moonlight nights with Cullen had awakened within Josephine a deep vein of passion that tore through her soul. And to her shame, she had found passion to be an intimacy of her spirit. If her mind understood that Wade wasn't Cullen who she had given her heart, Wade had opened a door to this intimacy. With her husband, she had accepted this part of herself, allowing if only for that moment to forget the world around her.

Understanding suffused through her. Wade was of her world—a world of which only she would be truly happy being who she was—a deep born Southerner whose convictions and beliefs bore from the land and the people.

Jo paused at the railing along the Battery. She had always loved the view of the harbor. Ships filled the harbor with flags flying from a multitude of countries. Sea gulls flew overhead in the cloudless sky as the sun set.

"What are you thinking, my love?"

"How content I am." She looked up at him and smiled. "How there is nowhere else I want to be than here."

Wade wrapped his arm about her and pulled her close against his side. There they stayed until the sunset.

* * * *

The beginning of October brought cooler days, though the heat in the city rose. The climate against Lincoln had escalated further, with claims that the South would never be the same if the *ape* was elected. Despite the fact that the Republican platform allowed slavery to exist, only it would not support the expansion.

Jo found it confusing because one of the most respected members of the community, Wade Hampton, had proposed the same compromise. His opinion had been met with hostility. Charleston seemed well beyond listening to any concession and was in a temper for a fight…toward the North.

The mood in the state was festive and joyful. Jo had watched Wade attend a different social event almost on a nightly basis. If it wasn't a rally, it was a dinner. Tonight, they were hosting a dinner party, not the small engagements that Wade and she had hosted in the past few months. It had not been her choice.

Wade had arranged for one last dinner before the family withdrew back to Magnolia Bluff. Kathleen had been the one to interfere and created the need for a much larger gathering. *Lord, that woman tried her patience!*

Tired and uncomfortable, Jo sighed. It promised to be a long night. Rosa had finished styling her hair, but there wasn't much more she would do with her appearance, not with her ever-growing belly. Staying in her mourning black, she had taken to wearing high-waisted gowns suited to her advancing condition, but little could be done to hide her pregnancy.

"You must promise me you will be on your best behavior, Jo," Wade said. Staring at himself in the mirror, he straightened his waistcoat.

"If I must, but I can't abide the woman, Wade. She is most infuriating…acting like she is mistress here!"

"Calm yourself. Do I need to remind you that she is only in the house because you relented? I would have left her where she was." A small laugh escaped him. He moved to her side. "My love, why hold anything against Kathleen?"

"Why do you ask that?"

"Because she is miserable here in Charleston. If the truth be known, do you not believe that Andrew regrets soundly his decision to marry her? I, on the other hand." He took her by the shoulders and looked into her eyes. "Thank God for Kathleen every day. For without her, I would not have you."

Her face softened upon the utterance. "You think you can sweet-talk me into—"

He lowered his face to hers and kissed her once, twice…three times until she forgot that Kathleen even existed.

"I don't know what I will do now that your time is drawing near," he whispered against her lips. His hand touched her swollen belly. "I will have to learn patience."

"I have over a month more. You aren't leaving our bed?"

He laughed, loudly. "I love you, Josephine Montgomery. Most would insist."

"Should I?" she asked genuinely. "I don't know about such things."

His smile widened. "I will not leave our bed." He kissed her once more. "Come, we have guests."

The answer pleased Jo. She wrapped her arm about her husband's and began their descent to welcome everyone. She smiled up at him as they walked down the stairs.

She wanted to tell him everything she was feeling, that she couldn't sleep without him holding her. She had never admitted to him that she had a desperate need to feel protected against her dreams that haunted her.

Perhaps she didn't know how she felt. Miss Hazel returned to Charleston last week. She had so desperately hoped for good news, but all that Miss Hazel told her was that due to Gillie's injuries, Gillie couldn't write. Miss Hazel said there was nothing more she could do for her. Gillie understood she needed to come home to help care for Jo and the baby.

It should have made her feel better...it didn't. She couldn't shake the feeling there was more no one was telling her. Hurt lingered for Gillie...for Cullen. She tried to push him out of her heart, but he was a constant ache...a void within her.

She clung to Wade with a need that had sprung within her to escape that void. She questioned whether the need originated from Wade's proclamation of his love for her or the life that was growing within her. All she understood at this moment was she felt safe within Wade's arms.

* * * *

The house was pulsating. Voices, loud and boisterous, echoed throughout the gathering with the same fever-pitch tension the city held. The hubbub of voices conveyed confidence in the Southerner strategy.

Jo sat quietly beside Mother Montgomery and the other matrons of the community in a line of chairs against the wall in the drawing room. Dinner had been a success, but her head pounded. If she heard one more "Yee-aay-eee" coming from the study, she would scream.

Tired and exhausted, she wanted nothing more than to retire for the night. It would not happen. She saw the affair lasting well into the early morning hours. A loud laugh drew her attention.

As she glanced back over her shoulder, she saw Kathleen in the doorway with Wade, who had emerged from the study. She drew in a breath to contain her ire. Already Kathleen irritated her, dressed in a low-cut sapphire gown that accentuated her bosom in the most indecent fashion. Why, she was a married woman! *Oh, good Lord!* The woman placed her hand on his arm and laughed up at him in a manner that made her heart hammer so hard she thought it would burst.

"For shame!" Turning, Jo smiled. Grace Ann had sat beside her. Behind her fan, Grace Ann smirked. "The nerve of the hussy!"

"She is quite shameless," Jo conceded as she opened her fan as well to conceal their conversation.

"Why ever did you let her back into your house?" Grace Ann said more as a statement than a question. "Mr. Whitney said she needs to return back to the North. She is trouble, Jo."

"Little Fannie was sickly," Jo said in her defense. "Poor Mother Montgomery was quite distressed."

329

"You are too kindhearted. Why, look at her! Not to mention, she went after your best friend. It is said that the two of them are inseparable."

Jo glanced over the fan to look at Charlotte. Something was wrong with her dear friend. She knew her too well not to recognize that Charlotte wasn't the same toward her since she married. The thought crossed Jo's mind it might have something to do with her pregnancy. Like Grace Ann's situation, Charlotte had not been able to conceive.

"I believe it's time for you to be in bed, Mrs. Montgomery."

Placing the fan down, she looked up at her husband. Despite her back aching and her swollen feet, she suddenly didn't want to leave…not with Kathleen acting as if she was hostess.

"I can't leave our guests, Wade," she protested.

"I'm certain they will understand. You need to rest. Come, I will see you back to our room."

She realized she was not going to win the debate and accepted his hand, helping her to her feet. *Oh, mother of all! I'm huge!* When she looked up into Wade's face, she saw the amusement in his eyes. Suddenly a wave of pity swept through her. She fought back her tears. *Tears for only heaven knew what reason.*

Wade left after he tucked her in bed. Alone in the dark, her mind wandered to the goings-on downstairs. Tossing and turning, she slept little, wishing Wade would come to bed. Somewhere in the middle of the night, she awoke alone. She cried.

In the wee hours of the morning, Jo crawled out of bed, her wrap tight around her. Where was Wade? Her bare feet crossed the cold floor, but as she turned the handle of the door, a voice called to her.

"Josephine, where are you going? Do you need anything? I can call Rosa for you."

Startled, Jo clutched her heart. "Oh, Wade!" she cried. "You scared me so! What are you doing in the chair?"

His hair lay plastered to the left side of his head. He wore his nightclothes and had pulled a blanket around him. He looked most uncomfortable. "I didn't want to disturb you." He yawned as his long legs stretched out from the blanket. "Do you feel alright? It is not even light outside."

"I was looking for you." For some unknown reason, her voice faltered. Tears welled. "You weren't in bed…You would rather sleep in a chair than with me?"

"Oh, my dear." He took her in his arms and embraced her tightly. Kissing the top of her head, he murmured, "I didn't want to disturb you. You were tossing and turning. Here." He swept her in his arms and placed her back into bed. "Now, stay where I put you."

He eased in beside her and kissed her.

"You looked so miserable in that chair…but you can't sleep with me?"

"I don't think I'm going to win this talk if we continue." He snuggled next to her. "I told you I wouldn't leave our bed. I won't. It is only I think living in Charleston is disturbing you. I believe you need peace and quiet at the end of your confinement. Would you like to return to Magnolia Bluff?"

"Alone?"

"No," he assured her. "I will be there. I can travel by boat the days I need to return to Charleston."

Jo said nothing more, not wanting to admit she wanted desperately to be away from the city. Her anxiety eased to know she would be going back to their home—the place her child was conceived, the place her child would be born and raised.

* * * *

Josephine slept through most of the journey back to Magnolia Bluff. True to his word, Wade had brought her home, along with Mother Montgomery and baby Fannie.

"You are not mad with me for wanting to leave Charleston?" Jo asked when the carriage turned down the lane toward the plantation house.

A smile flickered across his face as he reached over and caressed her face. "No, never. You should not worry about anything but our child. I was born here. Now my child will be. This is our home…his heritage."

The carriage came to a stop and the door opened. Wade exited first and extended his hand to her. A chill was in the air, but the day was bright. Glancing upward, Jo soaked in the sight. Sunrays streamed down from the heavens as if God smiled down upon them.

She looked upon her husband's smiling face.

"Welcome home, Mrs. Montgomery."

* * * *

Fall took on a deep hue of vibrant colors as the leaves began to fall. The fields had been harvested and the garden pruned for the upcoming winter. The wonderful aroma of apple pie filled the house.

Jo had been at Magnolia Bluff for two weeks. How quickly she had fallen into a routine with a newfound confidence. Her days were spent managing the household, knitting and sewing for the baby, and taking long walks. Oh, how she loved her strolls!

Wade accompanied her most days but when he wasn't available, he made sure Rosa went with her. He wouldn't allow her to go out alone. When he would go into Charleston, he would leave early and return late. He had only stayed over once.

Miss Hazel moved into the main house. With Jo's time growing near, her presence gave Jo a sense of comfort that her mammy would be there for the delivery. Miss Hazel had seen that the nursery had been opened up and prepared, putting Jo's mind at ease.

Early on a Thursday morning, Jo was engaged in knitting a blanket when the dogs began to bark. Wade had gone hunting with his grandfather before breakfast. At first, she assumed they had returned. Making her way to the window, she was surprised to see a carriage approach. The vehicle stopped—Charlotte and Jenna exited.

Jo made her way to the door and waited for the two to be announced. Before either woman had time to step into the parlor, Jo shrieked, "Charlotte!"

Her arms went around her old friend. Before she realized it, both of them had succumbed to tears. Sniffling back her sobs, Jo took a step back from Charlotte and then hugged her once again. "Charlotte, I'm so glad you have come." She gently smoothed back the loosened tresses of her friend. "It is unexpected."

"I hope you're not angry." Charlotte winced slightly. "I had to see you."

"I'm so glad that you have come."

Jenna walked in without comment and hugged Jo. "It was my idea. I suggested to Charlotte it would do her good to come back to Magnolia Bluff."

"It has certainly lifted my spirits to see both of you." Jo took Charlotte by the hand. "I'm so happy to have you here. You are staying for the birth?"

"I don't know," Charlotte said tentatively. "Arthur said I could come, but he wants me back by the end of the week."

"He will survive for a few days, I'm certain." Jenna shrugged in the most nonchalant manner. "He had no choice. I needed you."

Confused by the exchange, Jo asked, "Needed her? Why?"

"It is Anna," Jenna began. "She has another fever and wants Momma. Andrew is seeing to her. I promised her that Charlotte and I would come and help you and baby Fannie so Momma could go back to

Charleston. Although, it took some convincing for Charlotte to accompany me."

Looking back at Charlotte, Jo pressed, "You did not want to come?"

"Why ever would you think such a thing?" Charlotte declared, but she blushed and lowered her gaze. "Oh, Jo, I'm so sorry, but it was only…Arthur has wanted me to keep my distance. It was only because Andrew and Jenna insisted so…"

"Why would Arthur want to keep you away from me?"

"Understand, he is only looking out for me, Jo," she said with such sadness in her voice. "He doesn't understand how close we…were once. I think he was worried that there might be a scandal…"

Jo blinked in surprise. "Arthur was concerned that I might taint your name? Charlotte, we are family."

Tears came to Charlotte's eyes. "Arthur…he looks after me." She shook her head, finding it hard to come up with the words she wanted to say. "He let me come today to see you." Her voice carried higher. "But I…I can't stay."

Jo leaned back in an effort to restrain the urge to unleash her temper against a man who wasn't even there. Instead, she said, "Why, Charlotte, you love Magnolia Bluff, and I would love for you to be with me during my confinement. I'm certain, Wade will insist. Arthur can also come and stay. Wade said that the hunting has been the best it has been in years. I will have him send word to Arthur."

Charlotte looked over at Jo, but shied away when Jo's eyes met hers. "No…no, Arthur is expecting me home…he would be angry."

"Expecting you home? You only just arrived!" Jo reached over and squeezed Charlotte's hand. "Have you missed me as I have you?"

"Oh, Josephine, you have always been a good friend. Much more so than I deserve." Charlotte released a tremulous sigh. "I wanted to come. Truly I did and Arthur agreed when Kathleen suggested I talk to you and beg forgiveness for Andrew."

Immediately, Jo fumed. *So Kathleen was behind this!* It should not have shocked her, but to use Charlotte in this manner…to have gone to her husband! It just made no sense.

"Forgive Andrew? I don't understand. You did not come to visit, but to plead for Andrew?"

Charlotte seemed befuddled and hesitated before she continued. "Do you not believe it is a shame to hold to being angry at someone when you seem so much happier with Wade? Look at yourself. You can't deny that you would have been miserable married to Andrew. Don't you believe everything ended well for everyone?"

"Dear Charlotte, you don't know everything that happened…the humiliation…the pain…all because of Andrew's selfish act. Do you not know what happened when I returned…Harry Lee…what he did to Gillie…Cullen." She caught her breath. "It killed Papa." Jo had not meant for her emotions to run away with her.

Charlotte began to tremble again. "Oh, Jo, I didn't mean to upset you. I know nothing of what happened to Gillie…or Cullen." Her hands shook. "It is you…you seem different now than you did before you left. It's in your eyes."

"Of course it is, silly," Jo said with a sudden light-heartedness in a vain attempt to deflate the rising tension. "I'm going to have a child. It changes all women."

"No, it's more than that. There's a fire in your eyes that wasn't there before. To be honest," Charlotte said, "before you left, I was worried about you."

Jo studied her friend for a moment. She was different. There was a fire inside her, a motherly instinct to protect her babe. Her need to shield her baby wasn't something she could talk to Charlotte about, or anyone for that matter.

Losing patience, Jenna said, "Charlotte, do not hedge the truth. The nerve of that woman to press upon you to bother Jo during her confinement! You shouldn't allow it."

"Arthur says that Kathleen is family and that she needs friends. She has been treated poorly since she arrived. She is Andrew's wife and doors have been closed to her because of you, Jo."

"With reason, Charlotte," Jo said, aghast. "But it was not my actions, but hers that have closed doors. Darling, she married my fiancé and the letter she sent to my dear Papa…"

"Please, Jo, how was she to know that he would have a heart attack? She feels awful and wants nothing more than for you to forgive her. It is unfair to blame her for your loss."

"Not blame her?" Jo questioned, confused at her friend's insistence on forgiving that woman. Anger swelled, she pressed, "Why would I not blame her, Charlotte? All she had to do was tell me Andrew had married her. Why would she send a letter to my father? I was in Philadelphia. Why? If you know her so well, tell me why?"

Charlotte rose and then faltered. Jenna immediately stood and wrapped her arm about her. Jo was slower in her response, but helped Charlotte to the settee. As she lifted her legs, Jo caught sight of Charlotte's ankle.

Swollen and bruised, Jo wondered how Charlotte walked. "Charlotte, you are injured. What happened?"

"It's nothing," Charlotte insisted. "You know I'm such a klutz. I tripped down the stairs. That is all."

"It's not all, you silly girl," Jo declared. "You are going to bed immediately."

"No." Charlotte's eyes widened…fearful. "I—"

"We will not take no for an answer. Will we, Jenna?" Jo glanced over at Jenna. "Rest. I will go have your rooms prepared and inform Mother Montgomery of your arrival."

Jenna followed Jo to the door. With her hand on Jo's arm, she halted Jo's progress. "It will do Charlotte good to get away from Charleston for a time."

"What is wrong with her?"

Looking back over her shoulder, Jenna leaned down for Jo's ears only. "It is whispered that Kathleen was seen with Arthur, walking in the Sawyers' garden last week…alone."

Jo's heart sank. *Poor Charlotte! Poor Andrew!* "I swear! What is wrong with that woman?"

"I don't know," Jenna answered. "But I believe it will be best for Charlotte to stay here."

"But of course," Jo agreed. "I will have Wade send Arthur word. He would not dare go against Wade."

* * * *

The last few days had been a pleasurable time for Josephine. Though Mother Montgomery had returned to Charleston to care for Anna, she had sent word that Anna's fever had broken. It was her hope to be back at Magnolia Bluff before the birth.

While her mother was away, Jenna had made it her mission to see that Jo's burden around the plantation had been eased. Charlotte had taken to overseeing the care of Fannie. Jo took joy in watching Charlotte playing with Fannie and decided it was what Charlotte needed—a baby of her own.

Jo saw Charlotte return to a semblance of her former self. Color returned to her cheeks. At times, she even smiled. It did not go unnoticed by Jo that Charlotte had not even mentioned Arthur, and Jo didn't press. She did not want anything to disturb the peace she had found.

Awaiting her time, Jo spent her days with a growing anticipation. She had come upon the realization that Wade was the Wade of old: easy mannered, gracious, and charming. His care and concern for her was evident to everyone. She took comfort with him by her side.

335

The sound of a rapidly approaching horse interrupted Jenna's play on the fortepiano. Wade rose, but heavy footsteps followed by a loud pounding on the front door, led to a stout, medium height man bursting into the room.

Immediately, Jo recognized Arthur Bowles. He held a hat in his hand, uncovering his unkempt hair. He looked quite disheveled; his waistcoat was unbuttoned and his cravat hung loose. It was obvious he had traveled fast and hard.

Moreover, he reeked of whiskey on both body and breath. His stubble face transformed into a reddened rage when his eyes caught sight of his wife, who seemed frozen in her chair. "Charlotte, why did you not return? I told you…"

Jo watched mortified as the man rushed across the floor and pulled Charlotte to her feet. His expression hardened; his eyes blazed with pure rage. A painful moan escaped Charlotte when he raised his hand. For a moment, Jo feared the awful man was going to slap Charlotte before Wade seized hold of the outraged man and hauled him away from his cousin.

Jenna swiftly took Charlotte into her arms in a protective manner, placing herself between Charlotte and her husband. Grandfather Montgomery rose and stood between the women and the enraged husband as another barrier.

Wade spun Arthur around and faced the man, eye to eye. "I warn you now, sir, to contain your temper or you will sorely regret your actions. You will not now or ever raise your hand to a woman in his house."

Arthur sneered. "She is my wife. I will do with her what I will."

As he pulled him up by his lapel, Wade barked, "She is my cousin and this is my home. Make no mistake about it. You will not treat a member of my family in this manner under my roof."

Arthur scoffed. "Do not lecture me when you have sorely ill-treated one of your own. A sweet, kind soul who has no one. You and your family have turned your back on one in need…so do not lecture me."

Wade wasted no time in questioning who Arthur spoke of; the whole of the room knew who he meant. Wade laughed. "You are a fool if you believe Kathleen to be the innocent party."

Indignant, Arthur drew himself up to full height. His bitterness remained unrestrained. "Kathleen is your family! The poor woman has been treated abominably. Living in a strange city that holds animosity toward her because she was born north of the Mason-Dixon—"

"Please don't," Wade demanded. "Don't say another word. You need to sleep off your bottle of courage."

"Courage?" Arthur's voice rose. "Are you questioning my courage? I assure you I have already signed up to fight those damn Yankees. Have you?"

"Surely you jest! Why is everyone so fired up about secession? To fight a war? It all seems so silly to me. Why would anyone want a stupid war?" Jo stated forcefully, having enough of Arthur's nonsense.

"I am not surprised at your sentiment. It is whispered you are a Yankee sympathizer." Arthur sneered with righteous anger. "If Lincoln is elected, no good Southerner will be happy until Yankee blood is spilled. Would you like that, Josephine Montgomery? How will you feel when your lover has taken up arms against the South?"

Wade's eyes narrowed dangerously. "Watch your words. You are talking to my wife."

Arthur huffed. "Was she not set to marry that damn Yankee cousin of yours after Andrew jilted her? I hear he's done gone and signed himself back up in the Navy for the Union. Didn't tell her, did ya, Charlotte? Ya said that your Jo would never side against the South. I tell ya she has… It's blasphemy! Why, I've heard it said she's a nigger lover."

"You little man! You don't know me, so don't try twisting my actions." Jo's eyes blazed and bore into him. "Do not question my loyalty. I have no doubt that we, Southerners, are drenched in tradition of honor and loyalty. Our men are brave and courageous, but I do feel there is a need to change…it is ours to make right. But if you question where I stand if secession comes, make no mistake about where I'll be. I have a Rebel heart and can be no other."

"Do not call yourself a Southerner! Nothing more than a filthy little—"

Arthur could not utter another word. Wade's right fist slammed into his jaw. The man fell where he stood. As he crawled up on his knees, Arthur held his bruised jaw.

"I will tolerate no more!" Wade roared and grasped hold of Arthur's arm. "You, sir, have crossed the line, attacking what I hold most dear. I will not have you slander my wife."

Arthur shook Wade off with a violent jerk, but the fool got no further. Clayton Montgomery had already summoned Saul.

"Take him where he can sleep it off." Clayton gestured to Saul, who stood in the doorway. Then, he turned to Wade. "It will do no good to beat him up tonight. We will address these issues when he's sober."

Jo watched while Wade followed behind Saul, certain he was shielding her from the drunken man. She was certain he would have shown no mercy to the man if Grandfather Montgomery hadn't stopped him, but she hadn't time to contemplate Arthur's fate. She had her own issue to content with. Charlotte clung to Jenna much like a child to her momma.

* * * *

"I…told you…I should never have returned," Charlotte wailed. The poor dear shook so hard she could barely stand. Her face flushed with apparent embarrassment; she lowered her gaze.

"No, he won't, Charlotte," Jo assured her. "Wade won't let him. Tell me, darling, what is wrong."

"No…no…" Charlotte insisted, wringing her hands together in a nervous manner.

Jo maneuvered her rounded belly to Charlotte's side and grasped hold of her hands. "Trust us, Charlotte. We love you…there is more you need to tell us."

"Oh, Jo." Charlotte sobbed. "I can't. He's my husband."

Jo wrapped her arms around her and stroked her hair. "Talk to me."

The room sat in silence. Finally, Charlotte said with a blank, inscrutable expression, "I envy you, Jo."

"What is wrong?" Jo pressed. "Don't deny it again. Jenna and I are worried."

"You won't understand," Charlotte murmured. "You are loved. That was all that I wanted to be…was loved. Andrew acted so despicable, yet Wade rode in like a knight in shining armor. I wanted that knight…after Harry Lee. I thought Arthur was…like Wade. Your husband loves you. Despite what Kathleen told me, I can see it in the way he looks at you."

"My situation was…is…complicated. But now, after everything, yes, I'm content."

"I wish I was more like you. You are so strong…I'm not. I have tried to be a good wife, but nothing I do makes him happy. He was so caring and wonderful before we married. He proclaimed he loved me…I thought he did…I can't make him happy." She halted and began to sob.

"In your marriage? The way it is between a man and a wife?"

"Mother told me that marriage was to be endured…but Jo…" Charlotte paused again, but pulled up her sleeves. Deep purple bruises covered her bare skin. Her trembling hands released the material and let it fall back over her wounds. "He hurts me…in ways I can't describe…I dread his nightly visits… It was why I became friends with Kathleen. It made him happy and he left me alone…I'm going to go to hell…"

338

"You aren't going to hell, my sweet Charlotte..."

Charlotte withdrew from Jo's embrace; she gulped for air as tears streamed her face. "I could have endured if he only let me keep my baby..."

"Charlotte?"

Charlotte's eyes took a faraway look. "I told him I was with child and...and...he punched me...kicked me until...I lost my baby... He threatens me...his mother knows and she turned her back to me. Told me I was no better than his first wife."

Jo found it hard to breathe...hard to believe. How could this have happened? "You are not going back," Jo said firmly.

"You won't be able to stop him. He's my husband."

Jo didn't have an answer. She only knew Charlotte was not going back.

* * * *

When the tale was repeated to Clayton Montgomery, Charlotte quickly recanted the story, protesting she had over-exaggerated. Assuring her family it was her fault. She shouldn't have said a word. But Grandfather Montgomery would have none of it.

Clayton Montgomery refused to send his granddaughter back to her abusive husband, no matter what the law dictated. A protective net was cast and a plan put into motion.

Josephine entered into the bedroom she shared with her husband. An orange-yellowish light had barely appeared on the horizon and Wade had readied for the day, having only to tie his cravat.

"She is set," Jo said. "Do be patient with her, though. She has not stopped weeping."

"I will," Wade assured Jo as he finished with the last tug on his cravat. He crossed over behind her and wrapped his arms around her prominent belly. "It will be for the best. She needs time to heal where Arthur can't find her. Cousin Sarah won't ask any questions. Charlotte will be safe in Savannah."

"I know." Jo grasped his hands and leaned back against him. Poor Charlotte! How unfortunate she had been in love. The thought crossed her mind it could have been her as she remembered Holt Miller, but it had not been her fate.

"It is you who I worry about," he said in a tender voice. "I don't want you to be concerned. I will see to Charlotte's needs and return before the birth."

Jo turned around and forced a smile. "I will be well looked after. Jenna is here and you know well that Miss Hazel will see to me, along with Rosa. Go."

"Grandfather will tell Arthur that I have taken Charlotte to her mother's. He will not question. Men such as he are cowards."

"Do you suppose his words hold truth in them about me? Do people really believe I am not loyal? Are there whispers about me?"

"No, my love." He reached over and caressed her face. "I feel it stems from his association with Kathleen. Nothing more than her jealousy. I fear she believed Andrew's situation different than it is when she married him. I have been too lenient toward her. That will come to an end.

"I don't want you to worry about anything but our child." He leaned down and kissed her. "Let me tuck you back into bed."

"I will miss you," Jo confessed with a sudden intensity that shocked her. "Come back to me."

"Darling, I have no desire to be anywhere but with you. I will be back within the week."

Jo crawled back beneath the covers. Already the bed seemed so lonely. Sadness enveloped her for Charlotte, but that was not all that bothered her.

Wade had been wrong, ever so wrong. A new worry had emerged, one she could not simply dismiss. Arthur's words haunted her. He spoke as if the war was a certainty...he spoke of her lover...that he had reenlisted in the Navy, which meant Cullen was prepared to take up arms against his family...against her and the child she carried.

The hurt she had pushed to the far corners of her heart resurfaced, along with an excruciating ache. She understood the need to move on...they had no future...but to reenlist in the Navy? To prepare to take arms up against the South...his family...her?

She had not heard from Cullen since that dreadful day...but this message she understood clearly—the love she thought they shared had been nothing more than an illusion.

Chapter Seven

Outside the small Carolina coastal town of Georgetown, Cullen prepared to meet with his cousin in a quiet, rural churchyard. Andrew had promised to rendezvous by five thirty. That would give them an hour together before he had to return to the ship.

Cullen had given the matter a great deal of thought before he reenlisted. He was once more Lieutenant Cullen Smythe in the US Navy. In his last meeting with Commander Davis, a plan had been put into place, a plan that he himself had devised…a plan that needed his cousin's cooperation.

Long hours had been spent devising the minute details of the undertaking. Cullen had come upon the idea of using the Underground Railroad as a network to help spy upon the activities of the fanatics calling for secession.

When he had proposed the idea of using the Underground Railroad to Commander Davis, he held all the confidence in the world that it would work. The route and people were already in place to integrate into this Southern stronghold.

The threats of secession had not been taken lightly by the military. Cullen's plan would go into effect the moment Lincoln took office—eyes and ears into the thick of Southern hostility, the ways and means to communicate, and a route to come and go.

Careful negotiations had been debated between his father and those connected with the Underground Railroad: secrecy had to be maintained but most important, the links in the network would never be expected to spy, only provide what they had been doing for the runaway slaves.

The immeasurable danger in this mission could not be underscored, but it would be no more than what the Underground Railroad had faced in the past. One of the largest obstacles faced by the network would be integrating their agents into the communities. They needed someone who would be accepted and then fade into the background while gathering information.

A volunteer had stepped forward, Gavin Mitchell. Mitchell came from Virginia before setting up residence in Philadelphia. Posing as an engineer for South Carolina Rail Road, he would help maintain the rail lines. His Southerner heritage would give him the cover he needed to travel freely in the countryside.

Normally, the Navy would have taken full control of a mission, but secrecy was of the utmost concern and importance to protect the Underground Railroad. Knowledge of the links would be limited to only a select few, which meant that a guide would be needed to introduce Mitchell to the landscape and the intricacies of the system. They had found their man—Heyward.

As Andrew had done with the Underground Railroad in Charleston, he would be needed to head this network. Cullen now had to convince Andrew to do so. It would not be an easy task.

The day had been dreary and overcast. The rain from the night before had drenched the area; the ground beneath Cullen's boots was wet and soggy, but it was peaceful here. No one would disturb their talk.

The presidential election was within the week. Time had become their enemy. The wait was not long. As he looked down the lane, Cullen saw a horse and rider. Andrew had come.

"Good God, you're not suggesting that I could do such a thing?" Stunned, Andrew's jaw dropped. "Impossible."

"It is a simple plan. The organization is already in place," Cullen said. "No one will be in any more danger than they are now."

Andrew's hesitation did not surprise him. The rebellious youth had changed. His cousin's appearance had altered in the last few months. He was thinner; his cheeks hollowed. He looked as though he hadn't had a good night sleep in ages. Cullen did not have to ask the reason why. Andrew's marriage had come with a high price—his dignity.

Andrew's boot kicked the ground. "You have asked the wrong person. Even if I had the desire to do so, I could never do what would be needed."

"I disagree. For years, you have helped runaways."

"You know this is different. I know you are angry with the family, but I can't turn my back on them," Andrew said stiffly. "I am a physician. My conscience allows me to help people in need—"

342

"Your conscience? Where was your conscience last year?" Cullen snapped the sarcastic rebuke. "Do you truly believe I want to see *my* family harmed?"

"What do you expect me to think?"

"I would expect you to know the person I am." He paused. Losing his temper would not gain him an advantage. "There will come a time when you will have to choose a side. If you do not believe that, you are a fool."

"I have a wife and child to think of..."

"Then you should. You are worried that you are betraying the family. I understand well the convictions of our people...*our people*. What I question is the inability of the leaders to comprehend that they are living in the past. Change is coming, whether or not you want it."

"Nothing has happened, Cullen. Secession has been threatened for years."

"These are not idle threats. If Grandfather and Wade are so foolhardy to support secession, I pledge to you that I will protect the family. If you do this, the family will be protected...the legacy that Grandfather has taken such pride in...Magnolia Bluff."

"I can't, Cullen. You don't understand."

"That you are questioning yourself? What has become of the man you were...the man who placed the needs of others before himself? I know what I'm asking of you. I know it will not be easy, but my father has faith in you. Do not turn your back on what you believe in."

"Can you not see? I don't know what I believe in anymore." Andrew's voice was splintered.

"You do. I also know you have the courage to face the challenges. If it comes to be...this split between the North and South, you will be needed. Sacrifices will be made. Have I not made my own sacrifice?"

"A sacrifice made because of me."

"It is not why I am here. I cannot help but be angry...I will not deny that, but make no mistake about it. I am doing this to help my family. I am not betraying you. I'm doing what I have to to save the family."

"You sound so certain, but so do they."

"Right makes might." Cullen quoted Lincoln. "Secession is treason, Andrew."

"I don't want to make a rash decision." Andrew breathed out deeply. "I need time. Give me a few days. When I return...Wade has requested my presence at Magnolia Bluff..."

"We need to put this into place, Andrew. I can meet you there next week," Cullen said. "Mitchell is going out with Heyward to get the lay of the land. He will be heading up this mission. They will be leaving shortly. I will arrange to pick them up at Heady's dock."

Andrew shook his head. "That will not be a good idea. You must know that Josephine is at Magnolia Bluff."

"I will never deny that I care for her, if that is your concern, but I would never do her harm. I'm duty bound to respect she is married to Wade. I would not interfere in her life…not after all she has gone through…not when she is expecting his child."

Obvious relief flooded Andrew's face. "I wasn't certain you knew about the baby."

Something in Andrew's voice caused him to pause. "Andrew," Cullen queried. "Why are you going to Magnolia Bluff?"

"It is of no importance. It is almost November, Cullen. Most withdraw back to their plantations."

"Not this year, Andrew. I would imagine they would not leave until after the election," Cullen stated. "I can think of only one reason why Wade would request you. Being out on the plantation, it would take time to send for a physician if needed. Is Josephine's time near? Why would you keep it from me?"

"I am not keeping anything from you. It is only Wade is dealing with another family issue— Charlotte." Andrew looked straight into Cullen's eyes. With a small shrug, he said, "He has to be away for a few days and doesn't want Jo alone with only Grandfather. I will make arrangements to meet you when you go to Heady's dock. There is no need for you to go to Magnolia Bluff. It would serve no purpose."

Cullen nodded in a slow motion. "You are certain Harry Lee isn't a concern? I heard Wade had dealt with him."

"Harry Lee is in Mississippi. He is not a threat."

From the information Cullen had gathered, Wade had kept to his word, and Cullen would not have expected less. Wade was an honorable man, as was he. It had been the reason he had stayed away from Jo, giving her a chance for happiness.

But he knew Andrew well enough to realize that he withheld something. What, he wasn't certain…but he sensed it was about Josephine. His feelings had not diminished for her, and he doubted they ever would. He had left her in Charleston because he believed it was for her best. He could not deny she had never been far from his heart.

Perhaps he was making more of Andrew's words than was there. Perhaps he wanted an excuse to see Josephine. Perhaps it was a need for closure. Whatever the reason, he was now determined to see her.

* * * *

344

With the dawn, Josephine awakened from a deep slumber. Burrowed deep into her covers, she dreaded leaving the comfort of her bed. The night had been spent in wondrous dreams of her baby.

The last few days had been consumed with worry about Charlotte. Last evening, her mind had been relieved. She had received word from Wade that Charlotte was safe.

Cousin Sarah has welcomed Charlotte and understands her predicament. She will be well looked after until other arrangements can be made. Do not concern yourself with Arthur. As we predicted, he headed straight to Columbia. He will not be returning to Magnolia Bluff. I am in Charleston and will return after the election results come in unless you have news for me. Then I will return immediately. Your loving husband, Wade.

The baby moved and she smiled. Soon…soon she would be able to hold the little one. Finally, she swung her legs over the side of the bed. She crossed the floor and stood at the window.

Outside, the sun broke over the horizon with the promise of a beautiful day. She breathed in deeply. The day was warm for November and the view seemed to take on a splendor with the sunlight streaming brilliantly onto the garden. The majestic Virginia live oak opened wide its arms in an impressive array.

The old gray moss hung down, littered by a spray of color with cardinals and yellow finches settling in the branches. Overhead, she caught a glimpse of a great white egret. She leaned against the window with her arms crossed over her enlarged belly and drank in the sight.

"A glorious morn, Miss Jo." Rosa entered into the room with a wide smile on her face. In her hands, she carried a tray upon which breakfast had been prepared, a pile of buckwheat cakes with syrup. "I was saying to myself it would be a grand day for one of your walks, but I can open up the window here for ya if ya don't feel up to it. Let in the fresh air."

Rosa sat the tray on the table. After she cracked the window, she walked over to the armoire. "You won't want to miss a moment of this weather, Mistress. Do you have a preference on what you would care to wear today?"

A wide grin graced Jo's face at her maid's tease. Her wardrobe consisted of only black gowns at the moment. Her maid's jovial mood was contagious. "I will take the black."

A smile crossed Rosa's face. "Black it will be. Come now and eat."

"Why ever are you in such a good humor this morning?" Jo questioned, but then she thought of the election. *Was Rosa hoping that devil Lincoln would win?*

"Nothing more than blessed with another day from the good Lord," Rosa replied. "Now mind ya, I would like nothing more to sneak out this morning for a brisk walk. I do feel the day calling to me."

Taking a bite of her breakfast, Jo glanced back over at her maid. "Do you? I think I would enjoy it as well."

"Well, Miss Jo, if you finish up, we could get back before Miss Jenna gets up. She don't like ya leaving the house now with your time being so near."

"I feel fine," Jo said, but she understood well her maid's concern. Jenna had been like a mother hen around her as of late. "I believe I would enjoy a brief escape."

Josephine went through the garden arbor covered in the last of the late blooming roses. The path took her down toward the lush riverside landscape and dock. The pebbles crunched under her walking shoes. She could hear the birds chirp and flitter from one tree to another.

She rounded a thicket of shrubs along the river's edge. Rosa walked a foot in front of her and carried a long stick to alert her if some uninvited alligator decided to cross their path. Jo doubted it would happen. Most would be laying lazily out in the bright sunlight. *What a lovely day!* She was happy Rosa suggested an early morning stroll. She felt invigorated.

As she paused a moment, Jo stared out over the river. Wade had been right…everything had turned out for the best. She was enveloped in the safety of the arms of a man who seemed intent upon proving his love. Had she not promised God if Cullen and Gillie lived she would accept her life?

Deep in thought, she didn't hear the footsteps behind her, not until he was upon her. Abruptly, she turned and froze. Her heart caught in her throat.

"Hello, Magnolia."

The last person she expected to see stood before her. *Cullen—oh, dear Lord—Cullen!* At the sight of Cullen in his Navy uniform, her heart surged with love and fury. She could not bear it. For an endless moment, she said nothing; neither did he, seemingly unable to take his eyes from hers. Finally, she found her voice. "Cullen…what are you doing? What brings you here?"

With a long, heartfelt sigh, he said, "You do, Josephine. You do."

"No, Cullen, no…you can't be here. You have to go." Breathless, her voice faded.

"I'm not going anywhere until we talk. You can't deny me that."

Her mind raced. She glanced around; Rosa was nowhere to be seen. *Oh, good Lord! I am alone with Cullen.* She tried to protest, but it went unheeded. He ushered her straightaway into the garden house. The door hadn't closed all the way before his arms wrapped around her…his lips were upon hers.

Time evaporated…all that had elapsed—the months without word, the hurt…the pain—melted away…there was nothing…nothing but the two of them. Gentle and softly, he kissed her and then slowly broke from her lips.

Suddenly, everything she had told herself, had convinced herself was lost upon his touch…his presence. In that moment, she forgot everything except the love she had hidden deep inside her.

Slowly, she opened her eyes to find Cullen staring at her longingly. He touched her face and caressed it tenderly.

Unable to find her voice, she pushed back against him. She needed to think and couldn't in his arms. The baby moved. Instinctively, her hand went to the movement. She stepped back.

"You don't need to protect the babe from me," he whispered. "I love you. I have never stopped. You have to know I never wanted to leave you or ever felt so helpless in my life."

"But you did and I am married to Wade." Her voice was no louder than a whisper, yet echoed in the stilled room.

His eyebrows arched in a half frown. "I understand you must be angry with me. I have had my own to deal with…"

Her hand extended to pause his thought. She said in a low, steady voice, "I have never been angry with you…with the situation and all that happened…but never with you."

He took her hands and raised them up to him. He kissed each and entreated her, "Guilt gnaws at my soul, Josephine. Forgive me. You never deserved any of this."

"Of what? The life I have now?" She looked up at him, askance. "There wasn't another outcome. We both knew when we returned to Charleston. You could never live with yourself if your family lost their home, knowing that your happiness came with a selfish price."

She stared at him, at a loss for words. *Why, oh, why had he returned!* Just when she had convinced herself that he was only a memory…nothing more. Her heart toiled, but it would never do…never. She had to make him understand. She shook her head and continued.

"I wanted you to do the impossible. To make it all right, but the cruel fact of life is that we were never meant to be. Over time, I have accepted it." Her pent-up frustration seeped into her voice. "Accepted that there is a void within me, but why…why didn't you see me before you left? Why didn't you say good-bye?"

"I wanted to…believe me, I wanted to." His face hardened as if he relived the pain from that day. "I wasn't given the opportunity. Wade refused to let me. I told myself that it was for the best. What could I do? Tell you that I would love you forever? That I ache? I do love you, Josephine. It is why I am here."

"What do you mean?"

"I accepted the fact that you married Wade. I stayed away, but I can no longer. I have been lied to and deceived for the last time," he said with firm determination. "I came for you. To take you away from the madness that is descending upon Charleston. Let them have their plantation and money. Let them have it all. A war is brewing. I refuse to leave you in the midst of all that is happening and especially with my child."

Upon the utterance, she peered at him as her face flamed. Words tumbled out, one over the other. "Oh, no, Cullen. The baby's not yours. The babe is Wade's…it's Wade's."

His eyebrows went up in disbelief. "Do not lie to me, Josephine. I stayed away because I thought it was for the best. Do you not think when I heard you were expecting I did not ask when? I did nothing because I believe there were no consequences to the time we spent together. Do you believe I have forgotten the last time we made love? Seeing you now…tell me…tell me the babe is not mine!"

His words shook the core of her being. She cried, "Don't do this to me, Cullen. It's not fair."

He refused to stop and pressed on. "I remember every detail of our last night—every kiss, every utterance. How could you deny it is mine?"

Her eyes came back to his. "Do you believe that Wade waited to consummate our marriage?" Her heart sank. How hard this was! The pain evident in his eyes destroyed her inside.

He grabbed her. His hands on her shoulders gripped her so tightly that they hurt. "You let him touch you! You lay with him!"

Jo lifted her head up in a swift, fierce movement. She retorted, "He's my husband… husband! What would you have me do?" She recoiled against the wall and felt horror-struck. "How dare you? You sound as he did when he discovered his wife wasn't the virginal bride he thought he had married."

His eyes blazed at her, but in her next breath, she felt her legs weaken beneath her. She slid down against the wall to the floor. She dropped her head in her hands and sobbed.

"Goddamn it, Josephine. I didn't mean...only not so soon..." He rushed to her.

At his touch, she pushed him away. "Don't come near me. You have no right. No right to touch me. No right to ridicule me for my actions. No right to be disappointed in me. You left me...no matter the reason...you left me! I was desolate and alone. My heart broken.

"Can you not understand? Wade loves me. He has protected me and cared for me. He believes without question the child is his...he won't even consider that it might not be. I won't take that from him. He has given me back my honor and my child."

A stricken look on his face, he questioned, "Are you saying that you don't know who the father is?"

"God forgive me." She shook her head and said fiercely, "Cullen, but don't ever say those words again. Let me make it clear to you. I won't take this away from Wade."

"Even if the child is mine?"

She answered quickly, floundering in the confusion of bewilderment. "It's not. It has to be Wade's. It has to be. I couldn't do that to a child, not give it a name because of my behavior. He would be shunned for being a bastard. I couldn't do that...no matter my feelings. Don't you understand?"

The dam of tears burst and fell freely down her cheeks. He leaned down and tried to comfort her, but she would have none of it. "Don't touch me. I know what you think of me. I can't make this right for everyone...I wish I could...I can't."

She covered her mouth with her hand, but the torrent of emotions spewed forth. "Don't do this to me...I prayed to God that I would be a good wife to Wade if he would allow you to live and Gillie...Gillie...oh...how I have missed Gillie..."

Slowly, she looked back up at Cullen. "I've worried so much...Miss Hazel said she couldn't write..." She rambled incoherently. "But I know she is being cared for. Isn't she? You have seen her?"

Her eyes pleaded with Cullen for an answer, but he said nothing, only looking at her strangely. "Cullen...you have seen her...you took her back to Philadelphia with Heyward. You would have checked upon her. You would not have been so cruel."

"Josephine, you need to talk to Miss Hazel."

349

"No…no," she demanded and searched his eyes. His frown deepened ominously. Reaching over, she gripped tight his lapel. "What is wrong?"

"No one told you?"

Panic filled her and she shook her head. "I have written constantly so she would know I am thinking of her. Wade wouldn't allow me to go to Gillie. He said it was for the best until after my time…"

"Jo, calm yourself. It is for the best until—"

"No!" she screamed. "No…no…no! She is supposed to be happy with Heyward… She is free! Oh, Good Lord! I need to go to her…"

"It will do no good." Cullen reluctantly yielded. "She knew what you did for her. Heyward and Miss Hazel never left her side."

Her brows drew together in sudden worry…she knew. Trembling, she struggled for a breath as Cullen talked. The words jumbled together.

"Gillie was going to church…walked out in front of a carriage…there was nothing anyone could have done."

Her eyes blurred. Her mind ran rampant with a million thoughts. *There was more he wasn't telling her. Gillie's mother had died in the same manner.*

A sharp pain swept through her. She took a deep breath in but she knew before she exhaled. For a moment, she couldn't speak, but she gripped tight to Cullen's arm. Her face contorted as her belly hardened and contracted.

"The baby?" Cullen waited only for her to nod before he swept her up in his arms.

She felt his hurried step along the path to the main house. She couldn't allow him to carry her in to it… She couldn't think straight, but she realized that Wade would be furious. The pain ebbed.

"Put me down. Please, Cullen," she begged. Panic frightened her more than the pain that gripped her. "I can walk in myself. Please…don't do this."

He paused and sat her down. Her legs weakened and she reached for his arm to balance herself.

"I need to go in by myself. Please."

"I can't leave you, Josephine. Ask me anything else, but I can't leave you now. Despite everything you have said, I know you love me and only me. Return with me." He cupped her face tenderly. "Come with me now."

Frightened eyes met his. "If you know me at all, you would not ask such a thing." She took a deep breath. Once more, she grimaced in pain.

Desperately fighting the wave of discomfort, she spoke broken words. "I can't...I won't leave him."

"You are asking too much of me, Josephine. I had to leave you once before...it was not my choice...now you are asking me to walk away again from the woman I love who is having *my* child. Even through your words, I know—"

"As he...does." Jo paused. The onset of pain began again. She allowed him to hold her tight until the pain once more subsided...until she could find her words. "It is my burden to bear. Cullen, please. If you care at all for me, leave. You have to understand. It is not about you or me. It's about the babe. The baby comes before everything else..."

He peered at her sharply. "Tell me then you don't love me. Tell me!"

For a brief moment, she considered uttering the words. Her mind cried out—*tell him*. He would leave. Her legs swayed; her heart pounded...God forgive her. She whispered, "I can't...I could never."

A sudden warmth ran down her leg. She looked up helplessly at Cullen, forgetting about everything except her baby. Immediately, he swept her up in his arms and carried her into the house.

* * * *

Despite Cullen's unexpected appearance, Cullen's grandfather hadn't seemed surprised. Instead, Clayton Montgomery sat smugly behind his desk in the library and studied the cigar he held in his hand. Biting off the stub, he scraped a match on the bottom of his boot and lit it. With a puff on the butt, Clayton offered one to Cullen. "Take it. May help calm your nerves."

Cullen took the offering. The next moment, he exhaled smoke, but it had done nothing for his mood. He scowled. "What do you know about my nerves?"

"Figured, really." Clayton didn't take his eyes off his grandson. "I ain't as stupid as I look, Cullen, nor as insensitive as I appear. Just gonna give ya some advice. In the end, you will learn that it's better to live with decisions rather than regret. Remember the reasons all came to be and accept."

"You've got a lot of gall, Grandfather," Cullen replied gruffly. "Accept. You've never accepted a damn thing in your life. You manipulate everyone around you. And now you have the nerve to tell me to *accept*!"

Undaunted, Clayton stood and walked over to the decanter. He poured two glasses and handed one to Cullen. "Believe you may need this. Know I do."

351

Hurried footsteps paused in the doorway. Cullen's eyes flicked to the door. Jenna hesitated before she interrupted softly.

"Miss Hazel sent me down to tell you that the midwife, Mrs. Peters, is here, but you should make yourselves comfortable. It will be awhile. Miss Hazel said I wasn't needed in the room, but do you want me to wait in the hall, Grandfather?"

"It would seem the best course." He watched Jenna ease back out, closing the door behind her. He chuckled to himself as he turned back to Cullen. "If Mrs. Peters says all is right, it's all right. Best midwife in the state. Wade made certain. Also called for Doctor Flynn, besides Andrew. Don't think Josephine would let Andrew within the room, but I understand despite his dereliction of his duty, he had been quite impressive as a physician. Better to be prepared."

"If you say so." Cullen drank down the contents of his glass.

"From your tone, I take it you still blame me."

Cullen relaxed in the leather winged back chair and blew out smoke. For a time, he just stared at his grandfather. "Infuriated would be a better choice of words. And as I sit here, I'm becoming more so, wondering why I allowed it to unfold as it did. Why I put you and this family before what I held dear. Tell me, Grandfather, did my sacrifice satisfy you? Or do you need more? Do you want my blood also?"

"Boy, I never wanted any of this to happen. Never wanted my idiot son to wager my estate and lose. Never dreamed that Andrew would have done something so foolhardy as marry that Yankee woman." His voice held a sharp, clear edge. He drew a puff on his cigar, released a circle of smoke above his head and then pointed his finger at Cullen. "You, though, and Wade, both stood behind the Montgomery name. Even with that damn Yankee blood flowing through your veins…make no doubt, this is your home no matter where you lay your head at night. Your momma was raised here—you were raised here. You understood what it means to hold to our honor."

"Honor be damned! It was all about money and greed." Cullen cursed under his breath. "You're so blinded by this so-called honor. It is used every time someone wants an excuse for stupidity. Tell me, why did I have to pay for another's sin?"

"The innocent always pay for the guilty. Is that what's wrong with you, boy? Feeling you have been mistreated? Make no mistake about it, Cullen, you have not suffered any more than any other. What is more than likely is that you're not as innocent as you make yourself out to be."

Cullen gave his grandfather a defiant glare. "What the hell are you talking about?"

"You know exactly what I'm talking about. Wade told me that he offered to help you escape with Josephine. But you know as well as I or Wade…for that matter, Josephine…you couldn't live with the consequences of doing so. Knowing that you didn't release her, but let her cling to nonexistent hope until it was almost too late. It could have cost you your life."

Cullen wanted nothing more than to throw his glass at his grandfather. *How dare Grandfather! How arrogant! What have I done that was so wrong!* His anger kindled, he retorted, "Tell me, Grandfather, how all of this will fall upon my shoulders? This whole quandary. I want to know what I did wrong!"

"Don't be putting words into my mouth, son. I didn't say it was your fault, but you haven't been terribly mistreated like you're making yourself out to be. No, not by a long shot," Clayton said. "Gonna be mad at me…be mad at me. Ain't gonna change anything."

Cullen stared at his grandfather in dismay. "Your point?"

Clayton's lips twisted. "What kind of man makes love to a woman and leaves her to face the consequences?"

For a moment, he thought of denying it, but was acutely aware that his grandfather would not have made the accusation without proof. One of the servants probably saw him close the door when he was alone with Josephine and made the assumption. No matter. It would be a useless denial.

"I did not abandon Josephine. Do I need to remind you that you tricked me into bringing Jo back to Charleston with that damn telegram? If not for that trickery, she would be safely in Philadelphia as my wife."

"Was it trickery? I thought it was her papa's wish. She is a dutiful daughter…and wife."

Cullen realized that he should retreat and not respond. Instead, he blustered, "It sounds like there is something you want to tell me. What precisely is it?"

"I'm telling you that you have come on a fool's errand," Clayton said in a strained voice. "I'm not the only one who realizes the possibility the child is yours. I have no doubt Wade does as well. He has overcome any qualms and claims the child. It is his, Cullen. He will give the child his name…that is, unless you insist on making your presence known."

"Where does that leave me?"

"Not here. There is nothing for you here."

"This is my home."

"Not in that uniform!" Clayton banged his hand on his desk and leaped up. "It is you who has chosen to turn your back on your people."

353

"Alluding to what? That unless I agree blindly with your view, I cannot be considered a South Carolinian?" Cullen seethed.

"It is treasonous for you to reenlist for the sole purpose to take arms against your people."

"But in your eyes, it is not treason to call for secession? We see things quite differently, Grandfather, because I do not see your loyalty but your greed to hold to slavery for your own prosperity. Would it not be braver to admit that it is time for a change?"

"A true Southerner would never utter that trash!"

Cullen met his grandfather's angry eyes with his own. "It was you who raised me, Grandfather. I hold to the convictions that were instilled in me."

"Leave!" Clayton shouted. "You are no longer a Montgomery!"

"Because I don't *accept* that there is not another way besides secession?"

"I will not dignify that with an answer. It is not the reason you came. Know, though, nothing you say or do will make her change her mind," Clayton snapped spitefully. "I know Josephine well. She will never leave Wade."

"It must be hard playing God." Cullen spoke with ill-concealed disgust.

"You're mistaken, Cullen. Sadly mistaken. It's over and has ended the way it should have."

"So it does not matter whose child it is as long as your blood runs through it. You can sit on your throne and oversee your poor subjects. The way you see it, we are all your subjects, are we not?"

"It matters only that Magnolia Bluff was saved and the heritage preserved."

"You conniving bastard! My child doesn't need your damn plantation or your misguided concepts."

"I'm sorry you feel that way, Cullen. It is a shame. I had hopes you could at least take that with you if you believe the child yours. For I can guarantee you will leave alone."

"Go to hell!" Infuriated, Cullen walked out of the room and slammed the door behind him.

Cullen's nerves wound tight as he waited upon the veranda. His mind ran rampant with a million thoughts. *God, he wished he could turn back time!* He would have never let his conscience interfere with his decision. He would have taken her without looking back...but it wasn't his grandfather who haunted him—it was Josephine.

She had appeared resigned to her fate and her eyes pleaded with him to do the same.

His grandfather talked about duty and honor, but the only thing that kept Josephine within these walls was the ring around her finger. He had understood so well on that day. He had known what she would do, had to do, but with everything within him, he wanted another option.

There had been none. Was there any satisfaction from the knowledge she married Wade only to save his life and Gillie's? No, he thought miserably. He had failed her. The day he had left her, he had convinced himself that he could leave loving her…that they both would survive. Survive? Perhaps—or was it merely existing?

Josephine clung to her damnable pride and honor. Her words echoed within his soul…she would never place her needs before the baby. His grandfather was right. She would never leave Wade…

He breathed in deeply and took in the sight before him. He didn't know when or if he would ever come back. *God, he loved this place.* He loved the sounds, the birds singing, the leaves rustling in the wind; he had even missed the slaves singing while they worked.

The sun would set soon…a voice broke the stillness of the twilight. "Cullen."

He turned back to see Jenna. She gave him a tentative smile.

"It's over," she said simply. "A boy. A strong, healthy boy. They both are fine. I thought…I thought you would want to know."

"Thank you." He turned back to the view.

Cullen took no notice of how long he stood alone on the veranda while darkness fell around him. Soon he would depart…alone. Mitchell would be returning with the boat at midnight. Cullen had only one thing more to be done.

He took to the back stairwell and ascended to the nursery. He heard soft humming as he entered into the open door. The dim-lit room was warmed by a bright fire. The only other occupant rocked a small bundle, but halted when she caught sight of him in the doorway.

"Good evening, Miss Hazel."

"Lieutenant Smythe," she said in a soft voice. "I wasn't expecting you."

"I'm sure you were not," he replied and made his way by the fire. "I have come to see my son."

Miss Hazel studied him carefully with her large telling eyes, neither anxious nor nervous by his presence. She seemed in control, too much so. She grated upon his nerves. Shaking her head, she began, "I believe ya are mistaken—"

"Beg your pardon, ma'am, but I don't give a damn what you believe." Cullen held out his arms. "I'm not leaving until I hold my son."

She rose slowly with the infant, her reluctance evident. "Don't like it. Don't like it one bit, but ya was good to my Gillie," she said. "Well, sit down. If ya gonna hold him, hold him right."

Cullen obeyed and she handed him the infant.

"That's right." She held the little one's head until Cullen had his hand underneath it. "Cradle his head like that."

The moment his eyes fixed on the infant, his heart swelled. Never had such intense emotions gripped him so quickly…so strongly. Bundled up tightly, the baby's eyes were closed, but he squirmed and nuzzled against him. As he looked at the bald baby, he held no doubt it was his. He couldn't say why or how…but he knew.

With his free hand, he caressed the baby's soft cheek. The baby reached up and gripped his finger. "My God, he is beautiful and strong."

"A big boy," Miss Hazel agreed. "Miss Jo did a wonderful job. We were worried for a while, but she did it."

"She is well?"

"She needs to rest, but she'll recover nicely."

He nodded. "And the name?"

"Percival, Miss Jo said. Percival Wright Montgomery."

"It is a good name," he said solemnly. For a moment, silence descended on the room; the only thing heard was the crackling of the logs. Finally, he asked, "She is happy?"

"Lieutenant Smythe, I don't wanna hurt ya none. Honest, I don't. I know I owe ya a debt of gratitude." Miss Hazel sighed heavily. "She do seems content. Master Wade been good to her…real good. …Ya got it all wrong about the baby. Ya do. You shouldn't think such a thing."

"Are you trying to convince me or yourself? I know he is mine. No matter your words, my grandfather's, Wade's, even Josephine's."

"You are right, Lieutenant Smythe, it ain't my place to say. But I know that Master Wade won't be happy with ya here."

"I don't think, Miss Hazel; I know he would not," he agreed. "But we aren't going to tell him, are we?"

"You are leaving soon?"

"I'm not going to cause any trouble now if that is what you are asking." He looked up at her. "Remember this, though, Miss Hazel. I don't like it, but I will never turn my back on my own child. If he has need of anything, send word to me in Philadelphia. If I'm not there, my father will receive it. If I have to live with this façade, I will do what I can to look after my own."

"Yes, Lieutenant."

Cullen glanced down. The baby was sound asleep in his arms. "If you don't mind, I would like to stay here with him until I have to leave...alone."

He saw her hesitation...her worry that Wade would appear shortly. But he would be gone before such a time. He had no desire to cause Josephine more distress than he had already.

Ever so slowly, Miss Hazel walked out of the room.

THE WAR

Chapter Eight
Charleston

An abrupt chill had descended on Magnolia Bluff. By late December, the last of the leaves had fallen and had left only the pines to give color against the cold, gray skies. For the last couple of years, the Montgomerys' Christmases had been subdued.

The veil had been lifted and the plantation celebrated. The whole of South Carolina was in a festive mood. The good people of Charleston had been jovial since the night that Percival was born...when it was announced that Lincoln had been elected president of the United States.

Charleston pulsated with the rambling of secession and the declaration that South Carolina would make a stand. Lincoln declared that the Union would not be divided, but the fine people of South Carolina were not going to let no damn Yankee tell them what to do!

The whole of the state sat in suspense, not as to the outcome which all declared would happen, but as to when. It came. On December 20, the ordinance was issued. By Christmas Eve, the legal proclamation was proclaimed. South Carolina had declared its independence from the United States of America. They had seceded from the Union and the people were ecstatic.

The Montgomerys celebrated. The house burst into its full beauty with music and candle flames. Everyone was in a cheery mood: dancing, singing, proclaiming the virtues of South Carolina.

The New Year would be brought in with the declaration of the shining bright future of a new world for all within South Carolina. All around her, Josephine heard the echo of the hubbub of voices emulating the fever-pitch tension of the day. It was a dazzling announcement of a new wave dawning upon the South.

During the festivities, Grandfather Montgomery spoke openly about the plans for the state to form an army.

"We will not be alone for long. News is filtering in that other states are set to follow our lead—Mississippi, Alabama, Florida, Georgia, and Louisiana. We will have all the Southern states before the end of February. It is said that a convention will be convened in Montgomery to unify the South. No way them Yanks can stop us now!"

Josephine had not met a soul who didn't have their own idea about the conflict that surrounded them. She heard the proclamation that the Yanks were too scared to fight, but it was the assertion that if it came to it, there would be a war. It invoked fear into her heart.

Fear that invaded her newfound happiness and she was happy since the birth of Percival, far happier than she had been in the last year. Through the grinding agony of childbirth, pure joy surged as the pain washed away the moment her son was handed to her. Instantly, her heart melted. Never had she known such love.

There had been a short time when she had succumbed to tears shortly after Percival's birth. The sadness of the loss of Gillie overcame her, and she broke down in sobs. Miss Hazel would have none of it.

"Gillie would not wanca' to grieve. You did everything ya could for her. She knew that, dearie. She did and ya know better than anyone that she would have loved your little one. You have to take care of yourself so ya can raise him proper. Ain't asking ya to forget the precious girl, only choose to remember the good."

Jo prayed to God for Gillie's soul. For so long, she had not prayed to God, fearing that God had condemned her for loving a man before her wedding night. God had punished her by forcing her to live with the knowledge of the lingering doubts of Percival's parentage. But she held no doubt that God would care for her Gillie. Never had a sweeter woman walked this earth.

With every day that passed, she focused her attention on her son, promising herself she would never forget Gillie, but it wasn't only the loss of Gillie that bothered her.

Cullen's appearance that day had become a silent wedge between Wade and herself. He had made no mention of Cullen's unexpected visit or any consequences it may have caused. Nor had she revealed her knowledge of Gillie or asked him why he hadn't told her. Was it her own guilt that lay between them? Did he regret his confidence in declaring Percival his child?

Despite the worries on her heart, her sorrows were eclipsed by young Percival. He was adorable. He had lost his baby hair and had become quite bald. A happy, chubby little thing with rolls of fat upon his little legs, his large blue eyes seemed to be darkening. He had a way to make her forget everything but his soft coos when she cradled him lovingly in her arms.

Wade had been the epitome of a devoted husband and father. He had declared Percival the most perfect of babies and professed Jo looked splendid in coming through her confinement.

He had given her the most beautiful of charms as a gift for presenting him with a fine son. Moreover, he surprised her with a lovely emerald necklace for Christmas, quite extravagant.

She, in turn, had given Wade an engraved wedding ring with the date of their marriage and her initials. Since they had married, he had not worn one. The rush of the wedding had not allowed her time to choose a ring for her husband. Although not as lavish as his gifts, it had come from her heart and commitment to their marriage.

Sincerely touched by her sentiment, he vowed to her, "I will never take it off. It will connect us forever."

With that declaration, Josephine settled into her role as his wife and the mother of his child. Pushing the past behind her, she found a semblance of contentment.

The New Year began with the outward manifestations of celebrating South Carolina's independence with lavish parties and grand balls. Confidence exuded from the occupants of Charleston so much so that young and old were captivated by the excitement.

Change was in the air. No longer could Josephine ignore the inevitable. The papers were filled with rapidly developing news. The last being the Virginia legislature leaving a peace conference feeling insulted.

The whole family had returned to Charleston by the end of January. The Battery was crowded with parades of marching soldiers. The streets swarmed with people, who had flocked to the city in anticipation of the call running rampant within the state—war. Charleston was as tight as a dress ready to explode at the seams.

Josephine descended from her carriage alongside of Grace Ann, who had accompanied her to Miss Haney's shop. With all of the galas to attend, Wade had insisted she get a new wardrobe.

The attentive *auntie*, Grace Ann had become a most welcome fixture within the Montgomery household. Jo swore that Percival's eyes lit up the moment Grace Ann walked into the room.

"I swear he is the most beautiful baby Charleston has ever seen. That's what I told Mr. Whitney and he agreed," Grace Ann declared. "Why, I saw the most perfect pony the other day when Mr. Whitney and I attended the races. I told Mr. Whitney that we must buy it for Percy."

"Grace Ann, he is not even five months old."

"I can just tell he is going to be a fine horseman. Like his daddy is. It's in his blood."

Jo could not argue the point. Carolinians had great skill on horseback. Even in this state, Wade was renowned for his horsemanship and had been recruited by a friend of the family, Wade Hampton, to join a cavalry troop Hampton was organizing.

Hampton was a shrewd man by reputation. Grandfather Montgomery seemed to take great pride in Hampton's enlistment of his grandson. In preparation for the anticipated war, the unit had begun drilling.

Jo cast her eyes toward a dark, gray sky. A storm was gathering. Grateful it had not burst upon her while shopping, she scurried into the house. Her breasts ached. She had been gone too long from her son.

She slipped off her gloves; Olfus took them at the door. "You have a visitor, Mistress Montgomery. It's Dr. Montgomery's wife. Master Wade left explicit instructions for her not to be allowed entrance, but, ma'am...she insisted. She's in the parlor."

"It is all right, Olfus. I will see to her needs. Will you have tea brought in?"

As she exchanged glances with Grace Ann, Jo wondered when Kathleen returned to Charleston. She had developed a terrible reputation in the city after her dealings with Arthur had become common knowledge. Wade had not discussed Kathleen's departure in detail with Jo, but Jo realized the separation from Andrew was not amicable.

At the time, it had been the least of her concerns. She wondered what Kathleen hoped to accomplish. With Wade out for the day, Jo admitted she was glad to have Grace Ann by her side. Kathleen had a haughty arrogance that displayed itself when the woman was in ill humor.

The good people of Charleston were renowned for their hospitality. Most were good, kindly people, generous to a fault but they were also a stubborn lot. The rumor of Kathleen's improper relationship with Arthur, which had been whispered behind fans, had become a topic openly discussed. A black cloud hung over Andrew.

Once a lady was in disgrace, it was hard to find their forgiveness, especially when the one shunned expressed no remorse for their transgression. Homes began not receiving her.

To make matters worse, it was whispered Kathleen had facilitated a duel…and not involving her husband, but between not one, but two alleged lovers. One had been Arthur. He had been shot dead.

Charlotte had remained with Cousin Sarah. It had been deemed the best for her to recover, but it had been the last straw for Andrew. He had left his wife at their house in Charleston and made his main residence Magnolia Bluff while Fannie stayed in the nursery with Percival. Kathleen had disappeared until today.

Josephine entered to find Kathleen on the settee in the subtle elegance of the room. Kathleen's eyes were fastened on the door. She was dressed in a blue muslin gown; it was her usual rich apparel. At first glance, the sight of her momentarily unsettled Jo. This was not a cordial call.

"I'm sorry to have kept you waiting, Kathleen." Jo smiled sweetly. "But we had not expected you. If you would like to see your daughter, I'm certain…"

"It is not the reason I'm here." Her teeth gleamed at her with a false smile; her eyes darkened. "I came to talk with you, sweet sister."

"We have nothing to discuss."

"I believe that we do. You forget I was in Philadelphia when you came to *marry* Andrew."

An awkward silence followed. Confused, Jo wasn't certain how best to proceed. *What was Kathleen up to?* Jo was certain it would not serve her well.

"I declare, Kathleen, what on earth does that have to do with the price of eggs?" Grace Ann swooped down beside Kathleen. "Tell me, please. I would like to understand how you explain you married another woman's fiancé."

"I fear your dear cousin isn't the prim and proper little Southern belle that all you people down here think she is." Kathleen paused as Olfus brought in the tea service, but hadn't the good manners to wait until Olfus left before she continued. She tilted her head down and flashed a smile at Jo. "I came to make a bargain with you."

Jo lowered her gaze and poured a cup of tea. She had the sudden awareness that Kathleen had knowledge of her true relationship with

Cullen. Jo's raised eyebrow betrayed her bewilderment. She questioned, "What kind of bargain do you think I would ever make with you?"

"You are rich, my dear. I believe it will be quite easy to keep me quiet," Kathleen began. Quite smug, she folded her hands sedately in her lap. "Of course, I could simply tell of Cullen Smythe appearing at Magnolia Bluff the day your young one was born. I heard he came to take you away from here."

Jo's face fell like a stone. *Oh, mother of all! What did this woman know?* She sat and digested the information in silence while indignation swelled within her. She had been under no illusions about Kathleen. The woman was bitter, disillusioned, and jealous.

"Be warned, Kathleen, you won't get away with such nonsense," Grace Ann said contemptuously. "Do you think for one moment anyone would believe such an out-and-out lie? From you?"

"Come now, Grace Ann, I would expect better. Your poor brothers have been so mistreated by the Montgomerys. Where is your loyalty?"

"That is none of your affair!" Grace Ann shook her head ominously. "It is not my loyalty that is in question. I have never seen a woman act as fast as you and cause so much damage in her wake. Why, there is no house in Charleston that will receive you. For that matter, the whole of the state."

White-lipped, Kathleen stiffened. Whipping out the fan attached to her wrist, she fanned herself. She snarled, "I have seen and heard enough to know of what I speak. Everyone fawns over Jo as if she is a helpless soul instead of an infectious evil."

Jo shot a look of pure wrath at Kathleen, whose face broadened with a malevolent smile. She said, "It is not I who is evil, Kathleen. I have tried to be merciful to you. After all that you have done toward me, I allowed you into my home…cared for your daughter. But I will take no more. I want you to leave."

"I am not leaving until I get what I came for or I will tell my tale," Kathleen countered in defiance. "Have you told your dear family that you disappeared with Cullen Smythe while in Philadelphia? Why no one knew where you were? Ask Jenna and Anna if you don't believe me…Then he appears at Magnolia Bluff, begging for dear Jo to return with him. Makes me wonder who is little Percival's daddy."

The venomous words hit their intended mark. Jo felt her heart race madly. She clutched her hand against her chest to calm it, relieved only when she looked up. Wade stood in the doorway. His hardened gaze fixed on Andrew's wife.

"Kathleen, that will be enough. Don't hold another for your unhappiness." Wade's iced voice resonated throughout the room. "As Grace Ann said, no one will believe your nonsense. Since I would know better than anyone if Percival is my son, there is no doubt. Moreover, I will not hold to any notions otherwise."

A hushed silence ensued. An eerie sense of disaster loomed. Kathleen sat rigid in her seat. Jo sensed her nerves. Astonishment was written plainly on her face. Kathleen was frightened, as well she should be. Jo had never seen Wade so angry.

"Jo, Grace Ann, why don't you accompany me to the nursery? Percival just woke," Mother Montgomery, the most tactful of women, suggested. "I believe the men will deal with this matter."

Jo nodded absently. She hadn't even noticed Mother Montgomery enter the room, or for that matter, Andrew. One thing Jo knew well, of which Kathleen seemed to have no knowledge—a Southern family protects their own. Kathleen wasn't theirs, connected only by an unfortunate, embarrassing occurrence.

Grace Ann rose beside Jo and linked her arm into hers—a sign of a bond that was not broken.

Wade reached out and halted her. As he leaned down, he kissed her cheek. "Make no mistake. I will deal with this matter."

"I know," she whispered and gently squeezed his hand.

Behind her, Kathleen laughed. "You fools! I have had my fill of this life. Damn idiots, thinking you will better the Yankees you hate ever so much. Mark my words, you will all burn!"

Jo said nothing else, but quickly withdrew up to the nursery. Only then, while holding her son, was she to breathe again.

In the wee hours of the morning, Jo heard the door handle rattle. As she stood by the window, she turned to see it open and shut again. Wade had finally come to bed. His jaw tensed, but his eyes lay gently on her.

"I didn't know whether you would be sleeping."

"I couldn't," she confessed. She had tried, but it had been useless. "I was waiting for you."

Wade stepped close and opened his arms. She rushed into them and clung tight to him. Oh, how she needed him. He held her close until she heard the chimes of the grandfather clock strike two.

Breaking the embrace, he didn't release her, but held her by her shoulders. "Kathleen is no longer a threat. She is leaving soon enough back to Philadelphia. Andrew told her he wants a divorce."

Taken back by his utterance, she stared at him in disbelief. Divorce was unheard of in respectable families! It would make such a scandal!

"I told Andrew that he has our support. Enough is enough. The family has done all it can for the despicable woman. She has given Andrew just cause for divorce. It will not be hard to prove she has taken lovers."

"I am at a loss for words."

"I'm not." The rage for the woman sprang forth in his voice. "Goddamn Yankee! She disrupts all our lives. Seduces Andrew away from his duty and caused the unfurling of so many lives...then decides this life is not for her. I told her she would not receive one penny from me...or from my brother."

Her eyes widened. She said under her breath, "But what if she...?"

"She won't utter a word of her lies. She has no proof, only whispers that Cullen had been seen at Magnolia Bluff. I suppose from one of the servants, but it meant nothing. Everyone knows at one time, it was his home. Only Kathleen tried to twist it, but nothing will come from it. Kathleen has been silenced."

He sounded so confident...so assured. He went on. "Life in Charleston was nothing like she had envisioned. She had mistakenly assumed that Magnolia Bluff was Andrew's. It was a disappointment to her. She has already left...without her child."

She looked at him doubtfully. "I don't understand...we are keeping a child from her mother?"

"What do you think of me? I would not be so cruel. Kathleen made it clear she wants nothing to do with the child. She said she wants to leave this godforsaken land and everything that reminds her of it."

The revelation left her thunderstruck and yet, the actions didn't take her completely by surprise. A surge of compassion swept through her for the little one sleeping. It was inconceivable how Kathleen could leave her baby... *I would die if Percival was taken from me.*

She looked up to find Wade frowned fiercely at her. It wasn't over. *Had Kathleen filled his head with doubts?* She had no wish to push him further. Nevertheless, the time had come.

Her brows knitted in perplexity. She asked, "What more did she say?"

"Nothing more than I have not already heard."

She stiffened. *He knew Cullen had been at Magnolia Bluff.* He reached out and gripped her arm. She tried to pull away. "Wade, you are hurting me."

He ignored her plea. "Why, Jo, why? Why didn't you leave when Cullen came?"

Her eyes fixed on his, unable to break from his gaze. She had known this time would come. It had been inevitable. She said simply, "I am here because you are my husband. You told me once you knew me better than anyone because you are like me. Then you would know the answer."

"Do I?"

"Yes," she answered, turning his angry words aside. "I am going nowhere. You have given me the life I have always wanted. My son—"

"Our son." He lowered his face to hers and repeated, "Our son. No one...no one will take him from me...from us."

"I wanted to tell you that Cullen had come that day at Magnolia Bluff...but I was scared it would come between us. Then it was easier to pretend it never happened. But...now...I don't want any more secrets between us."

"There will be no more pretenses," he murmured huskily. "All I want is what I have with you, Josephine."

"Then know I love you, my husband."

The admission whispered in the air between them. The ghost of the past was no more. His gaze pierced hers and she saw only him...Wade...her husband...who with one look aroused her so effectively that her whole body trembled.

His face softened. Pulling her to him, he lifted her in his arms and strode purposely to their bed. He lowered her upon the mattress and muttered thickly, "You don't know how I wanted to hear those words."

His mouth dipped downward to hers. She accepted him readily and wrapped her arms about his neck. He kissed her again and again with an urgency...conveying his need for her. She met his with her own.

He rose on his knees. Somehow, they removed their clothing. She watched as he thrust the unnecessary garments away, leaving nothing between them but a deep, sensual intimacy.

Her hands moved down the hard length of her husband's body and slipped down his thigh. His arousal hardened with her touch.

"Slow, my darling," he whispered. "I want to savor every moment...every second with you as we are now."

"Is this the way love is supposed to be?" she asked, caught up in the fever of the passion they shared.

"If you mean, do I feel we are one...that our hearts beat with the same rhythm...that with every breath I take, it is you I live for...that my every dream is of you? Then, yes, Josephine."

He kissed her, taking her breath away with his fierce ardor. He touched her everywhere; his lips pressed hot against her perfect skin, eliciting gasps of pleasure that rose to begging cries. His mouth suckled at her breast while his hands lifted her hips and parted her legs. He slid his fingers into her, touching…caressing the core of her being.

In slow, rhythmic strokes, he brought her to the edge of ecstasy. She trembled beneath him when he moved in her, quickened and deepened his pace.

Breathless, she met his passion with a fevered eagerness. Gasps of desire escaped her as they joined in the intimate union of their bodies. Release sought together as one, man and wife. For Jo, she had found her haven in the safety of her husband's arms.

The sun rose in a clear sky. Jo had slept late. Her night and early morning had been spent in amorous lovemaking. Rolling over, she reached across the empty spot in the bed. *Where was her husband?* Her question was answered in her next breath.

Wade walked into their room, clothed in his dressing robe and holding Percival. He smiled at her. His hair was disheveled; stubble shadowed his face. He was not in a hurry to begin his day. "I held off our young son as long as I could."

Jo sat up and took the hungry baby in her arms. A moment later, a cooing Percival suckled at his mother's breast. Her gaze rose from her son to Wade, who sat on the edge of the bed with a tender expression.

"Happy?"

"Very." She beamed up at him. "Perhaps I shouldn't be. Not with poor Fannie without a mother…and the scandal that will ensue."

"Fannie will be well loved," Wade assured her. "It is for the best. I would not be concerned about the family being disgraced. The character of Kathleen is well-known. What's more, when it is discovered she has abandoned her child, she will be vilified and burned in effigy in the streets if not for the war on the horizon."

"I can't help but feel for Andrew."

"Andrew is going to withdraw back to Magnolia Bluff," Wade said in a calm voice. "But we have more to discuss. You are aware that South Carolina is in the midst of reconstructing. I have been asked to help."

Living within Charleston, Jo did not need to be told that it was a city on the edge, alive with anticipation: boundless celebrations, endless social events. Even Jo had been caught up in the revelry, but now Wade's tone was serious.

"I have been in meetings with Hampton about his legion he has formed."

Suddenly, the brightness of the morning dimmed. She asked dreaded question. "You are going to fight?"

"If it comes to it, Jo, it would be expected. I have military experience. Hampton is footing the bill for his legion, but even though he is one of the richest men in the state, more will be needed. I have pledged our support."

"I trust you."

A small smile formed on his lips. He opened his mouth as if he wanted to say something, but thought better of it. He rose and crossed the room to the window. Looking thoughtfully out, he sighed. "War is coming. It is inevitable. Everyone is anxious for it to begin. They have no understanding of what war is like. Grandfather calls Lincoln an ugly, grotesque ape who spends his time whittling wooden sticks and telling vulgar stories. I fear Lincoln is more clever and stubborn than we have given him credit for and we are underestimating him."

"Oh, mercy!" Jo cried. She had not heard one utterance against the war in this house. "You have misgivings?"

"I believe it would be foolish not to," Wade said in a low voice, his eyes fixed on the view outside. "You will not hear me talk in this manner outside of these walls. I will publically stand behind the stance that South Carolina has taken."

Wade turned back to her and met Jo's eyes. Jo paused for a breath as she tried to comprehend his meaning. She confessed, "I'm confused. I thought you wanted to secede."

"I don't question the succession, but the path we have taken from there. I don't like Davis. I find him to be quite lacking the leadership we need. He talks as though holding cotton over the head of the European nations will gain their help." His voice rose with his irritation. "No one wants to listen to what we are facing. I have talked in length with Hampton and his aides, who feel as I do. We have much to overcome. We should have been better prepared before making a move. The North has the best army in the world. They have ships and arms and are well organized. We are in confusion."

"Wade!" Jo cried, looking conscience-stricken. "Why are you saying these things? You are scaring me. Everyone says a war will be over quickly…that there may not even be a war. The Yankees don't like us anyway."

"Cullen."

"Cullen?" she asked, so bewildered and startled by the anger in his voice.

"Cullen," he repeated. The room stilled and he quickly made his way back to her bedside. "He has written me…several times. He has outlined in a quite detailed manner why he believes the South will fail."

"Why…why would he do so? Why would he write you?"

"My darling, loyal…dutiful wife. You were thrown into a situation you didn't ask for or want…but you need to know that Cullen believes strongly that Percival is his."

"He told you that!" Jo gasped in real distress.

"Yes, and more." Wade went on. "He wrote that he realizes you would never leave me, for your character would never allow it. You would never forsake your family's honor."

"Oh, Wade…I would never leave you—"

"I know." He reached over and caressed her face. "I am not questioning you. I only want you to understand I will not let you regret marrying me, Jo. I will make you proud."

"Wade, we talked of this last night…You have already made me proud. You saved me…"

"One day I hope you know the depth of feelings I have for you." He kissed her lips lightly and smiled down at Percival. He continued, "Cullen's concern lies with Percival, Jo. Understand fully, Percival will always be mine, but Cullen believes otherwise and has sworn to protect Percival. Cullen has threatened to take Percival if the violence escalates. He said clearly he would never allow his son to endure the horrors of a war. He won't sit idly by."

Dumbfounded, her voice faltered. "He's…threatened to take Percival from me…us?"

"I believe that is his intention," Wade said frankly. "But, Jo, don't fear. I would never allow it. I made it perfectly clear to Cullen what would happen if he attempted such an action."

She looked at Wade with eyes wide with fear. "What, Wade? What will you do to stop him?"

With his arms wrapped about his small family, he calmed her. He stroked her hair gently, but his words burned. "What I would do to anyone who threatens my family," he said bluntly. "I would kill him."

Chapter Nine

War fever had become infectious and spread rapidly across the South. The streets of Charleston were filled with drilling regiments in their gray uniforms with blue cockades and red sashes, and swords in sheaths buckled to their waist.

Soldiers and civilians alike sang marching songs. Citadel cadets had begun their own preparations. At night, practice shells lit up the sky like firecrackers at Christmas.

People were restless as they awaited war news. The cry came to reclaim their state from the Federal government. Carolinians wanted the Union troops out of the state...out of Fort Sumter. It had become a battle cry.

Fort Sumter had become the main topic of conversation at dinner parties. Kathleen had been forgotten. Wade had predicted the good citizens saw her as a leper and felt that Andrew was fortunate to have her gone. He had been correct in his assumption.

Focus centered on the reconstruction of government being formed for the new South—the Confederate States of America. Heated debates ensued to the point where some called for South Carolina to secede again from the Confederacy. It was uneasy times.

The arguments overflowed to the dining rooms. The bickering was endless.

"Damn Davis! Sending Beauregard! Beauregard acts as though he is a king to everyone in Charleston, but it is Colonel Whiting who is doing all the work. Beauregard takes the glory and benefit from the colonel's work."

"Does it matter who gets the honor? It is all of our honor. We have much to contend with. The *New York Herald* has written slavery must be extinguished, if in blood. Trying to incite the Yankees!"

"Mark my words. The fort will fall soon enough now. Anderson is burning blue lights, signs and signal for the fleet outside. Why, I heard we even intercepted a letter from Anderson urging them to let him surrender."

The bickering ended soon enough. When General Beauregard was brought into Charleston to lead the newly founded Confederate Army, he was met with opposition. The people of Charleston never had taken well to orders given by anyone they considered an outsider and Beauregard, from Louisiana, was definitely an outsider.

The serious, reserved man was short, standing only five seven, and thin. Dark-haired, he had a cropped mustache and droopy eyes. His stilted reception did little to ebb Beauregard's determination to drive every damn Yankee out of the South.

To Jo's surprise, the cries abruptly turned from revulsion to adoration. The arrogant, haughty general soon had had the whole of Charleston eating out of his hand. General Beauregard became their savior with the promise of leading them to the promise land—free of Northern interference.

Moreover, the general had taken quite a fancy to her husband, impressed with his Naval Academy days. "Wade Montgomery was made to be an officer. Men look up to him," Beauregard declared openly. "The South needs men such as him."

It scared Jo...the thought of her husband becoming an officer...the thought of him going into battle.

Nightly, the sound of regular shells exploding in the air resounded throughout the city. It made it impossible for Jo to get a good night's sleep. Then on Friday, April 12, the highly anticipated time came.

An eerie calm descended when St. Michael's bells chimed out four o'clock. Shortly after, a heavy boom silenced the anticipation of the moment—the time when the South would make their stand.

General Beauregard issued the order and the newly formed Confederacy's arms fired at the bombarded fort. The Confederacy had made a stance upon its right to exist—the fight for the rights of the Southern States—and had taken an aggressive position. Jo understood there would be no going back once the bullet fired.

Wade wasn't home. Anxious to see the response from Fort Sumter, he had joined the rest of the men of the city to watch the exchange. Jenna and Anna urged Jo to join them on the rooftop to watch. Jo declined.

She chose instead to spend the moment with her son. She crept silently into the nursery and watched him sleep. He seemed so peaceful, but she had a sudden worry. What kind of world had she brought him into?

The secessionist leaders had decided South Carolina's fate and declared that they had been left with no option but the one taken. Had the proud Southern people not the right to protect its way of life?

As she watched her son, Jo pondered what the conflict was truly about. Was it about slavery as the North proclaimed? No. But how could she explain her stance behind the South to her son in years to come when she so violently opposed the *peculiar institution*?

Over the last few months, she had searched her heart. It bled for Gillie, but she had come to the conclusion the new South in time would do away with the moral evil that encompassed the whole of slavery. It would be their right and duty to do so.

To Jo, it came down to one simple fact. The North made a power move over the South: the North's constant antagonism toward the South, to remove the power and rights that each state deserved. No, it was their honor: the whole of their lifestyle questioned, debased, and mocked by the Northerner radicals.

Wade's questioning words troubled her. It had to end quickly. She wouldn't consider another option. She got down upon her knees and prayed. She prayed to God for everyone: South Carolina, the Confederacy, Wade and...Cullen. *Cullen.*

She had pushed Cullen to the far recesses of her heart. She had to...or she wouldn't be able to live the life in front of her with Wade.

Papa had been right. Wade and she were of the same cloth. Each had sacrificed for the betterment of others, put their needs in front of their own. Her heart softened as she thought of her husband.

The weight of his family's burdens had fallen upon his shoulders. He protected her and gave her unconditional love...a life full of promise. She remembered how angry she had been to have been ripped from Cullen's arms...but it had not been Wade's fault. He had been a victim as much as she.

Fear emerged within her as shells exploded in the sky. Her heart was torn in two, much like the two who had been brothers...who now stood on opposite sides of this conflict. Her heart lived on the edge.

Oh, she wanted none of this! While cheers erupted outside, tears flowed slowly down her cheek.

Charleston celebrated. At 2:30 p.m. on April 14, Fort Sumter surrendered. Major Anderson had surrendered less than thirty-four hours after the first shot. With the action, the revelry of parades began.

Governor Pickens had a correspondent, William Howard Russell from the London *Times*, escorted around everywhere. Crowds welcomed anyone with a uniform of gray.

The *Mercury's* headlines read: "the Administration of the old Government may abandon at once and forever its vain and visionary hope of forcible control over the Confederate States."

Church bells rang. Everyone took to the streets, riding in open carriages, exclaiming the virtues of all things Southern. Hopes ran high for the newly founded Confederacy.

Jo chose to stay in the house with the children. She couldn't shake the ominous feeling that swept through her.

* * * *

The days after the surrender passed swiftly, like the fleeting hand of time. It became obvious that war was upon them and preparations had been made. Inevitably, the South now had to be ready to forcibly defend its right to exist.

How precious the moments had become! Never had Jo been more aware of how precious each moment had become with the threat of Wade leaving to join the fight.

With the morning light, the rapture of the night eased into memories. She wanted nothing more than to stay in her husband's arms and deny the inevitable day of its power against them.

Jo lay nestled in Wade's warm, loving arms. He ran his fingers through her rumpled hair as his breath brushed against her ear.

"The orders came down yesterday. Hampton's Legion has been called up to Virginia."

Josephine stilled. The moment she had dreaded had arrived. Wade was going to war.

"When?"

"Within the week."

She wanted to cry, but it would never do. Wade was courageous and brave. She would be the same. Breathing in deeply, she collected herself. "I will have everything prepared. Your uniform needs its buttons tightened." His strong arms turned her and she saw the pain of separation evident in his eyes.

"At one time, I would have been as the others, declaring the Yanks have had this coming and talking of all the glory to be found…" His voice faltered. "But all I feel is I don't want to leave you. How selfish am I?"

"We must be brave."

"My darling, I do not know how I can leave if you aren't brave." His voice resonated with his deep-felt love. "There is so much I need to say. I cannot help but worry. It maddens me that I'm going to protect my home. Yet when I do so, I will leave you unprotected."

"I don't want you to worry, Wade. I will handle everything. I will do my part as well."

"Then you will do what I request," he said solemnly. "Grandfather is old and despite his protests, his health is failing. Andrew is to be left behind. With his foot, he would be useless as a battlefield surgeon. It will ease my mind if you allow Andrew to look after the family while I am gone. He has vowed to do so."

At this moment, she would agree to anything. Andrew mattered little to her compared to Wade leaving her side. Jo crumbled inside, crying to herself. *If you must go, you must not die! You must come back to me!* She could never utter the words out loud. Instead, she kissed him lightly on his lips. "Don't let it be me who you worry about, Wade Montgomery. I will miss you when you are gone, but I will be here, waiting impatiently for your return."

"Then I have no option but to return." He embraced her tightly until they had no choice but leave the comfort of their bed.

* * * *

Three months passed before Josephine found her way back to Magnolia Bluff. She had left behind a city whose intoxication for the war had not waned. At the end of July, news filtered into the city that the Confederacy had won the first battle at First Manassas in Virginia.

The streets overflowed with excitement. Talk swirled the war would come to a swift end, echoing the sentiment that "one more victory and the war will be over."

Crowds would wait outside of the *Mercury* for news of the battles fought. It frightened Jo, for not only did the paper carry news of the conflicts, but also the list of dead and wounded.

There was no official system of notifying kin. A casualty list was sent to papers to be posted for all to see. It was anguish to read over the names. The human cost of the war was heartbreaking, shattering families with sorrow of the loss of a loved one. Most times, a letter of condolence would be sent to the family by the commanding officer. Rarely, a telegram was sent—only under special circumstances.

Jo's days had been spent with the other ladies, making uniforms for their brave men. Late afternoon was saved for walks with the babies along the Battery, accompanied by Mother Montgomery.

It had not been long after Wade had departed that Jenna had met a young man, Derek Elbridge. He tarried from a plantation in Georgia not far outside of Atlanta. As most young men, he had readily joined one of the legions formed in Charleston the moment the first shot was fired, worried the war would be over before he could reach Virginia.

Caught up in the war fever, the two young lovers wanted to marry, but Grandfather Montgomery refused to give his consent. At seventeen, Jenna was heartbroken and felt her young life would end if she didn't marry Derek immediately.

"Young lady, I'm not objecting to the marriage. I ask only you wait until he returns. It won't take long. Mark my word," Clayton stated firmly. There was no changing his mind.

Jenna fumed, but Derek refused to go against her family's wishes. Jo held him in high esteem for his actions. So it was that as Jo before her, Jenna had to say good-bye to her soldier.

The events of those months merged together. One day seemed like the next. In the gleaming sunlight, Jo watched Jenna say good-bye to Derek. He looked so handsome in his gray uniform. He reminded her of Wade headed off on his best mount with a sword Grandfather Montgomery had ordered for him.

She missed Wade terribly and lived for his letters. He wrote of his men and camp life, but never once did he complain. He shared with her his hope for their future at the close of each correspondence and told of his undying love for her.

His letters brought comfort, but without Wade to shield her fears of the future, the glaring inconsistencies of her life edged their way to her consciousness. Her longing was sharpened as the days lengthened.

The return to Magnolia Bluff had been earlier than previous years. Clayton Montgomery had enjoyed himself immensely in Charleston, but he had a sudden need to be home. Jo complied and packed up the babies, their nursemaids, and Jenna. Mother Montgomery had already planned a visit down to Savannah with Anna to visit Cousin Sarah and Charlotte.

The house was ready, as Andrew had been living there, but the nursery needed to be cleaned. Jo took to it early the following morning after feeding Percival. Lottie, Percival's nursery maid, took the babies down into the parlor while the rooms were scrubbed.

Jo hadn't bothered to wake Jenna. The poor thing was grieving Derek's departure. Despite the high spirits at the train station, Jenna had become disheartened.

As she wiped a window, Jo heard a shriek emerge from downstairs. Dropping her rag, she raced down the stairs. Before she got down the staircase, she saw Lottie holding Percival. Her heart calmed. Then she saw the blackies crowding around the foyer by the study's door.

She gripped the banister and hurried down. When she entered into the study, she found Clayton Montgomery, the patriarch of the family, sprawled out on the floor. His breathing labored, he lay unconscious.

As she knelt beside him, she looked up to find Amos standing there, looking helpless.

"Go find Dr. Andrew…now!" Jo demanded, but she knew as well as Amos it would do no good.

Clayton Montgomery passed away without regaining consciousness.

* * * *

In the twilight, Josephine stood on the veranda and overviewed the gardens. In the weeks that had followed Grandfather Montgomery's death, it had become her habit to take in the night air before she retired.

Sadness descended upon Magnolia Bluff. An era had passed with the death of the monarch of the family and the plantation mourned. The family had Clayton Montgomery's body taken back to Charleston and laid to rest in the family plot alongside his wife, Amelia. Despite her personal feelings about the man, he had loved his wife, who had died near over twenty years ago. He had never remarried, but had stayed faithful to her memory.

Most of the extended family managed to attend the burial. Andrew had sent messages to both Wade and Cullen to notify them of the death. No one expected their attendance.

In the weeks that had passed, Josephine noticed subtle changes. Though the slaves had showed the utmost respect to their master upon his death with their prayers and hymns, tension among the blackies had risen.

Andrew had assured her that there was nothing to be concerned about. It was to be expected with the war brewing around them that unrest would manifest itself, but at Magnolia Bluff it seemed to be mostly curiosity about the conflict. Miss Hazel had repeated the same.

It gave Jo a measure of comfort, but more weighed upon her. Rumors proliferated of a Union blockade along the Southern coastline. How were they supposed to transport crops or receive goods? The overseer, Barclay Laird, was optimistic about the yields in the fields but it would do little good if they had nowhere to sell their crops.

But her constant worry was her son. Word had trickled through the lines that Cullen served with the blockade. Magnolia Bluff was vulnerable, sitting along the Ashley River. Jo feared they were defenseless if the Union Navy attacked Charleston.

Andrew assured her that would never happen. Charleston was too well defended, but she remembered all too well Cullen showing up before Percival's birth without warning.

"Josephine?"

She recognized the voice behind her readily enough. Andrew walked toward her, limping heavily, which had become more pronounced as of late. Since his self-proclaimed exile from Charleston society, his appearance had altered. He had become rather unkempt. His wrinkled waistcoat needed cleaning; his hair was uncombed. He had grown a beard. Moreover, he had only left Magnolia Bluff for the funeral. "Jo, I have a matter to discuss."

"I'm sorry, Andrew, I was about to go check on the children."

His eyebrows lifted. "It will only take a moment and I fear I must insist."

Silently, she chastised herself. She was tired and had no desire to be pulled into a deep conversation. "Can it not wait until the morning?"

"So you can think of another excuse not to talk with me?" Andrew said in a solicitous tone. "I do not want to add to your burdens, Jo. I know what you think of me, but I assure you I want only to make amends between us...for Wade's sake."

"Is it necessary? I gave my word to Wade I would allow you to run Magnolia Bluff. But you must understand I only tolerate you because Wade insisted." She shrugged. "I accept your presence. I hope, though, you don't expect me to entertain you. I am sorry for your misfortune, but that is the extent of it. And I don't see the need to have only the most formal conversation. Now if you—"

"Jo, stop." He sighed. "I'm not asking you to forgive me. I cannot ask you to do what I cannot do myself. No, this has to do with the running of Magnolia Bluff."

"It is not necessary. As I said, Wade warned me, and I will not dispute what he has set up. He realized that Grandfather Montgomery was in ill health. He had no problem with Barclay as overseer—"

"Listen to me for a moment," he interrupted her. "I want only to let you know of a situation. It has to do with White Oaks."

Silenced, Jo stared at Andrew, frightened of what he would say. Yet, she had to ask. "Has something happened?"

"One of the bucks escaped. One named Thom."

"No!" Jo cried, flashing back to the time Heyward had escaped from Hoyt Miller. *Had they treated one of their slaves in the same manner?* She shivered. Afraid to ask the details...afraid not to. "Has he been recaptured? What are we doing?"

"No, he is gone. I did not raise the alarm. I felt it best at this time to keep the matter quiet. With the war upon us now, I fear there will be more episodes such as this, but I do not want to give rise to more runaways," Andrew said bluntly. "I believe it was an isolated incident and have treated it as such, but the overseer and I at White Oaks disagreed. I let him go."

"You felt it necessary?"

"Yes, and I would like you to trust me on this, Jo."

She studied him, serious and intent. Quite different in his approach with her than Wade would have been with this matter, Andrew had been direct and forthcoming. She was certain Wade would not have told her in an effort to *protect* her.

"I am going to send Barclay up to White Oaks. They will need an experienced overseer. I found a man to replace Barclay here. A Troy Gardner. A Virginian. He traveled down here in all that commotion back in the spring.

"He came to me as a patient. He had gotten injured being pushed through a window during one of the celebrations. An older man, he can't serve in the Army now because of his injury. Cut up his hand pretty bad. Can't pull a trigger."

"You believe it for the best?" she asked with a sudden appreciation that it was not her decision to make. Her stomach churned with the thought of disciplining any slave in a harsh manner.

She supposed it was not business for a woman to have to deal with, given their sympathetic nature. Jo wondered whether any other Southerner felt as she—that they were caught in a web of their own making, now not knowing how to untangle themselves in the mess they were in concerning slavery.

"There is one more thing you may find more to your liking. I received confirmation that Harry Lee and Buck are in Virginia with a legion from Mississippi. With Wade gone, I wanted to give you some comfort that your cousins will not be a worry."

Jo gave him a slight nod, but said nothing more. There would have been no need. She was certain her face betrayed relief. When she retired for the night, she felt her worries had lessened considerably. Everything Andrew had discussed seemed reasonable.

Her sole attention now would be directed on the care of the family and her son. With this hopefulness, she took up her pen and wrote to Wade.

* * * *

The stormy weather of the day before had calmed. The South Atlantic Blockading Squadron under Flag Officer Samuel Francis Du Pont had their orders. Du Pont, a cautious commander, waited until there were no unforeseen obstacles in their path before he gave the command to engage.

The fleet of seventy-seven Union vessels had disembarked from Hampton Roads ten days ago, not knowing their destination until the ships were out to sea. Secrecy being of the utmost importance, the captains of each vessel received a sealed envelope opened only after on the open sea—Port Royal, South Carolina.

Lieutenant Cullen Smythe, US Navy, first lieutenant and acting executive officer of the *Bienville*, doubted the efficiency of the attempt at secrecy since the *New York Times* had run the headline "The Great Naval Expedition" days before they departed, which gave the details of the venture, namely the seventeen warships headed south. Though, he doubted the Confederate Navy could withstand an assault even if they knew their destination.

It had been a chaotic week since their departure. A gale had splintered the convoy. Three ships had been lost, sunk or driven ashore. The gunboat *Isaac Smith* had to throw most of their guns overboard to stay afloat and the transport *Governor* went down.

A couple of days later, a vain but valiant effort by an inferior Confederate flotilla had tried to engage the force but had been driven back by the superior firepower of the convoy. It had done little to slow the expedition, but it had caused a problem to the mission.

When the *Isaac Smith* had thrown most of their guns overboard, the infantry had lost much of the ammunition needed for a ground assault. General Thomas W. Sherman informed Du Pont the troops would not be available for the engagement.

Cullen had slept for four hours out of the last forty-eight, but he was ready. He refused to think that he was about to fire upon the people he considered brethren. He held to the contention that the nation need not be divided, but he wondered whether men had gone mad. There would be no going back…he was about to do battle.

"We're coming about, sir!"

A rocket zoomed high into the galvanized sky, missing its mark, but his eyes followed it as the trail of a golden shower of sparks fell short harmlessly in the water. Cullen gestured to turn to port.

The ship's bow hammered into the rushing waves, cut in-between the other gunship to fire portside and maneuvered through the smoke streamed from the funnels of the battleships. Cannonballs arced toward their intended targets.

Counter shelling from the forts disrupted the movements of the ships, but Cullen held to his orders. He navigated his ship to fire again, far enough away from the guns of the forts. Cullen dropped his gaze inboard and watched the swirl of activity on deck. The tackle men were slewing the guns around.

The bow gun blazed; a reddish-orange tongue of flame shot across the water toward Fort Walker. Guns exploded. Another shell landed in front of the bow and sent a towering geyser of water into the air, which dowsed Cullen with salt water.

Giving no ground, Cullen stepped higher onto the ladder and yelled his orders to fire the broadside guns. He looked across the water through the smoke-whitened air; another cannon fired from the fort. The battle had only just begun.

The bombardment continued for over three hours. When the last shot fired, the Union had a decisive victory. Through an eyepiece, Cullen watched a steady stream of Confederates flee Fort Walker.

He walked up the stern to the pilothouse to inform the commander. By mid-afternoon, the Union flag had been raised over Fort Walker. Not only had the Confederates abandoned the fort, all the white folks in Beaufort had evacuated the area, in so much of a hurry that some had left their dinner on the table. When Union soldiers rolled into the streets of Beaufort, they found only one white man, a drunk sleeping in a back alley, who hadn't a clue what had happened.

Beaufort was now in control of the Union forces.

* * * *

Within three weeks since the capture of Beaufort, the Union had discovered it had been an advantageous win in more than one way. Strange how still a vibrant town turned. The white flight had left a brilliant opportunity for the Navy. Occupation of the town by Union troops was a tremendous gain. The harbor allowed entry to the largest ships and was in a central location…perfect for the base of operation of a spy network…directly in the heart of the Confederacy.

Cullen rode along the back road into the pines. Swift-moving thunder clouds threatened what had been a sunny, pleasant day, but the weather wasn't on his mind. He was set to meet Andrew and Mitchell at a remote cabin along the marshes northwest of Beaufort. He wasn't alone.

The night before, Cullen had rowed over to the *Wabash*. He had received his orders from Commander Davis, none to his liking. But like so many other things in his life, he had no control over the situation. The orders had come down from the secretary of war, Gideon Wells, himself.

Lieutenant Hugh McFadden, who had been aboard the *Ottawa*, accompanied him on his journey along with an Army man, Captain Eli Claiborne, under the command of General Thomas Sherman, who now had hold of Beaufort.

Claiborne was a tall man with a scar across his face from the battles he had seen in the Mexican War. A lifer, he bore from a small town on Long Island. He had an intense love for his country and no patience for the South, feeling a firm hand needed to be shown.

In front of Cullen, the cabin came into view. Smoke filtered out of the chimney, a signal that Andrew and Mitchell had arrived.

"It was his heart," Andrew said. "Wade was not there. He is in Hampton's Legion and is in Virginia."

Cullen sighed. He had received the news of his grandfather's death, but it had not seemed real until Andrew talked to him. Death was so final…never to reconcile their differences…never to talk again to the man who had raised him.

Showing no emotions, he walked over to the rickety table and sat in the hard, straw-seated chair. The cabin was old and abandoned, filled with only broken furniture, dust, and clutter left from the previous occupant.

"I have word for Uncle William," Cullen offered. "If you see him tell him, his home has been looted."

"You have been there?"

"I rode out personally. The slaves have ransacked the whole house. Even with my presence, the slaves reveled with their newfound freedom. One of the blackies was playing the devil out of Aunt Lydia's piano. Slaves dancing away upstairs…all over the house. It is the same throughout Beaufort. Debris from the homes clutters the streets."

"What am I to tell Uncle William?"

"Tell him that he has lost everything within Beaufort by his own foolishness. Who instructed the fools to leave their homes in that manner? I know it was not cowardice."

"It is my understanding that it was Reverend Walker," Andrew said. "He incited fear into the community."

"How stupid it had been for the inhabitants to leave their homes unprotected. The town has been plundered," Captain Claiborne said. "It does not bode well for any to return."

"Do not underestimate the people, Captain," Cullen said in an icy voice. "They may have been ill-prepared for this fight, but they won't make that mistake again."

"Lieutenant Smythe, I am fully aware of the challenge before me."

Cullen felt his bile rise. His plan had been put into place. Mitchell had been accepted in the countryside. The information gathered had already been fruitful: Mitchell had supplied the information needed for Fort Royal's assault.

The people of Beaufort had held a belief that the forts would protect them, but in reality the defense of the harbor had been inept. Mitchell and his informants had pinpointed the weakness. The cannons mounted atop the parapet at Fort Walker had left them exposed to enemy fire. Moreover, the cannons hadn't the range needed to do harm to the Navy's vessel.

Mitchell discovered several flaws within Fort Walker: the cannons were poorly sighted toward the harbor, the units ill-trained, and the gunpowder was of inferior quality. Given the information, Port Royal had become the target of the Union fleet.

"Speaking of challenges," Mitchell interceded. "Might I ask the reason for this meeting, given the need for extreme secrecy? I do not like being called away in this manner. It could raise questions."

"It will not be done so again," Captain Claiborne interjected and glanced over at Cullen. "All communications will go through the proper channels. This was a necessity."

Cullen met the captain's eye and glowered. He had a sudden dislike of the man. "This will be brief. I have been relieved of the duty of overseeing the network. It has been reassigned to Captain Claiborne."

"He's Army," Mitchell said stiffly.

Cullen's lips tightened and found it hard to say the words. "According to Secretary Wells, it does not matter. He feels it better served to have someone on solid ground to give directions to the network. All other resources will stay as they are. You have been re-designated for this assignment, Mitchell, to the Army, keeping your full rank and commission."

"I will be overseeing any needed arrangements extended by the Navy," Hugh offered with a sympathetic glance at Cullen.

"You?" Mitchell queried, making little effort to conceal he had not liked what he heard. "What has happened? I agreed to this mission because of Cullen. Now that it is proved its worth, the higher beings have pulled the rug out from under—"

"No," Cullen said austerely. "I have been reassigned, too. I asked for Hugh personally. With respect, my request was honored. The network will not be affected by this change."

"Reassigned? To where?" Mitchell's eyebrows rose.

"The Western blockade. I was told that Flag Officer Farragut asked for me personally. I am to leave immediately."

Mitchell turned to Cullen and ignored Claiborne. "Why? This makes no sense."

"It seems it has been a conditional request." Cullen shot a look over at Andrew. "For his participation in this venture. Now, if I could have a moment with my cousin... alone."

Cullen waited until the others left the cabin. Then he turned to Andrew, who sat across from him.

"I know you are upset, but I have my reasons...good reasons," Andrew said, not bothering to deny the accusation.

"Maybe I don't agree with those reasons."

"Oh, come on. I have complied with your bidding at great risk," Andrew argued. "I have made strides to solidify the network. I sent Barclay up to White Oaks and brought in one of your men, Troy Gardner, at Magnolia Bluff. The links are in place and Mitchell has integrated well. You have your network."

"I set it up to protect—"

"I know why you set it up, Cullen. Do you believe that Wade did not tell me? He would not have been that foolish as to have left and not protect his family. He told me you believe that Percival is your son and perceives you as a threat."

Cullen nodded in an absent way while Andrew's words sunk to the core of his being. Reprimanding himself for his oversight, he had not considered that his cousin would consider him a danger to those he had striven to protect. His gaze hardened.

His frustrations unleashed, he stood and pushed back against the table. "Do you believe I would harm my son? Why do you believe I have gone to the lengths I have...I won't have my son—"

"Hold that thought, Cullen." Andrew gestured with his hand for Cullen to calm. "I do not question your need to protect those you love, but this network is not about Josephine and Percival. For this to work, it was my belief that it needed someone not personally involved to head it."

"You question my honor!"

"Never," Andrew answered quickly and direct. "Over the last few months, I spent a great deal of time soul searching. I have made many mistakes, but I refuse to be bullied into another."

A scowl crossed Cullen's face. A retort lay on his tongue, but he kept his mouth closed.

Andrew stared at Cullen and frowned. "Tell me...tell me that you would put your mission above the needs of Josephine and Percival... That is the reason I made the request because, Cullen, I will not be party to you taking a child away from his mother."

"I would never! How dare you!"

"I dare because I know you!" Andrew's intensity matched Cullen's. The anger echoed in his voice, but then in the same breath, he calmed. "You cannot tell me that at the first sign of trouble you would not overreact...and put your personal interest above all others. I can't allow that...I understand...but in good conscience I can't..."

Andrew let his words fade and he paused. His eyes never left Cullen, though. Relentless, he went on. "He's my brother, Cullen. He has been the perfect husband and father to a son he knows may not be his. Yes, I do realize that Wade questions, but he has given Percival a name and loves the boy unconditionally. Percival is his, and I won't be a part of anything that will hurt him. I refuse."

The cabin became quiet. Cullen stared at the floor. Wanting nothing more than to cry out that Jo should have been his wife...Percival should have his name...if Grandfather hadn't interfered...if...

Slowly, Andrew shook his head. "This is for the best for everyone, including you. Percival is being well looked after. He is loved by everyone. I won't take him from Josephine—"

"Then she can come if the need arises. I never intended to leave her—"

"She would never leave Wade. You know that, Cullen. No matter how bad it gets. You are just going to have to live with it. I'm sorry. For once, I'm going to do the right thing."

Cullen cursed under his breath. "Wade has left his family...a war...a war is exploding around them..."

"That is not how he sees the situation. You need to leave them, Cullen." Andrew's voice softened. "They are a happy family. These are words you might not want to hear, but Josephine loves Wade. Take with you that Percival is loved greatly and lacks for nothing. Do you not know that most plantations fear rebellion with their slaves? Not at Magnolia Bluff. They would die to protect Percival and Josephine."

"Because they know you are running a goddamn illegal railroad on the grounds…"

"For Heaven's sake, do you take me for an imbecile? Only a few trusted know of what we do… No, it is more. It is the way she treats them…the way that Wade has. Heyward has not been forgotten, nor has Gillie. Miss Hazel has become a fixture at the plantation."

Andrew spoke but Cullen had latched onto words that cut him deep. He said, "She loves Wade…"

"Yes," Andrew hesitated, but stated firmly. "I believe she does. She has done what she must and you should do so, also. Cullen, you are family and will always be. It is why I tell you now for your own sake—move on. They are safe and will remain so. You can leave knowing you have done everything you can for the boy. Some things are out of your control. This is one of them…they are not your family."

Rage erupted within Cullen. He was furious and there wasn't a damn thing he could do about it…about any of it. He had no control. Damn the war. Damn the Navy. Damn Andrew…Wade and Josephine… Could no one understand his need to get his son out of this godforsaken war?

Cullen made no more arguments. It was done. He would fight the battle on a different front, but his heart would be left in Charleston.

Chapter Ten

Plantation life had changed, but had settled into a routine that gave it a sense of normalcy. Although the Yankee blockade had tightened, the war continued and had been successful for the most part. Slowly, the fear of a massive advance of the Union against Charleston eased, along with Jo's fear that Cullen would descend and take her son away.

The community had pulled together for the cause. The weeks went swiftly by, filled with not only the demands of the plantation but also helping with the war effort. The demands on the Confederate commissary grew.

Josephine's days passed pleasantly enough. She was surrounded by family and loved ones. Each shared a common purpose—caring for one another. Percival and Fannie were cared for so well by everyone on the plantation. The babies' laughter and glee shielded the house from any gloom that could have so easily overwhelmed the inhabitants.

Neighbors called, giving the semblance of days gone by. It wasn't. Despite the boisterous call for secession and the brave cry to lay down one's life for the Confederacy, the reality of the cost had begun to filter back into the community.

Up the river a piece in Summerville, Jenna had gone to the wedding of one of her friends, Kelly Eastley in Charleston, back in April. Her new husband, Thomas Kent, left for the war a few days after the marriage.

Last month, word came that Thomas had been killed in action. Less than a week later, Kelly gave birth to a stillborn and developed a fever. She died two days later. The whole family gone…as though they had never been.

Magnolia Bluff's rooms were filled. Besides Mother Montgomery, Jenna, and Anna in the house, Andrew had now moved into Grandfather

Montgomery's old room. An influx of visitors came and went. Charlotte had come for Grandfather's funeral, but had left shortly after. She had found comfort with Cousin Sarah.

To Jo's delight, Grace Ann had come for an extended visit. Though, Jo confessed to herself she gawked at her cousin's trunks, wondering whether she was visiting or moving in. Grace Ann had come to care for her surrogate son. When Grace Ann had offered her support during her pregnancy, Jo had thought it was empty words.

Grace Ann had a superficial quality about most everything except herself...except for little Percival. She had become quite attached to the little fellow, almost obsessively so. At least for the time being, Mr. Whitney had retired back to Whitney Hall. He seemed to understand Grace Ann's need to be close to Jo and the young one. For that, Jo was grateful.

"Miss Jo."

Jo looked up to see Rosa in the doorway. For an hour, Grace Ann and she had been watching Percival and Fannie playing. They seemed to love each other. Percival had passed his first birthday three weeks ago. He had walked early, even before Fannie. The two together waddled beside each other...so precious. "Yes, Rosa, am I needed?"

"It's Miss Anna," Rosa said with effort. "She ain't got out of bed this morning. Says she's cold, but she's hot on her head. Miss Anna done got a fever."

"Where is her mother?"

"Her done gone out with Miss Jenna to visit Mrs. Randolph. She told me to check in on Miss Anna later in the morning 'cause her begged off on going calling with 'em."

"I'll watch the little ones," Grace Ann offered. "Go see about Anna."

Jo followed Rosa up the stairs, disavowing the fear that seized her upon the mention of a fever...until she entered the room. She move quickly to Anna's bedside, but she needed not to feel her head.

Perspiration poured off her reddened face; the poor dear shivered uncontrollably. Jo leaned down and felt Anna's forehead with the back of her hand. Anna was burning up. When she pushed back Anna's sweaty hair, Jo caught sight of a rash that covered her neck, much like a sunburn.

"Oh, honey," Jo whispered, hoping she hadn't betrayed her concern. Anna grasped Jo's hand. "Oh, Jo, I feel so bad."

"I know, I know," Jo repeated and looked over at Rosa. "Send for Dr. Andrew. He's inspecting the fields with the new overseer and then send for her mother."

Weariness sank deep into her bones while nerves gripped her soul. Jo paced outside of Anna's door. Andrew had been inside with his sister for only a few minutes before he exited.

An ominous feeling swept through Jo the moment she saw the look on Andrew's face. Scared, Jo retreated a step. She had told herself that Anna was more susceptible to fevers. She had always recovered, but any fever sent trepidations throughout a household…with reason. In the low country, the mortality rate for fevers was high.

Andrew frowned and lowered his gaze. He said simply, "It's scarlet fever."

Darkness fell over the plantation. By the morning, more had developed a fever: two of the house girls who helped in the nursery and tiny, fragile Fannie. Relentless in his care for his loved ones, Andrew demanded his orders be kept in place to contain the fever. Andrew immediately quarantined the house.

The upstairs reeked of sickroom odors and medicine salts. Jo wanted nothing more than to throw back the curtains and open the windows, but Andrew warned it would be harmful to Anna and Fannie.

The whole of the house had been placed on alert. Jenna stepped in and performed the duties that Jo and her mother would have usually looked after. Grace Ann placed herself in charge of Percival and refused to come out of her room with the little one, not while the fever raged through the house. Mother Montgomery's attention centered on her daughter while Jo cared for little Fannie.

Two days after Anna took to bed, her fever broke, but the news was overshadowed with the failing health of small Fannie. The tiny one refused to eat and her cries had become faint whimpering.

Andrew's efforts contained the fever from spreading. Anna and the two house girls would survive, but for his own daughter he could do nothing more. In the wee hours of the morning, Josephine rocked the ill child.

Fannie's head burned with the fever. The only comfort the little one found came with constant rocking. Jo prayed. She prayed with the comprehension it was the only hope they had.

The sick baby girl's life was in God's hands now. Josephine sang to her: soft and rhythmical, soothing the small one. Then, the babe became strangely still and quiet.

Jo's voice faded off as she looked down. Tears streamed down her eyes as she realized the baby was no longer breathing. She must have cried out, for Andrew came running, but there was nothing more to be done.

The rains came. Torrential rains poured the day little Fannie was placed in the ground...so small...innocent. At the gravesite, the family stood as sorrow stricken figures against the gray sky. Aloof, Andrew stood by himself, unable to be comforted. The gloom couldn't be lifted, not even letters from Wade telling of the exploits during the victory at Bull Run in October.

Overcome with grief, the house fell silent with only weeping and wailing to be heard. How thankful Jo was her own child had been spared, yet her heart ached as if Fannie had been her own. For the last few months, she had been. The thought she would never see her smiling face again tore against Jo's heart.

Sleep evaded Jo. The memory of little Fannie haunted her. She eased out of bed. There would be no sleep. Throwing a wrapper about her gown, she went out into the hall to the nursery. Percival wasn't there.

Her heart stopped for a moment. Hastily, she made her way down to Grace Ann's room and opened the door. She breathed again as she saw Percival snuggle close to his aunt. He looked so peaceful. For the first time in days, a smile crossed her face.

While her time had been consumed by the sickness that gripped the plantation, Grace Ann had looked after her son with all the ferocity of a mother bear protecting her cub. She had a way with Percival and had not let him around the sickness...giving Jo one less worry. Strange how everything had changed since their youth.

Growing up, more than not Grace Ann had treated her like a poor relation. Their relationship had changed...so much had changed. The breach between Jo and Harry Lee had extended to Grace Ann. Though Grace Ann saw her mother often enough, the relationship with her father was strained.

Papa had once told Jo, "Friends come and go, but family...for better or worse, they are always with you."

It was what Grace Ann and Jo had discovered, making their bond closer in these times of strife. Without a sound, Jo withdrew. She had no desire to disturb either of them. She made her way back out into the dark hall and was halfway back to her room when she spotted Rosa at her door. "Rosa?"

"Miss Jo," her maid said in a low voice, easing back into the hall. "It's Dr. Andrew. Him in the study and…Amos thought he might need ya."

Jo readily followed Rosa down the staircase and into the foyer. A light burned beneath the door of the study. Jo paused before she turned the handle. "I will see to Dr. Andrew. Perhaps make a small tray of leftovers from dinner. I don't believe many of us ate."

"Yes, ma'am."

She waited until Rosa disappeared around the corner before she opened the door. Andrew sat behind the desk, silhouetted against the dim candlelight with a bottle of whiskey in one hand and a glass in the other. He was drunk.

His coat was flung over one of the high back chairs; his cravat lay on the floor. He wore his unbuttoned shirt outside of his breeches. Rather purple in the face, his bloodshot and glassy eyes met hers. He raised up his glass toward her and drank it down.

"I came to see if you have need of anything. I have sent for—"

"I have all I need right here," he interrupted her. He poured the last of the whiskey into his glass and then flung the empty bottle against the wall. "The way I have it figured, another bottle and the world outside these doors will disappear. Now if you will excuse me, Jo, that world includes you. I want to be alone."

Bending down, she picked up the bottle. "I will call for Amos. You need to go to bed and sleep this off."

"Oh, Josephine, I'm way beyond sleeping off my troubles." He drank down his glass once more. Squinting, he glanced toward the decanter on the table across the room. He stood, but stumbled and caught hold of the desk.

Jo rushed to his side and helped him to the settee. "I'm sorry for your loss, Andrew. Truly, I am…I wish there was something I could do to ease your pain."

"So you have no answers? The most gracious Josephine can't fix this…no, not this." He looked at her with a strange expression and then held out his empty glass in a mock toast. "This is to you, Jo. For reminding me what a failure I am. To you, Josephine, in your benevolence."

"That is quite unnecessary," Jo said stiffly. "I'll get Amos. You aren't yourself at the moment."

"Myself! No, for once I'm quite myself, Jo. Do you want to know what I feel? Do you really care? Or do you feel vindicated for my behavior toward you!"

In his current state, she doubted he was conscious of his words. "Don't be ridiculous, Andrew. You are family. I would never wish this on anyone. If it eases your mind, know I hold nothing more against you."

"You should," he said. "I have treated you abominably...all because of the love of a woman."

To her surprise, tears flowed unheeded down his cheeks. He wiped them back with his sleeve. She stared into the face of a grieving man expunging his demons.

"Kathleen...Oh, good Lord! Forgive me...I loved her...sacrificed my good name for the woman...and she threw it back in my face. Do you know what it's like to love someone so desperately and have them laugh in your face...telling you how pathetic you are..."

"Give it time. You will get over her."

"Time? Time won't heal the damage Kathleen has done." He hiccupped and then laughed mockingly. "Do you know the last words she had for me? She told me that Fannie wasn't mine. Oh, I suspected...but then she had the audacity to make sure I knew my suspicions were true. Taking pleasure in playing me for a fool...that sweet, innocent babe wasn't mine."

Slowly, he stood and stumbled over to the decanter. She made no attempt to stop him. He poured himself another drink and glared at her over the glass. "God forgive me! I couldn't even look at Fannie...I couldn't look at the child who was supposed to be mine. The spiteful woman took from me what should have been my joy...she made me despise that angelic face to the point I couldn't even bear to look at her...Lord Almighty...I hate her. Tell me, what kind of person have I turned into?"

Befuddled how to respond, she fell silent momentarily. Finally, she said, "I believe you've had enough." She crossed the floor and took the glass out of his hand. He jerked it back; the contents sloshed over both of them.

"Have I offended you?" he asked curtly. "Of course, I have. Poor Jo, caught in her own quandary. Whatever will you do when Percival grows up looking as his father? He already favors him."

"You're drunk," she said coldly.

"Not as drunk as I am going to be," he said unapologetically. He poured another glass and downed it. Slamming the glass down on the table, he looked back at Jo. "Did you think I didn't know that Percival is Cullen's?"

The statement was so unexpected. Startled, her jaw dropped. Bristling with indignation, she cried, "How dare you? Percival is Wade's."

"Without doubt," Andrew agreed in his stupor. "Wade has taken considerable pains to ensure there is no question of that fact. He is…is the happy, doting father and husband to pacify you."

"Be silent!" she cried, bewildered and deeply disturbed. "Do not say such horrible things!"

"No…no, you need to hear this." He stumbled over to her and caught her arm. "Don't you want to hear how I envy my brother? He has the woman he loves. No matter the cost to you…to him…to Cullen. He manipulated everything to his advantage… He has become Grandfather…dictating to us how to live our lives…only he didn't anticipate Cullen's desire for you."

"You are making no sense. I'm going to get Amos."

"Ah, running away from the truth," Andrew taunted. "I told you Wade would stop at nothing to have you or Magnolia Bluff. He did the only thing he could by sending that telegram to have you come home."

A deadly hush descended upon the room. His voice had held a remnant of his imbedded hurt, but resonated a desire for another to share in his pain by attempting to inflict hurt upon her. She would have none of it.

"You lie! Do not insult Wade with such an accusation. It was Grandfather Montgomery."

He laughed. "Is that what you believe?"

She got no other answer. He released her arm. Behind them, the door opened. Rosa stood in the doorway and stepped back to allow Amos entrance.

"I'll take 'im, Miss Jo."

Jo nodded and watched the big black man wrap his arm around Andrew, whose head slumped awkwardly down. Amos led Andrew out the door.

She stood and stared at the empty space for a time. Her mind reeled. Jo doubted Andrew would remember the night's events. She would not forget.

* * * *

Josephine walked through the next day in a blur. She felt angry, outrageously so. The night had scarred a memory on her soul—Andrew's drunken remarks. It tortured her heart.

I told you Wade would stop at nothing to have you or Magnolia Bluff. He did the only thing he could by sending that telegram to have you come home.

She had tried to reason with herself. Not only had Andrew confessed that Wade had expressed his doubts that Percival was his son, Andrew's words had been filled with innuendoes that Wade had inflicted the cruelest of tricks upon Cullen and herself. The question became— was it true?

Andrew had been extremely inebriated, but he had seemed so certain. Had Wade deceived her...and Cullen? Wade...?

An anger so deep embedded in her heart, so much so it hurt. She had believed Wade and herself to be kindred spirits, drawn together by forces beyond their control. Adding to her growing bitterness, she had allowed her heart to soften toward the man who readily accepted her son as his, knowing he could well be another's.

She had convinced herself that Wade wanted what she had—a stable, loving family. She believed he forgave her of an unforgivable sin...because he loved her, giving them a chance for happiness in circumstances beyond their control.

Oh, she had been a fool. She had allowed herself to have fallen under his charms. Had her heart swelled for a liar and a cheat? *Was Magnolia Bluff all he cared for?*

If Wade had tricked her so deviously, he had been masterful. If not for that telegram, she would be married to Cullen, with his child. Gillie...Gillie would be alive. Dear, sweet Gillie. *Oh, dear God, what am I to do?*

Poor little Percival was so confused. His mother was upset; his constant companion was gone. He kept looking around as if missing something, a pitiful, heartbreaking sight.

Miss Hazel sensed Jo's distress...not for the right reason, mind you...but it was there. It made it worse when she held her young son. Percival wailed and cried unmercifully, unable to be comforted by his mother.

"Now, Miss Jo, ya done gone and had a bad day. Why doncha get along and take a nap. Ya haven't slept for near two days now."

"I can't sleep."

"Then go for a walk. Miss Grace Ann and I will care for Percival. We will. Why, Miss Grace Ann treats him like he's her own. He ain't gonna lack for attention."

Jo made no more of an argument. She wrapped her shawl about her shoulders and headed out the backdoor. The late afternoon sun hung low in the sky; it would be dark soon enough.

The leaves on the trees laid scattered along her path. Only the green pines colored the woods, taking the path down by the Ashley, the same path she had taken when Percival was born. There would be no surprise visit today from Cullen. No, he was too busy fighting a war against her and what once had been his home.

As she neared the river's edge, a white egret flew overhead. She watched until it landed in the tall grass across the water. A freshet breeze stirred, giving the view a semblance of peaceful calm. She thought miserably it was only a façade…there was no peace to be found.

The crackling of the dried leaves and twigs told of another's walk. Glancing behind her, she sighed heavily. Andrew. She had no desire for another conversation. Her overwrought nerves could take no more. "Go away," she said before he had the chance to utter a word. "I have nothing to say to you."

"But I do to you."

Jo's scowl deepened as she waited until he was by her side. He had greatly altered his appearance since the night before with a much-needed change of clothes. He had shaved his beard off and left a well-groomed mustache.

"Andrew, I do not need to hear anymore hypocrisy." Her frown grew ominous. She saw his eyes fixed together in a stubborn manner. "I have been insulted by you for the last time."

"I deserve that." He faced her with fortitude blazed in his countenance. "It is not for me but Wade I ask you to hear me out. I had no right to unburden my conscience to you and in turn further do you harm. Honor demanded my silence."

"What has been said can't be unsaid."

"I do not deny that, but I gave my word to my brother. I know he greatly loves you. Anything done was motivated by that love. Do we not all make decisions at times that we come to regret?"

"His came with a high price. It cost Gillie her life…Cullen has ostracized himself from his family—" Abruptly, she stopped speaking. Her emotions toiled beyond the ability to talk.

"If Wade had not sent the telegram, I can't disagree that the outcome would have been different, but you can't blame Wade for Harry Lee's actions. Harry Lee had already kidnapped Gillie and Heyward. Whatever was done to Gillie and Heyward is not on Wade's conscience."

Jo was silent. Perhaps she had no reason to blame Wade for Gillie's death. No, it was more of a need that had emerged within her to lash out at Wade and hold him responsible for everything bad that had happened to her. As she blinked back welling tears, she struggled to find words. "Do not make light of his actions. He deceived Cullen...me. Our marriage is a lie...a lie. You can't undo—"

"I can't! I wish to God I could...because if you must blame someone for the whole of the mess, it is me! Me! Not Wade...not Cullen. I made a vow to rectify the wrongs I have done and once more have made a terrible error in judgment."

"Andrew, what do you want me to do? Act as if I have no knowledge of what Wade as done? Are you mad?"

"It is exactly what I'm asking," Andrew said in deadly seriousness. "I do not know if the words I uttered last night held truth to them. Grandfather slung them at me when he admonished me for the disgrace I had caused the family by marrying Kathleen.

"He proudly told me when emphasizing that Magnolia Bluff would survive because of Wade's actions. That Wade was a true Montgomery, doing whatever necessary—"

"That Wade had turned into him! Is that what he said?"

"I will not deny it was Grandfather's perception. It is not mine."

Her mood would not let her accept Andrew's attempt to soothe out his conflicting words— not with the anger that possessed her. "Wade caused harm with his actions. There are a wide range of consequences. I—"

Andrew imperiously stopped her. "Wade values honor above his own life; it would shame him for you to suspect him of such an action, whether or not it is true. This would destroy everything that Wade has worked for...for you...the family...Percival..."

His insinuation that Wade had claimed Percival without question was not lost upon her. Her mind reeled. "You ask too much."

"Do I? You know Wade. You made sacrifices, as did he, but before Clarissa, Kathleen... before Cullen, it was the two of you. Are you going to hold it against Wade for loving you...for doing anything to have you?"

"For Magnolia Bluff."

"No, you," Andrew insisted. "Your papa wanted Wade for you from the first. It was not a lie that he endorsed Wade before his death. It was your papa's wish because despite the claim of love for Cullen, could you have been happy anywhere but here? With Wade?"

"At what cost?"

"All actions have a cost, one way or another, but I sincerely doubt Wade's motivation was to cause Cullen harm. Wade wanted you. Can you hold it against Wade that he grasped at the one chance he had to have his heart's desire?"

"Yes…yes…yes! What he did was morally wrong. You are twisting your words to justify his behavior that has no justification. He destroyed Cullen's link to his family…your family. The family that you contend Wade wants so much to preserve."

"Did Wade's actions break the bond with Cullen? I highly doubt it. Cullen help cut the ties on his own when he decided to wear blue. This gulf between Wade and Cullen would have come, despite their feelings for you. It is out of your control, as this conflict that has swallowed us up in its hatred," Andrew went on loyally. "The past can't be changed. The question becomes what future do you want."

She gave him an uneasy glance. The last few days had weighed heavily against her. It occurred to her that now, as she was then, she was caught in a quandary. She gave no heed to the tears that escaped down her face. "I don't know much at the moment, Andrew. I hurt. Nothing you have said has eased that pain, but it is my cross to bear. Perhaps with time…"

"You do not have time, Josephine." Andrew reached into his waistcoat pocket and pulled out a telegram. "A messenger brought it this afternoon. It's from Wade. He is leading an expedition back into the area and will be home within the week."

* * * *

Josephine watched her son giggle and waddle across the parlor into her arms. Her heart swelled with a never-ending love. His hair had darkened, even darker than hers; his deep brown eyes were so huge and expressive and his infectious smile lit up a room.

There was no love greater than she felt for him. Then, as quickly as love surged through her, a sudden sadness gripped her. How unfair life was for her to enjoy this moment in time and it be denied to… She halted her thought. It was a useless sentiment. She could not undo the past, but long suppressed feelings toward Cullen began to emerge and stir up her frustration and anger.

Driven by her conscience, tormented silence haunted her about Cullen…what could have been…should have been. It did little to soothe her soul that it was she who had caused the strife between Wade and Cullen. Two men who had been closer than brothers. Two men who now stood against each other.

The dreaded truth was that she would never know what could have been if Wade had not sent that telegram. If indeed, he had sent the blasted message! She only knew the heartache the telegram had caused.

On the horizon, she foresaw other worries. Concern mounted around Charleston. The naval blockade of the harbor had begun to show its effects; the wet weather had greatly hampered harvesting the crops. Constant rumors of slave unrest added to the uncertainties. The community was fearful, especially after the debacle at Beaufort.

"I hear, Miss Jo," Miss Hazel said, "that 'em Yanks in Beaufort have opened it up. Yes 'um, for all to come and be free."

"And what, pray tell, do you want me to do about it? I have little control of anyone's behavior. If you are nervous to be here, I will ask Andrew to see if I can get you to Philadelphia."

"Ain't gonna go nowhere, Miss Jo. This is my home. Ain't gonna let no one take my place away from me. I 'ust worry about you, that's all."

"I'm not going anywhere, either," Jo assured Miss Hazel.

She said no more on the subject, but understood the warning that Miss Hazel had given her. No matter how the slaves were treated at Magnolia Bluff, they weren't free. There were chains that bound them to the plantation.

Take only one day at a time, Wade had told her before he had left. *One day: no more, no less.* Oh, she already hated this war. Her only wish was that it would be over swiftly.

Yesterday, more bad news filtered back to Magnolia Bluff. Their neighbors to the west, the Simmons, lost two of their sons in Virginia.

Holding her son, she moved over to the window. The sky suffused with a deep orange, a brilliant sight to behold. Her gaze held toward the lazing disk of the sun.

In the distance, a sight caught her eye. Wearing Confederate gray, riders emerged around the curve along the lane up to the house. Her heart fluttered. Sudden trepidation filled her.

Her husband had returned from war. She should rush down the stairs, but she hesitated, afraid she would not be able to conceal the doubt from his eyes…the betrayal that burned a fire in her heart.

"Jo! Jo!" Jenna dashed into the room. "It's Wade. He's home!"

Not waiting for Jo to respond, Jenna gestured for Jo to go in front of her out of the room. It would never do not to be the first to welcome her husband. Jo forced a small smile and picked up the hem of her crinoline-stiffened skirt.

The dutiful wife stood at the foot of the steps with Percival in her arms when the riders halted in front of the house. Wade didn't bother with introductions before he leaped from his horse.

Suddenly, she was in his arms…they were in his arms. Wade's full beard gave Percival only a moment's hesitation. His little arms embraced his papa as his father's attention turned to Josephine.

If Wade picked up on her reserved greeting, he gave no indication. He kissed her openly in front of everyone. He whispered, "Josephine."

Breaking from his lips, she finally uttered, "You are home."

"I'm afraid only briefly." He looked at her as though he had seen the gates of heaven open for him. "General Stonewall Jackson needed volunteers to secure more guns to take up to Virginia. I gladly accepted the mission and have been given leave to take a few days to check on you and my family. God Almighty, I didn't care what I had to do. Given the opportunity, I would have walked through hell to see you again."

* * * *

The Montgomerys sat down later than normal for dinner, but what a feast had been prepared. The family gathering had turned into a celebration, welcoming Wade's companions, Private Dennis Crocker from Savannah and Private Earl Riley from outside of Atlanta.

The men bathed and had been given clothes to wear while their uniforms were given a good wash. Pleasant chatter filled the rooms, the first hint of festivity the family had known for such a long time.

"Ma'am, you're as Major Montgomery has described ya'. It is no wonder he has talked of nothing else." Private Crocker heaped another helping of potatoes on his plate. He was a thin thing with curly reddish hair and kept nodding to Anna, who blushed prettily. "It's nice to have family to write ya' and all. Got my mamma and sister writing me. My pa don't write none. Lets my mamma write. Gonna go down to see them tomorrow. Major said we could have a few days at home 'cause the mission went so well. Snuck them guns right through the blockade—"

"Crocker…" Wade admonished. Pushing back on his chair, he lit a cigar. "The ladies don't want to talk of—"

"I do," Jenna interrupted. "I have questions about all that you do. Derek is in Virginia. I worry so about him. What is camp life like?"

"Camp life is hideous at best." Private Riley answered and took a sip of sweetened tea. "Sweltering heat in the summer, replaced by the damp and cold. Sickness is everywhere…" His voice faded, as if remembering the company he was keeping. He mumbled, "Sorry, ma'am."

Wade frowned. "Obviously, it is not home."

"But ya must have fought 'em Yanks," Jenna pressed, hungry for news. "The paper said you whipped 'em good at Manassas."

"Ya wanna hear?" Riley snapped, to Jenna's bewilderment. "Ain't nobody braver than a Reb soldier. In that is the truth. Brave and undaunted, facing our enemy without fear in our eyes. I was there at Bull Run, if that's what ya talkin' of." His head tilted toward Wade. "Followed the major there into battle." His voice tensed. "At one point, we were retreating, running into a dense wooded area, turning as we rode and firing. It was as if a hail of bullets rained down. Shells exploded around us, tearing through our ranks. Men fell around us as if they were flies…"

For a moment, his eyes glazed over…as if he stood back in the memory. "I rode with my best friend, Michael. We signed up together. The best shot in the county he was… We were rallying and formed a line of support. We started off and emerged from the woods. I watched as a bombshell struck Mikey's horse and body, and literally tore him to pieces. I couldn't do anything. I wanted to…but I couldn't stop…had to go forward. The explosions all around me…echoed with the groans of the wounded and dying. I had to push on…the enemy had to be pushed back. Blood…so much blood. It was splattered over the trees and soil…the ground strewn with dead bodies. Yet I kept on pushing until we had the advantage…I left Mikey…"

He lowered his head and said grimly, "We won. In the midst of all the confusion of the Yanks' retreat back to Washington, there were civilians who had come out to watch as if it was some damn picnic. My friend got blown to bits and they came out for a picnic. I went back and found Mikey. Buried what was left. Ain't no damn picnic."

Awe fell upon the room. No one spoke. Jo glanced at Wade with frightened eyes.

"Andrew," Wade interposed hastily, "I noticed riding up to the house that the plantation looks in good shape. Some around here look like they are feeling the effect of the blockade."

Jo caught Jenna's concerned eyes. Wade had diverted the conversation but the words echoed hauntingly in the room.

* * * *

An hour passed. As she brushed her hair, she sat at her bureau and pondered the day's events. The excitement of his return filled the house with a gaiety it had rarely seen in the last few months. She, too, got caught in the festivities. Wade was home and everything else seemed to be forgotten until this moment.

Alone in the stillness, she thought of all the things that she had wanted to say to her husband. So many things she wanted to ask. So many things she needed to know. It was only after Private Riley's outburst that the reality of the war suffused through Jo. The man was disturbed and tormented by what he had seen in battles.

Through the evening, she listened to Wade talk at length in an effort to make light of the burden the soldiers carried. She watched his mother, who couldn't take her eyes off him; his sisters hung on their brother's every word. Grace Ann had been no better, laughing at his jokes and stilted funny stories.

Jo caught Wade's troubled gaze, though he had quickly hidden it behind a façade of smiles and charm. Understanding suffused through her: he held back in an effort to protect the women from the realities that truly surrounded him at camp and battle. It scared her.

After what seemed an eternity, the door opened. Wade did not look at her immediately when he walked in, but closed the door behind him. How she wished she could shut out the world as easily.

"Andrew kept you awhile."

"We did not talk long," Wade confessed. Taking his uniform coat off, he slung it over the high chair. "I have been in the nursery, watching Percival sleep."

She placed her brush down; she turned around on her cushioned stool and studied her husband for a long moment. He looked tired. Moreover, his voice carried sadness in a faraway tone. "He loves you," she said simply. "He's happy to have his daddy home, as am I."

"As I am to be home." He sat on the chair and pulled off his worn boots. "While I watched him, I realized I have never seen a more beautiful sight. So peaceful. So innocent. He has grown so." Abruptly, he stopped. His blue eyes rose slowly until they met hers. "I'm sorry."

"For what?" she asked, confused, but something in his voice warned her to be cautious. She rose and knelt beside him. "What is wrong? Do you have a headache? I can massage—"

His boot dropped to the floor and he grasped her hands. "For having to manage on your own these last few months…enduring poor Fannie's death… I've had nightmares that something happened to you or Percival and I would be too far away…"

She shook her head and spoke softly, not sure what to say to ease the strain she saw in his face. "Wade, don't do this to yourself. You have made your family proud with your bravery and courage. You have done what you must. I have done no more than any other wife. We all do what we must for the cause."

"You have done me *proud*." He brought her hands to his lips. "You have been constantly on my mind since I have left. Forgive me, Josephine. I told myself I would not burden you with my guilt, but it weighs heavy on my soul. I cannot take this burden to my grave if I'm killed."

Stricken by his proclamation of his mortality, she cried, "Oh, don't say such a thing! Nothing can happen to you. Nothing, do you understand!"

"Please, Jo, I don't want to alarm you, but there is the possibility with each battle fought. I need to know. Do I still have your love?"

She could feel her chest tighten, finding it hard to take her next breath. Had Andrew told him his suspicions? No, Andrew would not have, not after pleading with her not to confront Wade. Lost for words that did not come, she remained silent.

"I ripped you from your lover's arms. You would have been married to Cullen if not for me and the cursed duty you felt. Oh, no, my darling, don't turn from me," he pleaded in an unsteady voice when she looked away, trying desperately to compose herself. "You need to know the man you married. I took great pleasure in winning you by whatever means. I loved you and even though I don't deserve you, I was the victor." He lifted her chin up and forced Jo to look at him.

She breathed in deeply and whispered, "What is wrong, Wade? Why are you talking in this manner?"

He pressed his lips tightly together. Obviously, the words came hard. "Andrew…Andrew confessed that in a moment of weakness, he told you that I had confided that Cullen believed Percival is his. I fear you may believe I have dishonored you."

Wade had detected her aloofness. Her heart stilled. This was the moment to confront him with *everything* she suspected…to inflict the pain she felt…to hurt him the way she had been hurt.

She withdrew out of his reach. Her reaction was instantaneous as frustration lashed out at him. "You humiliated me. You confirmed Kathleen's nastiness of accusations! How could you?"

His hand ran through his hair. He looked at her with eyes that reflected the depth of depression. A cold fear crept over his face. "It was necessary to protect you, Jo."

Filled with apprehension, she said in an uneasy tone, "I'm mortified, Wade. It was bad enough to have Kathleen accuse me of being a hussy, but to have my husband—"

Abruptly, he grasped hold of her arm and pulled her back to him. "Don't ever say that word…ever! Do you understand me? Never! It is

401

not what I think and I would never…never do anything to cause you harm in any fashion!"

The intensity of his tone took her back. His expression betrayed his distress. She could not ignore the truth that faced her—he was frightened of losing her.

"Why, then, Wade? Why would you degrade my reputation? How can I hold my head up in polite society anymore? What will be said about Percival? Will his name be tainted?"

"You have it wrong…all wrong. Right before I left for Virginia, Cullen wrote Andrew. Cullen warned him that he was going to do whatever he needed to do…to protect what he declared was his son! His son, Jo!" His voice rose higher; his grip tightened. "I had to leave. I had no choice, but I couldn't without taking care of you. Can't you see? It was the only choice I had to keep you safe."

Suddenly, his grip eased, but the alarm in his eyes didn't diminish. He went on. "Do you not know me, Jo? You are my life. I would never dishonor you. Understand. Andrew is my brother. I have to depend on him to watch over you while I am gone. It went no further, but there is more I need to say…to confess. Something you deserve to know. I can't live with myself otherwise."

The room stilled; her blood ran cold as trepidation grew. She looked at him and saw it in his eyes…he was about to affirm her suspicions. *Oh, Good Lord, it was true!*

His face rigid, he began, "After receiving news that Andrew had jilted you at the altar, my only thought was to get to you before Cullen could marry you. I did the one thing I could do to ensure your return…"

Her eyes widened in disbelief. She could keep quiet no longer. She cried out as the words rolled off her lips like a pained scream. "It was you! You…*you* sent the telegram!"

Jo tried to jerk away, but he caught her arm and swung back against his chest. She fought him, wildly hitting him with her fist over and over again. He ignored her attempt to dispense hurt upon him, letting her continue until she collapsed hapless into his arms.

Uncontrollable sobs shook her body. It had been a shock. Despite Andrew's warning, the admission wrenched her soul. Images assaulted her…images of Cullen's eyes staring accusingly upon her. What a fool she had been!

Her dark eyes hardened. She sneered. "You believe it will ease your conscience when in reality it will destroy the life I thought we had created together."

"Listen. It is all I ask," he said. "All I wanted was what I had. Before Cullen...before Clarissa...it was you and I. A love like we had isn't easily to be forgotten. Through everything, I never did. I never meant to hurt you. I confess I put honor and duty before us, but in that I had no choice."

Jo caught her breath. She could not argue that she too held to honor and duty, but she had never deceived another in a veiled attempt at the conviction. She railed, "Do not hide behind your honor to defend yourself. I won't have it! Let me go!"

"No." He stubbornly resisted her efforts to distance herself from him. "I want only to explain myself."

He gathered her close and tried to still her, forcing her to listen to him whether she wanted to or not. "My reasons went beyond honor and duty...it's the Montgomery legacy. I can't have you believing that I have shamed you to obtain Magnolia Bluff."

She glared up at him, but ceased to struggle. She straightened herself up. "If you can, convince me of your good intentions, because all I see is a greedy man much like his grandfather who would have done anything to ensure he gained his much-desired prize—Magnolia Bluff."

For a long moment, he looked at her. "Everything I have ever done, I have done for the furtherance of my family. You and I have been caught up in a tangled web of lies. It is for that reason I need you to understand my actions. I married Clarissa for one reason—to save Magnolia Bluff. I let you go to Philadelphia for one reason—to save Magnolia Bluff.

"When you went to Philadelphia, you lied to me and told me that your papa would disinherit you if you went against your engagement. Do you not know it tore at my soul to let you leave? I did it only for the family...not me. What did I have to gain? Magnolia Bluff would have gone to Andrew."

His tired eyes met hers. Her train of thought had differed from his on the matter. She had been hurt, but it did little to explain his deception. She said the words that burned in her heart. "What of Cullen? What reason did you have to cruelly trick your cousin?"

"Nothing I say will expunge my guilt toward Cullen. Make no mistake, I do not apologize that I have you, but that I deceived my cousin is something that I will have to live with."

"Is it that guilt which claims Percival?"

Out of it all, it had been the unspoken secret they shared. She stared at him, hardly breathing.

He was silent for a moment. Then in a calm, tired voice, he said with finality, "I have proclaimed Percival as mine. In my heart and soul, he is my son. It was by my actions that we married, which took you from my cousin. True, our union was your papa's dearest wish, but your papa would have accepted Cullen after Andrew's fiasco. It was I who could not have it, not when you were within my reach.

"I wanted you by whatever means necessary. I have always truly believed we were destined to be one. Moreover, I do not believe that Cullen could ever have given to you what would truly make you happy. You needed to be here…in Charleston…at Magnolia Bluff. It is who you are."

She wanted to scream that he was wrong. She had loved Cullen, but a remnant of pain surfaced as she remembered that Cullen fought for the North. He had chosen to turn his back on his family, the place of his birth…and her. Then slowly, the realization suffused through her that Wade's words held truth in them. Perhaps, he had known her better than she had known herself.

He sighed heavily. "I was so angry when I discovered that you had been with Cullen, but ultimately, I came to the realization I was going to lose you if I allowed that fact to consume me. I found that my love for you was deeper than my rage and discovered it's what we choose to let come between us that will define our marriage. I came to an acceptance that my life is better with you in it and would never be happy otherwise. God has shown me favor by giving to me the greatest gifts a man could ask for—a loving wife and a healthy child.

"Tell me, my darling, despite all that has come before us, have we not been happy?"

For a time, she said nothing. A million thoughts ran rampant through her mind and heart. The night had been sweet agony with having Wade home. There had been a barrier between them—the hurt and pain of the doubt that had lived inside her was much deeper than the insult of having Andrew know of her indiscretion.

Through the strength of Wade's conviction, she found the answer she sought. He loved her. He loved Percival. Moreover, Private Riley's words at dinner terrified her. It frightened her to imagine life without Wade. She could not bear a future so dismal. Her resolve faltered and with it, the wall crumbled.

A sudden consciousness swept through her that Andrew had been correct. She couldn't change the past, only the future.

The only future she had…the life she had known…the life she was born into was with Wade. It was a different love, perhaps, than she had

404

felt for Cullen, but she was a different person now. She gave herself up to Wade's joy and Percival's legacy.

"Josephine, my love, my life." His voice softened to a low whisper. "Tell me...have I ruined your life by marrying me?"

"No." She encircled her arms about his neck and embraced him fiercely. "You are as I am. I do not want to be anywhere but here with you and Percival. It is my only wish that we are a family...always."

She could say no more, for his lips were upon hers. Their lips blended with an impatient urgency. Overwhelmed with the passion he stirred, the world became his touch, his caress, and the rhythm of their bodies.

Jo snuggled into Wade's shoulder. Their coupling had been intense and quick. He had been almost apologetic. There was no need. She was happy, truly happy, which came with acceptance of her life as it was: a husband who loved her beyond measure, a healthy son, and the promise of a future...if the war allowed. She pushed back the thought, thinking only of the days before them.

Cullen was but a memory, the past. Her future lay with the man who held her tightly in his arms.

* * * *

With Percival in his arms, Wade walked over the side fields with Andrew. His small son had become his shadow in the week he had returned home. *God in his mercy, it was going to be hard to leave once more.*

He had briefly hoped to have been transferred to the defense of Charleston, but his orders arrived yesterday. He had been recalled back to Hampton's Legion. By this time tomorrow, he would be back on his way to Virginia.

"Before I leave, Andrew, I will show you where I keep the copy of the documents I signed. I should have done so before I left, but I assumed Grandfather would have shown you."

"Grandfather barely talked to me."

Wade shrugged, not surprised with the information. He went on. "I will admit, I signed them with the greatest reluctance. I have doubts we will ever recover what is owed to us by giving up portions of our crops to the Confederacy. No one knows what the government bonds will be worth by the time the war is over, but it is our duty."

"I had Gardner take care of the arrangements when you wrote to me about it after Grandfather passed. I knew Magnolia Bluff had pledged her crops. I just had no knowledge of where the papers were kept."

Wade stopped, turned and gazed at his brother. "I have been meaning to ask why you sent Barclay to White Oaks. I'm confused to the reasoning. Barclay knows Magnolia Bluff. With the slaves posing a threat, he would notice any change in demeanor or behavior. Nothing comes before the safety of the family."

"I can easily bring him back," Andrew said. "Gardner seems to have a way with the slaves. I haven't detected the slightest unrest, but it is yours to address. I don't proclaim to have the skills you have in running a plantation. If you want—"

"No, no." Wade swung Percival onto his shoulder. "Don't be defensive. I don't have time for this. It is only Barclay knows Magnolia Bluffs, the slaves, the land. I know that with the worry about revolts, I would feel better if Barclay was here. I don't know this Gardner."

"I do, Wade. Trust me and have faith in my ability to take care of everyone. I can assure you I have kept the faith."

"What does that mean?"

"That you aren't as concerned with a revolt here at Magnolia Bluff. You know your people. That is not your worry. Your worry has left the Carolinas."

Wade stared at Andrew, his expression altered, sterner, more intense. "Cullen. You are talking about Cullen?"

"I have held back on this information until today because I didn't want to ruin your homecoming. Know though, I won't lie to you. Cullen contacted me when the Yanks overran Beaufort. He was there. I saw him myself. I made it clear to him that I will never allow him to take Percival. I gave you my word that I would protect your family. I will keep it."

Wade's anxiety changed to relief. "You said he is gone."

"Transferred to the Western blockade. He sent word to me himself." Andrew paused a moment, as if carefully considering his next words. "Cullen has come to an acceptance of the situation. In his last correspondence, he only wanted me to know that if the need arose, I could send the whole family—Mother, the girls, Josephine, and Percival—to Philadelphia. Uncle Jonathan would take them in. He is not a threat to you anymore."

"You are certain?"

"I will protect the family. I swear, Wade. I haven't been the brother you have been to me, but I will make amends. I won't let anything happen to Josephine or Percival."

"I trust you, Andrew. It is Cullen I do not, but if he is not here, I doubt he can do much from his ship. I'm sorry, Andrew. It's just they are my life and it kills me not to be able—"

"I know, brother. I know. I will guard them with *my* life."

Wade let Percival down at the lawn's edge. Instead of walking, the toddler clung to his papa's leg until Wade picked him up again. Swinging Percival above his head, he had the little one giggling and laughing. Percival fell back down into his arms and hugged him tight.

He looked back over at Andrew. "Then I will leave with one less worry."

Wade did not sleep. He spent the night staring at his wife. Despite his desire to stop time, the morning dawned. With the greatest of reluctance, he rose.

Jo leaned against him. Fighting back tears in a battle she lost, she cried, "I can't bear the thought of all the lonely nights without you."

"Now, none of this." He wiped her eyes. "Be brave, my darling. I will return."

"I will try." She choked on her words. "Promise one thing, Wade, before you go. I listened to your men tell of your bravery and how you have distinguished yourself in battle. I'm so proud of you, but promise me you won't do anything foolish. Come home to me. I will survive, knowing you are coming back to me. Promise me."

"You have my word, Mrs. Montgomery." He leaned over and sealed the promise with a kiss.

Less than an hour later, he mounted his horse. The whole family stood on the steps. He smiled at his mother, his sisters, and his wife. *Oh, Lord, how lovely she looked!*

Jo wore the dress he had bought from a blockade runner after his mission had been completed, a white cotton tarlatan. Woven stripes were set in the bodice and skirt with a red satin ribbon intertwined into the cotton lace, worn over crinoline. A matching red silk belt tied in the back with a large bow.

The matching bonnet was secured with a floral ribbon. Tiny tresses of dark curls escaped and framed her lovely oval face. A vision to behold… He tethered back his horse.

With one last glance over his shoulder, he saw Percival happily waving good-bye in his momma's arms. His young son had no concept that his father wouldn't be returning for a while, but he did. He prayed fervently to God to watch over them until his return.

* * * *

With the descent of colder weather, the North had made no attempt for further skirmishes or battles. The Confederacy's winter quarters had been established outside of Centerville, Virginia. Makeshift huts littered the hillside.

Despite the hardship of being away from home, the men had taken the opportunity to rest. With no immediate battle looming over them, camp life had become tolerable. The ladies of the immediate community gave gifts of comfort to the officers: socks, comforters, and scarves.

The troops even enjoyed snowball fights and singing heartwarming songs around the campfire. Wade, himself, had imbibed in many lavish meals, accompanied by toast after toast to independence. His mind, though, was never far away from his home.

His worry concerning Cullen eased, but Harry Lee and Buck were never far from his mind. Before the war, he felt in control. Now, he had lost that advantage. The war had caused more havoc than the battles on the field.

Fortunately, Wade had discovered that the Haynes brothers had been assigned to an infantry unit under the command of Brigadier General Richard Garnett. Wade had the opportunity of making Garnett's acquaintance during his Navy days on one of his assignments. General Garnett, formerly of the US Army before he had resigned his commission to serve for the Confederacy, had agreed to keep a watchful eye on the brothers.

Monitoring the brothers had served to be beneficial. Wade supposed he shouldn't have been surprised that the brothers had already been on the verge of a court-martial. Each had been formally warned of actions unbecoming a soldier. Buck had even been demoted back to private.

From Garnett's report, Harry Lee and Buck were not cowards and had no issue in battle. Harry Lee had even received a commendation for his bravery at Manassas. Wade held no doubt that Harry Lee had no qualms in taking another's life.

Taking direct orders had been another issue. When ordered by their captain to do guard duty, the brothers had refused, which had led to an inopportune duel. Neither man who participated in the duel had been injured: Buck missed wildly, the captain intentionally fired wide.

Buck had been formally charged with insubordination. Harry Lee avoided the charge only because of his deeds on the field, but, Garnett assured Wade that there would not be another episode such as that one without more dire consequences. Buck had been transferred out of Harry Lee's unit.

Wade had taken comfort in the knowledge that the brothers had pressing matters to concern themselves with besides any revenge they might still harbor against his family. Still, Wade relayed the information on to Andrew.

Josephine's letters came regularly. He read and reread them every night. The last letter, she had conveyed Grace Ann had returned to Whitney Hall. Theodore Whitney had taken a fall from his horse. Grace Ann had immediately withdrawn back to her home to care for her husband.

Knowing how close Jo had become to her cousin, he wondered why Jo had not gone with Grace Ann. Reading between the lines of his wife's letters, though, he held to a lingering hope that it was her own health that delayed her venture away from Magnolia Bluff…that perhaps another life grew inside her.

At the end of January, Wade received an invitation to join General P.T. Beauregard for dinner, along with seven other officers. It was not unusual to dine with the commanding officers, but never had he received a formal request.

Wade had known Beauregard well from Charleston and had found the general had not lost any of his flair for the dramatic. The man had not lost his popularity among the men nor the animosity of President Davis, if the rumors held any truth in them. The night had not played out long before Beauregard made a shocking announcement to the men.

"Gentlemen," Beauregard explained shortly after the men had been seated. "Raise your glasses. I want to make a toast."

Wade eyed the general suspiciously, but complied. Beauregard smiled broadly and held his glass high above his head.

"I have declared myself a soldier for the cause and my country. Being a dutiful soldier, I am prepared to go where I have been placed…I have been called to the Western theater and have accepted my reassignment…on a couple of conditions. One of which are you men."

"Us, General?" Wade questioned, confused. "I'm under Lt. General Hampton's command."

"Hampton's Legion has been restructured." Beauregard glanced around the table. "Everyone here tonight has been reassigned under my new command. Drink up, my brave men. To the Western theater we go!"

On February 2, Major Wade Montgomery departed alongside Beauregard. As the train moved west, crowds met them at every stop with enthusiastic cries of encouragement and belief in the general who would lead them to victory.

* * * *

My dearest Josephine,

I am writing from our encampment in Corinth. Our division is to meet up with General Johnston within days and I do not know when I will be able to write again. Large factions of troops have been congregating, which means another battle will be faced. Beauregard has given us hope that victory against the Union is within our grasp. It is my hope, for I long to see you once more.

Your wonderful letter was delivered to me last evening. I hold it against my heart as a reminder of why I fight. I fight for you, my love, and my children: Percival, and the one you hold within you. Please do not blush at my frankness. The news of our impending arrival has filled me with great joy.

I write this as the breeze brings the soothing scent of honeysuckle. This is a lovely land we have gathered around: green rolling hills and warm, welcoming locals, who have renewed our belief in what we do is right. Their faith has become mine.

It is not easy...this war that is being waged. In my last skirmish, we overtook a Yankee encampment that was filled with an alarming amount of supplies that we have lacked: food such as fresh bread and cured ham. Their uniforms are not ragged, nor their boots' soles filled with holes from wear, and they seem to have a surplus of ammunition. Things that before the war, we had taken for granted. I have learned never to take anything for granted.

I hold to the belief that I serve my state and country and will endure the hardships of being separated from my loved ones as all soldiers before me. At night around the campfire, I talk only of the virtues of my wife and escapades of my son, who must be growing by leaps and bounds.

Do not let him forget his papa, who loves him greatly. And now you have added to my happiness.

I dreamed last night we had a daughter, the most beautiful of babies. You will laugh but I saw her quite vividly, a gorgeous little girl with curly blonde hair and the bluest of eyes. I saw her playing happily with her older brother and you were looking upon them both, smiling lovingly.

I will hold to that thought until I receive the news that both of you come through safely. Be strong, Jo, for me.

Yours forever, Wade

* * * *

Wade received his orders. Johnston and Beauregard had made the decision to move forward and become the aggressor. The losses at Fort Henry and Fort Donaldson demanded a quick response.

In the early hours of the morning, the Confederates prepared for battle. Easing up into Tennessee along the Tennessee River to Pittsburgh Landing, it was said that the Union commander General Ulysses Grant headquartered at Shiloh church.

Upon his steed, Wade saw the Union forces were before him, unprepared for an attack. Wade waited for the signal. It came in the distance as the sound of the drums called for action. Wade answered. With his sword held high, he repeated the cry that he himself had heard General Hampton use in battle: "Charge them, my brave boys. Charge them!"

With his unit at the front, Wade drove the charge. Rebel yells sounded. Discharge after discharge, one Union soldier dropped, and then another. Wade pushed forward. The Union line broke and the enemy was in disarray.

A hail of lead and iron filled the air with dark fire. *Load and shoot. Load and shoot.* There was no time to think, only react and push forward. Somewhere in the chaos, the Union had regrouped and mounted a defensive in a field along a road.

Unsure of his location and hazy about the local geography, he lamented the fact that he had no real orders after the initial attack. He would have to rely on his instincts in directing his men. Unwilling to give up their advantage, he urged his unit into the smoke and dust.

Time had become irrelevant. Around him, he heard the moans of the injured soldiers left on the battlefield, an echo of the overwhelming misery and suffering of the wounded. Confederate cannons roared in the distance. Heavy fire from both sides caused Wade to give pause as to which direction to lead his men. He could not see far in the fog of smoldering battle.

Finally, a courier arrived. "Major Montgomery?"

"I am."

"General Beauregard sent notice that General Johnston has fallen. He is now in full command. He directs your forces to the rear of the Union. They are in retreat."

Immediately, he gestured to the left in hopes his men would follow. It was not a worry. His men placed their trust in his leadership. Exhausted…thirsty, he refused to give ground and called out to hold the position at all hazards.

It seemed that the woods had become filled with cats on the prowl, popping out of nowhere to wreak havoc… Men fell, both Yankees and his brothers…then he saw a break in the defensive. Gray-clad troops swept through.

Never had he witnessed such a ghastly scene…such carnage. He watched his men rush toward the line of blue…into the hand of death…but his brave and courageous men fought on…until the blue sounded the retreat.

Dead and wounded lay where they fell, some on top of each other. He tethered back his mount and allowed his men to continue forward while he covered their rear. Around him, artillery burst…from the Yanks…from the Rebs.

As the last of his men charged forth across a stream, his eye caught sight of movement. In the water and mud, a body moved ever so slightly. A small form dressed in blue struggled to lift his head from the water, but a fallen soldier had collapsed on top of the boy, trapping him beneath the dead weight.

A cavalryman had been trained never to dismount in battle. For a brief moment, he thought of his training as a naval officer. It was easier, he supposed, shooting men from the bow of a ship. *You didn't have to see their eyes as their life drained from their bodies.*

Beyond the line of fire, cannonballs began to explode. He had to leave. In these perilous conditions, it was suicidal to stay…and then a muffle cry emerged from the boy.

Looking over his shoulder at his troops, he turned back to the boy. He hadn't a choice and leaped from his horse. He heaved the lifeless body to the side; he knelt down and rolled the youth on his back. Coughing and muddy, the boy looked up at Wade with fear wide in his eyes. Lord, he was young, with a baby face that had never seen a razor blade. "I'm not gonna hurt you, boy," Wade said. "How old are you?"

"Eleven," the boy uttered in a low, timid voice. "I'm the drummer boy…I got caught behind my unit…don't think I can't shoot…"

Wade was certain the boy could. Most drummer boys had dreams of becoming soldiers, but like most of the men fighting this day, the boy was scared. He probably didn't even realize that tears streamed down his face.

Not wasting any more time, he lifted the boy up and carried him up the bank. Fifty paces to their right, a shell exploded and shook the ground beneath them.

"It's all right," Wade assured the boy. "I'm going to see you through this. I have a boy, myself. Percival. He's much younger than you. The last I saw of him he was just learning to walk. His momma would have my hide—"

The sentence hung in the air. Another shell exploded, much closer. Wade wrapped his arms about the boy and used his body as a shield. Instantly, he felt a hot sensation in his back and then nothing.

* * * *

Spring blossomed at Magnolia Bluff. The flowers colored the landscape, from camellias to the hyacinths, but it was the honeysuckle that Josephine caught a whiff of in the breeze. What a lovely day!

Finally, she began to feel better, having been sick for the last few weeks. Morning sickness. Mother Montgomery said it was a good sign of a healthy baby. She prayed it was true.

As she sat on the veranda with Mother Montgomery, she watched Percival romp on the lawn, laughing and giggling. It did her heart good.

Andrew had been called to Charleston. He had left early morning and wasn't expected back until the end of the week. It surprised her, then, when she saw him walk up the path from the docks.

Suddenly, an ill wind blew and chilled Jo to the core of her being. Her eyes met Andrew's reddened ones. His forlorn expression spoke more than words. She knew…Oh, God, she knew. Her chest hurt, as if she couldn't breathe. No…no…no. She had to leave…if he didn't say the words, it wouldn't be true. But she couldn't move.

Mother Montgomery grasped hold of Jo's hand. Tears had already begun to fall.

Slowly, he walked up the steps and choked out the words. "I'm sorry. So truly sorry."

Her head shook in denial; she clutched her hands to her chest. His words blurred together. *Brave and courageous… Wade led the charge…he fell at Shiloh…He died a hero…*

Her head spun; her legs crumbled beneath her. She remembered little else until she woke in her bed, crying for her husband who would never return.

* * * *

The USS *Hartford* steamed out of the port of Havana. The *Hartford*, the command ship of the Gulf Blockading Squadron led by Flag Officer David E. Farragut, was a beauty of a war vessel. The almost three-hundred-foot wooden-hulled sloop of war was made for confrontation, having twenty-nine smoothbore guns on her broadside and twenty-two pound Parrott rifles.

Cullen had met up with his ship at the end of January. Shortly after the ship sailed from New York, President Lincoln had issued a General War Order Number One, appointing February 22 the day for a general movement of the Land and Naval forces of the United States against the insurgent forces. The intent was a full assault against the Southerner cause, an aggressive stance with the intent of using the full extent of the force the Union had at their disposal.

Under the new command, Cullen accepted his assignment under Flag Officer Farragut. His commander was a short, stout man with an iron face, notorious for strategizing every conceivable twist. The news that Farragut was to lead the Squadron had been somewhat of a surprise.

Not only was Farragut a Southerner who held to the flag, his reputation preceded him. Not given to the political overture, his decisions seemed based on what better served his country. From what Cullen knew of the man, Farragut hadn't the edge of those ambitious sorts…seeking fame to better themselves.

Rumors abounded on the ship that Farragut's foster brother, Commander David Porter, had requested the position. Some thought him better suited, but Porter had to settle for second-in-command. Cullen listened, but never offered an opinion. Much like Farragut, his focus was upon the mission and he cared little for idle gossip.

Beneath a dapple of clouds that covered the full moon, Cullen stood on deck while on duty. His thoughts ran rampant. Earlier in the day, he had received news of Wade's death two and a half weeks earlier.

Wade had died in the bloodiest battles of this damn war, Shiloh. A Union victory but he was told his cousin died a hero, trying to save a Union drummer boy. His bravery was respected by both sides—a truly courageous and valiant officer.

Never had Cullen felt so alone…his brother had died. As much as he wanted to deny it, it cut through his heart like a knife.

Cullen focused on Josephine—the woman who obsessed his every breath. He looked out over the dark ocean and saw her face. It haunted him…she had pleaded with him to leave her. She who held his happiness in her hands had turned from him and had taken their son…his son!

Vivid memories of his youth assaulted him…growing up in the realm of Charleston and Magnolia Bluff. He loved the land and the people. He had laughed along when he was kidded and called a Yankee. Now, the distinction stabbed him in the heart worse than if it had been a dagger—it cut him off from the world that once was his beloved home.

He wore the Union blue uniform proudly and believed deeply in what it stood for. What right had they to self-proclaim their independence? Had he not a right to his opinion, even if it differed from theirs? Was it not his home? No…they…his own family had ripped his claim of being a part of their home…their heritage…uncaring what they took from him.

Breathing out the cool night's air, anger and frustration grew inside him. His mind clamped upon the wrongs done to him. No, he would have no more of it.

His ire toiled as the ship cut through the rough waves. The love he had clung to for Josephine evaporated with the heat in his heart, replaced with an equally powerful emotion—hatred. Firm resolve filled him...he would right the wrongs and protect his son by whatever means necessary.

The *Hartford* would arrive at Ship Island early in the morning. Cullen's eyes lay solely on their destination. May God have mercy on their souls. For the South was about to face the fury of his anger.

PART FOUR

THE SUN RISES

Magnolia Bluff, Charleston
April, 1862

Dark days lay ahead; that was Josephine's only certainty. The shock of the death of the man she thought invincible had worn off and pain seared through her. A sense of relentless despair overwhelmed her with hopelessness.

The day before last, Major Wade Montgomery was laid to rest. A funeral service had been held for the beloved husband, father, and son. There had been no body to bury. To show respect for the life lost, an empty coffin was lowered into the ground.

Jo had watched dirt fill the grave. The past seemed only a blurred reminder of a way of life that had been so completely and utterly destroyed. She was left with the realities of the hard, rapacious world around her. The harsh reality of the war.

She felt she had fallen into a dark tunnel with no light to guide her. The weariness of the war drained her. She hated the talk of Wade's heroic acts. How brave and courageous he had been!

Had not anyone known that he promised to return?

How could he have risked his life so thoughtlessly!

He promised!

It was unimaginable that she would never see his handsome, smiling face walk into the room again.

She wanted nothing more than to see Wade lying lackadaisically in their bed and laugh at her foolishness. At times, she thought she could hear him and expected to turn around to find him there to comfort her. But there would be no comfort: only the haunting words…*he's dead— dead…*

He wouldn't be coming back.

Wade had died a hero at the Battle of Shiloh. For the longest time, she had not opened the letter from his commanding officer, General P.G.T. Beauregard. Finally, she forced herself to read the correspondence.

> *Mrs. Josephine Montgomery,*
> *It is with the gravest heart that I'm writing to inform you of your husband's passing. Major Wade Montgomery will be sorely missed. He was an officer of valor and courage whose legacy will be long remembered. Admired and respected, Major Montgomery in death showed us all how to live life.*
> *On April 6th, we took the Union by surprise by attacking them not far from the foothills of Mississippi over the border in Tennessee. In what is now been proclaimed as the Battle of Shiloh, your husband led his men into the glorious battle. He bore his position proudly and held it at all hazards.*
> *In the most dangerous of circumstances, Major Montgomery led his men on an assault against enemy lines. In the midst of battle, despite the imminent danger he faced, the major noticed the Union drummer trapped along a creek bank. He saved the lad, but in turn lost his life.*
> *His loss is felt by all. We lost many a good man that day…a day that had us on the edge of glory. Unfortunately, the next day victory was taken cruelly from us, but Major Montgomery did not lose his life in vain. He has inspired many with his bravery.*
> *I received notice of Major Montgomery's last moments from Union Captain Lawrence Bronson. The young drummer boy, Howie Albright, informed Captain Bronson of your husband's brave deed in detail. Know your husband did not die alone. The young lad did not leave his side and saw to it that his sacrifice was reported. Take heart that Major Montgomery's last thoughts were of you and your son. He loved you greatly.*
> *Major Wade Montgomery's courageous feat will not be forgotten.*
> *Respectfully, General P.G.T. Beauregard*

Numerous expressions of sympathy arrived. Each commended Wade's virtues, but none could do what she wanted most—bring Wade back to her. Jo took the letters and added them to the pile of letters that Wade had sent her. A silent tear fell down her cheek as she tied a ribbon around the packet. Kissing the top of the letters, she placed them inside the lap secretary.

Sitting behind her desk, she stared out the window. The sun shone brightly down upon the earth. It all seemed so strange. The whole of her world had collapsed. Yet, life carried on...the birds sang, flowers bloomed...she had no choice but to carry on and live each day.

Her children depended upon her. Percival and the new life that grew inside her had a great need of their mother. Jo pushed aside the overwhelming sorrow that welled inside her. She couldn't allow the ache that gnawed at her heart to consume her. Wade would expect her to be strong.

Wade's death had caused a huge void in her soul. Her protector...her lover...her husband was gone and no amount of mourning, crying, longing for his return would bring him back. Gone were any lingering secret doubts about the war, replaced by a simmering hatred toward all things Yankee.

Grief-driven determination gripped her tightly. She would not fail Wade. She would fight as he had done to maintain his legacy for his children.

Magnolia Bluff would survive.

Chapter One

Battle of New Orleans
April 24, 1862

Boom. Boom. Boom. The Western Blockading Squadron had taken relentless fire from Fort Jackson and Fort St. Philip for five days. Seventy-five miles downriver from New Orleans, the Confederate forts served as the city's major southern defense from a Union attack.

Heavily fortified, the Rebels were determined that the Union squadron would be unable to maneuver up the Mississippi River. The commander of the squadron, Union Flag Officer David G. Farragut, was just as determined to break through their barrier.

Over the last couple of weeks, Lieutenant Cullen Smythe had slept little in preparation for this naval assault. He had overseen escorting the Coast Survey unit along the river's passages. The indomitable task of surveying and marking the Mississippi's outlets had been fraught with danger.

Following direct orders from Farragut, the squad had been under constant fire from the forts and snipers as they charted every aspect of the locale. Surveying took time under the best conditions. Cullen had made certain that the unit performed their jobs safely under cover by marksmen.

Unlike most rivers, the muddy Mississippi didn't dump into the Gulf by one main outlet but five channels. Because of the war, the dredging that had once been tended to had been almost nonexistent. Farragut needed at least sixteen feet of water to pass through safely without fear of grounding a ship.

Farragut had become impatient at the impasse. The Western Squadron's mission was to take New Orleans and control of the lower Mississippi. The fleet waited on Farragut's orders to begin their assault at the highly valued prize.

From the intelligence gathered, the Confederates expected the threat to come from the north and held confident with their position of strength from their two strong deterrents south of the city: Fort St. Philip and Fort Jackson. Fort St. Philip sat slightly north of Fort Jackson and directly across the river.

Using that information and the precise charts that the Coast Survey prepared, Farragut had used every means available to take the forts by surprise. He had tree branches and bushes tied to the mast to camouflage the ships from a distance. Mortar boats began the assault and opened fire, hidden from view from the forts by a dense stand of large trees.

The ships had been equipped with chains suspended from the hull a few feet above the waterline to serve as armor against enemy shells. Sacks of sand had been heaped into the engine room to protect the engines. Yet, despite their surprise attack and constant bombardment of the forts, the Union squadron efforts had done little damage to the heavily fortified outposts. The Southern forts had held for over five days.

On deck, Cullen stood in his position as executive officer in front of the wheel. He watched one of the rowboats used to communicate between ships pull alongside of the *Kennebee*. As of late, there had been many such boats.

The light of the day would soon fade into night and fog would settle over the water. Cullen caught sight of the boatswain in his flare-legged blues, neckerchief, and black straw hat walk toward him. The bearded sailor acknowledged Cullen. "Sir, Commander Bell requests your immediate presence in his cabin. I am to take over your watch."

Despite Cullen's surprise at the request, he relinquished his post and made his way down below deck to the commander's cabin. After one knock, Commander Henry Bell responded and Cullen entered, closing the door behind him.

Cullen stood at attention. "You called for me, sir?"

The clean-shaven commander looked up from his desk and gestured for Cullen to sit. The gray-haired officer was a lifer, having joined the Navy in the early 1820s and had once served on the Board of Examiners at the Naval Academy. Cullen had been unfamiliar with him before becoming part of the Western Blockade Squadron, but the man had a reputation as a damn good seaman.

"Lieutenant Smythe, we don't have time to mince words. I have only just returned from the *Hartford* with new orders. The fleet is preparing to move."

Straight away, Cullen read Bell's expression. Although it came as no surprise, his commander wasn't happy with the news. The ramblings among the crew held truth to them. It had been rumored that Flag Officer Farragut wanted to race by the forts without taking them in an unheard of manner. Commander David Porter had been the one who had promised to take the forts with mortar fire...it hadn't worked.

"The *Kennebee* is in readiness, sir," Cullen stated confidently.

"Assuredly." Bell nodded. "Time is on the side of the Rebels. The longer the delay, the more preparations and help will come to the defense of the forts and New Orleans."

Bell leaned back in his chair and drew in a deep breath. His stern look left Cullen with the impression he carefully contemplated his next words. "Lieutenant Smythe, you have been commended for your performance as of late, but your behavior gives me pause."

"You have me confused, Captain. Have you called me here to be reprimanded?"

"No, Lieutenant, your performance has been exemplary. I wanted to talk to you about your time under me. When you volunteered for the Coast Survey venture, I gladly allowed you to participate. I heard nothing but praise for your actions. You maneuvered the men in and out of quite a few precarious situations.

"But I have been begun to notice that you have been quite aggressive in your actions since word came of your cousin's death. At times, I would venture reckless. I need to know if you have a total disregard for your own life or have always been so brazen."

A tightness in Cullen's throat allowed only a direct answer. "I fight for my country and family, sir. I want only to put down this rebellion."

"Calm yourself, Lieutenant, but I am no fool. I will confess I held a certain hesitation on delivering the news when it came shortly after Shiloh. I realize it was sent as a show of respect to you and your cousin, but I believe it has affected you more than you would care to admit."

"Sir, I would never allow my personal life to interfere with my duty."

"Lieutenant, you forget I myself am a Southerner. I, too, have family fighting for the Confederacy. It pains me. Remember, we are only human. This war has torn many a family apart."

"Sir, I only want this blasted war to be over and I will do whatever is necessary to ensure that fact."

Commander Bell nodded. "Then we understand each other, Lieutenant. Nothing should come before the mission you have been assigned. It holds too much importance."

"Mission?"

"Flag Officer Farragut has directed three of our best gunboats to open up the barrier to allow passage for the rest of the fleet: the *Itasca,* the *Pinola* and the *Onieda*. Farragut believes we will be able to make it past the forts without damage from the barrage of fire that will erupt at the forts. We, Lieutenant, are going to open up the way for our ships. Our objective is the obstacle that stands between us and the water passage up to New Orleans—the barrier."

Cullen remained silent, knowing well the barrier they faced. It outstretched across the river, made up mostly of old schooners chained together at their bows with anchors.

"Farragut has plans for taking two of our gunboats to supply cover for the *Pinola,* which will carry the explosives to blast our way through the barrier," Commander Bell continued. "It will be impossible to take out the entire barrier, but the objective is to open it large enough for all our ships to pass safely through.

"You may not be aware that Lieutenant-Commander Bemis of the *Itasca* has fallen ill. He will be unable to participate in the upcoming mission. A replacement needs to be found. Farragut wants a daring, courageous officer to command the *Itasca*. I assured him you were that man. Farragut agreed. Lieutenant Smythe, you have been transferred to the *Itasca* temporarily to captain the ship."

Astonished, he refrained from revealing the exhilaration that surged through him, sensing Commander Bell held reservations. He said simply, "Thank you, sir."

Bell's brows drew together in a frown. "Do not take this mission lightly, Smythe. There were objections to your appointment, mainly from Commander Porter. He cited your inexperience in command under fire and what he called your lack of *forethought*."

"Sir, I believe I am fully capable…"

"I did not say I had misgivings. In truth, I believe you are quite competent and brave. There were those who felt strongly that you were the right man for the job. High recommendations came from Reids and Kroehl. Kroehl is the explosive expert, so Farragut weighed heavily upon his approval, especially since you have already been working with him on the Coast Survey unit."

"But you do have your own reservations."

423

"Lieutenant, I have stated my concerns. I will say that it was mentioned that perhaps your position here in the Western Squadron was a political appointment. I say this only so you are aware. I believe one needs to know what they are up against."

The speculation did not shock Cullen. He had heard it before and would have been foolish not to recognize that some would consider his advancement due to his father's connections and not his own actions. It only fueled his resolve to prove them all wrong.

"When should I prepare?"

Commander Bell's answer came readily and direct. "Tonight."

* * * *

Shrouded in the cover of the night, preparations had been finalized. The constant firings had ceased on orders from Farragut and the ships had fallen back out of range of the forts, but the still and quiet did little to ease the tension-filled air.

A stiff wind brought a driving rain, which only served to further camouflage the operation. Readied, Cullen had his orders—provide the necessary cover for the *Pinola* to set the explosives and afterwards secure the open passage.

Cullen had once served under Commander Lane Graham of the *Pinola*, having been assigned to his ship shortly after the academy. Graham was an arrogant, egotistic man, who made commander at an early age, not much older than Cullen. He would do whatever necessary to ensure victory.

After meeting him again while serving under the Western Squadron, the years had done little to diminish the friction between the two officers, but the mission came before any irrelevant rivalry. The war gave little time for petty grievances. Moreover, with the greatest reluctance, Cullen had to agree that Graham was an excellent choice for this mission.

It was time. Flag Officer Farragut had come to see the mortar boats off on their quest. He sought out Cullen. "Lieutenant Smythe, we need this to be successful. Abide the result—conquer or be conquered."

"Rest assured, sir," Cullen affirmed. "The mission will be carried out."

The gunboats readied, Cullen took his place on board the *Itasca*. If the crew held any qualms of his newly acquired position, none were acknowledged. Each sailor understood the importance of their task and the need to have a commander who would show no hesitation if the need arose.

Stealthily, the *Itasca* rowed through the water under cover of darkness and rain. There would be no engines until the mission was complete. The longer the Confederates were unaware of their actions, the better chance for success.

Cullen stood before the wheel and monitored any activity from either fort. All was quiet as he watched the *Pinola* secured to one of the wrecked schooners attached to the barrier.

"Close the gap," Cullen ordered. "We may not have explosives, but we can work on the chains!"

The *Itasca* silently pulled alongside of the next stranded schooner. The crew began to use hammers and chisels to break the chains that held the barrier in place.

A sudden flame lit up the dark rain. A second flash roared and exploded. Fort Jackson had awakened. The Rebs had spotted the gunboats and began a heavy fire bursting forth across the water.

"Heads up, men!" Cullen cried against the wind. "Hold steady!"

Almost immediately, Fort St. Philip entered the barrage and the pace of bombardment stepped up. Cullen held back the command to withdraw, waiting until the last notch in the chain to that schooner was broken.

"Sir, the *Pinola*! The signal." The helmsman pointed toward the gunboat.

As he peered out over the water toward the *Pinola,* Cullen caught sight of the signal. The explosives had been set…but in the same moment, he saw the *Pinola* fall back.

Cullen looked back at the boatswain. "Fire up the engines, Mr. Collins. Prepare to be on our way."

"Aye, sir, but the men aren't finished with the chain."

A bright glow flickered in the rain-filled sky, followed closely by another one. The crew was working furiously, but they didn't have much time. The explosives would be lit in moments. Cullen had only seconds to make a decision.

Rampant thoughts ran swiftly through his mind. The chain wasn't broken, but it would be weakened enough to break after the explosion…the *Pinola* needed cover.

"Fall back," Cullen commanded. "We need to shield the *Pinola*."

No sooner than the order was given than Cullen watched the *Pinola* flounder and be pulled back into the flow of the river. Despite fighting futilely against a surge of wind, the *Pinola* was being swept away by the current.

Still flying under the sail, the *Pinola*'s engines hadn't fired up…neither had the explosives gone off. A shell exploded off their broadside. Cullen had no more time to waste. "Stand ready! We are going alongside. Mr. Collins, when we get close enough, toss the *Pinola* a line."

The thudding engines came up to speed. Guided in reverse, the stern shook. Through the midst of rain and smoke, the *Itasca* cut through the rough water toward the *Pinola.*

"Lieutenant!" the helmsman called from the starboard. "The *Pinola* is rowing back to the squad."

Cullen stared in disbelief. The barrier hadn't been broken...*Damn it*! Cullen cursed under his breath with the realization there had to be a problem with the explosives. They weren't going to be going off! Then it hit him...Graham was scrambling back to Farragut to make him the scapegoat in this fiasco!

Blood rushed to his face; his fist clenched. Farragut's words echoed within him—*Conquer or be conquered!* Conviction and determination surged through his veins. He wasn't returning without completing his mission. He had one option left.

In that moment, he cast his eyes upon his men. Their eyes, too, fixed upon him. Their mission had been compromised...on the verge of failure. Fort Jackson hadn't stopped its bombardment; the torrential rainstorm hadn't lessened...they had no explosives.

"Turn about!" Cullen commanded. "Turn about!"

"Sir," the helmsman cried over the wind. "The barrier? We'll hit the chains and be ripped apart!"

"Men, prepare! We are going to break that damn barrier! Ram where we weakened the chain... We will hit it head on!"

Nary a man said another word, but worked in earnest to turn the craft back toward the barrier. Their mission set before them, the brave men bore down and readied for the assault and the wind.

There was no going back once the decision was made. Committed, the gunboat gathered speed, aided by the wind. Smoke burst from the stack and dropped down, encompassing the ship in a haze. The rhythm of the engines steadily increased.

"Full speed ahead!" Cullen directed from the helm. "Hold steady!"

With momentum, the *Itasca* struck the chain. Immediately, the bow propelled out of the water. The engines grinded with a god-awful noise. Cullen was knocked down against the starboard bulwark. Managing to crawl to his knees, he heard the water rush against the hull and the bulwark trembled beneath him.

Spars and rigging clanged; a jolting crunch shook the ship. The chain caught on her keel, pushing the ship almost entirely out of the water. The *Itasca* hung in the air! The next moment, the gunboat crashed back down onto the surface, skimming the water twice before it came to a sudden halt.

Intact! The *Itasca* was completely intact! Cullen hurried back on his feet, desperately surveying the ship.

"Check the men, Mr. Collins!" he commanded, maintaining the elation that swelled within him.

In the pouring rain, shouts erupted from their companion ship, the *Pinola,* which had seen the whole of maneuver—the barrier was broken. The fleet could make it through.

* * * *

With Lieutenant-Commander Bemis unable to sufficiently recover from his bout with pneumonia, Farragut rewarded Cullen for his daring act and promoted him to captain of the *Itasca.* The crew supported Farragut's decision. Cullen's reputation had garnered him a position where men wanted to follow him into battle—a leader, brave and true…one who had courageously took a seemingly impossible risk and came out victorious.

Farragut offered Cullen one bit of advice. "Put your mission before all else."

The advice was well accepted. Cullen had a great admiration for Farragut, a man who stood by his convictions despite the possible repercussions. It was widely known that Farragut's stepbrother, Porter, coveted Farragut's position. Cullen held no doubt that Porter would see that Farragut was replaced if he failed to capture New Orleans.

In Cullen's mind, failure was not an option. As he stood on deck, he pulled out his pocket watch. Two o'clock. It was time. The tactical maneuver would begin.

In the darkness, the engines churned and smoke billowed from the stacks, clouding the river as the ships began their voyage through the narrow passage…one at a time. Within minutes, a vociferous roar erupted.

Fort Jackson and Fort St. Philip had been on high alert and wasted no time bombarding the advancing fleet. Guns flashed from the forts; rockets burst in the air. A geyser of a missed shot sprayed the *Itasca,* drenching Cullen on the helm.

Holding course, the *Itasca* made it through, as had the ships before it. The Confederate fire had essentially been ineffective.

"Captain, broadside!"

At the helmsman's cry, Cullen's gaze broke from the USS *Pensacola,* which had only just cleared the barrier. Over his shoulder, he watched the dreaded *hellish machine* materialized out of the smoky haze.

Momentarily, he could only stare. Never in his life had he seen such an intimidating contraption. Ironclad, the CSS *Manassas* had one smokestack in the middle of its rounded curving hull, looking like a floating cigar. Sitting low in the water did little to conceal its deadly weapon—a pointed iron ram. Its one intent was to stab holes in armor-plated ships

The *Manassas* paid no mind to Cullen's gunboat. Its intent lay with the larger Union fleet ships. Cullen had enough worries with the remainder of the Confederate fleet.

"Nine…ten at the most, sir," Mr. Collins reported as he walked to Cullen's side. "Your orders?"

"Fire!"

The order rang clear for all to hear. In turn, a continuous thunderclap began. His crew worked vigorously. The shell men rammed home the powder cartridges for the guns to fire; the tackle men swung their guns around to face their targets.

A cry rang out. "They're trying to board us!"

The efforts of the Confederates were for naught. Only three rebels made it to the deck and were instantly repelled, falling overboard into the dark, murky water.

Cullen's attention turned once more to the river. The Confederates began reckless efforts to bring down the Union fleet. The *Pensacola* had turned in time to avoid the *Manassas* and did an about-face and fired broadside at close range, hitting its mark.

Looming in the fog of smoke, Cullen saw a fiery raft loaded with wood and tar headed toward the USS *Mississippi,* intent on catching the wooden steamer on fire.

"Turn portside!" Cullen shouted back to Mr. Collins. "Aim and wait for my signal to fire!"

His boatswain stared at Cullen, confused until he saw the intent behind the action.

The raft was escorted by two gunboats. Cullen intended to take out the second one, which would force the raft off course.

"Hold steady…steady…" Then, at the precise moment, Cullen yelled, "Fire, men! Fire!"

Cullen looked across the water. Through the haze, his gun crew worked furiously. Recoiling from the *Itasca's* aggressive attack, a flame burst out along the Confederate gunboat. Wounded, the boat lost its course and floundered into the burning raft, which drifted to the riverbank and burnt out without incident.

428

The morning light brought a halt to the dash through the break in the barrier. The Union fleet had sustained little significant damage. Only three ships did not make it through; one gunboat, the *Varuna,* had fallen victim to Confederate fire. The two others, *Kennebac* and *Winona,* had got caught up in the lines and hadn't the time to make it through before the light of day.

Conversely, the Confederate navy had suffered greatly. After CSS *Manassas* had taken a hit from the *Pensacola,* it rammed the *Brooklyn,* but not fatally. Next, the CSS *Manassas* had followed behind the fleet until the *Mississippi* had had enough. The Union steam frigate turned on the *Manassas* and fired, hitting her broadside.

The *Manassas* ran aground. The crew of the Southern sea-bearing vessel evacuated right before the *Mississippi* turned its full force of the wounded ship. On fire, the *Manassas* slipped back into the water and floated helplessly down the river.

With no viable information of the defensive between the Fleet and New Orleans, Farragut moved ahead without the ground commander, General Butler, or Commander Porter. Both had stayed to secure Fort St. Philip and Fort Jackson.

But they were not needed. The Union fleet encountered little more Confederate opposition. Only once were they submitted to random Confederate sharpshooters, who found it more prudent to fall back after the USS *Hartford* fired two batteries of fire in their direction. The skirmish took no more than twenty minutes. It was the last of the resistance between Farragut and New Orleans.

Gathered intelligence from within New Orleans had told of a smug city confident in their strength to repel the Union forces. The *New Orleans Tribune* had boasted—

Our only fear is that the Northern invaders might not appear. We have made such extensive preparations to receive them, that it would be vexatious if their invincible armada escapes the fate we have in store for them.

The prediction had not been fulfilled. New Orleans had fallen.

Entering the harbor, Cullen was greeted by the sight of a city ablaze. Everything of value had been torched: ships, steamers, cotton, and coal. As the Union fleet rounded Slaughter Point, New Orleans for all intent and purposes was under Union control. The Rebels had withdrawn, leaving only an angry, desolate city.

Chapter Two

A glorious Southern sun shone down at its very hottest. Jo lay upon the settee that had been brought out on the piazza and took in the view on this fine June day. The garden was alive with a multitude of assorted flowers and scents. The arbor was densely covered by climbing ivy. Roses abounded in vibrant colors; fragrant gardenias encompassed the air with full blooming magnolias bordering the landscape.

Jo watched butterflies flit from one bloom to another in sweet serenity. In the midst of the picture, Anna sat on the ground with Percival in her lap. The toddler seemed captivated watching a small rabbit, scampering amid the rose bushes. So beautiful and peaceful, the vision looked like the hand of God had descended and painted upon a living canvas.

Across from Jo, Mother Montgomery sat quietly and darned Anna's dress. The days of extravagance were behind them. The Yankee blockade had tightened around Charleston. Luxury items had become hard to come by. Proclaiming that the day would come when they would need to make their own clothes, Mother Montgomery had brought the old loom down from the attic.

The dear woman looked up at Jo with her soft, kind eyes. "Do you care for some more tea?"

"I'm fine, Mother Montgomery." Jo sighed, setting the newspaper she held in her hand down on the table. "I swear, despite the headlines proclaiming our presumed success, my *Mercury* holds nothing but bad news."

"I quite agree. Jenna told me she read that *Beast* Butler's behavior in New Orleans is worse than those heathen Indians out West."

"How dreadful and quite unpardonable. To treat women so. Arresting them for laughing!"

"Darling, do you think it's wise to upset yourself over matters that you have no control?" Mother Montgomery looked over at Jo with a concerned expression. "Maybe it would be for the best if you didn't read any papers for a while."

"How else am I to know what is going on? The whole of our Mississippi fleet has been annihilated. It is disastrous…we live upon a river. What if their attention turns to Charleston?"

"Oh, dear! When have you become so faint of heart? My woman's instinct tells me we are safe here, but if you would feel better, we can move back into Charleston."

"No," Jo declared. "We need to be here."

Jo's hand went instinctively to her growing stomach. She understood Mother Montgomery's worry. War had seeped into their world and the blinding truth was undeniable. Everything that had existed in the past seemed so completely and utterly destroyed…buried with Wade.

The past was a distant memory. She had to face the realities of the cruel world she now lived. The proclamations that the war would end with the next victory had become quiet whispers, but no one dare speak against the deadly venture for fear of being called traitorous. Jo's fears went unspoken—that all the brave, courageous men suffered for a barren endeavor.

"Well, I stopped reading the paper after Mrs. King and Mrs. Langston were openly attacked in the paper for riding up and down the streets with their livery footmen while poor soldiers' wives sat on the sidewalks," Mother Montgomery abruptly announced. "I was aghast at the nastiness of the article. What more can they expect of us? Have we not footed the bill for this war? Mrs. Langston said that we get so little enjoyment, what harm is there in a brisk ride?"

"Some have said that the war is a rich man's venture and a poor man's fight, Mother."

Jo cast a glance over her shoulder at the voice. Andrew walked around the corner of the porch, followed closely by a somber Jenna. Frowning, his squared jaw tightened in obvious agitation.

Holding a handkerchief in her hand, Jenna patted her reddened eyes. Then she rushed around her brother and flung herself down at her mother's feet.

There was no need to know what the two siblings were fighting about. Jo knew readily enough—Derek. Last week, Jenna had received news he had been wounded in a skirmish and was recovering in a Richmond hospital. Jenna had been harping at her brother to let her go to her fiancé. Andrew had steadfastly refused.

"Oh, dearest Mother," Jenna cried with tears in her beautiful eyes. "Andrew is being unreasonable. It is not fair."

"What is it now, my dear?" Mother Montgomery gently stroked her daughter's head lying on her knees.

"Maisy told me that her mother traveled to Richmond and cared for her brother. It is not unheard of in these times. Mrs. Reese is still in the city. If I go now, I could stay in the same boarding house. Derek needs me! I will die if something happens to him!"

"Do not be so dramatic, Jenna." Andrew scowled darkly. "Since I am committed in my duties at the Charleston hospital, I have no time to travel and you truly cannot believe I will allow you to travel by yourself...a single young woman!"

"It is not unheard of these days! Maisy says that lots of women go nurse their injured loved ones. There are so many of our boys hurt and wounded...I could help the cause..."

"I spend most of my days at the Charleston hospital. If you want to help, you can do so there. I will send a telegram and see what I can do for Derek."

"I don't care what you say! I am going," Jenna railed. "Derek has no one else...not with both his parents dying of typhoid and his brother fighting Heaven knows where."

"Jenna, perhaps Andrew is right," Jo interceded. "I understand you are upset, but it is not reasonable..."

"Reasonable! I'm sick to death of being sensible. I have always been the obedient daughter, but if it was you, Jo...you would not be questioned! Not you! We have to keep Jo happy!"

Shocked by the venom in Jenna's voice, Jo's expression dropped. "Jenna, how could you say such a thing?"

"How can I not? If it had been Wade, no one would hesitate to go. Why is Derek different? He is as much family as you and has not put the family through what you have!" Jenna shouted, lifting her red, swollen face from her mother's knee. "Tell me that you would not! Do not pretend that you have no knowledge of what I say. Not after everything that has happened because of you!"

"Jenna, that is quite enough!" Mother Montgomery gasped. "Don't take out your unhappiness on Jo. We all have suffered these last few months."

Rising to her feet, Jenna would not be calmed. She lashed out. "Yes…yes, we have suffered, but none like Josephine. We have to suffer in silence. I will be silent no more."

"Lord Almighty, Jenna, hush!" Andrew said, sharp and direct.

An awkward moment of silence followed. Jo's eyebrows rose as she stared at her sister-in-law in disbelief. She understood that Jenna was distraught, but it was a mortifying thing to hear such animosity in her voice directed at her.

The siblings faced each other; their eyes locked. Then, slowly, the tense lines on Andrew's face eased. "Your anger should be at me, sister. Not Josephine."

Despite Andrew's words to redirect Jenna's emotions, Jo was on the verge of hysteria herself. Battle after battle, disaster after disaster had well-worn on her nerves, but, now, she had come to the realization that the family resented her presence.

She wrung her hands and glanced back and forth between the three of them. For a brief moment, comprehension swept through her. Why would they not? Had her papa not forced her union with Wade and threatened to take away their way of life if they had not complied with his proposal?

With Wade's death, Magnolia Bluff had fallen to her and her children. Reprimanding herself greatly, she had wrapped herself in a cocoon of grief, thinking only of herself…her children. Good Lord, did they not know they were her family…her only family? She choked back her own welling tears.

Taking a step back, Andrew rubbed his forehead as if his head hurt. His frown was deep and fierce. "I have tried to keep from you women our predicament, but it was foolish." His attention turned to his sister. "You have misdirected your anger. It is not just because it is not fitting for you to travel, but it is because we have to be frugal with our money."

"Are we paupers?" Jenna brushed away tears.

"No, of course not, but the war has caused us a hardship. We are in better shape than most plantations in the area, but Confederate money has dropped its worth and prices have risen dramatically. We have not been able to get our crops to market."

The news was not shocking to Jo. Already, changes had occurred on the plantation. White flour had become scarce and cornbread had replaced biscuits and rolls at meals, but Magnolia Bluff had been fortunate that food was on the table for every meal, most of it being harvested from their own fields. It was not only the family who had to be fed and clothed, but the slaves as well, stretching their limited resources.

Once what had been a profitable crop, cotton had dropped to five cents a pound. Rice had suffered a similar fate, commanding no price outside of South Carolina. The blockade kept the money crops to rot in the fields or cotton to be stored to be sold after the war.

"Surely, it is not as bad as all that, Andrew." Mother Montgomery fanned herself profusely. "You are scaring us."

"I do not mean to scare you, Mother," Andrew continued. "But you must face certain truths. Wade committed a great deal of money to two of Hampton's regiments besides what we committed to the government. It would be foolish to expect the government bonds to be paid back in the immediate future. We need only to be prudent."

Jenna regained a small bit of composure. Silent tears fell from her eyes. "Dear brother, my heart can't accept I can do nothing. I fear for Derek."

His head shook in a slow manner. Andrew said in a subdued voice, "I wish there was more that I could do."

Clutching her hand to her heart, Jenna visibly flinched and seemed to lose her balance. Andrew gripped her arm and helped her sit.

"I have to go to him." Jenna sobbed.

"Quite impossible," Andrew said firmly.

As she looked into Jenna's face, Jo saw herself. If it had been Wade, nothing...nothing would have kept her from him...if only Wade had been injured. What if Derek didn't survive his injuries? What would she have done to see Wade one more time!

From the corner of her eye, she saw Percival run up the steps to see what all the commotion was about, followed by a worried Anna. Poor Mother Montgomery could do little to comfort Jenna.

"I think she should go." Jo spoke in a soft voice, but all eyes turned on her, shocked and in disbelief. Jo reaffirmed her statement. "I think Jenna should go to Richmond."

****

The trunk was packed and locked; the tickets bought. Jenna was prepared to go north, accompanied by Rosa. The journey would be arduous; the railroads were in bad shape. Jo watched the carriage loaded up with Percival at her side. His pout proved the little one wasn't happy at being left behind.

Already seated, Andrew waited to take his sister to the train. The arrangements had been made. Telegrams sent. Mrs. Reese was to meet Jenna at the train station and Jenna was to stay at the same boarding house.

Good-byes said, Jenna gripped the carriage door and then hesitated. She ran back to Jo and hugged her tightly. "Thank you...thank you."

"Go and bring him home," Jo encouraged.

Standing with Mother Montgomery, Jo watched until the carriage was out of sight. A moment later, she felt her mother-in-law's hand grip hers.

"She will be fine. Have faith."

"I know she needed to go. It is hard, though..." Mother Montgomery's voice faltered.

A moment of silence ensued. Jo prayed that Jenna's journey would be safe. She would not be able to live with herself if something happened to Jenna now that she was the reason Jenna was allowed to journey to Richmond.

Jenna's bitter attack had stunned Jo, but the harsh words had woken Jo from the slumbered daze that Wade's death had caused. For so long, she had had Wade...before him, her papa...to protect her from the rapacious world about her. She had no one now...only herself.

She had wanted to cry out. *Have you forgotten that it was my inheritance that saved Magnolia Bluff?* Instead, she finally accepted the truth she had long denied—Wade was gone forever. It was now her responsibility to keep the family together.

Despite knowing that Jenna lashed out her hurt upon Jo, it was humiliating nonetheless to hear the words spoken about one's self. Pushing back her wounded pride, she did the only thing she knew to do to draw the family back together.

The gold coins Wade had left her in case she had need of them were hidden in her room. She reprimanded herself that she had not done so before. She took them all and gave them to Andrew for the family's use, alleviating the financial burden of Jenna's venture.

The final epiphany dawned upon Jo. The war was not only on the battlefield, but on the home front. Jo prepared herself for battle to maintain Magnolia Bluff and the family.

* * * *

Surprisingly, the summer at Magnolia Bluff passed peacefully. The war seemed a distant rumble. Somehow...someway life found a way to continue and sometimes joy filtered into the void within Josephine.

Jenna returned with Derek and the family rejoiced. For two and a half months, Jenna nursed the gravely ill man. Shortly after she arrived in Richmond, the two married at his bedside, not knowing whether he would survive or not. He had.

435

Derek had been shot twice: once in the back left shoulder—shattering his left arm—and once in the leg. He lost his arm. Moreover, he developed a life-threatening fever. Jenna never left his side during his long recovery and was thankful he improved enough to return back to Charleston.

The family celebrated, but Jo found Derek a different man than the one who had left so enthusiastic for the war. His appearance had changed. He had lost weight and his face was gaunt from his illness. Like so many other soldiers, he had grown a long, thick beard, but it was more than his physical features. Derek's once outgoing personality had become reclusive, dark and brooding.

Derek tried to be cordial and smiled to the point his face was fixed with a hardened expression of embarrassment and exasperation. A proud man, he had no desire to be coddled by the women on the plantation.

Only recently had Derek begun to leave his room and interact with the family. He had not added much to the conversation at dinner, but everyone was pleased with his company. His efforts gave Jenna hope he was healing.

As she neared the end of her confinement, Jo relaxed most evenings in the cool, languid breeze on the piazza. The sound of tree frogs and chirping crickets was laden with peaceful serenity. From her view, she watched her young son toddle behind his grandmother.

By the massive live Virginia oak, Mother Montgomery glanced over her shoulder and then nodded to her maid, Louise. Louise sat down a bundle package and to the delight of Percival, began digging a hole with a shovel.

"What is Mother Montgomery doing?"

Breaking her gaze, Jo turned to find a solitary figure in the open parlor doors, watching the scene. The next moment, Derek eased into a chair across from her.

"Our neighbor, Cora, told Mother Montgomery that she had buried her silver in case the dreaded Yankees invade."

A strange expression crossed his face. "But she is doing it in full view of everyone on the plantation."

A small laugh escaped Jo. "We haven't the heart to tell her that if the Yankees ever made it to the plantation, there would be little doubt that one of the slaves...or Percival...would show them exactly where she had hidden them." She looked back at the sight. "We have Amos dig it back up after Mother Montgomery comes in the house. We have used one excuse after another why the bundle appears back on the dining room table in the morning…there are only so many times you can tell her that the dogs dug it up."

"She doesn't question it?"

"I believe it is more of a distraction for her. We all have a need to find something to take our minds off the conflict."

"For me, it seems the war is so far away from here," he said in a distant voice. "It is my hope that it never rears its ugly face around these parts."

"It is impossible not to feel the effect of the fighting." Jo swallowed back her obvious pain of losing her husband and refused to let melancholy overwhelm her. "Our spirit will endure, for our cause is just."

"Do you not fear that it will get worse…much worse before it gets better?"

Jo turned back to her brother-in-law. There was no mistaking a distinct bitterness in his voice. "I wake each morning and face the day because it was Wade's wish and to ensure his sacrifice was not in vain. His children, family, and Magnolia Bluff are my focus. I have control of little else."

"You must realize that the war isn't going well for the Confederacy," he pressed. "In Richmond, the residents are frustrated and anxious, especially now with Lincoln's proclamation he intends to free the slaves."

Taken back by his frankness, she met him with her own. "I am not a fool, Derek. At last count, seventeen of our slaves have run off to Beaufort. Grace Ann wrote me that it is worse at Whitney Hall. Three hundred of their negroes have gone over to the Yankees."

"That does not concern you?"

"Andrew and I have made no effort to stop any who want to leave," Jo acknowledged. "If we tried to contain their leaving, it would only facilitate an undercurrent of resentment that we don't need."

Derek scratched his nose and twisted the end of his beard in an anxious manner. "Sometimes it feels hopeless…all of this. My sweet Jenna believes everything will work out…that everything will go back to the way it was." His voice echoed his despondent thoughts. "It is I who have been a fool. To come back here…marry Jenna. I am a burden. It would have been better if I hadn't survived."

"Dear God in Heaven!" Jo cried. Gripping her swollen stomach, her heart went leaden upon the utterance. "How dare you even think such a thing!"

Stunned by her reaction, he rose and waved his hand down toward her in a vain effort to calm the distracted woman. "Miss Jo, I didn't mean to upset you. It was only…"

Gasping for air, she breathed out with an anger she had no knowledge she held within her. "Do you not believe that I would not change places with Jenna quicker than a heart could beat? I …I have dreamed that it had been a lie…that Wade did not die…but then I wake and realize it is only a foolish dream and have to face life without him."

Shaking his head slightly, he pressed his lips together tightly. "Pardon me, Miss Jo. I am sorry for your loss, but I am a cripple. Plain and true. I will only add to your misery."

"You, sir, are part of this family." Indignation swept through her and she pulled herself to her feet. "I'm frightened to death, but look around you! Too many people depend on me…and you also. We need you…Jenna needs you!"

Derek bit his lip and his jaw hardened. With a blank expression, he said nothing, but walked backed into the house. Jenna appeared at the door and wrapped her arm about him. Glancing back, she gave Jo a questioning look.

Disheartened, Jo sat back down. *Oh, I have gone and irritated Jenna once more!* The poor man had not asked for the brunt of her veiled frustrations, but he had weighed on her already frayed nerves. How could he think he wasn't needed?

Jo looked back at Percival, who sat in the middle of the fresh turned dirt and played without a care in the world. She watched his face glow with his evident delight and with the realization these moments were too short-lived.

* * * *

The Earth turned. Another season had once more begun to transform the landscape of Magnolia Bluff. The September sunrays of the late afternoon filtered into the room, but Josephine was unaware of anything but this moment.

She basked in the joy of the sounds of the healthy baby girl she delivered earlier in the day. Her newborn's cry resonated through her like a song from Heaven. Her prayers had been answered and Wade's dream a reality.

She had picked out a name long ago for her daughter, Madeline Marie. She had thought Wade would have been pleased to have his daughter named after his mother. Never had Jo seen a more beautiful baby. Fairer than Percival had been, she was perfect, with ten little fingers and ten little toes and quite a strong set of lungs.

Cradling Madeline in her arm, Jo wiped away happy tears that escaped down her cheek as the baby suckled upon her breast. The ever resourceful Percival climbed up in bed and snuggled against his mother. The warmth that contentment brings suffused through Jo; she had her children.

Chapter Three

To the chagrin of the war-torn South, Lincoln held to his stance on slavery and kept his promise. On January 1, 1863, he signed the Emancipation Proclamation. According to the federal government of the United States, slaves within the rebellion states were freed. The South was outraged, but Jo heard that celebrations were reported in Beaufort.

Once the Charleston newspapers boasted the just and mighty Confederacy would vanquish their oppressors quickly and decisively; now questions in the Southern leadership began to be asked. While never questioning that the soldiers in gray had done their duty and honored their new nation, headline after headline boldly declared that the statesmen had forgotten the interest of the people they represented.

Nowadays, Jo gave little thought to politics. The plantation claimed all her attention that wasn't directed for her babies.

Life had a way of carrying on even with the war raging in the background. Magnolia Bluff entertained visitors and the family visited Charleston. Despite the drain on their resources, Jo resisted the urge to curtail the friends and neighbors from calling. Mother Montgomery took such pleasure with her friends and there had been so little that made her smile.

Magnolia Bluff seemed to suffer less than their neighbors. Jo credited Andrew. He had done such a good job of running the plantation in the midst of the most turbulent of times.

Relieving one burden on the family, Derek slowly began to take an interest in the demands upon the plantation. At times, he was still aloof and distant, but the dark moods had become less frequent. Quite determined, he had trained himself to use his one arm to do most tasks any two-armed man could do.

Jo found her days busy. She rose before sunrise and did not stop until well after she put the children to bed. Exhaustion would set in by late evening. The moment she laid her head on the pillow, she slept soundly—at least, until Madeline would wake for a feeding.

This night had been no different, except before she could ready for bed, Rosa informed her Andrew requested her presence in the study. Jo found him at his desk with his head braced between his hands. His eyes rolled up slowly on her entrance. His somber look caused her to slip quietly into a chair across from him.

"Josephine, word has come in from Whitney Hall. There has been a slave revolt."

Immediately, her blood ran cold. *Grace Ann!*

Andrew reached down and took hold of the telegram on top of the desk. He handed it to Jo. "There is not much information. Your cousin, Grace Ann, has been injured, but was fortunate to have survived."

Overwhelming relief flooded Jo that her cousin was safe, but as she read the telegram she was also stunned. Her hand shook while her eyes skimmed over the correspondence. *The house had been burnt to the ground. Louis, Peggy, Sarah, and two of Sarah's children had been killed.*

Andrew rose and stoked the fire in silence. Sitting the poker back against the hearth, he turned. "We should know more in the morning. I will make inquiries."

"I need to go to Grace Ann."

"We need to get more information before making a move," Andrew said firmly. "I cannot in good conscience allow you to go into danger, but we will do all we can to help your cousin."

Quietly, she excused herself and made her way back to her room. There was nothing more to be said, not until the revolt was put down.

* * * *

Death was in the air. The well-remembered mansion was in ruins, burnt to the ground. In the late morning, the sun's rays gleamed eerily down on the ruins, giving light to an unearthly quiet. Every building on the grounds, the stables, the cookhouse: everything was gone. Nothing of the magnificent plantation remained; only two bricked chimneys stood over the ashes as a memorial of what had been.

Jo walked along the edge of what had been the main house, horrified at the sight. The souls who died that heartbreaking night loomed before her. As she drew in a deep breath, she gathered up her courage to do what she must.

Despite Andrew declaring she had lost all common sense, Jo had traveled with him to Camden. She adamantly refused to be left behind when she discovered the revolt had been contained to the Whitney plantation and had been swiftly put down.

She had reasoned she would be in little peril, but along the journey, she, too, wondered whether she had ventured on a fool's errand. So much had changed since her last visit. Moreover, she had brought little Madeline with her. She had refused a wet-nurse for Madeline when she was born, so Jo had little choice.

Perhaps she had been irrational in her thinking, but she had an immediate need to see her cousin. In so doing, ignored the fact that the world around her had been spun on its axis. Despite the desperate desire to cling to a semblance of what had been, Jo could not deny what had been in the past as clear as black and white had become hazy and distorted.

The revolt at Whitney Hall had sent shock waves throughout the community. The countryside was besieged under a dread of the unknown. Fear encompassed the town, regardless of being in no immediate danger. Ramblings reverberated throughout the streets. *Damn Yankees, instigating slaves to kill whites! Heathens! We aren't safe laying our heads on our pillows at night.*

The people of Camden's fears were unfounded. The uprising had been contained at Whitney Hall to a group of unruly bucks. Furthermore, the slave patrol had been vigilant. Less than a day after the massacre, all of the rebellious blacks who had been credited with the attack had been captured and hung.

On her arrival, Jo settled Madeline at the Camden Inn with Rosa and then immediately sought out her cousin. A cry erupted from her throat when she first saw Grace Ann. She hadn't been prepared for the sight. The poor dear was battered and bruised; her shoulder sagged. Her face was scratched; one eye swollen, black and blue.

Grace Ann burst into tears and incoherent mumblings. Jo took Grace Ann in her arms and rocked her cousin, but she couldn't be calmed.

"I hear screams," Grace Ann bemoaned. As if reliving the moment, her hands covered her ears. "Make them stop! Make them stop!"

"Darling, it's over. Over," Jo whispered. Tears burned Jo's eyes, knowing she hadn't the power to stop the noise for Grace Ann. "Perhaps it would be best not to talk of it. I'm here. Let me take care of you."

"No...no," Grace Ann pleaded as she gripped frantically at Jo's arm. "I need to tell someone. I can't talk with Mr. Whitney.... He's worried about me and the children...he's lost so much...Oh, Jo!"

Jo wanted to say it was best to forget, but Grace Ann was inconsolable and calmed only after she had cried herself to sleep.

Throughout the night, Grace Ann would wake. Sometimes, Grace Ann would have to be reminded where she was; other times, she talked. Jo listened and her heart ached.

With the morning sun, Jo had traveled out to Whitney Hall to where she stood now—to salvage anything that survived the fire. Sadly, Jo looked over the pile of burnt rubble. There was nothing.

Charred remnants crackled under her foot. In her mind, she conjured up the house that had stood proudly only a short time ago. With each step, she heard Grace Ann's haunting voice recite the tale...

It was as most nights since Louis returned from the army. We were in the parlor, waiting for Mr. Whitney's presence so we could continue in for dinner. Louis was upon his four or fifth glass of wine, expounding on the failings of Davis and then the wine ran dry.

The house black stepped forward with another bottle. Cursing under his breath, Louis grabbed it. Immediately, the houseboy retreated as Louis threw the empty container at him. He missed and it shattered against the brick hearth.

"Louis!"

I turned to see Mr. Whitney in the doorway. It was obvious he was upset. His face was blotted red; his chest heaved violently.

"Ah, Father, you have returned. Now, finally we can eat."

"The ladies can lead; we will follow. There is a matter I wish to discuss with you in private, Louis."

"Where are your manners, Father? It would be rude for us to exclude our women. For shame!"

"Shame! You talk to me of shame! I have just returned from the banks of the Wateree River. Agy's body has been recovered...you do remember Agy!"

"The black wench from the kitchen," Louis answered caustically. "She drowned?"

"You tell me to my face you didn't know she walked into the river with her two small girls, who drowned as well. You bastard! After I threatened Davie, he told me the whole sordid tale! The woman could take no more from you."

"Father, you are unjustly condemning me. How is it my blame that a madwoman kills herself and children?"

443

"It was you who drove her to this! Willy is mad with grief. Now I will have to handle him. You have cost me much with your careless behavior."

Mr. Whitney's voice resonated within the room. He stomped over and jerked the bottle of wine out of Louis's hand. "Disgraceful. Your brother is fighting for our honor and you have behaved in the most reprehensible manner."

Louis grabbed back the bottle and shoved Mr. Whitney. "You are making too much of this. Upset with a dead nigger!"

It was then I saw a red glow growing out the window. Confusion turned quickly to alarm. The slave cabins were on fire...clamorous voices erupted. Then, without warning, Willy appeared in the room, holding a field knife.

He was a tall, black man, muscular defined even through his shirt. His white teeth and eyes glared with a frenzied look. Mr. Whitney screamed for us to leave the room. I did as I was bidden, only glancing back to see Willy lunge at Louis. A gut-wrenching cry cut through me as I ran out the door.

In the foyer, my heart froze in terror. Three more bucks had bolted in the front door. Danta, our butler, lay on the floor in a puddle of blood. Peggy refused to leave Louis. Sarah and I had no time to argue with her, but scrambled up the stairs. A strong hand grabbed my leg, sending me sprawling down.

Cries of fear...of pain surrounded me. I fought, kicking and screaming. A shot was fired. Then I was freed. Looking over my shoulder, I saw Mr. Whitney holding a pistol, still smoking.

Mr. Whitney yelled. "Run! Get the children! Don't look back!"

Frantic, I fled...leaving Sarah at the top of the stairs, running to save her children. Upstairs, the nursery girls helped me...thank God because there was no other help. The other house slaves had disappeared. I grabbed Mirabella and held Elijah's hand and we raced down the back stairs.

The children...all of Peggy's children...we saved them, even the baby. Sarah tried to save all of hers. The older ones got out, but Lord have mercy, Sarah and her youngest two, Teresa and little Joshua...couldn't be saved. Everything happened so fast. We ran all the way until the woods. Only then did we turn...the house was engulfed in flames.

Rising from the ashes, a story was spun of discontent slaves—striking out at their master and incited by Yankee propaganda—who had caused the revolt. The truth—that Louis had abused the slave girl, Agy, for years…had fathered children by her—would never be acknowledged.

Jo shuddered at the thought of what Agy must have endured to have chosen to take her own life and those of her daughters. The hopelessness…the bleakness. In turn, her husband, Willy, had struck back, violently and brutally.

He avenged his wife's death. In the end, Louis, Sarah, Peggy, and Sarah's two small children died torturous deaths, along with twelve faithful slaves. So senseless. So tragic. For what? It gained nothing. Willy and the four other slaves had, too, lost their lives.

"I'm sorry you had to see this." Mr. Whitney walked through the rubble to Jo's side. "I knew there was nothing that was salvageable. I hadn't the heart to break it to Grace Ann."

"It needed to be done. There is no need for her to see any of this." Jo spoke abstractedly in a low voice, looking out over the ruins. Silence followed.

Grief gripped her soul, encased in an overwhelming sadness. She had no more tears. Her tears had long dried, replaced with an endless void of her yesteryears.

"Spawn of Satan!" Mr. Whitney suddenly uttered under his breath, his face blank with consternation. "To lash out in such a rage! To kill innocents! It is this damn war!"

Jo made no response. She had known him as a kind and wise man. Strong in his silent manner. She had never seen this side of him. His rage scared her.

The fire's haze still covered his heart. Mr. Whitney saw only insolent slaves: unfaithful, unreliable, and vicious. Though, she could not deny that even the slaves at Magnolia Bluff were acting differently, as if they sensed freedom on the horizon, but she could never imagine them taking such a violent act.

Common sense dictated that she couldn't ignore that times had changed. Had not the massive defection of slaves in Beaufort shown that slaves were not as content with their situation as white plantation owners had proclaimed? The slaves had not only refused to join their owners and flee into the woods when the Yankees arrived—why, the Yanks themselves had to stop the looting and burning of their masters' mansions! Then the question became would open defiance become commonplace or Heaven forbid, as it had here at Whitney Hall, insurrection?

445

Andrew assured her that would never happen at Magnolia Bluff, but she had begun to wonder whether the South hadn't, in its own disregard of human life, brought down the wrath of God himself upon them.

"At times there is no reason, only the aftermath we have to find a way to survive," Jo offered, emotionally exhausted herself. "When Wade died, I had no choice but to focus upon Percival and the new baby. Their welfare and future is now mine alone to ensure. I don't have time for any other sentiment, especially one I have no control over. Perhaps, yours now should focus upon Grace Ann and her convalescing."

Mr. Whitney scowled. "Are you questioning the care of my wife?"

"I believe you are hurting. So is she," Jo asserted. "Grace Ann needs to heal and she can't do so here. She spoke to me once about your plantation in North Carolina. Small. Quaint. A wonderful place to raise children."

"Truth is, it has been a thought. At least, for a time until Whitney Hall can be rebuilt." His hand rubbed across his mouth as he sighed. "Peter telegrammed he's taking a leave and has already arranged for Peggy's sister to take his children. Grace Ann wants to take Louis's children as our own."

"I know it is her wish. I'm sure she will make a wonderful mother. Percival adores her," Jo said, fully aware that Grace Ann needed the children as much as the children needed her. "She hasn't said so, but I believe she is hurt that Aunt Sybil hasn't come."

"And well Mrs. Haynes won't," Mr. Whitney said in a strangled voice. "Her father has seen to that. I'm not sure you're aware that he disowned Grace Ann after I sided with the Montgomerys after you married Wade."

"No...Grace Ann never mentioned it." In silence, her eyes met his. There was an immediate understanding that Grace Ann, too, had paid a price. It was an upsetting thought.

"I'm certain it is not Mrs. Haynes's doing," Mr. Whitney said flatly. "Though, she sent a note. In it, she also informed Grace Ann that Buck had returned to the Groves."

"Buck—home? I had not heard..." Her voice trailed off. An old fear sharpened. She had not thought of her cousins in such a long time. "Harry Lee?"

"I heard a rumor that Harry Lee is in a Yankee prison camp, as I heard that Buck deserted."

Alarmed, Jo couldn't ignore the unbridled fear that filled her. Stumbling over her words, she asked, "When...when did he return? Do...you...?"

"I'm unsure, but would imagine it has been a couple of months. I have already alerted Andrew to the situation and he assures me that he is keeping a close eye on Buck. I would not be overly worried. I doubt Buck would make a move without Harry Lee. Moreover, despite that Wade is no longer with us, the arrangements he made are still in place."

She felt a chill up her spine, but also a sudden resolve that she would not be ruled by the fear her cousins inflicted by the mere mention of their names. She was a different person than she was before the war…unimaginable loss changes a person.

"You are not alone." Mr. Whitney reached over and squeezed her hand. "Go now and please tell Mrs. Whitney I will return by dark."

* * * *

The drive back to Camden weaved the carriage along a path of devastation. The row of whitewashed slave cabins was gone. The only evidence was the blackened spots on the ground.

As she looked out the window, she fought back melancholy as she studied the landscape. The sky darkened with the promise of rain. In her view, she noticed the split-rail fence broken and splintered; the slaves' garden patches seemed to have been trampled. The livestock pens were emptied. Odd for five slaves to have caused such damage.

At the end of the lane, a temporary shelter had been built for the homeless slaves…the ones who had stayed. Most seemed to have taken flight.

Near the creek's edge, the threatening clouds began to sputter raindrops. Suddenly, out of the woods, dogs ran wild on the trail of a scent. Barking madly, the pack swiftly crossed the water to the other side, followed closely by Johnnie Syms, Mr. Whitney's overseer, on horseback.

The carriage slowed to allow the overseer to cross. He turned and tipped his hat in a polite manner. Then an abrupt screech erupted: a cry for help. At first, Jo thought she imagined it, but another shriek, a gut-wrenching scream…from a child.

"Stop! Stop!" Jo pounded her hand frantically on top of the carriage over and over until the carriage halted.

Swinging back the door, she stepped out. Her eyes caught movement in the woods. Looking back over her shoulder, she called to the driver, "Don't sit there. There is a child out there!"

The old black man shook his head. "No, ma'am. Master says to getca back to town. Ya best get back in."

In front of her, Syms turned back to her. "Malcolm's right, Mrs. Montgomery. It's not safe for ya to go into these woods. Still rounding up the niggers who helped ole Willy."

Her heart pounded, but another cry pulled her out of the cloud of fear for herself. "Mr. Whitney would not allow me to go back alone if he was concerned about my safety…that is a child!"

Not waiting for an answer, she rushed by Syms and through the shallow water across the creek. The dogs' bark heightened as if they had trapped their prey. Climbing up the muddy bank, she tripped, but it served only to deter her momentarily. Ignoring her scratched, stinging hands, she made her way through the briars and bushes.

Abruptly, she halted. "Oh, my God!"

Riding up beside her, Syms said, "Mrs. Montgomery, I tole ya it would be best if ya returned to the carriage. I'll take care of this."

Shaking her head in disbelief, she steadfastly refused. "Call them off! Call them off now!"

"Mrs. Montgomery…"

Breathing hard, she shouted, "Now! This is atrocious! If you are a Christian man, call the dogs off the boy!"

His color was high; his face contorted. With the greatest reluctance, he whistled. The dogs' barking ceased. Behind him, four blacks ran up and grabbed the hounds.

Deeply disturbed, Jo ran forward toward the frightened child. The small, light-skinned child looked up at her. *Good Gracious! He couldn't be any more than five or six!* His terror-filled eyes widened as he recoiled from her touch. He wore only tattered pants and no shoes. Despite being covered in dirt and mud, she saw clearly his chest and arms were covered in bruises and wounds.

Jo wanted to wrap her arms about him and comfort him, but he had soiled himself badly. Instead, she offered him her hand. "Come with me. Trust me. No one is going to hurt you."

He said nothing, but the whole of his body trembled.

Turning, she shooed the dogs and men back with her hand. "Be gone. Obviously, he's not the one you are looking for…" As she looked into their faces, her words faded. "Surely not."

Syms dismounted and walked toward the boy. "I told ya, ma'am. It's best you go back to town and leave him to us."

She looked at him, and then back at the child. "I'm not going anywhere, not until you tell me what in Heaven's name is going on."

448

"His momma is the one who caused the whole revolt. Killed herself and babies. Got ole Willy all worked up. Can't have the likes of 'em around."

Aghast, she whispered, "He's a child."

"His daddy was sick in the soul. Ain't no cure for that. Ya look at the youngin' 'em eyes. He'll grow up and slit your throat..."

Interrupting him, she declared, "Don't you take that tone with me! I will tell Mr. Whitney what I have seen and he will deal with the likes of you."

He laughed, a coarse, hard laugh. "Ma'am, who do ya think gave me my orders?"

Her face fell; she felt nauseated. Oh, God in Heaven! That despicable man was lying. He had to be, but he would not shut up.

"The master retaliated against these niggers for the deaths they caused. Went on a rampage. Don't think 'em burnt down 'em own homes and trampled their own gardens. Wants anyone associated with ole Willy execu...punished. They hid that one...until 'em stupid niggers figured out that Tome boy would be the death of 'em. That he was a spawn of that she-devil. Began throwing rocks at the boy to keep him away. Ain't even wanted by his own kind."

As she looked down at the boy, he raised his head. His frightened eyes shone back at her. Oh, good Lord, she saw Gillie reflecting in them.

She straightened her shoulders back and held out her hand for the boy, giving him no choice but to take it. She whirled around and stared at the sadistic face of the white man. "I don't believe a word of what you said and if you think I'm leaving this child with you, you are sadly mistaken. If it is as you said, you can tell Mr. Whitney I have the boy. But I can assure you of one thing—nothing...nothing is happening to this child."

She made her way through the men and dogs, holding tight to the boy's hand, almost dragging him along. They did not stop until they reached the carriage and rode back to town.

* * * *

The morning after the incident, Jo had not left her suite at the Camden Inn, where she had sought refuge to think. She realized she could not leave things as they were, but Andrew had urged caution. *After breakfast...after breakfast, I will go see Grace Ann and explain myself.*

She had only eaten two bites of her eggs when she sensed an intrusion to her peace. When she looked up, she found Mr. Whitney in the center of the room. He barely glanced at her and appeared annoyed.

449

Pulling out a chair from the table, he sat and placed his hat down in front of him. She need not be told she was about to be admonished for her behavior the previous day. Suddenly, she felt like a young girl who had ripped and dirtied her good dress before church.

"Would you like for me to send for another plate?"

"No, it is not necessary. Are you finished? I would like to take a small stroll in the garden with you."

Something in his expression told her that she had no choice. Something she had never seen before in him, something ruthless.

"I have only to inform Rosa to care for Madeline."

Mr. Whitney waited impatiently, twisting his hat in his hand. When she returned, he accompanied her to a bench in the inn's dormant garden. A chill wind blew, but he made no effort to see to her comfort.

"I understand that you witnessed an unfortunate occurrence."

"I would say more of a disturbing sight, Mr. Whitney…one that I could not ignore."

Acknowledgment of that fact registered in his face, but his expression did not soften. "It would have been for the best if you had. You had no right to take the boy."

Her soulful eyes widened with shock. She wasn't certain she heard him correctly. "I did what I thought right, Mr. Whitney. You were not there and did not see what occurred. I'm not certain that Mr. Syms has been truthful with you. He…was chasing…the boy with dogs! The poor thing was covered in filth. Battered and…"

"That's enough, Josephine. I will deal with the matter. Now please turn the boy back over to me and we will forget this nasty business ever occurred."

"He is ill," Jo began.

"Let me remind you, he is not your concern. Don't believe because of our connection, I will turn my back on your actions. This matter needs to be dealt with promptly."

She looked at him and saw his severe countenance. His dark eyes narrowed. Slowly, she comprehended he did not care about her explanation, only a twisted revenge.

"Explain it to me then, Mr. Whitney, because for the life of me you have me at a loss. This is a five-year-old boy…"

"A slave…that nigger's boy…she destroyed my family. Killed my boy…my grandchildren."

A bilious sensation churned in her stomach. The words she had conjured to salve his anger suddenly struck her as useless. He was blinded by a merciless rage against anything and everything connected to the rebellion.

"Sir, I can't believe my ears. Surely, you are not suggesting holding the actions of others against a young lad." She took a deep breath in before her fragile courage wavered. "A lad who is obviously your grandson. You know this as well as I. Grace Ann told me herself on my prior visit. One look and it is obvious. Isn't it the reason why Willy…"

Abruptly, she realized her mistake.

Rigid in his seat, he said, "Watch your mouth, young lady. After all I have done for you, show me the respect I deserve."

"Mr. Whitney, I have always admired and respected you…why, I love you for all you have done for me…but this…this I can't accept. I won't."

"It is not for you to decide. Despite those damn Yankees' proclamation, my slaves aren't free. Don't make me go to the authorities."

"Would you? Is that why you are here? I know it couldn't possibly be the boy. He is only a means to expel the anger and frustration you are feeling at the moment." Confidence in her voice contrasted her trembling hands. She gripped them tightly, hoping he wouldn't notice. "You are lashing out your frustration…when your family needs you the most…"

Mr. Whitney seethed. "You have no right to assume you know me. Moreover, you have no right to talk of *my* family."

"Why, because I am only your bastard granddaughter?"

"My mistake was to have informed you of that fact," he said coolly, rising to his feet. "I will be back this evening. I will expect you to hand over the boy then."

A chill swept through Jo as she watched him walk away. Burning with indignation, she waited only until he was out of sight. Racing back up the stairs, she burst back into her suite.

"Rosa, send for Dr. Andrew."

* * * *

Josephine found her cousin in the nursery, rocking Peggy's youngest. No more than a few weeks old, the baby slept soundly in the afternoon's repose. Grace Ann glanced over at Jo, and then returned her gaze to the sleeping child.

"Dearest, whatever have you gone and done to cause Mr. Whitney's terrible mood?"

"I fear I have unintentionally offended him," Jo said, overcome with an overwhelming sadness. A silent tear streamed down her cheek.

451

"You will apologize, won't you? I know he has been a brute as of late, but it is quite understandable. Such a tragedy. I worry so about him."

"And I worry about you."

"There is no need," Grace Ann assured her in a soft voice, as if not to wake the baby.

Staring at Grace Ann, memories assaulted Jo, old ones…good and bad. Pushing back the emotions that threatened to overpower her, she leaned down and kissed her cousin's cheek. Grace Ann reached up and squeezed her hand.

Jo eased out of the room, descended the stairs and out of the house. Hurrying down the steps into the waiting carriage, she reached over and took her daughter from Rosa. Across from her, Andrew sat with the little boy lying across his lap.

"You said your good-byes?" Andrew asked.

Nodding, Jo could find no words. She wanted only to get back to Magnolia Bluff as quickly as possible. She would not be returning.

Chapter Four

Josephine walked onto the porch of the old cabin and paused before she entered. The sun waned, giving way to a still darkness. Lantern light shone under the crack of the door and smoke climbed the chimney. Miss Hazel had kept her word. She had come.

Not bothering to knock, she eased open the door. A slight smile formed on her lips at the sight before her—the small scared boy snuggled into the crouch of the old black woman's arms in the creaky rocking chair. Her dry, wrinkled hand caressed the small face.

His faint smile whisked her back to the day she had first seen Tome on the Whitneys' lawn, an innocent young boy loyally waiting by his friend until her mother came for her. She wondered whether his innocence was lost forever.

"Come in, child. Don't dawdle."

"You are quite right. We don't have much time." Jo shut the door behind her. "Andrew is giving Mr. Syms a tour of the grounds as we speak. We tried to hold him back until morning, but he wouldn't hear of it."

The Montgomerys' offer to pay for the boy had been refused. Instead, Mr. Whitney had sent his overseer to Magnolia Bluff to ensure the boy's return.

"Now, now, donca worry none. Ain't gonna let anything happen to this youngin'."

"We won't have a say if Syms finds him." Jo sighed. "Amos drove me over in the buckboard with Rosa. I don't know the exact details, but Andrew says he has made the necessary arrangements to get Tome down to Beaufort."

"When?"

"Immediately." Jo fumbled in her cloak pocket and felt to make sure the small envelope she brought was secure. She hadn't thought it would be this hard. Though unrelated by blood or color, the realization how much she relied on this woman swept through her. She swallowed hard. "Miss Hazel, I fear I have a request of you."

"Law, child, just ask. I ain't gonna refuse to help this young man."

"It's more than help, Miss Hazel." Jo drew up a chair from the dining table and sat. "I want you to take Tome north. Raise him yourself."

"Leave?" Miss Hazel's eyebrows rose in question. "This is my home."

"Oh, Miss Hazel, just do as I ask," Jo said in a much harsher tone than she intended. The last days had worn on her frayed nerves.

Tired. Exhausted. Her mind fought against her heart. Her Southern upbringing had taught her not to question what tradition had handed down. For years, she had accepted the peculiar institution, that in time the South itself would do away with it. Until then, she had believed that the blacks were in much better hands under their guidance. Now, everything had become confused.

"Now, Miss Jo, I'll take the boy to Beaufort for ya, but I'm sixty-two. I can't raise the boy and I ain't leavin' my farm." Miss Hazel looked sharply at Jo. "Already got runaways in the marshes waiting for me to abandon my cabin. Whatca think will happen? Won't have a home to come back to…"

Jo stood and slammed her fist on the table. "You don't have a choice!" Her voice trailed off and she stood in silence. Miss Hazel's eagle eyes met hers, which Jo had no doubt conveyed her fear.

With her emotions toiling, Jo walked over to the fire in silence. Taking a deep breath, she turned back to her mammy. "You have to go. I saw the devastation of a festered hatred. In turn, the revenge inflicted. Those men are here at Magnolia Bluff."

Jo gestured her frustration and waved her hands in front of her. Finally, she fell back into the chair and took her head in her hands. Endless moments passed, and then she looked up imploringly at the confused Miss Hazel.

"The loyalty and love for my home has not diminished, but it riles my temper not to be able to question an atrocity…as if doing so implies I'm betraying God, country, and family. But none of their threats will make me turn the boy back over to Mr. Whitney."

"Oh, Miss Jo, I knows your heart, but ya will make it worse for yourself. Ya and I know what Mr. Whitney is to ya. What if he…?"

"I have no control over his actions," Jo interrupted. "Only my own. He will do as he must, as I will do what I must." For a moment, time stood still. "That day when they were chasing Tome in the woods…when I took his hand, I looked in his eyes, I saw Gillie. I knew then what I had to do…what I couldn't do for her."

In all the years she had known Miss Hazel, Jo had never seen her cry. Her mammy had always been a pillar of strength. Today, tears welled in the old woman's eyes.

Sighing heavily, Jo regained a semblance of her composure. "There's more. Buck is back. Andrew assures me that Buck would not be foolish enough to retaliate at me directly. I myself doubt that Buck would have the backbone to try it by himself, but not to lash out to hurt me in any manner he had at his disposal—you."

For a moment, Miss Hazel paused before she answered. "I will go."

Relief mingled with sadness gripped Jo's heart, but she couldn't afford the luxury of being overcome with emotions. She took the envelope out of her pocket and moved over to her mammy.

"Amos is waiting to drive you down to Beaufort. He will stay to make sure that you make the necessary contacts for you to gain passage to Philadelphia." She squeezed the envelope into Miss Hazel's hand. "This will help. May God go with you."

Miss Hazel lowered her gaze at the young boy. "Now, Tome, tell Miss Jo thank ya for her kindness."

"Thank ya, ma'am," Tome said, trying to be all proper.

Jo stepped back and allowed the two to leave the cabin. She heard Amos greet Tome. Shortly after, the buckboard creaked and Amos snapped the reins to their old mule, Gus. She sat in the stillness until Rosa informed her that Andrew had come to escort them back to Magnolia Bluff.

* * * *

A slight sea breeze whisked through, rustling the budding trees of the low-country forest. Birds sang; wildflowers bloomed. Ignorant of the widespread conflict of the region, nature awoke from the dormant sleep of winter.

A festoon of Spanish moss swung in a slow rhythm, hanging from the water oaks. Heyward walked along the overgrown path down along the shoreline. Beaufort had become a safe haven for runaway slaves since the Union occupation.

North of the town, a refugee camp had been established for the contraband slaves. The area was overcrowded with crudely built shanties

455

and tents that had been quickly erected for the influx of needy. He searched for his mother in the chaos.

The tall black man trudged into the newfound community. Each step taken added to his frustration. These camps had become notorious for their lack of decent housing and food. Paying work was scarce and most of the inhabitants had no education.

"The information I obtained said she was down by the church." Lieutenant McFadden pointed to a small whitewashed building. "From what I understand, she has begun teaching reading at the missionary school."

As he turned the corner at the dirt road, his anxiety eased and affection warmed his heart. He caught sight of his mother, sitting outside of one of the hastily built shelters. A flock of children surrounded her as she held a book in her hand.

His anger had been vexed by the information Lieutenant McFadden had relayed only hours before—his mother had been a refugee for well over a month—information Captain Claiborne had seen fit to withhold from him.

Hell, if not for McFadden, he still wouldn't have known. He had enough of that damn arrogant captain and found him no better than any plantation owner he had ever known: barking orders at him, calling him nigger... Where was the respect that was supposed to come with freedom?

Over the last few weeks, he had come in and out of Beaufort at least three times. Claiborne made no mention of his mother, though Heyward knew well Claiborne had the information.

Heyward's days had been hectic. The network was floundering for the same reason this camp was overcrowded. The Underground Railway, in turn the foundation of their network, had been founded with brave souls willing to place their lives in peril to help others in need.

The fact that had been overlooked until lately: most of those souls in the Deep South were slaves themselves...slaves who now were able to escape. With President Lincoln's proclamation freeing slaves, hope was instilled into their lives for those who yearned for that freedom.

All through South Carolina, paranoia ruled the land. Men looked suspiciously over their shoulders at any stranger. Moreover, bandits, deserters, and runaway slaves littered the woods, waiting to take advantage of any lone traveler.

Heyward feared the network had worn out its usefulness and had become too dangerous to maintain. Mitchell had yet convinced Captain Claiborne of that fact.

His last trip into Beaufort, Heyward had been fired at by an unknown assailant in the woods. The bullet whizzed by his head. Walking barefoot with nothing but the clothes on his back, Heyward assumed that the thieves quickly surmised he was a worthless target and allowed him to move on without another attack.

"Heyward! My boy!"

His pace quickened and he walked briskly to his mother's side. Despite her height and frame, he picked her up and whirled her around. Her welcome laughter echoed in his ears as her arms wrapped around his neck.

As they slowly came to a stop, she clapped Heyward's cheeks. Her plump face lit up, smiling into his eyes. She repeated, "My boy! My boy!"

"Ma," Heyward began. "I would have come sooner, but I knew nothin' 'bout ya being here. No one told me. What happened? The last we talked, ya swore ya would never leave Magnolia Bluff."

"So much…so much," she began, but was abruptly cut off by a pull on her skirt.

Heyward looked down at the small boy vying for Miss Hazel's attention. Thin with the largest brown eyes, he was light-skinned, even for a mulatto. If not for his thick, tight curled hair, he could have passed for a white child. He wore ragged clothes and no shoes, but a large smile was plastered on his face.

Something about the eyes mesmerized him for a split second. *Lord Almighty!* For a moment, he swore it was as if Gillie looked back at him. Then it passed. Heyward shook his head in quick dismissal. Then the child spoke.

"Grammy Hazel…Grammy Hazel, is this my new pa?"

Heyward shot a shocked look over at his mother, who broke out into a long laughter. He watched his mother take the boy by the shoulders and face him.

"Yes, Tome, this is who we have been waiting for…my son, Heyward."

At a loss as to what to say, Heyward pointed his finger at the boy and then halted. As he stood in the middle of the hastily built shelter, angry confusion washed over him.

There was only one room. On either side of the single fireplace, an area served as makeshift sleeping spaces. Furnishings were meager, with only a crudely built table with hand-crafted benches as seats. A lantern sat in the middle of the table and served as its only means of light during the night.

"It was time, Heyward. Simple as that."

He had listened to his mother talk with only half of his attention. He had heard enough when she said Miss Jo sent her away. His repressed ire at the name of that woman surfaced. He said nothing for a long moment. Finally, he spoke. "I have been trying to getca out of there for months. Said it was too dangerous and you won't act until Miss Jo tells you to go."

"I told ya, son. The boy had to disappear."

Heyward wasn't a fool. He knew his mother. She had fought him on leaving her farm with every fiber of her being. Her home meant too much to her…it was hers. Not many black women in South Carolina could claim that honor.

Moreover, he didn't know a smarter, braver woman. She had manipulated and maneuvered anything and everything to be close to him when he was a slave. She had long maintained her farm, but that had been with the Montgomery blessing. With Wade Montgomery's death, the protection their name gave her weakened.

To be honest, he hadn't worried about her until lately. Most times, she was up at the main house with Miss Jo. Recently, though, his feelings had changed. The war hadn't gone the way the Rebs had planned. He feared the land would break out in chaos and give little thought to taking out their frustration on an old black woman living alone.

"I ain't saying he didn't haf to, Ma. I just don't understand what ya are doing here with him."

Her large, shrewd eyes looked over at the boy, who sat quietly on the lap of Lieutenant McFadden. "I tole ya, Heyward. It is time…time to be a family. Tome needs a pa. Ain't never had one. He wasn't claimed by no one at the Whitneys'. His ma's man wanted nothing to do with him. Most nights, he slept at the steps of their cabin unless someone took pity on him."

Her tone was subdued, but Heyward saw the workings of his ma's mind. She figured it would fix everything if the three of them formed some kind of family, but it wouldn't work. His ma was wrong on this one.

He wasn't the fatherly sort. At one time, he thought he could have been with Gillie, but Gillie was gone, along with any desire he had had for a family. His heart had hardened to the thought.

"What you are asking, I can't do, Ma. Besides, I can't leave. I got a job to finish," Heyward said in a grave, solemn voice. His eyebrow lifted as he watched the boy climb down off Lieutenant McFadden's lap and walk over to him.

"That's what Grammy Hazel told me," Tome said. "Said you are a soldier helping fight for our freedom. I want to do that too…just like you. I told Grammy Hazel she got nothing to worry about. I'll protect her from the bad man."

Heyward looked over the boy at his mother. "What bad man?"

* * * *

"Captain Claiborne, I believe it is best if we recall Mitchell. The network was collapsing even before Heyward asked to be replaced." Lieutenant McFadden glanced up as he saw Heyward walk into the tiny office. McFadden motioned for him to close the door.

Heyward had to stand because there wasn't another chair. From the look on Claiborne's face, the man was in no frame of mind to be hospitable.

"This network has been extremely beneficial to our intelligence. It would be ill-advised to dismantle it prematurely. We have this…" Claiborne clicked his fingers together as he had the name of the tip of his tongue.

"Jonas, sir," McFadden offered. "Let me remind you that the team worked well together because there were three of them. Once Heyward is discovered gone, I would recommend caution."

"Look around you, Lieutenant." Claiborne's tone was laced with sarcasm. "The streets are filled with refugees. I dare say that one more missing nigger isn't going to cause concern."

At the utterance, Heyward tensed. McFadden shot him a look of caution.

"There is no need to use such language, Captain," McFadden stated firmly. "Heyward has done a commendable job and has risked his life daily for the mission. He is also a volunteer who hasn't been paid for his work as was agreed."

"Which you reminded me last night, Lieutenant…of my being remiss. I assume that you visited General Sherman last night because he met with me this morning to make sure I had rectified the situation." Claiborne breathed out heavily and handed a pouch to Heyward. "You will find the papers are in order, including a written recommendation from Lieutenant McFadden."

Heyward accepted the pouch. Opening it up, he looked through them. He read enough to recognize that Claiborne had spoken the truth. Closing it up, he smiled. "Thank ya, Captain."

He wanted the good captain to know he could read. His mother had seen to that. He was not an ignorant soul. He had every intention of going back to Philadelphia to accomplish what he had dreamed of with Gillie.

His mother and Tome waited for him outside. The ship was leaving with the tide. They would be on it.

Over the last few days, Heyward had come to the realization that there comes a time in a man's life when he has to make a choice. For so long, he had tried to outrun the anger that lived within him, but there was only so far he could run.

There would be no more running.

He was taking his family, Ma and the boy, up to Philadelphia to start life anew. He had done all he could for the cause down here in the Carolinas.

Chapter Five

Children's laughter echoed on the piazza. Percival ran around his little sister, who sat in the middle of a pallet, laughing and giggling. Every few minutes, Madeline glanced around to ensure her mother's presence and then resumed being entertained by her brother's antics.

Jo soaked in the sight of her two wonderfully clever and precocious children. Madeline had a headful of unruly dark blonde ringlets, with the largest eyes as blue as the depths of the ocean. Unlike her brother, she was a painfully shy baby, quite attached to only a select few—her momma, grandmother, and brother.

Strange how the siblings were so different. Rambunctious and energetic, Percival was personable and outgoing. He had yet to meet a stranger. He loved animals and always had his daddy's dog, Duke, running after him.

The beautiful sunshine had given Magnolia Bluff a lovely garden this summer. The flowers were in full bloom: violets, roses, and yellow jessamine. The vegetables had also been plentiful, keeping the table filled with green peas, strawberries, asparagus, and potatoes.

Josephine realized they were fortunate. While not as bountiful as in the past, no one on the plantation was going hungry. The chickens supplied fresh eggs; the cows, fresh milk, which also allowed them to make yellow butter.

She wiped back the sweat from her brow. The sweltering heat had begun early this year, with no promise of the weather breaking until fall.

"Oh, dear, the heat is so unbearable. It has become impossible to sleep. The air is so heavy I find I can't breathe properly. I fear it is not healthy for the children or Jenna." Mother Montgomery fanned herself.

Looking over at Mother Montgomery, Jo could not argue with her. The unyielding warmth was oppressive. If not for the war, they would not be at Magnolia Bluff at this time of the year. Mother Montgomery had suggested they return to Charleston. Reluctantly, Jo had been considering it.

The heat wasn't the only deterrent on the plantation. The bugs and mosquitos had been dreadful. The mosquito netting had been the only saving grace at night, but Jo feared that too would become scarce soon enough.

In his constant need to keep moving, Percival ran into his sister and knocked her over, inciting an ear-piercing cry. Mother Montgomery rose and picked up the screeching child, immediately calming her.

Jo watched in admiration. There was a gentle dignity about her mother-in-law. Underneath her low, soft voice was a strong will, which cared deeply for her family. She never came out and demanded, but suggested. Jo realized she needed to heed Mother Montgomery's wish to go live in Charleston.

On the other hand, Derek had been quite vocal about the need for Jenna to find relief from the plantation. The poor soul had been so ill since she confided to Jo she was with child.

In the past, women in the family way would have been pampered along the coast with the ocean breeze to cool her; iced drinks to refresh her. Times had changed. Even going into Charleston would not alleviate all her discomforts, only ease them somewhat.

The Charleston of old had faded as it faced the harsh reality of war. There were no more cries that the conflict would be over quickly. The city that had sounded the call for secession and served as the face of the Confederacy had become paranoid, fearing the Yankees would descend upon them at any moment.

The blockade had drained its inhabitants. Provisions needed for everyday life had become increasingly difficult to come by. Moreover, the comforts afforded the rich now came with a stiff price. A pair of gloves went for thirty dollars, a pair of slippers for fifty, and that was for articles of clothing that in the past would not have been fit for their servants.

The blockade-runners had become the only ones to profit during this conflict. The once affluent and wealthy had learned how fast everything could change.

The lovely, charming city had become a shell of what it once had been. The great fire of '61 had blackened the streets. The residents had been unable to repair the damage, due to the lack of men and supplies. The war raged and silenced the church bells that once peeled throughout the streets.

Facing the inevitable, Jo had concluded she needed to heed Mother Montgomery's wish to go live in Charleston…at least for the summer. Derek wasted no time after Jo relented and had left earlier in the morning to inspect the logistics of the move.

Derek always made an effort to be polite to Jo, if not somewhat brusque, but was tension underneath the surface. Jo was keenly aware Derek had never forgiven her for the implied offense when he first returned to Magnolia Bluff. Jo realized he felt she had questioned his integrity. Consequently, she had not expected Derek's support when Andrew insisted on telling him about the incident with Tome.

"Times are hard enough. We need to rely on each other. We cannot keep a secret this sensitive. He is a part of our family and has a right to know."

At first, Derek seemed taken back by the tale, but in the end supported Jo in her decision to help the young Negro boy, despite the ramification it might mean to the family. "It is a shame. I greatly admire Mr. Whitney and understand his grief, but I also grasp why you could not turn your back on a child. We will endure any rumors that might arise."

Understanding suffused within Jo that Derek considered her empathy a weakness of being a woman, but it was an encouraging sign for the family. She remembered Miss Hazel telling her once that misfortunes will do one of two things: strengthen a family or split it.

Jo wondered whether it had more to do with Jenna's stance. Only the night before, Jenna declared, "I don't question our cause and know it is just, but I can't help but feel that slavery's time needs to come to an end."

"I do not disagree with you, my dear," Derek replied. "I doubt it will ever be the same after this conflict. We are fortunate here at Magnolia Bluff. The servants who have stayed are loyal and excellent. They are as much a fixture here as the family."

Jo realized that although Derek was raised on a plantation in Georgia, it was not as large or massive as the land owned by the family he had married into. He had become a great asset, not afraid of hard, physical labor.

She had discovered that Derek had an inner strength that emerged since his return. Gone was the thought of him as a cripple. His left shirt sleeve may have been pinned up at the shoulder, but that was the only indication of his handicap.

Not afraid to toil alongside the remaining Negros, Derek worked harder than ten men. The plantation had come to depend heavily on his guidance. He mended fences, tilled the garden, and saw to the livestock.

With most of Andrew's time and energy concentrated on the hospital in Charleston, Gardner had begun to come to Derek for direction on the care of the plantation. It was one less worry upon Andrew's shoulders.

For well over a century, the main cash crop on Magnolia Bluff had long been rice. They had not even attempted to plant the fields this year. There would be no cash crops. It would have been a useless venture. Instead, Derek's focus was upon Magnolia Bluff maintaining its ability to be self-sufficient.

The emphasis had turned to the other plantations under the Montgomery name to supply the needed cash crops; those grew cotton. Unfortunately, cotton had fared no better, commanding no price whatsoever. Derek reasoned that at least cotton could be stored and sold at a later time.

Long before the war, Jo would have fallen on her knees, praying and weeping, at the magnitude of problems that faced Magnolia Bluff. She had learned to take one day at a time, not looking ahead…just surviving the day.

Lost in her thoughts, Jo smiled over at her daughter, who made such a lovely picture with her grandmother. The little one reached up and touched Mother Montgomery's face in the most gentle of fashions with her chubby hand.

From the corner of her eye, movement caught her attention. Turning, Jo rose and walked over to the railing. Amos ran haphazardly across the back of the front lawn, flailing his hands over his head.

Rosa emerged from the back of the house and ran to meet him. Amos doubled over for a moment to catch his breath. Grasping the large black man by the shoulders, Rosa leaned over and said something.

Too far away to make out the words, Jo watched in confusion. Rosa glanced around in a nervous manner and then ushered Amos back the way he came. After one last look behind her, Rosa followed.

"Mother Montgomery, can you watched the children for a moment? There seems to be a disturbance of some sort."

"Oh, my," Mother Montgomery cried in a low voice, Madeline clutched to her chest. "Is it…is it the Yankees?"

"No…no, my dear. I can assure you I would not be going out to greet the devils," Jo calmed Mother Montgomery. "More than likely, it is nothing. I just saw Rosa head toward the barn. I hope it is not Ole Toby. Can't afford to lose another draft mule. Amos said the old mule was looking peaked last night. Do you need Anna to help you with the children?"

Obvious relief flooded the older woman's face. She shook her head. "I will bring the children in for a nap."

"Thank you. I'll be back shortly." Without looking back, Jo scurried down the steps. She didn't want to lose sight of Rosa, because she had lied to Mother Montgomery. Rosa hadn't headed to the barn but along the path to the docks.

Keeping up her pace behind Rosa, Jo focused on following her without being detected. Rosa turned off the trail, but made her way through the tall weeds along the riverbank. Terrified of running across a sleeping alligator, snake, or worse, Jo picked up her skirt and rushed through the undergrowth.

Breathless, she paused. Rosa had slowed and moved alongside Amos. Inching closer, Jo saw what had brought the two out along the river's edge. It was a man...a white man.

Instinctively, she walked up to Rosa and stared down incredulously at the unconscious figure. Sprawled on the ground, he faced upward as if he had been rolled over. He had no hat; his unkempt beard hung down to his chest; his disheveled brown hair tangled. He was a big man, but his face was thin and his cheeks sunken.

Covered in mud, he wore no uniform, but clothing of a working man. A once white shirt was tattered and torn; his pants ripped. He wore no shoes, but it wasn't his appearance that had her trembling. No, it was the blood oozing over his shirt along his waistline.

Groaning, his face contorted, writhing in pain. She eased ever so cautiously down to his side. All her instincts cried to run, leave him to his fate, but she did not. She reached out toward him.

"Lordy! Miss Jo, don't ya touch him."

Startled, Jo recoiled and clutched her hand to her bosom. Finally able to breathe again, she asked, "What happened? Do either of you know this man?"

"No, Miss Jo," Amos said. "I found him like this. Somethin' awful done happened. But ain't gonna worry ya none, not with Dr. Andrew and Master Derek gone. Went and got Rosa."

Glancing up, Jo saw the two exchanged nervous looks. Then she turned her attention back to the injured...dying man. The only semblance of life reflected was in his chest heaving heavily and the grunts of pain it took to make each labored breath.

Mustering up her courage, she reached over and pulled up his shirt. Easy enough now to see a gaping wound: he had been stabbed.

"Amos, did he say anything?"

465

Jo looked around; her heart hammered loudly. Everything was quiet, but caution had to be taken. Andrew and Derek both had warned the women numerous times not to show hospitality to strangers. There were miscreants who preyed upon the weakened state of plantations. Could this man be one of a group?

"Amos," Jo repeated and then demanded, "Amos, what did this man say?"

Most reluctantly, Amos stuttered, "He asked... for Dr. Andrew, Miss Jo...Dr. Andrew."

****

There had been no time to waste. Jo had Amos take the man to the sick cabin. She had her doubts that he would survive being moved even that short distance.

Jo stood nervously over the bed. *How could a man bleed so much and still be breathing?* She rinsed out the towel and placed it back over the wound, but again the towel reddened as fast as she held it against it.

"Hold it tight against it."

As she jerked her head around, she immediately breathed a sigh of relief—Andrew.

Throwing his hat on the hardback chair, he rolled up his sleeves and proceeded to take control of the patient. Silently, he worked in the hot, sweltering room. He asked only for Jo to retrieve his medical bag on his horse.

After what seemed an eternity to Jo, Andrew stitched up the wound. Finally, the bleeding stopped.

"It is fortunate I was returning to Magnolia Bluff today. I had only turned up the lane to the main house when Amos caught me." Andrew sighed and rubbed the back of his strained neck. "You didn't call attention to him, I hope."

"Of course not," Jo answered defensively. "Only Rosa, Amos and..." She glanced over in the corner at Lonnie, who sat with a muddled expression. "Lonnie. Amos told the others that Lonnie got hurt in the cutting back the overgrowth to cover. I don't think many of the other darkies will believe the story, but Mother Montgomery will."

"I doubt any of them will say anything. No one wants trouble and it is best for Mother and the girls to be unaware of his presence." As he washed his hands in the bloody water, Andrew nodded his head. "I understand the stranger asked for me."

"That is what Amos said." Jo nodded. "I assume he must know you are a doctor."

"It would be my assumption," Andrew agreed. "The roads aren't safe traveling alone these days. He must have gotten robbed and assaulted."

"That is what I was thinking." She eased over to the bedside. "Is he going to live?" The man's clothing was strewn over the floor. Nothing worth saving, Jo bent down to pick them up.

Drying his hands, Andrew shrugged. "He is in God's hands. I believe I have stopped the bleeding. He is lucky it didn't hit any vital organs, but he has lost a lot of blood. Time…time will tell."

"I am going to take his clothes and burn them. I'm sure we have something in the house that will fit him when he recovers. I need to return. Madeline will need to be fed." As Jo tucked the clothes in a bundle, a cigar case dropped to the floor from his pants pocket.

She reached down and picked it up. Opened, she saw three cigars, but the fourth had a note wrapped around it. Her fingers untied the string that bound it to the cigar. Her eyes widened in disbelief as she read.

The words and numbers blurred together. There were names of officers, suggested strategy of the leaders, and places of the Confederate defense in Charleston. The number of units stationed within the city and at the forts on the islands, the number of cannons, rifles, and ammunition that had arrived only in the last week…

Her hands trembled. Looking up at Andrew, she uttered with deep hatred, "He is a spy."

****

"Send for the sheriff, militia, whoever it is that will deal with this….this man." Jo's voice rang sharp with a rising anger. Aghast, she caught her breath. "Get him out of here…now."

Andrew moved swiftly around the cot where the unconscious man laid and took the paper from Jo. Something in the way he glanced over the contents told Jo she was correct in her assumption. The man was a Union spy!

"Well," Andrew said in a long, drawn-out manner as he scrutinized the paper. "It does seem as though he may have infiltrated our lines, but it would be his death to move him. I won't allow that."

"Allow that? You are not serious, Andrew. It is not a question. I want him gone. I thought he was a victim of a robbery along the roads. I will not be party…"

"Calm yourself." Andrew took her by her shoulders. "Whether or not he is the enemy, it changes nothing. It is my duty to care for him."

Jo wrenched herself away from his grip and backed up to the wall. Pointing at the man, she cried, "He is not my duty. Get him off the plantation."

Andrew shook his head slowly. "Jo, it's impossible to move him. It would be a death sentence. I know you. It's not what you want…to have a man's death upon your hands."

"Do not think my empathy extends to Yankees! Moreover, don't hold what I did for that poor black child against me. This is not the same thing! He…he is the enemy!"

"You don't know that. In his state, he can't defend himself. If you call the authorities, he won't get that chance. He will die before they get him back to Charleston in his condition. I ask only you wait…it may well be pointless. He may die anyway."

She shook her head vehemently and stared across the room, frowning. "They killed Wade!" Her lips trembled with the declaration, her hands clenched into a fist. "Wade's dead because of those damn Yankees. Never has there been a finer man who walked the earth and he's gone…gone because they killed him!"

"No, Jo, this godforsaken war killed Wade. Can you not see there has been too much death? It is all around us. I refuse to add to it and won't allow you to do so either."

"How dare you tell me to remain silent and harbor a spy!"

A long, deep sigh escaped Andrew. He glanced back over at the man, who fidgeted uncomfortably. Sweat poured off his brow. Grimacing, the wounded man clutched his side. Andrew rushed over and jerked the man's hands back from the injured area.

"Find me a rope," Andrew demanded from Lonnie. "We are going to have to restrain him so he won't open back up his wound."

Andrew watched Lonnie run out the door and then turned to Jo. "Help me. He is going to…"

Jo shook her head. "I told you…"

"I know him," Andrew abruptly announced, holding the patient's arm down by his side. He looked up at Jo. "From my time in Philadelphia…you may as well. He is Gavin Mitchell. Jo, he is a friend of Cullen's."

Taken back, she said nothing. *Cullen*…for so long she had refused to think of him. He had deserted her…taken the side of the enemy. Finally, she said in a voice that could barely be heard in the small cabin, "Why…why would he come here?"

"How can I say? He visited before the war with Cullen. As you said before, he knows I am a doctor…he had nowhere else to turn."

468

Anguish suffused within her. *What am I to do?* She had not time to contemplate the dilemma. Lonnie raced inside, empty-handed. "They're coming, Dr. Andrew!"

"Who, Lonnie?" Andrew asked, unable to leave Mitchell's side.

"Soldiers...Confederate soldiers are at the main house," Lonnie uttered, out of breath. "What's we going to do?"

Jo looked out the dirty window. *Oh, Good Lord, it was a whole unit!* She looked back at Andrew. She had no choice. She walked out.

****

Jo stood in the doorway for a moment. The sight she must have presented to the men. The front of her dress was drenched in blood; her hands, sticky and coated with the same liquid. She didn't care. She was in no mood to be hospitable...no matter whether it was the militia.

Lonnie hadn't been wrong. It was a unit of soldiers. From the looks of the weary men, they had been drudging through the swamps.

Immediately, she recognized the leader, Lucas McCoy. He was dressed in a ragtag Confederate uniform, as were most of the men. Their britches had holes in them; boots with the soles worn clean through; their uniform coats, faded and patched.

The sun bore down in the cloudless sky. Jo marched out toward them with her skirt swinging in the wake of her gait. She gave no mind to the men who reined in their horses around her.

"Good day, Mr. McCoy. What brings you out this day?" She tossed her head back. Bone-tired, she hadn't the patience to deal with this man...this abomination who helped Harry Lee kill Gillie...for that was what he had done, surely as if he choked the life out of her himself.

"It's Captain McCoy, Mrs. Montgomery," he answered solemnly, nodding his head slightly. "I hate to impose on you at this time, but we have been searching for a renegade. We fear we may have a spy in our midst. We have tracked him down to the river and have since lost him."

"And this has to do with me?" she asked with a venom that cut with contempt. "I can assure you I don't make a practice of taking in renegades, Captain. Now, if there is anything else you need?"

"I believe you don't understand my request, Mrs. Montgomery. We need to search your plantation. As I said, the trail ends..."

Fuming, her eyes flared at him. "You will do no such thing!" She lashed out at him, scarcely hiding the contempt she felt for the man. "I won't have my home turned upside down because you lost your prisoner or whatever he was. Why, so that you can find someone else to try to hang without a trial? No, Mr....Captain. You will do no such thing. I give you my word that no one is here."

"I believe what Captain McCoy is asking, dear cousin, is what have you been doing since you are drenched in blood and I myself stabbed the spy in the gut? Could it be you are sheltering a spy at Magnolia Bluff?"

The skin on her nape prickled as if evil breathed on her neck. Her heart lurched with fear. Breaking through the crowd of men, Buck Haynes rode up beside McCoy. His appearance had changed. His dirty hair fell down to his shoulders; his unkempt beard looked as though a bird had nested in it. Skinnier, his worn clothes hung loose about him, but his eyes…his eyes still held the same gleam of depravity.

She met those eyes with a scornful glare. "Get off my land, Buck. You are not welcome here."

"Can't, cous. I'm part of the militia now."

"Don't tell me they allow deserters into our militia!"

He chuckled and leaned back on his horse. "Tough words coming from a nigger lover—at least, that is what rumor has it."

Burning with humiliation, she felt her face go scarlet. *How had he found out about the incident at Whitney Hall?* An uneasy feeling washed over her. She supposed that it was inevitable that word would get out what she had done…more than likely twisted the facts, that she had betrayed Grace Ann and Mr. Whitney.

"I haven't a clue to what you are trying to insinuate. I am loyal citizen of South Carolina. Do not question my allegiance."

"Mrs. Montgomery," McCoy intervened. "Ain't here for no other reason than finding the fugitive."

With the back of her hand, she wiped her brow and looked back at the sick cabin. "My man, Lonnie, was out in the fields this morning with a swing blade. It got caught on a vine and he tried to jerk the swing blade off and was successful, except it went back at him, nearly cut his arm off. I've been tending to him all morning."

"You won't mind if we check it out."

"I do," Jo declared. "I gave you my word. It should suffice. I will not be disgraced at my home when we have sacrificed much for the cause."

"There is no need for your stance. I assure you it is a necessity."

"You understand perfectly my stance and my aversion to your presence," she retorted, riddled with disdain. "Can you tell me that you searched the Randolphs' place or the Middletons'? I sincerely doubt it. I believe you are here only to dishonor my family. If you even dare dismount, I will write to General Beauregard personally and tell him of your treatment of the family of his beloved major. I have a letter in his own hand stating the bravery and courage my husband displayed and the ultimate sacrifice he made for God, family, and country. I gave you my answer. Now, get off this land."

Jo refused to move.

Some in the unit began to withdraw. Another rode up to McCoy. "Told ya I saw signs of a boat pushed into the water. I swear he left by the Ashley."

McCoy started to say more, and then refrained. Instead, he turned to Buck, who was the only one who had not retreated. "Come on. We have more work to do."

Buck glared at Jo. "I'll be back."

She made no retort, but stood there on trembling legs until the last soldier disappeared out of sight.

****

Jo sat in the dark and waited. A door opened and closed. She made no movement to leave. Andrew was about to feel the brunt of her rage. Her anger flamed, fanned at Andrew, Captain McCoy…Buck!

Oh, Heavens to Betsy! She had lied to save a damn Yankee! Only after she had calmed down…after she had fed Madeline, hugged Percival tightly…had she comprehended the full extent of her actions.

Disaster loomed over Magnolia Bluff. The whole of the plantation was endangered while that Yankee recovered in the sick cabin. Everything that Wade had done…the sacrifice he made would be for naught if that blasted McCoy—or worse, Buck—discovered they harbored the spy.

"Jo, I got your note. Why are you sitting in the dark?"

She said nothing while Andrew lit the lamp on the desk. The room glowed in the dark as the lamp's light burned. He had not changed his blood-stained clothes, but he had washed up. Turning back to her, his eyes lit on the empty glass on the table beside her and walked over to the decanter.

"Would you like another? I find I need one myself." Andrew lifted the decanter.

Ladies of quality would never drink hard liquor in the presence of a gentleman. At the moment, neither was she a lady or Andrew a gentleman. She handed him her glass. "Don't dawdle. Out with it," she demanded contemptuously.

"There's not much to tell," he said, grimly, drinking down the entire contents in one-mouthful. "Mitchell's alive, but barely. I told Gardner what had happened. Had no choice in the matter. He is watching him now."

471

Jo grimaced. *Lord almighty! However were they going to keep him a secret if the whole of the plantation knew of his presence!* Her anger stirred. "I'm not taking a chance on getting caught with him. I don't care how you do it, but move him!"

Slowly, Andrew poured himself another drink and stared at it as he swirled the brandy around his glass. "I suppose I should tell you I'm grateful you did not turn him over to McCoy. I thought for sure it was your intention when you stormed out of the cabin."

"Spare me, Andrew. You know well enough I'm not that much of an idiot. McCoy would have condemned us all if he discovered the man. Why, I have no doubt Buck would have burnt Magnolia Bluff down! But I won't have it! I won't lose Magnolia Bluff over some dirty, lousy Yankee spy!"

"Stop! I do not need you hammering at me. I will handle it."

"You won't be able to if Buck…"

"Jo, I know." Andrew's manner eased. "I will not make light of the situation and surely not Buck. It will bode well for you and the children to move into Charleston, at least for the time being."

Terror struck her. "You are afraid of what Buck will do?"

"I certainly don't trust the man, if that is what you ask. Thank goodness, I heard that Harry Lee is in a prison camp at Fort Delaware. I doubt Buck will try much of anything on his own, but while Mitchell recovers…if he recovers…it is best you aren't here."

"We are set to leave for Charleston at the end of the week. Didn't Derek see you? He went into Charleston…"

"I have been so busy at the hospital that I've been staying there," Andrew answered before she finished. "But Mother mentioned it in her last letter. I didn't realize it was set."

"We will leave, but I want that *man* gone as soon as you are able to move him. I won't have Magnolia Bluff jeopardized more than it already has been. We don't need any suspicion upon us as Yankee sympathizers."

"Josephine, don't let Buck's words gnaw at you," Andrew directed, suddenly showing a little compassion toward her. "If it concerns you about what you did to save little Tome, don't. We need to do what we must and not be dictated by others' perception of what is right."

"You're wrong," Jo snapped. "We have to be concerned about what is whispered. Everyone is on edge…we have to do everything…everything to protect Magnolia Bluff. Wade…Wade can't be forgotten…"

"I, too, hold to Wade's memory. Trust me, Jo. I will do everything in my power to ensure Magnolia Bluff will be whole for Percival."

Emotions overwhelmed her. Abruptly, she wiped back a silent tear. "You understand my position. I want nothing more to do with that Yankee. You will take care of it without causing attention to the family."

"I give you my word." Andrew nodded in agreement and stood aside as she made her way through the door in silence.

* * * *

Rain pounded against the windowpanes. It had been relentless most of the night. Jo knew because she had found little sleep. She had been up most of the night with her daughter. The little one was teething. Finally, she had been able to lay Madeline down without her screaming.

She prayed Percival wouldn't wake up with one of his attention-seeking antics. He had been a terror the last few days. Mother Montgomery said it was the move into Charleston that had him riled up.

Jo realized it was more. Her son had picked up on her anxiety. An anxiety that would not be squelched until that damn Yankee was off her property.

The wind howled louder. Glancing down at Madeline, she assured herself her daughter was sound asleep. Rubbing her tired eyes, she needed to rest, even if it was for only a couple of hours. The morning sun would rise in less than three hours whether or not she had gotten any rest.

For the last week, Jo had worked endlessly to prepare to withdraw into Charleston. Derek would maintain residence at Magnolia Bluff. They could ill afford for it to be vacant of family. Andrew would reside when he wasn't at the hospital, allowing Derek the opportunity to be with his wife during part of the week.

Jo had not minded keeping busy. It drove back the thoughts that occupied her heart and mind. She survived each day by the continual chores that needed to be attended to…it was the only way she kept herself from feeling and it was not a luxury she could afford herself. Her heart would never endure if the hurt and pain that lived inside her soul emerged.

Above all else, her children needed her. She would do whatever was necessary to ensure their safety and well-being. They were her life…her reason for being.

If only Andrew would tell her what she wanted most to hear—that the damn Yankee was off her property. Then and only then would Magnolia Bluff be safe…the family would be safe.

If the truth be known, the whole thing gnawed at her. Something wasn't right. She couldn't put her finger on it, but she was certain it had to do with Andrew's reaction.

How quickly and efficiently Andrew had covered the tracks of the Yankee spy! She had spent the first few nights in dreaded anticipation. Too many people were aware of the man's presence: Lonnie, Gardner, Amos, and Rosa. Why, Andrew said they had even moved Mitchell to the overseer's house.

Yet, there had been no whisperings, no guarded looks. Even when McCoy had sent back a patrol unit—twice—there had been no indication of any abnormal activities. That alone had bothered Jo.

As she eased out the door, she made her way to the next door to the left. She had decided to crawl in beside her eldest to ensure he not walk into the nursery looking for her and wake his sister. When she looked into his room, there was no Percival.

The little hellion must have climbed into her bed. She sighed and walked into her room. Her heart stilled…he wasn't in her bed.

"Miss Jo, donca worry none. He's with Dr. Andrew."

Jo whirled around to find her maid in the doorway. She shook her head. "He doesn't need to bother his uncle. Can you…?" She paused. Something in Rosa's nervous eyes told her that Percival wasn't in his uncle's room; for that matter, he wasn't in the house. With an exasperated glare, she demanded, "Where is Percival?"

Rosa shifted from one foot to the other. Jo stared at her with fierce intensity. Rosa lowered her gaze. "Percy heard Dr. Andrew leaving the house, ma'am…"

"Oh, Good Lord! Rosa, tell me that he didn't go out with Andrew! In the dead of the night…in the rain!" Jo's voice rose to the point of hysterics. She knew…oh, Lord in Heaven, she knew exactly where he had taken her son…her son.

Immediately, she heard Madeline cry out. Jo gripped Rosa's arm with a strength she didn't know she possessed. "Stay with the baby. Do you hear me? Don't leave her. I will be back."

"But, Miss Jo, Dr. Andrew said he wouldn't be long…"

Ignoring Rosa, she wanted only one answer. "Do you understand me? I swear, Rosa, I will…"

"I will stay. I promise, Miss Jo," Rosa uttered in a low, cutting voice, pained from her arm being squeezed so tightly.

Releasing Rosa, Jo rushed down the stairs, pausing only to grab her cloak. Guided by the lights from the main house and the faint lights from her destination, she drudged along in the wind-swept rain through the mud and puddles along the path to the overseer's home.

Stomping up the steps in her water-soaked slippers, she barreled through the door without so much as a knock. The wind took the door and slammed it hard against the wall. Throwing back her hood, wet hair strands plastered her face, framing the rage in her smoking eyes. "Where is he?"

"Mrs. Montgomery?" Gardner emerged out of the door at the far end of the hall.

Whipping around him, she flew down the corridor…her hand on the handle of the door when it flared open. Andrew stood aside to let her enter.

"Josephine, he is fine…"

"You had no right…no right at all!" Her eyes surveyed the small room and lit upon Percival. Sitting in the middle of the bed, he was surrounded by small soldier play figures. He looked up at her and smiled.

"Looky, Momma," he squealed and held up a handful of the toys. Pointing to Mitchell lying in bed, he went on. "He gave them to me…said I could keep 'em." Percival stood, and then unsteady, toppled over, falling on the injured man.

"Percival Wright!" Jo cried and grasped hold of him, jerking him up roughly. "Get off that bed this instant. You know better…"

"It's quite all right, Mrs. Montgomery," Mitchell's deep voice said. "I asked him to join me. He has been quite entertaining. He is quite a remarkable young man. Inquisitive, bright, and obviously handsome. You have done a remarkable job. You must be proud."

"I am," she said curtly, wanting only to take her son back to the house, far away from this man. "Now, Percival, say good-bye. We need to return home. It's not acceptable to be out this late…you need to be in bed."

"Please, a few minutes more. Since you are here." Mitchell swung his legs over the side of the bed and stood. "I'm leaving. I wanted to thank you personally…"

Jo swept her son in her arms, not noticing for the moment that he had blocked her escape.

"Gavin," Andrew began. "Don't. I told you…"

"I know what you told me, Andrew, but she's here now. Just a few moments. That is all."

Not wanting to leave, Percival wiggled out of his mother's arms and cried for his figures. Andrew immediately launched forward to pick up his nephew's new toys.

Jo stepped back and stared at Mitchell. Her eyes shot through him like daggers.

Taking advantage of her silence, Mitchell went on. "I wanted to thank you for saving my life. I know…your reluctance in doing so, but the result was I lived and owe it to you. I will be eternally grateful."

As she looked at him standing before her, he did not resemble the man who almost died only a week before. Clean-shaven, the color had returned to his face. More so, his cheeks had filled in. Bare-chested, the dressing had been freshly changed. Wincing, he stepped toward her with effort.

"I did nothing more than I would have done for any poor soul. I can assure you had I known your mission, I might not have been so compassionate. Do not believe I will do so again. Now please excuse me."

"No, one moment. It's Josephine, isn't it?" he said, using her given name. "As I said, I am leaving and will not be back. I can't leave without at least trying. Cullen is a close friend. I can think of few I hold in more esteem than I do him so I won't mince words. Come back with me."

An awkward silence ensued. Still, Jo could not move. She glared at him with a hatred that stemmed from the fear of losing her precious son. She shook her head. "No…no!"

"Listen, please," he begged. "I don't have long, but surely you would want for your children to be safe. I can have you within Philadelphia within the week. You won't have to worry about anything other than your children. Cullen has set…"

"Cullen left me," she cried. "Mother of God! Do not play me for a fool! I know he has eyes on my son. We are not leaving!"

For a swift instant, she feared he would snatch her son and take him by force. Her chest swelled with indignation. "Magnolia Bluff is our home. My husband's legacy to his son, *his* son!" she declared forcibly. "Our fate lies here. It is who we are. I will not betray my husband— ever! Whatever we have to endure, we will, but we will never…ever leave what Wade gave to us…sacrificed for us!"

Andrew drew Percival up and handed him over to Jo. "It was only an offer. I told him it was useless. He only wanted to see Percival," he said in a low, soft voice. "Calm yourself. I will see you and Percival back to the house."

"You are making a mistake," Mitchell intervened, refusing to be ignored. "It is only going to get worse. We might not be able to get you to safety if you change your mind."

With Percival in her arms, Jo walked purposely to the door, turning before she exited. Her voice was strong. "It is you who are mistaken if you believe that I frighten easily. We have already endured much and will endure whatever God has set forth. I certainly don't need charity from a Yankee…any Yankee."

Chapter Six

Without much ado, Lieutenant Cullen Smythe accepted his highly decorated promotion to captain. He gave a brief thought that his father would be proud, but other than that, he cared little for his decorations. His concentration lay on his command, the *Itasca*, and their mission. A consumed man, he lived for battle.

New Orleans had fallen swiftly, but Vicksburg had been a different matter. Heavier fortified and better defended, Vicksburg had only fallen after an extensive siege. Farragut's fleet had supported the ground troops under the authority of General Ulysses S. Grant.

With this victory, the Mississippi River was under Union control. Another thrust in the heart of the Confederacy, cutting the western Confederate army off from the main troops and supplies. *One more victory...one more day until the close of this damn war.*

Rear Admiral Farragut had been recalled to Washington after Vicksburg fell, but Cullen expected him back soon enough. Most of his peers had taken leave when it had been offered and had gone to spend time at their respective homes, but Cullen had chosen only to take shore leave.

New Orleans had become a bitter disappointment. The people had been aggressive and hostile. When General Butler took command, he met their bitterness and resentment with brute force, which served only to infuriate the masses greater.

Then, to make matters worse, General Butler had in essence declared war on the ladies of New Orleans. Driven by the unyielding spirit displayed by the inhabitants, Butler had declared in no uncertain terms that the women of the city were no better than prostitutes and were to be treated accordingly.

Butler's men had taken it as permission to ravage the city. Butler had become known as Beast Butler. Although behind his back, he had, also, earned the nickname Spoons. The general, much to the defamation of the Union army, had a habit of stealing the silverware of the Southern homes in which he stayed. Last December, Butler had been removed from his command, replaced by General Nathaniel Banks.

Cullen supposed it was to be expected when one conquers a proud, stubborn people. If he allowed, the thought that these were his own people would gnaw at his very soul. Cullen had to remind himself of his commander's words. Farragut had declared that in all their actions *we are compelled to do this in defense of our people and the honor of our flag.* He believed in those words and held to them.

The war had become a bloodbath. At times, the reason for the conflict seemed a distant notion of a wrong against another. Now, the reason meant little. The moment they took up arms against one another, there had been no turning back. All that mattered was that the North was victorious at all cost.

Before the war, Cullen remembered the enormous antislavery sentiment in the North, but there had also been a strong anti-Negro attitude. Now, it had become plain that the white Northerners, although against slavery, had no wish to deal with the prospect of what freeing the slaves would mean. The politicians and their constituencies did not want an influx of ex-slaves into their towns and cities.

The North had not anticipated the massive slave escapes and with the flood of black refugees, there had been no plans about how to care for these newfound freedmen. Many escapees found themselves in worse physical conditions than they had known on the plantations.

They were herded into camps and set up in tents with rations in exchange for work. The blacks were put to work in much the way Southern troops used them: building fortifications, digging latrines, and cleaning the camps. Blacks frequently complained that their Union supervisors treated them worse than their former masters and overseers. In truth, many Union soldiers resented having to serve in the war, especially those who were draftees, and they blamed the blacks for their predicament.

No, Cullen reconciled, there would be much to be overcome after this war. First, though, it had to come to an end. The frustrating part was it seemed never-ending. Supplies to the South had to be low and morale had to be even lower. Yet, they fought on.

Like caged animals, the Rebels fought at Vicksburg, yielding only after a stranglehold on the city. After the fall of Vicksburg, Grant had a better understanding of the heart of the South, especially after making two frontal assaults on the city.

Losing heavy casualties, Grant backed off, deciding on a siege to cut off their supplies. The Rebs held out over forty days before they finally surrendered. With the victory came the realization that there would be only one way to end this rebellion. The heart and soul of the South had to be cut out by whatever means available.

Never a day went by without an overwhelming sadness washing through Cullen. Wade's death had cut him deeper than he wanted to admit to anyone, especially himself. His father's letter bothered him more than his father would ever know:

I feel deeply the loss of your cousin. He demonstrated the honor and dignity that they esteem to in the South. I know that his death must weigh heavily upon you. You were close to him and even though the war had come between you both, the loss will be felt greatly. Take heart, my son.

His father understood little of his feelings. The war had changed him. Would Father be proud of his son if he knew his son hated a dead man?

His frustration…aggravation…and concern grew with the last letter from Hugh.

There is much that has happened since the last I wrote. I found I was unable to do so until Gavin had recovered sufficiently. Cullen, he almost died. Claiborne is so headstrong he would not listen to me when I said I wanted Gavin pulled after Heyward left. Claiborne insisted Gavin at least try to see whether he could obtain any vital information before he gave up his cover. Gavin agreed, but was almost killed for his efforts.

It happened when Gavin was walking along King Street after making note of all the information he had collected. He was accosted by a group of ruffians led by one you know well, Buck Haynes.

Gavin had been betrayed by one of his own men. It seems that Buck had been searching for a way back into the militia in Charleston. Buck caught wind of Gavin's mission.

Jonas had introduced Gavin to an old friend, Sterling Lester, who worked down at the docks. He saw the supplies loaded up for the forts and listened to the men talk. Gavin was able to gather exactly what was going in and out…from blockade-runners and the railroad. Unfortunately, as good as the information was that Sterling supplied, he had a fatal flaw—his drinking. It loosened his tongue.

480

Buck got hold of Sterling...by the time Buck was done, Sterling had no tongue. I doubt Sterling held back any information he had. Thank goodness he knew nothing of our operation except for Gavin and Jonas.

When Buck ambushed Gavin, he stabbed Gavin in the struggle. Despite being severely injured, Gavin was able to escape up the river to MB, where by some twist of fate, he was saved by Josephine. She found him along the riverbank where he had swum ashore.

Andrew cared for him, but not before Buck rode up with a Charleston militia. Josephine saved them all by insisting the militia leave before searching the grounds. But I would be misleading you if I did not state she holds little love for anything connected to us Yankees. She has taken Wade's death hard and seems only interested in maintaining his legacy.

I saw her the night I went to retrieve Gavin. Andrew had brought Percival down at Gavin's request. It was good to see the boy. I brought him some soldier figures. It should ease your mind to know that he is growing tall and seems quite happy. I was able to hide outside the window before Josephine burst into the room quite upset, for Andrew had not informed her that he had borrowed her son for a little while.

Gavin used the opportunity to try to talk her into withdrawing back to Philadelphia. She steadfastly refused. But take heart, we are keeping an eye on your son, who, I will state, is a miniature version of yourself.

I have heard of your recent exploits and promotion. Congratulations...

Anger burned inside him. How dare she! Was she not free now? No longer bound by her ring and yet she stayed...refused to leave! Keeping his son within the boundaries where a war raged...with Buck loose to wreak havoc! No, he would take no more. He wrote back clearly and without reservation.

Take Percival out! Take him out now...with or without Josephine!

* * * *

"Momma! Duke loves being home!"

In the crisp November wind, Jo smiled at the sight of her son running around the front lawn. Holding a sleeping Madeline in her arms, she breathed in deeply. It was good to be back at Magnolia Bluff.

She swore if she never set foot in Charleston again, it would be too soon. *Lord have mercy on my soul!* She couldn't have taken much more of the city. The infamous charm and warmth of the inhabitants had been replaced with fear and paranoia.

There was no more festive entertaining. The focus now centered on surviving and helping the cause. Many a day was spent volunteering at the hospital, visiting a neighbor in need or comforting a family who had lost a loved one in this dreadful conflict. A stifling, overwhelming melancholy enveloped the city.

Occasionally, Jo glimpsed the old Charleston when she walked along the Battery with the children, sat on the piazza enjoying the cool ocean air, or attended church at St. Michael's.

There had been moments to celebrate. Shortly after Madeline's first birthday, Jenna delivered a healthy son, Eugene Samuel. Never had Jo seen such joy from Derek and found herself envious of the little family, but reprimanded herself greatly. She realized any happiness snatched during this time should be held to as long as possible, much like this moment... returning to Magnolia Bluff.

Jo shook off the guilt she felt by escaping Charleston. She had become so homesick for the plantation. All the horrible news coming from the battlefields had become wearisome and depressing. She had no desire to ever look at a newspaper again. On the lips of every person she had greeted was one sad story after another.

Moreover, most of the benevolent friends seemed to think that Wade's death was a badge of honor that she should wear proudly. If she was told once more her sacrifice had been needed, she would scream. She had sacrificed enough. She had lost her husband and found herself quite selfish in not wanting to lose more.

Despite the defiance that still ran throughout the city, Jo couldn't deny most felt the South was living on the edge of defeat. The poor souls wanted only to find a semblance of meaning to the price that was being paid for this war. Even in victory, it seemed the South suffered defeat, as was the case at the Battle of Chancellorsville. The city fell into mourning with the loss of General Stonewall Jackson.

Derek had declared that with Stonewall Jackson's death, the South was dealt a severe blow. The man had been a brilliant commander and leader. Afterwards, the news from the war seemed to be followed by one defeat after another, first Gettysburg and then news came that Vicksburg fell.

So many soldiers dying. Death...death...death. It was all around her. She could take no more.

"Master Percival's happy to be back."

Jo glanced over at Rosa, who had walked to her side. "I believe we all are."

"I'm just happy we arrived safe and sound. Ain't safe, I'll tell ya, to be on those roads, Miss Jo. Mark my words," Rosa stated soundly. "Now let me take that little one and put her down in her bed."

"Rosa, don't be overly dramatic. We were quite safe." Jo dismissed her maid's fear and relinquished hold of her precious daughter.

As she watched Rosa disappear into the house, Jo realized Rosa's apprehension came from eavesdropping on the prevalent conversation as of late—debating whether to return or stay in Charleston. Had it not been the same before they went into Charleston? Was there anywhere truly safe?

In truth, there was nowhere else Jo wanted to be and was content with the decision to return. But the last few weeks, the dinner table had been the center of debate about the situation.

Andrew held the concern that the family would be overwhelmed with demands upon their goodwill if they stayed in Charleston.

"It is the neighborly thing to do…to share what we have, but there are too many hands out in Charleston. We can't refuse. It will only cause ill will," Andrew said. "Moreover, I believe we need to be at the plantation. Already we have lost the kitchen building at White Oaks because we have no one living there."

"We would be foolish not to consider the dangers faced at being at Magnolia Bluff. There have been cases of homes being burnt to the ground," Derek argued. "I've heard of Yankee incursions."

"If we stay in Charleston, how are we going to stay self-sufficient?" Andrew countered. "I strongly feel the slaves who have remained want to continue to live at Magnolia Bluff. We have a responsibility to them as well. Furthermore, who's to say that the Yankees won't try to invade Charleston?"

Finally, the decision had been made and they were home! Jo couldn't have been happier.

She watched her son skipping alongside his Uncle Andrew, laughing and giggling. Since the day that Yankee departed, she found a newfound confidence in her brother-in-law. He had protected her and Percival.

Furthermore, Andrew had allowed Percival to become his shadow when he was around. For that, Jo was grateful. Percival needed a man's influence.

This had been the right decision. Jo felt it in her heart. Wade's spirit lived on within the boundaries of Magnolia Bluff. This was where he would have wanted his family. It was where they belonged.

Here the war did not exist.

Jo reflected on the past and drew strength from what Wade had given her—his love. She would hold on to it and live one day at a time, having faith Wade watched over them.

* * * *

Less than a month after their return, Jo made a request for the family to dress formally for dinner. It had been quite a long time since the family entertained. The days and nights had been consumed by the need to maintain the plantation and keep the family healthy and safe.

Surprisingly, her request had been met with unbridled enthusiasm…at least from the women. Anna and Jenna spent the better half of the afternoon readying for the night, much like they would have before the war. Mother Montgomery even promised to play a few pieces on the piano.

For the night, she took off her mourning and donned a flowing lavender taffeta gown with a dropped V-waist, lined with ruffles up the full skirt. Rosa twisted her hair back in what once had been fashionable. She studied herself in the mirror, remembering the last time she had worn it…at the last dinner party she had attended with Wade.

She wiped back welling tears; this was not a time for sadness. She wanted the family to enjoy the evening. Outside, a reddish glow reflected off the scattered clouds as the ball of orange lowered in the sky.

"Momma, you look pretty."

Jo turned to find her young man in the doorway. "I thought I had already put you to bed, my love."

"But I wanna go down with ya."

"Not tonight." Jo took his hand and led him back to his room. Tucking him into bed once more, she promised, "I will tell you all about it in the morning."

When she walked back into her room, she took the letter she received yesterday out of her top drawer. Charlotte had married and wanted Jo to share the news with the family. Charlotte had found comfort with a wounded soldier, George Williams. He owned a general store in Savannah and was the nephew of Aunt Mae on her husband's side. Moreover, to Jo's delight, Charlotte was expecting a baby.

Dearest Jo, I wanted you to share in my happiness, but with the war raging around us, I succumbed to George's desire to marry quickly and quietly. After my first marriage, I was so hesitant to marry again, but George is so different, loving and caring. He is as excited as I am about the baby. I know I should not be talking openly about such a private matter, but it is you, my oldest, most beloved friend.

Jo was certain that Charlotte was apprehensive about how society would take her marriage with the scandal attached to her first union. Perhaps in the past, Charlotte's worries would have been founded, but not today, not when death could lie beyond the bend. No, life needed to be celebrated each day.

Tonight was an opportunity to live just for the moment. There was no yesterday…no tomorrow, only this moment.

As she descended the staircase and into the dining room, Jo was delighted that everyone had followed suit. Mother Montgomery still wore black, but had changed to a white lace collar pinned with a cameo that her three boys had given her for Christmas many a year ago.

Anna sat next to her mother in a shimmering cream gown trimmed in a deep forest green. Jo was certain it must have been Mother Montgomery's at one time. Pearls adorned her neck as pearl droplets hung from her ears. The poor dear hadn't had the opportunity to enjoy dances and parties as had Jenna, not with her poor health and the war. Tonight, though, she shined.

Beaming in her much-worn rose gown, Jenna sat by Derek, who also dressed for the occasion in a borrowed suit that once had been Wade's. Rosa had altered it, shortening the pants and sleeve of the waistcoat. He looked quite dashing.

Jenna had confided that she longed to dance with her husband. He had been self-conscious of his missing arm, but in the confines of the family's eyes, Jenna hoped she would finally get her dance.

The table was set with the china that had been handed down from one generation to the other for a hundred years. Mother Montgomery had taken it out of hiding for the occasion. Crystal goblets were filled with wine. A hog had been slaughtered and fresh ham, potatoes, and dinner rolls filled the table. Not the most elaborate of meals, but never had one been more appreciated.

"You look lovely." Andrew rose and pulled back a chair for her. "Thank you for suggesting this night. It is a much-needed relief. Tell me, though, how long are you going to tease us? What news have you promised to share?"

"I see no reason to delay." Jo glanced over the faces of her family. Unfolding the letter, she began, "I want to say that the last few years

485

have been trying…We all have lost loved ones…those will never be forgotten.

"Saying that, I know that my dearest husband would not want us to mourn forever. I feel Wade is with us now and always. So let us smile tonight." She sniffled, trying desperately not to cry. The emotions weighed heavier on her than she imagined. "Family meant everything to Wade…he loved you all. Family shares in the sorrow, but over the last year, we have had the good also.

"Jenna married and we added a new family member." Jo smiled over at Derek, who raised his glass to her. "We have had children to add to the nursery. Each a blessing…and yesterday I received news from Charlotte she wanted me to share. She has married George—"

"Momma."

Chuckles emerged, for behind Jo, Percival stood dressed in his Sunday clothes. Half buttoned, his shirt hung loosely over his pants. He wore only one shoe, but his hair was gelled backed and combed the best he could to the side.

"Percival, I told you…"

Andrew stepped to Percival's rescue. "I think for tonight we could add a chair for the young man…"

Suddenly, the sound of horse hooves, thudding as swiftly as a frightened rabbit, resonated throughout the room. Everyone's eyes met. Immediately, chairs were pushed back and everyone rushed toward the parlor's front windows.

No news was ever good that was carried that swiftly. Neither was this.

Two riders rode hard onto the lawn. Galloping madly, one drew in the reins just in time to swerve from barreling into the front steps. Laughing, he slid off his mount and stumbled toward the entrance.

"Josephine Buchanan Wright! I've come to settle the score."

God help me! It's Buck! Frightened, Jo stood frozen with Percival clinging to her skirt.

Upon getting no response, Buck leaned down and picked up the biggest rock he could find. He threw it through the window. Glass shattered and screams emerged.

Instinctively, Jo covered Percival with her body. Ignoring Buck's taunts, she inspected her son closely. She could find no marks on him. Picking him up swiftly, she handed him to Mother Montgomery. The men had already stepped outside.

"Take him upstairs," she ordered hurriedly. Not waiting for an answer, Jo rushed out the door and ignored the cries of the women to stop.

She couldn't.

Buck had come for her...she had to get rid of the menace.

"What brings you here?" Jo demanded. Ignoring Andrew's attempt to push her back into the house, she moved forward. "You aren't welcome here. Leave and take your friend with you."

"Paying a call long overdue, dear cousin. I came to see you," Buck slurred and staggered up the steps. Tripping, he grasped hold of his buddy for support.

Jo recognized Buck's companion. One of the boys who hung out with Harry Lee—old man Harrison's boy, Gus. No-good varmint from all accounts, which explained his presence with Buck.

Buck reeked of liquor. His cheeks were reddened. He pointed a filthy finger at Jo. "We have business to discuss. Ain't going until you hear me out."

"I owe you nothing and I can assure you I don't want to hear a thing you have to say."

His head tilted back, his eyebrows rose. He pressed his lips together firmly and shook his head. "Now...now why did I think you would say that?" Holding up his finger for a moment, he reached behind his back and pulled out a pistol. He aimed it straight at Jo. "Now, like I said. Let's talk."

"Put that gun away, for God's sakes, man," Andrew demanded. "There are women and children here."

"Shut up." Buck turned and pointed at him. "Or I will make you shut up."

Derek raised the rifle he had grabbed before he rushed out of the door.

"Put that down, mister," Gus countered, holding his gun straight at the group. "Don't make me use this."

"What is wrong with you, Buck? Have you done gone and lost all your good sense?" Jo rushed forward.

"Ain't me, it's you. Want to know why I'm here...because I got no home. No home because of you! Grandpa Henry passed away last week and you know what I got. Nothing! Nothing.... 'cause it all went to you and all these Montgomerys."

"I didn't even know Grandpa Henry died."

"Don't care neither, by the looks of things. What do you have going on here? A party? And didn't even invite me!" Buck waved the pistol around. "Wonder what your family would say if they knew the truth about ya. Didn't think I would figure it out. Thought you were too smart for me...for all of us."

"Too smart for you? What on earth do you mean?"

"That you are a Yankee sympathizer. Yeah, it all fell into place. You sitting here pretty as you please. I know this is the place that Yankee spy came. Can't fool me. You, Josephine Buchanan Wright Montgomery, are no better than Yankee scum. You have betrayed everyone and I'm gonna make sure everyone knows!"

"You lie! You drunken fool! I would never betray the South...my home...my family."

"I'm done listening to you. It's time for all you to listen to me. Right now it's just me and Gus, but I'm going into Charleston and fetch McCoy. He'll see to things...right after I take what's mine. I need a home and this one will suit me just fine."

"Don't, Buck," Jo pleaded. "Don't do this. Go away. Sober up."

"Nah." Buck shook his head. "Want to show Harry Lee I am man enough. I'll show him when he gets home that I handled things just fine. You should be happy, Jo, 'cause I'm not gonna make you suffer like Harry Lee would. It will be short and quick..."

From the corner of her eye, Jo saw Amos come out of nowhere. He lunged at Gus, sending him sprawling on the ground in one direction, his pistol in the other. A gun blasted and Amos fell.

Clambering down the steps, Jo fell down beside the big man. "You shot him!"

"Ain't nothin' but a God damn nigger. Now get up, Jo! Ya gonna rue the day you took us on. Ain't got Wade to protect ya no more."

"Okay...okay, Buck. There's no need to get upset. You want a room for the night...food. Come on in. We'll take care of you," Andrew said in a soft, calming voice. He edged closer to Buck. "We were about to have dinner."

"I told ya to shut up," Buck snorted, raising the barrel up.

Then, suddenly, Buck paused. To Jo's horror, she saw the reason.

Percival ran out the door. Frantically looking around, he saw her. With outstretched arms, he bolted for her.

Too late, she cried, "Don't. Stay there!"

Buck grabbed hold of Percival by his shirt collar and lifted him off the ground. "Looky what I have here. Who's your daddy, boy?"

"Major Wade...Montgomery," Percival stuttered, confusion and fright riddled in his voice. He called out, "Momma!"

"Don't look at ya momma, boy! She ain't gonna help you now...not now...not ever!"

Buck's eyes grew dark as his hand encircled Percival's neck. Andrew lunged and slammed Buck back. Immediately, Derek snatched up Percival and headed toward the door. Tumbling down the steps, Buck and Andrew landed on the driveway.

Staggering up, Buck gripped tight his pistol. Enraged, he slurred, "Yeah, come on. Let's see what you can do, n—"

A shot rang out. Buck stepped once, then twice and fell face first on the ground. The entire back of his shirt oozed blood left by the shot that killed him.

Smoke curled slowly in the air. Jo lowered the gun. She couldn't breathe, but felt everyone's eyes upon her. Behind her, she heard a horse race down the lane. For a timeless moment, she stood there, unable to move.

Andrew crawled over to the motionless body and confirmed, "He's dead."

Befuddled, her mind painstakingly comprehended her actions. She had done the only thing she could to protect her son. She had killed a man...snatched up the fallen gun off the ground and fired at Buck...shot him in the back.

"Jo, let go. Percival is safe." Andrew untangled her fingers from the handle. "Rosa, come over and take Miss Josephine up to her room."

Somewhere in the distance, she heard Percival scream for her. The girls' voices...shrill, frightened voices...resonated around her.

Walking into the foyer, she saw her son crying against his grandmother. Hurried steps ran to her. Her eyes once more shone with a flash of clarity. She bent down and took her son in her arms.

She squeezed Percival tightly. When she glanced back through the open door, revulsion filled her as rage and fright melted away. Dazed, she felt Rosa's hand on her shoulder and followed Rosa up the stairs.

* * * *

It was a ghastly night. Percival cried and clung to her like a small frightened animal. He clutched her tightly and buried his head into her bosom. She spent the night rocking him and soothing his fears as her own grew.

Her small, brave little man. She tried to lay him down, but the moment his head touched the pillow, his eyes opened and his arms reached out for her. So, she held him throughout the night.

At every movement, every sound, her body was on alert. There was no rest for any. Mother Montgomery cared for Madeline and came in several times to check in on Josephine.

Rosa sat with her, unmoving on the chair in the back corner. She said nothing, but her presence calmed Jo.

At one point, Andrew came into the room. "Are either you or Percival harmed?"

She shook her head. "Amos?"

"He's resting. The bullet went through his shoulder. I believe he will recover. Derek and I are going out. We will be back in the morning."

Jo understood. They were disposing of Buck's body. *Oh, whatever am I going to do!* This was an awful mess! The lies Buck told last night disturbed her mightily, but the greater concern lay with Buck's drunken friend.

Gus had scrambled back to his horse and galloped away the moment Buck fell dead on the ground. He could be anywhere by now. What if he told the authorities she had shot Buck in the back? Would she be arrested for murder?

Six o'clock. The grandfather clock chimed and announced morning had arrived. Finally, she had been able to lay her sleeping son in her bed and change into her mourning black clothes. Straightening out her skirt, she watched Rosa ease back within the room.

"Miss Jo," Rosa whispered. "Dr. Andrew wants to see you in the garden. Don't ca worry. I won't leave Master Percival."

With the greatest reluctance, Jo stepped toward the door. Glancing back, she saw Rosa drag the hardback chair to the bedside. She took a deep breath in and looked around the room.

As it rose over the horizon, the morning sun gave light to the darkness. Through the window, Magnolia Bluff was awakening. The dew on the grass reflected off the sunbeams, illuminating peace and calm.

How beautiful and untouched it all seemed. Her hand held to the handle for a moment more before she exited the room she had shared with Wade...had loved...had given birth. So many memories.

She walked out.

Andrew waited at the foot of the stairs. Covered in mud and dirt, he looked exhausted. He handed her a cloak. "Come," he said. "Let's walk."

She made no protest and followed him out into the garden.

The path Andrew took led down to the dock and through a line of large live Virginia oaks. Jo noticed his limp seemed more prominent. What seemed forever, they walked. Finally, he paused.

Jo swore she saw tears well in his eyes, but he quickly rubbed his tired eyes and suppressed the emotion. As he looked back up at her, fear gripped her. Something was wrong...bad wrong.

He sighed heavily. "I wanted to talk so no one would hear us. There is so much I want to say...have to say."

"I'm sorry, Andrew. I know the predicament I have placed the family in with my actions. I couldn't...I couldn't let him..."

Andrew shook his head and reached over, gently taking her hand in his. "There is no need, Jo. I wish only it had been from my hand. You did what you had to do to protect your son. Make no mistake, Buck would have killed Percival, you, and any other who got in his way."

Releasing her hand, he stepped back and stared at her with a faraway, melancholy look. "I never told you about the day Wade called for me to treat Gillie. It was..." He paused, struggling to control his composure. "Horrific. Never have I seen someone who had been tortured so. The things...it is not necessary for you to know what happened, but that they did. Such a beautiful life. To have endured the pain...the humiliation. It solidified my stance on slavery."

"I have always known you have been sympathetic to the slaves' plight. It is why our slaves..."

"No, Jo!" he said, violently. "You don't. You don't know me at all. I have hated slavery and everything it stood for long before the war. It ate at my conscience. Oh, I listened to all the propaganda. But unlike Wade, who despite his misgivings, followed the call his state made upon him, I could not. Wade, like those who remain now, do so only by their sense of honor, not wanting to disgrace our country or family. He gave his life for all he believed in and none of that was slavery. Despite his heroic actions, his toil and suffering has been for naught."

His words scared her. Confused, her mind ran rampant, for it seemed he was confessing the sins of his soul to her. Her nerves shaken, she asked, "What are you saying, Andrew?"

Above her, birds twittered; the wind rustled through the leaves. Andrew stood deadly still.

"For what I am about to utter, you will hate me." His voice carried clearly and articulate. "I'm not asking for forgiveness, only understanding—one day. I told you when this whole dreadful business started that I lived only to redeem myself. I had much to atone for, Josephine, so much. Know, I love my family and all I have done I've done for them."

Jo trembled. Comprehension began to sink into her. For a long moment, she could only stare in disbelief and then abruptly recoiled. Her

491

hand clamped over her mouth, her eyes widened in disbelief. "You...you have been helping the Yankees!"

"I have done what I've had to do to protect the family. I'm a doctor who has pledged to uphold life and it is that pledge I have kept for everyone, Jo. Both sides." He lowered his gaze and looked down at his hands. "Believe me or not, I love my home and my family above all else. Grandfather called me a coward...said I had no backbone and had disgraced the family, but I believe with my actions, I have saved Magnolia Bluff and the family."

Jo slapped him, hard, and uttered in complete disgust, "You betrayed Wade and all he stood for."

His hand went to his cheek. "No, Jo," he snapped. "I've protected you and the children. They have become as my own. I did what I must to protect those I love, but it was not I who set this network up. Do you not know that Cullen wanted Percival out of here at the beginning of the conflict? Who do you think stood between him? Even now, I was prepared to stand again against them."

Color drained from her face at the mention of Cullen. Her heart faltered. "Why? What is going on?"

"An order came down to remove Percival. No matter anymore of my stance or whether or not you were willing to go with him."

"Dear God," she whispered. Her knees began to quiver. "No...no."

He rushed to her and took her hands in his once more. "Listen, quickly. I had to send word to Beaufort last night. I tell you all this because you have to go. All of you. After last night, I realized that there are things I can't protect you from. Harry Lee...what happens if Harry Lee returns?"

Her chest heaved; she couldn't breathe. *All the words he was saying.* Her body went cold.

"Jo, there is no other way. I wish it had been me who shot the bastard, but what if McCoy gets wind of what has happened? He would like nothing better than to throw you in jail, no matter if Buck deserved it or not. Too many people saw—the slaves, his friend."

"I would hang?"

"He would have difficulty proving murder without a body. We can always say that he left on his own accord...cast doubt on the way he died. Fell in the river, drunk. But they will never prove you shot him. Derek and I made certain Buck's body would never be found. Already, there is animosity growing around us, for we are faring better than most. You can't tell the Yankees the real reason I'm sending you at this time.

Even they can't know what has occurred. It is better to have all be buried with Buck."

"Sending me? Oh, Good Lord, what have you done?"

"They are here and are waiting. You won't be going back to Magnolia Bluff. I told them you discovered our scheme. They can't afford to keep you here."

"No." Her voice shook. Glancing around frantically for a way out, she saw shadows in the trees walk out toward them. "I won't go. I won't leave. I'll never leave my home. I won't betray Wade."

Andrew gestured and the two came forward. Jo rushed at Andrew and gripped tightly to his coat. "Don't do this. I will hate you forever for your betrayal."

His eyes broke from hers. "One day," he said. "One day you will understand. I do this to protect you and the children. After all this madness, you can return. You will have a home to return to and we will be here waiting."

"My children…my children!"

"They are going with you. Rosa has already taken them down to the appointed place."

It was the last she heard. She felt strong hands grip her arms. Her vision blurred through her tears. Someone said, "If you scream or make any noise, we will bind your mouth. If you fight us, we will tie you up and carry you."

She obeyed.

She had no choice…no choice at all.

Jo's only hope was the promise that her children would be with her.

Chapter Seven

"Momma…Momma," Percival cried. "We're on a ship…on the water!" Excitement rang in his small voice.

Jo felt none of it…she was petrified. The moment she stepped aboard the vessel, she realized it was a warship. Mortified by the stares of the sailors…their snickers…she followed her escort in silence. Poor Madeline clung to her as if her little life depended upon it, while Percival thought it a grand adventure.

Percival rambled on about each thing that caught his eye. Jo nodded in an effort to pacify him while she tried to comfort his crying sister, whose tiny fingers had dug into Jo's arm. All the strange faces and noises frightened Madeline.

Two weeks had passed…two long weeks. She had been taken down to Beaufort. As promised, the children were at her side. Never had she traveled in such discomfort.

First they were literally pushed into a closed carriage that provided a jarring ride along a bumpy road. At dark, they were transferred to a boat that sent them to the Union occupied town.

She had no answers to their fate, no news about Magnolia Bluff, no communication from Andrew. Nothing. A Captain Claiborne met with her, but he dismissed her readily enough when she refused to talk.

Isolated from town, the days passed in an overseer's house on one of the abandoned plantations. Their welfare and comfort had been seen to with Rosa packing a wicker valise for each of them. The children were allowed to play outside and along the shoreline. The only restriction was that they were not allowed to interact with the inhabitants of the town. It had been a quiet existence until soldiers came in the wee hours of the morning.

In an unusual chilly December wind, Josephine and the children were transported to a waiting ship. Once aboard, she was escorted to a small cabin, where she sat in wait.

The weather had cooled considerably. Assuming they were traveling north, she worried. She had no coats, gloves, or boots for the children. Suddenly, panic consumed her when Jo realized she had nothing except the clothes on her back.

A knock on the door startled her. As she moved to open it, Percival pushed a chair over to pull himself up to look out the porthole. Madeline screamed, afraid her mother was about to put her down.

The door opened. A tall, handsome officer stepped into the cabin, followed by a cabin boy dragging a trunk. A Navy man. Jo recognized the uniform. Moreover, the man seemed familiar. His blue eyes held a warmth; his smile, kindness.

Glancing over his shoulder, the officer saw Percival kick his chair out from under him. Immediately, he walked over and grasped hold of the little boy, who clung precariously to the porthole with his fingers as his feet dangled in the air. Percival squealed in delight as he was flung over the officer's head, touched the ceiling and then placed safely back on the floor.

Percival looked up at the man and asked, "Did you bring me more men to play with?"

"More men?" Jo asked in a failing voice. "Oh, no…you were there…"

"Yes, Mrs. Montgomery," the officer answered, taking his hat off and tucking it under his arm. "Lieutenant Hugh McFadden. You may not remember but we have met before in Philadelphia."

"Cullen." She stared at him, remembering.

"Yes, Cullen has been a trusted friend for many years," Hugh said. "I want to apologize for the inconvenience of withdrawing you from your home, but let me assure you, it was a necessity."

Grabbing Percival by his hand, Jo took a step back. "That is what I've been told."

He gave her a faint smile and opened the trunk's lid. "In here are some articles I thought you might have use for...women's and children's clothes. I know you weren't allowed time to pack."

With Madeline balanced on her hip, Jo quickly glanced over the contents. A pretty blue organdie, a pink taffeta, slippers, petticoats…from the look of them, everything was new. She looked up at him. "Where did you get these?"

"I didn't steal them from any defenseless Southern lady, if that is your inference," Hugh answered. "You will have need of them. I have another trunk with warm clothing for you and the children as well. Boots, gloves, mittens. I won't go into all the details, but I'm to escort you to Washington."

Jo shot him a suspicious glare. Abruptly, she questioned, "What is going to happen to us?"

"I'm to escort you to my commander in Washington. From there, they will be able to tell you exactly what is planned, but I would not worry. Your family in Philadelphia has been notified. I would expect that Mr. Jonathan Smythe will be in Washington to greet you."

Her eyes widened. "No...no! He will take Percival from me!"

Immediately, Percival ran in front of her and held out his hands, as if protecting her from the lieutenant. "Don't make my momma cry. I haf to protect her..."

Lieutenant McFadden knelt down on one knee. "No one is going to harm any of you. I give you my word."

"But you're a Yankee!" Percival spat the word at him as if it was the most dreadful thing in the world to be.

"Yes, I am, but I am a man of my word. I'll tell you what I will do. After I talk to your momma, I will take you on a tour of the ship. Would you like that?"

Percival looked pleadingly at his mother. Exasperated, Jo agreed, "If you are good. Now, let me talk. Sit on the bed and play with Madeline."

Hugh waited until the children were settled. "No one will separate you."

"Don't lie to me." Jo made an effort to keep her voice low. "What else am I supposed to think? I'm dragged from my home...taken against my will. Do you not know I have realized that Cullen has wanted to take Percival from me for a long time? That is his intention."

"I'm certain it will be an adjustment, Mrs. Montgomery, but no one wants to pull a child away from his mother," Hugh repeated. Lowering his gaze, and then looking back up at her, he went on. "I do have to emphasize that you can't say a word about the scheme you uncovered. It has been a secret known only to a few. There will be serious consequences for the ones left behind if it is revealed. Harm could befall your family. Magnolia Bluff burned. I would advise you not to say a word to anyone unless I tell you it's safe. Not even the commander of this ship knows the real purpose of our mission."

"Your mission?" Anger resurfaced...rage at Andrew's betrayal burned. "Your mission be damned."

"I don't expect you to understand—"

"I don't want excuses. I want to go home, Lieutenant McFadden. I want to take my children—"

"That's impossible," he stated firmly. "It will be better for you to accept things as they are. You and your children are safe and will be well looked after. Cullen will—"

Jo laughed, almost hysterically. "Cullen?" she cried. "He will take my child and where will I be? Tell me, Lieutenant McFadden. What is to become of Madeline and myself?"

"Cullen has well looked after his—"

"His son? Percival is not his son!" she hissed. Had she not been so scared, so nervous, she would have collapsed at the assertion, but now she did not have the luxury to worry about her reputation. "Percival is Wade's son. Cullen lost all claim when he left me. Can you not understand that he hates me? I do. I understand it well. He will be happy only when I'm destroyed and taking my child will do so. Please, Lieutenant, I beg you...don't let him."

"You are exhausted. Rest. I assure you that everything will work out. No one is going to take a child from his mother..."

"Don't lie to me. Andrew told me you were sent to take him!"

"Calm down," he replied, annoyed at the reference. "I would have never done such a thing unless absolutely necessary." Hugh sighed heavily. "This conversation is done. All I can tell you is, don't be concerned. Your welfare will be seen to. At this time, you have no other option but to sit back."

"What do you mean?" Jo countered, completely confused.

"It is with the greatest reluctance, I am to inform you that you are being held as a prisoner of war. I would surmise that an agreement will be made for your release when we get to Washington. Until then, there is nothing more to be done."

His words silenced her. She only managed a nod when Percival took the lieutenant's hand and walked out the door with him. Her knees buckled and she sat back on the bed. Madeline crawled to her side. Jo hugged her daughter tightly.

She whispered, "Prisoner?"

* * * *

The city of Washington frightened Jo. Not at all what she had imagined, the city reeked with a rank, foul stench. Moreover, she was once more alone with her children.

Lieutenant McFadden had departed the ship the morning they docked. She had not seen him since.

497

Without warning that night, she and the children had been escorted by a platoon of Union soldiers from the ship to this house…this room. A platoon…truly a platoon to escort her! What did they expect—for her to make a run for it with two children on her hip?

In the darkness, she had been taken in an old rickety carriage to this house on a crowded street. The house was in need of much repair. The paint was peeling off the building; the bottom step was broken. When she walked into the foyer, she paused in an effort to get her bearings of her new surroundings.

Her immediate thought was that the house needed a good cleaning. One of the guards pushed her from behind. Jerking her head back, Jo shot the soldier a hard look.

"Upstairs," he uttered roughly.

Grabbing Percival's hand, she held tight to Madeline in her other arm and climbed the stairs. A door opened and they were herded into this room. Comprehension dawned on her. She wasn't to live in the house, only this room—it was her prison cell.

The lock clicked. Releasing Percival's hand, she raced to the door. It was locked. Looking around, the room contained little. A bed, a small chest, and a writing desk. A couple of hours later, the trunks were delivered.

Jo had never been more thankful. The room was cold. There was no fireplace and the temperature outside was frigid. Bundling the children up in their clothing, the three of them huddled on the bed.

Days passed and the room grew smaller, especially with a rambunctious three-year-old. Percival couldn't understand where the life he had known before had gone: the lawn, his dog, the stables…his room. Everything he had known and loved, except his mother and baby sister, had disappeared.

For a time, he had been distracted, first with the house in Beaufort and then the ship. Now reality seeped into his world. Moreover, Jo worried about Madeline. Her darling daughter had become even quieter than normal.

She needed to talk with Lieutenant McFadden. Even being forcibly taken from her home in the manner she had been, she had not suspected she would have been treated in this manner and…the children! It broke her heart.

Food had been scarce. Adequate water had been supplied to wash, but the children needed baths…she needed a bath, but not in this freezing room. She had long forgotten how it felt to be warm. Moreover, their clothes had disappeared. Having given clothes to the guards to be washed, none had been returned.

"Momma, I'm hungry. I want to leave."

Percival pulled at her skirt. Jo wanted nothing more than to cry, but she couldn't succumb to the desperation of their situation. She leaned down to her son to give him the only comfort she could. He smelled. *Oh, Lord, he had soiled his clothes again.* Once more, Jo changed her son.

He screamed, being exposed to the cold and the freezing water. "Momma, don't! I can't button 'em. They're too small!"

"Please, Percival, you don't have a choice. There is nothing else."

Frustration overwhelmed her. The pants and shirt had been supplied by one of the guards. They were the last clean clothes Percival had. Madeline wasn't in much better shape.

Crying Madeline climbed down from the bed and clung to Jo's leg. Then Percival started to cry. Jo's stomach growled in response to the stress. Food had been aplenty at Magnolia Bluff compared to the rations she had received over the last five days. She had given most to Percival and Madeline.

Percival had readily displayed his temper numerous times. Jo had given up on the thought of controlling his temper as he fell on the floor, kicking and screaming and wanting to know why he couldn't eat, run, and where was everyone.

Truth be told, Jo wanted to do the same.

As she picked up Madeline, fear swept through her. Her daughter felt warm. *Oh, Lord above, no! Madeline had a fever!* Laying her daughter on the bed, Jo rushed to the door and pounded on the door, over and over again until her fist swelled. Abruptly, it opened and Lieutenant McFadden walked into the room.

"Lieutenant," Jo began. "Have you come to take us away? The children...they need attention. I fear Madeline..." Then suddenly tears ran down her cheeks. "Madeline has a fever. We haven't eaten...and are ever so cold."

McFadden shut the door and frowned. He went into his coat pocket and pulled out treats for Percival and Madeline. Percival screamed with delight and for the moment was content. Madeline held it in her little hand.

Shaking his head, he had the look of wanting to say something.

"This isn't what you envisioned? Surely, Cullen could not want this. Percival..." Jo choked back her tears. "You are going to take us away from this dreadful place...please, for the sake of the children..."

His eyes said otherwise before she heard his words. "Josephine, I'm so sorry...this has been a horrible fiasco. The war department is quite disorganized. I fear you have gotten lost in the paperwork. Unfortunately, my hands are tied." Glancing around the room, he went on, "These are totally unacceptable conditions."

Madeline began to cry once more. Jo picked her up, but even her mother's arms wouldn't comfort her. Jo turned to him with pleading eyes. "There must be something you can do. Madeline is sick...sick! They aren't feeding us. You..." Her voice rose higher to a fevered pitch. "You sent us here to die."

"No, no. This was never supposed to happen," he insisted. Pressing his lips together, he hesitated. "I need you to give me the children. They are coming for you. You are being taken to a military court to be charged formally."

A wave of despair swept through Jo. She felt as if her voice was paralyzed, but she managed to utter, "But I have done nothing."

"It is not what you have done, but what you know. I'm not deserting you, Josephine..." He dispensed with formalities. "We don't have much time."

She gave him a wrathful look, disbelieving the words she heard. Suddenly, her legs weakened and with Madeline in her arms, Jo collapsed to the floor. Immediately, Madeline screamed; Percival ran and hugged her. His small hands pushed back her disheveled, dirty hair, trying desperately to get hold of his distressed mother's attention.

"They are taking you to Old Capitol Prison. There's absolutely nothing I can do to prevent them. They are in all probability coming at this moment. But Cullen's father is downstairs, waiting in a carriage with Cullen's sister, Elizabeth. They came as soon as they heard. Mr. Smythe came for Percival, but insisted on Madeline as well. Prison is no place for children. I'm sorry. I can't begin..."

For a moment, she digested it all in silence. She held her hand up. "Stop, please. I don't want to hear it. Cullen...where is he?"

"At the moment, he is on assignment in the Gulf of Mexico."

Jo nodded. She was given no more time as the door flung open. Her gaze focused on Jonathan Smythe. He had changed little, dressed immaculately. Hat in hand, his eyes met hers.

He said nothing, for he caught sight of Percival. Immediately, his face softened. He had no need to say the words out loud; she saw it in his eyes.

"They are on their way upstairs. We don't have any more time." Jonathan's voice faded, as if apologetic for what he was about to do.

Jo drew in a deep breath and did as she always had and always would.

* * * *

Josephine straightened her gown the best she could before the soldiers arrived. The moment they entered with their weapons drawn, she was glad her children were no longer with her. She ignored the soldiers as long as she could. Through the dirty windowpane, she watched the carriage fade down the street. Her heart withered.

Voices carried around her. Someone jerked her to face the man barking the orders. She said nothing but stared blankly out in space. One of the soldiers reached down and grabbed her arm roughly. She jerked it back and slapped him.

He caught her hand. His eyes widened. "Looky, looky! Whatca' got here!"

Her wedding ring...the emeralds...glittered in the light.

He reached for it. The ring slid off her shrunken finger.

Jo grabbed for it.

He expounded a god-awful laugh.

Struggling to regain her ring back against his brute strength, Jo reached up to his face and dug her nails into it, clawing down across his eyes.

The Yankee slapped her hard across her face.

She fell down and hit the corner of the dresser.

He kicked her with his heavy boots. He jerked her up by her hair. The taunts began. "Southern whore. Hussy."

Defiantly, Josephine Montgomery raised her chin and held her head high. She would not cry and give them the satisfaction. Never! The Yankee scum! She wanted nothing more than to claw all their eyes out, but she hadn't the strength. She hurt so badly...her babies were gone.

****

Cloaked in darkness, Josephine was transported to the Old Capitol Prison. Originally a tavern had stood upon the ground, along with a hotel. The prime location on First and A Street led Congress to build a temporary brick capitol after the British had burned down the old one during the War of 1812. Before the outbreak of the present conflict, the building had been converted into a private school, and then a boarding house.

The huge rectangular, three-story building sat intimidating to all who walked by, but inflicted fear into Jo's heart. Her legs swayed upon her entrance into a long corridor.

501

"Take the wench back to the side, Louie. Ya know where the prostitutes go," the guard at the door yelled.

"Calm down, Sammy. Ever seen the lot of us escort a whore? Commander Graham sent us. Got ourselves a Southern bitch!"

The voice faded as the door opened at the end of the corridor. An older officer emerged and gestured for the guards to bring her to him.

"Mrs. Montgomery, I'm Superintendent Wood. I have been instructed to place you within a cell and I must apologize…" His voice trailed off. He reached over and moved her face from one side to the other. His cheeks reddened and shook his head. Snapping his fingers at one of the sentries behind him, he ordered, "Miller, get her some decent clothes, water, and food. She looks as though the wind would blow her away. She is supposed to be in court in the morning. Who did this?"

Not privy to the heated exchange, Jo fell in step behind the sentry. Two others followed her. The cell was on the second floor. No sooner than the prisoners perceived her, than she heard obnoxious calls from men with Southern drawls coming from the cells she passed.

Their words were no better than the Yankees', using the same coarse, vulgar expressions. She didn't even know the meanings of some of the words, but there was no denying the implication they held, the vilest slang as if she was within a brothel.

At the end of the hall, Jo was placed in solitary confinement. She would learn later that her room lay in a unit with three other rooms that housed Confederate officers. The prison was filled to capacity.

The young sentry gave her a sympathetic look. "Don't worry none, Mrs. Montgomery. I can't imagine they would hold you long. Don't have many women here. Ya haven't done nothing bad, have ya? From the look of you, can't imagine you have. I'll be back shortly."

He closed the door and everything became black, blacker than night.

Her life had become a never-ending nightmare.

****

The morning came. Then two more days passed without word of what was transpiring. Jo had been able to wash and change her clothes, but she had no mirror to check on her appearance. Though, she could feel the huge bump on her cheek had lessened.

Superintendent Wood informed her that her hearing would be this afternoon. *No matter what happens, I will be strong and face this challenge as Wade did.*

She had found little comfort in the quiet of her room. The small, quaint four walls at least kept her safe from the other prisoners. Superintendent Wood had allowed a brief note from Lieutenant

McFadden stating Madeline was well. Her fever had broken. The children would be in Philadelphia before Christmas.

Christmas! Jo had forgotten about the holiday completely. It mattered little. She took heart that her children were safe for the time being.

Her cell held a tiny window. If she pushed the stool across the room, she could look out. It overlooked A Street and a view of the people of Washington, including the vulgar Yankee troops that moved back and forth along through the road. They had caught sight of her. Their behavior left her no choice but to withdraw from the window and its view.

Jo waited with trepidation, not knowing what awaited her. She told herself that her nightmare would soon end. She had done nothing, but her confidence faded the moment the knock came to signal the time had come. The thick door opened to expose the soldiers sent to escort her for her trial.

In silence, she was transported by carriage to a military building two blocks over. She made no protest but followed the guards to a small room. In front of her there was one large desk that faced two smaller ones. She was guided to the desk on the left. To her surprise, an officer sat at the table. Immediately, he rose at her appearance.

A man of average height, he straightened his uniform jacket while he pulled back a chair for her. He had fair hair and a pleasant smile, but his eyes were marred by dark circles. "I'm Lieutenant Joel Boyd. I will be serving as your lawyer at these proceedings." He grimaced. "What have they done to you?" He reached for her.

She recoiled slightly. A sudden desire to weep encompassed her but Jo held her emotions.

He took her elbow. "Don't be afraid of me, Mrs. Montgomery. I'm here to help you. My anger is not directed at you, but anyone who would treat a lady in this manner. I need to know exactly what has happened. Obviously, you have been beaten."

Jo lowered her eyes. She wanted nothing from this man or anyone in a navy uniform. She didn't answer his question. She asked only, "My children?"

"Lieutenant Hugh McFadden informed me they are quite happy and have been transported to Philadelphia to be cared for by your family there. You have no worries concerning them, but I am certain they miss their mother. Lieutenant McFadden will be in attendance this afternoon, which, in my opinion, will not take long."

"They will let me go." Jo's voice faltered, hoping against all hope.

"That is my belief." He tilted his head to the side to get a better look at her face. "Do you have any idea of the charges against you or what you face?"

She shook her head. She eased down into the chair as she gripped tightly to the table's edge. "I only know I was forcibly taken from my home."

"I have been told you are being charged with aiding and abetment of the South," he said simply.

Confused, she asked, "Spying?"

"We will see what is their stance soon enough." He paused and glanced over his shoulder. Under his breath, Jo heard, "How the hell did Malcolm get in here?"

Jo turned and saw a man with a pad and pen in hand. *The press was covering her proceedings?* She looked back at Lieutenant Boyd.

In a moment of perplexity and confusion, she watched Lieutenant McFadden enter and take a seat behind her. She turned her gaze from him as a highly decorated officer entered from another door, followed by two other officers. He sat behind the large desk in front of her.

"General Gideon Benson," Lieutenant Boyd whispered. "He is in charge of the hearing."

General Benson quickly dismissed the reporter. "You will not come snooping into my hearing."

The dismissal did little to alleviate a new fear Jo developed—that her name would be plastered on the headlines to further humiliate and disgrace her and the name she carried.

General Benson was an older gentleman with a head full of white hair. His hands, wrinkled and dried from the days that had come before, held papers that he read over quickly. He grimaced. "So, Lieutenant Boyd what do we have here?"

Jo's shoulders straightened and her head tilted higher. She would hold to her dignity, if nothing else.

Lieutenant Boyd stood, taking an aggressive stance. "It is quite provoking to have one treated in the manner Mrs. Montgomery has obviously been treated. Taken from her home and her children. To what end does all this serve? She has done nothing wrong and we have treated her appallingly. To imprison a female in this manner is abominable."

"Lieutenant, sit down. I will say what is proper," General Benson exclaimed. He turned his attention to the one across the aisle from her, the prosecutor, a pompous arrogant sort. "Captain Johnson, you and I both know that she is not a spy. That charge is dropped."

Captain Johnson stood. Not exceedingly good-looking, he was middle-aged with a pot belly and long pointed nose. Jo could feel his eyes burn into her. Then, the craven-hearted heathen pointed to her. "Do not be fooled by her appearance. The only defense she has is the sympathy card. Secretary Stanton himself has expressed concern about the situation in a letter you hold. According to the war act, we can hold her indefinitely because it is vital we do so for the betterment of the Union."

Jo felt rage swell within her. Did he not realize that at any time over the last few days she could have given the information to numerous Confederate officers? She had more access to them in prison than she would ever on the street.

No matter whether they prided themselves that the rules were adhered to within the prison walls, the simple truth was that information passed freely. She had already been asked numerous times why she was confined. She had, as she had with the Union, given no answer. She had not even told them her name.

From the moment Andrew had sent her with McFadden, the life she had known was over. The quandary of the situation lay with the fact that if the information became common knowledge, she understood the consequences.

Jo was certain that Andrew would be executed if he wasn't able to escape, but it wouldn't only affect him, but the entire family, everyone...Jenna, Derek, Anna, Charlotte, and Mother Montgomery...even Grace Ann.

The shame and dishonor would lie on the heads of all of them. The most important truth— Wade would have died in vain. Above all else, she could never allow anything to take away from his sacrifice.

Magnolia Bluff would be no more. Pillaged and burned to the ground would be its fate. No, Cullen had put in place a well-covered operation to help the Yankee cause and now she would pay the price.

Arguing and bickering ensued between the lawyers. Jo's head hurt as she tried to follow the conversations. She wondered whether her reputation would be in shreds even if she walked out the door free of all charges. On one side, her family and the entire city of Charleston would know she had knowledge beneficial to the South and withheld it. On the other, the Yankees seemed intent to use her to advance their careers and enact revenge. She had been reduced to being used as a pawn.

"Mrs. Montgomery? Mrs. Montgomery?" General Benson called to her. "Lieutenant, see to the defendant."

Jo felt Lieutenant Boyd's hand on her shoulder. She jerked away and cried, "I hear you clearly."

"Good, for I want you to understand fully what lies in front of you," General Benson stated plainly. "I find the whole of this situation despicable." His eyes lay upon the captain. "I wish I had within me the power to throw you within a prison cell, Captain Johnson. To think we have been reduced to that, to imprison a lady without just cause!"

"Sir, there is cause. She has knowledge that…"

"I know why we are here, Captain Johnson. I'm also aware she has done nothing to cause herself to endure this fate. I question what this war has done to us all."

Jo's heart leaped with hope. *Was he going to let her go?*

"Stand up, Mrs. Montgomery."

Slowly, Jo eased upward, with Lieutenant Boyd standing beside her.

General Benson began, "I find this situation a trying one. Any other time, I would happily dismiss it, but it's not within my power. I'm afraid my hands are tied. Captain Johnson is correct that they can hold you indefinitely given the state of war we are now in. Unfortunately, due to the sensitive nature of your knowledge, I see no other recourse but to sentence you back to your holding cell until it is deemed safe to let you go."

"General Benson, I protest!"

"Sit down, Lieutenant Boyd!" General Benson demanded. "Mrs. Montgomery, you are to be held in your cell, but with the stipulation that your comforts will be seen to. You will be able to write to any you choose, knowing your letters will be read before they are sent. I can also assure you that whoever is responsible for your injuries will be dealt with properly. Where are her children?"

"They are being well cared for by family in Philadelphia."

Jo heard nothing else. She didn't even look toward Lieutenant McFadden as she was led away.

Back within the confines of her cell, the conditions improved. She was given books and embroidering to pass the time; paper and pen to write letters. Jo took comfort with the weekly letter from Cullen's father, who wrote about the children.

She sat alone in her cell. She hurt, so terribly, and was so utterly alone…so alone.

Chapter Eight

August, 1864
Mobile Bay

"Captain! It's going right at the *Hartford!*"

Turning quickly, Cullen surmised the signal quartermaster's assessment was correct. Through the thick, acrid smoke, the dreaded ironclad ram, the CSS *Tennessee*, emerged. The determined Southern vessel was surviving the constant duress on its assault toward the Union flagship, flying the Rear Admiral Farragut's blue pennant.

On the deck of the USS *Itasca*, the fighting sailors ran furiously to load and reload the guns. Their efforts were made harder from the barrage of fire from the forts and enemy ships. Clanks of the slings and relieving tackles resounded on the deck. The smoke was so dense, visibility was only a matter of yards. Nevertheless, the shadow of the CSS *Tennessee* loomed closer.

The Union fleet had taken a beating. Already Cullen had witnessed the unbelievable sight of the sinking of the USS *Tecumseh.* It had crashed into one of the dreaded torpedoes planted in the harbor while chasing after the formidable CSS *Tennessee*. After the explosion, confusion followed. The crew watched the inconceivable—the USS *Tecumseh* standing on her bow straight down in the water. Less than a minute after her stern raised high in the air, she disappeared into the sea. For a moment, all eyes gazed on the sight, knowing they, too, could share a similar fate.

Rear Admiral Farragut gave no one a chance to contemplate the loss. He swept the USS *Hartford* through the waters, right into the Bay.

Taking the lead, the commander's call rang out: *"Damn the torpedoes. Full speed ahead!"*

Cullen swore under his breath, knowing the waters were filled with torpedoes. Holding to the faith he held in Farragut, Cullen directed his ship to follow. With a glance over his shoulder, he saw that none of the fleet had faltered...staying the course. Through the barrage of shelling, smoke, and haze, he caught sight of the flag that flew above him, waving proudly...standing firm.

Suddenly, the question of why he had chosen the path he had...holding to the Union...was answered as he watched the stars and stripes flying. There was power in the red, white, and blue. He felt it radiate through him. He fought for the country he loved. His heart filled with faith in his cause and that his purpose was just.

Through the chaos and confusion, the CSS *Tennessee* reached the USS *Hartford*. Cullen screamed orders. Water sprayed over him from the constant bombardment. A pulley broke off and swung down. Cullen barely ducked in time.

"Straight ahead, Mr. Decker."

"Aye, sir!"

Cullen pushed his vessel alongside the CSS *Tennessee*'s stern. "Fire in succession and fire low!"

The eleven-inch guns were no more than ten to fifty yards from their objective. Alongside the USS *Chickasaw,* the guns fired again and again. Smoke rose from the battle explosions of dozens of cannons firing rapidly with devastating accuracy.

Through the smoke, a white flag emerged over the once mighty CSS *Tennessee*. Her stack was completely shot off; the steering chains destroyed. The battle was over in Mobile Bay.

* * * *

Captain Cullen Smythe stood on the main deck. The ship would dock soon enough. He would be in Washington before nightfall. Exhausted, he drank in the salt air. This he would miss—the feel of the sea beneath him. His three-month leave would begin the moment he set foot on dry land, but his intention to resign had already been made.

He had done his service to the country. He had a medal of honor to prove it for his part in the Battle of New Orleans. Moreover, Rear Admiral D.G. Farragut had given his blessing before Cullen's departure.

"Go home. We have done all we can do now. You have served with distinction," Farragut dismissed him.

Under Farragut's command, Cullen had served with the Western Blockade. Two long, hard years, but they had been successful. First with the blockade of New Orleans, then Vicksburg, and now with the victory at Mobile. The South could not stand much longer.

Over the course of the war, he had seen changes in the navy. Although the Confederates would go down in defeat—of that Cullen was certain—their ideas, engineering of their ships would be duplicated with the Union fleet. Gone were the days of the glory of the wooden ships. Ironclads had shown their military value.

Mobile Bay had long been in Farragut's sight and with the appointment of Ulysses S. Grant as Supreme Army commander, Farragut got his wish. Grant prepared to take the heart out of the South. Already, Sherman began his march toward Atlanta.

Cullen had served as a man possessed. Farragut had respected Cullen's fearless approach, courage, and bravery. Cullen's commander hadn't cared why...why Cullen had thrown caution to the wind or that Cullen fought like he had nothing to lose.

No one knew Cullen had tried desperately to get Josephine out of his head...and his heart. Over time, his heart had hardened; he hated Josephine as intensely as he once loved her. She had kept his son from him, denied him his right to claim him openly...and refused to leave Wade for him.

For the last eight months, Cullen had known Percival was safe with his grandfather. It had relieved his mind, especially now that the South was feeling the wrath of the Union. Less than a month had passed since he had gotten word of all that had transpired at Jo's trial. He hadn't gone into much detail with Farragut, but he had told him he needed to return to deal with a family issue.

On the last day of August, 1864, Cullen's eyes soaked in the sight before him— Washington. He had only a few issues to take care of at the state department and then he was headed to Philadelphia, his attention solely on his son.

* * * *

"What has happened to you, Cullen?"

Cullen shrugged as he poured himself a drink. "Would you like another? I find that I might indulge this evening. Tomorrow I go and see my son."

Hugh had met him down at the docks. In high spirits, Hugh had immediately taken Cullen to his quarters in Washington at a boarding house. He had been lucky to find an apartment with the shortage of housing in the city.

"You heartless son of a bitch! I have waited quite impatiently for your return. I have done everything you requested and now you are going

509

to walk away from her. Have you any idea…?" Hugh struggled to find his words.

Cullen had never seen Hugh so angry, but it mattered little to him. He gulped down his whiskey and poured another. "I have an idea that my son had been kept from me. She can rot in prison for all I care."

Shocked, Hugh's hands closed on the chair in front of him and thrust it to the side. He fumed. "You put her there!"

"If she wants to become a martyr, it is not my problem. I'm sure there is a place in Heaven for her. Some women are callous, cold-blooded creatures. Those you know how to deal with. It is the ones such as Josephine that you have to be leery of…she holds to her goodness and honor. She reels you into her web. She is the worst kind of woman."

Color rushed to Hugh's face. "You can stand there with a clear conscience…you who put her in this position to begin with! I took her to protect your damn scheme! To protect your home from destruction! To protect your family in the South. What if she talks? All will be for nothing!"

Cullen laughed. "If she was going to say a word, it would have already been plastered in every Southern paper. I know her. She won't say a damn word to protect the same home and same family honor. She doesn't want anyone to think she would betray the South. All is for her own gain, I assure you."

"Oh, yes," Hugh sarcastically spouted off. "She has plans of glory. She had it all planned out. She planned for you to use a system of spies on her plantation and to be discovered. She planned to be arrested to keep her silent. You do realize that Percival and Madeline were with her when she was taken into custody. I suppose you didn't hear that they nearly starved and froze to death when they first arrived in Washington.

"To keep prying eyes from her, she was placed under guard at a secret location…even from me! The war department was in such chaos they lost her paperwork for days before I found them. She gave her food to the children. She had no heat. Yes, she sat in her glory in a filthy six-by-ten room with two small hungry children. When I finally found her, Madeline was sick with a fever. So to further her newfound glory, she gave up her precious children to your father.

"She was transferred to the Old Capitol Prison…prison, Cullen! For over eight months, she has held to the little dignity that is afforded her in her cell. She has been beaten and the one thing she held dear to her they stole from her. Go, visit her, Cullen, and tell me that she has done all for herself. You God damn imbecile!"

Cullen sat the glass down, but his hand gripped it tightly. "What do you mean she was beaten and starved? Who would treat a lady in that manner?"

"The guards, you fool!" Hugh's cold eyes fixed on Cullen. "They thought her the enemy. The sergeant in charge of the unit stole her wedding ring before she was transferred. She fought for it. She was beat up for her efforts. They delayed her court appearance because of her black eye and bruises, but they were apparent even days later. Do you have any idea what she has been thrust into? Do you care?"

"Did they...?"

"Rape her?" Hugh answered for him. "No. Now Superintendent Wood has been put in charge of her care. She is in solitary because she isn't allowed to talk to anyone. Cullen, you didn't see what they did to her and the children. The baby is not quite two and she has been ripped from her mother's arms for over eight months because of me, because of Andrew, and because of you. Your son has not had his mother!"

Cullen scowled. "War is hell, Hugh. It is for everyone."

"But not by me. I have fought honorably. I know only that she saved Mitchell. I know that I'm the one who took her from her home when she pleaded for me to let her stay. She told me she wouldn't say anything, but do you know what was in the back of my mind? Do you want to know, Cullen?" Hugh snapped.

Staring at his outraged friend, Cullen made no reply and shook his head in denial.

"I thought I was doing you a favor." He laughed a cynical laugh. "I realized I couldn't take a chance on leaving her, but I thought all would end well. I thought you two could reunite now that she is free. She told me that you hated her. I didn't believe her. I made a huge mistake, but this I promise you, Cullen. If you don't make this right, I will."

* * * *

When Captain Cullen Smythe started his morning, the sky had been cloudless. When he stepped outside after his meeting in the late afternoon, gray clouds covered the sun. The wind smelled of rain. He hoped he would accomplish his intention before it descended.

He had expected this morning would have gone quicker. A sudden impatience bothered him. Secretary Welles had been quite thorough in his briefing. Cullen learned the use of Magnolia Bluff had been invaluable, that had been a certainty.

Josephine was another matter.

"I don't like locking up innocent people, but we didn't have much of a choice. In this situation, Captain, I feared that she would say something that would endanger the mission. We both know the consequences if that happened."

"Magnolia Bluff is safe from looting and burning from the Union forces as agreed?"

"Yes, Captain. It has been arranged that Dr. Montgomery will post a sign saying the plantation is being used as a hospital for typhoid fever when we make our presence known. It should divert attention away from seemingly preferential treatment from us damn Yankees."

"Secretary, I realize the issues Josephine presents, but I have serious concerns about keeping a mother from her children. Moreover, do not forget she saved Mitchell, reluctantly, but she saved him nonetheless. She is a lady whose only crime is being loyal to her home. I would like her immediate release."

"I would love to do so, but I can't simply dismiss the concerns surrounding the issue at hand or I would have already done so. She has to concede to silence."

"I believe I can take care of your objection, Secretary."

"Then be quick about it, Captain. Tell me—what is your solution?"

****

The agreement about Josephine's release had been made. Now, Cullen had only to convince Josephine. Hugh had offered to come with him, but this was something he had to do on his own.

In front of the Old Capitol Prison, Cullen exited the carriage and straightened his coat. "Wait," he instructed the coachman, handing him a token. "I shouldn't be long."

"Yes, Captain."

Cullen reached into his coat pocket and pulled the papers out as he walked up the front steps of the sprawling multistoried building. An ill-fitted uniformed sentry opened the door for him.

"I have come to speak with Superintendent Wood." Cullen glanced around. He had heard the horrors of prison life during the war and given what most prisoners of war were enduring, this wasn't the worst by far. But still—the thought of Josephine being housed in this place...

"This way, Captain," the sentry with pocked-mark skin called to him. Cullen followed across the creaking old floor. From an open door on the left, a voice barked, "In here, Captain Smythe."

"Come in, come in. Superintendent Wood." He extended his hand to Cullen. "I only just received word of your coming. I have to say I'm happy she is being released. It has put a lot upon me to keep her as I had been ordered..." His voice faded as he glanced up at Cullen's sullen face.

512

Wood breathed in deeply and accepted Josephine's release papers. "You brought the necessary orders. Good." He studied them only for a moment and pulled out a ledger. "Sign here and I'll have you escorted upstairs to retrieve the prisoner."

Cullen nodded. The quicker the better. He followed a sergeant up the stairs. The drafty, creaking building smelled, a mixture of sorts, disinfectant and foul odor... Heaven knew what else. On the second floor landing, a curt guard sat on a stool outside a room.

"Arty," the sergeant called out. "She's going home. Open up."

The guard knocked loudly on the door. He put his hand out. "Give her a minute. Always have to. It ain't proper."

Cullen wanted to push the door in. He didn't have time for this. Finally, the guard slipped a key in the lock and swung the door back. He entered.

A wave of guilt surged through Cullen. The cell was small with only a chair, a few books on the floor, and a slop jar to the far left. The unwashed window had no blinds or shades, but his eyes fixed on the small cot. A slight figure sat with her knees pulled into her. Her head lifted as he moved toward her. Her eyes widened.

By God, what had they done to the beautiful woman he had left behind! Her face was so thin. Her eyes had never seemed so large, but it was also the eyes that bothered him most. There was no light in them. "Josephine," he uttered.

"Captain, she don't talk," the guard offered. "In her sleep, sometimes she calls out for her babies."

Slowly, Cullen walked over to her.

Josephine recoiled from his grasp.

He reached over and pulled her to her feet. "I'm taking you out of here."

She shook her head. "I'm not giving in. I will never." No sooner had Jo uttered the words, her legs buckled. She swayed and then fainted.

Cullen picked her up. She was as light as a feather. He wasn't going to waste time in this hellhole. He said nothing to anyone else and no one dared to counter his intent. He carried her out of the prison.

* * * *

Washington was a crowded city: government officials, officials from foreign embassies, soldiers—lots and lots of soldiers—and the families of those men inhabited the capital. Cullen felt fortunate to have obtained a suite at the Carrington Hotel.

The carriage began to slow. He looked over at the unconscious Josephine, who fidgeted and grimaced as if in pain. Her eyes flittered, and then opened wide. She stared at him in silence, but did not seem surprised. He supposed she had expected him to show up eventually.

Suddenly at a loss for words, he said, "We are at the hotel."

Only then did she show her anxiety, nervously patting her dirty hair…her dress. "I can't go in the front door," she whispered. "Not like this."

"I'm sorry. We don't have a choice." He gave her no indication that a wave of sympathy swept through him. Her dress was somewhat clean, considering she had been sitting in a prison cell. But the smell of the place lingered on her. Her hair seemed plastered on her head in an unflattering manner. "No one will take notice. I will call for a bath immediately." Instantly, he regretted the words.

She glanced at him as if he had slapped her across the face.

What was he supposed to say? He sighed impatiently as the carriage door opened. After he descended the steps, he offered Jo his hand.

Cullen watched her call upon all her poise and dignity, bravely tilting her head back. He gave her his arm, but he had been wrong when he had told her no one would notice. Eyes fell upon Josephine in question. He patted her hand as he could hear whispers that joined the stares.

The desk clerk moved in such a manner as to intercept Cullen.

Thankfully, Hugh appeared at the counter at that precise moment. His arms filled with packages and a bouquet of flowers. "Don't go there, good man. A room has already been procured for the lady, who has endured much these last few months. You don't want to cause any problem with us, I assure you. You can send the manager, though. We do have a few requests," Hugh cautioned the desk clerk and smiled over at Josephine. "You don't know how good it is to see you. As you can tell, I have spent the morning accumulating necessities I felt you might need."

Hugh leaned over to Cullen. "We have two reporters looking for a story in the lobby. You need to get her upstairs as quickly as possible." Hugh gave Cullen the necessary time to scuttle Josephine to the stairs, and then he paused the manager who had appeared. "Now, I believe the lady will require a bath and quite a large meal. We will be celebrating. It is a good day."

The manager looked confused but Hugh had handed him a few bills. Glancing down at his palm, a large grin formed. "I will see to everything."

Upstairs, Cullen opened the door to the suite, keeping the door open long enough for Hugh to enter. Hugh hustled in, ignoring Cullen. He flung the packages down on the sofa, except for the bouquet of flowers, yellow roses.

"I know you have missed your flowers." Hugh spoke to Josephine as if he had known her all his life.

Her eyes softened upon the sight and accepted them. Her head bent down and took in a deep breath. The fragrance seemed to invigorate her. "Thank you."

Cullen stood to the side. Why the hell did it bother him so that Hugh had brought her flowers? Why the hell couldn't he act as Hugh? To make her believe she was as she was before they threw her into that hellhole. He watched as his irritation grew.

* * * *

Night had fallen. Hugh had long left, as had the doctor who Cullen had called. Biting off the end of the cigar, Cullen took a deep breath and lit it. Blowing out smoke, he stared out the window at the lights of Washington.

Again he waited.

Tomorrow…tomorrow his father was arriving with his son.

Was she sleeping, he wondered. The doctor had recommended an extended rest. "Physically, she should recover with rest and food."

"What is that supposed to mean?"

"It means she needs her children. That was all she kept saying."

Deep in thought, he didn't hear the door open behind him.

"Cullen?"

He turned. For a moment, he was taken back in time. Her raven hair, washed and combed out, hung down below her waist; her face soft in the night light. She had changed to a fresh nightgown that Hugh had bought for her. Another shortcoming he had failed in.

The white nightgown silhouetted her figure underneath. He couldn't take his eyes off her. God, he was in bad shape, for he wanted her. He must be a sick man.

He pulled the cigar out of his mouth. "Yes," he said curtly. "The doctor left something if you couldn't sleep."

She shook her head as she moved across the room. "We haven't talked…" She hesitated. "I know how you feel." She shook her head at him before he could deny anything. "Don't. I really don't feel like debating or arguing. My one concern is my children. I need to know what you plan to do about Percival."

"You aren't wasting time denying he's mine now?"

Her eyes met his. "Don't go there. Wade is his father. He gave him his name, an honorable name. Don't take that away to hurt me."

"He's mine," Cullen replied forcibly. "Do you know how I feel being denied that fact? Do you know what it feels like to have a child and not be able to acknowledge him?"

"I have had a long time to think." She sat down on the sofa. Her eyes locked on his. "What did you want me to do? Tell me? What could I have done differently to alleviate your pride, your hurt, your pain?" Her look prompted a blunt reply.

"You should have come with me. If not immediately, I would have come back for you."

Her eyes flared, the first response he had seen from her.

"How dare you? How dare you?" she repeated, fuming. The room fell into silence, deadly silence. Finally, she questioned, "Have you not thought once about how I felt? What do you think I felt when I was told I had to marry Wade? What did you do to stop it? You told me...promised me everything would be fine. You held me in your arms and told me you loved me. I held to that hope until it was almost too late. I did the only thing I could have done, but once it was done, I could not go back. If you thought differently, you never knew me."

Cullen shot her a stabbing look and countered, "I never wanted you to marry Wade. Do you think I gave a damn about Magnolia Bluff? I cared only about you. I wanted only you."

"Then you had time to take me away, Cullen, before you went to rescue Gillie. You had time..." Her voice faded. Her face fell into her hands.

For a long moment, Jo hid her face. Then she shook her head. "This will get us nowhere. If you don't understand I did it all for my child, for his honor...to be able to live with my conscience, there is nothing I can do to convince you now. I realized when Wade told me you were set to kidnap Percival from me how much you hated me. Now, my question to you is what is going to happen to Percival?"

The room seemed to tilt and blur. Anger burned in Cullen, but at the moment he didn't know whether it was at the woman in front of him or himself. He said soundly, "He will be with me."

Pressing her lips together, she sat back as pain swept across her face. "I realize that I am in no position to ask. I am homeless and have nothing but my love for my child. In truth, I don't know how I'm to keep Madeline and myself. I can't go back to Magnolia Bluff. I doubt I will ever be able to return after everything that has occurred. I have racked my brain, Cullen, trying to desperately come up with a semblance of a plan.

"I was hoping that maybe you could find it in your heart to find me a place of employment. I was thinking perhaps a housekeeper. I love to teach but I doubt I could find work as such in the North. If I could just be close to him…please don't take him from me."

Cullen frowned. "I don't believe finding you employment will be feasible. I was going to wait until in the morning, but you realize that there were conditions to your release. You don't think you simply walked out?"

As soon as the words came out of his mouth, he watched the whole of her body tense. He walked closer to her. She shrank back into the sofa, pulling her feet up to her much like he had seen her in the morning.

Jo shook her head. "No, please don't send me back. Cullen, please." She began to rock. "I haven't done anything. Please, let me see my children. I only want to see my children. I can't go on…"

What was wrong with her? He gripped her shoulders and pulled her up to him.

Her hands clutched his loosened shirt. "Please." Her eyes looked frantically at him. "Don't do this. I can't take more. I have lost everything except my children."

Suddenly, she withdrew. "Is that what you want? You want me destroyed. You want me dead!" Jo fell on her knees. Her mind wandered. She began to ramble. "Oh, my God! Madeline. Who will look after her? My baby. Will Percival know…?"

Bending down, Cullen pulled her back up to him. Hysterical, she kept shaking her head, mumbling incoherent words, not listening to a word he said in an attempt to calm her. Restraint lost, he shouted, "Shut up! Shut up!" He drew back his hand and caught himself only a moment before he would have struck her.

Shocked, her eyes widened in fear…fear of him.

God in Heaven! What had he almost done? He had come so close to hitting her…physically hurting her. The next moment, he pulled her to him.

Josephine pushed back with everything she had, but he was stronger.

She broke into sobs.

Cullen let her cry.

****

Cullen held her, his shirt damp from her tears. He had lost his sense of time…he didn't care. It had been so long since he had held her in his arms. How many nights on board ship had he dreamed of her? No matter what he had vehemently denied—he did love her.

517

It was himself who he hated.

He hated he hadn't taken her away the first night they landed in Charleston. He hated he hadn't given her an option when he had gone back for her. He hated to admit that damn honor and duty that she held to so fervently, he had also.

He had left her, not she him.

For the first time, he admitted to himself his own shortcomings. Was it his own jealousy that drove him? That she had chosen to make a life for herself and her child?

Or was it that Wade accepted Percival as his own?

Wade…oh, dear Lord…he was jealous of his cousin. Cullen thought he knew Wade so well. But to react the way Wade had and become the man he had died, there had to be only one reason: his love for Josephine.

The thought plagued Cullen—did Josephine return that love?

His own father had written of what a fine boy Percival was. His father knew; from his letter he readily understood.

I find I'm dealing with another young man as was his father, stubborn and with the distinct habit of never being wrong, but I find I have had experience with such a young man before and have used it to my advantage. He is bright, intelligent, and has a love for the sea, he tells me, but he is extremely worried about his mother. He has more than once explained to me that he is the man of the house and needs to protect his mother and Madeline. Madeline, now, is thriving. The first couple of weeks were difficult, given the fact we thought we might lose her. She refused to eat, but Elizabeth has formed quite the attachment to the little lady, and eventually the baby returned that love. Monica adores her also; she's quite a beautiful toddler. With all that has happened over the last few years, I have to say I have enjoyed the diversion. The house is alive again. The gloom that had descended down upon us over the last few years looks as though it's lifting.

Cullen felt Jo's hands push back against him as she tried to sit up. Gently, he pressed her back down to his chest. "Don't. Not yet." His voice was low and soft. "You're not going back to prison ever. I gave them my word that you would not reveal what is going on at Magnolia Bluff. That was enough for them to release you."

"Why would they allow such, Cullen? Why would they take your word for me?"

"Because, as your husband, I could speak for you," he said bluntly. "Father and Percival will be here in the morning. We will be married tomorrow afternoon."

"Oh," she whispered and then silence. They sat in the darkness. Neither said a word. Then she said softly, "You can't. My reputation must be in shreds with everything that has happened. I can neither go back home nor stay here without whispers and stares. I know Philadelphia…"

"Hush, Josephine. Stop. I know of everything that has happened. It's *my* fault. Moreover, I'm not going to throw the mother of my child in the streets."

He paused. Could he tell her he should have married her so many years ago? He should have taken her off the plantation after Wade died. That it was his biggest regret. But he said nothing.

Tears flowed freely against his chest. She whispered, "If this is what you want, Cullen. I will have my children?"

"Of course."

She wiped her eyes. "Could we go back to Rosemount? The children would love to go to the countryside and it's such a beautiful place."

Cullen's heart faltered with her remembrance of Rosemount. "I'm still in the Navy, Josephine. I don't know if I have time to take you there yet. The war shouldn't last much longer and I do plan to resign after my furlough. Give me some time to settle my affairs."

Josephine inhaled a steadying breath. "Of course," she said simply…dispassionately. "I understand." She turned away. "I believe I will retire."

As he watched her walk back into her room and shut her door, he said nothing else. Cullen stared at the empty space where she had stood and then he lit back up his cigar. His eyes focused on the glowing tip of the cigar.

Jo had always been full of fire and life, but being in prison had certainly diminished both. And he knew he was to blame. Could she…would she…ever forgive him?

* * * *

Cullen rose early in the morning to take care of a few errands before his father arrived. He had left Josephine a note explaining he would be back shortly. Thankfully, he had been able to get everything accomplished quicker than he first thought.

Walking down the corridor to his room, he reached in his pocket for his key. Suddenly, the door swung open and Josephine bolted out.

519

Startled at his presence, she recoiled, but then recognition lit in her eyes. Smiling broadly, she cried, "They are here! I've been waiting at the window. They are here!"

"Whoa!" He laughed and caught her by her waist. *By God, she looked beautiful smiling...happy.* "They will come upstairs. You will miss them if you go down."

"I hadn't thought of that." She stepped back into the room. Biting her lower lip, her face dropped with a sudden worry. "Do you think Percival will be mad with me or forgotten me?"

Cullen stared at her. Her confidence had all but disappeared. He reached over and touched her face tenderly. "He will be as happy to see you as you him."

Tears welled in her eyes, but the smile returned when down the corridor a call came out.

"Momma!"

Cullen kept his hand upon Jo's shoulder as not to have the reunion in the middle of the hall. But nothing could stop the patter of small feet running as fast as he could into the room. Cullen stepped back as the young lad ran in with his arms outreached. Jo clung to her son, hugging him tightly.

A strange nervousness gripped Cullen. He hadn't seen his son since the day he was born. He couldn't get a clear view. Percival's face was hidden against Jo's shoulder. All he saw was a headful of dark, thick hair after Percival's hat fell off.

Glancing over at the door, Cullen watched his father walk in, smiling brightly. When he extended his hand to his father, his father shook his head and pulled him into an embrace.

"It's been too long, son. Too long," Jonathan said. "Done us proud. Mother has told everyone about your medal of honor."

"It's good to see you, too, sir," Cullen acknowledged. "Thank you for bringing Percival. Jo has been upset being separated from the children."

Josephine drew her son back to get a good look at him. "You have grown a foot." She choked back her tears. "I can't even imagine how much your sister has changed since I've last seen her..." Her voice faded; tears flowed.

"Don't cry, Momma," Percival said, quite straightforward. "I'm here. I will protect you like I've protected Maddy. Isn't that right, Grandfather?"

Cullen caught Josephine's eyes widened on the utterance. His father's face colored a dark shade of red with an apology on his lips for allowing Percival to call him by that name, but it was the young man himself who had Cullen speechless. If there was any doubt of his parentage, it vanished upon the glance. It was like looking into a mirror. Percival had his nose, his chin…his eyes.

Percival stopped suddenly as he caught sight of Cullen in his naval uniform. Instinctively, Percival stepped back into his mother's arms, as if he was protecting her from him. Josephine smiled softly at her son…their son.

Her head tilted to the side, pointing to Cullen. "Percival, do you know who this is?"

Percival shook his head, but leaned against her. His small hands cupped her face so she could look only at him. "He's a Yankee."

"Yes, darling, but you remember when I said there were good Yankees, like Lieutenant McFadden and all the sailors on board the *Sovereign*?"

He nodded but his eyes were fixed on Cullen. He looked back at his mother.

"He's your daddy's cousin from Philadelphia. You remember when I told you the stories of the uncle you were named after? How he and your daddy got into lots of mischief? You remember I told you they had their cousin with them? It was Cullen. Remember I told you how your daddy saved me before we married and his cousin helped him? It was Cullen. He was there the day you were born. And now, Percival, this afternoon, he is to become your father."

Josephine stood with her hand on her son's shoulder. She slightly pushed him toward Cullen.

Percival jerked back rebelliously. Then he stepped forward himself. He eyed Cullen from head to toe. "Do you command a ship?"

Cullen knelt down, feeling his heart in his throat. He nodded. "I did. Now though, I feel it's time to concentrate on my family."

"You fought my daddy?"

"In the war, we were on different sides, but soon the war will be over. Then we all will be on the same side again and be a united country."

Percival glanced back at his mother, who nodded to him. He extended his small hand to Cullen. "It is nice to meet you, sir."

* * * *

In the late afternoon, Cullen exchanged vows with Josephine in a church that he had searched out that morning. Percival was there alongside the man who had already proclaimed himself to be his grandfather. Hugh stood as Cullen's best man. His father had brought the ring he had requested, a simple gold band, but it had been his grandmother's. When the preacher pronounced them husband and wife, Cullen leaned down and kissed his bride's cheek. It was done. She was a free woman and he had his son.

* * * *

A week had passed quickly. Soon Cullen would return to Philadelphia. He couldn't remember a more pleasant time. Percival had been constantly by his side and seemed quite impressed that his new father commanded a ship, even an enemy ship.

Cullen understood the necessity that dictated that he could never openly proclaim that Percival was truly his son, but he wouldn't contradict anyone who assumed he was. He took pride in the fact most assumed Percival was his as they walked around the shipyard. Percival was a handsome lad, if he said so himself, and quite intelligent, too much so at times.

Cullen took Percival aboard the *Pailulda*, the battleship he had returned on from his tour of duty. Percival climbed up high on the railing in a position Cullen was certain his mother would never approve. Cullen wrapped his arm about Percival's waist and looked out over the harbor.

"I like ships," Percival announced. "You like them too."

"I have all my life. My father commanded ships."

Percival looked up at him with inquisitive eyes. "Are you my real father?"

Taken back by the question, Cullen answered with a question. "Why do you ask that?"

"Ya' promise not to tell Momma?"

"If I do not need to tell her, I won't."

Percival lowered his gaze for a moment, and then looked back up at Cullen. "When they thought I was sleeping, I hear' 'em. Auntie Elizabe' said just look at the boy. He has to be Cullen's son. You're Cullen, aren't ya?"

Cullen nodded his head slowly.

Percival asked again. "Are ya? Are ya my real father?"

"I married your mother. So, yes, I'm your real father," Cullen said. "I knew your daddy very well. We were like brothers. He was a great man who was brave and courageous and did what many men would not do. I owe him greatly…a debt I can never repay."

Percival looked up at Cullen. "Can I call you Father?"

"I would like that."

"I don't think Momma would care," Percival said in deep thought. "Momma cries when anyone mentions Daddy…except when that mean man came. He talked about Daddy and scared Momma."

"Mean man? What mean man?"

Percival fidgeted. "It doesn't matter anymore. Momma said I was safe. The mean man wanted to hurt me, but Momma shot him."

Shot him? What did Percival mean? Josephine shot a man? Who? Cullen picked Percival up and placed him on the deck. Kneeling down, he pressed gently, "I need to know what happened, Percival. Do you remember his name?"

"He was so mad at Momma…he grabbed me," Percival said. "Momma said no Buck no…he hurt me…then Momma shot him." He shrugged. "He died."

"Your momma…what did she do then?"

"We left home. Momma said we had to…then Lieutenant McFadden took Maddy and me on his ship with Momma."

"I'm glad the lieutenant brought you to me," Cullen told his son. "Your momma is right. You are safe now. All of you are safe. I will make sure of that."

Percival smiled and reached up to take his new father's hand. Cullen returned his smile, but if Percival had spoken the truth, there was more going on with Josephine than he first imagined. He would deal with it soon enough. At the moment, he had his son with him…safe away from the dangers at Magnolia Bluff.

* * * *

Windows open, Cullen sat around the table in the hotel suite with his father and Hugh, cigars and drinks in hand. Tomorrow, he would return to Philadelphia with his bride and son. Josephine and Percival had already retired for the night.

"I will have to return to Washington periodically to be kept informed on Magnolia Bluff. With the fall of Atlanta, Sherman will soon begin his sweep across Georgia. I want to ensure that Magnolia Bluff does not meet the same fate as what is in store for those in his path."

"So it is official, you have resigned your commission?" Jonathan asked.

"I'm done. Farragut accepted my resignation." Cullen let smoke trail in a circle above his head. "I want to thank both of you for all you have done. I can't begin to tell you how—"

"Then don't." Hugh clasped Cullen's shoulder. "Don't like blubbering idiots when they drink too much and are too damn happy."

"Well, you're going to have to listen to me once more saying that I'm indebted to you," Cullen exclaimed. "If not for you, Hugh, I'm certain that the scheme would have backfired. It still could. We still need to tread carefully, especially now with Andrew supplying the information we are seeking."

"It is a brave thing Andrew is doing. Taking over where Mitchell left off. He is bearing a lot on his shoulders."

"Andrew knows the risks, Mr. Smythe," Hugh said. "He believes that the war needs to end and that the South will not win. What he does, he does because he knows it is the right thing to do. His conscience weighs heavily on him."

"I know the guilt he feels. It rages within me as well. When the war is finally over, it will take a lifetime for the wounds to heal...if at all," Cullen acknowledged.

"If there is guilt to be felt, it should be with the South's poor leadership that got them in this mess to begin with," Jonathan stated firmly. "And their damnable pride. So many lost over what should have never happened."

"I doubt many Southerners will hold that sentiment." Cullen tapped ash from his cigar. "Speaking of Andrew, you said that he has said nothing to you about Buck or a possible shooting."

"No. He only mentioned Buck when he talked of Gavin's stabbing," Hugh insisted. "Andrew told me that he would be keeping an eye on Buck. That he was dangerous, but nothing more. I will look into it further. I am to return to Beaufort at the end of the week."

"There is also Harry Lee. I need to find out where he is at, also. He could present an even larger problem if there is any truth to Percival's story."

"Why, though, would Josephine not tell anyone?" Jonathan shook his head.

"I will try to get the information out of Josephine when the time is right. I'm not sure she is in any condition to be pressed at the moment. One minute she is fine, the next weeping."

"Give her time, son. She has been through a great deal. When I had lunch with her yesterday, she was concerned whether she would get to see Madeline on our return. Why would she question whether she would see her child as though you are holding it over her head?"

"That is what I was saying. She has unreasonable fears...The first night, she thought I wanted her dead!"

Hugh frowned. "I would believe it would be expected. She was in a solitary prison cell for over eight months. Even though other women sympathetic to the Southern cause have been incarcerated at the Old Capitol Prison, such as Rose Greenhow and Belle Boyd, those women chose to walk in the prison yard when given the opportunity. I heard Belle Boyd flaunted herself. Josephine withdrew. She couldn't even go to the window after hearing God knows what shouted at her from the street.

"When I visited her, she was always on the cot, rocking back and forth. Her mind had to be affected. She is a proud woman. She needs time to regain her dignity."

Cullen ran his fingers through his hands. "I don't need to be told," he said. "I hold enough guilt within me."

"Hopefully in time," Jonathan said, turning the conversation back to the war.

Cullen stared at the closed bedroom door. He hoped so.

Chapter Nine

Josephine had woken this morning in such high hopes. Today, she was traveling by train to Philadelphia. More importantly, by evening she would be reunited with her daughter. Oh, how she had missed her baby! Since the moment she had handed Madeline over to Cullen's father, there had been a void in her heart.

She had worried so about her little girl. She hadn't wanted to give her daughter to Mr. Smythe, but at the time, she hadn't a choice…Madeline had a fever. She couldn't have kept her. Jo shuddered to think what would have happened if Madeline had stayed with her. No, she had made the right decision, but it had hurt…the last eight months had been so painful.

The joy she felt slowly dissipated over the journey. Across from her, Percival slept in Cullen's lap. Her young son had left her side to be by Cullen. It was absurd to hold it against Cullen that Percival had taken to him so readily. The child had never had Wade around…the damn war.

She felt like weeping. What was wrong with her? She should be happy she was no longer in that horrible prison. The children were safe and…seemingly quite happy. Why then did it feel like a black cloud descended on her?

No, Jo silently promised herself. This day she would be happy…she would have both of her children back in her arms. Madeline was hers and no one else's. There had been a bond between mother and daughter since the moment Madeline was born.

She refused to contemplate what Cullen had planned. There had been a time when she would have had her heart's desire to be his wife, but not like this. He married her for only one reason, Percival, and she married him why? Because she didn't have another option.

In all, the marriage was nothing more than a sham. He hadn't come near her since they exchanged vows, said nary a word. She pressed her lips together in thought. She had to accept what was given her…she had to be close to Percival and keep Madeline.

Josephine looked up to find Cullen staring at her. She broke from his gaze and stared out the window until the train slowed at their station.

****

Jo's frayed nerves could not take much more. She had spent so much time thinking of her children. She had forgotten her in-laws, Cullen's stepmother and sister. Monica Smythe had been kind to her on her last visit to Philadelphia, but much had happened since that time…moreover the fact that Elizabeth's best friend had been Kathleen. The closer the carriage came to Cullen's home, the greater her anxiety mounted.

She could only imagine what Cullen's family must think of her! She had not had one correspondence from either Cullen's stepmother or sister during her imprisonment. The only letters she received from anyone had been from Jonathan Smythe.

The carriage pulled to a stop. If not for Percival's excitement, Jo would have panicked.

"I want you to see my room, Momma," Percival cried, reaching for his mother's hand.

"Patience, my boy," Cullen said sternly. "I want to reiterate with you our conversation. You remember what I told you."

Percival pouted. "Not even for tonight? Momma will be lonely."

"Your mother will be fine," Cullen said. "Big boys sleep by themselves. Go now. I'm certain your mother is eager to see your sister."

Jo stared intently at Cullen. How dare he tell her son he could not sleep in her bed! Percival had slept in her bed while they had been in Washington! Cullen had not even discussed his decision with her.

Cullen met her stare. "It is best not to start a habit that will be harder to break later on. He doesn't need to be babied any longer."

A protest lay on her lips, but Percival pulled at her hand. "Come on, Momma."

She could not help but smile at his eagerness and walked into the grand home holding his hand. Jo expected her daughter to greet her, but Madeline was nowhere to be seen.

Monica Smythe greeted the travelers. She had changed little since the last time Jo laid eyes on her. The woman looked exquisite. She wore a dark green gown buttoned up to the collar, which was adorned by a cameo. Her skirt was hooped but dainty, not flaring out as had once been the fashion. Emerald earrings dangled from her ears. Her hair was pulled back fashionably in a net.

Cullen made his way to her side and kissed her gently on each cheek. She embraced him readily enough.

"It is good to have you home, Cullen. You have been sorely missed." Tears welled in her eyes. "You must tell us all your adventures."

Jonathan walked over and took his wife's arm. "Monica, you must not forget our son has a wife now."

"Of course, I have not forgotten." Monica turned to face Jo. The warmth in her voice faded to a still coolness. "Josephine, it has been awhile."

Awkwardly, Jo stood in the middle of the marbled foyer. Forcing a smile, Jo said, "It is nice to see you once more, Mrs. Smythe. You have my heartfelt thanks for the kindness you have extended to my children."

Monica raked her eyes over Jo. "Percival has been a dear and of course, we were not going to let that poor darling, Madeline, go homeless," she said haughtily. "While her mother was in—"

"Monica," Jonathan lightly reprimanded. "Jo has looked so forward to reuniting with her daughter. Let's not go there."

Jo felt her chest heave. She comprehended well she had been insulted. Gone was the woman who had only shown her warmth and kindness. That was before Jo had married Cullen's cousin…before Percival had been born…before the war.

"No, let her finish." Jo flung her hand derisively. "I was in prison. There is no use denying it." Her voice rose higher than she intended. Immediately sensing his mother's distress, Percival pulled at her skirt.

"Momma," he cried. "What is prison? Is that where they kept us in that cold room without food? Is that where you were? They wouldn't tell me. Did they hurt you? Why did they…?"

The look exchanged between Cullen and his father did not go unnoticed. Quickly, Jo fell onto her knees. Percival hugged her tightly. "Oh, precious, I'm here now and that's all that matters," she said, calmer than she felt. "Why don't you show me—"

"Why doesn't Percival tell his grandmother what he did on his trip? What of the ship I took you upon?" Cullen said crisply. His frown was fierce. Not giving his son a chance to respond, he picked up Percival and handed him to his father.

Percival glanced back at her. Jo forced a smile, which dissipated quickly when she faced Cullen.

"I believe we need to talk." He gripped her arm tightly. Not giving her an option, he dragged her down the hall and into the study. Slamming the door, he released her.

"You hurt me."

He ignored her. "What was that supposed to mean back there? Why would you say something in front of Percival that would obviously upset him? Don't you know that he had dreams and nightmares when he first came here? Do you want to bring them back?"

Jo stiffened. Any confusion she held about their marriage was clarified in that moment. *Lord, what have I done! He hates me.*

She made no response. There was nothing she could say that would soothe his feelings toward her. It hadn't been her intention to cause her son any anxiety. Holding her aching arm, she walked toward the door.

Cullen would have none of it. He whirled Jo around. "Answer me."

"Let go of me and never touch me again." She jerked her arm free and took a step back. "Explain to me why it is acceptable to insult me in front of my son, but not for me to state the truth. Maybe you should have thought this marriage through before you said your vows.

"I warned you that there would be consequences to marrying me. Tell me, Cullen, exactly what do you expect of me? Do you want me to hang my head and speak only when spoken to? I'm not sure I understand your rules." She swung her head back in a defiant manner. "Where, should I ask, is my room or do I even have a room? Tell me because obviously I've missed what my position is in this house!"

His eyes bore into her so intently she feared he could see into her soul. She could take no more. Her emotions were on the verge of unraveling. She had a strong need to see her daughter. Once more, she started toward the door.

"No," he said.

She paused and glanced back at him.

Cullen shook his head. "No, I don't expect you to hang your head down. I apologize. This father thing is new to me. I reacted to his needs. I was insensitive to yours. Mother was out of line, but we have to be prepared for such a reaction. It will be worse when we leave this house."

"You're wrong." Jo met his gaze. "It couldn't be any worse. I see it in your eyes. You're ashamed of me. You have your son and obviously your father and mother assume he's yours to only further sully my reputation."

She reached for the door handle. This time he made no effort to stop her. She wanted him to stop her…tell her he wasn't ashamed of her…that he would protect her from whatever she faced. He did nothing.

Picking up her skirt, Jo raced up the stairs to find her daughter. In the corridor, she heard giggles and laughter. Slowly, she walked toward the merriment. Halting in the doorway, her heart fluttered at the sight.

The room was bright and airy. Painted pink with white trim, the matching curtains were pulled back, letting in the bright sun. A white crib with pink covers lay against the wall. Toys littered the floor. Two china dolls sat on white bookshelves above a large doll house next to a rocking horse.

Sitting on the floor, Elizabeth played with a toddler with a headful of dark blonde curls. Jo couldn't take her eyes off her daughter. Tears blurred her vision. She had been so worried about her little one.

Oh, my, how she had grown! She is so lovely! Madeline walked around in a circle, laughing. Elizabeth hid her face behind her hands and said, "Peekaboo."

Giggling, Madeline's eyes sparkled; wobbling, she fell back on the floor. Startled, she began to cry. Instinct took over and Jo rushed inside, but Elizabeth was closer. She picked up Madeline and soothed her. Jo's heart faltered hearing Madeline cry, "Momma, Momma."

"Now, now, everything is just fine. You silly goose," Elizabeth said and had Madeline laughing within seconds.

Jo bent down on one knee. "Oh, Madeline! It's Momma. I've come back for you."

Madeline screamed. Jo wrapped her arms around her; Madeline screamed louder and pushed back frantically against her. Picking her daughter up in her arms, Jo desperately tried to soothe her, but the toddler would have nothing of it. She went limp in Jo's arms.

"Now, now, Madeline." Elizabeth pried Madeline out of Jo's grip. "You are fine."

Feeling as if her heart had been ripped from her chest, Jo watched her daughter calm in Elizabeth's embrace. The little one hid her face in Elizabeth's shoulder and refused to look at her mother.

"I'm sorry, Josephine. Madeline has formed quite an attachment to me since she arrived. She was so…so sick. I'm sure it will comfort you to know, I didn't leave her side and have cared for her as if she was my own."

The softness of her words did little to ease Jo's frustration. She wanted her daughter back in *her* arms…she wanted to comfort *her* daughter. Jo raised her chin, chagrined at the circumstance she now found herself.

"Words cannot fully express my feelings. My children are my life and I am eternally grateful for the wonderful care they have received, but I am their mother. I do know how to take care of my own children."

"Josephine, this is Mrs. Finnegan. She is Madeline's nanny." Elizabeth handed Madeline over to an older woman dressed in a gray gown with a white apron and cap who had hurried into the room.

The heavyset woman smiled tenderly at Madeline, who made no resistance to the exchange. Mrs. Finnegan patted Madeline's back and asked, "What would you like me to do, Miss Elizabeth? I was under the impression it was going to be a slow introduction back to her mother."

"I'm her mother. She does not need to be slowly introduced to me!" Jo's voice rose. "Now hand her to me!"

Mrs. Finnegan looked over to Elizabeth, who gave a small nod, but without another word, left the room more than a little miffed. Jo's triumph did not last long.

Over the course of the next hour, things went from bad to worse. Madeline stubbornly refused to allow her mother to come near her no matter what Jo tried. Mrs. Finnegan seemed confused on how to handle the situation. Madeline quickly realized that her crying disturbed her mother and screeched louder. Exhausted, Jo sat down, defeated, on the floor.

Mrs. Finnegan walked over and picked up Madeline. "If ya don't mind me saying so, don't worry yourself none, Mrs. Montgomery. The little one loves you. I've seen it before. She's mad with ya, that's all. Mark my word, it will pass and she'll come around. But it may be best if you gave her a little space and start things first thing in the morning."

Jo stared at the woman in disbelief. Her own child was mad at her! Madeline acted as if she hated her…hated her for abandoning her. What had she expected? Madeline had been ripped apart from her. What kind of mother was she!

Elizabeth walked back into the room. Looking at Jo with eyes filled with pity, she took Madeline back in her arms. "Again, I apologize, Josephine. Mother and I had discussed the best way to handle your return. It seems it wasn't communicated to Cullen. This whole scene could have been avoided. Mrs. Finnegan is correct, though. Perhaps it is best we begin again in the morning."

Jo made no more protests. She rose to her feet and made her way out into the hall. Leaning back against the wall, she clasped her hand over her mouth in dismay, heartbroken.

In the nursery, she heard Elizabeth tell Mrs. Finnegan it was time for Madeline's nap.

"Yes, ma'am," Mrs. Finnegan agreed. "Gonna take a good one after that scene. Poor little thing. So confused, probably wondering what is going on. Shame, just when she seems so settled now. Hope Miss Madeline don't go and get sick again. Wonder if we could talk to the missus and see what we could do."

Jo's hand clutched her stomach. *They were going to keep her daughter from her? No, no, they couldn't!* She refused to let them. She wiped back tears and straightened her dress. She had to talk with Cullen.

At the foot of the stairs, voices resonated out into the foyer from the parlor, clear and distinct voices.

"You are going to have to do something, Cullen. She is causing a scene upstairs with Madeline. She isn't a fit mother. The poor child's scared of her. Does that not tell you something? Oh, why did you have to go and marry her? You could have easily set her up in a small house somewhere and she could have visited the children if she wanted."

"Mother, don't! Jo has been through a lot, all of which has been my fault…it's my responsibility to fix everything."

"Gibberish! You served your country with honor while…"

"He didn't have a choice, Monica," Jonathan said. "We will make the best of it."

"What do you mean he didn't have a choice?"

"Mother, if you must know, Hugh was set to marry her if I didn't. If it wasn't Hugh, it would have been someone else. Look at her. Some fool would step in to save a damsel in distress. I wasn't about to let anyone raise…"

Jo heard Cullen's voice fade off, but his meaning was clear. *His son.* He was not going to let anyone else raise his son!

"Oh, Cullen, does this not make my point more relevant? What kind of woman is she? One look at the boy and everyone will understand why you had to step in and marry her. Your poor cousin, to be deceived in such a manner! Oh, I don't know how we are to slant this. Not only did the papers in Philadelphia speculate as to why she married you but everyone in Charleston is questioning her character!"

The papers? She had been in the papers? *Oh, Heavens, what had they said about her?* The clock struck three. Josephine stared at the door in front of her. She could not stand another minute in this house.

She wanted nothing more than to run blindly out the door, but her children…abruptly she stopped and stared in disbelief. Blinking, she took a second look.

A distinguish black gentleman stood in the hall, dressed in a black suit with a white shirt and black bow tie. He gestured for her to follow him.

Jo hesitated only a moment. Easing down the foyer, she glanced back over her shoulder. No one was around. Turning back to the man, she cried, "Heyward, is it truly you?"

"Yes, Miss Jo," Heyward answered. Out of nowhere, he asked, "Would you like to go visit Ma…now?"

"Oh, yes, please. I would like that more than anything."

* * * *

Heyward rode the streetcar on the front platform with the driver. It riled his blood. Colored people weren't permitted to ride in the car, no matter how well-dressed, how much money they had, or how well-behaved.

He had learned over the last few months to control his temper about such matters. Ma said it would take time to change, but she didn't understand how it irked him the way white folks looked down on him.

Since his return to Philadelphia, he had become a well-respected member of the community with the help of William Still. Still had helped him invest his money when he had first arrived in this city and had overseen it while he was away working for the Union army.

Mr. Jonathan Smythe had hired him as a clerk, which only served to further his aspirations. He had a son now to look after. He never wanted Tome to ever question his integrity.

His son…Tome. He would admit he had first fought the idea of taking Tome in as his own. He had enough to worry about. Having a family had been the furthest thing from his mind. For the last few years, he had been consumed by his need to expel his helplessness in Gillie's death. She haunted his dreams…until he saw Tome. He swore he saw Gillie reflected in the young one's eyes.

Did he believe that it had been Gillie who guided that poor soul to him? Foolish, he supposed. Foolishness he would never admit to. Yet, he took comfort in the thought.

Tome was officially his son. It had been simple enough. He claimed him as his own down at the courthouse when the small family arrived in Philadelphia. With Still's help in finding a house to buy near his own family, Heyward began to feel a part of the world he now lived.

Moreover, the look on Ma's face when she saw their new home would be etched in his memory forever. The modest whitewashed house had black shutters, flowerboxes in the windows, and a small wraparound porch. The garden in the back was big enough for Ma to grow her vegetables.

"Lordy! Lordy! Never thought I would live in a place like this. I thought my farm just right for me. I was so proud of it, but this…this is my home…home with my boy. My boy."

Ma…After all these years…there were no ties that bound them anywhere but to family. He gave all the credit to his mother. She had struggled mightily to keep them together. He didn't know how she had managed what she had. When he was sold off to the Montgomerys as a boy, he never thought he would ever see her again.

Life had fallen into a pleasant routine. Ma's days were occupied with Tome, church, and the garden. She had already made so many friends. The Stills loved her. Many a night, he would come home and find they had guests for dinner. Ma would entertain them by sharing one story or another of her interesting life.

The war still raged in the South, but Heyward had already begun his life anew…until word came about Josephine. *Lord, the woman was a thorn in his side!* If it was not Gillie running to her beck and call, it was his mother.

Ma's affection for the lady tore at him. When the news came that Miss Josephine's children had arrived in Philadelphia without their mother, Ma was taken by surprise. Something wasn't right and Ma was worried. Miss Jo would never abandon her children willingly.

Heyward knew the lady well enough to discern the truth behind his ma's words. He also realized that Mr. Cullen wanted Percival out of South Carolina. He had been prepared to slip the child out of Magnolia Bluff if the need arose. It had been part of the mission.

Regardless of his feelings toward Miss Josephine, he had interceded with Mr. Smythe on his mother's behalf and arranged for Ma to visit Miss Josephine's children.

Mr. Smythe had kindly allowed a visit to soothe Ma's fears, but it accomplished nothing, only escalated Ma's uncertainties. The moment the little boy saw Ma, happiness exuded from his being. He ran up to Ma quick enough and hugged her soundly. The baby had been another issue. The young Miss Elizabeth had refused to let Ma even hold the little one and only allowed her a brief moment to see her, to his mother's chagrin.

"Lord Almighty, Heyward, did you see that…that youngest lady would have had me thrown out. Won't let me around Miss Madeline, no matter that young Master Percival leaped into my arms. Acted like I was some type of leper. Don't like her…not one bit."

Heyward made no comment. That was the way it was up North. The uppity white folks. Not Mr. Smythe per se, but, definitely, Mrs. Smythe and her daughter, Miss Elizabeth. Neither had any patience for those they thought beneath them and colored people were well beneath them.

Shortly afterwards, he had begun to hear whispers at his work. Mrs. Smythe would drop by. From his office, he watched the husband and wife disagree. At one time, she had even slammed down a newspaper on his desk. Unable to make out fully what the arguments were about, he heard certain words: *papers, it will come out, scandal.*

Heyward confiscated the discarded newspaper. It hadn't taken much to put together that they were discussing the mystery woman briefly mentioned in a paragraph on the folded back page. It was conjecture that the state department was holding a Southern woman in the Old Capitol Prison for suspicion of spying.

He realized that reporters reached for anything to make a story. Speculation abounded, but in the end the story seemed to die. The fear that it would become common knowledge that Miss Josephine had been in prison petrified Mrs. Smythe.

Heyward had been summoned to the Smythe house by Jonathan Smythe on his return from Washington. When he arrived this afternoon to meet with his employer, he heard Mrs. Smythe distinctly crying, "The speculation will turn into headlines. They will certainly label her a Jezebel!"

Voices echoed out into the foyer. It was then he saw Miss Josephine come down the stairs. She looked perplexed, bewildered, and hurt. There was no way she had avoided hearing the harsh words. A surge of pity swept through him for Miss Josephine.

He made a decisive decision…one he knew he would soon come to regret. He was not one to dismiss common sense…but it just wasn't right.

Giving no thought to proprieties, he offered Miss Jo an opportunity to see his mother. She, in turn, followed him without question. Her only desire was to see her mammy.

Heyward directed Miss Jo to walk behind him as he led her from the streetcar stop. His house set three blocks over. Miss Jo made no complaints.

Opening up the gate to the walk, he motioned Miss Jo to the back of the house. He held no doubt of where Ma would be. Walking around the side of the house, Ma knelt in her garden, transplanting a lilac.

Ma looked up and her face beamed. "Miss Jo! Well, don't just stand there, child. Come give your Miss Hazel a hug."

Overcome with complete joy, Jo fell into her mammy's arms and wept.

* * * *

Heyward walked through his front door, well aware that Mr. Cullen wouldn't be long behind him. He had waited at the corner of the street until he spotted the Smythes' carriage coming up the avenue.

Looking out the side window, Heyward saw Tome was playing with his friends in the neighbor's yard. His attention turned to the voices coming from the kitchen. The women had not ceased talking since he had left them over an hour ago.

He had found he needed time alone to think. Miss Josephine's appearance had brought back memories.

As he stood in the doorway, the two were so engrossed that neither noticed him. He watched them. With the greatest reluctance, he admitted a truth he had always known, but refused to acknowledge—the two women sincerely cared for each other.

"I feel so lost, Miss Hazel, like I've fallen down an abyss and can't find my way out." Jo heaved a tremulous sigh.

His mother sat back and took a sip of her tea. Reaching across the table, she squeezed Jo's hand. "Now, Lordy, I would too if I was dealing with those women. I tried. I did. When the childlin' first came. Went to that house. Heyward told me not to try. I understood why when I got there."

"Elizabeth treated me the same and I'm Madeline's mother." Miss Josephine nodded. He saw her look over at his mother and smile. "Oh, Miss Hazel, I've missed you so."

"I have thought of you often," Ma said, but adding sorrowfully, "But it ain't the same, Miss Jo. You had a need to see me this afternoon, but it can't happen often, if at all."

"You can't mean that." Jo looked dubiously at the older woman. "I need you."

"Ya know I speak the truth. The world we knew is no more."

Miss Jo's face betrayed she readily understood. Society stood as a wall between them. Swallowing back her tears, Jo asked in a quivering voice, "What am I to do? I can endure no more. It haunts me…being locked up away from my children…my children…I—"

"Don't, Miss Jo. Don't go no further." Miss Hazel heaved a sigh. "It ain't right…to have kept you locked up that way, not able to see ya childlin', for no reason."

536

"It ain't never been right to treat people like animals," Heyward stated soundly and stepped into the room. "We have problems. The Smythes' carriage is driving down the street."

Miss Josephine lowered her gaze in a defeated manner.

His mother would have none of it. "Miss Jo, you look at your old mammy and listen carefully," she said in a commanding voice. "Don't ya ever give up those childlin'. Not now…not ever. Look at Heyward and me. I never, ever gave up hope."

A hard knock on the front door interrupted the visit. Heyward went over to greet his uninvited guest. Opening up the entrance, it was as he had known. Mr. Cullen had come to collect his wife, none too happy by his expression.

Mr. Cullen waited until Heyward invited him inside, but he was unable to completely mask his temper. He asked in an icy voice, "Is my wife here?"

Ma would have none of it. Walking over to Heyward's side, she exclaimed, "Why, Master Cullen, come in. Come in. Miss Jo and I were just finishing up tea. Now, sit right down there at the table and have a cup. You, too, Heyward."

Heyward watched his reluctant guest make his way to the kitchen. He caught his mother's arm. He had to know. In a low voice for only her ears, he asked, "Is it true? Did I hear Miss Josephine correctly when she first arrived?"

"What, Heyward?"

"Is Buck Haynes dead? Did Miss Josephine kill him?"

Chapter Ten

Josephine sat in a tomblike silence on the carriage ride back with Cullen. She wanted to be anywhere other than with him, but she had no choice. He had cast his net and she had been caught within.

No sooner than the carriage halted in front of his magnificent home, Cullen whisked her upstairs to a small, but elegant bedroom…on the other end of the corridor from the nursery and her children.

The room was painted a soothing blue with matching drapes and bedcovers. An armoire sat in the far corner across from the four-post bed. The furniture was mahogany with a couple of embroidered, cushioned highback chairs around a hand-carved accent table. A thick beige Persian rug with blue designs covered the wooden floor.

Despite the comforts of the room, it might as well have had bars on the windows. She felt it nothing more than the prison cell she had only been released from.

The door slammed. Cullen's voice rang sharply in the room. "Little fool!"

She had had enough of being reprimanded for her actions. Turning her back to him, she walked to the window. Before she had time to push back the curtain, he whirled her around to face him, his anger fueled by her refusal to address him. "You can't disappear in that manner! Is this your way of getting back at me? To embarrass me and my family?"

Her own ire sparked. "I thought you had already done so by marrying me!"

His face rigid, he released his grip and stared at her. "You are not ignorant, Josephine. You know as well as anyone proprieties have to be followed. You…you left with…"

"I know." Jo raised her chin defiantly. "I am not a child to chastise. I had a deep need to see my mammy."

"You are not in Charleston anymore. There are—"

"Stop," she demanded. "I did not mean to embarrass you. It was not my intent, but if you insist. I'm sorry...I'm sorry I embarrassed you...I'm sorry that I married you...I was so wrong...ever so wrong. I had thought there was some semblance of feeling for what we had, but I was mistaken. I want to leave with my children. I want only my children."

"It's a little too late for that. You are in this marriage whether you want it or not. If you think for one minute—"

"You would allow another to raise your son? I believe you have made it unambiguously clear, but what of me? Tell me...tell me what you want me to do."

"It is obvious that you overheard a conversation that was not meant for your ears," he said hesitantly. "You're right. I may have reacted to the situation, not thinking all the way through..."

"Through?" Her brows arched in a half frown. "You hate me, Cullen. Tell me what I'm supposed to do. I'm in a city that is unforgiving to a Southerner. I have no friends or family. My children, that are my life and the reason I agreed to this sham, have been ripped from me."

"Don't be overly dramatic. You are my wife, Josephine," he pointed out. "You are acting as if you are being tortured. You have wealth and status. I'm certain in time you will adjust."

"I don't want wealth or status." She buried her face in her hands. Her voice was barely a whisper. "I never have. I have done everything to protect my children and Magnolia Bluff. Everything. I have tried to live up to the expectations placed upon me...I have failed..."

"What could you have possibly done that would make you say something so foolish?"

"You don't know...you don't know what I have done." Her hands shook; her voice faltered. Suddenly, she was reliving the moment back at Magnolia Bluff. "I didn't know what else to do...he had Percival. I was so frightened he would hurt my son...I saw the gun on the ground...then he was lying on the ground...dead...I never wanted to leave my home...Andrew said I had to...I killed a man..."

The room became deadly quiet. Abruptly, she stopped and collapsed down on her knees, staring down at her hands as if blood dripped from them. "He wouldn't stop. He wanted to hurt me by harming Percival..."

Cullen's brows drew together in sudden worry. He knelt beside her. "So Percival wasn't being dramatic when he told me a bad man tried to kill him. Don't you think it's time to tell me the real reason Andrew felt it necessary to send you north? Don't try to deny. After all these years, Andrew would never have slipped up unless it was intentional."

She refused to look up at him with troubled eyes. "I tried to protect Percival, Cullen. I swear. I…did the only thing…I shot him…"

Taking her hands in his, his voice calmed. "Josephine, what happened? I need to know."

Silent tears streamed down her face. "It was Buck," she said in a low, wavering voice. "He rode up to Magnolia Bluff with Gus Harrison and accused me of ruining his life. Grandpa Henry died and the Groves was lost to him and Harry Lee. He was going to make me pay.

"It became chaotic. Amos lunged at Gus. I remember Amos knocking him over and then Buck shot Amos. Andrew came at Buck…it was at that moment Percival appeared, trying to get to me. Oh, Good Lord, Buck grabbed him. I saw Gus's pistol at my feet. The next thing I remember, I had a gun in my hand and Buck lay dead."

She clutched her bosom. Her body trembled. "I killed him…Cullen. I shot him in the back…they will say I'm a cold-blooded murderer…Andrew and Derek took care of the body, but Andrew said too many people had seen it happen. He said he couldn't take a chance with Harry Lee. If he returned, he didn't know if he could protect the children and me…"

"Ssh," he said softly, wrapping his arms about her. "Andrew did right. I promise you are safe. The children are safe. Trust me, Josephine."

She shook her head. "You don't understand. Harry Lee is coming for me, Cullen, bent only on revenge. I see him in my dreams."

"Did Andrew have any idea where Harry Lee is or was?"

"I'm not certain. Buck mentioned a Yankee prison camp."

"Harry Lee will not harm you here," Cullen promised. "Josephine, it is I who have much to apologize for…I should have pulled you and the children out from Magnolia Bluff after Wade's death. I should have done a lot of things."

Jo leaned into his strong arms. Her energy drained, she took comfort in his embrace, if only for a moment.

* * * *

Before dawn, Josephine woke. She had spent a restless night, but had awakened with a renewed determination. Cullen avowed she had the status of his wife. She was about to assert that status.

Seeing Miss Hazel encouraged Jo and reminded her of whom she was. Jo dressed with the help of her new maid, Mary, a young Irish immigrant. Jo liked her well enough, she supposed. The girl seemed eager to please, which served Jo well this morning.

Today, she was going to reclaim her children. Mary scrambled to keep up as Jo walked soundly down the hall straight to the nursery.

"Do you think this is wise, miss?" Mary said with her thick Irish brogue. "I think it's just brilliant to want to have your daughter near you, but, I tell you, ma'am, I know Mrs. Smythe and she won't like this none."

Jo was not going to debate her intention with her maid. She never lost a step and continued onward into the nursery without knocking. Her eyes fixated on the crib where her daughter slept. Easing down gently, she lifted Madeline into her arms. Sleepy, her daughter cradled her head on her mother's shoulder. Jo hummed "Hush Little Baby" as she used to sing to her.

"Mrs. Smythe, what…?" Mrs. Finnegan came in the side door, tying her wrap around her. "You can't—"

"I can," Jo repeated soundly. "Would you be so kind as to see to Madeline's breakfast? She will be down in my room. Mary here is going to help me gather what we will be needing."

Mrs. Finnegan hurried out the door. Jo had no doubt to where, but her attention lay on her child. "Now, my precious one, what would you like Momma to change you into for the day?"

Madeline smiled sleepily. "Momma."

Jo's heart swelled as she dressed her daughter. *Oh, the word was like a song from the angels!* The translucent peace did not last long.

"Josephine!"

"Why, good morning, Mrs. Smythe," Jo greeted her mother-in-law, who obviously had been wakened out of a sound sleep. The older woman had not taken her usual care before leaving her bedroom. Her braided hair hung over her shoulder and she still wore her nightclothes.

"Josephine, you can't simply take Madeline out of her room in this manner…"

"I am her mother," Josephine said firmly. "I have decided to look after her myself. I won't need a nanny. I am perfectly capable of doing so. I cared for my children at Magnolia Bluff."

Looking down at her child, Jo smiled. "Are you ready to go?"

Madeline looked adorable dressed in a pretty rose printed cotton dress with her white drawers showing under her skirt. Smiling broadly, her daughter's small arms reached out to her. Enormous pleasure washed over Jo. She gladly took her back into her arms.

"That may well be, my dear, but you are now in Philadelphia," Monica retorted. "You need to learn—"

"I believe you will find I'm a quick learner, Mrs. Smythe." Josephine tried a gentle approach. "I am sure you can understand my need to have my daughter close to me. I was telling Mary I want to move the crib into my room…"

"You're what? You're not taking Madeline into your room," Monica exclaimed. "It's unheard of."

"I believe I can do what I want. Thank you." Jo quickly relinquished her mild manner tactic. "Mary, we will bring only the necessities at the moment."

"Wait until I tell Cullen," Monica huffed and walked out of the room.

Jo wasted no more time and whisked her daughter down the hall, followed closely by Mary, whose arms were filled with clothes that fell haphazardly on the hallway carpet.

Footsteps sounded out in the hall and halted in her doorway. Cullen walked into her room, his jaw set; his brows furrowed.

"Do you want something, Cullen?" Jo held Madeline tighter.

Suddenly, Madeline cried out in delight and pushed against her mother. Her brother ran into the room. His hair disheveled, he hadn't even taken the time to put his slippers on his feet.

"What are you doing, Momma?"

"Madeline is moving into my room so I can look after her for a while."

"That's not fair." Percival pouted. "I can't. So she can't either."

"She's younger than you," Jo reminded her son. "But don't think I'm going to ignore my boy. I have missed you both terribly. I have so much planned for us to do."

Clearly annoyed, Cullen said, "Don't do this, Jo."

Madeline wiggled out of her mother's arms. She reached over to her brother, who took her hand and helped her climb up on their mother's bed, as happy as you please. The two siblings sat together in wait for the promised day to begin.

"I'm hungry, Momma," Percival declared. "When are we going to eat?"

Oh, good gracious, she hadn't thought what she would do after she had the children. She had prepared for a battle, but now the skirmish was won. Whatever was she going to do with two children in her small room?

"It seems I won't be getting anymore sleep this morning. Why don't I have a tray of food sent up for us?" Cullen asked.

Jo glanced over at Cullen and gave him a small appreciative smile.

From his perch, Percival cried, "Breakfast in Momma's room! Maddy, isn't this fun!"

Madeline giggled; Percival laughed. Jo sat on her bed and embraced her children.

* * * *

Josephine frowned. The last few days had not gone as she had planned. In truth, though, she had no plan except to hold on to her children.

Looking around her room, it was a mess. Toys littered the floor; clothes were strewn in a pile behind the door. A quilt covered the two highback chairs and table to form a tent that she and the children had played in.

The three of them had lived within the four small walls, much like they had done when they arrived in Washington—with a few significant differences. They could come and go as they chose and food was aplenty.

Jo had taken the children out for walks in the park with Mary. Elizabeth had even joined the little group. Gone was the arrogance that had raised Jo's defenses. Elizabeth asked with the greatest humility and seemed quite sincere with her apology.

"It was not my intent to keep Madeline from you," Elizabeth explained. "I worried about her because she is so sensitive. Of course, I would never keep a child from her mother."

"As I do not want to keep you from my daughter," Jo relented. The poor thing seemed quite upset. "Your care for her is evident."

The children loved being outdoors, but for the last two days, it had rained…and rained. The room had become their world. Pushing back errant strands of hair from her face, Jo began to pick up the toys.

Stepping on one of Percival's toy soldiers, she heard a crunch. She picked up her foot. To her dismay, she had crushed it soundly. Percival was going to be upset. He knew every piece he had.

She wanted to cry. Already her son was distraught and it was all her fault. Why had she pressed him while he was playing with his soldiers…why? She should have made light of Percival's play. How confusing the war must be on the young boy.

It had not stopped her. When Madeline tried to grab one of her brother's men, Percival grabbed it back. "No, Maddy, no. Momma, make Maddy put back my Rebel soldier!"

"Can she not play with you?" Jo asked.

Percival shook his head. "No, she doesn't like to die. She cries."

"Percival! Don't be mean to your sister."

543

"I'm playing Father," he announced proudly and held one of the figures over his head. "He's the greatest officer in all the war. I'm going to run over all of 'em Rebs!"

Taken back for the moment, she wasn't certain she had heard him correctly. "Your daddy was a brave and true soldier…a hero, Percival, but aren't you forgetting he was a Confederate?"

"No, Momma. Father was in the Navy. He says the war is almost over and the South is going to lose."

She knelt beside him and took one of the figures in her hand. She smiled at her son. "You are talking of your new father, but you should never forget your real daddy, Percival. He was courageous and…"

"Father said he was." Percival reached for the toy in his mother's hand. "But Father is my real daddy. I know, for he told me."

Heaving a weighty sigh, she pressed, "You're mistaken, Percival. You may want him to be, but your father died…"

All her resolutions to maintain a positive approach when dealing with the different sides of the war dissipated. Her loyalty to the South…to Wade…had not faded. She realized the futility of arguing with an almost four-year-old. Moreover, she would be attempting to convince him the man who had just proclaimed himself to be his father…the man he worshiped…had lied to him.

Ignoring her common sense, she endeavored into reasoning with a child too young to understand the concept. All he understood was his mother's attempt to take away what he wanted most dearly—a father…his real father. The man who died years before held little meaning to him, only talk in the empty air.

Soon, the argument spiraled out of control. Percival was adamant in his claim of who his real father was and Jo just as adamant as to who he was not. A senseless, meaningless quarrel. Another time, another place, she would have handled everything differently, but she, too, was a child clinging to a semblance of the past.

Opening up the toy chest, Jo leaned over to take the figure out of Percival's hand. "I'm sorry to disappoint you, but it isn't fair to your daddy. Until you can…"

The next instant he slapped her; the next, she slapped him back…not hard, but reactionary. He stared blankly at her—a look she would never forget. He cried and ran blindly out of the room.

Jo had made no attempt to rush after her son. She was well aware where he had headed. She well imagined her mother-in-law would be up shortly to inform her of her shortcomings. She had sent Mary down to check on her son.

Her maid had returned saying he was with Cullen. Her heart sank. He was safe, but the world she was so frantically trying to adhere to was slipping from her hands. She had no idea what she was going to do.

"Josephine."

When she looked up, Jo saw Elizabeth enter the room. Outstretching her arms, Madeline ran over and hugged her tightly.

"I hope you don't mind, Josephine," Elizabeth said in a nervous manner. "I have arranged a small surprise for you."

"Surprise?"

Elizabeth lowered her gaze down to Madeline. "I wanted to do something nice for you. You have been through so much. Being thrown into prison…I could never have survived. I'm not that strong."

"If you don't mind, I don't want to talk of it."

"Of course." Elizabeth smiled and looked back up. "I was hoping I could watch the children for you this evening…just for a little while so you can take a nice long bath."

"That sounds so wonderful, but…"

"It is set. I had Mary draw you a bath," Elizabeth went on. "If you don't mind, I will take Madeline downstairs. Mother has missed her. Percival is already with Cullen. You can enjoy a little time to yourself."

Jo hesitated, but decided it would be for the best…if she could trust Elizabeth.

* * * *

In the bathing chamber across the hall from her room, Jo sank into the tepid water. A brief reprieve, she had time to think clearly. Admonishing herself greatly, she had let her emotions get the best of her.

How had her life come to this point? How she missed Wade! Wade had taken care of her every need, loved her and cared for her. He had known of her weaknesses and accepted them. She wiped back the tears that escaped down her cheeks. She didn't have time for self-pity.

But…had she not done the same when she had lost Cullen? Cullen—who she had loved with the whole of her heart—had married another to save him. Dare she hope to rekindle that love?

A long-buried longing had re-emerged with Cullen's appearance. Along with this feeling came a sadness. The realization that time had changed his love for her and replaced it with a hatred toward her. He had become vengeful—intent only on making her pay for having a life with his cousin.

Cullen had relented to let her have her children in her room, but she could not live this way for much longer. The question lay not of what she

545

had to do, but how. For her own sanity, Jo knew she had to leave, but she was trapped.

She had not asked, but it was apparent even while she lived at Magnolia Bluff that her fortune was lost. What little she had went toward Magnolia Bluff. Whatever happened to her, it must survive. Wade had left Magnolia Bluff to Percival in his will—the ultimate declaration that Percival was truly his son.

Jo had never complained at Magnolia Bluff and missed it terribly. They didn't have much over the last couple of years, but she was content with the children. They were happy. It was home. A home they couldn't return to, not with Harry Lee out there somewhere.

Here—here she was a foreigner—a hated foreigner—but whatever she had to endure, she would do so to keep her children and protect them at all cost. Silently, Jo swore one day her children would be able to return to Magnolia Bluff.

Mary knocked softly and entered. She placed the contents of her arms down on the table in front of Jo. "Mrs. Smythe, I have some clean clothing I believe will suffice."

"Thank you," Josephine said. "That will be all."

She exited her much-needed bath and toweled down. She caught sight of the lotions on the shelf. She rubbed the lotion into her freshly bathed skin and savored the sumptuousness of her bath.

Looking at the nightdress Mary left, she wondered where she had obtained the apparel. They looked familiar: a white silk nightdress with a matching wrap and new soft and dainty undergarments. Slipping it over her head, she let it slither down her body, clinging to her curves in the most provocative manner.

A slit up the side of the gown displayed her naked leg. She remembered…it had been part of her trousseau she had picked out when she thought she was to marry Cullen. He must have saved her trunks…which meant she might have more of her belongings.

Jo dried her long, raven hair until it was damp and then brushed it until it glistened in the candlelight. It fell well beyond her waist, so she left it down until she could have Mary braid it. Tying the wrap about her, she walked back into her room.

With her hand on the handle, she told herself she would make it right with Percival. She wanted nothing more than to hug her son and simply put the incident behind them.

She opened the door. Immediately, all the confidence she had garnered vanished. The room had been cleaned…moreover, it was immaculate. The floor was bare of toys and clutter. The crib had been moved—all evidence of her children had disappeared. She had been tricked!

Seething, she turned back toward the door, but it was blocked. Much to her consternation, Cullen leaned casually against the doorframe.

Indignant, she cried, "Get out of my way!"

"I think not, my dear." He walked into the room and shut the door. "It's time we talk."

Venting her despair, she pressed, "Where are my children? What cruel trick have you played upon me?"

"Josephine, truly, you couldn't possibly think you could camp out in your room forever. Don't blame Elizabeth about Madeline. I told her to do so. The small one is being quite well looked after. Several people have missed her terribly."

Jo whirled around to face him, but immediately she realized he had no intention of letting her leave the room. She caught her breath. He was too close. His unbuttoned shirt hung loose over his trousers, revealing his hard, muscular chest. She took a step back.

"She is mine!"

"Calm yourself, Josephine. No one is taking your children. I tried to give you time to realize that your children still hold you in their hearts. You can't imagine that anyone could ever replace someone so dear."

Her eyes burned with the sting of tears. "Don't do this to me, Cullen. I understand well how much you hate me. Now you have the power to inflict enormous pain. You have my children."

"I have no desire to cause you pain, Josephine." He threw his hands in exasperation. "Can you not see that I have tried to give you time to come to grips with everything around you? Do you not realize I know how much you have lost?"

"You are concerned about what I have lost?" she quipped sharply. "You who plotted to take my son from me? You who told him that you were his real father? How could you do such a thing?"

"I talked to him before we married. He asked if I was to be a real father to him. I answered him truthfully. He is a child who can't understand fully."

"No!" she said adamantly. "Do not skim on the surface of honesty. You have made it clear to everyone that Percival is your son!"

"For your information, only a few trusted souls know the truth from me," he said in a voice void of inflection. "Though I bear responsibility for your predicament, there is nothing I can say that will undo what has been done. I will not deny he has my look, but people can only speculate. Wade made certain of that.

"He made it clear to everyone that Percival was his son. If you fear he will be labeled a bastard, it will never happen. Wade gave him his name and by leaving Percival Magnolia Bluff, he left no question." He moved to her side. His fingertips cupped her chin and he turned her head so she faced him. "I won't take that from Wade. I told Percival what a great man his daddy was, if you must know. I told him his daddy did what most would not and I owe him dearly."

Jo looked in his eyes. He reached back and ran his fingers through her hair. Immediately, she was aware of a warming sensation that surged through her body, spawned only by his simple touch. It was too much to bear.

"Wade loved Percival, Cullen…"

"I know," he whispered, so close she felt his breath against her skin. "I realize he loved you, also, but what gnaws at my soul is you loved him in return."

Lowering her gaze, she couldn't look at him. His words could not be denied. What did he want her to say—that Wade was a ghost that stood between them? She looked back up at him. "I loved him, Cullen, but—"

He placed his finger over her lips. "Don't say anything…not yet. I have something to show you." He reached for her hand; they walked across the room. As he drew back the large curtain that hid a door, he asked, "Have you not wondered where this door led?"

She would have been foolish not to realize it was connected to his room. Husband and wives having separate bedrooms were unheard of in the South. She had held the belief she had been placed beside Cullen for appearance's sake.

Opening it wide, he gestured for her to enter. It was a lovely room, rather large with a fire burning brightly in the hearth. A gold-plated mirror hung over the fireplace. The walls were a deeper, darker blue than her own. A finely carved writing table angled near the window.

The aroma of a warm dinner hung in the air, hovering over a table set for two in the far corner. Close by was the huge four-post bed. It had been turned down.

He came up behind her before she could utter her confusion. His arms wrapped around her waist, he pushed back her hair and kissed her neck.

Startled, she turned in his arms. Confusion reflected in her eyes.

"The children have been taken care of for the evening." He reached over and caressed her face gently. "I wanted this night to be about us. I know you believe I have set to punish you for some unknown reason, but, in truth, I wanted to give you space to come to terms with what had happened to you. I was told it would take time for you to recover, but I don't think there is any more time without losing you. I don't want to lose you, Josephine."

"Cullen, I don't know what to say," she gasped. "I thought you hated me."

"Never. I have never stopped loving you," he said in a ragged whisper. "You need to know everything that I have held within me. The torture I have endured first of losing you…and now with you so close. I wanted to tell you and then everything became so chaotic. I…Oh, Josephine."

Her stunned expression shattered into one of astonished surprise. They stared at each other for a suspended moment. Cullen lowered his mouth on hers. She abandoned all restraint and gave herself up to her long suppressed desire.

Her breath caught as his kiss deepened. After so many years apart— all the protest to the contrary—emotions so long restrained, repelled for self-preservation—unbridled passion was unleashed in the night much like a tide that broke against a dam.

Josephine was lost in his musky scent; his hard body pressed against her. Barely breathing, she looked at him. Reaching up, she touched his face to outline it with her fingers. He was real…it wasn't a dream.

He took her hand and kissed it. "Forgive me, my love. Pray, forgive me. I love you. I need you."

Her eyes locked with his, as if frozen in time. Both afraid to move, to breathe for fear all would vanish before their eyes. He cupped her face gently in his hands.

"I have seen you every time I closed my eyes. Your face has haunted me. So beautiful, so lovely, laughing up at me. You so innocently trusting me. I would awaken with the realization that you lay beyond my grasp. I allowed jealousy to gnaw at me. I told myself all I wanted was to have you back in my arms just once.

"Before every battle, I would dream of you. Your lips on mine, warm and eager. I have a thousand visions of you in my heart. I clung to them.

"Now, God help me, I have tried to convince myself it is all for the boy—that part of me that has clung to you was dead—that same idiotic part that told me I could live without you the day you married Wade. I can't. I've tried and find I'm only half a man. Forgive me, Josephine."

Josephine's breath left her in a sudden gasp. She leaned up to him and whispered, "Love me, Cullen. Don't let me go."

She kissed him fervently, caught in a fierce tide of passion. The result was inevitable. The kiss served as a bridge from yesterday to this moment. He swept her in his arms and laid her on his bed. All else was forgotten except their need for each other, a merger of man and wife, heart and soul together as the years melted away.

The crackling fire burned. He stopped kissing her for a moment, long enough to soak in the sight of the woman who had haunted his dreams for so long. He took the hem of her nightdress and peeled it from her body.

Her raven hair shimmered down in waves over her bare skin, enticing a tightening in his loins. He touched her, sliding his hand downward over her body and then sweeping it upward between her thighs, invading her most sensitive places.

Her breath caught as her hand fluttered over his tautly muscled chest. She moved her hand slowly down to his hard shaft and closed her fingers ever so gently around it. His breath caught on her caress, driving him crazy with need.

"Slow, my darling, slow. I want to savor every moment."

Leaning on his elbow, he touched her breasts; his fingers circled them, pulled at the tingling tips. He dipped down and his mouth claimed her nipple, intensifying the insatiable hunger deep within her.

She encouraged his assault. He lowered his kisses, claiming her body as his domain. His lips burned with the flame of desire over her stomach and hips, her thighs and mound. Soon she rocked with an unbearable throb, writhing with a sweeping sensation that coursed through her body.

She caught his shoulders and drew him up to her.

"I want you, Josephine, only you," he murmured huskily.

The whole of her body burned with a desire that he had ignited. "Take me. Don't torture me more. I need you…you…Cullen…please."

He answered her plea. His naked body covered her and she rose up against him. Their fevered kisses blended as their own bodies became one.

He entered her; his harsh breathing rasped near her ear, while her own quickening gasps escaped involuntarily from her inner being. She felt his hardness press against her pulse and her senses reeled in ecstasy. He moved in a rhythm that she matched. She knew this and wanted it. Throwing her head back, she almost wept as his final thrust filled her. Waves of bliss suffused through her, but it was more than pleasure shared. He had reached into her very soul and reclaimed what had been lost from the years apart.

The sweat on their bodies glistened in the firelight. Their passion spent, they collapsed in each other's arms. Since he last had her in his arms, he had been a man possessed with a need to fill the void within him. Searching for fulfillment, he had braved battles and faced death many times. None had brought him the answers he sought.

Deny the fact as much as he had, he had to acknowledge it had always been Josephine. She was the part of him that was missing. Sated, he pulled her to him and basked in the serenity of the peace he had finally found.

* * * *

Josephine stretched languidly beneath the comfort of the warm down-filled comforter. She had slept soundly for the first time since she had left Magnolia Bluff, forgetting for a moment she wasn't alone. A hand reached out for her and pulled her close to his naked body.

She turned in his arms to find him smiling broadly. Her eyes sparkled as his mouth found hers. She whispered, "Is this real? Am I going to wake up finding all a dream?"

"If it is, then I never want to wake up," he said. "There is so much more I wanted to say, explain and then I lost all restraint."

Her eyes searched his. "There is nothing to forgive, Cullen. I don't want to talk of things in the past. I'm afraid."

"Afraid? I am never letting you go…"

"Not of you, Cullen, but the world outside those doors. I don't think I could survive being ripped from you again. I am weak. You don't know what I felt when you left. I had waited for a miracle that didn't come. I pushed all my feelings aside to survive. Now you have broken through the barriers…if you don't feel…I couldn't…I won't endure…" Her words faltered.

Tenderly, he kissed her.

She whispered against his lips. "I love you, Cullen. I can live with everything if I know I have you."

"You have me," he murmured huskily. "You always have."

Chapter Eleven

The war raged on within a broken nation. The newspapers were filled with one battle or another, but the feeling held it would not be much longer before this horrific conflict would come to an end.

Despite the ongoing fighting, Cullen had never been more content. Over the last few weeks, Josephine had begun to heal. He had his love, his child, and his family.

Problems lingered. Josephine was fragile, so fragile, but she was making an effort and trying to find a place in his world. He had her moved into his room. He should have never had her in another room. She belonged with him.

The sight of Percival when he had come down the stairs in tears that fateful morning forced him to act. No longer listening to the advice of others, he did what he had wanted to do the moment he had taken her for his wife.

Percival had, at his father's insistence, apologized to his mother for his behavior, although muttering under his breath that Cullen was his real father. Josephine chose to accept his effort without a rebuttal.

Madeline had been another issue in which Cullen had found an acceptable solution. Mrs. Finnegan would stay on as the nanny while Josephine cared for her daughter in the room that once was hers. Josephine's worries eased with the easy access to her…their daughter. Wade had cared for Percival as his own; Cullen was determined to do the same for Madeline.

Elizabeth and Josephine's friendship seemed to flourish. He wished he could feel the same about his mother's relationship with his wife. The dealings between Josephine and his mother…there were some things that were harder to overcome.

The friction between the two hadn't eased. Cullen doubted it would in the foreseeable future. In the spring, he would take Josephine and the children to Rosemount.

Now, his home was filled with the aroma of cookies and evergreen. Christmas was upon them and he had never known such contentment. The sight of his wife moving about the drawing room, exchanging gifts she had taken such care picking out, warmed Cullen's heart. He had taken her out shopping after much persuasion that his money was hers.

She had asked him a million questions about the likes of everyone, even the servants. He had let her do all she wanted and enjoyed every minute of it, for she smiled and laughed. Moreover, for the first time he had picked out gifts for his son and Madeline, which made Josephine tear up at his effort.

Nothing compared with her reaction to the present he had given her in bed before they readied to go downstairs. He had picked out a locket, a gold locket with a heart encircled with vines. Inside he had placed a picture he had taken of the children, leaving the other side empty for another picture, one he wanted with her, engraving the back with *Yours forever, Cullen.*

While she stood in the mirror and admired her gift, he pulled out a small box. Looking at him oddly, she opened it and gasped at the sight. He had hunted down the emerald wedding ring Wade had given her…that had been stolen from her. An impossible task, but he had been determined. It had cost him both favors and money, but he had been successful. Overwhelmed, she wept happy tears.

Gone was any lingering jealousy he held toward Wade. In a way, the ring signified a healing. Now, he thought of the Wade he had known in his youth without the anger and rage that the war had wedged between them.

Cullen watched Madeline toddle over to Josephine with her stuffed bear. Josephine hugged her tight and sent her over to her Aunt Elizabeth, who laughed joyfully. Percival played with his soldiers in the floor. His parents sat on the sofa, looking happier than he had seen them in a long time. Cullen finished his drink and sat down to play with his son.

* * * *

In late January, news of the war filtered back to Cullen, not unexpectedly, but he tried to keep most from Josephine. General Sherman had made his move from Atlanta through South Carolina, destroying almost everything in his path, a path that diverted from Magnolia Bluff.

Devastation lay throughout the South with the trail that Sherman left. It was a calculated strategy to strangle the life out of the South, a harsh reality to the cursed war. The stubborn, prideful Southerners had steadfastly refused to contemplate surrendering. The Rebs had fought for over three years without supplies, ammunition, food, guns… The war should have been long over, but someone forgot to tell the Rebs.

Cullen understood, not at the beginning, but during his time with Farragut. The Union had been lukewarm in its attempt at the beginning of the war, feeling torn in fighting their own. The South had never had that issue. The Rebels felt they were fighting for their way of life—their families. They fought with what was most dangerous—their heart, a dangerous opponent.

He understood it had come only when Lincoln had taken the stance that the war needed to end and instructed Grant and Sherman to have the South feel the full wrath of the North. Shouldn't the responsibility of all actions of this bloody godforsaken war hold consequences? The only way to conqueror the South's undying spirit was to strangle their heart and cut it out.

Cullen had never doubted the stance he had taken. He believed fervently in the Union and believed just as strongly that they were in the right in the sight of God. The Union needed to be preserved. But unlike most he fought beside, he loved the land he battled. Despite everything, he loved Charleston, the people and his family.

He had long ago given up on pretending to have all the answers. Those days had passed with each battle and the good men lost. He sighed as he looked at the telegram in his hand. He had to make a trip to Washington.

Looking back over his shoulder, he watched his wife donning her new apparel for their night out at the theater. She had finally agreed to go out socially. He wanted this night to be perfect.

Josephine looked stunning in the blue silk faille evening gown, worn off the shoulder with a bodice cut low across her full bosom. Abundantly decorated with white silk braid and blue ribbon, the exquisite dress had a row of decorative bead drops. The hem was edged with silk ribbon pleated with handmade lace.

She peered over her shoulder, lightly touching the string of pearls he had given her. She smiled. *My God, she looked lovely!* His mind easily pictured her wearing nothing but those pearls. Tonight, he would make his fantasy a reality.

He tucked the letters into his desk drawers. The news could wait. In truth, he doubted he would even mention the letter that arrived from Andrew with news of Magnolia Bluff. Cullen saw no reason to share the correspondence with his wife and spoil her evening. The news would only sadden her.

Cullen,

Magnolia Bluff has survived. Though, I am over laden with guilt, not only over the way I have kept Magnolia Bluff from being burnt to the ground, but Josephine. I had no choice, but that knowledge has not eased my conscience. The papers have painted Jo a Jezebel with her marriage to you, believing she has betrayed Wade. I take solace in the fact that Magnolia Bluff and the family has endured. I am committed to overseeing Magnolia Bluff and the estate until Percival is old enough to take over his inheritance. Mother misses the children desperately. She doesn't understand why Josephine left. Again, it bothers me that Jo can't defend herself. Mother doesn't comprehend the danger Jo would have been in had she stayed, the danger the family would have had to face. As to your concerns about Harry Lee—I understand he died not long ago in a Northern prison camp, Fort Delaware, dubbed the Fort Delaware Death Pen. You might be able to confirm the information since it is the Union which held him. As always, I will keep you informed to the best of my ability. Andrew

Tonight, though, he refused to think of anything except his lovely wife. The theater awaited. At first, Mother had suggested the Arch Street Theater, but he had immediately rejected that theater when he realized what was playing—*The Southern Rebellion by Land and Sea*. Instead, he chose *The Black Creek* at the Walnut Street Theater. To his joy, Josephine had allowed him to invite the Mitchells along and had even seemed quite eager to include them.

He held up her pelisse of vivid black velvet with a matching fur collar and placed it around her shoulders. She turned to adjust her hat, a large brim black velvet hat drooped fashionably front and back. A red-dyed ostrich plume ran over the top and trailed down the nape of her neck. He snuck under the brim and stole a kiss before they exited out of their room.

"Later, my darling," he promised.

"I shall be thinking of it all night." She rewarded him with a brilliant smile. She took a step forward and then halted. "Do I have time for one more…?"

"No, my dear. They won't sleep if you keep checking on them. The children are being well looked after," he assured her. "Come. We have a delightful evening in front of us."

"We do, don't we?" She intertwined her arm in his. "Let us go. We don't want to be late."

****

The carriage tracked through the newly fallen snow until it pulled to a stop in front of an elongated brick building with high arched windows with a sign which proclaimed it *Walnut Street Theater*. Gas-lit lamps lit up the entrance and patrons bustled around the grille of the ticket booth. A poster hung outside the door: *The Black Creek* starring Edwin Booth.

Cullen had watched his wife in conversation with Diana Mitchell with deep satisfaction. The gist of their discussion centered on the most effective manner of discipline for young boys. Diana and Gavin's young son was only a year older than Percival. The semblance of normalcy appeared on the horizon.

His arm rounded Josephine as they walked up the steps of the theater. As they entered into the lobby of the magnificent theater, she tensed, aware of the curious eyes upon her. His arm tightened about her waist.

Jo gazed up at him. Her bright eyes reflected her resolve to enjoy her evening. She was prepared and readied to face the world with him by her side. Smiling down at her, he led her into the auditorium.

****

Josephine had to admit she was enjoying herself greatly. After everything she endured when she left Magnolia Bluff, she would have never believed she would be happy again. He loved her and she…well, she realized she had never stopped loving him.

In the far recesses of her heart, guilt lived. What right did she have to happiness in the midst of such a horrible war? Wade was dead; the South had been devastated. Jo remembered what Wade had told her— *live one day at a time*. She would do so.

The noisy smoke-filled auditorium quieted when the usher announced the play would begin. Cullen squeezed her hand gently in assurance as boys carried long poles down the aisles to adjust the gaslights. The footlight candles shimmered on the stage as the piano player began to play. For the next hour, she became enjoyably immersed in the play.

When the lights came on for intermission, Jo worried briefly that Cullen might feel the need to introduce her to his acquaintances. But when they entered the lobby, he asked only if the women would like refreshments.

Josephine watched Cullen engrossed in conversation with Gavin.

Touching Jo's arm, Diana leaned over to her. "I believe they like this time to talk themselves. If you ask me, men gossip more than we do, except they call it *discussions*."

Laughing lightly, Jo suddenly halted. She saw Kathleen, her former-sister-in-law, sweep-down the stairs on the arm of a distinctively commanding figure of a man, an army colonel from the bars on his collar.

Kathleen cast her gaze toward Jo's direction. Jo cringed when Kathleen advanced upon her with eyes narrowed. Tilting her head to her escort, Kathleen whispered to him. He released her arm and took a step back.

"Are you well?" Diana asked.

Diana's words seemed to have resonated from far away. Jo made no response. All her attention lay upon the woman who came toward her, the woman she had hoped never to see again.

The years had been kind to Kathleen. Dressed in an exquisitely coiffed taffeta gown, her light brown curls were swept upward in a fashionable trend. She had gained a mature, womanly allure.

"Well, Josephine, you seem to have done well for yourself," Kathleen sneered, stiffly smiling. "Come...come now. Don't be shy around me. Are we not family?"

"Once, long ago. You know well enough that you are not an acquaintance I wanted to renew." Jo gave the woman a bland smile. "Now, if you will excuse me."

Kathleen stepped in front of her to block Jo's way. "Josephine, I can't let you go so quickly. It's been years, although if the truth be known, I remember all as if it were yesterday."

"I, too, have those same memories." Jo's eyebrows arched in amazement of Kathleen's brazen manners.

"Oh, it's no secret of our connection here in Philadelphia, if you are wondering. There are no secrets between us. Why, I heard a nasty rumor that Cullen rescued you from the depths of... oh, what did I hear...prison." Her voice carried a soft, husky quality within it as she continued. "We will have to get together for tea. I have always been fascinated with the tales I have heard about prison life. Tell me, Josephine, how did you survive? How many favors did you extend to be so well looked after?"

Jo's cheeks grew hot with indignation. Rage boiled within her. Only the knowledge that Kathleen was baiting her kept her composed.

"Let's go find the men, Josephine," Diana kindly suggested. "They must be missing us…"

Kathleen reached out and grasped Josephine's arm. "Oh, my dear, don't be in such a hurry. We are no longer in strict and stuffy Charleston where I was the outsider. No, you are here in Philadelphia. Now you are the outsider. The good people of this city will never forgive Cullen for marrying a Southern heathen. They will never accept you."

"Are you saying that I need to apologize for being Southern? I will never do so. I love my home, but my duty lies beside my husband. I want nothing more than for all the troops on both sides to return home safely. There has been too much death." Josephine spoke in a tone much stronger than she physically felt. "I have always tried to live my life honorably and with character. That is how during these difficult times I survived. How do you?"

"This isn't about me."

"Is it not? Why can I not question you and your integrity? You are a coward for attacking me in such a manner."

Kathleen shrugged indolently. "Words are what I have found most Southerners hide behind. And now you hide behind your husband. I wonder how your fellow Southerners feel about your betrayal. You talk of honor and character yet display none of which you speak."

Exasperated, Jo fought the urge to scream at her. Instead, she uttered in a low, forceful voice, "You know nothing of me."

"I know enough." Kathleen smirked. "And so will the rest of Philadelphia soon enough."

"It is sad, Kathleen. I feel nothing for you except repugnance. It is beyond my comprehension how one can coldheartedly abandon their child. You never once answered any of my letters I sent about your darling little girl. Never once inquired of her health or well-being." Jo choked back her emotions. "She died in my arms…your beautiful little girl. I paid to have a letter sent urgently to you. I never heard back. That is what I find unforgivable. Fannie was so small, so innocent. What could she have ever done to harden your heart so? No, others may question me, but not you."

Kathleen's eyes narrowed with hatred. "This is far from over, Josephine. It won't be long until Cullen realizes the enormous mistake he has made. Not long at all…"

"You are sadly mistaken, Kathleen."

Jo turned to see that Cullen had walked up behind her. His jaw was set; his brow furrowed. He snarled, "Leave my wife alone from your barbs or you will sorely regret it."

"Tsk...tsk...tsk, Cullen. You should know I don't take threats kindly," Kathleen warned crisply and took a step back with a smile, although it held little humor in it. "We'll see who regrets what."

She said nothing else, but turned back to her escort. The next minute, the two exited the theater. The intermission was long over. One of the ushers announced the doors would be closed, for the play was about to begin.

"Come. We'll go home." Cullen's arm went protectively around her.

She placed her hand on his arm gently and shook her head. "I'm not going to let her ruin my evening."

"Are you certain?" He looked over at Gavin, who seemed to be waiting for their decision.

"Yes, most definitely." Josephine managed a smile. "The play is delightful, as is the company we have. Besides, you promised me a night out."

The four returned to their seats. The play went on. Delightful as it may have been, Jo's mind was far away. She could not simply dismiss the ominous feeling that Kathleen had provoked within her.

* * * *

Reflecting on the evening, Josephine sat at her vanity and stared into her beveled mirror. Mary unfastened her gown. It would have been a wonderful night if not for Kathleen. She could not deny that Kathleen's words had disturbed her. *How did Kathleen know she had been in prison?*

In the carriage on the way home, Cullen assured her that she had no fear that it would become common knowledge. He would make certain of it, insinuating he would find where Kathleen learned of the fact.

"You were wonderful, my love," Cullen asserted. "I even saw some kind smiles while we walked by."

She would not have disputed his statement if not for that brief encounter with Kathleen. Perhaps after the war, she would not feel as much as an intruder at social functions. However, if anyone found out she had been in prison, no matter the reason, she had little doubt any smiles would be dispensed her way.

Mary reached over the gown's shoulders to slide it off.

"That won't be necessary. I will help my wife."

559

In the mirror, Jo saw her husband's reflection in the doorway, his waistcoat and cravat removed. His dark eyes caught hers, leaving little doubt of his intent. The evening's confrontation had been forgotten; his mind was not on anything other than his obvious desire.

Jo gave no notice of Mary, who nodded slightly, and quickly exited.

Cullen closed the door and came over behind her. "Would it surprise you that I have a vision of you wearing my gift?"

"I am wearing them now." She smiled alluringly, touching the lustrous pearls that cascaded around her neck.

"Not as I want to see them worn."

He reached down and lifted her to her feet. His arms encircled her and pulled her back against him. The power of his touch warmed her; his fervent kisses on her neck sent a torrent of sensations surging through her.

His hands moved over the silk that covered her breasts, intertwining his fingers in the strings of the pearls. As he slipped the gown off her shoulders, he pulled the material down to her waist. He ran his hand up her pantalets and pulled them down, making her shudder. Soon he had dispensed with all the layers of clothing between him and his fantasy. She stood as he desired, with nothing but the pearls against her skin.

A large smile formed on his lips, staring at her in the mirror as his hands claimed her with firm strokes along her stomach, hips, and thighs. Dipping down, his kisses scalded her neck. Slowly, almost languidly, his caresses sent rippling waves of pleasurable sensations crashing through her.

She turned to him to accept more. He complied and lowered his head down to her breasts. As he suckled on one, and then the other, she closed her eyes and basked in his maddening kisses. Pausing only a moment, he led her to their bed.

He looked down at her longingly, fumbling with the buttons on his shirt. She helped him shed his clothing, worked at the fastening on his pants. Gently, he pressed her back on the bed and covered her with his naked body.

Their tongues tangled, enthralled in the essence of their passion. She responded with abandon. Sliding her fingers through his hair, she pushed him on his back and then straddled him.

As she rode him, the pearls hung down over her naked breasts in the most provocative manner. Aroused to the point he cautioned himself. He needed to give her pleasure, compelled to give her pleasure, before his own.

He flipped her, returning her to her back. "Hold your arms over your head and spread your legs."

She objected to nothing and he wanted everything. The anticipation of the coming pleasure curled in her stomach and flared in an overwhelming heat at the core of her being. He gave her pleasure with his mouth and tongue, but he took his own in hers.

He tasted her and savored her every gasp and groan of swelling passion. She came hard, thrashing and screaming. He took her then and filled her with the hunger he held for her…only her. Each thrust sharpened wanton sensations, taking them to a plane of ecstasy that erupted into exquisite relief.

Afterwards, Jo snuggled into his shoulder and he drew her closer. Beyond this night, he took solace in the love they shared and knew they could face the world outside these doors. This was as it should be. Josephine and him together.

* * * *

On Monday, Cullen rose early in the morning, the memories of Josephine's beauty and passion fresh on his mind. He would rather have lost himself remembering the long hours of incredible pleasure she had given him, but he had tasks to complete before he left for Washington on the afternoon train.

He had decided that he would move his family out to Rosemount when he returned from his trip. Most times, the house was not open until summer, but he saw the desire in Josephine to leave the confines of the city.

Kathleen was not the only resident of the city who held prejudice against Southerners. The city's bias toward their Southern brothers swelled. There was no need to expose Josephine to those sentiments more than need be.

In time, the rift that had divided the nation would begin to heal, but not until the war officially ended. President Lincoln had been inaugurated for another term a couple of weeks before. His first term had been spent diffusing the age-old practice of slavery. That, in turn, had caused the bloodiest, most horrific of wars, pitting brother against brother, family against family. Now, President Lincoln faced another gargantuan task: leading the nation out of the darkness it had fallen into and into the nation he envisioned.

Despite the earliness of the day, he found his father already at work in his office. His home office was situated in the back of the house with a separate door for any necessary visitors, such as the one sitting in front of the desk.

Heyward appeared deep in thought, rubbing his hand over his chin. He looked up when Cullen walked across the room.

"Cullen," Jonathan said. "Heyward has come with some disturbing news."

"What has happened?"

His first thought was something had happened to Miss Hazel. He prayed to God she was well. Jo took solace in the fact that her mammy was close at hand. Cullen came to the realization that it was useless trying to separate Jo from Miss Hazel. He had relented and withdrawn his objections to Jo visiting Miss Hazel.

Yesterday, Jo had even gone down to the Baptist church and donated supplies for the injured black soldiers. Miss Hazel had directed her energy into helping the wounded men who often received inferior medical treatment.

Granted, he had been furious when Jo had left with Heyward in the manner she had when she first arrived. There was so much already weighing against his wife, she didn't need any gossip about being escorted through Philadelphia with a freedman.

In truth, it had been more. He had been jealous of her love for her mammy...her need for someone other than himself. Not to mention, he had been abrupt with Heyward.

"Yesterday when Miss Jo was leaving after her visit with Ma at the church, I noticed a figure lurching in the alley. He looked like a vagabond, dressed in rags, heavily bearded. The man's hat brim was pulled down to his eyebrows, leaving most of his face in the shadows, but I swore, Mr. Cullen, when he looked at me, it was Harry Lee. I ran after him, but he disappeared."

Cullen faced Heyward. "It is a relief to me that you are keeping a keen eye out for Miss Josephine. I am deeply appreciative. Moreover, this gives me a chance to apologize to you for the last time we talked."

"It's not necessary," Heyward said. "I'm more concerned about the welfare of my family and Miss Jo. I refuse to lose more to that man."

"Then I can relieve your mind." Cullen walked over and sat on the corner of the desk. "Harry Lee is dead. He was captured and held as a prisoner of war at Fort Delaware. Andrew informed me of the fact and I telegraphed a man I know down at the state department. I just got confirmation from Captain Gibson, the fort's commander, that Harry Lee died of smallpox last year. It's over."

"You're sure?"

"Gibson said he saw a copy of Harry Lee's death certificate. Again, I apologize. I should have relayed the information to you."

Heyward shook his head. "I could have sworn it was Harry Lee."

"The son of a bitch is dead, but it does not mean that others aren't out there gunning for my wife. You have brought up a good point. There are many in the city who hold hard feelings toward any Southerner. Someone may have set their sights on Jo. Maybe I shouldn't leave today."

Jonathan held up his hand and shook it slightly. "I don't think it's necessary. I will see that she is looked after. If she goes out, I will send Ainson with her, and I will alert the coachmen and footmen to be on guard for any suspicious activity."

"If I see that man again, I will let you know," Heyward said.

A knock on the door disturbed the conversation. Elizabeth slipped her head in the room and smiled. "Father, Mother wanted me to tell you that Roger Dukett is in the drawing room. Were you expecting him this morning? He says you were supposed to discuss his government contract for uniforms."

"Oh, yes. I promised to send a note to Senator Cowan on his behalf. It seems that the government requisitioned another order for the troops and rescinded it after it was delivered. I fear we will be addressing more of these issues if the war is truly coming to an end." Jonathan turned to Heyward and Cullen. "I really must go and see Roger. Is there anything else, Heyward?"

"No, sir. I have to get back to the Chestnut Street office."

"Then I will see you there this afternoon. Thank you, Heyward. Your attentiveness is appreciated." Jonathan rose and nodded to Cullen. "I assume I will see you before you leave."

"But of course." Cullen answered his father, but cast a thoughtful glance toward Heyward, who had made no movement to leave. He had known Heyward a long time. Despite the class differences, the two men knew each other well.

Heyward had been one of the main reasons Cullen's network had worked. He also knew something else bothered Heyward. "Are you going to tell me what else is troubling you?"

"Not sure," Heyward stated honestly. "I'm used to being dismissed by others, Mr. Cullen. Not you."

"I am not dismissing what you saw," Cullen replied. "I would not. Remember it was I who helped you rescue Gillie and saw firsthand the damage the man inflicted. I certainly would not play light with the information if I thought for one minute it wasn't truly Harry Lee."

"I suppose I could have been wrong, but I tell ya, something is going on that I don't like. I can feel it."

"What are you talking about?"

Heyward nodded to the door. "Miss Elizabeth, there. She's friends with that devil woman Dr. Andrew was married to?"

"Miss Elizabeth was good friends with Andrew's wife at one time, but not now, especially after what that woman put my cousin through. Miss Elizabeth told me herself she cut ties with her."

"You believe that?"

"I have no reason not to." Cullen's eyebrows rose. "Do you?"

"I saw 'em, Mr. Cullen, more than once, together. One time walking down Walnut Street arm in arm. Then last week, a carriage drew up at your father's work. Miss Elizabeth got out, but I saw that woman in the carriage."

Cullen couldn't deny that the knowledge disturbed him. He didn't try. "Tell me again what you saw...in detail."

* * * *

"Oh, Cullen, I'm so sorry." Tears spilled down Elizabeth's cheeks. "I should have told you, but truly I didn't want to upset you or Josephine."

"Elizabeth, this is inexcusable." Cullen shook his head. "Whether intentional or not, you gave information to Kathleen, which she attempted to use against Josephine."

"I am weak, for in the end I couldn't tell her no...not in the state she was in," Elizabeth cried, lifting her head up. Wiping back her tears, she rose from the sofa and gripped Cullen's sleeve. "She played against my sympathy. I thought she had changed like she claimed. I was foolish to believe her. She was relentless. I told her many times to leave me alone."

"That is true, Cullen," Monica intervened. "I witnessed one of Kathleen's tantrums...here in the drawing room. Why, I had never seen such a display! She pulled at her hair and fell to her knees, weeping and crying she had no one else to turn to for comfort. I heard Elizabeth send her away."

"Elizabeth, do you comprehend the havoc Kathleen wreaked over Charleston and my cousin? She blatantly carried on numerous affairs, pauperized Andrew, and left her infant daughter behind without blinking an eye."

"Stop, oh, please stop, Cullen. I didn't know. She told me that the Montgomerys ripped her daughter from her arms and refused to let her have her. That it was Andrew having the affairs...that she was cast aside because she was a Yankee...but it wasn't until after her father passed away and news came back that her daughter died that I gave in..."

564

Elizabeth's voice cracked. Releasing Cullen's sleeve, she fell back into her mother's waiting arms. "I'm so ashamed."

Monica patted the back of her disturbed daughter. She looked over at Cullen. "She is sorry. I will make sure that woman won't set foot in this house again and Elizabeth will not associate with her anymore. Is that not right, Elizabeth?"

The distracted Elizabeth did not look around, only nodded. Falling back into her mother's arms, she wept.

Cullen frowned deeply. He had no choice but to accept his stepsister's apology, but with reluctance. He was disappointed Elizabeth had fallen back under Kathleen's spell.

In the end, Cullen left Monica to deal with Elizabeth. If she didn't, he would when he returned. He would not have Kathleen in their lives.

He had to prepare to leave within the hour and wanted to spend the time with his wife and children. He left the room.

Chapter Twelve

Just before dusk, a warm southwesterly breeze sprang up at the exact moment when Josephine exited the carriage. The buffeting wind whipped at her and tore at her bonnet. Hampered by her petticoats, dress, and cloak, she lagged against the force.

Turning, she reached up and gripped her bonnet tightly. Abruptly, she halted. There in the shadows between the houses was a strange man with his hat brim pulled down low over his eyebrows. He wore a large brown overcoat and his beard hung down to his chest. Even from the distance between them, she felt his eyes burn into her.

Catching hold of her skirt, she looked back. He had vanished, lost in the shadows. Good gracious! She had gone and let her fanciful imagination get the better of her.

Entering the house, Penniford, the Smythes' butler, was at the door and took her cloak, along with her bonnet. Immediately, she forgot the storm brewing outside as she was greeted to the sound of her children laughing in the drawing room.

Josephine walked in and smiled at her son playing with his sister. Elizabeth and Mrs. Smythe sat on the sofa, enjoying the sight themselves.

"I told you they would be content." Elizabeth's voice was soft and reassuring. "How was your visit with your friend?"

"Quite enjoyable," Jo acknowledged, patting her unruly hair back down. "Diana was quite hospitable. She invited over her two sisters as well. It was a lovely tea." Jo didn't add that it was a nice gesture on the part of Diana to include her, making her feel welcome in her new surroundings.

"I'm glad you are beginning to start calling on friends. I was thinking I would like for you to accompany me over to the Jancys' next week." Mrs. Smythe met Jo's gaze.

Touched by the invitation, Jo quickly agreed. "I would love to go."

"Then it is set." Her mother-in-law displayed no emotion at her acceptance, not even a small smile. "Penniford just announced supper would be in half an hour if you need to freshen up."

"Thank you. I believe I do." Jo glanced over at her children, who hadn't even looked up at her entrance. "I believe they are happy. You seem to have a way with them, Elizabeth."

"It is mutual," Elizabeth murmured, handing Percival one of his men that Madeline had thrown. "I truly enjoy them both."

Jo studied Elizabeth for a brief moment. She had to admit Elizabeth had gone out of her way to make Jo feel more at home since the episode over Kathleen. It would not come as a shock if it had been Elizabeth who suggested her mother invite Jo to the Jancys'.

Moreover, Elizabeth seemed at ease with the children. Her face lit up when they came into a room. Although never could she be considered a beauty, her appearance had greatly improved over the last few days.

She didn't know whether it was confidence or maybe she had found the happiness she sought in the children. *She needs children of her own. When Cullen comes home, perhaps I can set her up with one of his friends.*

"My dear." Mrs. Smythe halted Jo's progress out of the room. "In the foyer, you will find a small package Cullen sent."

"Thank you." Jo hurried out. On the table, as her mother-in-law had stated, sat a small package. She opened it quickly. It was a book from Cullen with a note.

Thought you might find this of interest. I know I heard you talk of the author, Charles Dickens. One of the wives of a fellow officer recommended this book, A Tale of Two Cities. I thought it might help pass the time until I return. Be patient. I have only to take care of a couple of more issues and then, my darling, you will find me constantly by your side. I miss you and the children, but will return as quickly as I can. Yours forever, Cullen

Languorously, Josephine walked up the stairs with the book in hand. Two weeks had passed since Cullen had left for Washington. Her nervousness in his departure had diminished, although she missed him dearly. She hoped his apprehensions about her had eased. He had almost canceled his trip because of his fear for her.

"Go, my love. Have no doubt I will be well looked after. There will never be a perfect time for you to go. There will always be one thing or the other. We can't live our lives in fear of what might be."

Cullen had gone with the greatest reluctance. She missed him so, but she had survived with the knowledge that soon he would return.

* * * *

The early morning sunlight filtered into the dining room. Sitting across from Elizabeth, Jo noticed her sister-in-law had scarcely touched her breakfast.

"Are you certain?" Elizabeth wrung her hands.

At first, Jo thought Elizabeth had been startled by the news, but now she swore Elizabeth was displeased. Holding the telegram in her hand, Jo made light of her confusion. "This is the best news, with Cullen returning earlier than he thought. I would have assumed you would have been delighted since you have devoted so much time with the children and myself."

"Of course. Of course." Elizabeth nodded. "It is only...I shouldn't say anything...but I had hopes of surprising the two of you. It is disappointing after all the careful planning to hear that my brother is returning early. Tomorrow you say."

"Surprising us? Oh, Elizabeth, what have you done?"

"If I told you, it would completely ruin the surprise," she said with a look that told she was at odds with herself on how to proceed. The chimes of the grandfather clock in the foyer rang eight times. She clasped her hands. "Oh, my! It is getting late. If Cullen is returning, then I have so much to do." She pushed back her chair and rose. "I might be able to pull it off, yet. We'll see."

"Elizabeth, you haven't eaten. I hope you aren't—"

"Don't worry, Josephine, I will make it perfect for you." Elizabeth strolled over to the door. Muttering to herself, she went on. "Yes, yes. I believe I can still have everything set."

Jo frowned. Although she appreciated Elizabeth's effort in trying to rectify her mistake in confiding family secrets to Kathleen, she had no desire to have a party in her honor, which was what she assumed Elizabeth had been rambling on about.

She appreciated everything Elizabeth had done. Truly, she had, but she was in no mood for a celebration, nor did she want to hurt Elizabeth's feelings. Oh, she missed Cullen terribly.

****

The golden sun tinged a reddish glow and loomed over the horizon. The day was done. The children had bathed and prepared for sleep. Jo had promised them an extra half hour of playtime before she put them to bed. Mrs. Finnegan watched over the children while Jo sat in front of the fire in the bedchamber and read *A Tale of Two Cities*.

She was almost done with the book and looked forward to finishing tonight. She had placed the mantel clock on the table in front of her. If she didn't, she would lose track of time and the children would be up after their bedtime.

Sensing a presence in her room, Jo looked up and saw Elizabeth in the doorway, wearing her cloak and gloves. She gestured for Jo to follow her. "It's been prepared."

"What?"

"My surprise," Elizabeth said, ill-concealing her excitement. She walked over and took Jo's hand, urging her upward. "You have to come with me now, though. Yes, you need to come with me. I have to show you."

"Elizabeth, it is late and I need to put the children to bed. Can it not wait until morning?"

"No!" Elizabeth's eyes widened. "No, no, no. You have to come now. I have the carriage waiting out back."

"Carriage?" Jo rose slowly, placing her book carefully in her seat. "Elizabeth, I'm not going out tonight. I'm sorry—"

"But you must. You must," Elizabeth repeated. "I have already checked in with Mrs. Finnegan. She will put the children to bed."

"I have to protest. I always tuck the children in at night—"

"It is Kathleen!" Elizabeth brusquely announced. "You need to come and see what I have done for you."

"Kathleen?" Jo stared at Elizabeth in confusion. Her sister-in-law scared her with her intensity. "Elizabeth, you need to calm down. Tell me what you have done."

"No," Elizabeth stated firmly, seemingly outraged at Jo's refusal. "You will ruin the surprise. You have to see it for yourself."

Jo gently put her hand on Elizabeth's arm. "Let's go see your mother..."

Elizabeth jerked her arm back. Her demeanor manner suddenly changed. She stated in a flat, dry tone, "It is you who doesn't understand the magnitude of Kathleen's hatred toward you. She is crazed. She told me she is going after your mammy. She intends to do her harm."

"Miss Hazel? Kathleen may be vindictive, but to harm another?"

"Kathleen plans to go to the authorities in the morning and accuse Miss Hazel of stealing a necklace of hers. You know as well as I that at the least she will be arrested. Jail won't bode well for a woman of her age. It is why I have the carriage readied. We must go and warn her. I would go myself, but I doubt she would believe me," Elizabeth urged.

"We have to tell your father." Jo spoke her thoughts out loud. "I need to check on the children, get my cloak."

"I have your cloak." Elizabeth grasped Jo's hand. "I have already told Father. He has sent for Heyward, but I thought we could go and collect your mammy. She can stay in the servant quarters until the matter is settled."

"But, of course," Jo agreed and followed Elizabeth. In the hall, the children's laughter echoed. She hesitated. "The children."

"Are fine," Elizabeth answered without hesitation. "It will only upset them if you tell them you are going out. Mrs. Finnegan will care for them. Come. We won't be long."

Trepidation filled Jo. Something wasn't right. Suddenly, she wished desperately Cullen was here. Sighing heavily, she realized logically she should wait until Mr. Smythe and Heyward responded to the threat, but she would never get any sleep if Miss Hazel was thrown into jail.

Josephine nodded. "I'm ready."

As she pulled back the curtain of the carriage, Jo saw the sun waned in the distance. It would be dark soon.

Turning back to Elizabeth, Jo asked, "Whose carriage is this?"

"I borrowed Kathleen's," Elizabeth said with pride in her voice. "Is it not the most ingenious move? Now, Kathleen can't go out."

"Kathleen's? Oh, Elizabeth, it will only serve to infuriate her more," Jo admonished. "Perhaps it will be best if you go back. We can use our carriage. There is no need to be so secretive. I would feel more comfortable."

Elizabeth sat back and said nothing. Jo stared at her sister-in-law. Elizabeth acted oddly, more so than usual. She had been so happy when she first came into her room with the news…

"Elizabeth." Jo broke the silence. "What was the surprise you prepared for me?"

The carriage slowly drew to a halt. Glancing out the window, Jo pressed harder, "Where have you taken me, Elizabeth? This isn't Miss Hazel's."

"No, it isn't." Pulling the hood of her cloak over her head, she had her hand on the handle of the door. She paused. "You trust me. Don't you, Josephine?"

A sudden overwhelming sense of foreboding swept through Jo. Slowly, she eased down the steps to the sidewalk. When she looked one way and then the other, Elizabeth had disappeared.

"Elizabeth!"

She stood in the middle of the street lined with homes of prosperous men. The mansions were impressive, sitting side by side with scalloped gables, latticed dormers, and terra cotta angel faces. Most presented brick façades with bow-front windows and secured with a high scrolled wrought-iron fence.

Where am I? Jo turned to call out to the coachman, but froze. The man leaped off his perch in front of her. Recognition sent goading spurs of terror cascading through her...blinding all reason.

Laughing, the man took his hat off. His face was thinner; his hair longer with a disheveled, unkempt beard. His eyes had not changed and they stared straight into hers. Death had no hold on him. He had walked out of hell for his revenge.

Good Lord, save me! It was Harry Lee!

Harry Lee raised his right hand to doff his hat, while his dark eyes took in her troubled state. His face hardened imperceptibly with a sneering smile.

Pale and shaken, Jo whirled around and stumbled backward. He reached for her; her knees buckled beneath her and she collapsed. Bending down, he pulled her to her feet.

"It will do you no good, my dear cousin, to fight this. A lot of time and hard work has been spent for this moment to occur."

His hand clenched tightly on her forearm. She fought back, wrenching from one side to the other.

"You just have to struggle. Don't you?"

She screamed, but the sound of her voice was muffled by his hand clamping down over it with a cloth. Suddenly, everything went black.

* * * *

Exhausted, Cullen was happy when he finally arrived back home. It had been a long day. After he had sent the telegram to tell Josephine he would arrive tomorrow, he had decided to forego the last official dinner. He had had enough of ceremony and war discussions. He had taken the last train back to Philadelphia.

The meeting with Welles had been productive. Magnolia Bluff had survived. Andrew had set up the sign as a hospital in front of the main house, saying the plantation had a typhoid epidemic. The excuse had worked. Speculation was bound to circulate, but nothing could ever be

571

proved. Now, all that needed to be done was to corner General Robert E. Lee and end this damn war.

Cullen hurried into the house and was greeted with silence. Taking off his coat, he saw Penniford round the corner.

"Mister Cullen." Penniford extended his hand to take his coat and gloves. "It is good to see you home."

"Thank you, Penniford. The house seems quiet, too quiet."

"Your parents are out for the evening. We weren't expecting you home."

"I took the train today. Is my wife in our room?"

"I haven't seen her since this afternoon. I assume so. The children are asleep in the nursery."

He headed upstairs to their room. He opened it to a dark stillness. The book he had given her lay on a chair, with a throw blanket lying on the floor. *Strange*. He walked through to the nursery where Madeline lay sound asleep. He tucked the blanket around her curved little body.

Outside the room, loud voices echoed in the hall. Cullen made his way to the noise. The door to his son's room was open. Looking in, he saw the room cluttered with toys littered on the floor, the bed covers thrown off the bed.

Percival stood in the middle of the room and stomped his foot. "I can't go to sleep until Momma kisses me. She always kisses me good night." His voice ranted with an inflexible determination.

"It is late. I have told you that your momma will kiss you when she returns. She wants you in bed." Mrs. Finnegan's exacerbated voice railed.

"I want Momma!"

"Percival?" Cullen walked into the room. Immediately on the sight of his father, Percival ran and flung his arms around him.

"Father, they won't let me see Momma. I want to see Momma." Tears flowed down his cheeks.

"Of course, you can see your mother." Cullen stared over at the nanny. "Why is my son so upset, Mrs. Finnegan? Where is his mother?"

Mrs. Finnegan looked at him with tired eyes and then looked at Percival. She shook her head. "I'm sorry, sir, but I haven't a clue where Mrs. Smythe has gone."

****

"Josephine, where are you?"

Cullen walked the house, pausing at doors to check all the rooms. Holding Percival's hand, he halted in the foyer when he saw Penniford strode toward him.

"I'm afraid Mrs. Smythe is not in the house, sir. Mary said the last she saw Mrs. Smythe was with Miss Elizabeth, walking down the servant stairs."

"I told ya. I told ya. The bad man took her!" Percival wailed to the point his small body shook.

"Percival, calm yourself. I will find your mother," Cullen assured his son, but fear grew within him.

Mrs. Finnegan stood behind him. "For the life of me, I wish I had asked Miss Elizabeth where she was going, but I didn't think Mrs. Smythe was with her. The last I saw of Mrs. Smythe, she was reading, having promised the children they could stay up an extra half hour. She never came to put them to bed."

"Did you not think that odd?" Cullen pressed. *Where...where could Jo have gone?*

"Mr. Cullen," Mary said in a timid voice.

Occupied with his thoughts, he hadn't even noticed she had walked up. "Yes, Mary."

"I have been racking my brain with where she could have gone. I heard her talking with Miss Elizabeth. She said something about Miss Hazel. Does that help?"

Cullen felt the first sign of relief. "Penniford, send a note over to Heyward and Miss Hazel and see if Mrs. Smythe is visiting."

"I have already taken the liberty of sending messages to Mr. Heyward's home and also, your father at the dinner party he is attending," Penniford said.

He nodded. Josephine's visits with her former mammy had not gone unnoticed by the servants. In truth, the servants probably knew their lives better than anyone.

"Father," Percival said with growing frustration. "I saw 'em from the window. I saw Momma get in with Auntie 'lizabeth. I saw his gun."

"Percival, what gun?" Now his son had his full attention. Cullen knelt to his level.

"The man who drove the carria'. He climbed back on top and pulled back his coat and patted it. The men who took Momma before had guns, Father."

"Listen, carefully, Percival. I will find your mother. You go back to your room with Mrs. Finnegan and go to sleep. I will have your momma back in the morning." Suddenly, he hugged his son, tightly. He pulled back, mussing his son's disheveled hair. "You can sleep in our room with Madeline. Will that make you feel better?"

573

Percival nodded, but eyed his father questionably. "But, Father, why did Auntie 'lizbeth said she was going to be my new momma?"

A chill shot through Cullen. "When did Aunt Elizabeth tell you that?"

"Not to me, Father. She talks to herself. She's funny, ex'pt she's been talking that everyone will be happy when it's done."

The gnawing fear turned to panic. *Lord, Kathleen had gotten to Elizabeth and caused her to betray her family! What was happening?* He knew only he was going to find out.

Cullen stood and turned to Mrs. Finnegan. "Take him into my room and lock all the doors…Madeline's also between the connecting rooms. Only open it to my parents or myself. Do you understand? Do not leave them!"

"Yes, sir." Mrs. Finnegan nodded. Water welled in her eyes, telling of her own worries. "Don't worry about the children. I won't let anything happen to them."

He swallowed hard. "Penniford, tell Father everything that has happened when he arrives." He paused to watch Mrs. Finnegan rush up the stairs. "Follow me."

In the study, Cullen pulled out a tin box and unlocked it. He checked to make sure it was loaded and handed it to Penniford. "Take the pistol and guard my children's door. Don't let anyone in except Father or myself, especially not my sister. Do I make myself clear?"

Conscious only of the need for haste, Cullen withdrew the other pistol. *God, what had happened to Josephine?* He didn't even know where to start. No, that wasn't true. He knew exactly where to go—straight to Kathleen.

With his loaded pistol in hand, he headed for the door. Grabbing his coat, he pushed his hat on his head. Briefly, he glanced up the stairs. Suddenly, he heard rapid footsteps pound into the foyer. Turning, he saw Heyward hurrying to catch him.

"Mr. Cullen, I received a note asking if Miss Jo was visiting. Figured something must be wrong. Ma sent me to check. Seems we were right." Leaning over, Heyward drew in a deep breath. "Do you want help?"

"I don't know what we face."

Heyward straightened himself up to full height. "Don't matter."

For a brief moment, he stared at the man, grateful for his offer. "Let's go."

Chapter Thirteen

Josephine woke to a repugnant odor mingled with musty, stale air. Lying on the floor of the cavernous room, she looked about, but saw little. It was dark and dank. Groggily, she crawled to her knees. Slowly, her eyes focused to make out shapes and forms.

Rising to her feet, she felt her way around and bumped into a table, a chair, and finally curtains. She jerked back on the material, desperately trying to get any light into the room.

A moment later, a sliver of light from the streetlamps streamed through. It wasn't much, but the dim light allowed her to see her prison. Frantically, she pushed against the window, but it wouldn't budge. She needed something to break the glass.

Turning around, Josephine surveyed the room. In the dim light, she surmised it must have been a parlor, but the covers over the furniture told that no one had entertained lately. On her left was a fireplace with a mantel; looking straight ahead, French doors led to another room. Then her eyes lit to a sofa and a couple of chairs to her right.

There had to be something in the room she could use. Large and heavy enough to break the window, yet easy enough for her to lift. She stared at the French doors. Her heart pounded madly. She hadn't much time before her cousin would return…of that she had no doubt.

Feeling her way around the room in the faint light, she tripped over something soft and bulky and fell down on top of it. Pushing back off it, Jo rolled over to the floor. The stench overwhelmed her…until she saw what she had fallen upon…and then terror gripped her soul.

Jo could not tear her eyes off the figure. A woman…dead…laid in a pool of dried blood. She was dressed in an evening gown, but it was

575

ripped and torn. Her throat had been slashed; Jo could make out the cut where she could now see maggots moving within it.

Oh, God! Oh, God! She crawled to her knees and recoiled against a table. Covering her mouth with her hand…*Oh, Lord, it was sticky with blood!* Clutching her stomach, she threw up.

Jo wiped her hand with her sleeve. *I have to get out of here! I have to get out of here!* Rising, she stepped back from the body, only to feel another object on the floor. Turning ever so slowly, she looked down. Another body. She screamed…and screamed.

Suddenly, the French doors opened wide. Light filtered in, illuminating the room with an eerie glow. Jo could see everything clearly—she was living in a nightmare.

"Cousin, I see you have met your roommates," Harry Lee sneered derisively and closed the gap between them. "It has been a long time. You don't know how I have lived for this moment. When I thought I couldn't take another breath, I thought of you and found strength again to live."

"You're mad!" Jo shivered uncontrollably. Frantically, looking all around, she did the only thing she could…she bolted toward the open doors.

Harry Lee caught her and spun her around to face him. He slapped her with enough force to send her reeling had he not had hold of her.

Tasting blood in her mouth, Jo twisted and turned, fighting desperately to get free. His fingers bit into her soft flesh and yanked her up, so close she felt his foul breath against her skin. She cringed.

Laughing, he withdrew a long knife from his belt. "Don't think this is going to be quick. Oh, no. I haven't waited this long not to enjoy every minute of what lies ahead for you. I'm supposed to wait for your sister-in-law. She will be in shortly. She wanted to see you die in front of her, but it doesn't mean I can't begin my fun."

"Elizabeth?" Jo's mind reeled. *Timid, shy Elizabeth wanted her dead?* She didn't believe it. "You lie!"

He took the knife and ran it along her cheek, nicking her skin. She felt warm blood run down her neck. His uproarious laughter drowned out the horrid gasp that trembled out from her.

"Damn you to hell!" Josephine burst out.

"I suppose," he mocked. "But you will be there long before me."

He pushed Jo back against a table. She watched as he took off his coat and rolled up his sleeves. "I had better get comfortable. This is going to take awhile. I owe you so much, Jo."

"I don't understand," she stuttered, gripping tight to the table's edge to hold herself up. "You're supposed to be dead."

"Do I look dead?" He chuckled. His head nodded in the direction of the dead man. "Colonel Reginald Holly, a physician for the Union army, stationed at Fort Delaware. Didn't do much except sign death certificates. For a price, he signed mine and smuggled my *dead* body out of that hellhole."

"That makes no sense. Why on earth would he do such a thing?"

"Ask Elizabeth. She was the one who found him after she overheard your husband say I was in a Yankee prison camp. Seems Kathleen and your devious little sister-in-law set in motion a plan to get me out." Harry Lee snickered. "I didn't care. Didn't listen to half their tale about how hard it was to find me. All I cared about was that it got me out of there…got me back to you."

Harry Lee stepped toward her, swiping his knife one way, and then the other. "I hated you from the beginning. Imperious little tramp. Remember when you first showed up in Charleston, down at the Battery—you tried to save Gillie after I dropped her over the railing. Did you ever figure out that I could have pulled you out easy enough? I laughed and laughed as you tried to grab hold of my hand. Could you not tell I kept easing it back just out of your reach? I watched you fall backward, struggling to remain afloat, watching you go down and then…You have had all the luck, Jo. What with both Wade and Cullen coming to your rescue."

He tilted his head to the side and licked his lips. "There won't be anyone to rescue you this night…you should have never refused me, Jo. You should have married me."

"I would have never married you! All you wanted was my daddy's money." She spat at him.

He slapped her again. His eyes narrowed with hatred. "You hypocrite! You act so righteous and moral. You are no better than I am, cousin. You enjoyed the wealth and status your father's money gave you. You reveled in our family's demise. You stood along the side of the Confederacy until the tide shifted and you ran back to your Yankee lover."

"I'm nothing like you! Nothing!" She wiped her bleeding nose with her sleeve.

"No, you are worse. You are a God damn nigger loving bitch!" he countered with a scoff. "Besides, your daddy was a bastard! What will your loving husband say when he learns he has married white trash?"

Her face flamed. *He knew about Papa.* Why would he not have told the world? She stopped herself. She knew the answer: because his name would have been tainted as well. She retorted, "He already knows you are my cousin."

His eyes flamed his anger. His hand gripped the knife tighter.

Jo ran. This time she got around him, but he lunged at her and knocked her down. Sprawled on the floor, Harry Lee straddled her, boasting a triumphant laugh.

Her pounding heart caused a cold sweat to soak her body. Staring up at the knife, she realized she was trapped.

"Mr. Haynes, I thought we agreed to wait until I returned."

Harry Lee eased off Jo and stood. Jo frantically got to her feet and stared, unbelieving of the sight before her. Elizabeth smiled.

"Why on earth is she still in that dreadful room, Mr. Haynes? Please bring her out here. I'm sure she has plenty of questions."

****

Elizabeth was stark raving mad. There was no other explanation. Feeling helpless in her plight, Jo had no choice but to listen to the woman's incoherent rantings.

"Elizabeth, Elizabeth," Jo repeated, anguish riddled in her voice. "Tell me why...why did you trick me? What have I done to you?"

"Done," Elizabeth jeered and strolled across the room. Her eyes raked over Jo. Shaking her head, she said in a wistful tone, "Such a beautiful woman. No one should ever have been allowed all you have been given. Kathleen and I wondered why God favored you so. Two men who loved you dearly. Not one, but two?

"I suppose Kathleen was jealous. I, myself, had my fill of men after Jeremiah. He betrayed me, told me he loved me then left me. He should have never left me, but I had my baby to comfort me until Kathleen." She shrugged with a bizarre, creepy smile. "I don't know where he went...Mother said he went West with his family. He left me without a word. They paid him off...he used me for money and left me with shame...I loved him..."

Jo gripped her flailing emotions with grit determination to survive. She couldn't die. Not yet. She reached for anything to bring Elizabeth back to sanity. "You didn't deserve him. You need someone to love you and all will be forgotten. I will help you. Cullen will help you. But we need to go home to the children..."

"Ah, but that's the trouble, Josephine. The children." A nasty smile twisted her lips. "They are the reason you are here. Percival and

Madeline need a good mother who concentrates solely on them. How could you choose to stay in that dreadful prison and leave them alone?"

"I had no choice," Jo stated adamantly. "I love my children and have done everything I can to protect them."

"You should have never left them alone," Elizabeth said, as if Jo had not spoken. She went on. "They can't have two mothers. I thought when you arrived that everything would have been set. Madeline, sweet Madeline, she didn't want you. You should have left well enough alone, but no! You set upon yourself to reclaim her, trick her into thinking you loved her, but you don't love her as I do."

Elizabeth's voice rose and then abruptly she halted. She looked around Jo into the parlor. Walking over to the doors, she closed them soundly. "We don't want to disturb Kathleen. She isn't happy as it is."

"It's Kathleen in that room! Your best friend. You killed Kathleen?" Jo asked, losing her grip on her own sanity. The woman was insane! She had to get out of here…she took a step back.

"You sound like Kathleen," Elizabeth scoffed. "She had to be punished. She killed my baby. She took me to that god-awful place and they killed my little girl…it would have been a girl, you know. She came to me in a dream and told me she was coming to me. And she did. I had to protect her from Kathleen."

Jo's eyes widened with horror. *Elizabeth thought Madeline was hers? Oh my God, she's crazy!* Jo shook her head. "No, Elizabeth. Madeline is my daughter. She needs her mother. She loves you, but—"

"Shut up!" Elizabeth screamed. "You don't deserve them. I can't have you stealing my child from me." She winced. "I do regret what I must do, but it's for the children's sake. I'm afraid Cullen has to die also. He could marry again and then…" Her words faded, as if she thought of something else. "Regrettable. Rest assured I will tell them even through your faults, you loved them."

"Elizabeth, you can't do this."

"In that you are quite wrong, my dear sister-in-law. I have thought it all the way through. When Kathleen came up with this far-fetched idea of saving Harry Lee from being a prisoner of war, it all fell into place. She believed she could manipulate Harry Lee into doing her bidding like she did before, but I knew…I knew he must have hated her. She left their child with Andrew. Kathleen could never understand the connection a real mother has to her child."

Jo glanced over at Harry Lee. *Fannie had been his?* She felt faint. She uttered in a low voice, "Kathleen plotted against me all this time."

"Don't tell me that you didn't suspect her," Harry Lee snickered. "She was in on my little plot from the time I got to Philadelphia to stop your wedding to that sniveling little coward, Andrew. She wanted to marry Andrew and I you. Of course, you would not have survived long enough to see the end result after I inherited all that was yours. Kathleen thought I would marry her afterwards and she was going to be the belle of Charleston."

"She was married!"

"Minute details, I can assure you." Harry Lee shrugged. "Besides, I never planned on marrying her. Just needed her help to get at you… See all the trouble you have caused?"

Jo stumbled backward, shaking her head. This couldn't be happening!

"Elizabeth, listen to me. You can't trust Harry Lee," Jo pleaded in a mild, almost soothing voice. "He killed Kathleen…Kathleen is dead, Elizabeth. When he has what he needs, he will kill you…and Madeline."

Elizabeth appeared less than pleased. "No! No!" she cried. "Madeline is safe…safe."

Jo saw before Elizabeth. The barrel glistened in the room light. Harry Lee didn't utter a sound. He cocked the pistol and fired once. Immediately, Elizabeth clutched her stomach and collapsed to her knees. In shock, she looked down. Blood oozed out between her fingers.

Harry Lee strolled over even before the smoke cleared and aimed once more at Elizabeth's head.

"Don't," Jo cried. "For God's sake!"

Harry Lee slowly turned back to her. His eyes had turned dark; his smile caustic. He gave her a nasty look.

Jo wasted no more time. Not looking back, she rushed toward the door Elizabeth had entered. Falling against the door, her hands desperately sought her escape. Trembling, she tried to turn the handle. *It has to open…it has to…*

A hand gripped her from behind and thrust her hard against the wall. "Bitch!" Harry Lee snarled. "You ain't going nowhere!"

He clasped his hands around her neck, squeezing so she couldn't take a breath. When he suddenly released it, she gasped for breath. "Told ya' it ain't going to be quick, cus!" He touched her face and ran his hand down to her bodice. Gripping the material, he smiled smugly. "It's time for my fun."

She twisted back and heard the material tear. She became like a wild animal, kicking and clawing. Jo clawed his face, digging her fingernails deep in his skin.

Harry Lee's face twisted into a façade of burning rage unleashed upon her. He hit her with the back of his hand. Reeling in pain, she rolled to avoid another. As she scrambled to her feet, he caught her. A cry of dismay escaped her lips.

She strained to get out of his clutches. Abruptly, he released her. Momentarily stunned to be free, she eased back in a slow motion. He reached down to his waist and pulled his knife out. A god-awful sound emerged, and Harry Lee venomously snarled.

With the handle grasped tightly in his hand, he lunged at her. She tried to run, but he knocked her down, hard against the hearth. As she lifted her head, she felt the world spin. She remembered nothing else as darkness descended around her.

* * * *

Cullen was a madman. He heard Jo scream and the sound sent cold, merciless fury throughout his veins. He ran, leaving Heyward in his wake. With the strength of ten men, he rammed the door with his shoulder, breaking the barrier between him and Jo off its hinges. He ran in swiftly and as dangerously as a mountain lion ready to pounce.

On their way over to Kathleen's house, he hadn't known what he would face. When they exited the carriage, the blood-curdling cry answered the uncertainty.

The house sat in almost total darkness; only a few lit gas lamps glowed dimly in the foyer. The air, stank and stale, gave way to a home that had fallen into disrepair, evidence that little attention had been paid to the residence for a long time.

Immediately, his eyes caught light reflected under the doorway. Bursting through the door of what had once been a dining room, his heart sank. Josephine lay motionless in the grip of a ghost from the past. With his knife set to plunge, Harry Lee looked over his shoulder and grinned.

With his pistol aimed straight at Harry Lee's heart, Cullen demanded, "Put her down."

Moving the unconscious Jo in front of him, Harry Lee laughed. "Don't think so."

Not taking the chance of hitting Jo, Cullen lowered his gun and tucked it in his belt. For a brief moment, he contemplated his options. He had only one—he charged at her assailant.

Taken by the intensity of the attack, Harry Lee could do little to evade the assault. Cullen slammed him hard and dropped him down on the floor. Gripping tight to Harry Lee's arm, Cullen banged it against the floor until the knife dropped out of Harry Lee's grip.

With the strength of his mad rage, Cullen's fist knocked Harry Lee upside his jaw. Harry Lee drooped, but kicked Cullen back. Rolling to his right, he reached for his knife, edging ever closer until he grasped hold of it once more.

Cullen reacted as quickly. Both his hands held Harry Lee's, who was desperately trying to thrust the knife into Cullen. Cullen's eyes fixated on the bloody blade sidling closer. Josephine moaned, distracting Cullen. Harry Lee used it to his advantage and kicked Cullen back. Harry Lee's attention turned to the woman lying unconscious.

No time to keep Harry Lee from plunging the knife, Cullen lunged over Josephine, covering her with his body.

A shot rang out.

The room filled with a sudden eerie silence. Ever so slowly, Cullen looked around. Knife in hand, Harry Lee stood over him. Stunned, Harry Lee's eyes widened in disbelief. He dropped the knife and then collapsed.

With a smoking Remington revolver in his hand, Heyward walked over to the fallen body and turned it. Barely breathing, Harry Lee opened his eyes. Heyward knelt. "Look at me, you sonofabitch, and know who killed ya." Heyward reached over, took the fallen knife and plunged it deep into Harry Lee's chest.

Cullen crawled to his feet and picked up Josephine, holding her tenderly in his arms. Her body was limp. Her face was cut and bruised, but she was alive.

Outside, a commotion arose. Someone had called the authorities. They would be inside soon.

"Let me talk," Cullen said to Heyward, covered in blood. Cullen's eyes conveyed to the man…his friend…the depth of the thanks he felt. "Stay by me."

* * * *

Restless, Jo tossed and turned. Dreadful dreams troubled her. She felt as though she was drowning in a sea of memories. Struggling against wave after wave, she desperately tried to find a semblance of sanity.

Harry Lee leaned over the railed fence on the Battery. "Here, Jo, let me help you!"

Frantically reaching for his hand, she fell backward. Harry Lee laughed. His horrible, ghastly taunts echoed around her as water rushed about her. Gulping for air, a hand reached down and grasped hers.

"You're safe, Jo."

She felt herself being lifted out of the troubled tempest. "Wade...is that you? Oh, can you forgive me? I tried, truly I have, to hold to your legacy. It's been so hard...so terribly hard."

Leaning down, she felt his hand lightly caress her cheek and his lips breezed over hers. "It is as it should be."

He smiled his charismatic smile she had known so well...and then faded into the fog that now surrounded her. So thick and cloudy, she couldn't see. Until a light illuminated and the clouds parted. Jo's heart swelled on the sight of Gillie's lovely face...so brilliantly lovely.

"Gillie, forgive me...forgive me!" Jo pleaded, reaching out for her. "There is so much I need to tell you. I never understood...Oh, Gillie, don't leave me."

"I have never left you." The voice carried, so soft and soothing. "I never will."

The haze faded and then there was nothing. Her head hurt; her body ached. She had no strength. She tried ever so hard to open her eyes. Someone was beside her, but she felt no fear. Was it Cullen?

Tears fell down his cheek. *Oh, don't cry, my love. Don't cry.*

* * * *

Cullen gently wiped her brow. Jo hadn't woken up. *She should have woken up by now.* It had been almost twenty-four hours and she laid the same as when he first brought her home, wincing on her every movement.

The doctor cautioned Cullen to be patient. "She has been badly beaten, but it is the blow to the head that is the most concerning. The sooner she becomes conscious the better. There is nothing more we can do but wait."

Stubbornly, Cullen had refused to leave her side. She looked so white, so dreadfully white. He touched her cheek. "Come back to me, Josephine."

The whole of the house was in an uproar the moment he carried her up the stairs. Poor Percival. Cullen would never forget the look on his son's face when he saw his unconscious mother.

The hardest part, though, was telling his father about Elizabeth. In the midst of the bedlam at Kathleen's house, Elizabeth had been found alive. No one thought she would survive long enough to be transported to a hospital, but she had.

Moreover, she had become conscious, if ever so briefly. Father had said she confessed to all her misdeeds as though she were talking of going out for the evening. Without question, Elizabeth had lost grip with reality, insisting that Madeline was hers.

Elizabeth had ranted on to Father that Kathleen had plotted with Harry Lee before the war in a scheme to get Josephine's money. When she overheard that Harry Lee was in a Union prison camp, she made subtle inquires at dinner parties and discovered Colonel Holly would be of use to them. From there, Kathleen used her wiles to entrap the good colonel in their plan.

Harry Lee had been smuggled out and the devil was unleashed. Cullen was certain that Colonel Holly greatly regretted his actions. For Cullen held no doubt that when Harry Lee arrived on the scene, the madman devised his own scheme, which included Colonel Holly and Kathleen's deaths. The first of many Harry Lee planned, if not for Heyward.

Unfathomable that Elizabeth had been that devious to contemplate taking another's life. Now, she, too, clung to life. God forgive him, but he couldn't care less whether his stepsister lived or died.

Josephine moaned. *Lord, she must be in pain.* One of her eyes was swollen shut; the side of her face had been cut where Harry Lee had run his knife down her cheek. Her neck was bruised from having a hand around it, but she would survive. She had to survive.

"Father," a small voice called from behind him. "Can I come in?"

Looking over at the door, he watched Percival ease into the room. Cullen wondered how long his son had waited outside. He opened his arms wide for his son to climb into them. He hugged Percival tightly.

"Miss Hazel, you can enter also," Cullen said, knowing she, too, had been waiting in the hall. "She would want you here."

The old black woman made her way in and shut the door behind her. She pulled up her own chair to the other side of Josephine. She said nothing, but words weren't necessary. They never were between Jo and her mammy.

Percival's small hand reached out and touched his mother's face. "Is she gonna wake up?"

"Yes, son."

Percival turned to his father and stared into his eyes. "Did you get him, Father? He won't hurt Momma again?"

"He won't hurt anyone ever again."

Percival nodded, content with his father's answer. He sat on the edge of the bed with his father, refusing to leave when Mrs. Finnegan tentatively tried to coax him out without disturbing Josephine.

Percival had a need to be by his mother. Cullen understood the need and, strangely, he needed his son by him. Time grew late. Percival fell asleep in his father's arms. Cullen laid him at the foot of her bed. He stood to gather a throw to wrap around Percival.

"Cullen?" A weak voice whispered in the still of the room.

Rushing to Jo's side, he kissed her forehead and took her hand in his. "Rest, my love. Rest. Everything has been taken care of. You have nothing to fear."

With great effort, Jo tried to nod. She grimaced as a sleepy Percival climbed toward her. Cullen reached over to grab him. She shook her head. "No, he's fine."

Her arm rounded his small frame into her shoulder and he laid his head against her. She glanced over and saw Miss Hazel. She smiled. Looking back at Cullen, she asked, "Madeline?"

"She is waiting impatiently for her mother, my darling."

Wincing, she nodded, but seemed satisfied with the answer. "I'm so tired."

"Sleep. I will be here. We all will be here when you wake." Cullen choked back tears. He stroked her hair as her eyes closed once more.

* * * *

Threatening clouds darkened the skies. Over the ocean's horizon, a storm brewed. Blustery winds whipped about Josephine, hindering her stroll along the beach. She gave the impending rain no heed nor did she give thought to the force of the waves that crashed on the rocks.

Two weeks ago, Cullen had brought her and the children to Newport, a beautiful seaport town in Rhode Island. The house was a beautiful manor that overlooked the cliffs. At first, he had taken her to Rosemount to heal, but in the end, he decided the whole family needed to escape Philadelphia for a time.

She halted and faced the ocean. Back and forth, the tide rolled in and out, closer and closer to her. She didn't move as the water covered her feet and waves sprayed around her.

Though her wounds had healed physically, a gloom enveloped Josephine she couldn't dismiss. So many deaths haunted her.

Elizabeth was gone. Poor, disturbed Elizabeth had succumbed to the gunshot wound less than a week after being rescued. Her mother had been devastated, blaming herself for not knowing how sick her daughter had been, but in truth, no one had suspected Elizabeth capable of such evil deeds.

That knowledge had not stopped Monica Smythe from unleashing her hurt and anguish at Jo the day of Elizabeth's funeral. "Elizabeth would be alive today if not for you. Why…why did you have to come into our lives?"

Cullen dismissed the rantings of his stepmother. "She doesn't mean anything she said. She was only lashing out her pain. Unfortunately, you bore the brunt of it."

In time, Monica Smythe had apologized for her outburst, but the doubt lingered in Jo that perhaps Elizabeth would have been alive if not for her. The thought gnawed within her that, not only Elizabeth, but others suffered because they were associated with her. Faces…so many faces haunted her…*Wade…Gillie.*

Almost six months had passed since that horrifying night. So much had happened. The war had ended. In April, the South had surrendered, unconditionally, with Lee at Appomattox Courthouse; followed closely after by the assassination of President Lincoln. The days before the nation were uncertain.

Her beloved South had lost. She remembered how confident and enthusiastic Charleston had been at the beginning of the conflict. Now, the life they had known was no more. The brave souls had fought the damning war thinking they were fighting for a purpose—honor. Lives, so many lives had been given for the cause without reason. *Wade…*her heart crushed within her. She had failed him so terribly.

Guilt weighed upon her. Why was she here in comfort instead of paying for her sins…sins that God had deemed everyone should pay—both North and South—and pay greatly for their transgression in acceptance of that horrendous practice. None had been spared his wrath: those who benefited, those who accepted, and even the ones who turned a blind eye. The sole source of brightness throughout these tragic years had yielded only one thing—the abolition of slavery.

Magnolia Bluff survived. The family survived, but that, too, had come with a price. Jo doubted she would ever be able to return. The hatred spawned toward the Yankees extended to her, though not to Cullen. She had been painted a minx by Charleston society. Cullen was a loyal soldier, respected by his peers, even if it was on the side of the enemy.

For so long, Jo had thought the letters she had sent to Mother Montgomery, Jenna, and Charlotte had gotten lost due to the war and aftermath. It wasn't until she read a letter Andrew had sent Cullen that she fully understood that she had truly been shunned.

It is unfortunate. I have tried to reason with Mother, but she refuses to listen. The atmosphere here in Charleston lends to their discontent with Josephine. The rumors and whispers have done their damage that I can't undo without confessing the whole truth. Guilt is heavy on my conscience knowing I'm responsible, but I can't explain Jo's silence while she was in prison. To be honest, I did not realize how important it would be to maintain our secret indefinitely. Regrettable that Jo suffers from our actions.

A couple of months after the war, Cullen felt it his duty to travel down to Charleston. Although not welcome with open arms, no one turned their backs on him. He stayed with his family and secured Magnolia Bluff from the taxes that were draining most of the other plantations.

The South had been inundated with carpetbaggers who showed little sympathy toward Southerners. Cullen insulated his family from the backlash, even offered help to a few of their neighbors. More importantly, the secret shared between Andrew and Cullen had been kept. Wade's legacy to his son had been saved.

Jo kept reminding herself it was not her, but Percival's legacy that was of the utmost importance. Her disgrace meant little. A small sacrifice to maintain what Wade had fought to keep for his son. Reprimanding herself greatly for indulging in her own sorrows, she fought the surge of grief that swelled in her. The long denied acknowledgment—she greatly missed her home and the family she left behind.

But she had Miss Hazel, only now her mammy had a life different than Jo's. As she had in the past, Miss Hazel had stayed by Jo's side until she recovered. Afterwards, Miss Hazel went home to care for Tome. She had a life outside of Jo.

At the time of her abduction, Jo had not realized that it had been Heyward who had killed Harry Lee. Cullen hadn't told her until much later. He had wisely chosen to keep the information a secret.

There had been no doubt she owed her life to Heyward, but there was also no doubt that they could never reveal the truth. Cullen took credit for killing the assailant. No matter that the death had been justified: even in Philadelphia, it would not do to admit that a black man killed a white.

Heyward could live the rest of his life with the knowledge he avenged his wife's death, but Jo suspected it only gave him a semblance of peace. What he truly wanted, he couldn't have. Gillie was never coming back.

Moreover, Harry Lee's true identity was never acknowledged. The authorities determined that he must have been one of the Confederate soldiers held as a prisoner of war at Fort Delaware who held a grudge against Colonel Holly. In his quest for revenge, he followed Colonel Holly to Philadelphia and massacred not only Holly but everyone in his path.

There had been no mention of any devious plot to kill Jo or that Elizabeth was also a culprit instead of a victim. There had been no scandal, only an outpouring of sympathy for poor Monica Smythe.

The question that burned inside Jo was not whether God would forgive her, but could she forgive herself? Her conscience gnawed at her. She had tried so hard to do what was right, but in the midst of everything that happened, everything had gotten so confusing. With every move, her actions had consequences.

A wave crashed upon her, drenching her soundly. Startled for a moment, she gasped for air. Another broke over her. She didn't move.

Suddenly, a hand jerked her backward with such force she would have fallen to the ground had not strong arms grasped hold of her. "My God! Josephine! Could you not hear me?"

The rain-driven wind gusted. She tried to turn away from him, but Cullen would have none of it. He reached over and cupped her face in his hands.

"Josephine! Josephine!" he cried against the wind. "What are you doing? Father sent for me because he was worried about you. Josephine, look at me." Staring into her eyes, his voice softened. "What are you doing?"

Her gaze lowered, but he lifted her chin up so her eyes met his desperately pleading eyes. Pushing back against him, anger rose within her. She shouted, "I wanted only to feel again! I want to feel."

"I want you to feel again…for me," he cried. "Come back to me, Josephine. I need you. The children need you."

He wrapped his arms around her. He declared, "I love you. I will never stop loving you, Josephine. I need you so desperately…"

"I don't know if I can. I want to…"

He leaned down and pushed back her rain-soaked hair from her face. His lips claimed hers with a kiss that left no doubt of his desire for her. Breaking from her, his lips lingered. "I know you love me, Josephine. I know it. I'm not going to let you go."

"How can you love me? What right have I to be happy?"

"The right that we should have never been parted. I'm not going to let you go down this path any longer for some nonsense feeling of guilt. We were supposed to be together before this cursed war. It was right then…it is right now. You aren't responsible for the actions of others. It is not your fault we survived."

Her trembling lips whispered, "I want it to be as it was…I just don't know how to fix this. How can I, Cullen, when every time I close my eyes I see their faces?"

"Let me be your strength. Lean on me and don't push me away. I'm not going anywhere." Through the wind and rain, he refused to let her go. "You need to fight, Josephine, for the life in front of us. The past…leave it. It can't be undone. We have everything we need as long as we are together."

Searching her eyes, he went on. "Remember when I pulled you out of an ocean storm once before? You asked how can it be? It can be because fate has destined us to be together. We have been through too much to lose it all now. I love you, Josephine. Tell me you love me too. Tell me and we will survive whatever is before us…together."

She reached out and touched his face, his handsome face. Everything in her being cried out to him. It had always and would forever. She tilted her face to him. "I do love you, Cullen."

He needed nothing else. He swept her off her feet, out of the ocean, out of the storm and into his arms.

Epilogue

Rosemount
October, 1884

Driving sheets of rain slashed against the windowpane. Josephine watched until the precipitation dwindled to where the autumn leaves illuminated within the swirl of gray mist.

For over nineteen years, her life had been happy and content with Cullen by her side. For most of the year, Rosemount was her home and escape from the hustle and bustle of Philadelphia. Moreover, it had been a wonderful place to raise their family.

But to survive, she found she had to block out the memories of her past. Now, with the mere mention that her eldest child had accepted his inheritance, the past flooded back. A vivid reminder that hidden deep within her soul there was a semblance of the person she once was.

At times, Josephine had almost vanquished thoughts of Charleston and Magnolia Bluff. Then this visitor arrived and a sudden remembrance surfaced of her youth. Her chest tightened. She didn't want to be pressed so. She turned from the window and sighed.

Across the elegant drawing room sat her anxious guest. For a moment, Jo did not speak, but studied the young lady.

Annalee Williams was a pretty, young thing. Her brown curly locks were piled loosely on top of her head, with bangs curling above her large green eyes. She wore a dress meant to impress of emerald brocade fashioned with two narrow pleats on the underskirt and trimmed with white embroidered ruffles.

Jo thought she favored her mother, except when she smiled. Her face radiated a confidence Charlotte never had. The exuberant look upon her face betrayed the innocence that only the young hold.

"How is your mother?" Jo settled herself on the floral upholstered sofa.

Drawing in a deep breath, Annalee answered, "Momma is well. She said I couldn't come all this way and not call on you. I have heard about you all my life, Miss Josephine. You don't mind me calling you Miss Josephine, do you? Forgive me, but it's how Momma talks of you but she calls you…"

"Jo," she said politely. "No one calls me Jo much anymore. Another time and place."

"Momma told me stories about the two of you when I was growing up, Miss Josephine." Annalee pressed her lips together in a manner as if pondering her next words. "I was wondering. Do you think of us at all? I mean, you live so far away. How do you do so?"

Josephine looked strangely at the girl. Her words had cut sharply. Yes, the feelings were still within her. No matter how hard she had fought to suppress them, never to let anyone know or suspect they still existed.

"To live up North after the war or away from everything I had once held so dear?"

The poor girl seemed frazzled at her answer. *Were there tears welling in her young eyes?* Oh my! She hadn't meant to distress the young woman. Then, comprehension dawned upon her. Percival! Josephine reached into her skirt pocket for a handkerchief and handed it to the poor thing.

"Oh, what you must think of me! Momma says that I'm too bold by half! She says it will be my downfall for certain. Pray, forgive me, Miss Josephine," she rambled on. "But I love Percival so. Momma says it won't last and I will be miserable forever! It would be best to break it off now."

She sniffled ever so softly. "But in truth, Miss Josephine, I will be miserable forever if I never see him again. Daddy has threatened me if I marry Percival. He told me he would cut me off as if I never existed. I told him I didn't care, but I don't know if I can do as you…to walk away from the only home I know…" She paused and wiped back her tears. "But…" She swallowed. "I love my home, Miss Josephine. My family. Percival says it is up to me. He can't make me leave everything behind, even though I know he thinks I should without a thought. I don't know what I should do."

Josephine's expression softened on the girl. She reached over and patted the girl's hand ever so gently. "I don't know what to tell you, my child. It isn't for me to say. I have only my story. I don't think it pertains

591

to you. We each have to make decisions and only then can we live with ourselves."

"No, please don't do this to me," she pleaded. "You don't know what I have done to come here. I have pulled old Miss Creighton along upon this trip to see you and only you. I know you can help me. I feel it within me."

The girl withdrew from her chair and eased down by Josephine's side. Taking Jo's hand in hers, she laid her head upon Josephine's knees. "Please. I want to know how you feel. There is no other who can come close to what I ask or understand. For are we not Southern women? No one else can understand the pull upon us. To make choices between what we hold upon our hearts. Loyalty to a home in which we love so dear and a life we so desire. Please, Miss Josephine, talk to me of how you feel now after all this time. Would you now make the choices you made in your youth?"

"Choices can't be undone, only lived with," Josephine whispered. Decisions made so many years ago had dictated her life today. Some she had had control over; the others she had not.

She wondered briefly whether she would have done things differently. She did not think she would. Of course, it was a senseless question. One could not go back in time.

Sounds of a carriage rolling to a stop before the house silenced Jo. Cullen was home. A few moments later, he appeared in the doorway with their youngest in tow.

"My dear, Quentin told me we had a visitor." Cullen released the young lad, who giggled and ran over to his mother.

Hugging her, the dark-haired five-year-old said, "Grandmother wanted me to ask if we have company for dinner."

"Tell Grandmother that we will indeed have a guest and to have Penniford make a room up for her as well. Can you do that, my sweet?"

"Yes, Momma." Quentin smiled at their visitor and scooted out the door.

Cullen walked across the room. Leaning down, he kissed her cheek. Jo's eyes lingered on her handsome husband's face. After all their years together, he still made her heart flutter.

"Darling, have you met Charlotte's daughter, Annalee?" Jo turned back to their guest, who had returned to her seat and tried her best to compose herself. "Annalee has traveled all the way from Charleston with the most wonderful news. Our wayward son is not lost. Percival is at Magnolia Bluff."

* * * *

592

Magnolia Bluff

Once more, Josephine walked the grounds of Magnolia Bluff. She had arrived for Percival's wedding to Annalee Williams. Over the years, she had never returned, knowing time had done little to diminish the wound the war had left. Memories lived long in the South. Most still considered her a traitor.

In that, she had lived with. Along with the knowledge that Magnolia Bluff endured the onslaught of reconstruction. The reality of the South's restoration had been a harsh road to travel. Charleston had been devastated. The city itself needed to be rebuilt. It had never recovered from the fire of '61. Every bridge and trestle had been destroyed; the depot burned. Even the train tracks had to be re-laid.

Plantations had changed. Many families lost their farms due to the taxes owed. Carpetbaggers swept down and took advantage of the desperate situation. Dark days had descended upon the South. Most in the Carolinas had found the best way of enduring was sharecropping. Rice was no longer a feasible cash crop. Soon, it was replaced with tobacco, cotton, and corn.

The circumstances had been no different for Magnolia Bluff. The plantation had not been profitable for years. Taxes had to be paid; a feasible cash crop had to be found. Life for the once affluent Montgomery family had become a struggle.

Wade had left Magnolia Bluff to Percival in his will. The rest of his estate was to be divided between his children and Josephine, but the once hefty inheritance had dwindled due to the financial burden of the war.

Through the years, Cullen had traveled several times down to Charleston and made the arrangements to help Magnolia Bluff survive the war. Andrew had overseen the everyday affairs of the estate. Slowly, the family had begun to recover.

The reality of the world around Josephine had made the dream that Percival would take his place as master of the plantation fade. For years, Percival had displayed irresponsible behavior, which sorely tried his father's nerves. He had steadfastly refused to go to the Naval Academy and had not distinguished himself in the family business.

With the greatest reluctance, Percival had agreed to go to Harvard. Josephine was thrilled he had completed his years at the university. The whole immediate family traveled to Boston for his graduation. But instead of returning to Philadelphia after the festivities with his family,

Percival had disappeared, leaving a note for his mother not to worry about him.

She assumed that Percival was trying to prove himself to his father. Now, it seemed that Percival had his own ideas about his future.

The night Annalee had made her appearance at Rosemount, Josephine approached the subject with her husband within the confines of their bedroom.

"Percival told you where he was." Josephine said it as a statement. In truth, there was no need to ask a question when she already knew the answer. She saw it in her husband's eyes.

"He asked me not to tell you."

"And you agreed?"

"He did not want to hurt you," Cullen said. "I have known for a while he wanted to live in Charleston. When he disappeared after his graduation, I deduced it was his destination. I confirmed it with a telegram to Andrew. I did not know about his intentions with Miss Williams, although it does not surprise me."

Josephine couldn't deny the hurt Percival inflicted by keeping from her his plans. Granted, she had seen little of him the last couple of years, what with school and traveling during his vacations, but she never suspected his trips had been to Charleston.

Both of her older children had had their own share of difficulties finding their place in the world. Their connections to the South had left them with a feeling of alienation, belonging neither to the North or South.

Josephine inhaled a deep, steadying breath. "I am not a child, Cullen."

"That is not a question, my love," he asserted. "I did not tell you at first because we were dealing with Madeline. Afterwards, I confess it was easier not to refer to Percival's intentions."

Josephine paused at the mention of her oldest daughter…her stubborn, willful daughter who at one point seemed hell-bent on self-destruction. That was, until Hugh McFadden had taken matters into his hands by marrying her.

Oh, she had no desire to relive those days. Cullen had ranted endlessly when Hugh announced his intention to marry Madeline. Then, Jo had known. Without telling Cullen, she had gone to Hugh for help.

Her beautiful, confused daughter had thought herself in love with a scoundrel…a married man, who had quite taken advantage of Madeline's innocence. When the man broke off their relationship, Madeline became obsessed with the rejection to the point where she wanted to confront the wife.

Aghast when Madeline finally confessed the details of the affair, Jo had no one else to turn to but Hugh because Cullen was away on business. Having only recently retired from the Navy as a commander, Hugh had not hesitated.

Hugh handled the situation and a scandal was averted. Moreover, less than three months afterwards, the once confirmed bachelor married her daughter. Reservations of Madeline marrying a man over twenty years older than herself fueled Josephine's doubts. But over time, her fears were allayed. It became quite apparent that Madeline adored Hugh. Her daughter had become a different person, content and had only just become a mother herself to the most precious, beautiful baby girl, Corinne Margaret McFadden.

"Cullen, Madeline hasn't been an issue for quite some time. What are you trying to tell me?"

His hesitation wasn't lost on Josephine. She pressed. "You have known he wanted to live in Charleston for over two years?"

"I realized the time would come, but I wanted Percival to tell you himself."

Percival had not.

Not until his fiancée had come north to meet her. Jo assumed Annalee's questions must have been answered. For now the whole family was here at Magnolia Bluff to enjoy the impending nuptials.

Jo visited Miss Hazel before she departed. The dear old woman had just turned eighty, half blind, but still worked in her garden and cooked for Heyward, no matter that Heyward had hired her a housekeeper.

"Lordy, child, got nothing to hang your head about. Why, them down there should open their arms to ya! I got no doubt ya helped every one of 'em after the war," Miss Hazel declared.

Jo could not argue with Miss Hazel. She never could. Miss Hazel never lost faith and had thrived in her adopted home. Active in her church, Miss Hazel had become a pillar of her community.

Miss Hazel's joy was her family. She beamed when she talked of both Heyward and Tome. Heyward had become a successful businessman in his own right. He had his own cabinet works, H&T Wright Company, not to mention his real estate dealings. Though, Heyward had never remarried. Jo doubted he ever would. His heart still belonged to Gillie.

Tome had grown into a fine young man. He had done his pa and grandmother proud. Last year, not only had Tome married a lovely young lady from his church, he had become a physician. Never had she seen such happiness illuminate from both Miss Hazel and Heyward.

"You would not hesitate to go back South?" Jo asked for a direct answer.

"If I was able, I would go with ya, Miss Jo." Miss Hazel met her eyes. "Have faith, child, it is as it should be. It is, you know, what Master Wade wanted…young Mister Percival at Magnolia Bluff."

After all this time, the mention of Wade still upset Jo, but she knew Miss Hazel was right.

Walking along the path beside the Ashley River, memories flooded back to Josephine. With the passing of time, the place had changed, but in a strange way had stayed the same.

The house looked no different, strong and proud to have weathered the storm. From Jo's understanding, it had been the only plantation that had not been burnt to the ground in the surrounding area.

The slave cabins still stood and housed those freedmen who hadn't wanted to leave. They were paid now for their services rendered. Amos had taken over Miss Hazel's place at her request. He had raised his family there.

Rosa had not left and was now employed as the housekeeper. Grace Ann had told her that there were rumors about Rosa and Andrew, but Jo gave it no mind. Observing the two of them together when she first arrived, Jo would not doubt the rumors to be true. There was something in their eyes when they looked at each other.

Although she had never returned to Charleston since the war, she had seen most of the family when they visited Philadelphia. Andrew had been the first to travel north after the war. He sought her out immediately when he arrived at Rosemount.

"I have not had a moment's peace since you left. I promise you I thought it was for the best. I just had to apologize. I beg your forgiveness."

"There is no need to ask forgiveness, Andrew," Josephine said. "You did what you felt you must for the family. I hold nothing against you…not now. I found Cullen again. I could not have asked for more."

Somehow making it right freed Jo of a heavy burden that weighed on her soul. Soon, the bridge was healed with Mother Montgomery, Jenna, Anna and eventually, Grace Ann.

Grace Ann had reached out to her not long after Mr. Whitney passed away. She confessed she had known something had happened between Mr. Whitney and Josephine, but respected her husband's wishes by not communicating with Jo. Grace Ann said she never knew the details, but whatever it was seemed to have haunted him until he took his last breath.

Sadness descended upon Josephine at the thought. Death was a finality that could not be crossed.

Josephine stood on the riverbank and stared reflectively at a great blue heron who had settled in the tall grass with a fish in its beak. Engrossed in her thoughts, she hadn't noticed her husband walk toward her.

"I thought I would find you out here instead of resting." Cullen walked up behind Jo and wrapped his arms about her. He held her for a moment as they soaked up the scene before them. Finally, he spoke. "Its beauty still amazes."

Her heart swelled with emotion, not only for the memories this place evoked within her, but for Cullen. This had been where he had been born and raised alongside his cousin Wade as if they were brothers.

"I'm here," he whispered. "Always and forever yours…if that helps."

"More than you know." She clutched his hand tightly. She loved this man! He knew her better than she knew herself, reminding her of what they shared. Nothing…absolutely nothing could diminish their life together.

Turning her to him, he leaned down and kissed her. A moment later, their haven was invaded by the screech of children.

With reluctance, Cullen released his wife and whirled her around to face the onslaught of happy faces. Jo smiled, watching their children bound down the path with their Southern cousins.

There had been a time when Josephine thought Percival and Madeline would have been her only children. Over six years passed after she married Cullen before she had Jonathan, named after Cullen's father, followed two years later by Theodore and then the next year, Alice. Quentin's appearance five years ago had been a surprise, but a most welcome one considering the doctor told her there would have been no more babies after Alice.

Percival walked alongside Quentin, who ran excitedly up to his mother's side.

"Percy showed me his horses, Momma. He says he will teach me to ride like he does."

She looked up at her eldest. Tall and lean, her handsome son had never outgrown his father's look, more so than any of her other children. His thick, dark hair was cut short; his brown eyes large and inquisitive. Unlike Cullen, he wore no mustache, but was clean-shaven. Most found him quite charming with the most disarming smile, which he had learned at a young age to use to his advantage.

"I look forward to seeing his horses," Jo responded. "Uncle Andrew said that Percival has an impressive stable."

"Uncle Andrew said it is in my blood," Percival said. "Dad was a renowned horseman."

"Wade was," Jo acknowledged. "He would be proud."

His arm extended to his mother, Percival asked, "Would you like to see them now?"

Jo looked at Cullen, who nodded. "Go. I want to show the children around where I grew up."

Percival walked in silence until his father and children disappeared from sight. "I am glad you are here, Momma."

"I wouldn't have missed your wedding, my darling child."

"Despite your protest, I know it was hard on you to come."

She couldn't deny his words. "You are my child. There is nothing I wouldn't do for you."

"I have heard. Uncle Andrew has told me. He admires you greatly for what you did during the war." He paused and nodded toward the garden. "Do you mind if we take a few minutes away from everyone? Father knows I wanted a moment to talk to you in private."

"I would like nothing more."

"Come, then. Grandmother has added to the gardens since last you were here."

The garden was beautiful in the autumn. The roses lent to the fragrance of the stroll. Jo had forgotten how many flowers were still in bloom this late in the year. The hydrangeas were covered in blue blooms and soon the budding camellias would lend its beauty to the landscape.

"You have not told me what you think of Annalee. She has been so anxious since she visited that you might think less of her. I told her that you would not. I hope you don't. I want you to like her, Momma."

Josephine looked over at Percival. "She seems a lovely girl and quite in love with you."

"As I am with her," he acknowledged. "She had reservations. Afraid her father would cut her off for marrying me. But when she came back from visiting you, her fears about us had been put to rest after seeing you with Father. I, also, allayed Mr. Williams's objection. He didn't want his little girl moving up North. I told him I was going nowhere. This is my home."

"So you have made up your mind."

"The place calls to me in a way I can't explain. I have known for a while it's where I belong. I knew even before Howie Albright visited Magnolia Bluff."

The name sounded familiar but for the life of her she couldn't place who he was. "Who?"

"The drummer boy who Dad gave his life to save at Shiloh. Howie came here with his son, looking for me. Said he dreamed often of coming here and felt the need to do so. Although a brief encounter, it was etched into his memory forever. He recounted Dad telling him about his home and his love he had for his family. Howie wanted me to know Dad's sacrifice wasn't in vain. That he had lived his life holding to the courage and honor that Dad showed before he died."

For a moment, Percival paused. "I didn't need Howie Albright to tell me this was my home. I felt it the moment I returned to Magnolia Bluff, but his visit help reinforced my decision to live here. I know all you and Father have done for me but…this is where I was born…it's where I belong…at Magnolia Bluff. I need you to say I have your blessing. I need you to say you understand."

She looked up at her son, realizing he had heard the call of the land. She understood his desire to live and raise his children along the banks of the Ashley River. He had become the man Wade envisioned. "My darling son, I have no right to deny you your heritage. You have my blessing."

He leaned over and kissed her cheek. "I love you, Momma…one more thing." He reached in his waistcoat pocket and pulled out a letter. "This is the last letter from Dad. Howie found it in his pocket after he died. He kept it all these years. It's yours."

He left her alone. A long silence ensued. She stood motionless and stared at it. Finally, she sat on the bench. With trembling hands, she opened it. As she read, she could almost hear Wade's voice…feel his presence.

It is quiet here tonight, my love. Only the crickets and bullfrogs disturb the silence. I revel in the stillness, knowing it will not last. The men know that in the morning we face a monumental task. We have been told the odds are against us, but as it has been from the start of this blasted war, we will do what we must and fight.

Once more I face my own mortality and my worries mount. Not for myself, but you and my children, Percival and the one that as of yet has made his appearance. I have learned that life is not about making an impact on the world as we know it, but on the lives of those you love. I wonder what impact I have made on yours, but I have a need for you to know what you have done for me.

If I die in battle, know I have found my true happiness in you. My feelings for you have been unconditional and for you to have returned my love has been the greatest gift I have ever received. My love is eternal and is not bound by time, for there is no end.

My thoughts are always with you. I miss you more than you can ever know. I miss the way you smile when I walk into the room, the way you laugh. I even miss the way you cry over the simplest of things.

When I first met you, you fascinated me with your unique view on life. I thought you charming, if not a little strange in the way you treated both Gillie and Miss Hazel. You looked beyond the color of their skin and saw them as people. I have had time to think on all the things in my life and have come to a realization that the world would be a better place to live if we all judged others by their deeds and not by their appearance. I have determined that it must have been the way your father raised you. It is my desire for you to raise our children in the same manner. I want them to see the good in all people, for I have seen the worst.

I sometimes catch myself daydreaming about home. I see Magnolia Bluff so clearly. The old oaks with their Spanish moss swaying in the wind, the horses running wild in the pasture and you standing in the garden surrounded by the blooming magnolias. It gives me peace.

If I have no more tomorrows, I want Percival to be proud of the man I was. I don't want him to ever question my loyalty, honor, or my duty to my country, God, or family. In the end, it is all I have to give him. Tell him to hold to Magnolia Bluff. It will be his, his home, his legacy...

Looking up at the moon, I wonder if you, too, are staring up into the same night's sky. When you look among the stars, remember me...

Clutching the letter to her chest, she remembered the world that was. That world was gone, but Wade's legacy would live on forever. She saw it in her son's eyes for his family and his home, grasping the knowledge that Wade had left behind the greatest legacy of all—love.

THE END

Just a little reminder...if you enjoy the Southern Legacy books take a moment and leave a review! It means a lot to Indie authors!! Thank you!! Have a wonderful day!

Touch base with me at
Website: www.jerrihines.org
Twitter: @jhines340

Books under Jerri Hines:

The Southern Legacy Series
Belle of Charleston, Book One
Shadows of Magnolia, Book Two
Born to Be Brothers, Book Three
The Sun Will Rise, Book Four

Winds of Betrayal Series:
The Cry For Freedom
Embrace of the Enemy
Kiss of Deceit
The Heavens Shall Fall
Set Fire To The Rain ~ Coming Soon!

Tides of Charleston Series:
The Judas Kiss
The Promise
Another Night Falls

Books Under Penname Colleen Connally

Secret Lives Series:
Seductive Secrets
Broken Legacy
Seductive Lies

Boston's Crimes of Passion
Fragmented
Framed~ Coming Soon!

Books Under Penname Carrie James Haynes
Dreamscape
Whispers of a Legend Series—Shadows of the Past
The Path Now Turned
Vision of Destiny
Time of the Nuxvenom

ABOUT THE AUTHOR

I'm a Southern gal that has lived the last thirty years near Boston with my Yankee husband. The funny thing is that as a Southerner I know I'm Southern; he hasn't a clue he's a Yankee. I believe in love and the power it holds. It is the reason I write romances. My fascination for history has inspired many of my books including the Winds of Betrayal and Tide of Charleston Series both set during the American Revolution. My Civil War saga, Southern Legacy, is my latest series. It is a serial made up of Belle of Charleston, Shadows of Magnolia, Born to Be Brothers and the dramatic conclusion, The Sun Rises.

I, also, write under the pen name Colleen Connally. Secret Lives, a historical romance series, is riddled with romantic suspense and a touch of paranormal. Fragmented, Book One Boston's Crimes of Passion, marks my first contemporary suspense thriller.

I am also a supporter of The Home For Little Wanderers in Boston and the Alzheimer's Association.